I0817775

AN ECHO OF TITANS

THE BLADEBORN SAGA, BOOK THREE

T. C. EDGE

COPYRIGHT

First edition: September 2021
Cover Design by Polar Engine

Previous book in the series:

The Song of the First Blade (Book 1)
Ghost of the Shadowfort (Book 2)

CONTENTS

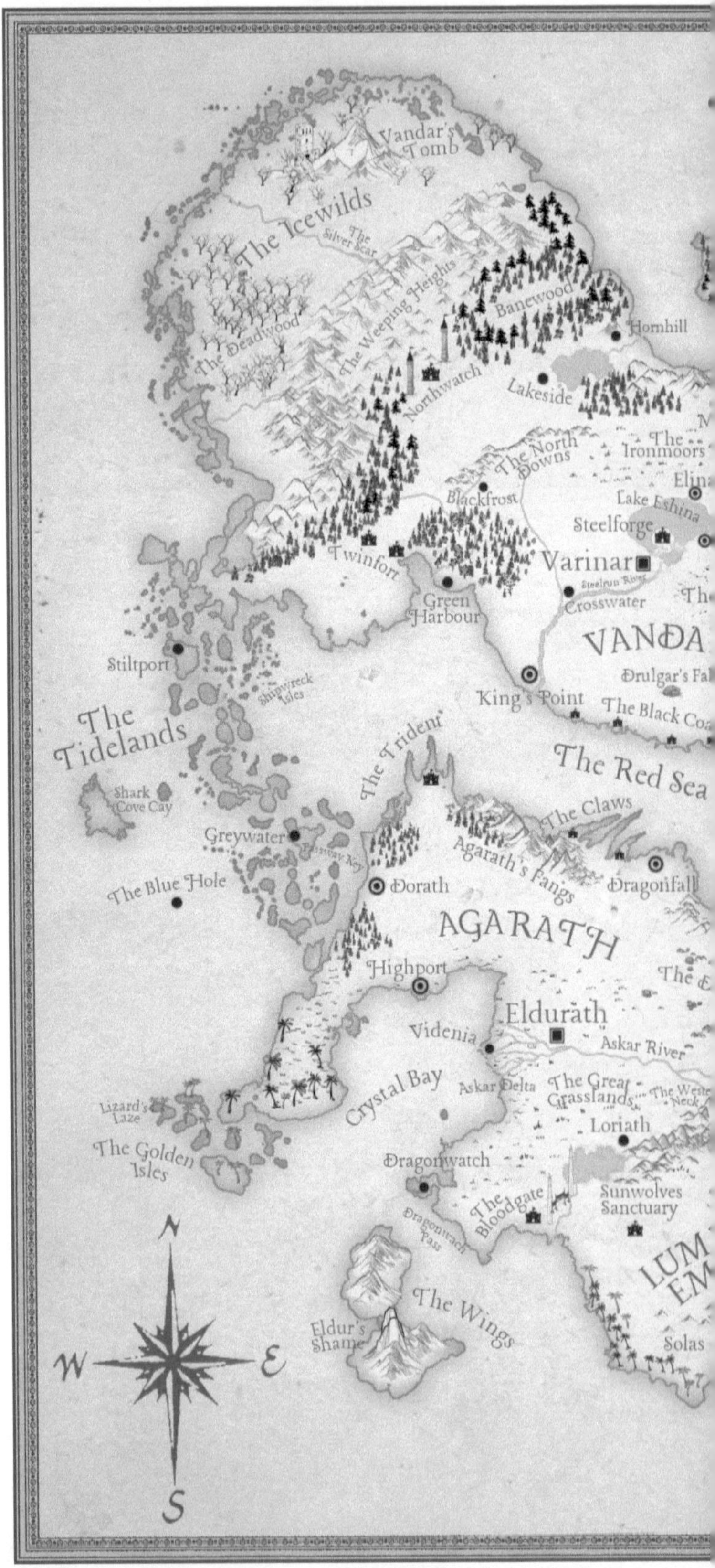

Vandar's Tomb
The Icewilds
The Silver Scar
The Deadwood
The Weeping Heights
Banewood
Hornhill
Northwatch
Lakeside
The Ironmoors
The North Downs
Blackfrost
Lake Eshina
Steelforge
Twinfort
Varinar
Steelrun River
Green Harbour
Crosswater
Stiltport
Shipwreck Isles
King's Point
Drulgar's Fall
The Black Coast
The Tidelands
The Trident
The Red Sea
Shark Cove Cay
The Claws
Greywater
Runway Key
Agarath's Fangs
Dragonfall
The Blue Hole
Dorath
AGARATH
Highport
Eldurath
Videnia
Askar River
Crystal Bay
Askar Delta
The Great Grasslands
Lizard's Laze
Loriath
The Golden Isles
Dragonwatch
The Bloodgate
Sunwolves Sanctuary
Dragonwatch Pass
N
The Wings
Eldur's Shame
W
E
Solas
S

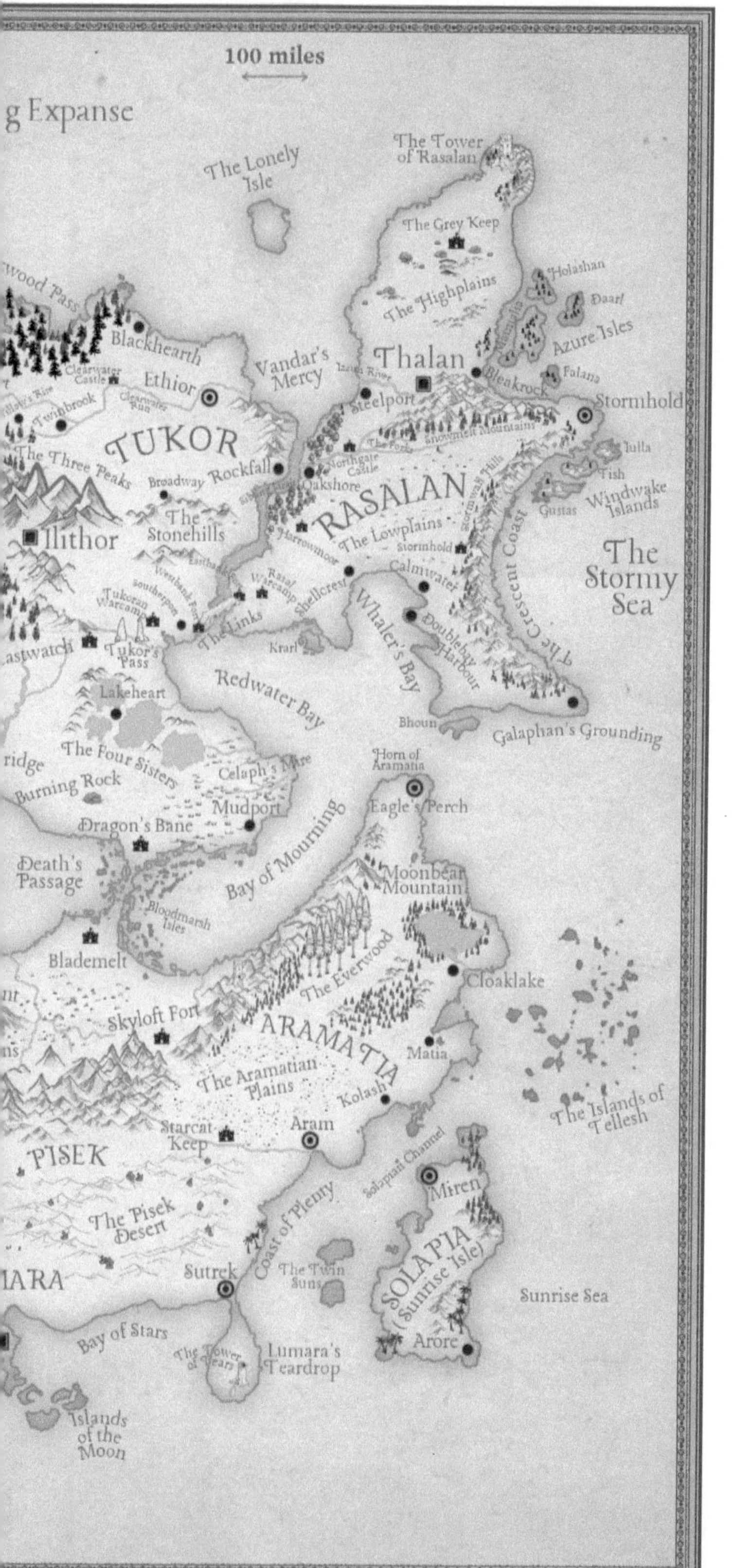

100 miles
g Expanse
The Lonely Isle
The Tower of Rasalan
The Grey Keep
The Highplains
Holashan
Daarl
Azure Isles
Falana
Thalan
Bleakrock
Stormhold
Vandar's Mercy
Steelport
Blackhearth
Ethior
Twinbrook
TUKOR
The Three Peaks
Broadway
Rockfall
Oakshore
RASALAN
The Lowplains
Tulla
Tish
Windwake Islands
Gustas
The Stormy Sea
The Crescent Coast
Ilithor
The Stonehills
Harrowmoor
Stormhold
Calmwater
Shellcrest
Doublebay Harbour
Whaler's Bay
The Links
Krarl
Tukor's Pass
astwatch
Lakeheart
Redwater Bay
Bhoun
Galaphan's Grounding
Horn of Aramatia
Eagle's Perch
ridge
The Four Sisters
Burning Rock
Celaph's Mire
Mudport
Dragon's Bane
Bay of Mourning
Death's Passage
Moonbear Mountain
Bloodmarsh Isles
Blademelt
The Everwood
Cloaklake
Skyloft Fort
ARAMATIA
Matia
The Aramatian Plains
Kolash
The Islands of Tellesh
Starcat Keep
Aram
PISEK
Solapian Channel
Miren
The Pisek Desert
Coast of Plenty
SOLAPIA (Sunrise Isle)
IARA
Sutrek
The Twin Suns
Sunrise Sea
Bay of Stars
The Tower of Tears
Lumara's Teardrop
Arore
Islands of the Moon

PROLOGUE

The host marched down the outer colonnade, armour clanking on the pristine white stone, banners fluttering splendidly in the breeze. They showed a blade thrust down before a mountain, silver on blue, their rich cloaks sewn with the same royal sigil in delicate silver thread. King Ayrin went afore them, resplendent in his royal raiment, his crown of miniature godsteel blades framing the curly black hair of his head. Behind came the finest knights of his father's order, proud men of his blood, survivors of the war.

"It went well, I thought," came a silvery voice behind her. "The boy has much of his father in him, but not *too* much, I hasten to say. I feel confident he will keep the peace."

Queen Thala, founder of the realm of Rasalan, nodded as she watched from the balcony of her palace. "Ayrin has a temperance his father did not. I loved Varin much as you did, Ilith, but he was always hot in the head. His son will rule well, I feel. He will lead his people through an age of expansion, and flourish where his forebears failed."

Ilith had a soft little smile on his face. "Is this speculation, Thala, or foresight?" he asked her. He wore the colours of his kingdom, umber brown and emerald green, his clothing wrought in leather and fur and modest for a king of such esteem. Of the Five Followers of the preeminent gods, Thala had always liked Ilith the most. How could she not? He had helped build her city, after all, as he had Varinar and Eldurath and Lumos too, and all before finishing his own.

She returned his smile. "It does not take a prophet to see that Ayrin will make a fine king, Ilith. This world we built has been scarred and seared, and now is the time to heal. Ayrin knows this. He will rebuild, as we all must."

"Ash is a good fertiliser, I hear," the blacksmith said.

"Then the Black Coast should become particularly prosperous."

They shared a laugh. It had been time enough now since Drulgar the Dread had razed the southern coast of Vandar to the ground that they could jest about it, without feeling *too* heartless. Over a hundred years, in fact, since that fateful day. A century filled with death and destruction and the great suffocating shadow of war. *But that was over now,* she told herself uneasily. *Over...until the next time.*

The Vandarian host were still making their way between the columns, toward the marble steps that would lead them down into the city. In the harbour of the Izzun, their great war galleons were moored, broad and bulky ships with three wide decks and four soaring masts and flapping sails of silver and blue. They had dominated the anchorage for a week, during which Thala and Ilith and Ayrin had held their royal conferences. Much had needed to be discussed. The War of Fire and Steel was over, but the dividing lines had been set. Thala had hoped Lumo would come, but alas no, the Moon Queen of Lumara had been beset by her own civil difficulties, chiefly led by her brother Sola and his belligerent warmongering ways. North and south were ostensibly at peace, but it would not last long, Thala knew. She had seen stirrings in the Eye of her master already, wars a hundred years distant, a thousand years off, wars that would unfold again and again between north and south for many millennia to come.

They will call them Renewals, she thought, sadly. *And there will be a full score of them before this is done...*

She drew a breath of cool autumn air, and forced her face back into a smile. It was Thala's wont to get morose when she looked too far ahead. It had been a parting gift from the great god Rasalan to lend her a portion of his power, the Eye through which she saw so much, yet her curse was not to share it.

Instead she kept a diary, a book into which she wrote down what she'd seen, to be passed down to her son and heir at her death and not before. Rasalan had decreed she use his Eye to watch and not interfere, yet Thala had understood the meaning behind his words. This book was to be her mouthpiece, through which she might communicate through time. *And time is a concept they do not truly understand,* she thought. Her master had, and he alone among the gods. *And he passed that power to me.*

"How long do you intend to stay?" she asked Ilith, as King Ayrin and his host disappeared down the steps. A chorus of cheers greeted them as they entered into the city square at the foot of the hill, echoing up toward the palace. Thala smiled. All the north had stood in awe of Varin, yet his youngest son was to be loved just as fiercely.

"If you want rid of me, Thala, do feel free to say." Ilith grinned impishly. He'd always had a light and teasing way about him.

"To the contrary, you're welcome to stay as long as you like. You might even send for some of your Forgeborn. I have statues I'd like to raise, and this palace you built me...well, it could do with an upgrade, don't you think?"

"You wound me, cruel queen. I have always considered Thalan some of my greatest work."

"I'm sure you say that to all of them." She smiled back at him, the wind rustling through her long golden hair. Once it had been bright as starlight but now she was starting to find strands of grey amidst the tresses, and there were more wrinkles on her face than she would like. "I hear you're building a fortress in the mountains. Far away to the north, near the coast. Black towers and impenetrable walls and magical protections, they tell me."

"They tell you true," Ilith said, nodding. "Forgiving as Ayrin is I am not so naive as to think that this peace will last forever. He will have sons one day, and who's to say who they'll take after, their father the peacemaker or their grandfather the warrior?" He gave her a searching look. "Or perhaps you already know?"

She gave that no reaction, for not even Ilith could know of what she'd seen. *It would only keep you up at night, sweet king*, she thought, for half of what she saw in the future was fire and blood and death.

"You cannot say, I understand." Ilith turned his eyes beyond the balcony. The crowds gathered in the square below were chanting now for the new Vandarian king, praising him for bringing peace after a hundred years of war. "All the north is weary of war, but that hunger will return," he intoned. "When it does, the Vandarians will seek vengeance for Varin's death. It's just a matter of time."

"And that's why you're building this great black fortress of yours? As a haven to shelter your people?"

"I can't rely on the Vandarians and their Bladeborn forever, Thala. My people are stonemasons and smiths, not soldiers."

Just wait, she thought, but didn't say. One day the Bladeborn men of Varin's blood would spread across all the north, founding houses and lands and castles of their own, and Tukor would be well stocked.

"I would hope that Ayrin honours his father's oath to protect my people should we come under siege," Ilith went on, "but there is sense in taking matters into my own hands too. This fortress...it'll be well hidden, unreachable by dragonflight, protected from their molten fires. Just please don't ask me to build one for you, Thala. It has taken a great deal out of me." He sighed. "I'm starting to feel my age."

She laughed gaily at that. "You've lived for thousands of years, Ilith. I should think it would tell eventually."

"It has, but only in these last two centuries. Mortality is such a rotten thing, don't you think?"

She smiled. They'd all lost their grip on everlasting life when the gods fell two hundred years ago. "In actual fact I think quite the opposite. Mortality has a radiance to it that an eternal life cannot match. After too many centuries the same faces and places do become rather drab."

A neat laugh slipped through Ilith's lips. "My face is among them, I'm sure. I can't say I've ever been much to look upon. Varin, though... goodness he was a handsome man. Ayrin looks much like him, don't you think? Less so than Elin did, but the resemblance is still strong."

"Quite strong, yes." She saw the smile begin to slip away from Ilith's face. "You miss him, don't you? Varin. His is a face that is hard to forget."

"I miss him more fiercely than I can say," sighed the kingly blacksmith. "What happened that day at the peace parley...I still dream of it, Thala. I can still see *them*, coming up behind him. I see Lori's black blade. I see the look in Dor's eyes, red and hateful, so full of vengeance. I see them driving that steel through Varin's back, and the blood, there was just so much of it..." He lowered his eyes.

Ilith had chastised himself for not acting, not confronting Eldur's sons, but what could he have done? It was only them in the pavilion that day signing the peace accord at Death's Passage; she and Ilith, Varin and Lumo and Lori and Dor, who'd come in their father's stead after his defeat to Varin at the Battle of Ashmount that had brought the war to a close.

"If you had tried to fight, they'd only have killed you too," she told the Tukoran king, as she had many times already these last months. "And then your own son would have been in just the same position as Ayrin, choosing whether to renew the war for vengeance or sue peace with their father's killers." She reached out, gripped his arm. "I'm glad you stood by, as I did, Ilith. We could not have stopped Lori and Dor from killing Varin that day. It was...fated. For better or for worse."

And now the seeds of war have been sown, she thought, for what Eldur's sons had done that morning would reap a bloody harvest one day. She had glimpsed it already. Glimpsed the next Renewal to rise, two hundred years hence, when Ayrin's eldest son Amron stirred all of Vandar to war. Amron would be much like his grandfather, Thala knew, quarrelsome and combative, and singularly gifted with the blade. He would raise Vandar's armies and seek vengeance for Varin's fall, beginning a war that would blaze for a dozen long years, spreading its smoking shadow across the world.

And later, much later, several thousand years from now, there would be another Amron, named for Ayrin's son, who would play an important part as well...

She looked at Ilith with a soft expression on her face. By the time the next Renewal stirred the first Bladeborn houses would be claiming lands in Tukor, and King Amron, son of Ayrin, grandson of Varin, would call upon his neighbours to fight. *But it will not be you on the throne, my sweet king,* she thought. Ilith's own life would end a little more than eighty years from now. *And might I tell him how and when? Might I confide in him what I've seen?*

She turned away from the Forgeborn king and turned away from that thought. It was not her place to meddle so directly. But *indirectly*, she could do...

That night, the Queen of Rasalan returned to her private sanctum and sat gazing into the Eye. It rested upon a plinth of pale yellow stone, its surface tessellated with diamonds and squares and circles in shades of blue. They were the colours of her kingdom, sun yellow and ocean blue, and in the centuries to come a Bladeborn Order called the Suncoats would emerge to help defend her realm. She'd glimpsed them in her visions, as she had a thousand things, and would sometimes sit for hours, even days, getting lost in a world out of time. For almost two hundred years she'd devoted herself to the mastery of her art, looking through the veil and beyond. Yet for all that mastery, she saw only what Rasalan willed. This was *his* Eye, *his* vision. She had always been, and would always be, only a servant to her god.

And Rasalan has shown me the way, she knew, watching the pupil grow wider. The Eye was quite large, a metre wide and half as tall, oval shaped and a vivid blue, with branches of golden veins, yet it was the pupil that held the sight, that black window at its heart through which she'd seen so much. As she gazed at it, it would begin to grow and expand, dilating, and Rasalan's vision would come forth to swallow her. And across the years, she'd begun to see a pattern. She'd begun to understand.

So she'd started the Book of Thala, the diary that would be her voice, through time. With her swan feather quill she would sit here scribbling, coding her messages and instructions for the future monarchs of her line. Because one day, she'd seen, the calamity would return. The twin tombs would tremble and the world would rip asunder, and the spawn of Agarath would swarm the skies. *All the world will burn,* she thought, *and the heavens will fill with ash, blotting out the sun. The trees will die and the oceans will dry and all foul things will come forth.*

It was Thala's design to help stop it, she and her pen and her book and her Eye. By the time it came to pass, she would be long dead and turned to dust, but here in her sanctum, she could put the pieces of the puzzle into place.

A puzzle that others must figure out, she thought, *else all the world will fall.*

1

Elyon

3,350 Years Later...

The great hall of Harrowmoor was full of nobles and knights, and a hundred banners had been hung to signal peace in the north.

At the heart of them, draped above the main stage, were the banners of the three northern kingdoms: the speared leviathan and rising sun of Rasalan, the blade and mountain of Vandar, the crossed hammer and sword of Tukor. And below them stood their leaders in attendance. Lord Donal Paramor for Rasalan. Prince Rylian Lukar for Tukor. And Dalton Taynar for Vandar, now prince and heir to the realm.

Elyon's throat was tight, his head weary. He stood beside Lord Wallis Kanabar, who wasn't in a merry mood himself. Nor were Lord Shorton or Lord Fullerton of the Lakelands, or the sundry minor lords and knights of East Vandar, all gathered here at Harrowmoor to complete the ending of the war.

"It should be you up there, Lord Kanabar," Elyon said. "This is *your* army, not Dalton's. These men are of the lakes and rivers and marshes, not the Ironmoors."

"All men of Vandar are his to command now," the red-bearded

Lord of the Riverlands said. He was dressed in rich blue robes and dark brown leathers, though wore a full shirt of godsteel mail on top. Many others were the same, and not taking any chances, after what happened at the parley some weeks past.

"You'll not contest it, Elyon?" asked Lord Denis Shorton, who wasn't short at all but tall and willowy with a long thin nose to go with it. It gave him a nasally voice and bookish appearance. "By rights your father should now be king, and you prince of Vandar. It sets my teeth on edge to see Dalton up there, lording it over us."

Lord Francis Fullerton of Lakeheart agreed with a firm nod. He was a toadish man, squat and homely, with wide thin lips and a broad bulbous nose. The pair had both raised thousands of men from the Lakelands to join Lord Kanabar's army for the invasion of Rasalan, though would be returning south with them soon, Elyon knew. *As will we all.* The war in Rasalan was done now and for that at least they could be thankful. It would allow them to focus their attentions on the south alone, as they should have done from the start.

"I'll offer no challenge," the heir of Daecar said. He was clad in his rich blue Varin cloak over wrappings of subtle leather armour, and felt stiff and tired and in no mood for this pomp and ceremony today. "If King Ellis decreed Godrik Taynar his heir, what can I do?" Last night a hundred men had called out in challenge to that news, and Sir Dalton had waved every one of them off. "Godrik is king now," Elyon went on. "If there's a challenge to be made it'll happen once the war is done. Civil war among the greathouses won't serve anyone right now."

"I quite agree," intoned Lord Kanabar. "We can bleat all we want, but it'll make no difference. When all the world is falling to war, it doesn't much matter who sits the steel throne. Any king, be he Ellis or Amron or Godrik, will make winning the war his focus. Every house in the north is rallying to that cause, great and small, lord and knightly. Forget the throne, and forget Godrik Taynar. We can muster the men of the east to make this right once the south is dealt with."

By which point, half the men in the room will probably be dead, Elyon thought.

The host from Tukor and Vandar had arrived some ten minutes ago, crossing the snowy moors from the siege camp south of the fortress, passing through the huge walls and grand gatehouse, the brutal barbican that they'd tried and failed to win. But they hadn't had to in the end.

Late last night, the white banners of surrender had been raised above the walls and towers. Elyon had been in the infirmary at the time, still recuperating from his recent flogging that had cut ten deep scars across his back. It was the first revelation on a night full of them. Two kings had fallen, Elyon had gone on to learn, and two others raised to replace them. Prince Hadrin of Rasalan had replaced his wise old father Godrin on the throne, and bent the knee to Janilah. Godrik Taynar had been promoted from steward to king, and was sitting the steel throne in Varinar. For a few crazed moments Elyon had been led to believe his father Amron would be king, but that hadn't lasted long. No...it was House Taynar who had seized the throne, and the rule of the Knights of Varin besides.

Elyon found his eyes on Dalton Taynar, standing grim and pale and sleek as a sword on the raised stage, gallantly dressed in his gleaming silver armour and Varin cloak. *Prince Dalton, First Blade of Vandar,* he thought bitterly, though the Sword of Varinar was absent from his hip. Dalton's first proclamation as prince had been to strip Vesryn Daecar of the title, and take it for his own, but there'd been one last twist to that tale that none had expected...

Vesryn had gone rogue. He'd fled the camp, taking the Sword of Varinar with him, and so far as the early reports were saying, no one had spotted him since.

"Dull Dalton best get used to not sleeping," said Lord Kanabar, looking over at their new prince. "After what he put Vesryn through, denying his claim to the Sword of Varinar, constantly prodding and poking and challenging him...well, I've half a mind to think that Vesryn may turn vengeful."

Elyon gave a tired nod to that, but it wasn't just Dalton who'd caused Vesryn to turn his cloak and flee. His own words rang out through is head. *You don't deserve that blade. You are no uncle of mine.* Those had been his parting words to Vesryn after the truth had spilled from his uncle's lips last night. The truth of his part in Aleron's death, and his father's maiming, and the treachery that had befallen their house. *Jonik,* he thought. It was the name Vesryn had given to the Shadowknight, the assassin, the man who'd posed as Fitzroy Ludlum during the Song of the First Blade. *My brother,* Elyon thought, his fingers balling to a fist. *Jonik...*

"He must have overheard what was happening in the longhouse," offered Lord Shorton, his many chins wobbling as he spoke. "He'll have overheard Dalton proclaiming his father as king, and himself as the new First Blade, and thought it better to run." He gave out a troubled sigh. "I fear he's truly lost now. To desert from his duty? To steal the Sword of Varinar? You'll excuse me for saying so, Elyon, but that speaks of madness to me."

Madness, and grief, Elyon knew. *You are no uncle of mine...*Those words had driven Vesryn off as much as the threat of losing the blade. Vesryn knew Elyon would bring the truth of it all to his father now. He knew that his wife Amara would learn of his treason, and his dear sweet niece Lillia too. And what was Vesryn without them? *All he has now is that blade,* Elyon thought, *and he isn't likely to give it up.*

"They'll track him down eventually," Lord Kanabar asserted. "True enough, Vesryn had grown paranoid, but mad? I'm not so sure."

"Madness is a descent, Wallis," said lanky Lord Shorton. "None of us can deny that Vesryn was on the way down..."

"But nowhere near the bottom. There's time to arrest his fall if he wills it. So long as he realises his folly and returns the blade, Dalton may be kind enough to overlook it."

Lord Wallis Kanabar was a pragmatist, but that sounded wholly naive. "He's a dead man walking," Elyon said in counter, his voice dull as a stone. "As soon as he hands back the Sword of Varinar, Dalton will have his head on a spike for treason. Vesryn knows that. He'll cling to that blade until his dying breath, believe me. He has nothing else to live for now." Those words brought Elyon a series of questioning glances, but he had no intention of sharing.

"Then Dalton best be doubly careful," Lord Kanabar said. "A man who's got nothing to lose is a dangerous man indeed. And the Sword of Varinar...it makes a man something more. If Vesryn decides to come for Dalton, I'm not sure there'll be much he can do about it."

Dalton knew that too. That was why he'd recruited Sir Brontus Oloran as his captain and second-in-command, and the mountainous Sir Taegon Cargill to be his chief bodyguard and protector. Both of the Varin Knights were currently at the bottom of the stage, fully armoured in interlinking godsteel plate, watching the crowds. And a number of others had been posted about the doors too, should Vesryn pay a visit. Sir Quinn Sharp and Sir Marcus Flint and Sir Ramsey Stone, who'd backed Dalton's claim to be First Blade all along. All would watch him now, night and day, but Lord Kanabar was right...if Vesryn came, it mightn't matter.

The proceedings went on, as the assembled lords and knights of the north waited patiently around the great hall. It was a dull formal affair, though soon the ale would break out in a bid to loosen things up, and the music would start playing, and the tension would ease. Already the skins and drums and strings were gathering in the galleries, the servers rolling out barrels of ale and mead. There were fifty tables set out here, long and thick, and a dozen hearths were burning warm around them. The hall was fit for a thousand men. Even with tenscore in attendance, it seemed almost empty.

Eventually, the three leaders upon the dais turned to the audience. There was something slightly queer and insincere about it all. When kingdoms and greathouses warred in the north, and then came to peace, this was always the custom. The leaders would chat on show of their lords and knights and show them how friendly they were. It was all rictus smiles and false words, but custom was custom, so it was observed.

"I say we have peace," called out old Lord Paramor, clad in a blue-dyed ermine cloak. It was clasped at the neck by a golden brooch shaped into a kraken, its long twisting tentacles clinging to the fur. "Peace in the north. We have peace!"

The crowd gave out a muted roar, mostly from the Rasalanians present.

"I say it too," called out Prince Rylian Lukar right after. "We have peace, I say!" He was dressed in green and brown, favouring simple attire as ever. Sometimes Rylian looked as much a humble traveller as a prince.

Another cheer followed, rising from the Tukoran contingent.

Then it was Prince Dalton's turn. "Peace," he cried. "I say it myself for Vandar. Peace in the north. Harmony between our kingdoms!"

A rustle of noise followed, mostly from Dalton's sycophants and bootlickers. Elyon stayed deathly silent. And with that, it was done.

The morning was ambling into afternoon by then, though in that windowless hall it wasn't so easy to tell. Up in the galleries, the fiddlers and pipers and drummers started playing, and a hundred famous songs were crooned. Each barrel of ale was tasted and tested before the tankards were filled and passed around. Sir Mallister Monsort joined them. "Curious," he said when he saw the poor tasters ushered in. "You would think we could forgo all that, now that we're at peace. We *are* at peace, aren't we? I'm sure I heard that somewhere." His lips twirled into a playful grin.

There had been poisonings down on the south coast, at Shellcrest in particular, and several hundred Tukorans had suffered less than pleasant deaths as a result. "Just a precaution," Elyon said, feeling less inclined to jesting than Sir Mallister right now. "They can waffle on about peace on stage, but tensions are still running high."

"And the dividing lines are still up, by the looks of it." Sir Mallister gestured to the crowds. They were gathered in their cliques and coteries. Kastor men here. Lake and Riverlanders there. Lord Paramor and the lowland lords keeping to themselves. "I suppose it'll take time to mend rifts."

To that end, Prince Rylian could always be counted on to bring people together. He and his dashing princely sons, Robbert and Raynald, were beginning to move through the crowd, breaking up the cosy little cliques. Foes would need to become friends if they were to defeat the Agarathi and their allies, and by the news coming from across the Red Sea, the Patriots of Lumara were gathering their strength too.

An ale found its way into Elyon's grasp, once the tasters had done their duty and stumbled away half drunk. That began the toasts. First Lord Kanabar raised his goblet to peace in the north. Then Lord Fullerton took a moment to remember those who'd fallen during the siege. Lord Shorton followed, toasting a speedy end to the coming war, and victory for north against south. Sir Mallister raised a cup for his friend, Sir Warren Condor, who'd been killed during the parley a month ago. Elyon proposed a rich long marriage for King Hadrin and his bride-to-be, Amilia Lukar, with no lack of irony. He'd learned that from Vesryn last night, and the thought still repelled him.

It seemed Sir Mallister wasn't aware, however. "Gods be good, no wonder Hadrin called for peace," he said. "Many a man would hand over the keys to their kingdom if it meant being wedded to the Jewel of Tukor."

"It sounds like you have a liking for the pretty little princess, Sir Mallister," japed Lord Kanabar.

"I am only human, my lord." Sir Mallister's golden hair was shining under the high swinging lanterns above them, his eyes a sparkling blue like his sister Melany. If there was a more handsome man in Tukor, Elyon hadn't seen him. "My sister is the princess's lady-in-waiting, as you know. By consequence I have spent much time with the pair of them, and have taken to guarding Amilia on occasion in the past. I will not lie, my lords. I had hoped to catch her eye during the times we spent together, but alas she showed no interest."

"Punching above your station, perchance, Mallister?" came the voice of Sir Rodmond Taynar, as he stepped through the crowds. He gave the Emerald Guard a smile. "You and Amilia would make a fine pair to look at you, true, but you're hardly highborn enough to snare her." He spoke in jest, and Sir Mallister took it well.

"How true that is, Sir Rodmond. Though my dear sister did manage it, with Elyon here."

"Half of the eligible young women of Varinar could say the same," laughed Rodmond. "Elyon has never been choosy with his matches." That wasn't true at all. All the women Elyon had courted and bedded in Varinar were typically beautiful, young, and of fine highborn stock. He saw no profit in engaging with Sir Rodmond on it, however. "So how's the back, Elyon?" the young knight went on. "I noticed that your stitches opened up last night, with everything that happened..."

They'd spent a week together in the infirmary, Rodmond recovering from a bolt he'd taken to the belly at the parley, and Elyon from the ten licks of the lash he'd been given for killing Sir Griffin Kastor. Which he didn't do, of course, but no one else except Vesryn knew about that. "Nurse Aliss stitched me back up last night, when things settled down," he told Rodmond. "And your gut?" He looked at the skinny young man's stomach. Rodmond wasn't tall, nor large, nor especially comely. He had his uncle Dalton's look; narrow-faced, sharp-chinned, and dark-eyed, though was of a decidedly more friendly disposition. "I hope you didn't set your recovery back?"

Sir Rodmond Taynar dared a pat to the belly, then winced. "It's... tender, but manageable. I doubt either of us will be able to swing a sword for a while, though."

Elyon nodded, as the others began to disperse, moving into the crowds to mingle. All across the great hall, voices were rising now above the music. As expected, the ale was having its desired effect, causing the cliques to separate. "So, are you still just 'sir', or should I be calling you 'prince' now, Rodmond?"

Elyon had always liked Rodmond Taynar, despite the long rivalry between their houses. He was affable, cordial, and had never much liked that he was his uncle Dalton's heir. He'd confided in Elyon as much last night, as they watched the banners of surrender rise up upon the towers and walls of Harrowmoor, pure white against the heavy black skies. Rodmond's father, Grayson Taynar, had been Dalton's younger brother by a year. He was only nineteen when he'd sired Rodmond, before going off to war, where he was badly wounded at the Battle of Burning Rock. Those wounds had killed him eventually, and seeing as Dalton had no sons, that made Rodmond his heir. *A role he's never favoured,* Elyon thought. *And yet now it isn't just a greathouse he's second in line to inherit, but a kingdom...*

"A prince..." Rodmond said quietly, a bemused little expression on his face. He took a long slow sip of his ale, then said, "I rather think that it should be *you* who's a prince, not me, Elyon." He gave a wry smile. "Just don't let my uncle hear me say it."

Elyon leaned in. "So you think my father should be crowned king?" he enquired. "I take it you weren't aware of all this... that Ellis had named your grandfather his heir?"

Rodmond shook his head. "I had no idea. But then again, I'm not completely surprised either. Ellis Reynar was always an immature king, wasn't he? And your father had lost favour with him these last months. I could see Ellis writing Amron from his line of succession out of spite alone." Rodmond had another sip, then glanced through the crowds toward his uncle, flanked by Sir Taegon and Sir Brontus. "But you know...you might be able to use that if you wished to challenge my grandfather's claim. You could point out that Ellis wasn't in his right mind when he wrote the decree. I'm sure you'd have lots of support. All of East Vandar would be behind you. So would your own men across the North Downs. And you'd have House Amadar too."

He would. Elyon's esteemed grandfather was Lord Brydon Amadar, head of one of the most powerful greathouses, and his mother Kessia Amadar had been the most beloved woman in all the north. That made Elyon half an Amadar himself. And there were other greathouses who'd support the Daecars too in a fight for the crown. Lord Porus Pentar of Redhelm certainly would, giving him the backing of the South Downs as well as the North. Along with the Lakelanders, Riverlanders, and Marshlanders of the east, they'd have enough to challenge the Taynars and their allies. *If,* he thought, *we sought to.* But he nor his father would, he knew. And he was surprised Rodmond was even suggesting it.

He said as much. "Your uncle would flay you living if he heard you speaking like this, Roddy."

Rodmond seemed unconcerned. "My uncle will never know unless you tell him. And he wouldn't touch a hair on my head, anyway. Leastways not until he has a son of his own."

"I don't imagine that'll happen any time soon," Elyon japed. "He'd have to lay with a woman first."

"Quite." Rodmond let out a bark of laughter. The dark circles around his eyes told Elyon he'd not slept much either, and his hair was typically tangled and unkempt. *Hardly princely,* he thought, but Rodmond Taynar had always been a scruffy sort. "So I suppose you've heard the news about King Hadrin and Amilia? Is that what you were talking about when I arrived?"

Elyon nodded. "Sir Mallister was about to profess his love for the princess, I think. Probably best that you intervened before he made too much of a fool of himself."

"And...how do *you* feel about it?" Rodmond pressed. "She was to be your sister-in-law. Now she'll marry that ugly old paper king."

"I'm trying not to think about it, to be honest," Elyon admitted. "Hadrin was once betrothed to my mother, you know? It's why people think he sought to kill my father, and destroy my family. Some sad old vengeance for stealing her away."

"I did hear a rumour about that," nodded Rodmond. "I suppose he gets his prized beauty in the end, though."

"A beauty *and* a crown, the two things he's always coveted." Elyon's skin crawled at the thought. *First my mother, then Amilia, who should by rights have been wed to Aleron by now.*

"There are rumours he killed his father himself," said Rodmond. "Cut King Godrin's throat as he sat in his solar with his pipe and papers." He glanced into the crowds. "Did I overhear Mallister say a man would hand over the keys of his kingdom to marry Amilia? Well, it seems Hadrin would lower himself to patricide and regicide for the honour too."

"At least we can all agree that it's Janilah who truly rules here," Elyon noted. "Not Hadrin."

"*Here*, certainly," nodded Rodmond. "Amilia won't take long to overpower that weaselly wretch. Rasalan was born a queendom, so it makes sense that a woman should rule." He grinned, and took a sup of his ale.

"And in Vandar?"

Elyon watched Rodmond's reaction. The young knight turned his eyes aside, then gave a shrug. "Far as I see it, Janilah would prefer for Ellis to have remained king. The man was a weakling, Elyon. But my grandfather?" He shook his head firmly. "You've met him...you know what Godrik Taynar is like. He's a hard old man, a proper man of the Ironmoors, and has never cowed to anyone. If Janilah wanted to control Vandar, he'd have been far better keeping Ellis on the throne." Elyon rather agreed, unless there was something else Janilah was getting from the bargain. "Anyway," Rodmond went on, "I suppose you can question Sir Nathaniel about it when you see him, if you think something untoward happened to our king. And Sir Gerald and Sir Alyn too, if you like. They were all there when Ellis fell from the balcony, after all. They swore it was an accident, but who knows. Perhaps they're hiding something?"

Clearly Rodmond was enjoying playing devil's advocate, though Elyon was quite sure that he'd get nothing from the three Greycloaks. Sir Gerald and Sir Alyn were both men of the Ironmoors, sworn to House Taynar, and Sir Nathaniel was an Oloran, a longstanding ally to the Taynars. *If Ellis was murdered, none of them will speak of it,* he thought. *Janilah has them all at heel now. He's got the whole bloody north in his pocket...*

He sunk another good portion of his ale, gulping eagerly, and decided to set the topic aside. He was too tired for all this conjecture. *But, there was one thing Rodmond had said*...He looked at him with a frown. "When do you imagine I'll get to question them, anyway?" he asked. "They'll all be returning to Varinar to protect their new king, won't they? And I'll be heading south to defend the coast. Hopefully as soon as possible."

Rodmond shook his head. "We have a certain wedding to get

through first. I'm told that half the lords and ladies in the north will be gathering for it. King Janilah wants to unite us, so far as my uncle Dalton says."

Elyon blasted a sigh. "Isn't this enough." He gestured to the crowds, a great blur of colour and noise. "Look how happy we all are? Look how *united.*" He planted a false smile to his face, and pointed to his lips. "See. Happy faces, Rodmond. Aren't we all so bloody happy."

Rodmond looked at him quizzically. "Are you quite well, Elyon? Been overdoing the roseweed have you?"

The feigned smile slipped from Elyon's lips. "So where's it to be, this wedding?" he grunted. "Ilithor, I'm guessing?"

Rasal royalty typically wed at the holy site of Galaphan's Grounding, at the southeastern tip of Rasalan, between the ribs of the ancient leviathan Galaphan who'd washed ashore there a thousand years ago. The ribs alone were said to be as tall as redwoods, the skull as large as a great stone longhouse. Elyon had always wanted to see it, but knew Janilah would never allow his granddaughter to be wed there among the water gods. *No, it'll be Ilithor,* he knew, *safe and high in the mountains.*

Rodmond confirmed it. "Ilithor is well positioned," he said. "We'll not take long to get there, and once it's all done and dusted, we can all hurry on down south to slay those Agarathi and their dragons." He smiled. "And anyway, don't look so perturbed. It'll give us a chance to complete our recovery. And I imagine your family will come too. Your father and sister and auntie. I know how dear they are to you."

That changed things a little. Elyon longed to see them again, but... "I'm not sure my father would wish to attend," he said. *And he'll be like to murder Janilah if he does,* he thought. Apparently Vesryn wanted that too, so far as he'd said last night. *And me,* he thought. He'd admitted that to Saska when they'd shared their first night in his tent. He'd confided in the girl everything, in fact, every dark secret he'd kept to himself. His thoughts ran to her a moment, wondering where she might be. *On a ship,* he hoped, *fast on her way south. Lancel and Barny will confirm as much as soon as they return...*"My father won't want to watch Hadrin be wed, less to the daughter-in-law he should have had," he elaborated, keeping the rest of his thoughts to himself. "I suppose Lillia and Amara might come, however."

The last he'd heard, Amara, Lillia, and Jovyn his squire had returned to Keep Daecar in Varinar, leaving his father to continue the muster of the North Downs and Daecar banners. It was Amara who'd informed him of that. According to her note, they'd decided that Varinar would be safer than Blackfrost, should they come under attack. The old seat of House Daecar was built mostly of timber, and inadequately provisioned with defensive walls, scorpions and weapons that might slay a dragon. Varinar, on the other hand, was purpose-built to defend against Agarath's winged spawn. Returning there was a wise course.

Still, the whole thing seemed impractical to Elyon. *Weddings during war? What was the point?* As far as he saw it, it was an entirely unnecessary and expensive distraction. *Unless Janilah has some other intention?*

He put the thought aside, weary of the speculations, and decided to do his duty as heir to House Daecar, and mingle. Spotting the small old figure of Lord Donal Paramor nearby, he carved his way through the crowd toward him. At his side was Sir Wallis, his eldest son and heir, dressed in his golden surcoat, and bearing on his chest the merman of his house. Elyon felt a quickening thud in his chest. The music seemed suddenly quieter. The last he'd seen of Lord Paramor had been at the parley, where his third son Sir Brendan had been slain.

"My lord," Elyon said, bowing before the man. "I wanted to come and tell you personally how sorry I am for your loss." He felt the eyes of the nearby nobles and knights on him. "I tried to tell him, Lord Paramor. Sir Brendan...I tried to tell him to retreat, but..." He looked to the figure of Sir Wallis, a man of middling height and build. He was in dyed-blue leather beneath his yellow surcoat, his countenance perfectly pleasant, if plain. "When you called the retreat, Sir Wallis, I tried to tell your brother. He didn't listen. He couldn't hear me. I..." He trailed off.

Sir Wallis gave him a genial smile. "Brendan was hard of hearing," he said, with some measure of courtesy. "You're not to blame for his impairment, Elyon, it was with him since his birth. Nor can you be counted responsible for his lust for the fight. He was always a headstrong man."

His lord father agreed. "Indeed he was." The old man's white-bearded face was in a kind smile, his blue eyes flecked with gold. "You've not been cursing yourself over this, I hope, Elyon? Brendan's death was not of your doing."

"My uncle..."

"Nor your uncle's," said the Rasal lord at once. "I do not blame Vesryn for protecting you, or putting the Sword of Varinar through Brendan's back. My son died by his own hand, Elyon. Deaf or not, he knew the retreat had been called. He merely chose to fight on. And that is not your fault."

No, it was Lord Cedrik Kastor's, Elyon thought, and old Lord Paramor knew that too. Though the parley had been tense, and bitter words had been shared, it was Lord Kastor's bellowing call to 'slay them all' that had sparked the affray, and led to Sir Brendan's death, Sir Rodmond's wounded gut, and the slaying of several Emerald Guards and Suncoats besides, with Sir Mallister's mentor Warren Condor being one of them.

Still, Elyon was grateful for their remarks. "My thanks, my lords," he said, with a bow. "It is some solace that we can move forward, as friends and allies again."

He sought to tend to other wounds after that. Across the hall, animosities were being soothed and rifts patched up, and he thought it best he try to do the same. First he went to Prince Dalton, dropping his head into a bow before him. Dislike Dalton Taynar though he did, he had no intention of widening the breach that had opened up between them. "I hope the difficulties you shared with my uncle will not extend to me, Prince Dalton," he said, giving him the proper respect of his new title. "I have every intention of serving you, as our new First Blade and prince."

Dalton gave him a curt nod. "My thanks, Sir Elyon. I hope the same. Perhaps you might prove it to me somehow?"

"Of course." He paused. "How?"

"By helping me track down your uncle. He has become a severe threat, to me and many others. I warned you all along that he was losing himself to the Sword of Varinar, did I not? This is not how I wished to be proven right, but..." He set his dull dark eyes on him. "Do you know where he's gone?"

"No," Elyon said, without hesitation. "If I knew I would tell you. I have no loyalty to him now."

Dalton's thin black brows lifted up. "Oh?"

I shouldn't have admitted that, Elyon realised. He searched for a suitable lie, then said, "We had a falling out last night, before we gathered in the longhouse. It was why he was absent when you announced the death of King Ellis, and your father's ascent to the throne..."

"And this quarrel? What was it about?"

"Several matters. Among them my relationship with Lady Melany Monsort, of which he never approved. But most of all, I questioned his hold on the Sword of Varinar." He looked into Dalton's beady eyes, hoping he would buy the lie. "I had come to see that you were right, my lord. He didn't take it well. I fear I contributed to his disappearance."

Dalton grunted, then considered that at length. To his flank, the hulking form of Sir Taegon Cargill loomed, some way north of seven feet and layered in lobstered godsteel. Dalton looked up at him, then back at Elyon. "Your uncle's mania will only worsen the longer he is on the run," he said. "Each day he will grow more dangerous. I would have you stay close to me, Sir Elyon. If you do not know where you uncle has gone, so be it, I believe you. But there are other ways you can serve me."

Elyon understood. *He thinks he'll be safer with me near him. That Vesryn won't attack if I'm there.* "I will do as you command," he said, realising he had no choice. He was a Varin Knight and under Dalton's orders. Heir to House Daecar or not, he had no recourse to deny him.

Next, he determined to speak with Lord Cedrik Kastor himself. Ever since arriving in Rasalan, he'd fast hated the man, for myriad reasons. That wouldn't change, but he could lie well enough. *Lies and lies and lies,* he thought. His whole world was full of them. "I am sorry for Sir Griffin," he told him. "I tell you true, Lord Kastor, what happened that night in my tent is something I'll always regret."

Yet it isn't Sir Griffin's death I regret, he knew, *but the fact that I had to send Saska away because of it.* He'd found her in his tent over Sir Griffin Kastor's body, a dagger in her hand dripping blood. And there'd been another body there too, the burly soldier called Borgin whom Saska had slain as well. He wished it hadn't turned out like that. He had ten scars on his back for it, and had been forced to throw Saska into a wagon and have Lancel and Barnibus secret her to the south coast. *Silver and blue,* he thought. She was still in his dreams and waking thoughts alike. *I hope she's safely free of this place. Free of the north forever...*

"In the spirit of peace, I suppose I shall accept your apology, Sir

Elyon," the vile Lord Cedrik Kastor allowed. Around him were his lickspittle lords and knights. The mean old Master of the Moorlands, Lord Gershan, with his hooked nose and crooked back. His captain and commander, Sir Gavin Trent, broad-chested and blustery of voice. Lord Huffort of Rockfall, quietly spoken but imperturbable, with his lantern jaw and short coarse hair, balding on top. "It will all be for nought, however, if my men return with news of this Aramatian spy that you kept hidden in your tent. I've got good Sir Cleon Marsh on the case now, scouring the southern roads and reaches for her. And curious, too...I've been told that two friends of yours among the Varin Knights have been missing ever since that night. Sir Lancel Greymont and Sir Barnibus Warryn." He tapped a finger on his pale lips. "Most curious indeed."

Elyon had expected this eventually. "My uncle sent them away on a private errand, I believe," he said.

"What errand?"

"A private one, and not one he ever told me about. Unfortunately he isn't here to speak of it."

"Most unfortunate, yes, and most convenient too." Cedrik Kastor had a cruel handsome face, with a slim nose, sharp jawline, and high cheekbones. A face Elyon wanted to crush under his fist for the things he and his father had done. "I'll await news from Sir Cleon, then. There are circumstances around my nephew's death that still do not add up. I'll get to the bottom of it eventually, Sir Elyon."

Good luck with that, Elyon thought. He bowed and left him there.

Afterwards, he decided to speak with Prince Rylian. They shared a strong relationship through Elyon's father, but hadn't spoken in some days. Elyon wanted to know what he thought of his daughter's upcoming nuptials. "I suppose a king is a good match for her," he said to the sightly, rusty-bearded Prince of Tukor, as they stood beside a table laden with trenchers of food and flagons of wine, ale, and mead. His sons and some of the younger knights were settling eagerly into a drinking game nearby, and Robbert and Raynald would no doubt seek to stir up a bit of brawling later, as was the Tukoran way.

"I thought your brother was a better match, personally," Rylian said. "I longed to see what a son of Aleron and Amilia might become. He'd have been as Varin reborn; a warrior without equal. There's no stronger blood in the north than that of the Daecars and Lukars, you know."

"I imagine a few of the other greathouses would argue with you there, my lord." Elyon smiled, but sensed some melancholy in the prince. His own marriage to Lady Clarris Kastor was a political match, and had never been a happy one. *Perhaps he wants different for his daughter?* "Amilia will make a fine queen, though, wouldn't you say?" he probed.

Rylian mustered a smile. "She will. She is as her grandfather born. She'll take well to ruling."

Elyon chanced a question then. "Did you know of these plans to wed her to Hadrin? I would expect that you, as Amilia's father, would have been central to such discussions?"

It was a leading question, and Rylian knew it. "You know I didn't, Elyon. And you know my feelings about Hadrin." He closed a fist. "I'll congratulate my father on some fine political manoeuvring when I see him in Ilithor. But beyond that..." He seemed to decide better of furthering that thought. Rylian despised King Hadrin, and all of this... the selling off of his daughter to secure a kingdom...Elyon could see it irked him greatly.

"Your father deserves much praise, my lord. This marriage will secure a lasting peace, and save thousands of lives and months of fighting." That much was at least true. But it didn't change the fact that Rylian had been left out. That was what had cut to the core of him; Janilah's refusal to keep him in his counsel. And that was what Elyon would use. *I will prod and poke,* he thought. *I can scheme as well, Warrior King.*

"As I say, Sir Elyon, my father has manoeuvred the pieces well. And it's clearly a game he excels in. I'll talk with him about it in Ilithor." He took a sip of his ale, and returned with a smile. "You'll be coming too, of course. It'll be your first time to the White City, will it not?"

"The first I'll remember, yes," Elyon said. "I believe my parents took me there once as a toddler, though you were away on campaign at the time. I have always longed to return as an adult."

"Well, we shan't remain here long. I've called for most of my army at the coast to return, and our navy will be sailing up the Sibling Strait, to ferry us across to Tukor. It will expedite the journey, if we don't have to go south via the Links."

"So we'll travel through the Stonehills?" Elyon asked.

"We will. And they're not so stony or hilly as they sound. We'll make good time when we get going. The wedding won't be for some weeks. Plenty of time for the north to gather."

"And the south," Elyon said. He looked into Rylian's proud eyes, brown and swirling green. "As we make merry, the Agarathi make war. I'm unsure of the wisdom in that, my lord."

"Weeks, Elyon, we're only talking weeks. And we'll have all our soldiers and commanders at the forts and castles, defending our borders." He put an arm around his shoulders. "Don't worry so, my boy. The Agarathi are some way from mounting a full attack. And it's quite possible they'll realise the folly in this war and call for peace, now that the north is united."

Maybe that's true, Elyon thought, *but your father won't let that happen.* Janilah never wanted a united north as a deterrent to the south. He wanted it so he could take it for his own. *It's the world he wants,* Elyon knew. *Not just the north. The whole damn world.*

He said none of that, though, and merely smiled and raised his goblet in a toast of peace, as Rylian followed, and then drank long and true. The hall was growing drunk and merry now, a setting Elyon once craved. He'd unruffled a few feathers, taken some of the weight off his back, and began building bridges.

All as a good heir should, he thought. *I wonder if father would be proud?*

2

Janilah

The late King Ellis Reynar's body lay upon a bier in the crypts beneath the Temple of Ilith. It was a temporary resting place for the former King of Vandar, before his body might be transported home to Varinar for burial.

The corpse had been put together as best as the acolytes could, though Janilah couldn't imagine it would have been pleasant work. When he'd thrown poor Ellis from the balcony, the Craven King had met the courtyard below with force enough to explode him. The white stone had been painted red, and chunks of skull and brain were still being found, he'd heard. "The puzzle of his body is incomplete," his natural daughter Cecilia had jested. A tasteless joke, but one to make him smile all the same. He did rather dislike the weaselly Vandarian king.

Princess Lyriss was still sobbing, as she clutched at her mother's waist. Janilah had been kind enough to provide private escort to the two grieving women, though hadn't expected them to linger so long. They'd been standing beside the bier for over an hour now, and the little toothy princess's miserable sobbing hadn't abated once. He sympathised, of course, but his sympathy had its limits. It was *only* Ellis Reynar, after all. A king yes, and a husband and a father. But a weak king, a weak husband, and a weak bloody father.

"My queen." His voice whispered into the silent chapel, as he stood a little way behind them, his old gnarled hands clasped before him among the folds of his heavy black mourning cloak. They were alone; the three of them, and the corpse. "I would counsel we leave your husband to his rest. He will be hearing this from the Eternal Halls, the Hall of Kings. It would be better if he didn't see the princess so stricken."

Queen Elitha Reynar was a rather more sturdy sort than her daughter. She hadn't shed a tear since entering the quiet stone chapel, dimly lit around the sides by candles, but had stood staring at her late husband's ruined body and face with a stoic, solemn expression. "Does the sound of women in grief trouble you so, Janilah?" she asked him, holding her daughter in her arms. She turned to look at him. "My husband is dead. He can neither hear us, nor see us. But if you have other matters to attend to, by all means do leave us. I will take Lyriss from the chamber when her tears run dry, no sooner. I have never considered it healthy to curtail grief, for the sake of convenience."

Janilah held his scorn. Vandarians of high birth weren't prone to showing their emotions freely, a fact that Elitha herself exemplified well. But her daughter had clearly taken after her recreant father. "As you wish, Elitha. I shall say no more, until you wish to depart."

She gave him a blunt nod, and Janilah withdrew a couple of steps into the shadows. His honour demanded that he remain with them until they were ready to leave, having provided escort. So on the wait went. Another ten minutes turned to twenty, and soon enough a further hour had passed. *The candles will have burned down to their wicks if this goes on much longer,* he grumbled to himself, as the tapers flickered about the wall niches and sconces, casting dancing shadows on the walls.

Perhaps this is my penance, he mused, as he endured more of Lyriss's soft weak sobbing and sniffing, and her mother's regular repetitions of 'there there' and 'let it out' and sundry other trite remarks that were intended to give the girl comfort. It was a small price to pay for murdering the man, he supposed, but the longer it went on, the more he wished he'd thrown the princess from the balcony too.

Eventually, when it seemed as though he might just spend the rest of his days down here in the dimness, Lyriss gave out a final great sniff, wiped her nose and eyes, and then nodded up to her mother. "I'm OK now, Mother," she said. "I…I think I'm ready to go."

Well praise the gods, Janilah thought.

"Are you certain, my sweetling?" asked the queen. "I'm sure if you wish to stay longer, good King Janilah will allow it." She glanced over. "Would you not, gracious king?"

Janilah bowed his head. "Of course," he said, through gritted teeth. "Do take as long as you need."

Lyriss chewed on her lower lip, and took another look at her father. The only solace was that his face hadn't been too badly wrecked by the fall. He'd landed on his back, shattering the base of his skull, and snapping every bone in his body all the while, but that face…that weaselly little face…well, it had managed to escape mostly unscathed. "I did have more stories," the horsey-faced princess said, as her mother stroked at the tangled nest of frizzy hair atop her head. "There was the time he took me onto Lake Eshina, and we fished for hours and hours. I spoke to a merman that day. One of the flipper folk. It was a great day."

"I remember that day too, my little sweet. You were so very excited." The queen played along, though Janilah was starting to feel that she was doing all this just to torture him. "Was there anything else? Any other stories you'd like to remember?"

That was the Vandarian custom, to tell stories of the dead in order to better remember them. Sometimes they didn't even need to be verbal. Lyriss hadn't been speaking much, after all. She'd mumbled occasionally, but mostly her stories were in her head, as she stood and thought of the fond times she'd shared with her father, and no doubt Queen Elitha had been doing the same. It all derived from how the Varin Knights honoured their dead. When a Son of Varin fell in battle, his brothers would tell tales of his valour and gallantry, the great duels and battles and victories he'd won. It was all to honour his memory and persuade Varin to offer him a better seat at his Table.

And one day I'll have a Table of my own, Janilah thought. King Galin Lukar had been promised that when he'd journeyed to Vandar's Tomb over three centuries ago. *Win the War Eternal, and I'll raise you as divine,* the spirit of Vandar had told him. Galin had gone on to conquer Tukor and win himself a kingdom, and for three hundred years since, his line had been trying to fulfil his vision. *And now I hold the torch. Now I light the way.* Janilah had always thought of himself as Galin's true heir, the only one to fully share in his vision. *It was I who found Ilith's ancient forge. I who uncovered the secret of the blades. I who worked tirelessly to gather the north beneath my wing, stoke the flames of war with the south. Me, me, me,* he thought. *And one day I'll be rewarded for it all. One day I'll be divine...*

"Good king?" Janilah withdrew from his thoughts and found Queen Elitha standing before him, wrapped all in mourning black. "We are ready to leave, Janilah." She peered at him. "You seem lost to a thought. Recalling memories of my noble husband, I hope?"

"Of course." His voice was a little hoarse. "I have many happy memories of Ellis." *Throwing him off the balcony, in particular*, he was sorely tempted to say. "Sharing his company these last weeks was a joy, before his untimely passing."

"I'm sure." Elitha turned to the low stone door. The ancient chapel was shallow of ceiling, though the halls above within the Temple of Ilith were grand and capacious, supported by white fluted columns and decorated with grand statues and depictions of the gods in tones of gold and silver and white. "Well, shall we? You can tell us of your fondest memories of my husband on the way."

He led the way out, trying to muster a valued memory of Ellis Reynar as he went...something...anything he could pass as being fond. It was a struggle. So much as he appreciated Elitha's stolidness and stoicism, he had felt quite the contrary for her spineless little husband. He was craven, witness, weak and servile, and throwing him from that balcony had been a pleasure. *A dark mark on my honour, yes, but a pleasure all the same. And not something that could have been avoided*, he knew. Godrik Taynar had made quite sure of that.

"I recall Ellis as a young prince, when he visited Ilithor with his father Storris," Janilah finally said, as they worked up the stone steps, moving toward the upper chambers. "He was so eager and full of life; I liked him immediately. I took him for a walk upon the bridges around the palace, and spoke of the towers and keeps, the castles and temples and courtyards, and all the great kings of the past for whom they were named. He was a curious young man, and turned out to be a wise young king. His passing is a wound to the north. One of so many we have suffered."

And how many have you inflicted? was the question he saw in Queen Elitha's eyes. His lies weren't fooling her, he could see that plainly enough, though if she had suspicions she wasn't likely to voice them.

No, it is her daughter she lives for now, her daughter whom she wishes to protect, and she'll keep her mouth shut to ensure that happens. They walked along for a few silent moments, sharing their private exchange through a series of polite smiles and little glances. *She is a dutiful mother, first and foremost, and will be seeking a good match for the girl. Well, perhaps I might just give her one...*

He took the queen aside when they reached the main temple chamber, bordered by statues and busts that filled the walls all the way up to the high vaulted ceiling. There were more statues within the alcoves too, accessed through pillared arches. Each was of a god or spirit or saint, and people were on their knees before them, praying by candlelight. "Your daughter is a sensitive girl," Janilah said, as Princess Lyriss was ushered away by an acolyte. The Greycloak commander, Sir Nathaniel Oloran, awaited her near the exit to the hall. "Perhaps I might help brighten her spirit. A betrothal to a prince, perhaps, to give her some succour?"

"Which one?" Elitha asked him instantly. "Robbert or Raynald?"

Janilah smiled at her forthrightness. "Which would you prefer?"

"Robbert, obviously. He will be king after Rylian."

"Quite. And Robbert it is."

The queen raised her eyes. They were about the only attractive thing about her, clear and sharp and full of wit. Her face was otherwise sow-like, with an upturned nose and ample cheeks, and a little too much chin. "You'd allow it?" she asked. "Even now, after..."

"Ellis's death does little to change things, Elitha. Lyriss will remain a princess, always, and Reynar has always been a great and storied house. A betrothal would serve us both, I feel, and give all of Vandar something to celebrate after the tragic fall of their king."

Elitha expressed a contemptuous smile. "I am not certain that our *new* king will be quite so happy, Janilah. Godrik Taynar will see it as a slight. I'm sure he expects Robbert to be wed to a maid of his house..."

"Who?" challenged Janilah. "Godrik's line is empty of maids of eligible age. His only living spawn is his son Dalton, who is himself childless, with no daughters to his name. And the next generation of the main Taynar branch is equally sparse. Dalton had a brother Grayson who perished after the war, but he had no daughters either, only a son, Sir Rodmond, who is Dalton's heir so far as I understand it. Now I'm sure there are girls of appropriate age within the lesser

Taynar branches, but they're hardly suitable for a prince like Robbert, are they? But Lyriss? She's perfectly suited to wed my grandson."

"Well I'm glad you think so. Though I will have to convince Lyriss that she isn't in love with Wendell Taynar first." She smiled up at him with that piggy face of hers. "A childish infatuation, and no more," she explained. "The boy is of a lesser Taynar line, so no one shall care when he's cast aside, and I've been reliably informed that Prince Robbert is most gallant and fine of face. Lyriss will forget all about Wendell when she looks upon your grandson, I'm sure."

Janilah forced a smile to his face. *Why is this lesser Taynar boy even being mentioned? Marriage has nothing to do with love,* he wanted to inform the queen. *And love between children isn't love at all.* "They will have an opportunity to meet prior to Amilia's wedding," he told her. *And if anyone will need convincing of this betrothal, it'll be Robbert not your horse-faced daughter,* he thought bitterly. Robbert was indeed fine of face, gallant, gifted, and second in line to the Tukoran throne besides. And who exactly was Lyriss Reynar? *This woman should be begging me for this favour, not quibbling over some lovestruck whelp.*

"And when is this wedding to take place exactly?" she asked. "I feel it would be rather insensitive to sidestep into such festivities so soon after my husband's passing. We must observe the mourning rites, Janilah."

"And we will. The wedding won't take place for some weeks. King Hadrin still needs to travel from Thalan, and my son needs to return from Harrowmoor."

"Of course," she said. "I quite forget that Rylian is the father of the bride. You do cast a shadow, Janilah, that makes one blind to those who stand behind you."

He considered the remark, then said, "My shadow offers shade, Elitha, that guards against the *southern* sun, and the glare from Agarath grows particularly fierce of late. Those who'd rather not be burned do tend to fall in line behind me."

She seemed to like that, judging by that porky smile. "Yes indeed. And I would hope that Lyriss and I will be afforded the same protections when we join your family?"

"You'll have all the protections you need," he told her, because that was what she craved most of all. With King Ellis dead, she and Lyriss would lose the protection of the Greycloaks as soon as King Godrik

Taynar arrived. "Lyriss will come and live here in the palace, and you will be welcome to join her. I will permit you to return to Varinar after Amilia's wedding, to handle affairs with Ellis, but after that you must return. Ilithor will become your home, Elitha. And I would expect the full support of House Reynar, and your banners, should my position ever come under attack."

"Attack? Now don't tell me you live in fear of a coup, Janilah."

"I fear no such thing. These are standard terms of an alliance, that is all."

"I see. Though it does seem to me that kings are dying with alarming regularity of late. I suppose that alone is enough to make one paranoid."

It might, he thought, *if I hadn't been the architect of most of them.* But he got the sense that she knew that already. "House Lukar and House Reynar have a long history," he merely said. "This will be but another weave in our tapestry..."

"And those terms go both ways, I take it? Should our lands ever come under attack, you will of course send men in support?"

"You'll have our full protection," he repeated. "No one will trouble your house once the betrothal has been announced."

Not that it was truly her house. Elitha Reynar was born an Oloran, and that was another reason for him to secure her support. The Taynars and Olorans were long term allies of one another, and Janilah had made sure to side himself with them both. So far the Taynars had gotten the better of the bargain, so it was important to continue to sweeten the deal for the Olorans where he could. This would help in that regard, and would secure Reynar support as well, a traditional Daecar ally. Ellis had already begun to pull away from the Daecars, after his well documented tiff with Lord Amron, and this would finalise that arrangement. The weaker the Daecars became, the better, so far as he was concerned. They remained the most likely to derail his plains. *And that I'll not allow.*

"I would have you wait to tell your daughter until a later date," Janilah went on, as he turned and began leading Elitha through the temple. "Out of respect for your husband." The acolytes all bowed as they passed, wrapped in black robes opposed to their typical white. Some of the other worshippers and mourners present had wreathed themselves in similar raiment, and would be permitted visitations with the king's corpse now that the queen and princess had left.

"That would be best, yes," the dowager queen replied. "I will give her a few days to grieve her father first. By then I would hope Prince Robbert will be on his way here."

"They'll not be long at Harrowmoor. I would anticipate them arriving in a fortnight or so. Most should be gathering by that time. I expect the nuptials to occur within the month."

"That will allow plenty of time for mourning," said Elitha. "Very good, my king. It appears you have it all figured out."

He did, leastways the matters he could control. But there were others beyond his grasp that remained frustratingly unresolved. "I only hope this will soften the terrible blow you've suffered, Elitha. We can discuss the details later, but for now..."

"Say no more. You have other matters to attend to, of course. Do see to them, Janilah. It looks like Sir Owen has been awaiting your return."

She gestured to Sir Owen Armdall, one of his six sworn swords, who was standing patiently in the courtyard dressed in his mantle of brown, white, and green over glittery godsteel mail. As Elitha took Lyriss off to tend to their private affairs, escorted by Sir Nathaniel and the Greycloaks under his charge, Janilah stepped over to join Sir Owen. The young knight was tall, lean, and unnervingly loyal, as with the other five who comprised his personal guard. He shifted uncomfortably as the king arrived. "What is it, Sir Owen?" Janilah asked.

"News, my lord, from Harrowmoor," the sworn sword said. "I wanted to inform you earlier, but...you were in the crypts, and..."

"Tending to the queen and princess, yes. What news do you refer to?"

As the knight prepared to speak, a small host of nobles came shuffling past them, making for the grand arched temple doors, each of them wreathed in black. Janilah turned to face them as they shambled by, accepting their bows and words of greeting, and giving back as appropriate. Only once their footsteps were echoing through the cavernous temple interior did he turn back to Sir Owen. "Is this something to be discussed privily?" he asked. The sworn sword nodded. "Then come with me."

They made their way from the front courtyard, and into the

adjoining passages that linked the Temple of Ilith to the palace, high up in the western reaches of the city. Within a few moments they'd found themselves within a private balconied chamber, giving ranging views across Ilithor. A snowy wind was blowing, loud enough to drown their voices to anyone who might pass, though these passages were commonly quiet and rare-used. "Go ahead, Sir Owen. Speak."

Sir Owen shifted his weight. "It...it seems that Vesryn Daecar has gone missing, sire," he said.

Janilah's left eye flinched. Vesryn Daecar going missing wasn't unto itself a problem, but there was more to it, he knew. "And the Sword of Varinar?"

Sir Owen swallowed, the apple in his neck going up and down. "It appears he took it with him, my lord. It's thought he learned he was to be stripped of his rank and office and abandoned his order and duty. Search parties have been mustered to find him. He'll not evade capture long."

Janilah turned away, setting his hands to the cold stone balcony edge. He gripped so hard his knuckles whitened, nails all but digging into the marble. *First a nephew, now an uncle,* he thought, his mind conjuring a horrid image of the boy Jonik, and the betrayer Vesryn, standing side by side, laughing. *I knew I couldn't trust him. I should never have put the Sword of Varinar in his hand.* "Do you have the note with you, Sir Owen?"

He heard the knight shuffle forward and hand him the scroll. The broken seal had the markings of Lord Lewyn Huffort of Rockfall, whose third son, Sir Edwyn, was another of Janilah's sworn swords. "This was sent to Sir Edwyn?" he asked.

"Yes, sire," answered Sir Owen. "The crow arrived from Harrowmoor an hour ago. Sir Edwyn was scheduled to stand watch beneath the steps to Tyrith's forge, so passed the note to me to deliver to you." He paused. "I wanted to inform you immediately, but didn't feel it appropriate to interrupt you in the crypts. I'm sure the blade will be retrieved in time."

"Are you, Sir Owen?" Janilah turned to him. His sworn swords were privy to large parts of his plans, but weren't permitted to give him counsel lest he asked for it. "How are you so sure?"

Sir Owen dropped his gaze. "Apologies, sire. I was only..."

"Trying to help, yes." Janilah took a breath. There was no sense in taking this out on Sir Owen, who'd always been stalwart in his support, as the others had. "And I'm sure you're right. But do not underestimate Vesryn Daecar. A cornered animal will bare its teeth, Sir Owen, and Vesryn's fangs are long with that blade to hand." *It gives him fangs and claws both, and a mind to stir violence,* he thought to himself. He looked back at the knight. "When are you set to gather in your council chambers?"

The Six had their own personal chambers where they arranged the running of the palace and city guard, as well as the other duties Janilah gave them. "Not for two nights, my lord."

"You'll meet this evening," Janilah commanded. "It's paramount that you reconsider your security protocols in light of this. Vesryn may seek to strike at me. Ask yourself how he might do so. Does he know of our secret routes? Could he infiltrate the city, the palace, without our knowledge?" He stared into the man's blue-green eyes. "Security must be watertight as we near my granddaughter's wedding. I'll not have Vesryn Daecar interfere. Make this a priority, Sir Owen. I trust you and the others to see it done."

"Of course, sire." Sir Owen stood straight and tall in his godsteel mail and multi-coloured mantle, his dual longswords at his hips. Their hilts were shaped as tree trunks for the Oak of Armdall, the crest of his house. He was perhaps the finest of all his sworn swords in skill, though all were much alike. *But if Vesryn comes?* Janilah felt a ripple of something approaching worry. *No matter how tight my grip becomes, there is always something that slips through my fingers.* The boy Jonik had gone as far south as south could go, and might Vesryn do the same? *Or worse, sink the Sword of Varinar to the seas, or toss it down a chasm, and hide it from me forever...*

That fear was enough to break a cold sweat upon his forehead. It would disrupt and cripple all his plans. *If a single blade should be lost...* He could hardly consider it. He had the Mistblade, had bought the Windblade for a crown, and had Gerrin chasing after the Nightblade. The Frostblade's location was in the Book of Thala, he was sure of it, and that was fast approaching in the custody of Sir Kevyn Bolt. But this he'd not expected. This could ruin it all.

With the letter still in his grasp, he quickly ran his eyes across Lord Huffort's words. The Lord of Rockfall was currently serving in Lord Kastor's northern army, though was a powerful figure in his own right, and had a great deal of influence across the east of Tukor. By his account, Vesryn's armour was missing too, which would make him all the more difficult to subdue. *But not impossible.* "The best foil to a First Blade has always been the bow," he said to Sir Owen. "The advantage of the Sword of Varinar is that it can cut through anything, so range is your ally." He looked out over the balcony. "Station your best bowmen around the palace grounds, entrances and exits in particular. Crossbowmen too. Make sure they all have a full consignment of godsteel tipped bolts and arrows. It takes only one to drive through a breastplate or helm."

"Very good, my lord."

Janilah returned to his chambers at that, working his way to the highest reaches of the palace where his personal apartments were situated. Dalton Taynar would be in charge of the search for Vesryn, but that wouldn't do. *He'd been foolish enough to let him escape with the Sword of Varinar in the first place. Why should I trust him to mend the mistake?*

When he reached his solar, he found his bastard daughter Cecilia already there. "You do get around, Cecilia," he said. "Are you here for a reason, or merely to gossip?"

"Is gossip not a good enough reason, Father?" she tittered, clinging to a flute of sapphire wine. "I was interested to hear how it went with Ellis, is all. I hear you were in the crypts for over an hour. Does the good king not begin to smell yet?"

"The chapel is well stocked with fragrant candles," he told her. "The acolytes know how to fight off the reek of a rotting corpse."

"Of course." She was perched on the window seat, with views over the city and mountains. There were few finer vantages than up here to take in the wonders of Ilithor. "I spoke with Amilia earlier. She seems to be coming around to the idea of this marriage."

"For which I thank you." Cecilia had helped to make Amilia see the benefits of the match. Lady Melany Monsort had also been tasked with the same, though didn't have Cecilia's silver tongue. "Amilia will have a fortnight to brace herself before Hadrin arrives," the king continued. "Once he's put an heir in her, she can forgo any further duties to the man."

"And if he's not capable of...*performing*? I've heard alarming reports of Hadrin's infecundity, Father."

"From where?"

"Here and there."

"Rumours are of little value to me," Janilah said, as he drew out quill and parchment from a drawer in his desk. "We'll find out soon enough whether Hadrin can sire an heir. And if he cannot, there are ample men who'd happily fill in for him."

"Many and more, yes. Half the men in the north would be most delighted to open Amilia's legs." She grinned. "Was this your plan all along?"

He looked up at her, as she preened at the window seat, wrapped up all in black wool and fur. With one hand she held her wine, and with the other toyed with a tress of hair, curling it about her finger. "It was always an option," he admitted. "But no, I would prefer Amilia's child be of Hadrin's blood, and a son preferably. Hadrin is direct of Thala's line, and has the power to command the Eye of Rasalan. Such a thing has its uses."

"That is terribly long-term thinking, Father. I've heard that Hadrin himself is too doltish to command the Eye. If you wish to make use of that power, you'll be waiting for Amilia's spawn to come of age. That is some way off."

"By which time I'll be dead." He could see that was what she was thinking, and she wasn't wrong either. Janilah was half way through his sixties and not likely to live long enough to watch his great-grandchild grow tall. But that didn't matter. He was securing the future of his line. "I want this house to rule for a thousand years once I'm gone," he told her. "Tukor, Rasalan, all the north and south besides."

"A bold ambition, to be sure, but a worthy one for a man like you."

He regarded her a moment. "But one you believe I'll fail to achieve?"

"I didn't say..."

"You didn't need to. It's written on your face, no matter how well you try to hide it." He stared at her. "You doubt me? That I'll gather the Blades?"

"The boy Jonik. My...my son..."

"Will be caught in time, and the Nightblade retrieved. I have the Mistblade. Taynar will hand the Windblade to me when he arrives. The Book of Thala draws near, Cecilia..."

"And you're certain the Frostblade's location will be hidden therein?"

"It must be." That sounded too uncertain. *Too much like faith,* he thought. But it was all he had. No other scroll or book or piece of parchment pointed to its location. "My scholars will be scouring the tome as we speak. They will provide report when they return with Sir Kevyn. I expect them to have a location for me."

"And Dalton Taynar will hand over the Sword of Varinar willingly, you suppose? He is the new First Blade, is he not?"

Janilah turned his eyes down to his blank parchment, and dipped his quill into the ink pot. "A hiccup on that front, and one I am seeking to resolve." He began penning his letter to Lord Huffort, until Cecilia's expected query interrupted him.

"What hiccup?"

"The Sword of Varinar has gone missing. Vesryn Daecar has taken it." He spoke in a perfunctory way, and continued writing. "He disappeared last night, I'm told. I'm writing to Lord Huffort to make finding him a priority. He's best placed to take charge of the search."

Cecilia shifted forward in her velvet-cushioned seat. "But surely the Vandarians are already doing that?"

"They are, though I don't trust them to see it done. Dalton Taynar let Vesryn escape from under his nose. He is a liability, Cecilia, and as ever I must oversee matters myself. Lord Huffort has several thousand of his own men at Harrowmoor, serving beneath Kastor banners. With the war won he can send his best men on the hunt. The more I put to this task the better."

"You're afraid he might come here?" Cecilia saw.

Afraid. Janilah didn't like the word. "I have nothing to fear of Vesryn Daecar. My concern is that he'll hide the Sword of Varinar from me, and make sure I never find it. He knows I seek the Blades. He might consider concealing the sword a more subtle vengeance than coming here to slay me with it."

He continued writing the letter, and ignored the rest of the questions Cecilia posed. Eventually she gave up speaking and relaxed back into her cushioned window seat until he was done. Once finished he folded and sealed the letter and summoned Sir Owen to take it to the rookery. As soon as the knight was gone, Cecilia chanced another query. "And if Lord Huffort's men should find Vesryn first?"

"I've ordered them to take his head."

She raised her eyes to that. "Is that wise? The Vandarians will feel aggrieved. Vesryn is theirs to punish."

Janilah almost laughed. It was hardly a concern. "No one will care. If the Knights of Varin are first to find him, they can do with him as they please, so long as Dalton Taynar brings me that blade, as his father promised he would." He gave her a quick look. "And I suppose you have cautioning counsel to that as well?"

"Well, I would imagine it less than certain that Prince Dalton would happily pass you the blade, given the struggles you have had with Vesryn. And..."

"And your son, yes. Struggles that I'll soon overcome."

"And if the Vandarians should learn what you're doing?"

"The Taynars know what I'm doing. They rule Vandar now. Godrik *will* hand me the Windblade, and Dalton the Sword of Varinar, lest Lord Huffort finds it for me first."

"The Taynars aren't all of Vandar, Father. If others should find out..."

"Then what?" he grunted, sitting rigid at his desk. "What exactly do you imagine they can do to me, Cecilia? Raise an army against me? Who? The Daecars and their allies? During wartime with the south? If the Vandarians are going to quarrel over anything, it'll be their throne and who should rightfully sit it. But they'll do no such thing until the south has been subdued, by which point none of that will matter. So stop fretting. I enjoy your counsel, and even value it at times, but when it turns to cynicism and these carping concerns, I find myself wearying of you." He looked her in the eye. "Now I'm sure you've got other matters to busy yourself with. And I've got more letters to write. Leave me."

She slipped from the window seat and set down her flute of wine. "As you wish, my lord. Mayhaps I'll pay the king's corpse a visit. I could do with a little giggle after this."

"Be respectful, Cecilia," he warned. "If you go down to the crypts, hide that bloody smirk. I had to do so for an entire hour. I'm sure you can last a few minutes."

"And how onerous that must have been for you, Father. I will of course try my best."

With those words, she fluttered from the room, leaving Janilah to his letters, and the ruling of the north.

3

Lythian

The skies were a heavy sheet of ashen grey, too thick for the sun to pierce. Beyond the hillside the valleys rolled into the mists, clad in fir and larch, weeds and sedge. Captain Lythian Lindar looked out to the southwest as the afternoon drained away, his eyes set deep and true into the distance, his ancestral blade Starslayer clutched between his fingers.

"You believe all this?" Borrus Kanabar asked him, standing at his side. Both men had been tended of their latest cuts and bruises, clad in boiled leather and robes of dark grey wool. Only the day before, they'd been facing their deaths in the Pits of Kharthar. Now they stood here, hundreds of miles away, within the company of outlaws and knights, lords and princes driven by a single quest.

"I'm not sure," Lythian answered, his voice hoarse and dry. After weeks of starvation and dehydration they were being carefully weaned back onto solid foods and liquids under Kin'rar Kroll's dutiful care. "I have never taken Kin'rar for a man of fanciful thoughts, and Marak is as pragmatic as they come. If they have bought into this..."

"Tethian's mad as his bloody father," Borrus cut in. They were standing alone and could speak plainly. Both men had been given the morning and afternoon to consider their course. To join Prince Tethian of Agarath, or call upon Lord Marak's oath of honour to return them home to Vandar. Borrus was clearly leaning toward the latter.

But me? Lythian wondered. He'd dreamed last night that all the world was burning, and hadn't stopped thinking about it throughout the day. It had been with him since he woke, cold and stiff and huddled beside Borrus in the ruins of the old castle here in the wilderness of the Western Neck. It had been on his mind as Kin'rar brought balms and bandages and a physician to tend them. They had spoken with Prince Tethian again that morning, and it had been with him then too.

"Maybe," Lythian finally said. "But Marak and Kin'rar and all the others here? It isn't madness that drives them all, Borrus. They truly believe in it."

That Eldur is alive, he thought. That was their purpose, to raise the demigod from the dead. Tethian believed he'd been entombed in the Wings over three millennia ago, going there to die with his dragons. And yet he hadn't died, so far as the prince said. "He lives on, in a state of suspension," Tethian had told them earlier that morning, once they'd been given a chance to rest and recover after their turbulent rescue from Eldurath. "He awaits us, my friends. We will bring him back together, so he might bring the world to balance. The Soul of Agarath and the Heart of Vandar. The old gods live *through* them, and the Renewals happen *because* of them. I told you last night...the gods *are* war. If we are to end the War Eternal, the Soul and Heart must be controlled. Only Eldur can command the Bondstone. Only the heir of Varin can command the Heart of Vandar."

Lythian had so many questions to all that. "The Heart of Vandar was split," he'd said. "The Five Blades...most of them are lost or stolen. The Mistblade and the Frostblade...no one knows where they are. And the Nightblade...it's been taken." Only the Sword of Varinar and the Windblade were safely kept, the former in the hands of Vesryn Daecar, newly serving First Blade, they'd heard, and the latter safe in the Steelforge vaults.

But Tethian had merely smiled. "They will come together," he'd said. "It is foretold. The Blades will be combined, as one, and the Heart of Vandar restored."

"Foretold? By whom?" Borrus had demanded.

"Pullio, Wise Master of Highport," said Tethian. "He lived almost a thousand years ago. I have long dedicated myself to his teachings. And others since. Quarl the Blind of Videnia wrote of the balance too. Of the Heart and the Soul, Vandar and Agarath, and the balance that must be sought to end the War Eternal. That was six centuries past. And the famed Skylady of Loriath, Misha the Magnificent, who uncovered much truth during her rise from humble to highborn during the Days of Dread."

Lythian had heard of the Skylady of Loriath, but not the others. "And which of them spoke of Eldur living in suspended animation beneath the Wings?" he'd queried.

"All." Tethian smiled, relaxed and warm. "And others besides have told of it, my own master Sotel Dar among them, who you will shortly meet. All have shaped my teachings, and my purpose. They have sharpened my resolve like an axe on a whetstone. Quarl the Blind wrote that the gods had never truly fallen, that they lived through the parts of themselves that they left behind. He had no eyes to see, but he saw more than most. And Pullio the Wise saw even more. For eight decades he read and wrote and preached of all he'd found. But history does not recall him. In his time he was prominent, but now much of his wisdom has been ignored and expunged from the record. It was not what the kings and lords of Agarath wished to hear. Peace with the north? An end to the war? No, my friends." Tethian shook his head. "No, to most here that is unpalatable. And is it not the same for you?"

"There's been more peace between our kingdoms than war," Borrus had said to that. "This'll be what? The Twenty Fifth Renewal? In almost three and a half thousand years. These wars don't last a hundred years each, Prince Tethian. A few years at most, and sometimes no more than months. We're at peace a lot more than we're at war."

That was true, of course. The longest Renewals might last for a decade or more, but most were a lot shorter, and in between, peace was sewn and sought. But never for long. Never for good. Tethian said as much. "We seek to end the cycle forever," he told them. "For this the Heart and Soul must be controlled, and peace sued between those who master them."

"Eldur and the heir of Varin?" Borrus tried not to scoff. "You say these augurs of yours wrote and spoke of Eldur's fate, but what of this heir? I have heard nothing of him, I'll confess. King Lorin had no children when that kraken dragged him down to the depths, leastways none that I've ever heard of. Pray tell, good prince, how you know of Varin's heir when we, Varin Knights as we are, do not."

Tethian smiled. "I will refer again to the teachings of my mentors and guides, for they have always been more wise than I. Each spoke of the rise of Varin's heir, and the balance that must be struck. But who this heir is, I do not know. As with the Blades, he will come forward in time." He smiled again. "It is foretold."

Borrus hadn't looked convinced by any of that, though Lythian was more inclined to listen. He'd mulled on everything Tethian had said throughout the morning and afternoon and now, as he stood with Borrus on the hilltop, looking out over the wilderness, it was time for him - for both of them - to come to a decision. "What should we do?" he asked, staring to the undulating hills, each depression between them filled with a soupy grey mist. "Would it not be better that we have one hand on the reins, Borrus? If we leave, we'll have no way to control what happens."

"Eldur's dead, Lythian," Borrus asserted. He refused to believe otherwise. "This is a fool's errand, and these men are a bunch of unctuous lickspittles, following Tethian blindly like this Quarl he so revers. I don't imagine Marak believes a word of it. He was always devoted to Dulian and now he's here to protect his son. That's it."

"And Kin'rar?"

Borrus flung out a hand. "Who bloody knows? Kin'rar never made mention of all this when he plotted to murder Tavash, did he? Let's be honest, he's got nowhere else to go, now that he's been branded a traitor. They're probably hoping they can convince Tethian to give up on this folly. Or more likely they're just humouring him." He nodded at that. "Yes, that's it. They'll go with him to the Wings, find nothing, and then convince Tethian to take the crown instead. I'll bet both Marak and Kin'rar are hoping for just that, to put Tethian on the throne where he belongs."

"Then might it not be better that we stay and help? I'm sure they could use a couple of Varin Knights if they're going to overthrow King Tavash. And you'll have your share of Agarathi blood."

"I've had my share and more. And I've had enough of working with these Agarathi too. Didn't work out too well the last time, did it? Tomos is dead, Lythian. We need to go home and report what happened to Lord Pentar, if nothing else. He deserves to know what happened to his son."

"He'll find out soon enough. We can make more of a difference here, Borrus."

"You believe that? Truly? Look around you, Lythian. We were abandoned to that bloody dragon-cell for how many weeks? Starved and humiliated, and forced to watch Tomos die. Why didn't they come sooner? Why didn't they break us from our cell?"

Lythian didn't have much of an answer to that.

"Because they don't really care, not about you or me, and certainly not about Tomos," Borrus went on. He flung out an arm. "And what they're planning to do with us, the gods only know. I sense something sinister here, Lythian."

Lythian disagreed. "I trust both Marak and Kin'rar," he said. "And we've been given a choice to leave, if we wish it. There's nothing sinister at play, Borrus, you're just being paranoid. Prince Tethian only wishes for us to be united, as he has said. He wants us to help him find this heir of Varin, no doubt."

"*Heir of Varin*," Borrus repeated in a scoff. "Now don't get me started on that. King Lorin *had no children*, Lythian. That line is broken."

"We can't know that for sure. Perhaps Lorin sired a child in secret? He was known to have rich appetites, Borrus, for wine and war and women most of all. Who's to say he didn't have a son?"

"*Me*. I bloody well am, Lythian. If he had a son he'd have to be at least forty years old by now. Where the hell has he been hiding all these years?"

"I don't know."

"No, you don't, and nor does Tethian by the sounds of it. You say he wants us to be united in this, but I say we're just being used."

"I disagree. Our support would be symbolic."

"Our support, yes. Our support in unleashing a terror. Eldur, Lythian. *Eldur*! The name's a curse in the north, one to give children nightmares, and you want to help raise him from the dead? No...it'll be our undoing, the undoing of all the north. This is nothing but a bloody trick. End the War Eternal?" He scoffed loudly. "No, Tethian wants to *win* it."

"That isn't true, Sir Borrus." They turned and found Prince Tethian emerging from the castle ruins of the old bailey, wreathed in his crimson cloak emblazoned with the ancient crest of Eldur; a black dragon head encircled by eight fiery rings. His youthful tan face was formed to a handsome smile. "I have explained my purpose, and now I will have your decision. I must apologise for interrupting, and overhearing, but it would seem to me that you, Sir Borrus, are of a mind to leave this place?"

Borrus cleared his throat, and straightened himself out. "I didn't mean to insult you, Prince Tethian."

"Of course not. You have suffered and are quite entitled to speak your mind." Tethian gave a good humoured laugh. "Your thoughts are those shared by most, I would say. Do not apologise for them. I should not have intervened without warning."

Behind Tethian, Skylord Ulrik Marak marched, mantled in a dark crimson cloak over his Body of Karagar armour. Skymaster Kin'rar Kroll followed, grey-caped to match Neyruu's graceful silver tones. With them was a woman, and one Lythian immediately recognised. He'd been told she was in camp, but hadn't yet had a moment to see her. "You know my cousin, Talasha," Prince Tethian said.

The woman was wrapped in red, and smiling elegantly, olive-skinned and inky haired. That hair was a luscious swirl of curls, twisting past her ears and neck and shoulders. For a moment Lythian stared, taking in the shape of her full lips and mouth, the frame of her soft rounded jaw, her burnished brown eyes that glowed with flecks of red. He'd met her only the once, at a garden party in Eldurath, but she'd left her mark on him, warning him of her brother, Tavash, and the hold he had on the king.

"So *this* is Talasha," Borrus said. He gave Lythian a look. "Your beauty comes afore you, Princess."

"So kind of you to say, Sir Borrus. I recall seeing you in the terrace gardens of Eldurath, before all this horror unfolded, though it is no surprise that you didn't see me. Your attentions were being drawn elsewhere, after all." She teased a smile. "Many pretty girls in Eldurath joined you in your bed, I'm told."

"We were well hosted...at first." Borrus dropped his head into a bow. "But Lythian sullied himself with no such sin, I assure you. He is the best of us, we always say."

"The best of *all* the Varin Knights?" she asked, sending Lythian a quick smile. "How impressive."

"In matters of honour, yes, I would say so," said Borrus. "As you can imagine, it sat ill with him when he was asked to murder your brother. It sat ill with us all." He gave Marak and Kin'rar a hard look.

"Tavash is of no consequence," Prince Tethian said to that. "His time atop the dragon-skull throne will not last long."

Lythian was still looking at Talasha. "When did you leave the city, my lady?"

Kin'rar gave answer. "I fetched her the night our plot to kill Tavash failed, for fear she would be considered a part of our collusions. It would not have been safe for her in Eldurath after that."

That was putting it lightly. Tavash was rumoured to have murdered his own mother, and had been behind the murder of his uncle, King Dulian, too. Killing his sister seemed perfectly likely for a kinslayer such as he.

"Tavash has always loved me fondly," Talasha said in that smooth sultry voice of hers. "But I thought he loved our mother too, before he threw her from the balcony. And your father, Tethian, before he had his throat cut to the bone. In the end, it was the throne he loved most dear. Let them share in one another's embrace, while they can. It will be a short dalliance, as my cousin says."

The daylight was starting to fade, a blush of pink and purple sinking into the deep grey clouds out west. Through a rare breach the sun shone down, as though illuminating the way forward. Tethian didn't miss it. "Eldur calls us," he said piously, turning to look that way. "But will you join us in our quest, my friends? Will you show solidarity in this great duty we share?"

"No," said Borrus without hesitation.

"Yes," said Lythian, a half heartbeat later.

The Agarathi turned to face them. Talasha's lips were in an inviting smile. *And is that why I agreed with such speed?* Lythian had to wonder. After a moment's thought, he realised it wasn't that. He'd come to this decision already, after hearing what Tethian had to say that morning. *If I leave now, I'll regret it. I have to see this through, no matter where it takes me.*

"It would seem we have a disagreement, my prince," said Kin'rar, his lean face shaped to a grin. He brushed some loose strands of tangled black hair from his eyes, sweeping them behind an ear. "Can you not be convinced to remain, Sir Borrus? For Lythian's sake. And mine. I feel we bonded on the ride here from Eldurath last night. Even Neyruu will miss you, I feel."

"I imagine that quite unlikely." Borrus returned, unsmiling. He looked at Lythian with a fierce glare. "You truly wish to stay?"

Lythian gave him a nod. "I do, Borrus. I...I feel I must."

"Then you're as mad as the rest of them." He stepped in closer and took Lythian's arm. "This isn't about *her*, is it?" He gave Talasha a glance, and lowered his voice. "Because she reminds you of..."

Lythian tore his arm away. The suggestion angered him. "You know why," he bit. "We've spoken on this at length, so don't pretend you don't. I feel we can make more of a difference here than adding our blades to a fruitless war."

"Well I don't." Borrus shook his patchy-bearded chin, the skin of his cheeks sallow and sickly beneath the sprouts of brittle hair. "If you go to the Wings all you'll find is rock and bone, and a whole bloody host of wild dragons. And that's the best you can hope for, Lythian. Because Eldur...*if* he's still living..." He shook his head. Eldur was a dark demigod to Vandarians, a figure to chill the blood of even the stoutest of men. "He'll bring calamity to the north. There won't be a man alive who can stop him."

"He will need no stopping, Sir Borrus," chuckled Tethian, amused. "I have told you this several times. Eldur will be a saviour, not a menace as you seem to think. He will be our salvation, from an eternity of war."

"It's best he leaves," grunted Ulrik Marak, staring at Borrus through his deep dark eyes, the right cut through with a savage scar that ran right up into his cropped grey-black hair. "He cannot be trusted. Eldur will be weak when we find him. This man may see a chance to put some godsteel in his heart."

"His black bloody heart," Borrus said. "But good idea, Marak, perhaps I'll stay after all. I'm grateful you think I'm potent enough to slay a demigod."

Marak huffed to that. "Kin'rar can fly you this very night to the south. I see no reason to delay your leaving."

"*South*?" Borrus's brow swept into a frown. "No, Marak, you have things all turned around. Vandar is north of here. I'll be going north, Kin'rar, if you please."

"You'll not go north from here," Marak told him firmly. "There are too many dragons, too many eyes. South is safe." He pointed that way. "The hills bleed into the saltflats of Lumara some twenty miles from here. You can be taken to the coast, where you'll be able to find a ship. We will even give you coin for passage..."

"Oh you will? How generous. And what purse is my departure worth to you? Or Tomos...how much will you pay for his life?"

"You blame us for his death?"

"No, he doesn't..." started Lythian.

"I do," cut in Borrus. "Of course I bloody do. You used us, and abandoned us. Tomos is dead because of you. And you, Prince Tethian. Because you're too craven to take your throne..."

Marak drew a dragonsteel dagger, but Tethian's hand went up. "Calm, Ulrik. His words are fair. He has every right to express how he feels." He took a short pace forward, his fine crimson cape as airy as a breath. "Please, Sir Borrus, do feel free to vent, if it will help you. Call me craven again, if you wish it. Call me a coward and a cur. I will take upon my shoulders every insult you can muster. Some I may even deserve. But do remember that I serve a higher function, and am a servant here, not a prince or a king."

"The world has enough servants," Borrus returned bitterly, as a misty breeze blew in from the west. The clouds filled in again, shutting out the sun, and the world seemed suddenly dark and shadowed, cold and grim. "But do as you please. I claim no right to tell a man how to title himself. But one right I do claim." He looked at Marak again. "The right to demand you honour your bloody oath, Marak. *North*. You said you'd take us north."

Marak's mouth twitched angrily. "I told you I'd help you get home. I will. By taking you south to the coast where you might barter passage on a ship..."

"A voyage that will take weeks. And I hate the blasted sea."

"I care not. This is the bargain, Sir Borrus. Things here have changed, and it is the best you will get. Kin'rar can make preparations immediately. Neyruu is still strong to fly."

"She is," confirmed Kin'rar. Neyruu had come away unwounded from the escape from the pits, whereas Marak's bonded dragon Garlath had suffered several nasty wounds from his fight with Malathar, Vargo Ven's brutish beast of a drake. "We can fly under cover of night, and land in the hills outside Solas," Kin'rar went on. "It is the closest major port from here."

"I have heard Lumara grows dangerous for northmen," Talasha put in. "The Patriots are creeping from their hiding places, it's said, and stirring every major city to rioting. I'd hate for Sir Borrus to be in peril. Has he not earned some succour after so long in chains?"

"All the world is in peril, Princess," said Marak, standing broad and grand upon the soggy brown earth at their feet. "But Kin'rar will make sure Borrus gets to the docks in one piece..."

"I don't need a godsdamn chaperone," Borrus insisted, looking like he might just storm off. "I'm rested and fed and have four feet of godsteel for company. The hills beyond the city will be fine. I'll make my way to the docks on my own."

"You're sure, Borrus?" Lythian remained uncomfortable with all of this. "Will you not think on it another night? Rest a little more? The dawn may bring clearer thoughts."

"My thoughts are clear enough. The dawn will only delay my return home. And I don't mean to stay here a moment longer than I must."

He is set, then, Lythian saw, with a note of sorrow. Borrus was obstinate at the best of times, and his mind was not for changing. "Well then..." He found himself lost for words. They'd been through so much, suffered through so much. *Is this it, truly?* he wondered. *Does our journey together end here?* He shifted on his feet, wishing there was another way. But he couldn't see it. "Borrus, I..."

"I'll bloody well miss you too, Lythian." The big man wrapped him in a hug, then shoved him away. "We part here, my friend, and I'll see no tears from you. If you're set on this mad course, so be it. I just hope you're not making a mistake."

And that was that. Before he quelled or questioned himself, Sir Borrus Kanabar turned and marched away, returning to the shadows of the ruins. Lythian watched him go, a part of him wishing to go with him. But a greater part knew he had to stay.

Kin'rar stepped over. "I will see him to the coast, Captain," he promised. "Do not worry for him. He will find himself safely home."

Lythian nodded, as Borrus vanished beyond the trees and crumbled walls of the old keep. "Tell him to find a ship going east," he said. "The route past Solapia and the Telleshi Isles will be the safer course."

"I will tell him," Kin'rar said. "You will see him again soon, Lythian. Borrus has proven himself quite unkillable. He'll survive the trials to come."

And will I? he wanted to ask, but didn't. He smiled wanly instead, and watched Kin'rar fade into the shadows of the ruins, through the larch and fir and tangled weeds. Firelight flickered back there, where the other outlaws and apostles gathered. There were dozens here, all bought into this holy crusade. Men gathered to Tethian's cause over the years, living with him in exile as he waited for his time to rise...

Lythian felt a hand take his, warm to the touch. "You are doing the right thing, staying here, Captain Lythian." Talasha's voice was as beautiful as her face, a balm to his ears after weeks listening to the mob, heckling and harassing him night and day. He thought suddenly of how awful he must look to her. When they'd first met he was garbed in fine clothing, his cheeks shaven and full of colour, his curly chestnut hair neatly cut. Now he'd turned gaunt and grim, his eyes hollow, his skin sour, his face embraced by a rough stained beard. She pressed her hand to his cheek now, as though sensing his doubt, his pain. "We will get you cleaned, and restored," she whispered to him. "Will you let me shave you, Captain? Do you trust me not to cut you?"

"I trust you," he croaked. It was the first tenderness he'd felt in months. He had to turn away, to look back out over the hills and low-slung mountains, wreathed in tall black trees poking from the mists. He took a long moment to brace his spirit, then asked, "Do you believe in all of this, Talasha? What your cousin is trying to do?" He glanced over at Tethian, who stood aside with Marak in conversation. He did have a way about him, a certain glow, a certain spirit. He could quite understand how people would be drawn to his vision.

Talasha was looking over too. "I believe *he* believes it," she said, "and that is good enough for me. My cousin was always thoughtful, Sir Lythian. He loved books as a boy, and never sought vengeance for his father's fate. Peace is in his blood. I believe he wants to end the war, not win it."

Lythian nodded as he stood staring out across the valleys and hills. The last of the light was receding, the clouds darkening and falling, it seemed, low and heavy above the tips of the mountains. Behind them, he could sense Borrus and Kin'rar already moving away through the ruins and the trees. Neyruu would be back there somewhere, curled up among the rocks, waiting to be summoned to the skies.

Lythian sighed, as he waited. It took a further few minutes before he heard a familiar *whump* of dragon wings beating the air. Then it happened again and again, *whump, whump, whump,* growing louder and closer still. Lythian turned his eyes up as a sleek grey shape swept over the treetops, bearing on its back a brace of men, silhouetted against the fading dusk. A mournful smile gripped at his weary whiskered lips. *Goodbye, Borrus,* he thought, watching his burly bald friend slip away into the clouds, blurring into the gloom.

And all of a sudden, he felt terribly alone.

4

Jonik

The night was dark and damp, an unseasonable chill in the air. Jonik stepped through the swirling mist that choked the sandstone alleys, wreathed all in black, his hood pulled up over his head. His right hand remained within the folds of his thin woollen cloak, clutching the hilt of the Nightblade. The Sun City of Solas was not a friendly place for northmen. *I must be on my guard, always,* he thought.

A clatter of laughter preceded the coming of a group of men, tramping around a bend in the alley ahead. These passages were tight and narrow here in the deep recesses of the city, and poorly lit besides. The occasional firelight flickered among the fog, given off by lanterns set in wall niches, but mostly all was dim and eerie. The approaching group held a single torch among them for illumination, each enrobed in lightweight linens weaved in dark grey and black. At their hips hung crude weapons, fastened to their belts; machetes and sickles and daggers and dirks.

It wasn't safe to move about unarmed here now, and the rioting in the city was making everyone wary. The clash of ideologies had created a fertile breeding ground for thugs and louts, and looting, robberies, and rape had become all too common. The Snakeways, as this twisting network of alleys were known, was particularly dangerous. Shopkeepers had been killed defending their stores, or left to pick through the wreckage once the pillagers were done. Women had been dragged to dark alleys to be defiled. The culprits were rarely men of militant persuasion, or those affiliated with the Patriots of Lumara. They were merely opportunists, base men seeking some reward as the city fell to civil conflict.

Are these such men? Jonik wondered, as the group approached. He watched them coming his way, their voices rumbling out in heavy drunk tones of Lumaran. The accent was deep and rich, less rough than Agarathi, though not so light and musical as the Aramatian lilt. Jonik's grasp of it was worse than poor, though their suspicious eyes and openly hostile looks told him he'd fast become the topic of their discussion.

Just keep walking, he thought to them, eager to avoid a quarrel. He'd heard tell of multiple clashes over the last few days, as the rioting in Solas descended into bloodshed, and northmen were in most peril of all. Only a week ago, a pair of humble Rasal merchants had been beaten to death for no other reason than their ancestry, and others had fallen to the same fate. As the men drew nearer, Jonik pressed himself to the sandstone wall of the alley to let them pass. With his hood up his northern features were well concealed, though to men like this it might not matter, not if they felt inclined to rob him. *Or try to,* he thought. *One wrong step will be the death of them all.*

By luck or judgement, however, not one of them made a move. They jostled past, huffing and sneering, swigging from clay bottles as they went. A couple of inches north of six feet, and wide-shouldered as he was, Jonik had enough menace about him to be better avoided. The men thus passed in a fog of grunts and gruff remarks, and continued on their way.

Smart choice, Jonik thought, turning and pressing on down the alley, swatting away the flies that buzzed about the streets as he went. They were thicker during the day, though continued to linger at night, a constant menace that the locals tended to ignore, but Jonik found infuriating. "I'll slay you all," he rasped, flicking a particularly determined one away. He moved beyond the firelight of a nearby torch and deeper into the shadows, escaping them. Arriving at an intersection of five alleys, he stopped in the small dark quad where they merged, gathering his bearings. Jonik had heard that many of the large southern cities had winding warrens of lanes and alleys like this, and the Snakeways were never less than troublesome to navigate for a man uninitiated to their routes and ways.

He took a moment to himself, thinking through the directions the old crone had given him. "When you reach the Five-Fingers, take the second lane on the left," she'd told him in a croaking Lumaran accent, though her grasp of the common tongue had been excellent. "Then straight down, and take a right at the end. That'll bring you to the old market. It'll be empty this time of night. Pass through and you'll travel a wider street, lined with red awnings." She'd been polishing the bar of her tavern all the while, sucking on her lips between sentences. "There's an old well at the end. Pass that, turn left. You'll travel down a long tight alley. At the end you'll see a door painted black, with a silver snake coiling around a golden sun. Intimidating place, oh yes. Might find them there." She'd shrugged and continued burnishing the wooden bar. "Or not. Lots of rough men here in Solas. But Karlesh... yes, he is said to visit that place often."

Karlesh. It was the name she'd given when Jonik had described who he was looking for. "A man with a hook for a right hand," he'd told her when he'd arrived at her musky old tavern, inhabited by a short order of cloaked and burly men. "And perhaps you know of another, some seven feet tall, with a mane of black hair? Or a man with a missing ear?"

The old woman didn't know about the man with the missing ear, but the giant she named as Bardook, another well-known thug. Three days ago, Emeric Manfrey's estate had been razed and burned to the ground, his staff murdered, his beloved Brewilla among them. Before they'd arrived to witness the death and devastation, they'd been passed on to the road by a roving band of men they took as Patriots of Lumara. Those were the men whom Jonik and Emeric were hunting. *Karlesh. Bardook.* Jonik had names and a location now, and it was time for him to deal some justice.

Still, the old crone had sounded a warning. "You'll want to be careful," she'd said to him, as she'd sucked on her lips and polished her bar. "Bardook is a known savage, yes. He once pulled a man's arm straight out of its socket, I have heard." She'd cackled a laugh, her once-black hair now pure white, and quite striking against her dark brown skin. "Northmen aren't safe here, not now. I would leave, or you will find yourself armless. And Karlesh...do you know how he got that hook for a hand? He is Lightborn, old blood. Tried to bond to a sunwolf once and had his hand chomped off for his efforts." Another bitter laugh escaped her. "But he's handy with the hand that's left, that you should know. Swings a sabre as well as anyone. And there are many other dangers here in Solas. Many men who might kill you if they see the tone of your skin. Better that you leave. You will find only death if you challenge these men."

"I'll be fine," Jonik had said, fingers holding the hilt of the Nightblade beneath his cloak.

She'd smiled, her rumpled lips drawing back to unveil the only four teeth she still possessed, poking out through her soft pink gums. "Bladeborn?" she'd murmured, peering at him more closely. "Ah yes, I see that now. No other man would feel safe here. But even so...be on your guard. If a mob spot you, you will have nowhere to go. These lanes are tight. And these men are fearless. They will close in with blades and blunts and no godsteel will be able to chop through them all." She'd studied him a moment longer, then asked, "These Patriots... what have they done to deserve your attentions, exactly?"

"They murdered a score of innocents and destroyed a friend's estate. We seek justice."

"Then you'll need to go higher than Bardook and Karlesh. They are soldiers only, cutthroats-for-hire. The orders come from above."

Jonik was aware of that. Upo Utappa, Emeric's friend and the local harbour master at the docks, had told them all about the hierarchy of the Patriots of Lumara, an organisation that stretched right across the empire, from Lumara to Aramatia, Pisek to Solapia. "I hear that a man named Iru Zon leads them here in Solas?" he'd said.

The crone had nodded to that. "His grandfather's grandfather founded the Patriots a hundred and ten years ago. Helio Zon was his name, the former City Master here. Iru Zon isn't Master of Solas, but he's of ancient blood, and sunlord of his house. He is a Lightborn of much power and influence. To target him would be the death of you."

Or him. "Is he here in the city?"

The crone spat into her rag and gave the bar another wipe. "From what I know, yes, but he won't be for long. There are rumours that the *warmoot* is being called. The rulers will gather soon at the Tower of Tears to decide whether we will go to war."

"The Tower of Tears. Is that in Lumos?"

The crone cackled derisively. "You northerners know so little of the south. The Tower of Tears is at the southern tip of Lumara's Teardrop, south of Sutrek. It is a holy place, where the leaders of our nations gather, monarchs and nobles and warriors all. Empress Valura will preside." She ran her old rag down the bar. "I fear she will bend to the Patriots' demands. With them in one ear and the Agarathi in the other, she may not have a choice. Otherwise it will be civil war here. Better we go to war with the north than ourselves, would you not say?"

"I'm Tukoran. What do you think?"

Another laugh wriggled out of her old wrinkly throat. "You go ahead and kill Karlesh and Bardook if you find them," she'd said. "They are feared around here. These streets will be safer with them gone."

He had every intention of doing so, and told her just that, before he thanked her for her help and took his leave. Now he was following the crone's directions, weaving his way through the tight alleys and lanes, battling the flies and avoiding the attentions of the thugs and looters such as he could. He reached the old market and found it deserted as she'd said it would be, carts and high-sided wains sitting to the side, emptied of their wares. Some looked to have been looted, others packed up until tensions calmed down. Spoiled fruit littered the square. The flies buzzed and swarmed in thick black clouds, humming around the refuse.

Jonik pressed straight on, pacing down the awning-lined street. It was more open than most others, a wider thoroughfare through the Snakeways. Some people stood at their windows, watching as he passed. Down a side-street, he spotted a huddle of scavengers picking through a pair of corpses, searching for spoils. Whether they'd done the killing themselves he wasn't sure. He gave it no mind, pressing on. Elsewhere he heard the rough bitter noise of a fight; the thud and thunder of fists and feet. He saw the commotion when he passed another street, as some half dozen men brawled outside a tumbledown store. The glint of dark iron caught the firelight as a short blade punched into a man's side, and after that, the fists and feet were replaced by daggers and dirks. Half the men had suffered knife wounds by the time he'd moved on.

Soon enough he was at the well. It sat alone at a meeting of three alleys, though looked old and dried up at a glance. There was some blood smeared atop the stone lip and he wondered what had caused it. Perhaps someone was thrown inside? He took a quick peek over the top but after a few short metres the interior was swallowed up by a darkness as black as tar. It wouldn't be the worst place to hide a body.

He took the left lane, as the crone had told him, and continued down a tight alley that seemed to go on forever. High sandstone walls rose up either side of him, as a pervading blackness closed in. He decided to join it, blending into the darkness as he gripped the handle of the Nightblade and let its ancient magic fill him. It would be better not to be seen here, should a group of men approach from ahead. The old crone didn't know what blade he bore, but she was right about the dangers of the mob in tight spaces such as this.

Eventually, he came upon the sight of the black door, painted with a silver serpent coiling around a golden sun. It was one of several signs that the Patriots of Lumara used, Jonik knew, in order to display their safehouses; an invite for zealots to enter, and for all others to stay away. The silver serpent was a representation of the goddess Lumara's warring, scheming side; the golden sun was Sola, one of Lumara's greatest generals and followers, and patron of the city in which he currently stalked. Jonik swung his eyes left, then right, to make sure he was alone on the street. Beyond the black painted door he could hear the rumble of voices and laughter. Cruel voices. Cruel laughter.

Do they joke about Brewilla? he wondered. *About Puli, and Kestan, and the other twenty men and women murdered on Emeric's estate.* Half of them had been locked away and burned to death. The rest had been hacked up and butchered out in the gardens and groves. A couple had been tossed, bloodied and cleaved, into the fountains and ponds to redden the water. Jonik could still picture the devastation. The burning villa and outbuildings. The smashed statues and walls. The trampled flower beds and razed fields. He could smell the thick stink of death and smoke, the caustic reek of blood and burnt flesh. He could hear the terrible screams of Emeric Manfrey as he rushed in through the doors of the villa, calling out Brewilla's name.

And her face. He could remember that too. Dark and beautiful, but somehow peaceful despite the horror of her passing. Her body had been half charred, but her face had been untouched. In the few days since, Jonik had learned more of her. She'd worked for Emeric for a decade, running his house, becoming his wife in all but name.

Twice now the exiled lord had fallen in love with a southern girl, and twice they'd been taken from him. First by Lord Modrik Kastor, who'd found out about Emeric's romance with a southern servant in his house in the north of Tukor, and exiled him for it, stripping him of his lands and titles. That had led him here, to Lumara, where he'd lived in peace for many years...until now. Until only a few short days ago, when the exiled lord's entire world had been dismantled and destroyed.

Jonik's lips were in a snarl as it all passed through his head. The old crone hadn't been wrong... the likes of Karlesh with the hook for a hand, and Bardook the burly black-maned giant were soldiers only; weapons to be swung. They had blackness in their blood, true, but the order would have come from above. But who? Iru Zon, the noble sunlord? Another lesser leader among the ranks of the Patriots? The organisation was a sprawl of lords and lowborn alike, half of whom liked to keep their allegiances unknown. Only now, with war stirring with the north, were they likely to unveil their true leanings. And any number of them could have been behind the razing of Emeric's estate. Any number could have given that order.

Jonik drew the Nightblade from its pitch black scabbard and rapped his knuckles against the ash-wood door, knocking on the head of the silver snake. He heard grunts and a barked order, then footsteps, then bolts. The door was heavily locked; three bolts scraped in their holdings, one after another, before it swung open, revealing a bronze-skinned man who looked of Aramatian heritage, bearing a serrated machete and wearing a patchwork of leather armour. His brown eyes shifted left and right down the alley, as Jonik stood perfectly still before him. Then the man frowned and turned back, shouting something into the room. Jonik didn't need to know the language to understand.

He cannot see me. As the man turned, Jonik slipped silently past him, stalking away into a corner of the tavern. Inside it was well lit compared to the lanes and alleys beyond, though still dim enough for him to hide. A few faint curls of black smoke swirled about him, but no more. *I must master the blade,* he thought. He wasn't far off, but in full daylight, the eagle-eyed would be able to spot him. Turning his eyes around, he counted eight men in attendance, sitting at the bar and tables nearby. A further man stood behind the bar, serving drinks.

The guard at the door shrugged and slammed it shut, pulling the bolts, one, two, three. Jonik smiled. *I have you all now.*

His eyes went from man to man, though it didn't take long for him to spot the one called Karlesh. The hook for a hand was something of a giveaway. He was resting it on a table, as he sat back staring suspiciously at the exit, stiff and upright. By his framing he looked their leader, and the crone had said he was Lightborn too. *Not a gifted one,* Jonik thought, looking at that curved shining hook. *If he had rich magic in his blood he'd still have a hand, and a bonded sunwolf besides.* He was probably Lightborn in the same way that Captain Turner was Seaborn, though there was something noble about his posture and bearing. He was younger than Jonik had expected, mid twenties perhaps, smooth-skinned and clean-shaven, with short black nappy hair and dark deep-set eyes. Beyond his obvious disfigurement he was handsome and neat-featured.

Jonik continued to scan the others. Bardook wasn't there, not in that room at least. There was an arched passage leading off it, leading to a second chamber, and he could hear more voices back there. He ghosted through silently, invisible, and found another host of five men in leather and linen, sharpening blades on whetstones. A set of timber stairs gave access to the floor above. Jonik crept up, careful not to creak a board, and found several more rooms for storage and sleeping. Some beds and bunks were occupied by snoring men. To Jonik's count, the safe house was occupied by some twenty Patriots. *Some twenty corpses,* he thought.

He returned to the main room, at one with the shadows, a thrumming thrill reaching through his body, fizzing fingers clutching at his chest. There was something intoxicating about being here among them, unheard and unseen.

"I will kill you all," he whispered, as the mens' voices filled the room. But one heard, a gaunt-faced man nearby with coarse black stubble filling his cheeks. He looked in Jonik's direction and frowned. *I am here,* Jonik thought. *Right here in front of you, murderer.*

"I will kill you all," he said again, and now the laughter was stopping, now more of them were hearing. Karlesh looked his way, staring right through him at the stained sandstone wall behind. Jonik walked to the other side of the room, quiet as a creeping cat. "I will kill you all." They turned. Chair legs scraped against the stone floor. Men were on their feet, calling out in panicked tones. "Every one of you will die this day." Steel was drawn, singing from sheaths. Out came Karlesh's polished sabre, as he surged to his feet. The guard at the door was waving his machete in Jonik's direction, though Jonik wasn't there anymore. He was right behind him. "I will kill you," he whispered into the man's ear, as he cried out in alarm and spun, and swiped.

But Jonik was gone. Away across the room. Huddled in a far corner, grinning. From the arched passage the five others came rushing in, bearing newly sharpened steel. Upstairs the floorboards were creaking as men woke from the commotion. Only then did Karlesh's voice came hurrying out in the common tongue. "Who's there? Who...who are you?" The others were cawing in Lumaran, Piseki, Aramatian. Their leader waved a hand and hushed them. "Who...who is there? Who!"

"Death," Jonik whispered, unleashing his hissing rasp. "Death come for you, Karlesh, lest you answer my questions..."

"Questions?" Karlesh's eyes bloomed in fear, flashing around the room, trying to find him. "What...what questions?"

Jonik moved again to confuse them, making sure his voice came from a different place each time. "Where is Bardook?" was the first thing he asked, and as soon as he'd asked it, he was gone again, slipping to another part of the room. The men were all closing in as one, huddling at the heart of the tavern, turning outward with brandished blades. Tables and chairs were kicked over to make room, to form little barriers. Jonik merely laughed, a soft bitter sound. "Where is the giant with the black mane?"

"Upstairs. He's...he's upstairs, sleeping."

He wasn't, not anymore. At that very moment, the giant lumbered sleepily into the room, unclothed above the waist. Thick long hair tangled about his barrel chest, a series of scars slashed across his rippling torso. They looked like claw marks from some southern beast. He bellowed out a confused barrage of questions in Piseki, and he had the look of them too, more chestnut-toned of skin, with wavy hair and a stubbled lantern jaw. In his grip a huge khopesh sword hung, curved and cruel, with a savage horn at its tip. When he got his answer from the huddled crowd of men he gave out a great barking laugh, and broke into the common tongue. "A ghost? There is a ghost here?" He laughed again, loud and raucous, and Jonik was laughing with him.

"Ghost. Yes, I'm a ghost," he said.

All of a sudden Bardook's laughter stopped. "Who said that?" he demanded, his voice a great booming thing. He pointed his khopesh to the corner where Jonik stood, unseen. "A ghost?" He took a pace forward, looming tall and broad. "Bardook the Strong is mighty enough to cut through a ghost..." He swung his blade at the empty air, and Jonik swung back with the Nightblade. A moment later half of the khopesh sword was clattering to the floor, split as if by magic, leaving only ten inches of severed steel poking out from Bardook's grip. The giant's eyes widened and he lumbered back in fright. The rest of them shrieked, as half of them made for the door, hauling at the bolts.

"If you leave this place you will die," Jonik hissed to them. Several took heed of the warning and backed away. A pair of others were still scrambling to unlock the bolts and escape out into the night. *I cannot allow that,* Jonik thought. He was on them in a flash, swinging for their necks. The rest of the men watched in abject horror as a pair of heads were cleaved from shoulders, spinning through the air, spraying blood. The terror that filled the room was a song to Jonik's ears. A blissful lullaby, and the Nightblade was humming, laughing in his grip.

He moved the bolts back into place. "Karlesh. Bardook. Both of you have been accused of murdering innocent estate workers a day's ride north of here. I am sure that others within this room took part in the same massacre. I am here to find out who gave the order. Tell me what I need to know and the rest of you may be spared."

May. He used the word on purpose, for he had no intention of sparing any of them. All were Patriots. All were complicit. Whether taking an active part in the butchery at Emeric's estate or not, they'd have done just as bad elsewhere. Other northerners had been targeted, and seen their estates and lands razed and destroyed, Upo Utappa had told them. The Patriots were a plague. And Jonik was part of the cure.

"I know nothing of this." Karlesh was finding something, some courage. He spoke firmly, as the group huddled close, holding their blades out in a defensive arrangement. "We are not murderers. We are humble men. Many of us work at estates ourselves."

Jonik slipped in and pressed the Nightblade through the chest of another man, twisting. The Patriot slumped to the floor, blood pulsing from his heart. "Each lie will bring death. Tell me true, who gave the order?"

The men were losing their faculties, and some the control of their bowels. The stench of piss filled the air. One began sobbing manically, then struck out in Jonik's direction, slashing wildly in a crazed and sudden assault. Jonik dropped down to a knee, and swung, taking away his legs. The Patriot collapsed to the floor, blood pumping out from the stumps, shrieking. The rest screamed and howled in horror, backing away. The stink grew a great deal worse.

"It was him!" one wailed, pointing at Karlesh with a shivering finger. "He...he gave it. The order. Him. It was *him*!"

Karlesh snarled and slashed, swinging his sabre at the man, cutting off his ear and a good thick slice of cheek. After that an anarchy descended, as Bardook led the charge, rushing out to where he thought Jonik to be, snatching a studded flail from a table and swinging it around his head. Several others followed him. Behind, Karlesh was stabbing wildly at the man who'd pointed the finger at him. Others were once again making for the door.

It was devolving beyond what Jonik could control, and perhaps he'd pushed them too far. One was screaming 'ghost' and 'shadowfort' and sure enough, they knew it was him by now. *Took them long enough,* he thought, ducking beneath Bardook's swinging strike, and cutting off his right arm. The giant wailed and clutched the bloody stump, as Jonik made for the door where several men were scrambling to escape. He saw no other way now, other than to kill them all. The Nightblade was puffing black smoke, gleeful and wanton, as the bodies piled up on the floor. He completed the rout, then turned, scanned. Karlesh was gone. *Must be a way out the back,* he realised.

He gave chase, hurrying through the arched doorway, leaping over bodies and limbs and pools of black-red blood. He gave a swish and cut Bardook's throat for good measure, to make sure the giant's day was done, then chased through the building, following Karlesh's bloody footprints. They led him through a rear door and into another narrow alley, and there he saw the Lightborn, sprinting off into the night.

He was on him in a heartbeat, flowing up behind him like black mist. He drove the Nightblade through the back of the man's shoulder, forcing him to the dirty stone floor in a puff of dust and dead flies. *They'll feast tonight,* Jonik thought, as he fogged back into form, his cloak and hood, body and bones emerging through a shroud of black mist. At his feet Karlesh was scrambling, reaching forward with his working arm. His fingernails were ripped free as they scratched at the stone pavings. Jonik drove the Nightblade through the back of his calf, pinning him to the earth. The man's howling sunk into the depths of the dark damp alley, as a fine mist filtered down from the sky. "The name," Jonik growled. "Who gave the order, Karlesh?"

The Lightborn was wheezing into the dirt, spitting blood. "The Abyss awaits you," he spluttered. "It's the Long Abyss for you, *freak*."

Jonik smiled. "Brazen. Are you not afraid to die?"

"I'll rise to the stars. I'll join the light. But it's darkness for you." He managed to turn his head, looking up as Jonik stood above him. "I've heard of you. The Ghost." He spat a glob of crimson spittle onto Jonik's black boot. "The darkness will take you. I will live in the light, forever. I've nothing to fear from you."

Jonik turned the Nightblade, rending the man's flesh open. "The name."

Karlesh shrieked, then began smashing his own head against the stone...*crack, crack, crack*, to try to knock himself out. Jonik pulled out the Nightblade, dropped to a knee, and wrapped his fingers around the man's neck. He pressed his head down onto the stone to still him. "You murdered my friend's love. You butchered his loyal staff. You destroyed everything he held dear." He twisted, turning the Lightborn's head to face him. "*Who* gave the order, Karlesh? Tell me who and I'll ease your passing."

The man's eyes were watery and weak. A gash had been ripped open on his forehead, leaking blood. But still he managed to mumble, "Me...I...I did. My order. It was...mine." His eyes drooped and rolled, as the blood fled through the wound in his shoulder, running in rivulets down the street.

Jonik gave a sigh, stood, and pressed the tip of the Nightblade to his neck. "Go join the light then," he rasped. "Your can watch your cause burn from the stars." He pushed the blade through the back of his neck, and left him for the flies to feast.

5

Saska

Rikki Bowen, the ponytailed captain of the caravel Steel Sister, was looking at the King's Wall perplexedly. "Do you ever take off that armour of yours, Sir Ralston?" he asked the giant, clad in steel from heel to neck. "I've not seen you free of it all trip, save your helm. Must make using the privy difficult." He gave a good natured laugh. "And other matters besides, hey lads."

Some of the nearby crew chuckled to that, as they pulled at ropes and rigging. Unsurprisingly, it was Bawdy Bron Bowen, one of Rikki's cousins, who laughed loudest of all. Sir Ralston didn't look so pleased.

He said nothing, though, as he stood firm and fixed at the gunwale across the quarterdeck, glaring at captain and crew in that withering way of his. Half the men aboard the Steel Sister were still giving him a wide berth, though the rest were beginning to get used to his glowering presence. Those tended to be Captain Rikki's relations. The ship had been his father's, he'd told Saska, and it seemed very much a family enterprise.

"Half these here men are kin to me, you know," he'd said on the day they'd set sail from Shellcrest. He'd gone on to point them out, one by one. "That there's Lanky Larry, the tall one. He's my uncle on my father's side. And there's Bawdy Bron, Larry's son. Loves a ribald joke, does Bron. We got Kevin the Con too, he's another cousin of mine from my mother's younger sister." He'd gestured to a man half way up the mainmast, patching a sail. "Good sailor, but better conman, is Kev. When he's not here on this boat, he's at some port-town swindling some fool out of their money."

"Sounds charming," Saska said.

"Aye, he seems to think so," Rikki laughed. He had a windburned face, with black hair tied into a tail behind his head and a deep widow's peak. He was handsome for all that, though, with that fine gritty stubble and constant impish grin. He'd gestured to another couple of men he called 'Ralph the Mouth' who liked to talk a lot, and 'Tanner Twelve Teeth', distant relatives both. "Not seen Tanner for a year or so. He was Tanner Ten Teeth the last time he came looking for work. Lost another couple since then."

"Not a popular man, I'm guessing," Saska put in. "To have had twelve of his teeth knocked out."

"To the contrary, he's a barrel of laughs is Tanner. You'll see. Got a story and song for everything. But loves a bare-knuckle brawl too. He's good as well, despite the name. Big lad, and quick as a snake. Says he wins ten bouts for every tooth he loses. And see that old man?" He'd pointed out a wizened old figure hunched upon a crate on the main deck, nimbly tying knots to fashion a net. "That's my grandfather, Old Hob, wisest man in the world. You're lucky you came aboard, Saska. He'll tell you your future if you're lucky."

She'd been mildly intrigued by that. "He's a prophet?"

"Of sorts, aye. Likes to read the birds and the clouds. Lots of wisdom up there, he says. And beneath the waves too, we Rasal believe. If you fetch him a certain piece of coral, he'll see your future in the grooves and pits. Been going around the world for over sixty years on this ship. That's sixty years longer than little Billy here."

Billy was the last of the family members he'd introduced, and Rikki Bowen's ten year old son. He had the exact same look as his father, only without the stubble and with a shallower widow's peak. Cute hardly did him justice. He'd even grown his hair and tied it back behind his head, and was wearing an identical replica of his father's white flappy shirt, tan sailor's breeches tied up at the knee, and a piece of crimson cloth wrapped around his forehead.

"I'm Billy," the boy had said proudly. "And this'll be my ship one day."

"It's a fine ship." Saska smiled down at him. "Thank you for allowing me on board."

"That's all right. We don't usually allow girls on here, but you're really pretty, so it's OK."

"That's sweet of you to say. And you're very handsome, Billy."

"I know. Handsome like my pa. Who's that big man with you?"

"His name's Sir Ralston Whaleheart. He's a knight."

"He's *huge!* Is he the King's Wall? Is the king dead, pa?"

Rikki gave a grave nod. "Aye, son, tragically so. But enough questions now, hey. Let Saska settle in."

Saska had settled in just fine after that, and for the last five days, little Billy had taken to following her and the Wall around. She didn't mind one bit, and was happy to field many of his questions, though could tell his presence rankled Sir Ralston, who looked like he wanted to swat him like a fly. "You can hide in your cabin if you want," Saska had teased him once. "I'm sure Billy won't be able to get you in there."

"I'm your Wall," he'd responded in that thunderclap of a voice of his. "I have to protect you."

"*Here?* What's likely to happen to me?"

Nothing was the short answer. The captain and his men were harmless, and besides, Sir Ralston had given her a godsteel dagger the day they'd set sail, replacing the one Lady Marian have once given her. "A gift from King Godrin," he'd boomed, presenting it. It was a beautiful blade, subtly curved along its length and lit a pale blue, with ornate markings inlaid into the pommel and haft. On closer inspection, Saska had seen that those markings were symbols. "What does it mean?" she'd asked.

The Wall gave no answer.

"It feels old." She ran her eyes over the steel, the cross-guard, the hilt. A fine blue mist rose like dust from the blade's edge. "Is this regular godsteel?"

The Wall gave no answer.

She sighed. "Do you know *anything* about this blade?"

"King Godrin asked that I give it to you."

"That's all?"

The Wall gave no answer.

That was just Sir Ralston. Saska had managed to extract from him his orders, but little else. "I am your Wall now," he'd told her that first day, and hadn't said much else since. She'd wondered if Godrin had told him where to lead her, or whether to lead her at all, but he'd simply told her that he was her defender now. "I am to protect you, not guide you," he'd said.

"So you don't know where we should go?" She was planning to make for the city of Aram, of course, and see if she might find out more about her mother. She hoped Ranulf would be there too, though if he was, finding him wouldn't be so easy. "Godrin never said anything about that?"

"He told me to protect you. He told me I'd find you at the docks. He told me to give you that blade."

"And that's all?"

He'd nodded, and said nothing.

Saska had come to see that Sir Ralston's use of language was limited. He wasn't stupid, no, just unbearably untalkative, and equally dedicated to his duty. Even now, as she stood at the helm with Rikki Bowen and his doppelganger son, the giant was watching, always watching, as he loomed at the side of the quarterdeck, his back against the gunwale. "Well, you might want to think about removing that armour of yours soon, Sir Ralston," the captain went on, glancing over at him once more. "The days will be getting warmer, believe me." It was already quite balmy, but further south it would become sweltering. "No sense in you cooking to death in that steel suit of yours. I think you'd make the lads more comfortable if you took some of it off."

"I removed my helm the day I came aboard," the Wall protested.

"Aye, you did, and we're all grateful for that." He had a sardonic twist to his lips. Sir Ralston Whaleheart wasn't a particularly comely man, with that bald head and scarred face and the ever-present scowl that made it all the worse. "But how's about you take off those greaves and cuisses and get yourself into a nice loose pair of breeches, at least? That'd be a start, and would give your unmentionables some room to breathe."

"And make using the privy less burdensome," japed Bawdy Bron, who was giving the sterncastle a good scrub with a mop. "You all in proportion, Sir Ralston? Bet you could fill a bathtub taking a piss."

The Wall gave no answer.

"You should take my pa's advice, *Giant*," said little Billy. "He knows best on this ship. And I want to see your muscles. I bet you've got big muscles under all that armour."

"Bet he's big all over," said Bron. "It's that third leg of his I want to see."

"Enough of that now," said Captain Rikki. "We've got a lady present, Bron. You'll fasten your tongue when she's here."

"I mean no harm by it, Coz. You know me. Got a fascination in such things, is all."

"Well fascinate yourself elsewhere. Now off with you. The main deck needs a wash too."

Bawdy Bron grumbled off at that, as Sir Ralston watched him go with a murderous look in his eye. He gave that out liberally, to be fair. Saska sidled up to him. Little Billy followed. "Cousin Bron's an idiot," the boy said. "Pa only keeps him around because he's family. You ignore him, Giant. Or give him a slap if you want. That'd be funny. I'll bet you can slap a man dead."

"That and more. He chopped the head off a dragon once," said Lanky Larry, striding up to the sterncastle on those long spindly legs of his. He took several steps at once, though was still dwarfed by Sir Ralston by well over a foot. "Heard tell of that years ago, not long after the war." Larry was more thoughtful than his son Bron and less inclined to lewdness. He had a more unassuming way about him, and was Rikki's first mate and quartermaster both, seeing to much of the crew's day to day runnings.

"Is that true?" Billy's eyes were big as boiled eggs, as he craned his neck skyward to the Wall. "You killed a *dragon*?"

Sir Ralston's mouth twitched. "It was only a little one."

"Not the way I heard it," said Larry. "Twas no Vallath, but a big enough dragon all the same. Lopped its head clean off in a single swipe, the singers say. Always thought it a little fanciful till I saw you leap aboard, Sir Ralston. There can't be a bigger man than you in all the world. Nor a stronger knight. Makes me wonder what you're doing on our humble vessel. Escorting young Saska to the south, of course, but that makes me wonder who *she* is. Someone important I'll wager, to have you watching over her night and day."

"I've asked her," said little Billy, folding his arms. "I've asked her a hundred times, but she won't tell me."

"Aye, and that's her right, son," said his father. "These highborn folk are under no obligation to go explaining themselves to the likes of us."

"She's not highborn," the boy insisted. "She's southern."

His father laughed. "And she can't be both?"

Billy chewed his lip and thought on that. Then he said, "I suppose. Her eyes did change colour. Does that mean she's Lightborn, pa?"

Captain Rikki looked bemused. "Now what are you talking about, boy?"

"Her eyes." The boy pointed. "They were brown when she first came aboard. Now they're blue, and getting brighter every day. And her skin's lighter too."

"Skin gets darker in the sun, not lighter," said Lanky Larry. Then he gave Saska a good long look, and said, "But you know what, the tyke's right. You do seem a little peaky, girl. You sick from the sea, are you?"

"But her eyes." Billy was looking at his grand-uncle like he was an idiot, though he looked at most of them like that. "Her eyes have changed. Hasn't anyone else seen it?"

"I have," came a cheery voice from above them. Kevin the Con was up in the sails again, peering down from the mizzenmast. He had a shock of blond hair, long lithe muscular limbs, and a crafty twist to his mouth. Saska might have liked him if she hadn't been told he was a conman. *And I suppose that's the point,* she thought. *It's that easy charm that he uses to trick people.* "Not much gets past me," Kevin went on, as he reefed a sail. "Pays to be observant in my profession, and Billy Boy's right, she had eyes like mine when she came aboard. Pretty hazel eyes, aye." He grinned disarmingly. "But they're blue as sea and sky now. Something odd about that. Girl's got some magic to her I reckon."

"It's a potion, not magic," Saska said to that. She'd had enough of them talking around her. It was time to set the record straight. "And it's fading, that's all."

"A potion, you say? Well a potion *is* magic, Saska." Rikki Bowen raised a single black eyebrow. "Now don't tell me you brewed it yourself? Not many who can do that, lest you're some Seaborn mage."

"I know a bit of alchemy," Saska admitted. She'd proven herself quite good at brewing potions when studying at the university in Thalan, under Mistress Tufnell's care. The woman was a Seaborn mage herself, and had invented some of the magical brews that Marian and her agents used to change their appearance. "And my skin was darker because of a lotion I used." She looked at every one of them. "*Don't* ask me why, because I'm *not* going to tell you. I'm trying to get away from all that. And any man who says different will have Sir Ralston to answer to."

The men accepted that, though Billy just looked hurt. "That's mean. We're only curious. You don't need to threaten us." He looked aside and folded his arms a little tighter.

"I know, kiddo, I'm sorry." Saska went down to a knee and put an arm around him. "But we all have our secrets, right?" she whispered. "Things we don't want people to know?" She smiled at him in a teasing way. "I'll bet you've got a few of your own."

The boy nodded firmly. "I've got *great* secrets. The best you'll ever hear." He gave her a devious look. "I'll tell you mine if you tell me yours."

She had to laugh. "You're not going to trick me that easily, Billy." She gave his earlobe a little wiggle. "And you're not so crafty as Kevin just yet."

It was turning to afternoon, and the air was ripe with the scent of salt and fish. Above them, the azure skies were poor of clouds and rich of sun, its glare beating down onto the baking decks. Some of the crew worked barefoot, their soles hardened to the heat and splinters that only folk of the sail and sea could endure. Others were bare chested, tanned and weathered by the sun and salt-spray, their fingers heavily callused by the wet ropes and rigging and nets they handled daily. It seemed an arduous life to Saska, sailing back and forth between north and south, hauling crates and casks and barrels from one port to the next, but a wholesome life too.

It made her think of Ranulf, of all the adventures he'd had. He must have told her about a hundred of them during their time together, and likely had a hundred more in reserve. *And how about the adventure we shared,* she thought. The old prison wagon in which they'd met. Their rescue by the hand of Lady Marian. Their journey across Tukor to Blackhearth, and voyage across Vandar's Mercy. The nights in the library of the university, where he'd told her of her secret past, the past that she still doubted, but was now determined to discover for sure. Leshie and Astrid had been involved in much of that too, and Leshie in particular was never too far from her thoughts.

Perhaps I'll see her again soon as well? Her lusty little friend had gone off on the ship with Ranulf and Vincent Rose, but who knew where she was now. *She was always an impetuous one,* she reflected fondly. Lady Marian had asked Leshie to spy on Vincent Rose's criminal activity, but it was anyone's guess whether she would. She could very well have joined him instead, or decided to run off on some other adventure of her own. *Or maybe she's with Ranulf? Maybe I'll see them both in Aram, and we'll all be reunited?*

It was an optimistic thought, though others weren't so fond. *Elyon*...She couldn't muster much joy when she thought of him, leastways for the manner in which they'd parted. Strange as it was, she missed him most of all. But then, that wasn't strange at all, not after the time they'd shared. Time spent abed together. Time spent alone in his tent. Time spent sharing secrets...those secrets that she'd never spill to little Billy, oh Elyon knew them all. *All but one,* she thought. She'd not told him about her royal heritage. About her mother the dead princess, and her grandmother the reigning Grand Duchess. About the fact that she mightn't just be Bladeborn, but Lightborn too, with godly blood of the north *and* south.

Most days she tried not to think about all that, though. It was easier during daytime, when she spent all her time on deck with Rikki and Billy and the Bowen clan and crew. But at night those thoughts crept in, lurking in the shadows of her cabin. She would lie alone on her uncomfortable little bed and think of it all then as the ship groaned and rocked on the waves, and when she slept it would get even worse, for waking at least she could control her thoughts, but when she drifted to slumber there was no defence against her dreams. Dark dreams, like the one she'd had out on the Lowplains with Lancel and Barnibus. Dreams of the men who'd tried to rape her, the men she'd been forced to kill. Dreams of that cloaked figure bursting alight. Of the cities and forests and mountains all burning. Of the dragons swarming like starlings in the skies...

She woke most nights drenched in sweat, her heart thrashing in terror, her voice hoarse. Two nights past she'd found Sir Ralston there, standing in the doorway, his shadowed figure looking much like the cloaked man who haunted her dreams. "I heard noise. I thought..."

"I'm fine," she'd rasped. "Just a dream, Sir Ralston. You don't need to stand guard here."

But he did. He stood guard on her every night, and every day, and only the gods knew when the man slept. But those dreams, those terrors, they reminded her of Thalan, of when Leshie and Astrid had woken her from a nightmare once. She'd been screaming in her sleep and hadn't realised it. It made her worry that she did it every night, that the crew might hear and think her mad, or taken by some dark spirit in the way only superstitious seamen could. So she'd asked the Wall, and his great head had swung side to side. "You are usually quiet. You toss and turn and mumble, but do not scream. But you need not fear any longer, my lady. I am here to protect you. I am your Wall now."

But can you protect me from my nightmares? she'd wanted to ask. *Can you protect me from my past?* He couldn't defend her against things that had already happened, against the memories scarred into her mind. By day she could keep them shackled, but by night they ripped free of their fetters, every dark shade and shadow of her past free to assault her all over again...

"Come here, Saska. We're getting our first good view of Aramatia." The voice pulled her from her thoughts. She squinted across the stern-castle deck and saw Captain Rikki waving her over to the helm. Beyond the Steel Sister, some way south, she could see the distant framing of land. Leaving the Wall to his holy vigil at the gunwale, she joined the captain at the wheel. "Here, take a look through this."

He handed her his monocular. It was a long cylindrical device used to magnify distant objects using a series of prisms and lenses. Typically, Saska would just use her godsteel dagger to enhance her vision, but was rather hoping to avoid the crew knowing about all that. She pressed the monocular to her left eye and closed her right, as she'd seen Rikki do. In an instant, the distant lands seemed a great deal closer. She saw high rough cliffs and crashing waves and a towering fortress built into and atop the mountainside. A colossal sculpture had been hewn into the rock in arresting detail; a bird of prey clinging to the outcrops with its talons, wings spread wide, hooked beak staring out to sea. "It's an eagle," Saska realised.

"Eagle's Perch," Captain Rikki told her. "Northernmost fortress in the south. Quite a thing, that stone eagle. They got something similar at Dragonfall across the Red Sea, but dragons instead of eagles, of course. The one of Drulgar is bigger, but I've always preferred *Calacan*, the *Eagle of Aramatia*. The legends say the bird was the goddess's closest friend, that they were inseparable. Suppose it's why Aramatians love their birds so much."

"You get them all over," put in Billy. "Statues and sculptures of eagles. And griffins too, they're cool. But I prefer the sunwolves and starcats. And the moonbears. They're the best. Their mountain isn't far, is it pa?"

Captain Rikki patted the boy's head. "A good long way south of Eagle's Perch, son," he said. "You can see it from the Bay of Mourning, over on the western coast, away off in the distance. You know of it, Saska? Moonbear Mountain?"

"I've heard," Saska said. "It stands alone, like Vandar's Tomb, right at the northeastern tip of the Scales. Have you ever been?"

Father and son burst out laughing. Saska waited until they were done.

"Begging your pardon, my lady, but none so low as us would ever dare venture to that mountain. Only those of the richest Lightborn blood go there."

Little Billy Bowen gave a shrug. "Which she is...maybe. Those eyes, pa. They changed colour, remember."

"Because of a potion, Billy. We talked about that."

Billy chewed his lip. "So...Lightborn's eyes *don't* change colour, then?"

"Not that I've heard, son."

The boy seemed disappointed.

"You don't have to be Lightborn to go there," Saska told them. "I know a Rasal man who adventured there once. He told me all about how he trekked into the foothills and spent several days in camp, trying to find a moonbear to study..."

"Which he never did, elsewise he'd not have been around to tell you that tale." Rikki Bowen looked far from convinced. "Was this man trying to get in your skirts, my lady? He wouldn't be the first to try that old trick. Many a man has told a fanciful tale of bravery to try to a get a fair maid abed."

"And you're one of them, I'm sure," Saska japed. She'd long since learned that it paid to tease these men, if she wanted to get along with them. "Was that not how little Billy was conceived?"

"Gods be good, she can read my mind. Now close your ears, son, while I tell our lady guest of the night you were sired." He cleared his throat. "It all began some..."

"Pa, shut up. No one wants to hear it. I want to know about this adventurer." The boy turned back to Saska. "Who was he? Someone famous?"

"So he always told me," Saska said, smiling. "His name's Ranulf Shackton. I can see you've heard the name."

The captain gave a smiling nod. "Aye, we know about Ranulf Shackton, my lady. We love him around here, don't we Billy? My boy loves an adventurous sort."

"As all brave boys should," Saska said to him.

"Exactly." Billy was grinning broadly. "There was a singer once. He came to Shellcrest when I was seven. Is that right, pa? Seven?"

"Aye, seven."

"Seven I was," went on Billy. "That was three years ago. I'm ten now. Did I tell you?"

"When we first met," confirmed Saska.

"I forget." Billy scratched his chin, as his father liked to. "Anyway, the singer. He sang all night about Ranulf Shackton. All his adventures. And then he came back the next night and sang again. All new ones. And then again. A whole week he was singing. Not one of the adventures was the same."

"I always supposed that Master Shackton must have paid the man to spread his legend," jested Rikki.

Saska laughed. "I'd not put it past him."

The land was growing a little clearer now, though they were likely to remain some way off the surging strand. Saska knew the route well enough from the maps she'd studied at the University of Thalan, and Captain Rikki had taken her down to his own cabin at the start of the trip to show her and Sir Ralston which way they were planning to go. There had been a whaleskin chart laid out on his desk, stained and frayed at the edges, but intelligible all the same. He'd prodded his finger at Shellcrest. "We're here," the captain had told them, as if they didn't already know. "We're gonna sail south, right through Whaler's Bay, and past the Horn of Aramatia. If the winds are right, it'll only take us some four or five days till we see southern land. After that, we'll hug the east coast such as we can, right down past the Cloaklake and the Telleshi Isles, and ease through the Solapian Channel. That'll get us to Aram in, I don't know, some two to three weeks, depending on the vagaries of wind and wave." He'd smiled. "Does that suit you both?"

It suited them just fine, and they were about on track with Captain Rikki's estimations. Eagle's Perch was set right on the edge of the Horn of Aramatia, and they'd taken just the five days to get here. And those five days had been clean sailing, unencumbered by bad weather or outside interest. For the first day or two, Saska had been worried that the massacre of Sir Cleon Marsh and his men at the Shellcrest docks might have brought a Tukoran galleon or two down upon them, but that had never materialised. They'd slipped free of the net and were on their way. *To Aram,* Saska thought again. *And then*...well, she didn't quite know.

By nightfall the cliffs were as black as tar, still lingering away to starboard against the star-strewn skies. It was calm, the air still as stone, the waters lapping light and gentle against the hull. Some of the crew took themselves off to sleep in the communal spaces below; spaces that Saska never wanted to see, given the fetid reek that swept up the corridors from that way. The rest stayed up on deck, playing dice and cards and other games by moonlight, gambling over this and that. Kevin the Con was the architect of much of it, and had invented several games himself. "Only does it to steal our money," Tanner Twelve Teeth grumbled to her, shaking his head. His voice had a whistling quality to it, as it stole through the gaps in his grin. "If he takes my well-earned coin, he'll get my well-earned fist. We'll see how he swindles old ladies when I rearrange that handsome smile o' his."

While all that was going on, Captain Rikki invited Saska and Sir Ralston into his cabin. The giant had to bend to get through the door, something that always brought a chuckle to Rikki's lips. "My sincere apologies, Sir Ralston, but a man like you just wasn't built for life at sea."

"You'd find it easier getting around without your armour on," Saska suggested, with a shrug.

The Wall's only response was a grunt.

"You might want to spin that suggestion into an order, my lady," Rikki offered, as he rummaged around in a drawer. "He'll have no choice but to obey you then, so far as I see it."

Saska chewed on that a moment. "He's sworn to protect me, not follow my orders," she told him.

"That's not what his face says."

The captain was right. Sir Ralston had turned awkward. Or his version of it anyway. "Do you?" Saska asked him. "Do you have to do what I tell you?"

"I am sworn to protect you. I am..."

"My Wall now. I know. But the rest?" She peered at him. "Remove your left gauntlet."

"I..." He hesitated.

"Go on. I want to see you do it."

"My lady, I..."

Saska could see it was making him uncomfortable, and more so than she'd realised. "It's OK. I'm just teasing you, Sir Ralston. It's how they all do it here. I'm sorry if I overstepped."

"Of course not, my lady. It's just...my armour. I do not imagine you will like what is underneath."

She hadn't expected that, nor had Rikki it seemed. The captain completed his search of the drawer and set down a bottle of something brown on his desk, in the company of three chipped and stained glasses. He contemplated Sir Ralston a moment, as though he knew something Saska didn't. "The war took its toll on you, I'll bet, Sir Ralston?" he said in a sympathetic voice.

"It took its toll on many." Even when the giant whispered, the entire room seemed to shake. "I came away with my life. A life I dedicated to..." He trailed off, clenching his huge scarred jaw.

"King Godrin," Saska said softly. *He grieves for his king,* she realised, *and here am I giving him scorn*. "His death must have been hard on you. Did...did you know he was going to die? When he sent you away, did you know?"

"My king told me only what I needed to know. To find you at the docks. To protect you, my lady."

"But why?" She stared up at him, though could see she'd get no answer. "He never said, did he? He never told you why?"

The Wall gave no answer.

"King Godrin was always full of riddles," Rikki said, as delicately as he could. He set about filling the glasses. "I've heard a thousand tales about the man. Tales of his wisdom and his kindness, but his foresight most of all. He was well loved, Sir Ralston, I say that with all sincerity. It must have been an honour serving him all these years."

"It was."

"Then a drink to him? A toast. You do drink, don't you, sir?"

"No." The Wall managed the thinnest of smiles. "But I will make an exception this once."

So they raised their cups to the late king, and shared stories of the man that only Sir Ralston had truly known. Rikki spoke most of all, of course, despite having never been within a thousand yards of him. The singers worked a strong trade in Rasalan, and it wasn't only Ranulf Shackton they sang of. And all the while, Sir Ralston said not a word. He just stood, his bald head pressed against the wooden ceiling above them, listening with a fixed grimace of grief.

"Well, I suppose I ought to stop talking now," Rikki Bowen finally said. "I half forget why I brought you down here now." He thought a moment. "Ah, that's it." He refilled and re-raised his glass. "We've crossed the border, good sir, my lady. Consider us in the south from now on."

6

Elyon

"You saw her leave?" asked Elyon. "You're sure of it? She was on the boat?"

Sir Barnibus nodded. He was still dressed in lowly traveller garb, roughspun wool and fur and dark brown leather boots, and had grown a short beard during his time away from camp. "The Wall got her safely aboard, we saw." He looked to Lancel, similarly dressed, though without the beard. His sandy hair was darkened by grease and sweat, and neither looked like they'd washed in a week. "The ship sailed off through the harbour right after. Then we had to leave, lest we get spotted."

It was a fair bit to unpack. "The Wall?" Elyon asked. "The King's Wall, Sir Ralston?" He'd heard a rumour that Sir Ralston had abandoned his liege lord, but it never made much sense to him. He'd been at Godrin's side ever since the war. There wasn't a man more committed to his duty in all the north. Both knights nodded. "You're sure?" Elyon went on. "You saw his face?"

"Didn't need to. We saw his *height*," said Lancel.

"And his swords," added Barnibus. "He's got those two huge greatswords, with the fin cross-guards and whale-head pommels."

"And armour. That greathelm, with the flat top and eye slits." Lancel gave a shudder. "Gods, makes him look a beast. And the way he chopped up those men..."

“What happened?” Elyon had only just received them in his tent, and it seemed the pair had rushed back from Shellcrest as quickly as they could, judging by their unkempt appearance and weary eyes. *And a good thing too,* he thought. Outside, the remainder of the siege camp south of Harrowmoor was being pulled down, and Lord Kanabar’s army of Riverlanders and Lakelanders had already moved off toward the Links, beginning the long march south to help defend the Vandarian coast. *Or begin our own invasion, now that we’re united.* That was the new rumour circulating through the ranks: that Janilah was using Amilia’s wedding to bring together the northern kings and great-lords, so he might propose a preemptive strike on Agarath before they could stage their own.

Barnibus and Lancel set into their explanation. It seemed that a knight of House Marsh, Sir Cleon, had accosted them as they prepared to put Saska on a ship called the Steel Sister some five mornings ago. A tense exchange had turned to blood and death when the King’s Wall appeared from nowhere, butchering Sir Cleon and his men as Lance and Barny mopped up those who tried to flee.

“They’d passed us on the road, halfway to the coast,” Barnibus explained. “We’d managed to get rid of them by giving them whiskey and wine from the wagon, but one of them recognised Lance...”

“But he couldn’t place me, not at first,” put in Lancel. “We thought we were free of them until they showed up at the docks, just as we were escorting Saska to the ship. There was a town crier cawing out about Godrin’s death and crowds of people everywhere. The Wall must have hidden among them, though quite how he did it at his size is beyond me...”

“He took care of most of them,” Barny said, taking over, “but we had to kill a few to make sure we weren’t recognised. If it got back to Lord Kastor that we were helping the girl...”

He didn’t need to explain. “You did the right thing,” Elyon told them. “I’m in your debt for this, both of you.” He considered them for a second, then asked, “I suppose you know about what’s been happening here? About Ellis and Dalton and Vesryn...”

“We heard about Ellis’s death on the road.” Barnibus shook his fleshy bearded cheeks. “They say he fell, but I can’t believe that. Not even Ellis Reynar was dolt enough to fall off a balcony.”

“He was drunk, apparently,” Elyon said.

"Ellis? Drunk?" Barnibus wasn't believing it. "He was hardly a known sot. This has Janilah's stink on it, surely."

"But why?" asked Lancel. "Why kill your lapdog, and put a wolf in its place? Godrik Taynar's not going to come to heel like Ellis, Barny. I don't see what Janilah has to gain by raising the Taynars to the crown."

Barnibus let out a grunt. "Should be your father sitting the steel throne, Elyon. He'd make a great king, a noble king, by the gods he would. And you a bloody good prince too, I say. Like Aleron would have been. But Dalton?" He shook his head, untethering a few flakes of snow from his locks of dirty brown hair. "I suppose he's going to come snooping about asking where we've been, now he's prince and First Blade both."

"So you heard about that too?" asked Elyon. "About Vesryn?"

"The soldiers told us," Lancel explained. "We crossed paths with some of Rylian's men, coming back from Calmwater. Told us the lot."

"Did they know who you were?"

"Don't think so. We were dressed like this and they never made mention of it."

"Kastor was asking about you both as well," Elyon informed them. "I told him Vesryn had sent you off on a private errand. He might ask you himself now that you're back. I suppose he'll have heard about Sir Cleon's death by now as well."

Barnibus didn't look concerned by that. "The Wall was said to be prowling the Lowplains, massacring bands of Tukoran soldiers. Sir Cleon is just another victim of the giant's wrath, he and his men. No reason for anyone to think otherwise."

Elyon considered it all for a moment. A brisk east wind was blowing outside, pulling at the loose folds of his tent. He could see a heavy snowfall starting to come down beyond the flaps as men worked to pack up the tents and pavilions, dismantle the longhouse and palisade, douse the firepits. Most of the highborn lords and knights had taken up residence in Harrowmoor under Lord Paramor's invitation, as they prepared to head west to Ilithor. Elyon was thinking about that now. About the wedding he was required to attend. About Prince Dalton Taynar's order to remain close, should Vesryn have a mind to slay him.

"We're leaving for Ilithor tomorrow," he finally said. "Amilia's to wed King Hadrin." Their faces said they'd heard about that too. Both had spent a lot of time with the Jewel of Tukor during her courtship with Aleron in Varinar. It seemed a lifetime ago now. "You should get yourselves washed and shaved, and pay Dalton a visit. You'll find him holed up in Harrowmoor with Sir Taegon and Sir Brontus and a half dozen others for company."

"Vesryn?" Lancel asked, understanding.

"Vesryn," Elyon confirmed. "Dalton fears he'll return to seek vengeance, and has me standing guard for him half the time too, along with a full score of Bladeborn bowmen. Sir Roy Gaveston is leading the hunt for him by Dalton's order, though I've heard that Lord Huffort's got a full dozen search parties out there trying to find him too."

"Lord Huffort of Rockfall?" asked Lancel.

"The very one."

"He serves under Kastor banners," said Barnibus, frowning. "I'm supposing Lord Cedrik must be in fear of a reprisal himself."

Or Janilah, Elyon thought. *I will not walk to his drum, not anymore,* Vesryn had said of the Warrior King the night he'd fled. *I have a mind to go there myself. I have a mind to kill him.* Elyon hadn't spoken a word of that to anyone. *Because I want him to try,* he thought. *I want him to succeed. And if he should die in the attempt, so be it.*

He turned from the bitter thought. He hated his uncle for what he'd done, but did he want him dead, truly? It was easier not to think about that. For all he knew Vesryn had crawled under some rock somewhere, to while away the rest of his days with naught but his precious Sword of Varinar for company. There were a thousand abandoned settlements out on the Lowplains where he might be hiding, a thousand little woods and groves, a thousand old mines and tunnels and caves. He'd been missing for five days now, and Elyon had heard no report of a proper sighting. How far could he have gone in that time? When they'd searched the camp, they'd found that he'd taken his destrier Sunsilver with him too, a magnificent chestnut stallion, swift as he was strong. The last confirmed sighting had been the stableboys who tended the beast, and one had been dragged before Prince Dalton the morning after Vesryn disappeared to give his testimony.

"He came out of nowhere, m'lord," the pimply faced youth had said, his voice a squeaky nervous thing. "Just leapt atop him, and rode away. Sunsilver, that is. Took off south, I saw. No more than a flash and he was gone."

"The horse was saddled?" Dalton had asked.

"Aye, m'lord." The boy had shuffled on his feet. "We'd saddled him up for the peace parley. The horses weren't long back before Lord Vesryn reappeared."

Vesryn had been among the host that rode out to meet the Rasal lords after the white banners of surrender had gone up around Harrowmoor. When he'd returned, Elyon had gone to find out what happened, and that's when the truth of Vesryn's deceits had come out. He'd left soon after, by the stableboy's account.

"Did he say anything?" Prince Dalton had wanted to know. "Anything at all?"

"Nothing, m'lord. Just took the horse and bolted. Had a cloak on, but was armoured underneath, I saw. And had his sword with him too. The big gold one."

"We know. That'll be all."

They'd learned little else since. One of Kastor's sentries had recalled seeing a rider flee into the moors to the south, but wasn't certain if it was Vesryn or not. With the surrender at Harrowmoor, all the camp had fallen to revelry that night, and it seemed no one had been paying attention. Nor had they found any tracks. There had been a lot of coming and going to the siege camp and trying to sort out one set of hoof-prints from another was all but impossible. Now, there were several hundred men dedicated to the search, and word had been sent for every watchman, soldier, guard and sentry at every tower, keep, fort and castle in Rasalan to be on the lookout.

But still nothing, except the theories. A dozen had sprung up pertaining to his whereabouts. Some said he was in the Oakenwood just to the north of Harrowmoor. It would be easy to reach and easy to hide in, and was a known hunting ground for outlaws. Search parties had thus been sent there to look. Others suggested he was making for the Snowmelt Mountains or the Stormwall Hills, where he might hide till his dying days amid the rocks and clefts and caves. Men were being mustered to watch those ranges should Vesryn appear. A popular thought was that he'd gone south, and was seeking to barter passage to the Telleshi Isles. The archipelago was a known haven for vagrants and wayfarers, and many a man had gone there to seek peace and escape a wicked past. The entire south coast of Rasalan had thus been alerted to Vesryn's possible presence, and the garrisons Rylian had established there were beginning to join the search.

There were others of a more fanciful nature. One spoke of a secret life. Vesryn had a concubine out on the Lowplains, it posited, and a brood of bastard sons and daughters besides. He was to lay down the blade and take up the hoe and begin his second life a humble farmer. Another man drunkenly said he'd had a heart-to-heart with Vesryn once, and learned of his aching desire to leave behind his life of service, and take to the sea, living off its bounty and hunting leviathans in his spare time. The sotted fool was a lowly Tukoran soldier who'd been summarily hauled before Prince Dalton to elaborate. When it turned out he was only fibbing for attention, he'd been stripped of his tongue for telling lies.

"We'll be off then, Elyon." Barnibus and Lancel were making for the tent flaps.

Elyon blinked from his thoughts and looked at them. "Right. I'll, um...I'll see you at Harrowmoor later then. I'm just arranging a few things here."

Lancel pulled back the canvas flap, and a squall of snowy air blew in. "Oh actually, there was one more thing," he said, as Barnibus prepared to step through.

"Go on."

"Saska had one request of you, before we sent her on her way."

That perked Elyon up. "What was it?"

"Something about a boy she once knew. I forget the name." Lancel looked at Barnibus for support.

"Del," Barnibus said. "She asked that you see if he's in camp. The labour camp, probably. He's just a lad, sixteen years old I think. She said she'd told you about him already."

Elyon remembered. "He used to live with her on the farm she worked at. Up near Twinbrook in northwestern Tukor."

The pair frowned at one another, and Lancel let the flap fall shut. It fluttered in the breeze. Inside the tent, the braziers were unlit, and the interior had a grey grim feel to it, cold and lifeless. But some of Elyon's things were still here. His books. A couple of garments the stewards hadn't collected yet. He could have had them packed up and conveyed to Harrowmoor easily enough, but wanted to come out here one last time. To have some time alone to think. Of her. Of everything. And that's when his friends had returned.

"So that's where she came from?" Barnibus asked. "Northern Tukor?"

Elyon had to smile. They'd been requested not to probe into Saska's life, partly to spare her and partly for their own good. *They're fine men,* Elyon thought. *Honest loyal men, and my brother always knew it.* He had few allies around him now, though knew he could rely on Lancel and Barnibus, and this proved it as much as anything. "You got her name from her at least," he said. "How long did it take for her to give it up?"

"Oh, only four or five days," Lancel said, with that wide handsome smile of his. "Was the same day we ran into Sir Cleon on the road. She'd been silent as the grave before then. Got talking after, though, even if she never spoke about herself."

That wasn't the Saska Elyon knew. The first night they'd met, she'd unloaded all of her secrets on him. *Well, not all. She never told me who she was really,* he thought, and that still vexed him.

"She mentioned a Kastor soldier called Don Mears too," added Barnibus. "Said you'd written about him in your notebook, and thought he might know this Del."

It was possible, Elyon supposed. Don Mears had been a sentry guard where the labour camp was situated at the first Kastor warcamp. He'd not seen him since, though, and for all he knew he'd already left or been killed sometime during the siege. "I'll look into it..." He was starting to remember how Saska's face looked when she'd told him about Del. How fond it had been. How she loved him as a brother. And the others she'd lived with in the little farming village of Willow's Rise, just east of the Hammersong Mountains. Her kindly old master, Orryn, and his chubby sweet daughter Llana. Del had been an orphan boy whom Orryn had taken in when he was a pup, and Saska had joined them when she was just fifteen, having endured years of abuse under the cold stone roof of Modrik Kastor's keep. *And he had a limp,* Elyon remembered. *Orryn. A limp on his right leg from an old farming accident. And Del...he was shy and tall, with black messy hair.* He was surprised he remembered it all. But then he remembered most everything that had passed through Saska's lips. Words and whispers, and kisses all...

He coughed and shifted as the memory passed, striding over to the counter opposite the bed. He grabbed his swordbelt and and fastened it about his waist, with a wince.

"How's the back?" Lancel asked him, watching. "We heard about the flogging."

"Healing," Elyon said, as he pulled on his heavy grey winter cloak, mantled over his Varin blue.

"You got ten, we were told," Barnibus said. "Ten too many, we figure, for something you didn't do."

Elyon stopped in his fiddlings and looked at them. His eyebrows twisted into a frown. "She told you?"

"Didn't need to. We figured it out. Had to be a reason why you were protecting her, right? So we put two and two together and got a dead Kastor knight...by *her* hand, not yours." Barnibus stopped and checked Elyon's reaction. "So it *was* her," he saw. "Saska was the one who killed Sir Griffin?"

Elyon saw no reason to lie to them. And even if he had a hundred, they'd earned the truth. "Sir Griffin tried to have her raped by that oafish brute Borgin," he said. "She was only defending herself, but you think Cedrik Kastor would have seen it that way? I had no choice. I took those licks happily and would take a hundred more if it meant seeing her safe."

"Noble," said Barnibus.

"You did the right thing, El," said Lancel.

"I should never have put it on you," said Elyon. "It was my mess and I..."

"You never did," broke in Barnibus. "It was Vesryn who gave the order to escort her south. And he's nowhere to be seen." He stepped forward. "We're in the clear, Elyon. Lance and I know what to say to Prince Dalton, and let's be honest, he'll not much care with the shadow of Vesryn looming over him. And Cedrik Kastor? The man can rot. He's got no power to question any of us, you least of all as heir to House Daecar. We're in the clear," he said again, "and Saska's long gone from these shores."

And with the King's Wall for company. Elyon couldn't figure that part out, the whys and hows of Sir Ralston's sudden appearance. "We should get going," he said, giving them both a grateful nod. "I'd best ask around about this Del before the whole camp disbands."

They stepped out into the bracing wintry wind, into the yard around which the highborn men of Vandar had arrayed their pavilions. Half were gone now or going fast. Vesryn's tent had been put to the flame after being searched for evidence. It sat as a blackened heap of charred support poles, timber decking, and melted hide, half hidden in snow. Further down the hill, huge swathes of land had been churned and muddied where the River and Lakelanders had arranged themselves in their neat columns and rows and rings. "We noticed they'd left," said Barnibus, as they padded across the snow. "Did Lord Kanabar go with them?"

Elyon shook his head. "He's coming to Ilithor with us, for the wedding. Lords Shorton and Fullerton are leading the army south."

"And your father?"

Elyon had been asked the same question by a hundred lords and knights already, half the Varin Knights included. Every one of them wanted to know if the great Amron Daecar would be returning to the fold, but Elyon's answer was always the same. "I'm not sure. My father is busy mustering the men of the North Downs and the journey to Ilithor is long. I wait in suspense of his crow."

But he wasn't waiting, because his father wasn't sending a crow. All communication Elyon had with his family went through Jovyn and Amara, and latterly Jovyn had been taken out of that equation. For whatever reason, Amara was taking charge of the dispatches now. He was eager to find out why when they met again in Ilithor.

He parted with the two Varin Knights as they arrived at their own tents, which had been left standing until their return. By Elyon's recommendation, of course. "I'll see you at Harrowmoor," he told them. "And I'll never forget what you've done for me."

He sealed it with a firm grasp of each man's wrist, before turning and making his way down the gentle hillside. Where Lord Kanabar's army had pulled poles and left, Lord Kastor's assemblage from northern Tukor were still packing up to march. Theirs was an ugly encampment, haphazardly arranged in their separate houses and colours. Half of the men were Kastor's Greenbelts, but the rest were drawn from the other greathouses of North Tukor, vaguely considered the lands north of the Stonehills and Three Peaks. There were the Hufforts of Rockfall, the Gershans of the Moorlands, the Swallows of Blackhearth, and beneath them served other smaller houses, both lord and knightly, and the men sworn to them, spearmen and shieldmen and axmen all.

It said something about Lord Cedrik Kastor's rule that his camp had been so awkwardly pitched, with little to no continuity between the houses. The Hufforts were neat and tidy and the Gershans took up too much room, and the Swallows were the opposite, far too tightly packed. Some of the men serving the banners of one house had somehow found their way into the midst of another, for no reason Elyon could think of. *No wonder they brawl so often,* he thought. With neighbours rubbing so close and treading on each other's toes, there was always likely to be friction.

He didn't rightly know where to start, as he worked through the refuse of tents and tarps, shoulders tight against the buffering white winds. The air clattered with the sound of hammers, the crunch of axes, the puffing pants of labouring men. *But it's labouring boys I seek*, he thought. searching out the barrack tents in which the boys had huddled, somewhere off to the south. As he went he passed a half dozen cloaked men taking a break from their work. They were warming their hands at a fire, handing around wineskins. Elyon heard one make mention of the Wall. "Butchered a knight of Rockfall down in Shellcrest, I hear. He and the score of men he had with him."

"Score? I heard it were a hundred," grunted another man.

"He was a Marsh, the knight," said an old figure with a thick grey beard. "Sir Cleon, I heard him called, son of Lord Malcolm Marsh. And he had a dozen men, not a score or a hundred. You whelps exaggerate every bloody story."

"I heard he had someone with him," said another with a patch on his right eye. "Someone half his size, though isn't everyone? They got on a ship..."

"And the ship sank," broke in a burly man, with a burly laugh.

The old man shook his head. "He didn't get on a ship. The King's Wall, on a ship? Why? He's out for vengeance for Godrin. Not a one of us is safe. No a one..."

"A giant and a madman," said Eye-patch. "Ain't the Wall enough to worry about. Now we got that rogue First Blade too."

"Mayhaps they're together?" posited the first man, his gaunt hollow face poking out from his hood. "Maybe they're going south to win us the war? You ever think of that?"

"You ever think at all?" asked the old man. He let out an exasperated grunt. "You're just trying to wind me up, I can tell..."

The gaunt man laughed. "Better that than being called stupid, I s'pose."

"You've been called worse, I'll bet," boomed the burly man. "Face like that." He started laughing.

"Rich from a man with a face like a sow's backend."

The big man stopped laughing. "You take that back. I got a nice face, I do."

"Nice to a lusty hog, mayhaps."

It didn't take long for the fighting to break out, though by that stage Elyon had long since given up listening. His mind had turned to the Wall again, and Saska, and just why he'd been sent to help her. The rumour had been that he'd abandoned King Godrin's service, but more likely he'd been sent away. *To protect her,* he thought, *by the command of a dying king. Or am I overthinking it?* It was possible Sir Ralston had chopped up Sir Cleon and his men for no other reason than them being Tukoran. That he boarded the same ship as Saska might only have been a coincidence. *But I doubt it,* he decided, as he pushed on through the winds. *There's something bigger at play here.*

He put it to the back of his head and kept on through the camp, stopping occasionally to ask the soldiers where he might find a lanky boy of sixteen summers with a mop of messy black hair. "Boys were camping at the south perimeter," one broad-faced Moorlander told him, as he furled his tent, and packed it onto a wagon. He had on his surcoat a brown serpent coiling around a green hill; the crest of House Gershan. "Some are in Harrowmoor, acting servants and the like. Rest'll be dotted about helping the men with their tents. Might have trouble finding him, milord. My mind conjures an image of a needle and a haystack." He shrugged and continued his work.

He wasn't much wrong about the boys being dispersed. Many that Elyon had taken for full grown men were in fact boys of fifteen or sixteen, dismantling tents, loading carts and wains, hauling weapons and supplies. The white winds and heavy cloaks weren't doing much for visibility, making it hard to spot the difference. He saw one such youth and marched over. "I'm looking for a boy of sixteen summers, lanky with messy black hair." The boy he was querying had much of what he was looking for. Not quite of Elyon's height, but close enough, and black-haired to boot. "His name's Del," he added, peering at the youth. "Do you know him?"

"No sir. Not heard that name. Del you say?" He thought on it some more. "No, sir, not ringing a bell."

"You're serving under Gershan banners?"

"Yes, sir. I was enlisted from Thackton, a village out near Lallymoor. My father said I needed to do my part in the war."

"And is he doing his part?"

"He's a cripple, sir. Broke his back falling off a horse. But was a soldier in his day. A pikeman and a good one."

"I'm sure of it," Elyon said, with grace. "You've not heard of Del, but perhaps you know a soldier called Don Mears, a sullen faced sentry. Serves Lord Caldlow of Broadway."

The tall boy shook his head. "Sorry, sir. Most of the Caldlow men are off yonder, past those rocks. You may want to ask there."

Elyon took the youth's advice. Lord Caldlow himself was too old to march to war, but had sent a thousand men to join Kastor's army under the command of his son, Sir Kristof, an oafish knight of limited skill, but handy when wielding a bottle. "Is your lord commander present?" he asked a soldier bearing the Caldlow standard - three grey hills framed against a starlit sky.

"Sir Kristof? No, milord. He's in Harrowmoor getting sotted most like."

"No matter then. Perhaps you know Don Mears. A sentry guard with a sullen face."

The man pursed his lips and leaned on a support pole he'd just pulled from the earth. "Name tickles somethin' in my head, sure." He shrugged and said, "Think he died in the siege, milord."

"Died?" Elyon repeated. His mind went to his one and only interaction with the sullen sentry. He'd seemed a decent man, and had spoken of a wife and three girls back home in his village near Broadway. *Now left without a father,* he thought, sadly. "How did he die, pray tell?"

"Fire, I think. An exploding barrel o' pitch from a trebuchet caught him and a few others. Nasty way to go to be sure. One survived. Got horrible burns on him, but he might be able to tell you more than I, milord. He's over..."

"No need." Elyon was thinking of Don Mears's rotten luck. Only about five hundred men had died during the siege, or one in a hundred from the fifty thousand camped at Harrowmoor's door. Most of those had fallen when Lord Kastor tried to take the gate in a craven assault. The rest died in bits and pieces during the long weeks of testing the outer defences. Don Mears must have been one of them. *Poor bloody man.* "I'm...looking for a boy as well. Tall, sixteen, black hair." He felt enervated by the news of Don's passing. It just seemed so wasteful. "Name's Del. Have you heard of him?"

The man shook his head. "Can't say I have, milord. Lots o' boys in camp, and some out on the plains too if the rumours are true. A few deserted, the night we took the fort," he said to Elyon's questioning frown. "Ran off the same night as that traitor Vesryn." He spat to the side.

Clearly he doesn't recognise me, Elyon thought. "How many?" he asked. "Boys, that is. How many of them deserted?"

The soldier shrugged. "Group of a dozen or so went missing, as I understand it. Few others have been slippin' away over the last weeks too. Happens. Some o' these boys are treated poorly, milord, and can't hack camp life. Especially since all them Rasal girls were released. Only got worse for the prettier lads then, if you catch my meaning."

The thought was abhorrent. A scowl swept over Elyon's face. "Boys are being abused?"

The soldier backtracked. "Aye, er, one or two. Not seen it myself, o' course, but you hear things...sometimes. Some o' these men here, they're hardly more than beasts. Have cravings, they do. And with all the highborn moving to Harrowmoor...not been anyone to tell them no."

Elyon had to take a moment to compose himself. He closed one fist and then the other, squeezing tight to purge his anger. "These boys. Have any been caught?"

"Unsure, milord. Lots o' villages out there that'll need good labour and whatnot now. Sure they're thinkin' o' finding gainful employment out on the Lowplains. Or just somewhere to hide, until the army leaves."

Well they'll not hide long, Elyon thought, *with everyone out hunting Vesryn*. Any boy caught deserting would be hanged. *And might Del be one of them?* He had to put it down as a possibility, as he left the soldier feeling in need of a stiff drink. Don Mears dead. Boys being defiled.

Elyon had been a central part of the drive to free the captive Rasal girls from the Kastor encampment a couple of weeks ago, but it seemed his efforts had only opened the door for more abuse. The tall boy from Thackton might have volunteered for the army, but most others wouldn't. Not Del, certainly, so far as Saska had told him. He'd been taken against his will like most others of his age, and now they had to contend with *this*? His stomach felt twisted in knots. *If I find him, I'm damn well taking him,* he thought. He'd wondered what he might do if he found Del, but that sealed it. *I'll take him under my service, and teach him the blade myself.* The boy wasn't Bladeborn but it didn't matter. He could still learn to swing steel and defend himself.

But the next hour stole away that hope. No one knew the boy. He spoke to a hundred soldiers, squires, and stableboys and not one of them had heard the name Del. Being lanky, black-haired, and sixteen was little to go on. There were hundreds of sixteen year olds in the ranks, and lanky was a relative term. As he worked through the wintry winds, he started to think that Del had been given another name. Or provided one himself. *Or more likely he isn't here,* he thought. *He's probably at some other camp, or maybe even dead already...*

He was lost to those thoughts when a hand caught him on the arm. "Sir Elyon Daecar?"

He turned. Before him stood a man of stout build and middle age, cloaked in stained black wool. The dark whiskers on his cheeks were sprinkled with grey and there were several deep ruts engraved on his weathered forehead. Elyon drew his arm away. "That's right." He peered at the stranger. "Who's asking?"

"Roark, sir."

Elyon regarded him, scanning for any crest or livery. He had no colours to suggest an allegiance. "OK, Roark. What do you want?"

"A privy conference, sir. Between you and my lady."

"Your lady?" Elyon hadn't seen many ladies out here. There were few in a warcamp, besides the washerwomen and serving wenches and such, and they weren't really ladies at all. "Who?"

"Lady Marian, sir, of House Payne. She's been seeking to confer with you, about..."

"Saska," Elyon finished for him. Lady Payne had been Saska's mentor, the one to send her into this dreadful snake-pit of a camp. He'd made attempts to find out if she was stationed in Harrowmoor during the siege, but those efforts had come to naught. "Where is she?" he demanded. He could feel a fresh anger rising in his throat, hot like bile. "Is she in the fortress?"

The man called Roark shook his head. His eyes moved left and right, as they stood amid the surge of labouring men, ghosts in the cold white mists. "We have commandeered a tent nearby, Sir Elyon. If you'll kindly follow me."

Elyon had little time to collect his thoughts as they picked their way through the wreckage of the warcamp. Within a minute or so he was being ushered into a supply tent still standing among the Huffort lines. There were two further men standing guard outside, one big and burly with a dented shield on his back, the other more youthful and lithe and mild of appearance. Inside was a fourth soldier, standing with his hand on the hilt of his blade. His face was flat and set to a scowl. Saska had made mention of these men, Elyon remembered, though their names escaped him. They were sellswords in the service of Lady Payne and had helped her flee Tukor some months ago. For that at least he was grateful.

At the heart of the tent stood Lady Marian Payne herself, wrapped in a sleek grey lambswool cloak. She was taller than Elyon had expected, near a match to his six foot three, with a slender face contoured of high cheekbones and a sabre-sharp jaw. Beneath her slim brows lived a pair of pale blue eyes, cold as a winter lake. Her thin lips turned into a courteous smile as he entered. "Sir Elyon, we find you at last. My men have spent the last two hours looking for you."

"They should have started in the Vandarian camp, Lady Payne." Elyon pushed forward his right foot and dropped his head into a bow, to fulfil his gentlemanly duties. "I was in my own tent until recently."

"I see. I'm quite sure Roark checked there?" She turned to the sellsword, who shrugged. "Well no matter, you're here now. I've been meaning to speak to you..."

"About Saska?" Elyon cut in. "Yes, I know."

"You do." She smiled. "Well of course you do. And I can see you're in no mood to bandy civil words."

She has a good read on me, Elyon thought. Though that was no surprise, given the woman's profession, running a network of spies and assassins. "Saska was of the opinion that you were in Harrowmoor during the siege," he said. "She told me that you promised her you'd remain close, and on hand to extract her if she needed it. I made what furtive efforts I could to find you, but heard nothing of your whereabouts." He looked into those cold blue eyes. "I trust you were in Harrowmoor all along?"

"I was," she said, though it sounded like she might be lying. "As I'm sure you can understand, my orders come from higher up the ladder."

"Like your order for Saska to assassinate Lord Kastor?" he challenged. When she offered no response, he added, "Killing Cedrik Kastor would have achieved nothing, you understand. The task was folly from the start, and I made sure to prevent Saska from attempting it once I took her under my care. It would have been the death of her, my lady."

"Perhaps you underestimate the girl? She is more capable than you realise."

"I know just how capable she is." He was thinking of Sir Griffin Kastor's corpse, slashed at the cheek and groin and punctured through the throat. "But quite how you thought her qualified to slay one of the most gifted swords in the north is beyond me. She is still only young, and new to the use of godsteel."

"I am aware, Sir Elyon. I was there when she first discovered herself to be Bladeborn. I was there to train her, to instruct her, to guide her. I was there..."

"To send her to her death," he broke in. "And I was there to save her from it." A dark thought came to him. "I know of Saska's past with the Kastors, living in the shadow of their abuses. I know of her desire for vengeance. A cynic might say you took advantage of that, Lady Payne. A cynic might say you exploited her."

"A cynic would be wrong," she said coolly. "I gave Saska every opportunity to recant, but she was adamant she see through her duty. Do not think yourself the only one to care for her, Sir Elyon. Not once did I want her to leave my side."

"You're to say someone else gave the order?"

"I'm to say that we don't yet know what will come of what has happened here. But in that our knowledge remains incomplete, and that's the reason we have sought you out. Where is Saska now?"

"On a ship sailing south," he told her. A part of him wanted to deny her the knowledge, but what purpose would that serve? No matter his thoughts on the woman, she was Saska's mentor, and had saved her life twice. She deserved to know. "To Aram, I'm told."

"By whom?"

"The men I sent to escort her to the coast. Both are trustworthy and loyal, and have just informed me that they saw her board a merchant caravel called the Steel Sister out of Shellcrest five days past." He stopped a moment to read her. "They tell me she wasn't alone. The King's Wall appears to have joined her."

Marian Payne gave no reaction, but for a tiny little twist to her lips. "I see," she said. "We had heard rumours that Sir Ralston was laying siege to bands of Tukoran men. This gives light to his true function. King Godrin must have sent him to protect her."

"*Must* have? So you don't know for sure?"

She shook her head. "King Godrin must have foreseen all of this in the Eye of Rasalan. There is trouble in Aram, and across the Lumaran Empire. Saska would not have been safe alone."

"And she'll be safe with Sir Ralston? A man his size only draws attention. The Patriots of Lumara will see a prize in a man like that. So far as I see it, Saska would have been better alone. With her colouring she'd have blended right in."

"Until she opened her mouth. Saska can mimic an Aramatian lilt well enough, but she knows nothing of the language. She is of mixed heritage by birth, and northern by upbringing. No, Sir Elyon, she'd not have blended in. At least with Sir Ralston with her, most men will think twice before getting anywhere near."

"Well I'll not question you on that, my lady. I've not had the pleasure of meeting Sir Ralston, but I've heard stories aplenty of the man." The one of him decapitating a dragon in a single swipe came most to mind, a tale Elyon had always enjoyed as a boy. He thought back then to what Saska had said the night he'd sent her away. "Saska told me she'd been cast out of Aram once," he recalled. He glanced to Roark and the flat-faced man, standing at the tent flaps behind him. "Do you know what she meant by that? We shared a lot during our time together, but she never told me where she was from. She never told me of her parents." Now it was Lady Payne's turn to share glances with her men. "You know, don't you?" Elyon pressed. "Her mother. She's in Aram?"

"Her mother is in the stars, Sir Elyon."

He frowned. "Dead?"

She confirmed it with a nod. "That is the suspicion at least. In truth we don't know for sure who Saska's parents are. She told you of Ranulf Shackton, I presume?"

"At length."

Marian Payne's smile was quite arresting when it came into bloom. "Of course. Saska was greatly fond of Ranulf, as are many who spend time in his company. During her weeks studying in Thalan, Ranulf often took to the university library; a second home to the man when not on some adventure. He had a particular interest in Saska's ancestry and came upon some information that pointed to her southern lineage."

"What information?" Elyon asked.

"An adoption record, most pertinently. One that detailed an infant girl of southern skin tone and vivid blue eyes, found in the town repository of Broadway."

"A slave," Elyon said. He knew how the Tukorans liked to dress up their shady practice. It was like putting a silk dress on a sow; no one was deceived. "She told me she worked in Lord Caldlow's household when she was a little girl. I take it he was the one who bought her?"

"Through his aides, yes," she said. "Apparently the child was found in the hands of a maidservant from the palace in Aram. She had been given a directive to return the infant to her father in Ilithor, though the record gave no name. Further to this was a rumour Ranulf had once heard when visiting Aram himself, regarding the death of Princess Leila Nemati, daughter of the Grand Duchess. This rumour spoke of her dying in childbirth, which is common, as you know, when birthing powerful Bladeborn."

Elyon knew that all too well. His own mother had died the same way. "I'm familiar with that, yes," he said, stiffly. "So you're saying that Saska may be this child? The bastard daughter of a southern princess and northern lord?"

"That is the theory, yes."

Elyon turned away, thinking. *An outcast,* she'd said to him that night she'd killed Sir Griffin. *A maid. A spy. I'm Tukoran and Rasal and Aramatian all at once. I'm nobody*. But that was a lie, he knew, and he'd known that all along. *But a princess?* He'd not expected that. She wasn't a legitimate one, perhaps, but a girl of royal blood all the same. Royal *southern* blood. *Lightborn* blood. He turned back to Lady Payne. "Did King Godrin know about this?"

"King Godrin forgot in a day what most men learned in a lifetime, Sir Elyon. He sent Sir Ralston to protect her for a reason. He believed that Saska would be important in helping to build bridges between north and south."

"Because she's Bladeborn and Lightborn both," Elyon said, thinking again of his dream where she'd faded to silver and blue. He'd taken that for her father being Vandarian, but perhaps he'd been wrong. Perhaps the blue was her Bladeborn side, the silver her Lightborn? House Nemati was Lumosi Lightborn, he knew, descended of Lumo, Mistress of the Moon. It made sense, and none at all. *Because it was just a dream. Nothing but a dream.* He cleared his throat. "Will you follow her, now that you know where she's gone?" he asked. "Try to take her back into your service?"

Marian Payne's head went rigidly left and right. "No, I shan't follow, nor have her resume her service. It would seem my training of her has served its purpose, for now. I shall be marching south, with the men mustered by my lord uncle. He wishes me to lead them." She smiled a sour smile. "A woman leading five thousand swords and shields. What an oddity that must be to a man like you."

"No oddity at all," Elyon returned. "I have my little sister Lillia training with godsteel as we speak. I have no issue with women being trained with the blade."

"To better defend themselves, I'm sure. But I wonder how you'd react if ever you saw your little sister leading the Daecar banners into battle. *War is no place for a woman.* Isn't that what you Vandarians believe?"

"All the north believes it," Elyon corrected. "Even here in Rasalan, it is unusual to see a woman in combat, my lady." Women couldn't join the Suncoats, and were thus ushered into the more clandestine operations of agents and spies and assassins. But if ever there was a woman to change one's mind on a woman's place on the field, it was the indomitable Lady Marian of House Payne. "But for what it's worth, I would gladly fight at your side." He gestured to Roark and the other man, and the pair standing guard outside. "These men of yours clearly respect you, and I've heard that many others, knights and lords and kings all, feel the very same. So let your doubters huff and quibble, my lady. When they see you in the van, garbed all in steel, they'll be glad you're with them."

"Damn right," grunted the flat-faced sellsword. "Never served a better leader, nor a finer fighter. I don't give a sod that she's got nought dangling between her legs."

Marian smiled to that. "Thank you, Quilter. Eloquently put, as always. And you, Sir Elyon, I am grateful for your words. You are a forward thinking man, it would seem, and rare among the lords of these lands. I can see why Saska might have enjoyed your company. But it leads me to wonder how *much* she enjoyed it." She had a suggestive look on her face. "You have a reputation, I've heard."

Elyon had to laugh. That 'reputation' followed him around like a bad smell, but by the Steel Father was it exaggerated. "You're asking if I took her to my bed?" he asked, going right out and saying it. He turned to examine the faces of the men. Outside, the younger one at the flaps was listening intently.

"He was in love with her," Roark said, pulling the flaps shut. "Lark, we call him, for his singing voice. Sweetest thing you'll ever hear, if you get a chance. Tried to seduce our Saska with it one night, but to no avail. Suppose she was waiting for a man like you."

Elyon shook his head. "It wasn't like that."

"How was it?" asked Marian.

"Good," said Elyon, unable to stop himself. "*Very* good, actually."

Marian's hand was on the hilt of her blade. "Care to discover if what you've heard about me is true, sir?"

Elyon showed her his palms. "A jest, and a crude one," he said. "But you did rather set me up."

"He's not wrong there," Quilter chuckled. "And we *were* told he had a tongue on him, my lady."

"Yes, we were," she said, eying Elyon again. "Now *without* the sordid details, Sir Elyon, tell me how it happened." Her blade showed another inch of misting steel. "I'm asking you quite plainly if Saska was abused."

That put an immediate end to the fun. "No," he said, almost reaching to his own sword. "You would ask that of me?"

"Yes, but not *about* you. I'm not accusing you of doing anything untoward, sir. My accusations are for Lady Cecilia Blakewood, who has a reputation of her own. So tell me now and tell me true...did she make Saska suffer?"

"Sexually, no. Emotionally, yes." He closed a fist. "The woman is a witch, some devious spawn of her father. You might want to reconsider your uncle Tandrick's orders, my lady, and join me in Ilithor for your new king's nuptials. A woman with your skills? You could slay Janilah and that bastard of his both."

"Treason, Elyon," Marian Payne said. "The north is at peace. There are no spies and assassins among us anymore."

"Tell that to my new First Blade. He is quite convinced that my uncle is out to kill him."

"I've heard. He even has you standing guard on him sometimes, does he not?"

Elyon nodded. "I'm hoping his paranoia will relent in time. I have never much cared for Dalton Taynar, my lady; he makes for dour company at the best of times. But for this wedding, I'd be going south with you to join my uncle Rikkard at Dragon's Bane. I would sooner find myself on the front line of a war than stationed at Dalton's side."

Marian Payne managed a small graceful laugh. "A shame. I would have liked to ride with you. I'm sure there's much and more for us to discuss, about Saska, and other matters besides. Our thoughts do seem in alignment on certain persons of interest, and the treacheries they have committed."

"Like your newly crowned king?" Elyon suggested. "It's widely rumoured that he had a personal hand in his father's death."

"I've heard the whispers, Sir Elyon. And those about King Ellis as well. The north is now ruled by a trio of traitorous kings, let me say that quite plainly. Yet the puppet master is, and always has been, Janilah Lukar. For many long years he sat in rivalry with King Godrin, and of course he thinks he's won. But I think different. Even after his death Godrin's plans will continue to unfold. The last laugh will be his, I assure you. It is just a matter of time."

Lady Marian Payne moved for the first time at that. Throughout she'd stood still and tall before him, holding court in the confines of that empty supply tent, but now she paced forward, long-legged strides closing the gap between them. "I will see you at the southern coast, I hope," she said, standing face-to-face with him, height-to-height. “Do hurry down once your dealings in Ilithor are done. I shall report to your uncle Rikkard that you fare well, if I should see him.”

“My thanks.” He dropped his head to a bow, and once again his right foot went forward. “It has been enlightening, Lady Payne. I bid you and your men a fond farewell, and safe travels on your onward journey.”

She left him at those words, gliding gracefully out through the flaps of the tent in a swirl of silver and grey. Her men followed, marching along behind her two by two, as she bled into the fading light of the dismantled camp. Elyon took a moment to himself before following. It would be back to the fortress of Harrowmoor now, back to the guard of Prince Dalton. But he still had something to do first. Something for the girl in his dreams.

He stepped out into the brisk dusky air, and continued his search for the lanky boy named Del.

7

Jonik

The little sandstone office of Upo Utappa sat beneath the shadow of the outer city walls, looking out across the harbour of Solas. Out there, a hundred ships were docked at the wharfs and jetties and riding the rise and fall of the waves at anchor, large and small. Cogs and caravels, galleys and galleons, skiffs and barges all bustled about the sparkling seas, while across the port deckhands and dockworkers laboured beneath the sun, pulling ropes and carrying crates and patching up lengths of sail.

It was another blazing day, and Upo's sparsely furnished office was stifling. It had in it only a desk, a small side table with a pair of old wooden chairs, and several shelves stacked with scrolls and accounts and the sundry documents the little harbourmaster kept. Jonik wiped a hand across his chalky brow, removing several beads of salty sweat as the conversation continued.

"So it's confirmed, then?" Emeric Manfrey was saying. "The warmoot is to take place at the Tower of Tears?"

Upo Utappa gave a nod, as he sat behind his old palmwood desk. He was a small man of middle years with skin of dark umber and an aversion to hair. He had none of it, so far as Jonik could see, not even eyebrows to frame his genial eyes. About his bony frame was a loose yellow linen tunic, embroidered with the crest of Solas; a circular golden disc, surrounded by a pattern of silver rays. "Yes," he said to

Emeric's question, his voice warm in the tones of his people. "I have been assured of it by several different sources. Many are travelling there as we speak by way of horse, carriage, and sail. It is a concession to help end the violence here and across the Empire. Empress Valura has no choice but to hear the Patriots' plea."

The old crone at the tavern in the Snakeways had told Jonik as much several days ago, and Emeric had learned of the same during his own investigations. "I suppose not," he agreed. "What do you imagine the outcome will be, Upo?"

"War," the diminutive harbourmaster said. "I'm afraid it can only be war, Emeric. The Patriots have expressed their full strength, and have more adherents than anyone let themselves believe. It is said both sunlords and moonlords from here to Eagle's Perch are rallying to them, and many Lightborn Sunriders and Starriders also. Even those with pacifist leanings know there is little choice but to side with Agarath, my friend. This news from the north has confirmed it, I fear."

That news had filtered through over the last couple of days. It told of a shift in power in Vandar and Rasalan; the fall and rise of kings. War between Tukor and Rasalan had come to an abrupt cessation and the entire continent had fast united. Now the fear all across the empire was that the Warrior King would drive forward his advantage while the south fell to civil discord. Emeric seemed certain that would happen. "Janilah Lukar will not waste this opportunity," he said, dressed in a basic brown tunic and light breeches of cream. "His line have always had their eye set on a southern invasion. Some posit that he manipulated the last war, by having King Horris Reynar murdered when the Vandarian royal delegation was in Eldurath. We all know what happened after."

"We do," said Upo, "but that is not a rumour I have heard."

It was widely known that King Tellion of Agarath had Horris Reynar killed, Jonik recalled. Leastways that was the northern understanding of events. The Agarathi ever claimed otherwise. To them Horris Reynar fell to natural causes, dying of heart failure as he slept. Like Upo, Jonik had never heard of Janilah's involvement. He looked at Emeric with a single raised brow. "I've not heard it either," he admitted.

"No, because not many would dare repeat it," Emeric told them. "Men who did tended to wind up dead by way of *unfortunate* accidents.

Mine own cousin, Sir Gerlan Stonewood, was one of them. He was the eldest son of Lord Stonewood, a lesser Vandarian lord, and my dear old aunt, Lady Lucilla Manfrey. At twenty Sir Gerlan joined the Greycloaks, and when King Horris travelled to Eldurath with his delegation, my cousin was there among his protective guard. But when he returned..." Emeric shook his head. "...he was never the same. There was something dark in him, some secret he wouldn't share. But one night I got it out of him, when he came to my castle and we got into our cups. He confessed to me that King Horris had never been slain by Tellion's men, but poisoned by his own. Men secretly under Janilah's employ, it was thought. Sir Gerlan recalled nothing of our conversation the next morning - or pretended not to, at least - and when I asked him of it, he returned to the official account that all the north was repeating."

He gave out a sigh. "It was the last time I ever saw him. Next I heard, he'd hanged himself in a barn on his father's lands. Suicide, they called it, but I knew my cousin, and he'd never have dishonoured himself or his family by taking his own life. He was murdered, I'm certain, as were many others back then, to hide the truth of what truly happened. I've known ever since that Janilah was behind King Horris's death."

Upo was nodding thoughtfully. "Not news to surprise anyone, I wouldn't say, and now it seems history repeats itself, my friend. First Janilah saw to the slaying of Horris Reynar, and now he does the same with his grandson, Ellis."

Emeric Manfrey nodded darkly and walked to the open stone window, turning his eyes out over the azure seas, heaving with hulls and a rocking forest of masts and flapping sails. While their nights had been spent in the city in search of the men who'd murdered Brewilla, by day they remained on the ship where they rested and trained, or here at the docks where they gathered information from the sailors and seamen, deckhands and dockworkers, traders and merchants who came in and out of port. It was how they came upon some interesting happenings, and the fishmarket was particularly productive, where stories and secrets were traded as readily as cockles and clams.

Jonik had heard many rumours there. There was talk of trouble in Eldurath, of rioting in the Pits of Kharthar. He'd heard of pirates roaming the open seas, of outlaws roving the lands, of growing unrest at the Wings. Something was stirring there, they said, and word of wild dragons attacking ships and caravans were becoming more common. One had even landed just outside the city, a week or so ago, some sleek grey dragon appearing in the dead of night, rumour said, before leaving only a few minutes later.

But it was the rumours of the Patriots of Lumara that most interested Jonik, and the many powerful lords in their ranks. Iru Zon and Elio Krator and Pal Palek among others. They were the heads of the snake, the men most responsible for the atrocities befalling northmen across the south. "This warmoot," Jonik said, as the exiled lord stared out over the harbour. "Might it not present an opportunity, Emeric? If all their leaders are there together..." He didn't need to say the rest.

"I'd caution against that," put in Upo Utappa, sitting at his desk. "You are but two men, against a military order. What we are talking about is quite different to what you've been doing so far, my friends. Laying siege to a few Patriot safehouses is not the same as slaying their leaders. Not only will each be heavily defended, but these men are powerful Lightborn themselves, with fearsome mounts for company. You may kill one, or two perhaps, but what will that truly serve?"

"Justice," breathed Emeric Manfrey, staring out over the docks. "We still do not know for sure who gave the order to raze my estate, Upo. Need I remind you that twenty of my staff were murdered, including the woman I loved."

"I know, my friend, and I can feel your pain. It is why I have sought to help you, despite the dangers it brings me and my own family. But you have slain many dozens of men now, and I wonder when it is enough. How long will this butchery go on before you are satisfied?"

"I want the man who gave the order. That is all."

"Jonik reported that it was Karlesh," Upo said. "Did he not tell you that with his dying breath, Jonik?"

"He might have been lying," the former Shadowknight offered.

"Or he might not," went on the little harbourmaster. "A man like Karlesh would be eager to please. He was young, from old Lightborn blood, and cruel. A good man to rise through the ranks of the Patriots. It is quite possible he mustered men to do this himself to win favour. Other northmen have seen the same treatment, and you were well known here, Emeric. Bardook. Ligrillo. Tix. Maxar. You have killed all you have discovered to be involved in this plot. Is that not enough?"

Emeric had no answer. He had nothing left now, save this hunt for Brewilla's killers. He'd lived here for over a dozen years in exile, having had his life in the north destroyed, and now the same had happened again. *He is a man of no nation, like me,* Jonik thought. *We walk this path together now. This path of destruction and death.*

"Karlesh could have been protecting someone," Jonik said, drawing Upo's eye. "Do you think it's possible the order came from Iru Zon?"

"No." Upo folded his skinny arms. "No, I do not. Iru Zon would not treat with a man so low. If he gave the order it would have passed through a dozen lips before reaching Karlesh's ears."

"But it still may have come from him," Emeric said, turning. There was a dark weariness in his eyes, a thinning of his cheeks. Emeric had lost his appetite for supping and slumber both, eating little and sleeping less over the last week. "I might find some rest if I put Sir Oswald's blade through his heart, Upo."

"Sir Oswald, yes. One of the greatest ever First Blades. A man who killed two dragons in single combat. A legend of your people, I know." He levelled Emeric with a reproachful look. "What would he make of this?"

"Of what?"

"Of this quest for vengeance. Does it not lack honour, Emeric? You were an Emerald Guard once. Is this not against your oaths, to hunt and slay and assassinate as you have been doing."

"I gave up on those oaths when Modrik Kastor stripped me of my land and titles. I am an exile, Upo, bound to no land, no order, no oath. And honour? There can be honour in justice, old friend. For that is what I seek. *Justice*. Not vengeance."

"Justice has been sought and served." Upo Utappa stood from his chair. "Karlesh is dead. So are the rest. Every man you have identified as being there that day have joined the blackness of night, forever dark for their sins. And you have heard nothing of who gave the order, save what Karlesh said. Now I say this *must* end, Emeric. I can have no further part in it."

"I understand." Emeric's lips forged themselves into a grateful smile. "You've done more than enough, Upo, but we will leave come the morrow. I know we've taken up space in your harbour too long."

"Space on the water is not what concerns me." Upo's hairless eyebrows creased to a frown. "Where will you go? East, I suppose?"

"East is the only way, my friend. I might find rest in the Telleshi Isles. They are a haven for lost souls like me."

"Then I advise you both carve out a home there. Take these men of yours and let this war pass you by, then consider what to do next." He gave Emeric Manfrey a doubtful look. "But I can see that will not happen."

"You never know," said Emeric, as he stepped forward, and the two clasped shoulders in farewell. "You never know, old friend."

"Yes, and that is what frightens me." Upo shook his head, though there was some levity back in his eyes. "I will see you off in the morning, Emeric. Whichever path you take, by sea and sail or steed and stone, I pray it bears you well."

They parted with the little harbourmaster at that, Emeric and Jonik stepping back out onto the port and toward the busy jetty where their skiff had been docked. They got a few bitter looks as they went, but were quite used to those now. Jack and Braxton were waiting in the rowboat, lounging beneath the mid afternoon sun upon the seating planks. Captain Turner and Soft Sid had rowed over with them too, though the pair looked to be absent. "Gone down to the fishmarket," Jack o' the Marsh explained when Emeric asked of their whereabouts. "Captain wanted lobster for dinner. Went to see Mugro about it."

"Captain Turner should be saving his coin," Emeric said. "My own coffers won't sustain us much longer, and we'll need provisions for our onward voyage." He turned his eyes eastward. "Sid went with him?"

Jack nodded confirmation. If not accompanied by a Bladeborn, Soft Sid was the next best thing to a bodyguard. At his size, few men would dare interfere with them. "They've been a while, though," the burly Marshlander was quick to add. "Was expecting them back by now. How'd it go with Upo?"

"He confirmed the warmoot is happening, as we'd thought," Jonik said. "The Empire will unite in war with Agarath against the north. If we think it's been difficult being here up to now...well, it's going to get a whole lot worse." He glanced over at Emeric. "Does that about sum it up?"

"I'd say you've hit upon the essence of it, yes."

"So we're leaving?" asked Brown Mouth Braxton, as he sat up on the rowing seat, and shielded the sun from his eyes.

"On the morning tide," confirmed Emeric. "We've done all we can here, and I'm inclined to say we've outstayed our welcome. Upo has been far too kind, and I've taken advantage of his generosity too long. It's time we sailed east, but we'll need our captain for that." He looked down the harbour. "Jonik, accompany me while I look for Captain Turner. We'd best make sure he's not gotten himself into trouble."

Jack o' the Marsh was fast on his feet. "I'll come too," he said, leaping deftly from the skiff for a man of his size. The rowboat lurched on the waters as he removed his weight. "Feel like stretching my legs."

Emeric nodded. "Braxton, wait here, if you will. We shan't be long."

Leaving Brax to resume his sunbathing, the three stepped toward the fishmarket a little further up the waterfront. They worked past the busy wharfs and jetties, past the looming Sun of Solas that shone ever bright at the heart of the harbour, a brilliant beacon for passing ships. The bustle was continuous. Porters went up and down from the cogs and caravels, pulling wains and wagons, conveying casks and crates and bolts of cloth. Sailors here between journeys made for the city gates, where the brothels and bars and bazaars awaited.

There were soldiers too, with their silky sunshine robes and studded leather tunics and those big round gilded shields they carried, the metalwork inlaid with the city crest. Those soldiers were here to protect the docks and harbour markets from the violence in the city, though had failed on that account once or twice. On those occasions, bloody skirmishes had broken out, the first involving a Vandarian merchant out of Mudport and his sellsword guards, and the second a bitter affray between locals who shared contrasting outlooks over the war. In both cases, some half dozen men had been killed, though Jonik had heard the Mudport merchant managed to get to his ship in time and flee, less a few unfortunate mercenaries who'd more than lived up to their terms of service.

Overall, the trouble in the city had been kept largely to the Snakeways, though, and over the last couple of days it had turned from a boil to a simmer, as the city guards took back control of the streets. Now it would likely stop entirely. The Patriots had gotten what they wanted in forcing Empress Valura into the warmoot, and there was no sense in them stirring further violence. *No, it's time for them to unite, as the north have,* Jonik thought. *It's time for the Last Renewal.*

When they reached the fishmarket, they found it typically busy. Though termed a fishmarket it was rather more, in truth, and all sorts of wares were bartered and traded. They stopped on the outskirts, looking through the confusion of carts and stalls, sellers and shoppers. It was a maelstrom of noise and colour and movement, stretching along an expansive length of the waterfront beyond the larger jetties and wharfs. Beneath the city walls to the west, a system of alcoves and covered colonnades had been built to be used for private, long-term storefronts. Along the harbourside, half the fishmongers sold directly from their little boats. Between them were the carts and stalls, where Mugro ran his successful operation trading lobsters, clams, prawns, and secrets. They headed to him first, and found him in characteristic mood, calling his deals of the day in competition with the other traders who'd pitched themselves nearby. "Ah, my friends," he said when he spotted them. "You seek more lobster, yes? Or is it information you desire?" He grinned that playfully pudgy grin of his. "More fishwives whisper me their secrets for kisses. I have more news for you, yes, more news from afar if you have the coin."

"We need no more fisherman's tales from you, Mugro," said Emeric. "It is the captain of Invincible Iris we seek. Jack said he came to you for lobster."

Mugro nodded. "Lobster, yes, he bought three."

"Where is he now?" Emeric demanded.

Mugro raised a stubby finger, pointing toward the city walls. "He went toward the arcade with the silent giant. He wanted spices, I think, for my delicious lobsters and prawns."

"Spices and *rum*," Jack muttered. "The rate Turner and Brax get through it, we'll be needing more soon."

"Ah yes, rum is sold in there too," put in Mugro. "Good rum. The best rum. I know a man who can give you good price. A half sickle for his name." He smiled and looked directly at Jonik. "You like hearing names from me, yes? I have more for you. Many more."

Emeric didn't look interested in furthering the discussion with the man. "Jonik, Jack, why don't you check the arcade. I'll search elsewhere. We know what Turner's like with his gambling." He needn't say anymore. Captain Gill Turner had a weakness for betting and around the market there were many such opportunities.

They split again, walking away from Mugro's attempts to coax more coin from their pockets. Eventually the lobstermonger gave up and continued calling out his wares, adding his voice to the constant din and chatter. "So Emeric's satisfied, then?" Jack asked as they went. "This whole vendetta against the Patriots...it's over?"

Jonik shrugged as they worked through the alleys and lanes between stalls. "He still wants the man who gave the order. I don't think he believes Karlesh would have raided his estate without leave from a higher power."

"Could be anyone though," Jack said. "There are dozens of high-born Patriots in Solas, let alone the rest of Lumara and the other southern nations. Or maybe the order came from elsewhere."

"Like?"

"Well, a certain warrior king comes to mind. I'm sure he's heard that Emeric's joined you in this quest by now, and what better way to punish him than have a few southern sellswords raze his estate."

Jonik didn't give that option much credence. "Janilah holds no sway down here. You think the Patriots of Lumara are likely to follow his orders? Come on, Jack. There's no reason to think he's involved."

Jack o' the Marsh bobbed his burly shoulders, his muscular arms exposed beyond the cream linen vest he wore. "It wouldn't have to be a direct order," he said. "A letter to the right person and word could easily trickle down into the ears of a man like Karlesh." He could tell Jonik wasn't buying it. "Fine, it's unlikely," he admitted. "But you might want to give it a little more thought, maybe suggest it to Emeric if he hasn't considered it himself."

"Why?" Jonik asked. "What purpose would it serve?"

Jack frowned to that, as though the answer was obvious. "It would consolidate your enemies, Ghost. You want vengeance against the Shadow Order, and to free those like you from their chains, don't you?"

Jonik begrudgingly nodded. He always found himself confessing far too much to Jack o' the bloody Marsh. Only a few nights ago he'd given in to the Marshman's questioning and admitted that his own path would take him back to the Shadowfort eventually. He'd even spoken of his recurring dream. The one where he stood in the mountains with Jack to his right and Emeric to his left, and Turner and Brax and the rest beside them, and then a dozen more, a hundred more, a thousand more, all ghosts in the darkness, men he was destined to lead in his bid to take the Shadowfort for his own, cast out the masters and the dark evil menace that lurked there. *The Shadow King,* he thought. Even to Jonik, who'd grown up among those black towers, the figure was mostly myth, but he'd always heard the whispers. That there was a darker presence there beyond the Shadow Masters and their council. An ancient evil that the masters themselves served.

"I'll take that surly silence as a 'yes'," Jack went on in his carefree way, as they continued past a glaring Piseki costermonger and a Lumaran boy selling bread and sweet cakes from a cart. "So you want to return to the Shadowfort for vengeance, and Emeric's busy trying to find his own justice against the Patriots of Lumara." He shrugged. "Well, seems that Lord Emeric's achieved his goal there, so why not get him turning his eyes back north?"

"By suggesting to him that Janilah is behind what happened?" Jonik gave that a derisive snort. "Emeric has no love for Janilah anyway, Jack. And if he wants vengeance against anyone in Tukor, it's the Kastors."

"For exiling him? I know. But Lord Modrik Kastor's over three years dead, Ghost. Emeric can hardly blame his son for what happened to him. Going after Lord Cedrik isn't the answer."

"And going after King Janilah is? There's no man more powerful in the north, nor the south most likely. And just how does getting Emeric to target Janilah help me? It's the Shadowfort I want. Not Ilithor."

"You want justice," Jack came back at him. "You want the men who made you a weapon. Then you want Janilah Lukar. It's obvious that he's been behind everything you've been forced to do, given what we've heard. So once you take the Shadowfort, and win yourself an army, you might just want to turn your attentions to the Warrior King too."

Jonik had wondered that as well, in truth. Janilah Lukar did seem to be the man behind the curtain, manipulating everyone to his will. But still... "That's a lot to be doing, Jack," he said, with something of a weary sigh. "I'd need that army first. Emeric's a start, but I'll need a host more Bladeborn before I even consider heading back into those mountains."

"True enough. I suppose the rest of us aren't much use in a fight against Shadowmen." They were coming along, though. Jack had a natural skill with the blade and young Devin was showing good progress. With Emeric's mind clouded by his grief he'd given up training the two in the blade, leaving Jonik to take up the mantle. The main deck of Invincible Iris had become their training yard this last week, and even Grim Pete had joined in once or twice, now that the world was falling to war. "We'll have to find sellswords, I guess," Jack went on. "Though that's not so easy without coin to pay them."

"We have the blades," Jonik noted. "The ones we picked up on Passway Key."

Those blades had been taken from the half dozen cutthroat mercenaries Lady Shark had sent, men Jonik and Emeric had easily dealt with. They'd had among them a sleek scimitar, several broadswords, and a greatsword too that a mighty brute had wielded. In the right hands they could be useful; unfortunately neither Jack nor Devin nor any of the rest had but a drop of Varin blood in them. In the end those blades were useless lest they found willing Bladeborn to join them in their cause, and those were in short supply around here.

"You're suggesting we sell them?" Jack asked.

"It's a thought," admitted Jonik, because that was the other option. "Mugro did tell me he knew a man who'd be willing to buy them. A northern merchant based on Solapia called Vincent Rose. Emeric's heard of him too. Not a man you can trust, but one who has an ear in everyone's business, apparently. Might be worth paying him a visit on our way east."

They turned a corner, wending between carts of cloth and clothing, as the city walls loomed ahead. The arcade was established along this stretch of the external defences, accessed through pillared archways of chipped yellow sandstone. Beyond were some hundred semi-permanent stores, erected beneath the vaulted ceiling and out of the sun's blazing glare. It was a relief to escape the heat. Even the short walk along the harbour front was burdensome for Jonik, having grown up in the frigid climes of the high Hammersongs. A dozen scents filled his nose as he turned his eyes around. The rich warm smell of leather being worked. The aroma of perfumes, popular among the highborn ranks here. The sharp tang of spices from all across the south.

"So where shall we start?" asked Jack, looking left and right. "Spices? Rum? Gambling dens? They play dice and cards in the alcoves here, I've heard, and we know how Cap Turner likes a flutter. There's also a popular game where men gamble over the length of their manhoods." He looked into Jonik's eyes. "No joke. They actually do."

"If that's the case, then it's a good thing he's got Sid with him," is all Jonik said to that.

Jack laughed, the sound echoing under the arches. "Probably why he brought him along in the first place. It'd take the Sword of Varinar to geld the man."

Jonik gave out a raspy snort. Sid was rather well-endowed, it was true. And then he thought of all the bastard boys up in the mountains, those stripped from their mother's breast and raised in darkness, raised as weapons. Most of them had been gelded too, lest they had strong enough blood to sire sons for the order. Jonik had been lucky in that regard and still had all the bits between his legs, but it wasn't so for the rest. His laughter curdled along with his expression. "Let's ask around," he said. "Maybe someone will have..."

He cut himself off and turned his eyes to the right. With a hand beneath his cloak, clinging to the hilt of his godsteel dagger, he'd heard it. *Knives being drawn.* The sound was unmistakable. Further down the colonnades he saw a group of men, five in sum, approaching a single figure lying on his side within a shallow niche in the wall. The man was sleeping, by the looks of him, and drunk. A clay bottle of something lay beside him, dribbling out a brown liquid. Jonik could tell by the shade of his skin that he was northern, though it was hard to be sure, filthy as he was, his cheeks dressed in a patchy reddish-brown beard. The drunk was large by the look of him, garbed in a roughspun grey cloak, and the men had clearly spotted an easy prize.

"Wait here."

It was all Jonik said. A moment later he'd left Jack behind, pacing swiftly behind the group as they closed in on their prey. They were still a couple of metres from the drunk when Jonik offered a polite word of advice. "I'd leave him be if you want to walk out of here alive." Every one of them turned, unveiling the faces hidden beneath their hoods. To Jonik's surprise, every one of them was light skinned too. "Who are you?" he demanded, eyes scanning and seeing the faint silver mist now rising from the mens' blades. *Bladeborn,* he realised. *Godsteel.* He took a short step back to give himself room to fight. Out came his own dagger in one hand and the Nightblade in the other. He searched their faces for one he might recognise. *Shadowknights?* was his first thought. *Gerrin's finally caught up with me.* But no, he saw no one he knew, and Shadowmaster Gerrin certainly wasn't among them.

The men ignored Jonik's question. Their eyes fell instead to the black misting blade in his grasp. "It's him," one growled. "The Ghost..."

"The blade," said another. His eyes glowed eagerly beneath his cowl. "Grab it."

They moved in at once, one slashing out at Jonik's chest, a second following right behind with a thrusting jab. *Assassins,* Jonik realised, as he side-stepped their attacks. *Cutthroats on our trail.* He and his friends had accumulated many admirers over their weeks on the run, and this was the latest batch. *The latest batch to die,* he thought, as he swung the Nightblade down and took off the arm of the first attacker, slicing it clean just below the shoulder. The man gave out a wheezing shriek as his arm dropped to the floor, still clinging to his godsteel blade, which hit with a heavy *clunk*.

A clunk loud enough to wake the drunken stranger, apparently, because a moment later he was lurching to his feet in a sudden swift motion, and pulling a great misting sword from beneath his rough-spun cloak. Jonik caught sight of a glint of swirling steel as the drunk swung in a brutal strike, hacking one of the men in half at the shoulders, as easy as that. The next man went down just as feebly, the drunk dropping low and swinging through his legs first, then standing up tall and taking off his head, which went rolling away through the nearest arch and out onto the sunbathed market. The crowds screamed and fled upon seeing it, but above the noise the drunk's voice bellowed free.

"I was having a bloody good kip there!" he roared, as the last two sellswords swung at him. Jonik decided to stand by and observe, slipping the Nightblade away. His dagger would be fine should he need it.

He didn't.

The drunk man was a savage, and clearly expertly trained. Even sotted and half asleep he despatched the final two mercenaries with alarming proficiency, carving one open at the belly and splitting the second from navel to neck in a blustering upswing. In an instant all were down, and the market had deserted of shoppers and sellers. The drunk gave out a grunting roar, shook his head as though still waking from his stupor, then turned his eyes on Jonik. "You're one of these?" he demanded, in a slurry voice. "You'd...you'd try to kill a man as he slept!" He stepped forward in a lumbering gait.

Jonik stayed put. "I'd *save* a man as he slept. You're alive because of me, sir. You owe me a life debt."

"A life debt!" the drunk spluttered. "For what?" His eyes went down to the jumble of bodies at his feet, their blood draining out through the gaps in the cobbles, a deep dark red in the shade. "*I* killed these bloody men, not you!"

He was older than Jonik had first realised, a good decade senior to Emeric by the look of his haggard face. There was something about him that was familiar, though. "Only once you'd awoken," Jonik said, all calm. "Before then they were about to kill you, until I intervened. They must have seen your blade." Jonik gave it a look. There was a flowing watery design to the cross-guard, and small blue and green jewels encrusted into the hilt. Flashes of red light showed on the length of the steel. "It looks valuable." *And I'm sure I've seen it before*, he thought.

"It's more than valuable, boy. It's bloody *in*valuable!" He bent down and picked up his bottle of rum or whiskey or whatever he was drinking, and had a long swig, then threw the empty bottle aside with a loud crash. "That one's still alive," he said after, pointing with that fine broadsword of his. It was the man whose arm Jonik had taken off, down on his knees trying to stem the flow. "That's all you did. You took his arm. I took four heads." He swung nonchalantly and cleaved the man's head clean off his shoulders. "Make that five. You'll not get a bloody life debt from me for that."

"Then you have no honour," Jonik told him, and apparently that was the wrong thing to say.

"HONOUR!" the drunk roared. Spittle came surging from his lips and his eyes were veined with red lightning. "There's not a bloody soul here with any honour! For days I've been looking for passage off this heap of sun-baked shit and not a single bloody captain will take me!"

"Do you have coin?" Jonik asked, wondering why he'd not encountered the man before.

"Coin? Coin!" He pulled a pouch from his pocket and threw it at his feet with a dull clunk. "Coin enough to get drunk and little else, it seems. Apparently I'm to spend the rest of my days drinking rum beneath this rotting wall. Not much of an end is it, for a man like me? What?" His eyes were blaring. "What!"

"There's blood soaking into your coin pouch," Jonik said.

"Bah!" The drunk picked it up again, almost keeling over as he did so, and thrust it into his pocket. How he slew those men in such a state was beyond Jonik's comprehension.

"I have a ship," Jonik told him. "We're sailing on the morning tide. Agree to that life debt right here and now and you can come with us." He was thinking of his quest. *A man like this might be useful*, he thought. "Or you can drink yourself to death right here, if you'd prefer. It's up to you." Jonik stepped forward, holding his dagger, the Nightblade hidden in its sheath among the folds of his airy cloak. The drunk clearly hadn't noticed him wielding it. "You speak of honour. I'll have your oath by godsteel." He reached out with his spare hand and waited for the man to consider it, though he seemed in no fit state to be making decisions of such gravity.

"If it helps, I saw the entire thing," came a voice in the meantime. Jonik didn't need to turn around to find Jack o' the Marsh there, faithful as ever at his right side. "He did save your life, sir. He saw those cutthroats stalking you from a way off and rushed to help. By your honour you owe him."

The big old drunk took in Jack, blinking through his bleary bloodshot eyes. "You're a man of the marshes," he said, half disbelieving.

Jack smiled. "I am. And proud to say so. I hail from a village near Mudport and used to fish the Mire as a boy. East Vandarian to my bones, sir."

"Yes, I...I can tell." The man's cracked lips peeled open into a trembly smile. He looked suddenly close to tears. "I thought all the northmen were gone from here. You...you have a ship, truly? You can take me north. Take me home?"

"We can," Jonik said, still holding out his hand. The man made to put the pouch of coins in his grasp, but Jonik shook his head. "Your debt is a life, not coins. That's how you'll pay for passage."

What has this man been through? he was thinking. And still he was trying to place him.

"A life for a life," the sot said, grunting. He considered it a second longer, then seemed to see no option but to relent. "It doesn't look like I've got much of a bloody choice, does it. Story of my life recently...but as soon as I kill for you, or save your life, that's my debt fulfilled. Yes?"

"Those are the terms," Jonik said, as though he'd done this a thousand times.

"Fine." The big man took his hand and shook once, then slid his meaty mitt away, leaving behind a palmful of dust and grime and slick sticky blood. "So you're Bladeborn, are you?" He perused the pair of them, still looking like he might totter over and collapse at any moment. "Both of you?"

"Just him," said Jack.

"I see." The drunk's eyes moved down to the hilt of the Nightblade. "Black haft. Unusual. And black pommel and scabbard too." He shrugged and peered forward lazily, leaning closer to get a better look at Jonik. "You look kinda familiar there, boy." He chuckled to himself. "Look a bit like Elyon, you know, just skinner and half as handsome. Elyon Daecar. You've heard of him, of course."

"Of course." Jonik's voice stiffened. Now it came to him. Now he knew. "You're Borrus Kanabar," he said. "The Varin Knight." *You were with my father*, he thought, his heart starting to rush. *You were there in Rasalan with him when I*...Even now, he could hardly even finish the thought. *When I made him a cripple.*

"Ha, well look at that," laughed the burly knight. "I'm still recognisable even after all this time. Covered in filth and half the size. That's good to know." He smiled broadly. It seemed so out of place, that grin, as he stood there over those five butchered corpses. But that was Borrus Kanabar, Jonik knew. He was said to have killed as many men as any knight during the last war. Killing came far too easily to him. And that was some cause for concern.

"Sir Borrus Kanabar," Jack was saying. "The heir to House Kanabar?" He looked shocked to see such an eminent man here. The Kanabars were the most powerful house in all of Eastern Vandar, and the lords of the Marshlands, where Jack had grown up, would be bannermen to Sir Borrus' father, Wallis. "What...what are you doing all the way down here, my lord? I took you as a drunken beggar when I saw you, I'm ashamed to say."

"No shame...no shame in that, boy. But this isn't the worst I've looked these last weeks, believe me. Long story," he said to Jack's querying look. "Long bloody story." Sir Borrus Kanabar licked his lips and rubbed his eyes. "So...this ship." He seemed to have trouble fully collecting his thoughts. Blinking, he took Jonik in again. "It's yours? Who are you?" Then his eyes fell to the black hilt of the Nightblade again, and he frowned at it for an extended moment. "Hang on. Is...is that..." He shook his head, and laughed. "That's not..." He looked up, and a cognisance returned to his eyes. "*You're* not..."

Jonik was wondering whether to just kill him right there and then, and add his body to the pile. This man was one of Amron Daecar's closest friends, after all. *When he finds out who I am...what then?* He had to balance that against the man's honour, if he still had any. The Varin Knights held their oaths sacred, though to look at him, he hardly seemed a Varin Knight anymore. In the end, he decided that the truth was best.

So out came the Nightblade, thrumming with that divine black mist as it slid from its black scabbard, and in an instant Borrus Kanabar was moving into Blockform, every muscle in his stricken body tensing. "Assassin," was all he managed to slur, eyes narrowing. "You're that bloody Ghost...that Shadowknight..."

"I mean you no harm, Sir Borrus," Jonik told him in an even voice. "But I quite understand your reaction." He held the blade aside, and low, so as to be unthreatening. "I have only one question for you - will you hold to your life debt and the oath you promised, or are we going to have a problem?"

Borrus Kanabar gaped. For a long, long moment absolutely nothing happened. "I..." It was all he could conjure. "I..."

"I've got a long story too, sir," Jonik told him. "Don't do anything rash until you've heard it."

"I..."

"We can return to the ship and talk this over, once you've rested. You'll come to no harm, I promise."

"I..."

"I'm glad we agree." Jonik smiled as cordially as he could. He gently slid the Nightblade back into its scabbard, then did the same with his dagger in a show of good faith. "Sheath your blade, sir," he said. "Enough blood has been shed for one day, I think."

"The city guards will be here any moment, Sir Borrus," Jack put in. "Sheath your sword and we'll get you safe to the ship. We have a skiff on the water nearby. It's not far."

Borrus Kanabar continued to stare at Jonik, with a new emotion behind every blink. Hatred there. *Oh, he wants to kill me.* Confusion there. *He's wondering why I'm here.* A bit of apprehension there. *He knows I'll kill him in a duel.* But most of all there was complete and utter fatigue. And in the end, that won the day.

Borrus Kanabar passed out right there on the cobbles, adding his body to the pile.

8

Amron

The bear was bigger than any Amron Daecar had ever seen, a monstrous white shadow lurking at the foot of the outcrop. "Quiet," whispered Rogen Whitebeard, his dark orange eyes peering over the lip of the rock. "Do not make a sound, and he will pass."

Amron clung hard to his godsteel dagger as he lay flush atop the black pillar of rock, stained white by frost and ice. The last light of the day was fleeing, and hadn't been with them long enough, the days growing short and shorter still. From the top of the outcrop the Icewilds spread out flat and far around them, pockmarked with surging formations of rock, gouged with chasms and clefts ripped deep into the earth. To the west, the horizon burned with a soft gold and crimson light where it met the cold grey sky. In but a few short minutes that light would fade into another long cold night. And the nights, just like everything else here, could kill.

Amron shuffled forward an inch, his black furs scratching at the rock and ice beneath him. Whitebeard glared as if the faint noise might attract the beast, but the winds were howling plenty loud enough to hide the sound. He looked over the edge. The bear was right beneath them, some twelve metres down the sheer drop, and four metres tall at the shoulder.

"We can kill it," Amron whispered. His breath frosted the air, joining the mists that swirled about them. The light was fast in retreat and with it went any lingering warmth. The sun was a miserly bastard out here, Amron Daecar had come to see. The further north they went, the more ungenerous it became, allotting them no more than a few short hours of light a day before plunging out of sight beneath the black horizon. Soon enough it would smile upon them a final time and fall beyond their sight for good.

Rogen Whitebeard's head shook within his ice-covered cowl. "It's too big, and too dangerous."

"I've killed bigger and more dangerous things before," Amron told him. The beast was nosing about the base of the cliff, scratching idly with its right paw. Those claws looked deadly, like to a disembowel a man in a single swipe. But a godsteel dagger through the top of its skull would be enough for it, Amron wagered. "I could jump," he whispered. "Put my blade through its head."

"No." Rogen Whitebeard had no time for heroics out here. "You're clad in fur, not godsteel, and these are his lands. We let him pass."

"And if he doesn't leave? We'll freeze to death if we have to stay up here overnight. We need to find shelter, Rogen."

"We're too exposed," Walter Selleck agreed, lying beside them. "And the weather's worsening." He said that too loud. The bear made a growly noise and looked up, and all three men planted themselves tight to the stone, stilling.

A long cold moment passed, until they heard the beast resuming its scratching and sniffing, trying to locate the source of their scent. "Did you never learn how to whisper, Selleck?" hissed Whitebeard. "Or do you not fear death as we mortals do?" Walter was not immortal, he was just lucky, and had styled himself the 'luckiest man in the world' for the blessing Vandar's spirit had bestowed upon him. It gave him a certain lack of care sometimes. *My light will protect us, and guide us,* he would often say. Pious words that a pragmatic ranger like Rogen Whitebeard would typically scoff at. "If you attract that bear again, I will throw you to him," the ranger warned, with a wolfish snarl. "Then Lord Daecar and I might use the distraction to escape."

"And lose my protection?" Walter's scraggly beard was coated in hoarfrost. Icicles clung to the sides of his moustache, hanging from within his hood, painted white by the fierce ice winds. "You'll not make it far without me, Whitebeard. I thought you'd come to see my value by now?"

Not long ago, Walter had indeed saved Rogen Whitebeard's life, when he'd tripped and tumbled down a snowy slope, and gone plummeting over the edge of a cliff. Quick as a whip, Walter had gone down with him, clinging to his legs like a limpet. They'd managed to land safely within a large bank of snow at the bottom of the sixty yard drop. A lucky place to land, to be sure, and all thanks to Walter, the man claimed. He liked to remind Rogen of it daily.

"I find myself weighing your use against your ineptitude," the ranger said, in a low growl. "At times like this I find myself wanting rid of you."

"For speaking a tad too loud?"

"For bringing that bear down upon us. You speak *too* loud *too* often. Out here, something is always listening."

Walter made to answer, but Amron cut him off. Now wasn't the time for their bickering, he knew. "I'm going to kill it," he said, coming to a decision. It was kill or be killed out here, so far as he saw it. He slid his godsteel dagger from its leather sheath, silent. Silver mist rose from its thin sharp edge, taken by the wind. He made to move, but Whitebeard's hand gripped his forearm tight.

"No." The ranger glanced back down at the bear. "If someone must be risked, it is me. You are in no condition to leap from this rock, my lord."

Amron bristled. He'd made it this far, despite his injuries. For weeks they'd been journeying north, across the Weeping Heights and this great white desolation, navigating the ranges and ridges, the slopes and scarps, the dark silent woods where the shadows and shades lurked, watching, always watching. "You forget who I am, Rogen," he told the ranger. "Need I remind you of my names?"

"I know your names, and I know who you are, Lord Daecar. A man with a weakened left arm and right leg. A man whom I am sworn to protect and guide into the darkness of these lands. A man who is too valuable to be risked. No, you'll not jump. If this bear must be killed, I will see it done."

"I'll not have you wager your own life on something I can do myself." Amron shifted forward a little more, judging the distance. The ranger's leather-gloved fingers gripped tighter at his wrist.

"*No*," he repeated, more firmly. "You will *not* leap from this rock, my lord."

Amron stared at him through his silvery blue eyes, crows feet reaching out toward his greying temples. The ranger had proven himself unbowed by Amron's rank and title, and not shy of giving orders. In any other setting he'd rally against that, but not here. He understood that this was Rogen Whitebeard's world, not his.

"Maybe...maybe we *should* wait," offered Walter, in a bid to break the tension. "As you say, Rogen, the bear may move off..."

"No." The ranger liked that word, they had found. His upturned amber eyes moved out over the darkening world. Frozen particles blew about them in the wind like a fine icy mist. "The winds are picking up, and a storm is coming. We need shelter, and we need it soon. In that, you are right, Lord Amron." He looked down to the foot of the cliff. "This bear will help provide it."

The ranger shifted forward, moving into a squat without a sound. His eyes narrowed, zeroing in on his prey. *A wolf,* Amron thought to look at him, watching as the man prowled forward, his dark grey whiskers coated white. It was how he got the name Whitebeard, for that permafrost that covered his face. The sun's last light was guttering out like a candle, shadows darkening upon the vast white world. Below, the great ice bear faded amid the mists and spreading pall of night. Sometimes, when the skies were clear, the long cold nights were not so black as Amron had feared. Moonlight and starlight would gleam upon the ice and snow, and make it seem as daylight to his eyes, even without the touch of godsteel to grasp. But other nights were different. When the skies were cloaked and clogged with cloud, an all consuming darkness would fall. This was to be one of those nights. The sort that all men feared.

A dull silver glow appeared as Whitebeard unsheathed his dark grey godsteel blade. Long legs hard as teak shuffled forward to the lip of rock, ready to pounce. The bear was a blurred shadow beneath them now, unaware of the threat above. It turned its head out toward the west, straightening its neck, as though watching the last light fade.

Whitebeard shifted forward, and leapt into the mists.

~

THE BEAST GAVE them sanctuary that night. After the ranger had leaped off the edge and put his blade through the beast's thick skull, he set about cutting it open, removing its entrails and insides, and forging them a shelter of bone and bear skin to beat off the bitter storm.

"Well it's rather cosy, if you ignore the smell," Walter Selleck pointed out in his cheery way. The bear-bone shelter had been skilfully erected alongside the outcrop, propped up with ribs and weighed with stones to stop it blowing away. Within his scaffold pack, Whitebeard carried a shelter of his own that they'd been using most nights, but a storm like this required something more robust. "Lucky the bear found us in the end, you might say," Walter said. There was even space to light a fire within, the smoke rising through a small hole cut into the hide roof. "Perhaps that's why I spoke so loudly earlier, Rogen. To lure it. Did you ever consider that?"

"Don't start, Walter," Amron admonished. "I think Rogen has earned a bit of silence from you for one evening."

"Evening, or is it still daytime?" Walter wondered. "I'm inclined to say that in any civilised part of the world, people would still be supping wine beneath a bright blue sky."

On the fire, some of their shelter was cooking, fat popping from the thick hunk of meat the bear had provided. Whitebeard had seen to that too, carving off the best cuts to cook and cure for their onward journey. He prodded the fire, glowering. "This bear should not have had to die," he said, in a voice thick with displeasure. "Beasts of this nature are too few. It shames me to butcher its body as such. I have no time for your jokes tonight, Selleck."

Walter was wise enough to know when not to push things. "How... how many are there left, do you imagine?" he asked, more sensitively.

"Too few," was the ranger's grunting reply. "And now there is one less."

Walter let a moment pass and then turned to Amron. "Have you ever seen a moonbear before, my lord?" he asked. "I suppose you must have, during the war. I've always wondered how large they truly are."

"A great deal bigger than this," Amron told him. "There were some Moonriders during the war, yes, though not many. Moonbears are rare and dangerous to bond for a Lightborn, but the effort is often worth it. Whenever one appeared at a battle or siege, they tended to turn the tide for the south. We lost many fights we might have won due to their interventions."

"I've heard it said that Bladeborn knights often prefer to duel dragons, if given the choice," Walter said. "I've always found that curious. A flying reptile with fiery breath and armoured skin seems more formidable to me than a giant bear."

"A common misconception," Amron explained, as the fierce winds tugged at the hide walls of the shelter. "Moonbears are far from regular bears, even giant ones. It isn't just that they're bigger. They have a special armour of their own, a crystalline structure to their fur that is every bit as durable as dragon scales. The moonbears, the sunwolves, the starcats...all have a magic to them. But the bears...they're unique. Bladeborn knights are weaned on stories of men matching up against dragons. Our histories are full of them, and it's not uncommon for the more stouthearted of knights to seek out such a duel. It's said that Varin takes a particular interest in them, for reasons that need no explanation. Slay a dragon and your place near the top of his Table is guaranteed. You will dine and drink with the dragon-slayers forever, they say. But to battle a moonbear and its bonded rider is different. Such occasions are rare historically, and thus we have not developed specific techniques to defeat them, as we have with dragons."

"So you never duelled one?" asked Whitebeard, hunched over the fire in his bundled leathers and furs.

Amron shook his head. "My father did, early in the war. He was part of the siege of Eagle's Perch, when King Storris sought to gain a foothold in the south. The siege was going well enough until a Moonrider arrived, charging our lines and scattering our forces at the head of a hundred Sunriders and Starriders. They're quite a sight in full flight, it must be said. My father was forced to abandon the siege and sail back to Mudport, though not before the Moonrider called him for a duel."

"I've heard this one from the bards," smiled Walter. "They say your father fought valiantly that day. That the moonbear twice had him in his jaws, ready to crush through his godsteel plate, and twice Gideon Daecar slashed himself free with the Sword of Varinar. He blinded the beast in the right eye, it's sung, before the Moonrider pulled the reins and fled for the fortress walls."

Amron had to laugh. "That was not my father's telling, but the singers do like to exaggerate, and paint our battles favourably. In truth the duel ended by mutual accord. The war was young and both saw profit in living to see a little more of it. It wasn't until the Battle of Burning Rock that they came together again, though they never met upon the battlefield that day. My father was too busy battling the Agarathi alongside King Storris, until Ulrik Marak came down on Garlath and slew them with his wingriders. They never got their second round."

"Who was he?" asked Rogen Whitebeard. "This Moonrider you speak of."

"A Lumosi Lightborn of ancient blood," Amron told him. "The Moonlord Justo Nemati, younger brother to the Grand Duchess of Aramatia. He's said to have perished of wounds he suffered that day at the Burning Rock, though the beast he rode did not. It returned to the sanctuary of its mountain, to live in peace, I've heard it said."

"A fate all war veterans deserve," Walter Selleck intoned. "Once their task is done."

"And when do you judge that?" Whitebeard asked sharply. It sounded like a challenge. "Has Lord Daecar not earned his retirement yet?"

"Many times over, for any normal man, but it would seem the world has need of him yet. He won a war, but not the *great war*. The War Eternal rages on, Rogen. The Last Renewal is upon us."

Rogen would usually show them his back at a comment like that, but with the ice storm raging outside, he had nowhere to go. "Not tonight," was all he requested. "Leave your preachings for another day."

Walter did just that.

They woke the next morning in darkness, though the storm had passed and the skies had stilled. Above them, a glitter of stars spread forth to the far horizon, the heavens softly coloured in shades of blue and purple and pink. At times like these it seemed the most beautiful place in all the world, distant and peaceful and far from the cruelties of man. Yet before the sun rose for its short arc across the skies, they saw evidence that such cruelty remained, even here.

"These are the bones of children," Rogen Whitebeard said.

They had come upon an abandoned settlement of sorts, shelters of stone and animal hide left to rot among a small scatter of rocks.

Amidst the remains of an old fire were piles of small blackened bones. Whitebeard took no time to judge who they'd belonged to.

"A sacrifice," he said. "To beseech their gods for game and good hunting. The more innocent the slain, the more bountiful the reward." He looked over the pile. "They must have been hungry, to have killed so many."

A chill climbed up Amron's spine. "When did they abandon the village, Rogen?"

"Abandon? No, they will return, in time." He shook a piece of hide canvas, the rough hairs clinging with ice and snow. "This is good material, and not to be wasted. They will range through winter in search of better hunting grounds, and return here come spring. They must have killed the children before they left."

A question was on Amron's tongue that he didn't want to ask. Rogen had spoken about cannibalism among the tribes, especially when the long winter fell and game became harder to come by. "Would they have eaten them? The children."

"Meat is not to be wasted," the ranger said, "but in this case, no, the sacrificial custom would prevent the flesh being consumed. They build pyres for their sacrifices. Fire is purifying, Lord Daecar, and the children are chosen young for their innocence. By the time the ritual is complete, the bones are all that remain."

"Which tribe?" Walter whispered, with a shudder to his voice. He looked as pale as the ice about them.

Whitebeard looked over the abandoned shelters. "It's hard to be sure," he said. "Sacrifice is common here, as is cannibalism. Some tribes take to it more eagerly than others, but when pushed to the extreme, there can be little choice. Often it depends on the leader. Weakness is not suited to these climes, and ruthlessness is often favoured. A sacrifice can thus serve a dual purpose, of appeasing the gods, and thinning the herd, so there are fewer mouths to feed."

Rogen Whitebeard had told them much and more of the tribes here, and the gods they worshipped. Many favoured animalism and a devotion to the natural world, though not all. The Deadcloak Clan of the Deadwood saw religion in the fur and hide garb they wore, worshipping every beast they slew to keep them warm through winter. The Crowmen of the Crag hailed the birds that garnished their black feathered cloaks. The Snowskins had grown adapted to the conditions more than most, with their white hair and milky skin, and developed a culture that worshipped snow and ice and the white world they inhabited. The Wild Weepers who prowled the northernmost ranges of the Weeping Heights were said to follow a dark spirit of the old age, some twisted form of one of Vandar's lesser gods. Rogen had spoken of them being particularly dangerous, raping and pillaging often into the smaller settlements that bordered the Banewood.

There were few tribes who took permanent residence at the heart of the Icewilds, though. Most stayed to the extremes and borders and would only rove across the wasteland when need drove them to do so. Curiously, none worshipped Vandar himself, despite existing so close to his tomb. According to Whitebeard, the tribes didn't go so far as that mountain. To them it was associated with the steel knights who would journey there to mine godsteel in days gone by, from whom they stayed well away. That persuasion had lingered. "The closer we get to Vandar's Tomb, the less we shall have to worry about the tribes," he'd said.

"Just all the other dangers, then," Walter had replied.

Those dangers had been ever present throughout the journey thus far, and the ice bear had been just the latest in a line of perils. Early on, they had been pursued by a pack of white wolves, only to find solace from them in a deep fissure in the earth. They'd ended up navigating an underground network of chasms for two days before returning to the surface, during which they'd found themselves under the watchful eyes of a darker menace; a shadowed figure that seemed to disappear each time they turned to face it, never unveiling its form. It wasn't something Whitebeard knew of. "The mind plays tricks in the darkness," was his only explanation. For two days they'd suffered through their fears that the shadow would take form, but it never had. By the time they emerged back into the white world above, it all seemed no more than a distant memory.

There was a stillness here that haunted them, when the winds failed to stir the air. Patches of woodland clothed the plains in places, sentinels and pines clad in white, and among those trees the winds always seemed to die. Then there was just the crunch of their feet on the packed snow, the labour of three men waging war with the wilds, the occasional caw of a crow or raven as they watched among the branches of the trees. Life was otherwise absent in those snow-clotted swathes of wood, though the sense of it remained. At times Amron would feel eyes on his back, and turn, only to find the cold and quiet behind him. At others he'd wake from his sleep in the shelter and be convinced they were surrounded. *They're out there*, he would think, though what 'they' were he'd never know. A tribe, a pack of wolves, a murder of crows, or worse? That thought was as deep as the cold in his bones, ever present, nagging in the back of his head. *We're being watched. We're being pursued.* Yet if they were, they'd seen no sign of it. On several occasions Whitebeard had ranged into the trees to look for tracks, only to return shaking his head. "If we were being followed, there would be prints," he'd say. "These lands play tricks, as the darkness does, my lord. The black and white can drive one to see things that are not there."

Long days had passed since they'd left the last patch of woodland behind now, as they continued on out across the endless white tundra. Here the winds were ever-fierce, blowing sharp and cruel into their cowls as they wrapped black cloth over their faces for protection. Visibility was often so poor that they could lose each other if more than a few metres apart. Those times were most dangerous of all; for to be split would be the death of them, Amron knew, and among the white winds, not even Whitebeard knew what lurked.

They pressed on through the scant hours of sunlight that day, forging ahead among the tall finger of rock that reached high and ominous about them. Some were thin as trees, jagged spears of stone that shot skyward from the earth. Others were wide and flat at the top, much as the one they'd scaled the day prior to escape the bear. Up there Amron spotted cairns of stones stacked atop the summits. "The Crowmen of the Crag bury their dead as high as they can," Whitebeard explained. "Mostly they keep to the foothills of the Weeping heights, but sometimes they range out here. When a man dies during a roving they will find the highest places they can to bury him, stacking him with stones and rocks. You will see many dozens of them, if you look hard enough. Some old. Some new."

Those burial cairns weren't the only signs that people wandered these lands. With daylight holding they came upon more bones, though these were of a beast slaughtered for its meat and fur, not children burned for the gods. The hide had been removed from the carcass, the bones hacked open for the marrow. Some of those were thick and long, suggesting a beast as large as the bear that gave them shelter. "These are greatyak bones," Walter identified, and rightly by the look on Whitebeard's face. "They're a distant cousin of the broadback, I've read."

"They are greatly less temperamental," Whitebeard growled, shielding his eyes from the icy sting of the wind. "Greatyaks pass for the best game you will find out here. They have thick coats that keep them warm through the winter darkness, and much meat on their bones. If one is killed it can keep an entire tribe fed for weeks. Sometimes they need but one to sustain them through to spring."

"This one was killed some time ago, by the looks of it," said Walter, kneeling to inspect the remains. "I recall seeing a small herd of them when I passed this way last time. They seem far too gentle for a place like this."

"Those horns of theirs say otherwise. They know how to defend themselves when attacked, Walter. Anything that cannot do so does not survive long out here."

"Including us?" the luckiest man in the world asked.

"Us most of all." Rogen Whitebeard led them on.

Dusk fell a little earlier that day than it had the day before, the hours of light seeming to pass in a blink. That golden haze drenched the west, infused with streaked vermillion, a pretty parting gift before the sun snatched back its glow. They pressed on in search of somewhere to shelter for the night, though more and more Amron was finding that Rogen Whitebeard had not yet passed these lands. He among all the rangers of Northwatch had ventured into the Icewilds most, but even so that experience was limited to the eastern expanses near the foothills of the Weeping Heights. By now those mountains were many dozens of miles behind them, a wall of rock beyond which the civilised lands of Vandar lay. Amron found himself at Walter's side. "Do you recognise these lands, Walter?" he asked. After another long day, the cold was getting into him, digging down into his bones. "Is any of this familiar to you?"

"No, my lord, I cannot say it is. But we're going in the right direction, I know that much at least."

"How can you tell? Even Rogen seems doubtful, sometimes. His certainty is betraying him."

"But mine is not." Walter nodded forward through the frosted air, as they continued past the towers of rock. "We need but continue northwest, my lord, and we'll soon see the mountain. When next the weather clears, it will show its face. Then we need but follow its beacon. We need but walk to its light."

An hour after that, Amron felt the gentle hum of running water beneath his feet. Ahead, cutting through the wide open plains was the Silver Scar, its surface frozen solid with a thick coat of ice. The evening looked to be a still one, the winds gentle, the skies alive with stars. Away to the east, the faint shadow of the Weeping Heights could still be spotted beyond the woods and lakes, and from up in those mountains the Silver Scar ran, wending west toward the sea several hundred miles away, its banks lined by great clumps of snow and old withered trees, their bare branches dressed in glittering ice. Whitebeard prodded his way to the banks, digging at the snowdrifts to find a safe way down. Amron followed. "How wide is it, Rogen?" he asked.

"It depends where you cross. Several hundred metres here, I would guess."

"And the ice is safe to cross?" Amron looked ahead with a mild trepidation. He was a man of grand proportions and had both a godsteel dagger and longsword at his hip, both adding to his considerable weight.

"At this time of year, yes. The ice will be some feet thick. It's perfectly safe."

Whitebeard proved right, as usual, as they stepped out onto the ice. It felt solid as stone beneath their feet, yet underneath it the river could be felt, flowing slow and ponderous downstream. Whitebeard took the lead, treading over the snow that had fallen upon the ice. In some places the snowfall appeared to have been brushed aside. Amron could see dark patches here and there, as though someone had broken through. "Those holes look fresh," he said. "Do the tribes fish the waters here?"

Whitebeard followed Amron's gaze. A frown fell upon his eyes. "They do. Ice-fishing is common, though you're right...those holes look fresh." His amber eyes searched about them, scanning. "We should make haste to the other side. Shadows...I sense shadows about us."

Those words were more disquieting than Amron Daecar could rightly say. Whitebeard was not a man unnerved by these lands, but suddenly he was pressing forward into a jog, making for the opposite bank.

Amron accelerated to keep up, as Walter followed behind, and in an instant his right thigh began to complain, thudding with a dull deep pain where the Nightblade had slashed him. Though his left arm was more seriously crippled, it was the leg that most troubled him out here. The discomfort was constant, the pain often keeping him awake at night when all he wanted was to sleep. By morning his leg would be stiff as steel and Walter would have to help massage the muscle back to health before they could set off. Movement and the scant warmth of the sun tended his ails until night came back upon them and the cold reached through his furs and wools and leathers and flesh, gripping at his bones. *But soon my ails will be gone,* he would think, when the pain grew so bad his eyes would water. *Soon Vandar will free me to walk and fight again.* The thought drove him on, day by day, but still there seemed so far to go...

A barking call ripped through the air ahead.

A crack of ice.

A splash.

Amron looked forward. Whitebeard had come upon an old fishing hole, the ice above it frosted thin and hidden by a light carpet of snow. His body was half submerged, his leather-gloved fingers scratching at the ice for purchase, trying to pull himself out. "No...stay back!" he called out, but too late.

Amron was already on him, reaching to draw him out, but in that moment the world gave way beneath him, the ice splintering and breaking up under his weight. Twenty stone of muscle and bone slammed down upon the ice, widening the breach. Amron felt his weight slide forward, the freezing flow of the river reach up to take him. His legs went in, and he spun and scrambled to grip the ice. The gelid waters soaked through his furs and leathers, a thousand tiny daggers stabbing at his flesh. Across the breach, Whitebeard was scrambling to escape the flow. Walter came rushing in to help, reaching down, but weighted by their blades, he'd never haul them out.

"My lord! My lord Amron!" he called out, as the water rushed up past Amron's chest, stealing the air from his lungs. He tried to call back, but his voice was a thin stilted gasp. He snapped a breath, then another, as the ice continued to give way. His left arm had no strength to hold on. His right leg had no strength to kick. And the godsteel blades at his hips were pulling him down and down, into the blackness below.

Steel sinks, was all he thought, as those anchors dragged him under. The river took him, the rush of wintry water pouring over his head, filling his cowl. He had a sense of Whitebeard dragging himself onto a thicker shelf of ice. Of pale shadows closing in from across the river. Of Walter Selleck calling out as the water rushed into his eyes, blinding him. Of the pull of the river, dragging him west, beneath the icy ceiling above...

White above, and black below.

Down and down he went.

9

Jonik

It was late morning by the time Borrus Kanabar emerged from below decks, rubbing his bald head and squinting in confusion as he stepped out into the sun. He took a good long look around, and then said one of the most obvious things anyone had ever uttered. "We're at sea."

They were. They'd been at sea all morning, and all of the night before. After slaughtering those cutthroats in the arcade, it had seemed sensible to expedite their exit from the city harbour, and Emeric and Captain Turner - who the exile had found deeply ensconced in a tense game of dice - had been in quick agreement. So they'd hauled Borrus Kanabar's unconscious frame to the skiff, gathered up the godsteel daggers the cutthroats had no further need of, pulled the anchor and raised the sails. Now they were fast on the move along the Sunshine Bay, heading east on a stiff favourable breeze. But all Borrus Kanabar seemed to know was that they were at sea.

"Right you are there, sir," called Captain Turner from the sterncastle, his tangled flaxen beard waving in the wind, tan coat flapping against his legs. "I trust you slept well down in the hold?"

Borrus Kanabar spun around, and looked up to the wheel where Turner stood. "I woke up among horses," he said, sounding hugely disgruntled by that fact. They'd elected to put him into one of the spare stalls, rather than in the communal sleeping quarters where the risk of him waking and causing trouble would be more acute. Jonik had scheduled a watch too, to make sure someone was always stationed outside the door, though had ended it at dawn when the crew arose. He'd expected Sir Borrus to have awoken by then, but apparently he was more drunk than he'd realised, and in need of a lengthy sleep. "Where's my sword?" the big Varin Knight demanded of Turner. Then he turned his eyes around the deck, where the rest were scattered here and there. "My ancestral blade. Red Wrath. Where is it?"

Jonik had taken that too, storing it with the rest of the godsteel blades he'd gathered. Their collection had grown overnight, the blades fetched from Lady Shark's men now added to by several godsteel daggers and a brace of shortswords. For all Jonik knew, those cutthroats might have been Lady Shark's men too, but it seemed unlikely. Either way it made no matter. They weren't Shadowknights, that was all Jonik cared about.

"It's safely kept," he told Sir Borrus, stepping down from the forecastle to join him. Emeric followed, along with Jack. Soft Sid was mopping the main deck nearby, Devin was cooking a pot of stew below, Brax was tending a rip in the foresail and Grim Pete was up in the crow's nest, as usual, peering down with those black beady eyes of his.

Borrus Kanabar glanced from one to the next, trying to piece it all together. "Safely kept? Where? That's my bloody blade, you impudent whelp. Hand it over right now."

"Not until we know we can trust you," Jonik said. He was unburdened of his cloak and wearing his black leather vest and breeches, the Nightblade at his hip. He had to wonder how much Sir Borrus recalled. "Do you remember me?" he asked, trying not to be too condescending. "I saved you from those cutthroats yesterday, and you swore a life debt to me in return. You made that oath by godsteel, if you'll recall..."

"Yes I bloody recall, *Shadowknight*." Sir Borrus's eyes went to the Nightblade, sheathed at Jonik's swordbelt. "An oath made with an assassin is meaningless. And I was drunk. The conditions weren't fair."

"They were fair," said Emeric Manfrey, stepping forward. He smiled through his sooty-black beard, his broad shoulders draped in his weatherbeaten green cloak. "We've met before, Sir Borrus, though you may not remember. It was over a dozen years ago now, at a tourney in Ilithor. I beat you in the joust, but you got your vengeance in the melee." Emeric could plainly see that Borrus Kanabar wasn't recalling it. "I'm sure you took part in many such tourneys back then. It was the last for me, however. I was exiled shortly after."

The burly knight frowned. "Exiled? For what?"

"I made the mistake of falling in love with a southern girl," Emeric explained. "That was enough for Lord Modrik Kastor to seize my lands and cast me out."

"Modrik Kastor..." the Barrel Knight repeated in a grunt. "If I had any saliva left I'd spit to the side. My lord father always cursed that man and his...*ways*." He scratched at a brittle patch of dirty hair on his cheek. "That would make you Emeric Manfrey, then. I've heard your sorry story, though only in bits and pieces, and the versions are always different depending on who you ask. The Kastor banners don't think much of you, but I suppose there's no surprise there. I heard you'd raped one of Kastor's women. A daughter or cousin or something, the details escape me."

Emeric turned still as stone. "I did no such thing. You've heard spurious tellings only, it would seem. But I'm not surprised that the Kastors would twist it like that, to better serve their ends."

"You'll not hear me disagree," Kanabar told him. "Though your choice of friends does rather put your tale in doubt." He glared at Jonik again, then his bloodshot eyes turned to Emeric's blade. "That sword of yours. I recognise the eagle-head pommel. Sir Oswald's, was it? The blade that felled Karlog and Bagazar."

Emeric shook his head stiffly. "Sir Oswald bore the Sword of Varinar when he slew those dragons, Sir Borrus. He was First Blade of Vandar at the time."

"Of course. It's a lot easier killing dragons with that big golden thing." Borrus hauled a breath of salty sea air into his lungs. "Gods I'm thirsty. I don't suppose you have any ale aboard, do you?"

"I'm sure we can help you with that." Emeric gave Jack a quick nod, and the Marshlander set off below decks, returning a few moments later with a wooden jug and iron tankard.

Borrus Kanabar took the jug, ignored the tankard. "Much obliged, boy," he said to Jack. "You were there yesterday too, I recall." He slurped down several huge swigs, then wiped his mouth of the froth. "You're from the Marshlands. A village near Mudport, you said."

"Marshbank, sir. It's built on decking mostly, where the marshlands get quite boggy."

"Yes, I know it. You catch good eel there, around Celaph's Mire. There's an inn...I forget it's name."

"The Slippery Eel?" Jack offered.

"Yes, that's it," laughed Kanabar. He took another swig, as ale dribbled through the crusts of filth in his beard, staining his roughspun tunic. "The Slippery Eel. Stayed there several times when travelling down the Lakeland Way. Best eel I've ever eaten. And that strange liquor they brew there...foul smelling stuff but packs a real punch."

Jack smiled as though he'd been there a lot himself. "It's distilled using eel's blood, Sir Borrus," he said. "Do you know the lands well?"

"Of course. House Kanabar may rule the rivers, but the men of the lakes and marshes are our sworn banners, boy. By rights I could demand your service, you know. Which lord did you serve under? Must be Lord Morley of Mudport, I suppose. Marshbank is under his jurisdiction, is it not?"

"I believe so, yes. We always considered Lord Rammas our senior lord, however."

"Oh he is. Rammas is Lord of the Marsh, higher ranking and richer than Morley, it's true. And you know who he swears fealty to? My father." Borrus looked over at Jonik with that. "Yet it seems you serve this Shadowknight now. Even you, Manfrey, or does he serve you? Or perhaps it's that great lackwit there with the mop who's in charge? Or that ugly little creature up in the crow's nest. Am I leaving anyone out here?"

"Me," called Braxton from the forecastle. "I'm the one with the rotten teeth, m'lord. Brown Mouth, they call me."

"Aye, we do," came Turner's voice at the helm. "A name o' my own thinking, lord, and most apt I assure you. And there's one more below decks cooking us up a nice lobster stew. Lad o' sixteen named Devin."

"Devin," repeated Borrus Kanabar. "That's it? No funny tag for the boy? I know how you seamen like your nicknames."

Turner laughed. "True enough. The lackwit over yonder is Soft Sid, and that creature up in the nest is Grim Pete. And a creature he is, you called it right. Horrible little man." He gave Grim Pete a wicked grin.

"I'm sure. And you are?"

"Captain Turner," said Captain Turner. "They call me 'Gill' for my Seaborn roots. Can dive some hundred metres deep and stay under for a quarter hour, no trouble." As ever, he was proud to relay that fact. "And I've heard o' your names too, don't doubt it. The Barrel Knight, aye, for your big burly chest. And one o' two perhaps less savoury names, that happen to slip my mind."

"Of course they do."

"You don't seem to quite live up to it anymore, if you don't mind me sayin'," Turner went on. He gave his own ample stomach a pat, his unruly flaxen beard catching the morning sunlight. "Thought you'd be bigger around the belly, from what I've heard. We've been wonderin' what's happened to you to put you in this godsawful state."

"Godsawful state? Now surely I don't look that bad?"

"Perhaps it's not for me to say. I'd not want to offend you, lord."

"Captain Turner is being polite, Sir Borrus," said Emeric. "The truth is you do look rather more bedraggled than befits your station, as I'm sure you know."

"I'm not blind, Manfrey."

"Of course. We can pull seawater up in pails to give you a wash, when you're ready. The smell is..."

"Better than it was," Kanabar interrupted. "Believe me. Not so long ago I was clad in a suit of shit, so this is a vast improvement. But that's the thing about captivity. The facilities are never so good as you hope."

Emeric took that up. "You've been in captivity, Sir Borrus? Here in the south?"

"Eldurath," Borrus muttered. "Me and Lythian Lindar both. I'm sure you know the name. The Knight of the Vale most know him by. And Tomos..." He paused a moment to compose himself. A wash of sadness came over him. "Sir Tomos of House Pentar, the Red Knight of the Helm. You may have heard of him too. The three of us were sent to Eldurath for peace talks some months ago by the man you maimed." Another fierce glare came Jonik's way. "Let's just say, things didn't go as planned. Poor Tomos was killed in the Pits of Kharthar several weeks ago. Lythian and I...we were rescued, eventually. And then we parted, a week past...or so." He shook his head and let out a sigh. "The days have rather merged together since then."

A short silence fell. They'd heard rumours of a breakout from the Pits of Kharthar from the merchants and fishwives at the docks. Some spoke of a riot in the crowds. Others of an execution that went wrong. There was even talk that some of the Fireborn had fought one another. That the legendary Lord Ulrik Marak of the Nest had gone rogue. They'd given it little mind until now, because half of all sailor's stories were either untrue or greatly exaggerated. But now they had a real life witness to it all.

"Why did you part?" came the first question, from Jack o' the Marsh. He lent a tender note to his voice. "You and the Knight of the Vale. What happened?"

Borrus could hardly muster a smile. "I've not the strength to discuss it, boy. Let's just say we had a disagreement."

"But you were rescued, you said," said Emeric. "By whom? We heard whispers that the Fireborn were warring. Were you part of that, Sir Borrus?"

"That's an exaggeration. A couple of Fireborn plotted against the new king, is all..."

"It was said that Sir Lythian slew King Dulian," called Turner. "Any truth in that, lord?"

Borrus Kanabar shook his head briskly. "Tavash was Lythian's target, but that's a bloody long story in itself." He pulled the jug of ale back to his lips, and supped liberally. Then he moved to a barrel beside the mainmast and sat down, slumping wearily onto the wooden lid.

"A barrel on a barrel, well wouldn't you know," said Turner, laughing. "Ah, course, now it comes to me. The Bloated Knight, heard that one for you too, lord, though doesn't ring true anymore. If it, er, ever did," he added, giving an awkward grin.

"One of the few positives of being starved for weeks on end," Sir Borrus said, sinking back beneath the shade of the sails. "Elsewise, I'd not recommend it. The Agarathi like to humiliate and break their prisoners before they execute them, Varin Knights most of all. Forget the shit and rotten fruit that we were pelted with for weeks, it was the bloody heckling that near drove us mad. And the heat."

"I'm sorry you had to endure that, Sir Borrus," said Emeric, with grace. "But I find myself wondering...how exactly did you make it all the way to Solas? It's almost a thousand miles from Eldurath."

"Flew," grunted the Barrel Knight.

"You...*flew*?" Emeric Manfrey sounded appropriately surprised by that. "How? Not on a dragon, surely?"

"Well I didn't bloody well sprout wings, did I Manfrey?" Borrus had another swig of ale, fast making his way through the jug. "I know how absurd it sounds. A Varin Knight atop a dragon? It's laughable, but true all the same. Got dropped just outside the city and spent a couple of days trying to get my way to the docks. Had to bloody the edge of my blade a few times, to be sure, but made it in the end. But no boats. Leastways none that would take me."

So it was him, Jonik thought. *That grey dragon Mugro spoke of. It must have been transporting Borrus Kanabar from wherever the hell he'd come from. Gods, the things that are happening. The whole world's spun upside down...*

"You shoulda just threatened someone," called down Brown Mouth Braxton, leaning at the railing of the forecastle. He smiled, but the sun was glaring bright behind him and sparing them the look of his appalling teeth. "Man like you. Who woulda said no?"

"Not many, I wouldn't imagine," answered Emeric, "but Sir Borrus has to sleep some time, Braxton. What about when he nods off? Those men he threatened might just slip a dirk in his neck. Even gifted Bladeborn are vulnerable when alone."

Borrus gave a nod to that, to suggest it was his thinking too. Then his eyes were on Jonik again, a snarl never too far from his lips. "I suppose I should give you some thanks for that. But I'll not say another word until I've heard your sordid little tale, Shadowknight."

"*Former* Shadowknight," the faithful figure of Jack o' the Marsh was quick to correct. "He broke free, Sir Borrus. The order is hunting him. And Jonik wants to..."

"Jack." Jonik gave the man a look to silence him, lest he say something out of turn, then looked back at the Varin Knight. He let a moment pass before speaking. "Jack's right. The order hunts me, Sir Borrus, for stealing this blade. What I did for them, I regret more than I could ever say. I will swear that by godsteel if you ask it..."

"What you did?" broke in Borrus Kanabar. "You mean crippling the greatest man in all the north? You mean murdering his son and heir?"

"Yes. For both of those things. I regret..."

"Words are worthless, Shadowknight." Borrus Kanabar lurched

back to his feet unsteadily. "And your godsteel oaths are shit to me. You have to have honour first. I see nothing before me but a traitor."

"A traitor to a vicious order of assassins," Emeric Manfrey said. "You would condemn him for breaking away from their service?"

"I would condemn him for hacking apart Amron Bloody Daecar. I would condemn him for slaying his son."

"Under orders and coercions you do not comprehend," said Manfrey, clinging firm to the pommel of his blade. "Jonik was under the persuasions of a Whisperer, sir. A mage he himself slew in a bid to break free of him. But first there was twenty years of darkness and torture and cruelty, an internment designed for the sole purpose of making a man a weapon. To break free of those bonds must have taken considerable strength. He should be celebrated, no censured, for that."

"Then you're a bigger bloody fool than I thought, Manfrey, and no wonder you were cast out from your castle. Southern girls are good for bedding, but not for wedding. Your father should have taught you that."

Emeric Manfrey's sword came out with a shrill song of steel. "You speak as Modrik Kastor once did. And I never got to have my vengeance."

"And you'll take it on me in lieu of him?" Borrus Kanabar didn't seem much threatened by Emeric's words. He even allowed himself a laugh and another full slurp of his ale. "Put away the sword, Manfrey. I have a habit of speaking out of turn and can only apologise if I've hit a nerve. When I tell of my family's disdain for the Kastors, I tell it true. You have an ally in me there, I assure you."

"But does *he*?" Emeric gestured sharply to Jonik. "You owe him a life debt by the godsteel oath you swore. The laws of gods and men demand your service."

"I've already told you what I think of that bloody oath. I was sotted and deceived. Had I known who he was I'd never have made it. And do you even want it, Shadowknight, wondering whether I'll slip my blade through your back as soon as I've met your terms?"

"That would be murder," Emeric told him plainly. "A dishonourable death on which Varin would look unfavourably."

"Yes, so the scriptures say. But maybe it'd be worth it for getting Amron's revenge."

"A petty vengeance for cursing yourself to a less illustrious seat at his Table. I don't see the value there."

"It would be far from petty, Manfrey. You do know who we're bloody talking about, don't you? The Crippler of Kings. The Slayer of Vallath. The Hero of the North. I could list the rest of his names if it pleases you but we'd probably be back home by the time I was done. It seems your memory needs jogging, after wasting away down here."

"My memory is quite intact. I know full well who Amron Daecar is."

"Do you? Do you *really*? And yet you're harbouring the scourge of his house." Borrus Kanabar took a heavy plod forward, nostrils flaring like a bull. "Did you even hesitate?" he demanded, looking Jonik dead in the eye. "When you saw him there in his tent at the warcamp in Rasalan, did you wonder for a second what the hell you were doing? *Who* you were doing it to?"

"I didn't know," Jonik whispered, his eyes falling to the wooden deck. *His death will save the world,* Gerrin had told him, over and over again, but that had only ever been a lie. "Not then..."

Kanabar hardly seemed to hear him. "And Aleron? You'd failed the first time, so you were given a second chance, is that it? Oh I've heard about that...even from Eldurath I heard it. How you impersonated some unfancied young Bladeborn and tricked your way to the final of the Song. How you hacked through Aleron's gorget again and again even when the bout was won. You murdered him, you little bastard. You defiled a sacred contest, and..."

"Killed my brother, I know."

A silence consumed them. It stripped away the whistle of the wind and the crash of the waves, the caw of gulls and creak of wood and the flapping of the sails in the breeze. Jonik stared at the decking in dark bitter thought. He could still see Aleron's eyes as the drugs took their effect, weakening him. See that last look of confusion as he cleaved through his armour and neck. Hear the spreading din of horror in the stadium as their beloved son's throat opened out into a fountain of blood. And the crack of thunder that followed, the thick sheets of black rain that fell, as though all the world was weeping, and the splash of Elyon's footsteps as he gave chase through the streets. He could still see him there, on his knees, sobbing rageful tears for his brother's loss. And begging. Begging to be killed, so he might go with

Aleron to Varin's Table. *A bond I'll never know,* Jonik thought. *A bond of brothers, true brothers, that I severed forever.*

Eventually he looked up, expecting to see a rage in Borrus Kanabar's eyes. But the man's face was strangely calm, as though he suddenly understood. "He was your brother," he whispered, staring at him. "You're...Amron's bastard son?"

Jonik stole a look around him. None of the others had known, yet there was something in Jack's face to say he'd worked it out. "I didn't know until after I attacked him in his tent," Jonik told them, his voice a quiet rasp. He felt suddenly shy under their attentions. This was meant to be his secret, his alone. *Why am I telling them? Why?* "I worked that out later, when I was in Varinar. My orders were always to win the next bout, the next fight. I had no idea that Aleron needed to die, not until the end. Not until that morning..."

"And you did it anyway?" Emeric Manfrey asked. The exiled lord nodded and answered his own question. "You had no choice, lest they kill you too," he said. "And take the Nightblade back."

And take the Nightblade back, Jonik thought, reaching to its hilt, needing its comfort.

"It's said Amilia Lukar is to wed King Hadrin," Jack put in. "Aleron was betrothed to her, wasn't he?" He already knew the answer to that. "Then it was King Janilah, we can all be sure of it. He needed Aleron to die so he might use his granddaughter to secure the Rasal throne. It's all been part of the same plot. Janilah's been manipulating it all from the start."

"Is that true, Shadowknight?" Borrus Kanabar asked, a deep-wrinkled frown on his face. "Was it...was it Janilah Lukar who gave the order?"

Jonik could only shake his head and say, "I don't know, Sir Borrus. My orders came from a Shadowmaster called Gerrin, who raised me. I can't say for certain who gave him the command."

"Janilah," breathed Borrus Kanabar. He thought about that long and hard. "Could be true...There's no man more ambitious, nor ruthless, than the Warrior King. I saw that during the war, with the way he ruled his armies. He was never afraid of sacrificing men for something greater. His line...the Lukars...they've been the same for centuries. My father always warned me to be wary of him. He said that the Lukars took Tukor once, but that wouldn't always be enough. That they'd want all the north, and then the south as well..."

"Well he's gotten his way then," Emeric said. "Janilah Lukar has the north, Sir Borrus. I suppose you've heard that already."

"Whispers..." Borrus nodded, slumping back down onto the barrel. "Yes, I've heard."

"This world has grown rife with treachery," Emeric continued on, "and clearly you yourself have suffered some of your own. As have I, with a recent loss, and Jonik...no matter what you might think of him, he's suffered more than any of us, and seeks only to make amends. What we need to know, right now, is whether you can be trusted to remain here in our company. Enough bluster, my lord. Jonik saved your life, and you swore him a life debt on the codes set forth by Varin. You'll either see it done, or be removed from this ship when we next make port. I do not imagine you will last long alone, should you part with us. So? What say you?"

"What say I?" Borrus Kanabar's lungs blew out a heavy whooshing sigh. "I say I have no choice. Fine. I bloody consent. Gods, Manfrey, you do love to go on, don't you?"

"If it means getting an answer from you, yes."

"Then you'll allow me my blade back?"

"No."

"No?"

"No. Not until the time comes as you'll need it."

"You'd deny the heir to House Kanabar his ancestral sword? On whose authority?"

"On his." Emeric pointed up to Captain Turner. "It's *his* ship, Sir Borrus, and while on it, you'll follow his rules."

Turner gave a shrug. "I take my orders from Lord Jonik here."

"*Lord* Jonik?" Borrus Kanabar didn't much like that. "He is *not* a lord, Captain Turner."

"Not in any official capacity, no, but in my humble eyes, aye he is. Any man who can wield a Blade o' Vandar is a lord in my book."

"And what book is that? A colouring book?"

Turner's yellow-bearded face twirled into a grin. "I see you have a tongue on you, lord, and not just for shoutin'. You'll fit in fine, I'll say. So long as you behave."

"I'll behave so long as there's sufficient ale and rum and whiskey to keep me happy. I *hate* long voyages. They're hardly any better than being caged." Sir Borrus turned to Emeric. "Where are we going anyway? We've got the coast to port so I'm supposing we're heading east?"

Emeric confirmed that with a nod. "West is too dangerous, though east may not be much better with what we've been hearing. We haven't yet confirmed our course. There are...options to consider."

"What options? Oh I see. You're wondering whether we should pass through the Solapian Channel or sail around the Sunrise Sea? The latter would be more wise, though longer. I can't see what other decision needs be made?"

"There are options," Emeric merely repeated. "We'll be sure to let you know what we plan to do once we've conferred, Sir Borrus."

"So it's like that is it? I'm to be treated as baggage? As nought but a naughty stowaway."

"You're to be treated as a newcomer to this group, who doesn't yet know what we have been facing, or doing, up to this point. You will be brought up to speed on that in due course, I'm sure, but I do feel we have shared enough for now. Jack, please make sure that our guest is comfortable, and well watered. Devin will be done with the lobster stew soon. He isn't much of a chef, but Captain Turner lost his cook off the Tidelands during a storm. Another story, sir, that you'll find interesting when we get to it."

"There was a kraken," put in Brown Mouth Braxton, grinning down from the forecastle. "Good tale, that one. Might make you appreciate the lordling here a little more."

The Barrel Knight didn't know what to make of that. "You...fought a *kraken*?" he asked, looking at Jonik in surprise.

"He might have killed it n'all, far as we know," Braxton said. "Drove that bulbous beast back down below, but who knows whether it died or not. All that inky blood? Might have drawn in the sharks...or something bigger."

"A tale for another time," Emeric said, putting an end to it. He looked at Jack again, who he seemed to have identified as being best suited to tend to Sir Borrus's needs. It made sense, with Jack being a Marshlander, and a genial sort besides. *He can speak of me,* Jonik thought. *Make the man understand.* He wasn't certain why he cared so much, but he did. *Because this is one of my father's closest friends,* he realised. *If he can understand, perhaps my father will too, one day...* "Haul some water for a wash as well, Jack," Emeric was going on. "And find him some clothes, if you can. You're not so different in size. Maybe you have something he can wear?"

"I'll see what I can do, my lord."

"Well then." Emeric turned back to look at Turner. "She's your ship, Captain. And your crew. I hope that all sounds OK?"

"Aye, we can spare Jack for a little while. Seas are calm enough and we're making good time. Not much else needs doing right now, lord."

And that was that. Jack set off into his assigned duties, Sid kept mopping the decks with not a care in the world to trouble him, Brax returned to patching the foresail, and Grim Pete remained hidden in his perch above them, watching the seas for trouble. That left Borrus Kanabar on his barrel, working hard on his ale, as Emeric moved to Jonik's side and drew him to the starboard gunwale. "Jack will bring him around," he said, confirming what Jonik had suspected. "Borrus Kanabar has a reputation for being belligerent and fast to judgement, but he's fair minded with all that when presented with the full picture. He'll learn to see your worth, Jonik, but that's of little great concern right now. It's where we go from here that matters most. Come to Turner's cabin later, and we can discuss it." And with that, he stepped away.

Jonik spent the next few hours alone in the hold, with only Shade for company. He'd grown to feel increasingly guilty over the horse's captivity here on the boat, a term that had gone on much longer than he'd expected. More than once he'd wondered whether to set him free. Not here, perhaps, in these southern climes, but in the north when they finally returned. *If we sail up the Sibling Strait, we could dock at Steelport, or even sail up the Izzun to Thalan. I could ride him to the Highplains and release him to his kin.* It was a thought both sad and hopeful at once.

He liked to talk to Shade, when they were alone. He did that now, updating him on what was happening. There was a wisdom in the horse's rich chestnut eyes, and Jonik had come to see that he understood their plight. "A few weeks," he promised him now, as he brushed his strong back flank, keeping it to a glossy shine. "A few more weeks and we'll be home."

He didn't know if that was true or not. Nor did Shade, he could see. The horse was alone now, which didn't much help his mood. When they'd landed in Solas, half the horses had been sold, and the rest had soon followed to help refill their coffers. Shade had come under much interest too. A dozen offers had come in to buy him, but each one had been swatted away. "He's not for sale," Jonik would say, no matter the sum. He would as likely to sell the Nightblade as sell Shade. "He's not for sale," he would repeat, when any one of the crew questioned him on it. Every one of them had done so, at one point or another, bar Sid. And every one had accepted Jonik's position and never asked again. *But they don't understand why,* he knew. *To them, Shade is just a horse.*

Even Jack had suggested he consider selling him, in his agreeable way. "He might thank you for it, Ghost. Horses don't do well on ships this long. And we've got a long way to go yet." Jonik had decided to ask Shade himself after that. The horse had lifted his chin and flicked his mane, as he tended to do when offended. That was all Jonik needed to know. The topic was put to bed right then and there.

"I'll take you up on deck soon," Jonik said now, still brushing. He did that too sometimes, to give the horse a breath of fresh air, and let him stretch his legs. He'd even taken him to the docks once or twice for the same, but it was never enough. *He needs to run, to gallop,* he thought. Though Shade possessed a gallant sense of stoicism, Jonik could still see the strain in his wise brown eyes. "When we land, wherever it is, I'll find you somewhere to run.," he said with all the conviction he could muster. "I'll make sure of it, I promise." The horse gave a gentle huff. It was the best that passed for a smile these days.

When Jonik met with Emeric later that afternoon, Shade was still on his mind. A non-stop voyage to the north might kill him, he feared, and he knew he couldn't live with that. "We need to make harbour somewhere," Jonik said firmly, as he, Emeric, and Captain Turner gathered around a map on Turner's desk. His cabin was small and cluttered, with a simple bed to one side, a cupboard for clothes, several crates of rum and whiskey stacked one upon another, and not much else. Behind his desk was a secret compartment in which Jonik had hidden the godsteel blades, Borrus Kanabar's included. The bottles of liquor clanked against one another as the ship rocked side to side. "We can't voyage all the way north as we are. We need supplies. Food, hemp, cloth to patch the sails, tar. We're running low on everything." He looked at the crates. "Except liquor."

Turner saw straight through all that. "You thinkin' o' Shade?" he asked, though it was more a statement than a question. "Aye, saw you go down below decks earlier, and not emerge for some time. You've got a soft heart for that steed, lord. It does you a service."

"He needs a break from this ship," Jonik said. He'd never been accused of being soft-hearted before. He wasn't sure whether he liked it or not. "And we *do* need supplies."

That was true. They'd been planning to gather them before leaving Solas, but with the drama with Borrus and the cutthroats, hadn't had much of a chance.

"We'll find somewhere," Emeric assured him. "There are lots of ports we can stop at, through the Islands of the Moon and along the Bay of Stars. If we haven't made harbour before then, we can land in Sutrek. But these are details. There is a larger decision to be made."

"Iru Zon," said Jonik, getting right to it. "You still mean to kill him?"

"My mind takes me both ways," admitted Emeric, after a moment's pause. "What Upo said yesterday...a part of me is inclined to agree with him. We have slain those who took part in the razing of my lands, and the murder of my staff. Twenty died, and we've killed more than that between us, Jonik. But this is not merely about numbers. An eye for an eye..." He shook his head. "Brewilla was worth everything to me, and many of my staff...Puli, Kestan...they were dear friends to me too, loyal and kind and longstanding in my company. I met Kestan during my first month of exile here. He helped me build myself a life, and was a business partner, not merely a member of my household. How can I weigh their deaths against the lives we have taken? I could kill a thousand Patriots and still find no balance on those scales."

"Such is grief, Lord Emeric," said Turner wisely. "It doesn't live well with logic."

Emeric nodded to that. "No, it doesn't. And I ask myself...would slaying Iru Zon change anything? Would it turn back the clock, and return to me what I've lost? This last week I have been consumed by a quiet rage, but back at sea I am starting to think more clearly." He drew a long breath. "I have been selfish, and reckless, in putting you all at risk. My vendetta against the Patriots of Lumara is personal, and mine alone. If I am to seek to further it, I will do so in the same manner... alone. I will leave this ship at Lumara's Teardrop and let you continue north, or wherever else you wish to go..."

"No," interrupted Jonik. "No, Emeric, you cannot leave."

Emeric Manfrey turned to him. There was a half smile on his face. "I said '*if*', Jonik. It is but one course before me." He placed a hand to the former Shadowknight's shoulder. "I am glad to hear you wish to keep me at your side. I know you have a quest of your own you yearn to fulfil. Your own justice you need to serve."

"For which I need your support," Jonik said, without pause. He thought of his dream. Jack on his right. Emeric on his left. "I have helped you seek vengeance. I would ask for the same from you."

"I know." Emeric looked younger all of a sudden, his cheeks fuller. That pall of grief looked to lift, just a little. "I have always known where your path would lead you, Jonik. And your adversaries...well, they are more properly defined than mine."

"The Shadowfolk?" asked Turner, with a shudder. "You mean to turn the tables on them, lord?"

"Eventually," Jonik confessed. "I must, Gill, or else I'll be running forever. And you will too." He looked to the door. "All of you. Everything we've done...you're all targets now. They'll not stop hunting me, and they'll not stop hunting you. That's how they work. No loose ends. No holes. The only way to end this is to go right to the source."

"To return home?" Turner said to that. "You wish to go back to the Shadowfort?"

"I wish to kill the masters, Gill, and any knight who might try to stop me. I mean to save the rest."

"Alone?" Turner was trying not to gape.

"He wouldn't be alone," said Emeric Manfrey.

Does he mean? "You'd..." Jonik swallowed to wet his throat. "You'd come with me, Emeric?"

The exiled lord smiled handsomely, his square noble jaw broadening beneath his thick black beard. "As you say, I owe you the same courtesy as you've given me. But I'll not be enough, not by a distance."

"Not by a hundred leagues," japed Turner, chuckling nervously. "Leastways not from what you've said, lord." He took up a glass of rum and threw the contents down his throat. "I'm Seaborn, aye, not Bladeborn, and not much help in a fight o' that nature. Nor's anyone else aboard this ship, but for the Barrel Knight." He looked at Jonik as though he'd just worked something out. "I see why you saved him now, lord. This life debt o' yours. You're expecting him to join you in your quest?"

"I don't think Jonik knew it was the heir of House Kanabar he was saving in the shadows of the arcade, Captain," Emeric said. "Nor do I think Sir Borrus will be willing to journey with us to the Hammersongs, life debt or no. He will be most eager to return to battle the Agarathi, I would say, given the treatment he's suffered at their hands. But as per his possible use...well, from a purely hypothetical position, yes, he'd be an excellent ally. Borrus Kanabar is considered one of the greatest swordsmen of his generation, not that you'd know it to look at him right now. But it's true. There wouldn't be many Shadowknights who could match him."

"Most Shadowknights are limited in their skill," Jonik said, to offer further context. "We're trained to strike from the shadows, not go man-to-man on the battlefield or duelling grounds. Only a handful are taught the five forms. I was given special training, for the strength of my blood, and the contracts I was likely to undertake. But not many are like me."

"And no surprise, given who your father is, lord," said Turner. He refilled his cup of rum, and had another taste. "I worked that out, you know. Right early on, I did. You got that Daecar look, after all, and soon as I saw you with that Blade o' Vandar, well...who else is famed for holdin' one? Can see why you didn't say anything, though. Not an easy thing to admit. Crippling your father and killing your brother. But you'll find no condemners hereabouts, lord," he was quick to add. "None at all. We all understand why you did it. We know you had no choice."

I had a choice, Jonik thought. *I could have refused. I could have run.* He'd done that anyway, so all that had changed was that Aleron was dead. He turned his eyes to the side a moment. *That demon. That Whisperer...*The creature had had a power over him, and it wasn't the only one at their disposal. There were others working for the Shadow Order, and that fed into the whispers of the Shadow King too. A darker menace controlling them all. *A menace I may yet have to face...*

The thought made him shudder. *Rumours,* he said to himself. *That's all they are.* The Shadowknights were told little and less, and only the masters would know if the Shadow King was real. It was thought among the lower ranks of the order that the Shadow Council determined which contracts they delivered, but was that true? Was there in fact a higher power lurking behind the curtain, pulling all the strings?

He cleared his throat. It wasn't for worrying about yet. "I just want to make amends," he managed, as Turner and Emeric awaited a response. *For that Janilah Lukar might need to die too,* he thought, *if he was truly the one who'd ordered the contract. But one step at a time...*

"Aye, but how, Lord Jonik?" queried Turner. "You two won't do, so far as I see it, and as you say, you can hardly rely on big Borrus Kanabar, can you?" Turner was thinking hard on it, looking at the map. "Mayhaps you'll find sellswords to help? They'll be hunting work with war on the rise, though finding anyone mad enough to march up the Hammersongs is another matter, I s'pose."

"Coin is a concern," Jonik told him. He'd been through this with Jack already only yesterday. "We'd need money to pay mercenaries, even if they were willing to join us."

"Them blades will help with that."

Jonik nodded. "They might." He turned to Emeric. It felt good to be unveiling his plans to them. First Jack, now Emeric and Turner. All seemed amenable. All seemed willing to help, in whatever way they might. A weight from lifting off his shoulders, little by little. "You said you knew about the merchant Vincent Rose. Do you think he'd buy them?"

"That man buys everything and anything. He could buy the world if he wished it." There was something resembling a snarl on the exile's face. "Rose is said to lack in scruples and rumoured to deal with the Patriots. Some of them are of mixed heritage, southerners with Bladeborn blood. He has been known to buy godsteel blades to arm them. I'm not sure I'd want to support *that* particular cause."

"No, of...of course not," said Jonik.

But there was something else in Emeric's eyes. Jonik let the exile think it through. That look tended to lead somewhere. "Vincent Rose is well connected," he finally said. "And there may be a way he can help us. We could satisfy Shade's need to stretch his legs, fetch supplies, and gather men for our cause all at once." He smiled, and nodded to himself, and when Turner asked, "how?", he merely said, "Leave that to me, Captain. You just leave that to me."

10

Lythian

Lythian Lindar was awoken from his sleep by a firm shake and a grunting voice. "Wake up, Lythian, you are needed."

His eyes broke open to the swarthy square face of Lord Ulrik Marak, down on one knee and furled in his deep crimson cloak over scaly leathers of charcoal black. It was not yet dawn, the sky as dark as pitch, clogged with clouds. A heavy fog had gathered about the ruins of the castle, hanging low and wet upon the mossy ground.

"What is it?" Lythian asked, confused by the early awakening. His mind was still full of his dreams, of the dancing that turned to dread. Most nights he was with Talia, his long dead wife, and the infant son he'd never named, dancing on that moonlit courtyard bordered by ruby-red maples, before the black wind closed in around them all and dragged Talia and the boy away. He shifted up against the pitted stone slab behind him, an old part of the inner wall of the ruined keep in which he slept, roofless and exposed to the starless night sky. Nearby, the soft sweet breathing of Princess Talasha could be heard, as she lay sandwiched between the two handmaids she had with her, Cevi and Mirella. Prince Tethian looked to be absent, as did Kin'rar. "The prince," Lythian said. "Where..."

"Prince Tethian requires your counsel," Ulrik Marak broke in. The scar that split his brow, from right eye to scalp, looked dark and twisted in the gentle light of a nearby torch, flickering in its iron sconce. "Come, he is waiting."

Lythian stood, still shaking away the lingering cobwebs of his dreams. He found his eyes upon Talasha once more, her bronze skin lit by the torchlight, curls of rich black hair spun around her ears and face. He had spent much time with her during his time here among these cultish outlaws, and had dreamed of her once or twice too. In those dreams, Talia's face would shift and change to Talasha's as they danced, and that black wind would never come. He had woken once to find her lying beside him, that beautiful golden face before his eyes. There had been a soft twinkle in her sultry brown eyes, mottled with specks of red. "You looked cold, Captain," she had whispered to him, with that smooth sensuous voice of hers. "I came to warm you. I hope that is OK?"

Lythian hadn't felt a woman's warmth in over fifteen years, not since Talia's death. Even lying beside one made him uncomfortable, as though he might weaken and forgo the vows he'd made to never love again, never sire another son. His unerring service to the Varin Knights had become his sole drive and duty, yet now...*what now?* he had to wonder. *The Varin Knights are changing, as is all the north, all the world. Might it be that I need changing too?*

He drew his eyes away from Talasha and filled his lungs with a breath of crisp cold air, pulling his grey cloak tight about himself against the chill. All those long weeks in captivity had taken their toll on him, but he was growing stronger again now, his vitality returning, his appearance tidied up. Talasha had taken care of that too, shaving his cheeks clean of that matted, scraggly beard, washing and neatening his light brown hair, tending to his wounds and the thousand little scars that now littered his body.

Stiff from his sleep, he reached and took up his blade Starslayer, hitching his swordbelt to his waist, taking a grip of the blade's hilt to further renew his strength. Lord Marak waited patiently for him to arrange himself. "OK, follow me," he said when Lythian was ready. "They are waiting within the woods."

They moved down from the hilltop, through the ruins of the ancient castle grounds, clogged by larch and fir, sprouts of sedge and thick wet weeds. Amid the lower ruins the embers of cookfires burned within the old yard, and here and there were soft lit torches where the sentries stood on guard. Sleeping bodies littered the stone floor, wrapped in roughspun cloaks of patched wool and fine rich mantles alike. Some were born high and others low, but all had bought into Tethian's vision.

They worked their way through the jumble of bodies and past what remained of the curtain wall. It had been eroded to hip height by now, as with most of the ruins, dotted throughout these woods amid the foothills. To their right, the forest sloped away eastward into a shallow valley. Left it flattened along a higher rise, where further on a craggy hummock broke out above the trees. Marak led Lythian in that direction, past several more sentries hidden in the foggy gloom, and through the edge of the treeline.

There a group of figures awaited. Prince Tethian. Kin'rar Kroll. The prince's faithful friend, Ashun Klo, whom he'd grown up with. The wise old scholar Sotel Dar who'd tutored Tethian in his youth and remained within his service. There were a handful of others, watching the trees, holding torches to fend off the darkness. Several men in cloaks and travel-strained clothes stood with a prisoner between them, a bag over his head and tied around his neck. His hands were bound in hempen rope, his garb poor, torn and bloodied in places. Lythian stepped forward to join the group. "My apologies for waking you, Lythian," Prince Tethian said. "I wanted to consult your wisdom, before we decided what to do with him."

On the far side of the hillock was a twenty metre cliff that ended in a cluster of sharp jagged rocks. It served as a manner of execution here, should a spy try to infiltrate their ranks, or one of the men turn to base behaviours and put his hands on one of the women, or murder another man in an affray. Such instances had been rare, but they had occurred, as the bloodstains and bones at the foot of the cliff would attest.

"Who is it?" Lythian asked. He was wondering why his counsel would be sought above the rest. Had a Varin Knight been discovered trying to find them? Was this a man of Vandar, of the north, that they held?

He had his answer a moment later. "Remove the hood," Tethian commanded, and one of his followers did just that. The patched woollen bag was pulled away and the face of Sir Pagaloth appeared before him, gagged and bruised and haggard. He looked sorrowful, swollen, his eyes down at the bare rock on which they stood. The last Lythian had seen of his former escort had been within his dragonmaw cell, on that stormy black night after Sir Tomos's death. *He could hardly make eye contact with me then, and still he cannot look at me,* Lythian thought. He turned back to Tethian. "What do you mean to do with him?"

"That will be for you to decide."

Lythian frowned at the prince. "Me. Why me?"

"Because you suffered most gravely from his betrayal, with the death of your friend Sir Tomos."

Lythian remembered Sir Tomos Pentar's execution. Dehydrated and starved and dressed in that mocking pasteboard armour, he'd fought off a dozen deformed drakes and even managed to slay a pair with the blunt iron sword they'd given him...

And then they'd eaten him alive.

Lythian closed a fist against the memory. The crunching of bones and rending of flesh and the cruel callous baying of the crowd. "He came to me," he said. "Sir Pagaloth came to my cell one night and confessed what he'd done. I did not blame him then and I do not blame him now. He has nothing to answer for."

Lord Marak gave a grunt. "You are too forgiving, Lythian. Pagaloth must be executed for treason. His betrayal saw Sir Tomos killed and many others that day we rescued you from the Pits, innocent women and children among them, trampled by the horde. All that blood and death might have been spared but for his disloyalty. And *still* Garlath recovers from his fight with Malathar. *Still* he remains too weak to fly."

"All of which is regrettable," Lythian said. "But it doesn't change the fact that Sir Pagaloth was told of a plot to murder a Prince of Agarath, and by compulsion of his honour, decided he had to unveil it. I do not count that as treason. Ulrik. He was only doing his duty as a sworn dragonknight of the realm." Before Marak might answer, he turned to the prince. "You sought my counsel, Prince Tethian, and you have it. If you choose to execute Sir Pagaloth for outing our plot - a plot that he himself saw as treasonous - I will have no part in it. To take his life would be unjust, I judge. Better to give him a chance to atone for the error he now knows he made."

Tethian nodded thoughtfully, holding his hands before him in a pious stance. "It seems we are torn on this matter of treason," he said.

"Kin'rar, it was you who spoke to Sir Pagaloth of your plans to assassinate my cousin. I will hear your thoughts."

Kin'rar nodded solemnly. The noble Skymaster was caped in grey as always, slim of face, black of hair, measured in his voice. "I sympathise with the position that Sir Pagaloth was put in, but I had trusted he would understand what we were trying to do. I only spoke to him of our plans to remove Tavash because of that faith, but despite that, he whispered our plot into Tavash's ear and look at what has come of it. The dragonlords have fast answered their new king's call to war. Their armies are mustering at Blademelt, Dorath, Dragonfall, and the Trident. It's said a thousand galleys and galleons clot the Red Sea, preparing for an invasion. That some of our Fireborn riders have started attacking towns and settlements along the Vandarian coast. All of this might have been avoided with a more moderate hand at the helm. Tavash's reprieve has doomed all the world to war."

Lythian might once have agreed with that, but no longer. "War would have been inevitable anyway, Kin'rar," he declared. "King Janilah would have made sure of that."

"Yes, I believe you are right, Captain," came the quiet croaky voice of Sotel Dar. The scholar was a venerable old man of seven and eighty, who'd spent his entire life studying dragon-lore. He had held a high office at the Nest for a large part of that, including the early years of Ulrik Marak's reign as lord there, investigating the true power and nature of the Bondstone and the ancient process by which man and beast were bonded. "This Last Renewal is inevitable now. Perhaps it always was?"

It certainly seemed that way.

"I can hardly believe I'm saying this, but perhaps it would have been better had Amron Daecar not been crippled and set aside," grunted Lord Marak. "He alone stood as a buffer against the Warrior King's ambitions. He alone might have stopped him."

"Ah yes, Amron Daecar," said Sotel Dar. "A name to strike fear in many of us here. It is a cruel world that has seen him crippled by such an act of treachery, but there is some balance in this too, I think."

"Balance?" Lythian wasn't understanding. "You're suggesting what happened to him is just, because of what he did to Dulian during the war? Forgive me, Master Dar, but I have to disagree with you. Amron showed Tethian's father mercy."

The old academic smiled. He had darker skin that most Agarathi, from a Lumaran grandfather, Lythian had learned, with a brittle white beard that hid the loose folds of skin on his wattled chin. White hair lingered on the very sides of his head, though the space between was more liver spot than anything else. Age had also stolen what limited height he might once have had. He was a tiny man to be sure, no more than five feet tall, thin and feeble and never without his faithful walking stick, shaped to a dragon's head on the handle, with a pair of gleaming rubies for eyes.

"Mercy, yes," he said, nodding. "Or cruelty? They are two sides of the same coin, sometimes, I think. You Varin Knights understand your chivalric codes of honour more than most. To be spared can be seen as a dishonour, can it not? To live beneath that mantle of failure is a shadow from which one may never escape. Now add to that the tearing of one's soul, for that is what happens when a Fireborn rider outlives their dragon. Dulian's bond to Vallath was forged strong as dragon-steel, and Vallath's loss made living almost unbearable. The prince became a king and that king lived in shadow. Why do you think Tethian never wished to bond his own dragon? He saw what happened to his father, and chose another path. A path that has led us here, Captain Lythian."

Lythian *had* wondered why the young prince didn't have a bonded dragon of his own, though that rather explained it.

"In the north, you saw my father's crippling...the loss of his legs... as his greatest torment," Tethian said mildly. "But of course that was never the case. Even without his legs he might have continued to soar the skies, had Vallath been living. But without him...no. He became half a man, his very soul and spirit split in two. It is the risk all Fire-born riders take when they bond a dragon, and not one I wished to chance. Many called me craven for it. Many cursed me for abandoning my duty. But I saw my duty as being elsewhere, as you have come to see, Lythian. It is a greater purpose that drives me. And these kings we speak of...Janilah, my cousin, the new-crowned Godrik Taynar and Hadrin of House Thala....none of them will matter when Eldur walks again."

A short silence took root among the host, and as ever Lythian saw that quiet stiffening of Marak's jaw, the subtle shift as Kin'rar glanced away. *Neither man truly believes it*, he saw, as he'd seen often during his time among them. They had not been long in Tethian's company, unlike Sotel Dar and Ashun Klo and many others who'd been with him all along. Tethian's teacher and childhood friend shared their prince's fervency, Lythian had seen, and Sotel Dar in particular was uniquely qualified to speak on the matter.

Two days after Borrus had left, the old man found Lythian alone by a fire, warming the chill from his bones on a cold dreary day. It was their first meeting, and they spent much of that afternoon telling one another of their tales. Lythian had learned right then and there that the scholar was convinced of Eldur's prophesied rise, a foretelling he had known about for decades. It had made Lythian wonder just whose quest it truly was; the prince's or his teacher's? "I helped build the foundation of Tethian's beliefs," Sotel Dar had explained when the question was put to him, "but he is the man to take us forward. His knowledge now rivals my own, I would say. First came Pullio the Wise, then Quarl the Blind, then the Skylady of Loriath. All added to the record that I studied, educating young Tethian when he came to me seeking answers. Now he takes up the torch, for his piety and his *blood*. It is a part of the prophesy, Lythian, that a man of Eldur's own blood be the one to revive him."

Sotel Dar had gone on to explain how he'd studied the Wings for many years, travelling there himself as a much younger man during Tethian's grandfather King Tellion's reign. "I explored many passages within the mountains," he said, "as others had before me. The Wings are much a mystery to us, even now, though the long decades of my life have given me time to understand them, such as I can. What do you know of them, my friend? What do they say in the north?"

"That they are comprised of two main islands," Lythian said, recalling his own studies. "Both are mountainous, with high cliffs and few beaches along their coasts. Reaching them is all but impossible, I have read, except by dragon-flight. All dragons are born and bred there, thus their name, though it's also said the islands are vaguely shaped as wings as well, I recall."

Sotel Dar gave a teacherly smile. "And the breeding of dragons. What do you know of this?"

Lythian had stroked his stubbly chin, newly shaven by Talasha the day prior. "It's said in the north that dragons are born from eggs, as with other reptiles. These islands provide a place for them to nest, and give them sanctuary when they are young. Only when they come of age are they lured to the Nest by the Bondstone, to be tethered to a Fireborn rider. Though not all dragons answer this call."

"Most don't, historically," Sotel Dar said, as he'd sat hunched upon a tree stump by the crackling fire, swaddled in threadbare red robes and leaning on his staff. Like Tethian, he had on his garb the fiery sigil of Eldur, as did many others in the party, stitching them onto tunics and jerkins, mantles and cloaks alike. "Some believe that only one in ten dragons ever leave the Wings. Others say the number is double or triple that, but all agree that less than half come to the Nest to be bonded. Most choose to remain wild and free, making their numbers impossible to define. Ever do our sentries stand vigil at Dragonwatch, but they can only make estimates of dragon numbers and activity. Contrary to what you may think, Son of Varin, many dragons do not need to eat often, but are sustained by the magic of Agarath. There are great fires burning beneath the wings, did you know this?"

Lythian shook his head.

"This we call the *Breath of Agarath*, great ever-burning fires infused with his lasting magic. Agarath's spirit lives on beneath the Wings, we believe, as Vandar's spirit lingers in his Tomb."

The old man began poking his stick at the ground, drawing a crude map in the dirt at their feet. It soon took a shape Lythian recognised, depicting the western half of the world. "If you look at where the Wings are, and where Vandar's Tomb is, you start to see that they are located at opposite ends of our world, south and north. These are the resting places of our gods, Son of Varin; the ever-burning embers of war. Sometimes they glow hot and we have our Renewals, and sometimes they cool and we have peace. But it never ends, not for good. This is why we must bring Eldur back, and seek out the heir of Varin. Only they can end the War Eternal. Only they can put out this flame."

Lythian had looked at that map for a long while, then said, "The holy cavern at the heart of Vandar's Tomb is known to be near-impossible to find. I imagine that the same will be true of the cavern in which Eldur rests?" His eyes went up to Sotel Dar. "Is that part of why you're here, Sotel? To be Tethian's guide into those caves and caverns? To show him the way to where your Fire Father rests?"

"It is a part of my function, yes," the old scholar answered. "There is no man living who truly knows the way, but of those who draw breath I am best suited to find it." He'd given Lythian a knowing smile, as though seeing what was in his head. "I'm not so frail as I might seem, my friend," he told him. "But should I weaken or be unable to navigate those tunnels and passages, we will have those who can help support me. You, I hope, will be one of them. A Bladeborn of your gifts will be a great asset to us. And that blade you bear also, should we find ourselves blocked."

So that's why I'm really here, Lythian had thought. *To cut through the rock if there are cave-ins and blockages.* He gave a rueful laugh. "Tethian spoke of the symbolism of my participation, but I suppose I have practical uses too."

Sotel Dar smiled. "A man like you has many uses in a place like that, I am certain."

Like sticking Starslayer through Eldur's heart, Lythian had thought. It was Borrus's suggestion, and Lythian had to admit, it had some merit. *Should we raise him to find him dark and dreaded, I will have no choice,* he knew. Though in such a circumstance, what chance would he have, going up against a god?

Upon the craggy hillock, the trial of Sir Pagaloth continued, as the barest hint of dawn began to peer over the edge of the world out east. Others had their say. Sotel Dar himself claimed that Sir Pagaloth be freed to join them, that all men should be given a chance to repent of their sins. Ashun Klo said the opposite. He was close as kin to Tethian, born of a powerful house, devoted to his liege. He was tall, slim, and more fair-haired than was typical for the Agarathi, with purple eyes and a narrow hawkish face. A cruel face, Lythian had come to see, and a dangerous one. His role was protective, shadowing Tethian wherever he went, leading his personal guard. He was said to be a supremely gifted fighter, and bore a pair of red-black dragonsteel blades at his flanks, either side of a glittering suit of black scale-mail armour that would offer him some protection, even against godsteel. To that end he spoke immediately out against Sir Pagaloth being allowed to join them. "We must consider him a possible threat and spy, given his *transgressions.*" His voice was as sharp as his high cheekbones and jaw, delivered quick and curt. "It is not worth the risk. I say throw him and be done with it." He wiped his hands for effect.

The men under his command echoed his sentiment. One of them, a broad-faced brute called Grumlo, claimed that Pagaloth was a warmonger and not to be trusted. "I know a man who served under Sir Pagaloth in Dragonfall," he put forth in a thumping voice. "He said he spoke often of the war, of the father and brothers and uncles he'd lost to northern blades and spears. He wanted vengeance, always. He wanted war." Grumlo sneered at the gagged man, who had no voice with which to defend himself. "That is why he spoke out to save Tavash's life. So he might have a chance to claim vengeance, and get his share of blood."

"I do not believe that for one moment," Lythian said in response. He didn't much like Grumlo or Rackar or Kartheck, or any of the other men under Ashun Klo's command. They were rough-faced and rough-voiced and rough-spoken, he'd come to see. "I spoke often to Sir Pagaloth when we travelled together, and when I was held captive in the palace in Eldurath. Not once did he show a yearning for war, as some of his men did. This rumour need be given no mind. I suggest this is hearsay at best and slander at worst, and nothing more than that."

"And I suggest *you* be thrown from this cliff too," Grumlo told him bitterly. He slammed the butt of his heavy black spear into the rock. "This man is *not* one of us, my prince. If your cousin had one thing right, it was executing him and that Bloated Knight for their crimes during the war."

"You should count yourself lucky that Sir Borrus is not here to hear you say that, Grumlo," Lythian said, all calm. "He would strike you through before you could spout another word."

"I do not fear that bloated pig," Grumlo came back.

"Easy to say with him hundreds of miles away," Lythian said. *And sailing east on a pleasant ship*, he hoped.

Kin'rar laughed. "Yes, I do fear you would have been *somewhat* outmatched against Sir Borrus, Grumlo. Only Lord Marak would be able to duel him fairly, as bearer of the Fireblade."

"That is my point, Skymaster," said Grumlo, seething. "The Knight of Mists walks among us with that blade of his all day and night. What if he should decide to turn on us? He should *not* be here, my prince. Throw him from the cliff, I beg you."

Tethian was smiling in that way of his, as though nothing much troubled him. "I thought it was Sir Pagaloth on trial here, not our honoured guest," he said, giving a chuckle. "No, we'll be doing no such thing, my faithful friend. Captain Lythian is a nobleman and knight of fine repute and will not do us any harm, nor we him." He turned to look at Pagaloth, and gave his final verdict. "I judge Sir Pagaloth to be the same. I called Lythian here to hear his counsel and it is *his* word I place most weight on. If he wishes for Pagaloth to live, so be it." He turned. "Is that your final decision, Captain?"

Lythian didn't have to take long to consider it. He gave a nod. "It is."

"Then remove his gag," Tethian ordered, "and unbind his fetters. I would hear what he has to say."

Grumlo did the honours, grunting all the while as he roughly pulled the gag from Pagaloth's mouth and untied his wrists. He took position behind him after that, as Ashun Klo drew out a single dragon-steel blade, black streaked with red. "Your prince has asked that you speak," Ashun growled. "So speak."

Pagaloth pulled a breath into his lungs. The black greasy beard he kept braided, sometimes in a double or triple-pronged fork, was a mess. It hung down from his chin and cheeks, twisted and unkempt. Where the ropes had bound his wrists red welts flared, and when his lips opened, a cracked and broken voice came out. "I...I only want to make up for what I did," he said. "I only want to serve."

"Then do it from your knees." Grumlo thumped him in the lower black with the butt of his spear, forcing him down before the prince.

Tethian raised a hand. "Control yourself, Grumlo. There is no need for violence." The guard grunted and drew back, turning his spear vertical. "How did you come to know we were here?" Tethian asked the kneeling man.

"I heard...I heard men speaking of it, the night of the rescue at the Pits," he croaked. "I left Eldurath the next morning, before dawn."

"You travelled all this way on foot?"

"He was on foot when I spotted him," Kin'rar Kroll said.

"You were scouting on Neyruu?" Lythian wanted to know. Clearly he was missing a few details, having been summoned late.

"When I returned last night," Kin'rar confirmed. He typically went out most days in search of something. News. Food. Threats. Neyruu was always kept busy. "I spotted a man ranging through the foothills some leagues to the west, heading in our direction. Grumlo and Rackar went out to fetch him and bring him here."

Lythian was starting to work out why Pagaloth looked so beaten.

Clearly Grumlo and Racker had put hands on him before they got him here.

"I had a horse, at first," Pagaloth told the prince, still on his knees. "A strong stallion, but he broke a leg fording a river in the Great Grasslands and I had to continue on foot."

"You have made good ground, then. Eldurath is a long way from here. Who spoke to you of where we were?"

"Men. I...I didn't get their names. I was there, at the Pits of Kharthar during the rescue. I saw a small group attacking some soldiers and gave chase when they fled into the crowds. I overheard them speaking, later, when they stopped. I...I confess I did not understand." He stared at the prince. "I did not know you were alive, Prince Tethian. The rumours...for years you have been thought..."

"To be dead, I know, and I would prefer that it stay that way for now." He looked at Sir Pagaloth firmly. "You were not followed?"

"No, my prince."

"And you spoke to no one of where you were going? Not your wife, your family."

"I have no wife, or family."

Tethian paused. "Your men?" he asked. "You were stationed in Dragonfall before you brought Lythian and his friends to Eldurath. These men, they were loyal to you, I have heard. Did you speak of this to them?"

"No, my prince, I said nothing."

"And you came here...why? Not for my cause, no. Not for Eldur. This is all new to you, you have said, and your face says it quite plainly too." Tethian gestured to Lythian. "This is for the captain, is it? To make up for Sir Tomos Pentar's death?"

Pagaloth's head dipped into a weary nod. "I made a mistake...one that I will have to learn to live with, I know. I would understand if you threw me to the rocks. I have considered death myself, for my shame. I thought I would find it coming here. I..." He looked around. The group was faintly lit by firelight flickering from the sentries about them. "I never expected to find...to find anyone out here. But I heard something about the Western Neck, and a camp, and a cause. From those men, I heard them before they saw me and ran. I knew I had to try. But now I'm here..." He looked again at the prince. "Eldur, Your Highness? You...you wish to raise him? He...he *lives*?"

"That is what we believe," said Marak.

"He lives," said Tethian, with certainty. He turned to look at the dragonlord. "He *lives*, Ulrik. Or do you still have doubts?"

"I am a pragmatic man, my prince. You know I will not believe it as you do, until I see him with my own two eyes."

Tethian smiled. "You are a warrior, Ulrik, and that limits your vision. But I will pull back the veil and show you the light, just as soon as Garlath recovers."

That would be a week or more at least. Special saddles had been built that would allow Garlath and Neyruu to convey a small host to the Wings, but for the time being they sat amid the yard, unused. And the wait went on.

"We are here to raise Eldur to the world above, and end the War Eternal, Sir Pagaloth," Tethian told him. "Much and more of this will not make sense to you, but in time you will come to understand." He paused again. "Your house name is Kadosk, I have been told."

"A house of knights, sire," Pagaloth confirmed. "My father was Sir Pagar Kadosk. He fell during the war, with his brothers, and mine."

"An awful thing," said the prince softly. "Not many can have suffered as gravely as you. What of your mother? Did you have sisters, sir?"

"One sister, my prince. She died before her sixth year. My mother lived through the war, but it took its toll. The loss of her husband and sons was too grave for her to bear. She took her own life, I am ashamed to say."

"No shame, Sir Pagaloth. It is a sin to take one's life, yes, but in such conditions one can understand. What happened to you after?"

"I was taken in by my father's sister, and took to my training. For some years I sought vengeance, it is true, but as I grew older I saw the folly in war. It is peace I seek now. To end the War Eternal...this is a cause I can live for, one to give me purpose again."

"Lies," grunted Grumlo. "Who can lose so much and not want vengeance? He is lying to you, my prince."

"If I wanted vengeance I would have taken it on Borrus Kanabar," Pagaloth said, stirring. "It was the Barrel Knight who slew my father and eldest brother in the war. I had many chances to seek amends when I led him across the Drylands, but not once did I consider doing so." He turned to the guard, and a little of that cold fire burned in his eyes. "You do not know me, Grumlo. Do not speak as though you do."

The oafish guard looked set to respond, before Tethian silenced him again. "One more word and you will be thrown from the cliff yourself, Grumlo. And these injuries Sir Pagaloth has suffered...I take it you were the one to inflict them?"

Grumlo withered at that. "I thought him a threat, my prince. I...I had to make sure."

"Well now we're sure. Be gone."

"But sire..."

"Be *gone*, Grumlo. Do not make me say it again." Grumlo dropped his head and trundled off, dragging his heavy spear and disappearing back into the woods. Tethian watched him go with a rare displeasure. "You may want to reconsider your choice of men, Ashun," he said to his friend and the captain of his guard. "I will not abide unfairness here."

"I will speak to him, my lord," said Ashun Klo, with icy grace.

"See that you do." The prince looked again at the man kneeling before him. "I understand you're a gifted swordsman, Sir Pagaloth?"

"I am capable, my lord."

"More than capable," said Lythian. "Sir Pagaloth may not have sought vengeance against Borrus, Prince Tethian, but they did duel once to first blood during our journey across the Drylands. Pagaloth came away the victor, if that is any indication of his skill."

"Sir Borrus was without godsteel in the bout," Pagaloth explained modestly. "And I sensed he was holding back at times, so as not to inspire further anger among my men."

"He said the very same," Lythian told him, "but Borrus Kanabar has been known to lie." He gave a fond smile. "It was a fair fight, and Sir Pagaloth won. Not many could say that of the Barrel Knight, Prince Tethian."

The prince considered matters a moment more, running a hand through his curls of black hair. "I think you have spent enough time on your knees, Sir Pagaloth. Rise and join us. You will be assigned to the service of the man you came here for. Captain Lythian, he is yours."

And with that the trial was done.

The host began moving off from the hillock and back down into the trees, making for the camp. To the east, dawn was starting to break, a sliver of red light glowing beneath the rolls of thick grey cloud. Marak pressed away in a different direction, heading into the valleys, as he often did, to check on Garlath. His dragon's pain was his, Lythian had grown to understand. "The soul-bond transcends bodies," Sotel Dar had told him. "This is unique among bonded Fireborn riders. When a dragon dies, a part of the rider dies too, and the same is true in reverse. A dragon shorn of its bonded Fireborn can become a pitiful thing, or a rageful thing, and will never be bonded again. The same thing happens if one or the other is injured. Their pain is shared, as is their mood. Do not expect Lord Marak to smile any time soon." Lythian never expected that anyway, in fairness, but true enough, Marak had been especially grumpy of late.

Soon enough the hillock was bare, but for Lythian and Sir Pagaloth. "You should rest, Sir Pagaloth," Lythian said to him. "You cannot have slept much since leaving Eldurath." *Nor eaten,* he thought, *to look at you.*

"Penance," Pagaloth explained, "for the torment I subjected you to. I have drunk little and eaten less on the road. If you will allow it, I might take a morsel now."

"I'll allow it," Lythian said, stepping toward the man. "And that penance...it's finished. I do not want you starving yourself on my behalf, Pagaloth. We have plenty of meat here. It would be better that you recover your strength for the days to come."

"As you have," Pagaloth said. "You look well, Captain. Better than when I saw you last."

"A corpse would have looked better, I'm sure."

"Just so." Pagaloth managed the feeblest of laughs. "I will eat, then. But..." He looked off down the hill, into the gloomy woods. "You are here by choice, for certain? When I saw the battle in the Pits, I...I wasn't sure what they wanted with you. It was for you whom I came, Lythian. To try to rescue you, if you needed it."

His earnestness was endearing, yet his worries unwarranted. Lythian placed a hand to his shoulder, giving him a gentle pull to lead him down the hill. "Let's get you fed first, Sir Pagaloth," he jested. "I don't think you're in any state to be staging a rescue just yet."

Smiling, they went off to break their fast, out there in the wilds of the Western Neck.

11

Elyon

"I'm looking for a boy of sixteen summers, lanky with messy black hair, name of Del. Have you seen him?" The serving boy gave a confused looked, then shrugged. "Right then, off you go." The boy shuffled away with his trencher of salted pork, moving through the billowing marquee. It was all a rather impromptu affair, and so the great flapping walls of the pavilion hadn't been properly fastened. There was something about the Stonehills that made driving stakes into the ground more difficult than on packed soil. Prince Rylian had told Elyon that they weren't so hilly or stony as they sounded, but that was rubbish. They were perfectly named, Elyon had found. About as hilly and stony as you'd expect.

He stepped through the colourful crowd of lords and knights to the next serving boy he saw. This one was carrying a large jug of ale that looked half the size of his body. "Careful there, or you'll topple over," Elyon jested. "Aren't you a little small to be carrying such a large jug?" He had an image of him trying to serve Sir Taegon Cargill, who stood over seven feet tall. Sir Taegon would have to kneel and the boy would have to use a ladder, and still he'd struggle to fill his cup.

"I'm thirteen, sir," was the boy's reply. That didn't make much sense to Elyon. The lad looked closer to three.

"Right, well, good for you." He reached down and down and down with his own goblet, so the little lying boy might fill it. Once he'd completed his duties, Elyon went into his pitch. "I'm looking for a boy, sixteen, messy black hair, about five times your height, probably. His name's Del. Do you know him?"

"I know a Del."

Elyon almost spat up the swig of ale he'd taken. "You *do*? A Del who's sixteen years old, tall with messy black hair?"

"No," the boy squeaked. "My Del's my brother. Dellard's his full name, but we call him Del. He's two years younger than me, sir. And shorter."

"So he's one year old and one foot tall?"

That was too far. The boy looked like he might cry. *Which makes sense,* Elyon thought, *seeing as he's a newborn child.* He judged it better to say, "I'm sorry, that was unfair. You're a strapping lad to be sure. Were you in the Kastor warcamp? I don't recognise you."

"I cooked stew," the boy said, nodding. "In...in the Huffort warcamp. My father's a fighting man, sir, but he went off with the army south somewhere." He looked suddenly distraught. "I still don't know where. No one will tell me."

"Mudport, most likely," Elyon said. "It's well protected, despite how it sounds. Lots and lots of ballistas for those nasty dragons, when they come sniffing around."

That cheered the boy up a bit, but in truth his father was likely to die. All the north was moving right now, the way Elyon had heard it, great heaving armies crisscrossing the lands like some enormous spider's web as they gathered in this city or that fort or marched south to defend the coast. *And here I am, heading for a wedding...*

"Well, if you talk to any other boys you knew from back at Harrowmoor, remember to ask about a boy named Del," he told the toddler. "Not your brother, but the tall one, with messy hair. If you hear anything, come to me."

The boy nodded and moved off, though of course he'd discover nothing. Elyon had asked so many people about Del by now that he was convinced the boy wasn't using that name. He only persisted with it because he didn't have another one, though he'd long since given up hope of finding him. In truth that hope had waned and weakened the very first day he'd begun his search back at the Harrowmoor camp, and had only grown more futile since. But Saska had asked that he look for Del, so he kept on with it anyway. It took no effort and made him feel better. And he'd even recruited Lancel and Barnibus to help as well.

He spotted them both across the stony-floored pavilion and marched over. "So...any luck?" he asked.

"Nope," said Lancel.

"What do you think?" said Barnibus.

And that about summed it up.

"Well, there's always tomorrow," Elyon said. "Keep trying. You never know when you'll get a bite."

"*Never* being the key word there," japed Lancel. "The boy's not with the army, El, that's clear enough. He's either dead or deserted, or at another camp somewhere. He was probably drawn into Rylian's southern army during the invasion, and garrisoned somewhere along the Rasal coast."

"Yes, I do suspect we were closer to him when we brought Saska to Shellcrest than we are now, you know," added Barnibus. All three were dressed in their Varin raiment, blue-cloaked and leather clad with godsteel daggers at their hips, which made a fine change to how the pair had appeared on their return to Harrowmoor some six days past. "You do realise that she'll never know you did this for her, don't you? It's noble that you're trying to track the lad down, Elyon, but I think it's clear enough by now that it's not going to happen. Forget him."

Forget him...and forget her, Elyon thought, though the latter would be a little more difficult, seeing as she continued to appear in his dreams. He gave no response, though. *If Lancel and Barny want to give up the search they can. I've asked enough of them already.*

A strong gust of wind pulled hard at the blue billowing canvas walls nearby, drawing their attention. "Feels like the marquee might rip free and take flight at any moment," Barnibus said, supping on his ale. "We'll be feasting under the rains soon, I'll wager."

The three moved to the nearest table and sat down, setting their tankards to the wood. Due to the last-minute nature of this particular feast, there had been little time to put down decking. That meant the tables had been unpacked upon the rough stony ground in a shallow valley between the hills, making them all uneven and askew. It made for a rather piteous setting, which rather suited the man they were gathered to celebrate.

Elyon said as much. "A feast hall to befit its king," he announced with a grim smile, looking toward the far end of the marquee. In a smart enough flourish, someone had had the sense to arrange the pavilion so that the top end included a bar of rock that doubled as a stage. The royal table had been placed atop it, from which the ratty, regicidal little figure of King Hadrin looked down upon his host, with Prince Rylian and Prince Dalton either side of him, and the sundry greatlords and ladies in attendance spreading to the flanks. "Makes you appreciate Dalton a bit more, doesn't it, looking at that," he went on. "He may be a bitter bastard, but he's bloody handy with a blade and commands respect for that alone. But *Hadrin*?" Even the name tasted sour on his tongue. "It still turns my stomach to think that Amilia has to wed that creature. It would have been bad enough for my mother, but that was decades ago. Now look at him. Dalton's hardly the stoutest man but he's twice Hadrin's size. Looks like he's aged a decade since last I saw him."

"Murdering your own father will age one prematurely," Barnibus offered darkly.

It was growing gloomy outside now, to complete their fourth day riding through the Stonehills. Two days ago, a crow had arrived, telling Prince Rylian that King Hadrin and his host were one day's ride ahead, and would await them at this very spot at the heart of the Stonehills, to travel onto Ilithor together. When Elyon had heard the news he felt certain that an event like this would be staged. Thus they'd arrived that afternoon to find this pavilion being comically erected, and the tables being clunkily arranged, a farce of a feast hall if ever there was one. The snickers had begun soon after. Even now Elyon could see the lords and knights of Tukor sniggering as they sat at wobbly tables, openly ridiculing the setting and layout and, most likely, the king they were here to honour.

I might feel sorry for Hadrin if I didn't dislike him so much, Elyon thought. The man was trying to appear lordly as he sat between Rylian and Dalton, but even with a larger throne to sit in, he looked a child between two men, old and ugly and with a spiteful little look on his face. Rylian and Dalton were speaking past him often, or turning to address the men beside them, arranged in order of rank, and thus the Rasal king was being largely ignored, to his displeasure.

Lord Paramor had been put next to Prince Rylian to continue healing the rift between their kingdoms, with Lord Cedrik Kastor on the old man's opposite flank. On the other side, Dalton had Lord Buckland for company, a big bear of a man with a huge black beard that rolled right down to his belly. He was the Lord of Northgate Castle up in the north of Rasalan, and would have defended his keep stoutly if the war hadn't ended at Harrowmoor. To his right side was the equally large Lord Wallis Kanabar, who looked happy enough to have found himself a good drinking partner. The two had been guzzling ale and laughing uproariously since their arrival.

Others at the table were some of the Tukoran lords, Lord Huffort and Lord Swallow, and several from the Lowplains who'd been at Harrowmoor under Lord Paramor's command, including Lord Browlan and Lord Maynard, otherwise known as the Oakenlord for his ancestral seat in Oakshore.

Behind them all were their banners, hanging from poles pitched into the ground. There was Rylian's royal standard of the crossed hammer and blade of Tukor. Dalton, now prince, had taken up the blade and mountain crest of Vandar, and Hadrin had done the same with the speared leviathan of Rasalan, set before the rising sun. The rest used the crests of their houses. Bears and mermen and stags and snakes. Even Sir Rodmond, being Dalton's heir and second in line to the Vandarian throne now, took his place up on that stage, with the Taynar banner fluttering behind him. But Elyon *wasn't* up there, and he could only see that as a snub. A snub he was grateful for, in truth, but a snub all the same.

A hand came down on his shoulder, and a moment later Sir Mallister Monsort was taking his place beside him, impeccable in Emerald Guard green. "Not on duty today, Elyon?" he asked, a teasing smile on his lips. "Now don't tell me Prince Dalton is letting you have some fun for once?"

"I'm sure he'll summon me for my nightly vigil," Elyon responded. That was how Dalton Taynar usually did it. He imagined himself more vulnerable at night and thus had Elyon on guard, typically with one of Sir Brontus or Sir Taegon for company. Brontus Oloran was the more bearable of the two. Not friendly, exactly, but he was happy enough to talk. Taegon Cargill tended to communicate in grunts and the occasional bodily function. The nights at his side were the longest and most malodorous, to be sure.

"Dalton ought to be careful, you know," said Barnibus. "It won't be long before people start calling him paranoid at best and craven at worst."

"They're already calling him paranoid, Barny," Lancel said to that, pushing an unruly lock of sandy hair behind an ear. "If Vesryn hasn't come for him by now, he's not going to. How does Dalton think he'd have crossed the Sibling Strait? Swam? With the Sword of Varinar at his hip? There's no surer way to guarantee a good drowning."

There had been no reports of skiffs or rowboats being commandeered either. If Vesryn had somehow crossed the strait, he'd have had to pay for passage from a sailor of fisherman or local merchant. Neither Sir Roy Gaveston, leading the hunt on Prince Dalton's behalf, or Lord Huffort of Rockfall, who had hundreds of his own agents searching for Vesryn by Janilah's order, had made mention of anyone giving Vesryn aid. "Lord Huffort controls the western coast of Tukor from Rockfall all the way south of the Stonehills," Elyon said. "There is no way Vesryn could have made it across the strait without being spotted, unless someone sheltered him." And even then it was unlikely. Every ship, large and small, coming across the water from Rasalan was being searched by Huffort's men. Nor had any affrays been reported, to suggest Vesryn had fought his way ashore. "My uncle didn't go west," Elyon said with certainty. "My best guess is he rode straight into the Oakenwood to hide and consider his next move. It's just north of Harrowmoor, dense, and a known haven for outlaws and bandits. I spoke with the Oakenlord about it earlier. He told me that there are wanted men among those trees who have been on the run for decades. We might not see my uncle again until he's into his seventies."

Sir Mallister gave a brisk shake of the head. "I always thought your uncle more heroic than that, Elyon. Overshadowed by your father he may have always been, but he fought valiantly in the War of the Continents, I've heard. I can't believe he'd just run and hide his way through the next Renewal. It would be a great dishonour to deny us the Sword of Varinar in this war."

Honour didn't have much to do with it anymore, so far as Elyon saw it. "Men can do terrible things to keep a Blade of Vandar, Mallister," he said, thinking of Jonik. He'd killed Aleron, his very own brother, and provoked the full rancour of his own dark order to keep the Nightblade. There was no reason to think that Vesryn wouldn't do the same.

For the next hour, the disgraced former First Blade remained the topic of discussion. The various theories as to his whereabouts were espoused and considered for the hundredth time, and all the while, Elyon found his eyes and mind drifting. When he spotted the drunken form of Sir Kristof Caldlow lumbering toward the exit, he rose immediately from his bench, bid his friends goodbye, and marched over to accost him. "Leaving so soon, Sir Kristof?"

The drunk heir to House Caldlow looked at him quizzically. He was not a pleasant man to look at. Small beady eyes peeked out from above puffy red cheeks, and between them was a wide nose all full of blackheads and broken veins. His hair was of a muddy colour, thinning and lank, and his physical form could best be described as awkward, with thin arms and bandy legs poking out from a circular body wrapped in an ill-fitting purple doublet of velvet, trimmed with gold. "Sir Elyon," he said, in a slur. "What...what do you want?"

"I can't come over to an old friend for a chat?" Elyon said, feigning offence.

"I...we've spoken maybe twice, ever."

"And have become fast friends in that time." Elyon smiled and snatched up a fresh jug of ale from a side table, and filled two cups. He'd been meaning to speak with Sir Kristof for some days, though was hoping to find him drunk when he did so. It would be better if he didn't recall Elyon's questions the following day. He raised his cup. "To your father's health. A shame he isn't fit to be here."

"Aye...the gout's done for him, Sir Elyon. Painful business." He clacked his cup against Elyon's then gulped down half its measure. Sir Kristof was a well known sot and sluggard, and not much of a knight. He would likely drink his way through this war at the head of the men under his command, and avoid the fighting as much as he could. "Got a growth in his neck besides. Some tumour, we're told. I expect he'll die any day." He hiccupped, then belched, then drank some more. "And certainly by the time...the war's...done," he said between more hiccuping.

Elyon put on a sad face. "I'm sorry to hear it."

Sir Kristof didn't look so sorry. He just shrugged and refilled his cup. "Is your father...coming for the wedding?"

Don't ask, Elyon thought. "I hope so," he said. He wasn't here to talk about his own father. It was Saska on his mind. "You kept southern girls in your household in Broadway when you were young, didn't you?"

Sir Kristof frowned to that. "Lots of Tukoran families did, especially back then. There's no shame in it...Sir Elyon." He glanced to the top table. "We're...not all...like the Kastors."

"I wasn't suggesting you were. No no, of course not." Elyon preferred to keep this light. He smiled and sipped his ale. "I'm just thinking of one southern girl, in particular. I heard you had in your kitchens once. A child of Aramatian lineage." He paused. "You probably had several, I suspect. But one with vivid blue eyes? Do you remember a girl like that, Sir Kristof?"

The man worked through the many drunken years he'd spent on this earth, then gave a nod. "The maids would talk about her," he said. "Big blue eyes, yes. She was just a tot, though." He looked to be getting a handle on his hiccups. "Think Father sold her on before her teens. Not sure where. The Kastors, maybe." He shrugged again. "But those eyes...yeah, I remember those eyes. They were rare enough to recall."

More rare than you realise, Elyon thought. *Lightborn and Bladeborn both.* "Do you know how your father came to own her?"

The drunk knight thought again. "Most were found at market in Broadway," he said. "But that one...something about the palace in Aram rings a bell. The staff liked to talk about it. The girl...she'd been found with a maidservant who said she served the Grand Duchess. She was raving mad, obviously. My father's men bought the infant off her, to be raised for work. The scullery wenches and washerwomen saw to that, I recall. She worked the kitchens when she was old enough, but Father never let her up into the house. None of the southerners were allowed up there."

Elyon kept a calm countenance. "This maidservant she was bought from..." *Or stolen from,* he thought. "You say she was mad. You didn't believe she was from the palace in Aram?"

The drunk shrugged. His lack of care was clear enough. "Maybe, maybe not. I never dealt with the hiring and firing of staff, Sir Elyon, and didn't speak to the woman." He chugged his drink down to its dregs.

"So the child's parents...you never knew who they were?"

He laughed at that, though it was a confused laugh. "No. Why would I? She was just a slave...or *servant*, I should say." He gave an awkward chuckle. "Why do you care anyway? This something about that girl you were said to harbour in your tent? That spy girl?"

"What spy girl?" He sharpened his voice.

"That...that one Lord Kastor said you had...in your tent." Sir Kristof frowned, unsure. "That was the rumour, anyway. Some of the men say you killed Sir Griffin to protect her..."

"Are you calling me a traitor, Sir Kristof?"

The man backed away. "No, I'd never."

Elyon stared at him, unblinking. Caldlow was a middling house of limited power and influence, and this man knew his place. "Good." He stared some more, to make sure that the sotted knight wouldn't say anything of this conversation. *If he remembers it.* "Now don't let me keep you, Sir Kristof. Enjoy the rest of your night." The drunk couldn't leave quick enough after that, scuttling for the exit.

Elyon watched him go. The world was tar-dark outside now and the rains were lashing harder against the fluttering canvas walls. He drew toward a brazier near the exit, warming himself as he considered things. Sir Kristof's testimony lined up well with what Lady Marian Payne had told him almost a week ago about Saska's heritage. *Lightborn*, he thought, *and Bladeborn both*. He'd always known Saska was part-Aramatian, but to be related to royalty made her something quite unique. She'd be able to bond a sunwolf or starcat, *and* bear godsteel all at once, and who on this earth could say that but she? There had been some over the years, of course. At certain points through history rulers of north and south had tried to secure a long term peace by marrying between their noble houses, but those were rare. Saska was probably the only person living who could claim both Bladeborn and Lightborn blood of that strength and purity. *Unique*, he thought again, *and no wonder I dream of her so often...*

A young man stepped in front of him, dressed in a yellow surcoat over glittery godsteel mail. Elyon looked him up and down. "You're interrupting, sir," he said. "Can you not see I'm deep in thought."

"My apologies, Sir Elyon. I have come to invite you to confer privily with the King of Rasalan, Hadrin of House Thala, direct descendent of the First Queen and Goddess by unbroken primogeniture."

Elyon's heart sunk. He'd been hoping to avoid having to speak with Hadrin tonight. *Or ever.* "Quite a mouthful," he told the young

Suncoat. "Do you have to say that to everyone you invite to speak with him?"

"I do, sir. I have been given the honour this evening of bearing the king's standard." He held that standard to his side, a tall banner hanging limp from a pole, the Rasal crest hidden among its folds.

"Standard-bearers typically ride with their hosts to war, and parleys, and such," Elyon pointed out. He'd seen the man moving around all evening, in truth, and had found it most unusual. "Strange to see one in a feast hall."

The knight seemed to agree, though wouldn't say so plainly. "My king wished to make an impression, I think."

"Well he's done that. I don't think anyone will forget this evening in a while." Even over the music, the flapping of the pavilion walls could be heard, cracking with the wind. One corner had even pulled free earlier, to a great chorus of laughter, before being hauled and hammered back into position. "What's your name?"

"Sir Francis Maynard, sir."

"Oh, a son of the Oakenlord? I rather like your lord father, Sir Francis. I find the Rasal nobility most agreeable." *Excluding your king,* he thought. "He spoke of having two sons. Are you the eldest?"

"I'm the second son, Sir Elyon, much like you."

Yes, but your older brother is probably still alive. He didn't let that thought fester long. "I understand that the Maynards and Bucklands are closely linked," he said. Oakshore, where the Oakenlord Ferry Maynard had his seat, was only about fifty miles from Lord Buckland's seat in Northgate.

"Yes, Sir Elyon. Lord Buckland is my uncle...my mother's brother. My mother was a Buckland before marrying my father."

"Yes, that's typically how it works." Elyon gave a cordial grin, hoping to delay things as long as possible. "You must be new to the Suncoats. You look a good deal younger than even me, Sir Francis."

"I'm eighteen, sir, fresh from the academy."

"And your brother?"

"He is some three years my senior. As your brother was you, I believe."

"You're quite correct. And your brother...he's a Suncoat, as you are?" Elyon understood both House Maynard and House Buckland to be generously provisioned with strong Varin blood.

"He is, Sir Elyon," confirmed the younger man. "He's stationed with the garrison in Shellcrest."

"I see. And you? Were you in Harrowmoor during the siege?"

"No, sir. I had been training in Thalan when the Tukorans invaded. I travelled south to Northgate after that, in a host of some five hundred, to help bolster Northgate Castle under my uncle's command."

Something clicked in Elyon's head. Saska had mentioned that she'd stayed with Lord Buckland for several days in Northgate, when she and Lady Marian Payne travelled south with her men. He wondered if Sir Francis knew them. "Do you know of Lady Payne?"

"Lady Marian Payne? Oh yes. A most formidable woman. She and my uncle are dear friends."

"She travelled with a girl of southern tone. Do you recall?"

"How could I not." The boy smiled youthfully. "A most comely girl, she was. Saska, that was her name if my memory serves. The castle seemed much brightened when she was there, and much darker when she left."

"I can imagine."

"My uncle was most fond of her too. She travelled south with Lady Payne and several men under her charge, some months past now. I suspect she must be with her now, as Lady Payne makes for Dragon's Bane."

She's not, Elyon knew. Though the part about Marian Payne was true.

"Well, I suppose I should take you to the king, Sir Elyon. He prefers to keep a tight schedule, and has many he wishes to see."

Knowing it would be churlish to delay any longer, Elyon followed Sir Francis Maynard through the crowded marquee toward the top table set on the shallow shelf of rock. By now half of the lords and ladies seated there had left to mingle, though Hadrin remained where he was, stiff and small in his oversized wooden throne. He was wearing his dark grey whale-skin armour, near as tough as Ilithian Steel, rough and pitted with a golden mantle atop it, fixed at the shoulders by black clasps shaped as squids. Between the two patches of grey hair that flanked his head sat a golden crown of simple styling, set with shells that sparkled a thousand colours in the lamplight. Elyon stepped up onto the shelf of rock and stood before him. "Sir Elyon Daecar, Your Majesty," announced Sir Francis Maynard. He stepped aside.

"Your Majesty," said Elyon, bowing low.

The flapping feast hall was loud with music and merriment. Both Prince Dalton and Prince Rylian had vacated their seats, leaving Elyon and the king to speak with a measure of privacy. Further down, Lord Kanabar's drinking competition with Lord Buckland had reached an impasse; both men were steaming drunk and passed out at the table. On the other side, Lord Cedrik Kastor sat neatly where he'd been all night, playing the perfect lord. He and Lord Paramor looked to have healed their rift, such as it was, in their bid to avoid further infighting.

"Is your father coming to my wedding?" asked Hadrin.

Elyon recalled that snivelly voice. A shiver went up his spine. "I am unsure, my lord."

"He hasn't written you, sir? I know that your sister Lillia is coming, with your auntie Amara. Why not Amron? Does he not wish to see me wed?"

"He is a long way from Ilithor. I do not believe he would make it in time for the ceremony."

"A long way from Ilithor, yes." Hadrin's narrow receding chin faded into his neck as he smiled. "A *very* long way from Ilithor, one might say."

Elyon wanted away from him already. Rarely had anyone caused his skin to prickle as this man did. "Our ancestral lands are far, yes. Not everyone agrees that a wedding is important at this time..."

"And the noble Lord Daecar is one of them, I'm sure. Just like his son and heir." The weasel king ran a slimy tongue over his oversized teeth. "I am told your uncle has stolen the Sword of Varinar. How typical of a Daecar, to take what he wishes. Your family have a long-standing history of living above the law. I hope you will correct that urge, when you come to lead your house."

Elyon bristled. "There is a longstanding history in your line as well, my lord. One of wisdom. And foresight. I'm told it ended with your father."

It was a common slur against the man. Hadrin had never compared favourably to his predecessor. His mouth twitched, and a shadow passed across his face. "Do you hope to match your father's achievements, Sir Elyon?" he then asked, through his teeth. "People said he was as Varin reborn. And my father's wisdom was oft compared to Thala's. Would you curse us both for being lesser sons of greater sires?"

It was an unexpectedly judicious response. "No," Elyon admitted. "Though some crimes do bring a curse, my lord." He took a moment to think. *Don't say it,* he told himself. *If you do, you'll not be able to take it back.* He let the urge pass, saying nothing.

The rat was having none of it. "What crimes are you referring to?" he pressed, a cold sneer driving up his top lip. "Do you have something you wish to say to me?"

"Nothing but congratulations and commiserations. One for your nuptials, and the other for your loss. It must be difficult, managing the joy of your betrothal with the murder of your father."

"*Murder*?" The word hung in the air. "My father died of natural causes. He was very old, Sir Elyon. At such an age, the heart gives out."

"Apologies. I must be mistaken. There was a rumour that King Godrin was killed." *By you,* he chose not to say.

"Rumours are weeds. They rise from dirt and die soon after, to be ever forgotten. My father died of a failed heart. Sir Munroe will attest to it, as will others of his guard."

Elyon glanced behind the king, where Sir Munroe Moore stood on watch, glad in full godsteel plate. He was the head of Hadrin's royal guard, and a traitor, if those rumours were true. "Ah yes, Sir Munroe. A man of perfect scruples. And what of Sir Ralston, King Hadrin? Does your father's Wall not wish to stand barrier to you too?"

"Sir Ralston is a traitor to my kingdom. He fled from my father's service and was last seen boarding a ship in Shellcrest, heading south. Some say it was his abandonment of my father that caused his heart to fail. But I'm sure you know this already. Many and more have been discussing it."

"It must have passed me by. But that is a severe loss. I'm sure Sir Munroe will do his best, but there is only one Sir Ralston Whaleheart."

"We don't all need a giant standing guard on us."

That seemed a small jibe at Prince Dalton. Sir Taegon was rarely absent from his side these days. "Quite. Though it does help, when you cannot defend yourself."

Elyon enjoyed that one. Hadrin was a Seaborn of rich blood, but no Bladeborn. Any man here with a drop of Varin blood would slay him for fun, and that vulnerability made the man paranoid and peevish. His face was a twisting web of insecurities, every wrinkle a weakness he was trying to cover up. "A king does not need to defend himself," he finally said. "He has others to do that for him."

That was true enough, though Elyon was growing weary of the joust. He sensed he might say something explicitly out of turn if he remained here any longer. He let a short moment pass before saying, "I am sure you have many others you wish to see, my lord. I would not want to spend too much of your valuable time."

"Well aren't you thoughtful. Stay right where you are." Elyon froze. He was halfway through his bow and about to step away. He looked back up to find the King of Rasalan sneering at him. "I am a *king*, Sir Elyon. You will leave when I say you can leave."

"A *foreign* king, on *foreign* soil." Elyon couldn't help himself. "I will leave when *I* will it so."

An ugly gurgle of a laugh crawled up the rat king's throat. "Well, it seems I was wrong. You are just as much a Daecar as your father and uncle and the brother you put into the crypts. Arrogant. Superior. Thinking you're above the law."

"There is no law that says I need to spend any time in your company. It is etiquette that compels me. And good etiquette must be earned." Elyon glowered. "You, my lord, have earned no such thing." He turned and prepared to step away. Then came the words that stopped him.

"I've seen him in the darkness. You'll never see him again."

Elyon turned. There was a cruel smile twisting on Hadrin's lips. A shiver climbed Elyon's spine. "What did you say?"

"You say the foresight of my line died with my father. It isn't so, Sir Elyon. The Eye of Rasalan is *mine*, and in it I have seen things." Up and up and up his lips went, as his smile grew ever more sinister. "I have seen your father, limping through the blackness. Oh, I don't expect to see him at my wedding, Sir Elyon, and never did. I don't expect that anyone will ever see him again."

Elyon lurched forward, slamming his hands on the table. People looked over. Sir Munroe took a step forward, hand on hilt. "What have you seen?" he demanded. "Where is he!"

"Dead," whispered the kingslaying king. He raised a hand to halt Sir Munroe. "To walk into the darkness can mean only one thing, Sir Elyon. Amron Daecar...is dead."

12

Saska

The Steel Sister sat at anchor off the rugged coastal cliffs, bobbing lazily on the clear turquoise waters some way down the northeast seaboard of Aramatia. Around them were a number of small rocky islets, each teeming with seabirds and lizards and seals, lazing beneath the midday sun, or fishing the rich reefs that cluttered the ocean floor beneath them. Half the crew were doing the same, spearing fish in the shallows, luring them with bait and lines, or duck diving deep to fetch oysters and clams.

According to Captain Rikki Bowen, it was a favourite spot for he and his family. "My father always liked to stop here on his trips," he told Saska. "We'd stay for half a day, maybe more, fishing the waters, gathering bird eggs, exploring the rocks and islands for debris washed up from passing ships." He was sat on the ship's figurehead - a busty woman in a sleek silver dress, reaching out to sea - with his legs astride her neck and dangling each side of her shoulders. "See how clear the water is, Saska. It's some fifteen metres deep here, between the islands, but the very best spots are further out. He pointed beyond the cluster of islets, toward the rough open sea. "There's a drop off, just out there where some of the men are swimming. Goes down and down and down it does. Never seen another reef like it. The Seaborn come here often to explore it, and gather the rich fruits at the bottom. Lots of treasures down there, aye."

"Like what?" Saska asked.

"Oh, a range of things. There are weeds and marine plants that only grow at certain depths, depths most of us mortals can't reach. And fish too. You heard of Death's Denial, I suppose?"

Saska nodded, as she stood at the bow of the ship. "It's a powerful stimulant. Made from the glands of deep sea serpents."

"Aye, precisely." Captain Rikki pointed again. "You find those slippery buggers on the seabed out there, several hundred metres down. That's how far the drop-off goes. And half way down you'll find drakeshells too. You know about those?"

Saska had learned about those at the University of Thalan too. "It's a red shell, shaped almost like a dragon's head," she said. "The Rasals shave the top layer of the shell, and make it into a powder. It's used for antiseptic and healing. Can speed recovery times from wounds and things like that."

She looked out to where the waters darkened and deepened, some fifty or so metres from the ship. A few of the crew were diving there, seeing how far deep they could get down the drop-off. Others were closer to the strand, exploring the shallow reefs between the islands, plucking corals and clams from the seabed some fifteen metres deep. A few were on the islands themselves, relaxing on the rocks like the lizards and birds, or splashing around in the surf where the waters weren't so deep.

"Ralph looks the best swimmer," Saska noted, looking out toward the drop-off. He was another distant cousin of Rikki's, lithesome and long-limbed, with big flippers for feet. He seemed to be able to hold his breath the longest, so far as she could judge.

"Aye, I'd say that's fair," Captain Rikki agreed. "Works out best for all of us. The only time Ralph ever stops talking is when he's holding his breath." He laughed.

That was true enough. They called him Ralph the Mouth for a reason. Sometimes at night she could hear him through the walls of her cabin, prattling on in the communal quarters until someone got angry enough to shut him up, often violently, as evidenced by the fresh bruises he sported the following day.

"We're all at home in the water, though," Rikki was going on. "There's a bit of Seaborn blood on my mother's side of the family, from way back when. Old Hob was a good swimmer in his day. He once went half way down the drop-off here and plucked a drakeshell from the reef, when he was a lad. Later, he began reading people's futures in the corals and such they brought to him. That's some Seaborn mage work, I've always thought. None of the rest of us have that gift, though. Suppose the blood thins each generation," he sighed.

Saska turned to look onto the main deck. Old Hob was Rikki's maternal grandfather, a gnarled old man of seventy five who'd spent almost all his life on this ship. He sat on the main deck all day long, trying knots and making nets, and muttering prognostications from the birds and the clouds. Apparently, the way birds flocked told him what weather was coming, and he could divine grander happenings from the wider world from their movements and behaviours, and the swirling shapes of the clouds. One night all the crew had gathered around him, when the winds had stilled and the ship had becalmed. "War," he'd croaked from the wooden crate he sat on, his body swaddled in a woollen cloak beneath the crisp night skies. "It'll be the worst...the worst since the Ashmount, since the demigods came to blows. The birds tell me. And the clouds..." He'd shaken his head, as though they were doing something unforgivable. "The world's gonna burn, I say it true. Something...something bad is coming."

It was all a little vague for Saska's liking, though had made her think of her dreams all the same. The dragons in the skies and the forests and mountains and cities all burning. The cloaked figure of doom who seemed to be behind it all. But that was just a dream, and this was just an old man with a head full of clouds and birds and stars and coral.

The crew hung on his every word, though. They went to him daily for news of their futures, though Old Hob always said the best detail was beneath the seas. "The skies give me news of bigger things," she'd once heard the old man say, when a young deckhand called Pretty Paul Parry enquired of his future. He was new to the ship, young and blond and girlish to look at, and unrelated to the Bowens. "But if you want to know *your* future, boy, you'd best dive down beneath the waves. Tis the bounty of the deep that will reveal your path. Corals, aye, corals and shells. Go fetch me one of those, and I'll tell you your future. You'll know the one when you see it. It'll be yours and yours alone."

The old man said things like that, Saska had come to see, and it was probably why Pretty Paul Parry was out there now, diving and diving and diving again in search of the right piece of coral. A couple of others seemed to be doing the same, though not every member of the crew bought into Old Hob's prophesies. Lanky Larry was one of them, the ship's second in command and Rikki's uncle on his father's side. "Not smart to meddle in such matters," he had said to Saska a few days ago. "The old man can go ahead and read the skies and seabirds, good luck to him, but I don't want my own future told. I wouldn't know what to do with it."

Larry was one of the more thoughtful men aboard, and Saska rather agreed with him. She hadn't spoken much to Old Hob as a result. *Some doors are best left shut,* she thought now, looking at the old man, as he tied his knots and made his nets, and occasionally glanced to the birds flocking about the islands. When he did he'd purse his lips, nod to himself as though realising something interesting or important in their movements, and then continue tying those knots.

She turned forward again to Captain Rikki. "You not going in for a swim?" she asked him.

"Might, in a little while," he answered, his legs hanging over the empty space beneath the figurehead. "But wouldn't want to show up the other lads." He grinned. "Not bad beneath the waves myself, you know. That's my mother's blood, the Hobs. She was Sally Hob. Married my father, Willie Bowen. The Bowen blood...no Seaborn in that so far as I know. Tis why Ralph the Mouth moves like a fish. He's a Hob not a Bowen." He turned back, and smiled. "And why little Billy here is such a good swimmer too. All comes down the Hob line."

She followed Rikki's gaze to find little Billy striding up to the forecastle, dressed in nothing but a pair of small brown breeks. Despite being just ten years old he walked about as though he was eight feet tall and thick with muscle. In truth he was closer to half that height, and slight as a sapling, with skinny arms and a little pot belly.

"You say my name, pa?" he asked, joining Saska at the bow. He went onto his tiptoes and looked over the edge. "Water looks nice. You going in, Saska?"

"We were talking about the Seaborn side of the family," Rikki told the boy. "From down your grandmother's line."

"Never met her," Billy said, offhand. "She died before I was born."

"Aye, that's true. My mother died young," Rikki explained to Saska. "I didn't know her well myself, truth be told."

"How did she die?" Saska asked.

"Sharks took her." Rikki shifted one leg over the shoulders of the buxom silver figurehead, then spun around to face her. "Old Hob worked this very ship with my father's father when he was a nipper. When he died, my pa inherited the ship, and he kept Old Hob on as his first mate. One day, Hob brought his daughter aboard. That was my mother, Sally Hob. She and my pa fell in love instantly, just like that." He clicked his fingers. "They got to starting a family soon after, and I came along, and together we all sailed the seas, the Bowens and Hobs together. As I say, my mother had that Seaborn in her from Old Hob, and liked to dive a lot. One day she went down and never came up. Later, we saw the blood, and the sharks. I was just a boy then. Still comes to my dreams sometimes, the sight of all the red, bubbling up from below."

Saska wasn't entirely certain how to react to that story, but to say, "That's...horrible. I'm so sorry, Rikki."

"Aye, but that's the sea. She gives and takes in equal measure and no man or woman, Seaborn or otherwise, will ever be able to tame her. Even now, we're at her mercy, Saska. Storms, krakens, pirates. Those sorts of things you can't control."

"We have the Wall now," little Billy said. "He'll protect us."

"Against pirates, aye, but storms and krakens? I think not, son. There's only so much one man can do."

"Giant can do *anything*." Billy slammed his foot on the deck. "He killed a dragon, Uncle Larry said. In a single swipe." The boy still talked about that endlessly, and harassed Sir Ralston on it to the point of torture. "Not even Varin did that."

Captain Rikki gave a good natured laugh. "Varin slew Drulgar the Dread, son, and who knows how many other dragons before that. One day, I'll sail you down the Red Sea and past Dragonfall. You'll see then."

"See what? The sculpture in the cliffs?"

"The very one, and you'll know just how big Drulgar truly was. Some say that sculpture's built to scale."

"It's not," Billy said. "I read in a book it's not. It's the singers who say Drulgar was like a mountain, but they exaggerate *everything*. I read Drulgar was more like that Vallath dragon, the one the Crippler killed. And he duelled the Wall once and lost. I read that too."

The boy clearly read a lot. "I didn't know Amron Daecar lost to Sir Ralston in a duel." Saska hadn't heard about that. She'd grown up thinking that Amron Daecar had never once been defeated.

"At a tourney once," Captain Rikki said in confirmation. "Twas one of the only losses Amron Daecar ever suffered, so far as I know. But he also defeated Sir Ralston on several other occasions. But let's not talk about that, or else little Billy will get upset."

"I'm bored." The boy climbed up onto the lip of the bulwark, ready to jump in. "*You're* boring me, pa."

Rikki gave Saska a look. "You see. He's taken your Wall as a hero, Saska. And for a while now he'll be the greatest man who ever lived."

"I'll have to tell him that," Saska chuckled. "He'll be touched."

"So, are you coming in then?" Billy was looking down at her. He had a peevish look on his face.

"Um...not right now," Saska answered, peering again over the edge. "I'm not used to water this deep."

"You can swim, can't you?" Billy frowned. "What sort of person can't swim?"

"I can swim just fine," she told the boy. "I've just never spent much time on ships, or swam in the ocean. I swam in the river near my village mostly, but that was quite shallow."

"What river?"

"Never you mind, boy," said his father in a stern voice. "You know Saska doesn't like to talk about where she's from."

"I don't see why." Billy was still looking at her. "Which river? There are some big ones in Rasalan. The Forks. The Izzun. The Marshway. There are loads."

None of those, Saska was thinking, though she'd travelled along and across them all at one point or another, when she'd gone south from Thalan with Marian and her men. Her thoughts were instead on the shallow tributary that flowed down from the Hammersongs, right past Willow's Rise. The gentle waterway where she and Del and Llana would spend their lazy summer afternoons, spinning stones and splashing in the shallows, and seeing who could swim across fastest, and get back to the other side first. She sighed at that thought. She was a long way from all that now.

"You leave the girl be," Rikki said when he realised Saska wasn't going to answer. "She's our honoured guest, Billy, and you're making her uncomfortable."

"I wasn't meaning to. It was a simple question, pa."

"A simple question to you, aye, but perhaps not to her. Who knows. Maybe she nearly drowned once, and is frightened to go out of her depth now? Happens more than a boy of ten will know. Even Rasals can turn from the seas if they have a close encounter with Daarl's Domain."

Billy chewed his lip in thought. "I guess." Then he let out a sigh. "First Giant refused me, now you have too. I asked him if he wanted to have a swim," he explained. "And Uncle Bron...he asked me to try to persuade you to go in. Some of the others did too."

"Now I wonder why they'd want that," Rikki said, glaring out toward the crew, as they dived and swam and fished around them. "I'll bet Bron said she should leave her swim-clothes in her cabin too."

Billy shook his head. "No, that was Kevin." He frowned. "Is that what they want? To see you naked, Saska?"

She didn't want to answer that question. It was all playful, of course, but it still made her think of Kastor and Quintan and the rest.

"I'll speak with Kevin and Bron later," Captain Rikki said angrily. "And they'd best hope I don't speak to Sir Ralston too. On that point, you shouldn't be pestering him so much, Billy. Godsteel doesn't go well in water. It's heavy, and it sinks."

"Yeah, well I hoped he'd take his armour off, *obviously*," Billy protested.

"He's said no a hundred times. Don't ask him again, d'you hear me? He'll remove his armour when he's good and ready, or never at all if he wishes it."

That wasn't strictly true. The Wall had now unburdened his legs of his sabatons, greaves and cuisses, and had removed his gorget and gauntlets as well. It left him in his breastplate, pauldrons, and vambraces only, to go with his newly clad breeches and the hood that helped hide his scarred neck. Scarring that Saska had learned covered his entire frame, with rips and tears, pits and burns making a ruin of his body from heel to head. Most of that had happened when he fought that dragon, though Saska didn't know the beast's name. In most duels with a drake, a knight would wear full godsteel plate, oiled to be fireproof, but that wasn't the case for Sir Ralston. He'd been caught unawares, and wore only his breastplate and helm, and when the dragon had breathed, Sir Ralston had burned. It added a further flourish to the tale. That of the giant flaming knight, hacking the head off a dragon, before his men could run in and douse him. *And this is the man protecting me,* she thought. *A hero worthy of Billy's praise.*

By the time Saska looked again, the boy was already leaping from the boat, disappearing through the clear waters in a graceful dive. Not a splash followed, and then off he went, swimming right down to the bottom, fifteen metres deep.

Maybe I should go in, she thought, watching. It was only a short swim to the nearest island and she'd never been uneasy in the water, in truth. Even when she had to cross the northern branch of the Clearwater Run, she'd managed it, despite the rapids and rocks, the fearful eddies and rushing white water that took some of the other soldiers to their deaths. She'd been on the run then, after killing Lord Quintan, and hadn't had much choice but to brave the rampaging river. If she could handle that, these calm waters would be nothing. She made her decision right then and there. "I'm going in."

She was climbing up onto the bulwark a moment later, already half regretting her decision. But down below, too many of the men had seen. A cheer went out when more of them spotted her. Even over on the nearby islands she heard her name ringing out. "Can't back down now," Captain Rikki noted. "You going in like that?"

She nodded. The other men were in naught but breeks, but she could hardly do the same. She was wearing boy's clothes; baggy white linen hose cut off at the knee, and a sleeveless beige vest, her olive arms bared to the sun. The black dye in her hair had been washed out now, though it was still quite short and scruffy after she'd shorn it off several months ago while on the run.

The cheering was still going on. It had some of the seabirds taking flight in alarm, and several grumpy seals were barking irritably and flopping down the rocks into the water to escape the commotion. The lizards just ignored it.

"Best do it quick now, Saska," Rikki said with a grin. "Before Sir Ralston sees you."

The Wall was having one of his short naps below, at Saska's demand, though all this noise was likely to wake him up if she didn't jump soon, and no doubt he'd try to put a stop to it. It centred her mind and she turned her eyes to the water, judging the distance. The men were still cheering her name, which wasn't helping, to be honest, and Rikki was trying to give her some advice through all that. "Just don't do anything you're not ready for; if you try to dive in like Billy did it won't end well. Just plunge in feet first, hold your nose and shut your eyes. Kick, and you'll be back on the surface in no time. And if you get into trouble, or panic, don't worry. We've got men all over who'd been more than happy to rescue you."

Saska didn't like the idea of being rescued, and that comment alone was enough to steel her. She was Bladeborn. She'd killed half a dozen men, lords and knights and deadly cutthroats among them. Marian was meant to have trained the fear out of her, but for whatever reason the drop suddenly looked as endless as the Long Abyss. It was ridiculous. When she'd sailed across Vandar's Mercy, she'd climbed the masts and endured the storm and faced her fears again and again. That was the whole deal. And here she was, fretting about an eight metre drop.

Enough, she thought, taking a full breath. It felt like she'd been standing there for an age, but in reality it was only a few seconds and if she jumped now, she still had a chance to save face. So she did. With a trembly leap off her tremulous legs, she hopped forward into thin air. The wind rushed, her clothes flapped, and an instant later her toes were touching water. Down she went, plunging down and down, closing her eyes and holding her nose. Bubbles rushed about her, all the noises above went dull, she kicked once, twice, and then up she went, thrusting through the surface to the sound of raucous cheering.

"Bravo, Saska, bravo." Captain Rikki was clapping from the figurehead above, calling over the noise. "You barely made a splash. Very nice, for a first go."

"You were *great*!" She spun, treading water. Billy was there beside her, having popped up from nowhere. "I was watching from down below. I knew you could swim really."

I never said I couldn't, she thought. But before she could say it, he was gone, duck diving out of sight in a perfectly obvious bid to show off. He reappeared a moment later, clutching a beautiful piece of blue coral. "For you," he said, taking a breath. "It's the same colour as your eyes." He grinned and handed it over, disappearing again. She wasn't quite sure what to do with it, so just clung on. A moment later Billy was back, his blurry figure clearing as he remerged from the seabed. He broke the surface and opened his little palm. There was another hunk of coral in it, azure blue as well. It was small with a white pattern of striations and pits, shining bright beneath the sun. "How about this one?"

"It's...beautiful," she said, kicking beneath her. Treading water wasn't something she'd done before, but it came naturally. "Like a gemstone."

"Like your eyes." He grinned again. "Do you think it's the one?"

She wasn't getting his meaning. "The one?"

"For my great-grandpa. Old Hob. He can read your future. There's a bit of coral for everyone, he says. A special one, right here around this reef. Though sometimes it can be a shell. I'll go look for those..."

"Um..."

He was gone again, and back again. This time he carried three separate shells in a variety of blue hues. "These?" He opened out his palms, easily staying afloat with his legs only. "Are you drawn to them?"

Above them came a call. "Doesn't work like that, Billy," said his father, watching with a grin on his stubbly cheeks. He'd removed the tie that kept his ponytail in place, letting his long black hair tumble down in twisting waves. "She'd have to find and fetch it herself. You can't be ferrying her every shell on the reef."

Billy chewed on that. "Fine. Well..." He looked at Saska. "Are you just going to stay here, or..."

"I haven't had much of a chance, Billy."

"Well come on." The boy took her wrist. "Take a breath. I'll lead you down."

"*Down*?"

"Down." He pointed through the water. "The good stuff is down there."

"It's fifteen metres deep." She wasn't liking being chaperoned by the boy. He seemed to think she could do anything. "Why can't we swim to that island?" It was the nearest one she pointed to, where several of the crew were lounging on the rocks. Lanky Larry was fishing with rod and bait, and Bawdy Bron was making a nuisance of himself with the local wildlife, chasing a seal.

"That's all rocks. The corals are down there. And the best shells too. Well…" He scrunched up his face in thought. "Actually the best stuff is out there, down the drop-off, but one step at a time." He gripped tighter and prepared to dive. "Come on."

"No, wait…" She pulled away. "I've never swum underwater like that. A metre or two maybe, but…"

"What's the difference? It's *only* fifteen metres, Saska. Just swim *down*. It's not hard."

"Not for you. I didn't grow up on a ship." She could hear the panic in her voice.

"Don't be a wimp. *Try* at least. Come on."

Try. Yes, I can try. "Fine," she said. "Just don't pull me. I'll follow…"

"You know how to duck dive?"

She frowned. "No, of course not. I just said, I've…"

"OK," the boy cut in. "It's simple." He began his brief demonstration. "Reach forward with your arms, roll your weight, and dive down. Your legs will go above the surface. Pull with your arms, like this." Her performed a stroke of some kind, in-to-out. "That will drag you down. Then when your legs are under, start kicking. Like this." He gestured below, demonstrating the right kicking technique. "Got it?"

"Um…"

"One more thing," said Rikki, observing above. "You'd best equalise as you go down."

"Equalise?" That was new.

"Aye." He pinched his nose. "It's about pressure…you don't need to know the science. Just blow, like you're blowing your noise. Your ears should pop."

That didn't sound particularly cheery. "*Pop*? What happens if they don't?"

"Your head will explode from the pressure," said Kevin the Con, swimming by with a rascally smirk. He stroked the water nicely too, damn him. Smooth water ran over his tanned lean limbs and shoulders. "And watch for the sharks as well." He made a biting gesture with his mouth. "And the sea snakes; they're poisonous."

"Shut up Kevin," bit little Billy, flicking water at him for all the good it would do. "You got what you wanted. She's swimming, isn't she?"

"Aye, but she's rather *overdressed* for my liking. Shift that shirt at least, sweetheart. The colour attracts the sharks, you'll thank me." He grinned in that way of his and swam off, before Rikki could shout down a reprimand.

"Is that true?" Saska looked down through the water around her. It didn't look like fifteen metres to the bottom, but she knew something about light and refraction. "About the snakes and sharks?" Captain Rikki's horrifying story was still on her mind. She could imagine the churn of blood bubbling to the surface.

"No, course not," said Billy. "He's just trying to scare you into taking off your shirt."

"Well..." said his father.

"What?" asked Saska, looking up. Then she looked down, searching for shadows and teeth. "There *are* sharks here?"

"Only little ones," Billy admitted, shrugging his little shoulders over the waves. "No bigger than me. They're harmless, right pa?"

"For a grown man, aye. If anyone should be worried, it's you, son. You're about the right size for them, I'd say."

"Yeah, and *I'm* not afraid." She could tell they were toying with her now. If there were proper sharks around here, it wasn't likely that Rikki would let his son go swimming. "The dangerous sharks don't come to shallow waters like this," the boy said. "They're out beyond the drop-off. That's where all the big nasty stuff is. The krakens and squids and sea monsters and such."

"Now why'd you have to go and mention all of that? I was just starting to feel comfortable."

"Good." He took that for truth. "Follow me. I'll go slow." He gulped a deep breath, and vanished.

Saska felt half exhausted already, but knew these experiences were good for her. She'd been through many and more with Marian and each had braced her spirit, made her stronger. So without thinking too deeply about it all, she went ahead and followed the boy's lead. She reached out with her arms, tilted her weight forward, ducked down, and pulled. When her legs sank below the surface, she kicked. Then she realised she still had her eyes closed. She opened them to a sting of saltwater, and all the world was a blur. Blinking several times, she cleared her vision such as she could.

Her next thought was; *damn refraction.* The bottom that had seemed so close above the surface suddenly looked leagues away, and the silence...that weird blurry lack of noise...it was all quite disconcerting. But there was Billy, turning back, urging her on. She pulled hard for another strong stroke, kicked, and felt herself descend. *Three metres, four, five.* Then she started to feel that pressure Rikki had talked about. Trying not to panic and turn back, she reached to her nose, blew, and felt a tiny *pop* in her ears. The pressure eased. After that she only had to worry about the air in her lungs, or lack thereof, and the sudden and inescapable urge to breathe.

You've only been under for five seconds, she had to remind herself. She could hold her breath longer than that, surely? A minute at least without practice. Maybe more if she pushed herself. She swatted all thoughts of fresh clean air aside and continued to pull herself down, kicking.

Six metres, seven, eight. Billy was right there with her now, smiling, making faces. *Nine, ten.* If anything, the water grew clearer, so clear she might have been looking through a crisp spring sky. That stinging sensation abated. She pulled again. *Eleven, twelve.* Some of the tallest growths of coral were near enough to touch now. The reef spread before her, an achingly beautiful confusion of colours and activity. Fish of all sizes and shapes sped here and there, some alone, some in shoals. There was a big green turtle languidly gliding among the rocks, propelled by a gentle stroke of its long, paddle-like fins. She saw her first shark, and almost rushed back to the surface, but Billy held her arm and shook his head. He gestured to watch. She did, as the sleek grey shadow moved right past them without any discernible means of propulsion at all. Billy smiled as if to say, "see, they don't care about us," and he was right. Nor was it so big. As long as Billy, yes, but slim, with half its length in its black-tipped tail.

It was only then that she realised she was at the bottom, a full fifteen metres down. Billy pointed to the corals and shells, scattered around the seabed in a wealth of shades of blue and green and red and violet, and all else in-between. He made another gesture. *Do any of them call to you?* she imagined he was trying to say. She thrust herself toward one that looked especially pretty, a glowing green chunk of rock pitted with tiny crimson jewels. She admired it for a time, wondering if it was calling to her. It was very pretty, yes, but that seemed all that had drawn her eye. And how lucky would she be to have plucked out the right coral on her very first go?

She began a short search, half swimming, half walking around the sandy sections of the seabed. At one point she pricked her foot on something sharp and decided it best to swim from now on. She found several other shells and corals that were as stunning as the last, but none called to her, whatever that meant. *And why do I care?* She didn't want her future told anyway. *Some doors are best left closed,* she thought. *And Old Hob? Really?* The only way to divine the future was by using the Eye of Rasalan, that ancient magical orb created and gifted by a god. The idea that an old man with a drop of Seaborn blood could see the future in coral was a little too farfetched for her. But still, there was no harm in looking. These rocks and shells were very pretty, after all...

It was about then that she noticed that she was all alone.

She looked left, right, back and forward, but Billy was gone. Her heart was clenched between tight cold fingers. Adrenaline surged through her blood. She thought she caught sight of red. Blood in the water? And a shadow. A shark. But it was just a little one again, gliding nearby, ignoring her. But still she couldn't find the boy. Still she was alone. Until finally she looked up, and saw him speeding for the surface. That didn't allay her fears. *What's he rushing from?* was her first thought. But all around her the reef was just as it had been. An other-worldly place of wonder and colour, chaotic and calming all at once.

She pushed for the top, feeling the first proper burn in her lungs, gliding easily up and up until she broke through into the world above. The voices of the men filled her ears. Gulls were cawing, seals barking, the waves crashing against the distant cliffs. She filled her lungs with a full breath of sweet pure air, smiled radiantly, and found both father and son looking at her with a look of deep vexation. "You lied," Billy was first to say, catching his breath as he bobbed like a cork in the water. "Why...why did you lie?"

"Lie?" she repeated. "What are you talking about?"

"There are acting troupes all over Rasalan that'd love to have you, Saska, there's no doubt there," said Rikki.

Saska looked up at the captain, entirely confused. "What do you mean?"

"You had us both convinced is what I mean," said Rikki, laughing. He'd removed his flappy white shirt, should he be required to dive in. Beneath was a tanned toned body well garnished with black curly hair. Those hairs made Saska think of Elyon momentarily.

"Might as well go to the drop-off...now we know," Billy chirped.

"This here...it's nothing for someone like you. We can go *much* deeper."

"No," Saska said immediately. Her mind was full of sharks of the big and bitey variety. "I'm staying here."

"But you can *dive*, Saska," said Rikki. "I mean, *really* dive. You've been doing this a long time, I'll wager. Billy comes up gasping for air and you just pop out as though you hadn't been underwater for three minutes..."

"*Three* minutes?" No, it hadn't been that long. "I wasn't down three minutes," she laughed.

"No, you're right. I'm sorry." Rikki Bowen nodded apologetically. "It was more like three and half, actually. Closer to four. Three is selling you a bit short."

They're joking. This is just another jest. She chuckled, because that's what you did when something was funny. "Stop toying with me. I thought I did OK for a first go."

Billy started laughing. "She just keeps going, pa!"

Rikki was looking at her a little more quizzically. "Aye, though I'm starting to think she's not joking, son."

But it was Old Hob who had the last word. When he'd arrived at the prow, Saska didn't know. But there he was, with his stooped back and creased eyes and the long grey beard that tumbled from his wind-burned cheeks. He looked down at her, pursed his lips, nodded, then merely croaked, "She's Seaborn, this one," before tottering away back to his crate.

13

Amron

Their cell was a cave, deep within a hollowed hill, lost within a network of tunnels and passages. Only one of those was large enough for them to pass through, though it was kept locked and barred at all times. Beyond the ancient iron gate, torches flickered, sending light down into their prison. It was the only light they'd had for some days now, ever since they were brought here from the river.

Amron sat wrapped in his furs upon a shelf of stone that served as a seat and a bed all at once. Their prison was some five by five metres, spacious enough, warm enough. Sheltered as they were from the elements beyond the hill, and with the flickering warmth of nearby fires to tend them, it had been a stay of relative comfort when compared against the previous weeks. The only problem was, they weren't going anywhere. And that was a grave problem indeed.

Amron coughed. A heavy hot pain rose through him, his lungs feeling as though they were filled with tiny pebbles, each made of molten rock. *That* was another problem. His time in the freezing waters of the Silver Scar had driven a fierce chill into his lungs that had further enfeebled him. *But at least I'm alive,* he thought, wheezing into the thick fur of his sleeve. When he'd been dragged down into those cold black depths he'd felt sure that was it, a chastening end to a chastening chapter in his otherwise storied life. *I should have stayed,* was his final thought, as the river embraced him, surging down his throat, into his lungs. *I should never have left Blackfrost. I should never have left my daughter...*

Then he'd felt hands on him, the strong gnarled hands of Rogen Whitebeard hauling him back up to the surface, kicking hard with those long, teak-tough legs of his. In that instant, Amron felt a surging will to live, he recalled, though his memory of the rest was only in fragments. The thick ceiling of ice that had greeted them when they'd reached the surface of the river. The desperate search to find the breach. The panic in Whitebeard's amber eyes as the urge to breathe grew too powerful, as he strained against that burning desire to gasp and let the gelid waters flow in. And the shapes...the shadows above them. *White shadows,* Amron had thought, staring up through the pale blue ice. And then the blackness swallowed him.

He'd awoken in this very cave some hours later, wrapped up in dry furs like a swaddling babe, Walter sitting over him as he came around. Across the cave, Whitebeard had already awakened, shivering violently as he lay garbed in layers of thick bear hide that their saviours had given them. It was then that Amron learned the rest of the tale from Walter. Those white shadows had cut a fresh breach in the ice using axes and spears of sharpened bone, dragging them both from the river. The water was pumped from their lungs, feeding life back into them anew. They'd coughed, spluttered, heaved and passed out once more, before being loaded onto sledges and dragged down here into this hollow hill north of the Scar.

"Our saviours have since turned jailers," Walter told him, when Amron asked where they were. "We're in a cave system of some sort, some miles from the river. I tried asking questions, but none would answer me. They seemed to recognise Whitebeard, though."

"Who were they?" the ranger had rasped, looking to the iron gate that marked the only way in and out. There looked to be a figure on guard in the adjoining cavern, furled in a heavy cloak, watching from the shadows. "Which tribe, Walter?"

"The Snowskins, by the descriptions you gave us," Walter told him. "I saw flashes of snow-white hair beneath their hoods. Some had glassy skin, pale as milk."

Whitebeard had settled a little at the news, releasing a breath. "Then we have been doubly lucky," he'd said. "The Snowskins *can* be amenable. I have had dealings with them in the past, as you know."

He had. Years ago, Whitebeard had broken his leg during a range and been found by the Snowkins and nursed back to health, under the care and attention of a kind girl called Elurra. It was a sorrowful tale he'd recounted once by firelight. A tale of love, and loss, and the grief that had followed him since. He'd visited Elurra many times after she'd restored him, earning a reputation among the men of Northwatch for these long lonely rovings he'd taken into the wilds. Yet none knew of the reason. None knew of the Snowskin girl who'd saved him. The girl whom he'd returned to, once, to find her dead, killed for refusing to couple with a man and bear his brood. Killed for the love she bore the lupine ranger from the south. Since that day, his dealings with the tribe had dwindled. "Some may recall me," he'd said, that first day in the cave. "Fondly...perhaps not, but...I cannot be sure. There are things that happened back then..." He'd turned away, and offered no further explanation, but to say, "We will be safe in their care, for now."

They had been, thus far, though despite Whitebeard's attempts to speak to them, none spoke back. The only times they saw their gaolers was when they appeared to bring them food and water, shoving wooden cups and carved trenchers through the bars, commonly bearing their own rations. As part of Walter's recital of events, he'd told them that their bags had been taken from them during the rescue. To keep them alive, the tribe had stripped them bare as newborns and covered them in dry furs. When Amron first awoke, he'd been surprised to find himself naked beneath those wrappings, though their own leathers and quilted wools, furs, boots and gloves and breeches had since been returned to them. Though their bags had not.

Nor had their blades. And Amron's, he'd learned, to his profound regret, had now been lost to the river forever. "I had to unfasten your swordbelt, to lessen the weight," Whitebeard had told him. "You were being dragged to your death, my lord. It was the godsteel or your life."

Now, only Whitebeard's dagger remained, though that too had been taken. "I saw them take it from you, when they brought us here," Walter explained. "One...he looked capable of wielding it. He was only young, and the leader of the group that found us, it seemed to me. He drew the blade from your sheath, Rogen, and was able to bear its weight for a short time. He struggled a little, but still...only a man of Varin's blood could do that. This Snowskin boy...he can only have been part Bladeborn."

If the news had come as a shock to Amron, Whitebeard had looked less than surprised. "Rangers have been known to lie abed with the tribespeople, in the past. It isn't common, but it has happened. The boy you saw must have descended from such a union." He'd frowned then, thinking. "He was the leader, you say?"

"He seemed to be, yes."

"Describe him."

"There isn't much to say. Men look much alike when bundled in white fur. But, he was a shade taller than most, I suppose. Well-built, for a boy his age. He can't have been much older than sixteen or seventeen summers, though I suppose that should be winters out here." Even in the gravest of times, Walter Selleck's sense of humour hadn't left him.

"It may be the son of the the *Snowfist*," Whitebeard had said after a short deliberation. "That is the title they give their chieftain, a man by the name of Stegra the last I knew. He was a large man himself, of an age and frame similar to you, Lord Daecar. I have not seen him for many years, though I know he had some Varin blood to him. Enough to wield a small godsteel dagger, at least. It would fit that this boy be his son."

If that were true, they hadn't yet confirmed it. Despite their attempts to call upon the boy leader to speak with them, not once had he come, and for many long days they had been confined to this cave, growing increasingly frustrated by their plight, and the long cold journey that still awaited them above. But with his blades lost and his lungs gripped by an aching chill, Amron had begun to wonder whether it might be time to turn back. More and more he'd thought it, and he thought it again now, as he sat there on that shelf of rock, coughing into his sleeve, wondering just how much more of this he could take. Across the cave, Rogen Whitebeard was sleeping, furled in black among the shadows. Against another wall, Walter Selleck sat in quiet thought, short legs crossed before him.

Amron rose from his shelf and shambled over. "My lord," the luckiest man in the world said, looking up, as Amron grunted his way to the floor, his ruined body flaring painfully in his left arm and right leg and within the very depths of his chest. "Does something trouble you, Amron?"

Amron gave out a huff. "Curious choice of question, Walter. There is much that troubles me, as well you know."

"Something new, then? You seem more dispirited than normal."

"I have lost my blades. That is a blow that non-Bladeborn struggle to truly grasp. It makes one feel half a man, weakened and vulnerable. Can you understand how that feels, for a man like me? To be here, in this place, among all these perils, with no way to defend myself?"

"I understand, my lord. You have lived your life as a shield for all the north. Indomitable and unbeatable. To have that taken away...yes, I know how you must feel. But I would ask what ails you, what is *new*? You have known about the loss of your blades since we were brought here. I can only imagine that was seven or eight days ago now, by the schedule of food and water being brought to us." It was the only way to judge the passing of the time. There was no sun, no moon, no stars. No way to know what time it might be, or how many days had passed, but for the rations that were shoved through the cold iron bars of their cell. Walter Selleck observed Amron for several long moments, then added, "You are thinking of returning to Vandar, when we are released. You think we should end our quest right here?"

"The thought has come to me," Amron admitted. "If we go on like this, we're sure to die, Walter. My lungs, I...I don't know whether I can face the cold again. We must be a hundred miles from Vandar's Tomb still. The thought of resuming our journey..."

"Is frightening, I know. But necessary. We have come this far, and cannot turn back. You will regret it forever if you do."

"Regret? There is much I regret. Abandoning my daughter for one. The daughter I was never there for. The daughter that Amara and Vesryn had to raise, while I was on the road, running from my grief." He vented a painful sigh. "She was the last person I thought of, you know, when I was drowning beneath the Scar. *Shame*, Walter. It was shame that filled me, for failing her. For the folly of this trip. For my selfishness, my ego..."

"Chastisement will get you nowhere, my lord. You must keep the faith, and look into the light." Walter placed a stubby-fingered hand upon Amron's arm. "Consider the positives. Consider how far we've come. Whitebeard's blade will be returned once they free us. And you have *me*, Amron. You have my protection, and.. "

"And that is a great deal more valuable than a blade at my hip,"

Amron finished for him. He spoke without sarcasm. "I know, Walter. Rogen may continue to doubt the mystic light you preach of, but I do not. Had the Snowskins come but a moment later, we'd have both drowned. Had it been another tribe, we'd all have been butchered for the spit. That sort of fortune has followed us for weeks, and that can only be down to you..."

"Then trust it. *Trust it*, Amron. Vandar's light will not lead us stray. It guides us to his spirit, through me. All that has happened thus far has been necessary, including this short incarceration. Perhaps the Snowskins have some part to play in our quest? Perhaps these days we've spent here have sheltered us from a storm that would have otherwise killed us, or a rival tribe, or some other menace lurking beyond this hill? We cannot yet see the full picture, my lord. All we can do is trust that it is still being painted, even when our backs are turned."

"What a way to wake," growled a voice across the cave. Amron looked over, as Rogen Whitebeard shifted up against the wall, the dark grey tangle of his beard running ragged from his hollow cheeks and chin. "It seems I cannot escape your preaching even in my sleep, Selleck."

"Oh I do apologise for waking you, Whitebeard. I suppose I must have been speaking too loud."

The ranger managed a grim smile to that. "You do seem unable to control the volume of your voice. Perhaps you might call to our captors and finally get that conference we've been seeking?"

Whitebeard in particular had been trying for days to get the Snowskins' attention, without reward. Walter returned the man's smile. "Gladly." He shifted to his feet and made quickly for the bars. "Hello...hello there," he called out, his words echoing off down the passages. "We'd be most appreciative if you might send someone with authority to speak with us." A figure emerged from the shadows of the adjoining cavern, cloaked in white and bearing a spear of bone in his grasp. "Ah, good man, please do pass on a message, if you'd be so kind. After a week here in this fine warm cave of ours...well, we *think* it's been a week, anyway...we're quite ready to speak with your leader. Please, do send word up the ladder. Unless of course you have the authority to treat with us yourself?"

The tribesman stared through the bars with a set of pale blue eyes, his irises barely visible within the whites that surrounded them. Like their milky skin and white hair it served to help camouflage them amid the wasteland in which they lived. Of all the tribes, the Snowskins preferred the long cold winters, growing adapted to their perils. According to Whitebeard, they had excellent night vision, and a natural resistance to the sting of the icy winds, when the world plunged to temperatures that no other man could bear. A long moment passed, as Walter stood face-to-face with the gaoler. Then, as the guard prepared to turn, and bleed back into the shadows, he let out an unexpected pair of grunting words. "I tell," he said, before marching away out of sight.

Amron and Whitebeard shared a look. Both pressed themselves to their feet. Amron knew that they spoke the common tongue here, though mostly in a broken, simplified form. "Did he say, 'I tell'," he asked, seeking clarification.

"I do believe he did," nodded Walter. He gave Whitebeard a sideward glance. "I suppose I must have gotten lucky, Rogen."

Still, no one would believe it until it happened. They'd had one or two false promises like this thus far that had led nowhere. After a quarter hour, they began to conclude that the Snowskin guard was playing a cruel trick on them. "He probably went to take a piss," Whitebeard growled, dropping back down into the little nest he'd feathered for himself.

Whether that or something else, he didn't return for some time. That quarter hour doubled, then doubled again, until they lost track of the passing of the minutes completely. Eventually, Whitebeard went back to sleep, and even Walter looked disappointed. "It seems our jailer has a wicked sense of humour," he sighed, trying to get comfy in his furs.

Amron did the same, returning to his shelf. They'd all cultivated their own little beds in the cave, such as they could, using their furs and wools. He made to settle down, as a fit of coughing roughed up his lungs. And in the midst of that fit, came a voice.

"You wanted to speak with me?"

Amron's spluttering wilted. He looked to the bars, where a man stood. Not a boy, certainly. This was a man of middle years, lined of face and large of frame. "Stegra," said Whitebeard, seeing him. He moved to his feet in an instant. "This is Stegra Snowfist," he told the others. "Chieftain of the Snowskin tribe."

The chieftain stood grand behind the iron bars, filling the width of the tunnel. His cloak was the pelt of an ice bear, body and head, the top of its jaw forming a hood. Long deadly fangs framed his face and ran right down past his temples to his ears. Between them were a set of fierce incisors, and beneath those a heavy beetled brow and a broad square jaw clothed in a thick white beard. Stegra Snowfist stared at Rogen Whitebeard through eyes like moonstones, a pale blue-grey, narrowed and sharp. "Blacksteel," he said, giving Whitebeard a name that Amron had not yet heard. "It has been a long time since I saw you last."

"Many years, Snowfist."

"Many years," repeated the towering tribesman. He glanced at Amron, then Walter. "Why do you come, after all this time? I told you before...*not* to come again."

Amron found himself struck by the man's voice. It wasn't just his strong grasp of the common tongue, but the power of it. A chill wind seemed to blow as he spoke, filling all the cave. "I had no choice, Snowfist," said Whitebeard. "I have my orders, as you know."

"Orders?" The big chieftain laughed, a booming sound echoing through the honeycomb hill. "You had orders to visit Elurra, did you? I was not aware of this. All those years you came to us, seeking her company, turning her mind to lands far from here. Were those orders, Blacksteel? Orders from your steel lord?"

"My mandate has always been to watch these lands for threats to Vandar. I will not deny I wished to see Elurra, but I often came for information as well. Do not pretend you didn't do well from the bargain too, Stegra. I bloodied my blade often for you, if you will recall."

Amron frowned. Whitebeard had told them nothing of this. "What do you mean?" he demanded. His voice was scratchy and hoarse from his coughing. He cleared his throat. "You killed for this man, Rogen?"

"I helped him with some of his enemies in exchange for information, yes."

"Why didn't you speak of this before?"

"It wasn't necessary. I had hoped to avoid any interaction with the local people. There seemed no sense in mentioning it."

"And these last days here? Gods, Rogen, you might have said something. To make us better understand..."

"And who is this one?" interrupted Stegra Snowfist. "This big man is the steel lord you serve, Blacksteel?"

"My name is Amron, Lord of House Daecar, former First Blade of Vandar, and you will free us from this cell immediately."

"I will?" Stegra Snowfist laughed. "Or maybe I will not. We are not in Vandar here, Lord of Daecar. These lands are of ice and darkness. Lands you steel men abandoned long ago."

"We seek passage only," put in Walter, shifting forward to draw the man's eye. "We are no threat to you, Great Snowfist." He bowed. "We are on an errand of much importance to our own lands. And one that may become important to yours, in time."

That got the chieftain's attention. "This little fat one speaks in riddles. What do you mean?"

"A threat," said Walter. "A darkness that will cover all the world is coming..."

"We live in darkness. This is no threat to us."

"And fire? Death? The doom of all days? We are entering the Last Renewal, Stegra of the Snowskins. If we do not prevail, you may be sharing these lands with dragons and worse, and much sooner than you know."

Snowfist laughed again. "Dragons do not like the ice, little man. And you speak of worse? We live with worse. And you will see worse, if you go any further." He gave a firm shake of the head. "If you continue to that mountain, you will not come back. I cannot allow your passing."

"So you know of our purpose?" asked Amron.

"Of course I know," the man declared. "What else would three steel men be doing out here? That mountain calls to you, always. Many have tried to reach it, and many have never returned." He shook his large head, skin and hair and hood all coloured in shades of white. "For your own sakes, you will turn back. There is evil in that place, much menace in the darkness and the depths. But you will not reach it anyway, no. The path you seek is shut."

The three Vandarians traded glances. *Evil...menace. Does he speak of Vandar's spirit, or something else?* Amron wondered. Whitebeard had told them that the tribes feared the mountain, and this...it sounded like superstition, and no more. *But, the rest of it...*"The path is shut," he repeated. "What do you mean by that, Snowfist? The *mountain* is shut? Is that what you're trying to say."

"I do not try. I succeed. I am Stegra the Snowfist, and that is my way." He looked Amron dead in the eye. "The mountain shivers, Lord of Daecar. It breathes, and it stirs. None of my kin dare go there, but I did, this past winter, with my son. He is fearless as his father, and wished to see it for himself. So we went together, and we saw..." He turned his eyes to each of them in turn. "There is no way into that mountain. Much of what you steel men built has come down. Walls. Tunnels. Caverns. Chambers. It has all collapsed, and trapped the darkness within, where it must remain. There is no way to reach its heart, if that is your wish. No good can come of you going there. Only death will you find."

The way is shut, Amron thought, with a dull throb of despair. "Is...is it possible, Walter?" He wasn't sure how to feel. For days he'd considered calling an end to their quest, but now...now he just felt hollow, empty, stripped of all hope. "Could the way to the chamber be impassable?"

And there in Walter's eyes he saw it. The first sign of his fraying faith. The first faint dimming of his light. "I...I am not sure, Amron. There...there are many tunnels, many passages." He nodded, firming. "We will find a way. We *must* find a way."

"You will not," Snowfist said. "There *is* no way, not to where you want to go."

"We felt shivers a year ago in Northwatch," Whitebeard put in, a thoughtful look on his face. "An earthquake, we supposed, coming from the far north. They have been reported to occur occasionally, though typically by rangers in the Weeping Heights. I've felt them myself on my ranges, though rarely have the tremors ever been felt so far away as Northwatch. So...what Snowfist says may be true. If the earthquake originated at the mountain...the damage it did...there may be no way in."

"There *is* no way in," the chieftain insisted, those strange pale eyes almost lost amid the bone white of his skin. "This journey of yours will not end inside that mountain. I know this because I have seen it, the damage that the shivers have done." He turned to Whitebeard. "And I told you, Blacksteel, *not* to return here. I warned you what would happen if you did."

Whitebeard gave the chieftain a hard cold look. "Then why haven't you followed through, Stegra? *Why* have you not yet killed me?"

"Because I have only just learned you are here. Had I been there at the Scar, I may have let you drown. My son…he was too young to have known you, back then. The sting of your betrayal has not scarred him, as it has me."

"I did not betray you," Whitebeard told him. "I only sought vengeance for what *he* did."

"You killed a man of my tribe."

"Because *he* killed Elurra!" A vein was emerging on Whitebeard's forehead, the cords in his neck sticking out. Not once had Amron seen him so impassioned. *Old scars can still hurt,* he thought, watching on as Whitebeard's past was opened up before them.

But Snowfist remained the model of calm, dipping his great bearded chin into a slow nod. "Justice," he said, in a deep cold voice. "Yes, justice it was…*if* you were a Snowskin. But you never were, Blacksteel. You were but a foreigner to our lands, a guest among us. You had no right to kill him."

"I had every right." He grimaced. "I…I loved her, Stegra."

"I know this. And that is why I did not kill you myself. Instead, I told you never to return. I told you never to pass beyond the borders of these lands. But here you are, right before my eyes. And now I must weigh my thoughts, and decide whether you will die…"

"Then decide," Whitebeard growled. "Take my life, if you wish it; I have never much cared to draw breath since her death."

"No," Amron said, as firmly as his ragged voice would allow. "There must be another way."

"We never intended to cross paths with you," Walter added, trying his best to diffuse things. "You commanded that Whitebeard never cross these lands again, as you've said, but he has others who give him orders as well, Great Snowfist. Lord Borrington of Northwatch is permitted to take his head should he refuse his commands. He had no choice but to lead us this way by his lord's word, and not once did he expect to come upon you or your tribe. I humbly beg you consider that, when you come to your verdict. He is a good man, a proud man, and a dutiful man most of all. Without him, all three of us would be dead."

Snowfist nodded thoughtfully, pulling at his thick white beard. "That may be so. Blacksteel was always well suited to these lands. That is why we liked him so...before he slew Bragga Burnside without my consent."

"Bragga," Amron repeated. "This is the man who killed Elurra?" When Stegra Snowfist nodded, Amron glanced at Whitebeard and said, "The man you call Blacksteel has told us this tale, though in truth we know little and less of what happened. By his account, this Bragga Burnside killed Elurra when she refused to couple with him. East of the Weeping Heights, that is considered murder, Snowfist, and punishable by death. It seems to me that Whitebeard acted only to settle the scales."

"I do not deny this. But he did so without my leave. Let me repeat that. *Without* my leave. Tribal affairs are dealt with by the tribe, Lord of Daecar. Blacksteel took Bragga's life without consulting us, and in doing this, earned his exile from these lands." He paused, his eyes gleaming with a pale blue flame. "A less kind Snowfist would have taken his head right then and there. But Stegra is more merciful."

"Merciful, *and* wise," put in Walter, with a thin placating smile. "To kill a Ranger of Northwatch would not have gone unnoticed across the mountains. By letting him go, you prevented more steel men from coming here. Very wise indeed, Great Snowfist."

Amron knew that wasn't necessarily true, and he rather imagined Walter did too. Rangers went missing sometimes during their rovings and never returned to Northwatch. In such cases others would be sent to search for them, but rarely would they be found. *There are a hundred ways to die out there,* he recalled his father Gideon telling him, when he stood at the window of the Commander's Tower as a boy, staring out over the mountains and the wilds. He'd experienced a fair few of those himself by now and could quite see how a ranger could go missing and never reappear. And Whitebeard? He ranged further than anyone, often disappearing for many months at a time. Robert Borrington had told Amron as such, and never quite knew when the man would resurface. *And that would make reporting him missing rather troublesome,*

Amron knew. By the time they realised he wasn't coming back, there would be no trace of him left to find.

Of course, Snowfist seemed quite smart enough to know all that as well. Still, he patted his thick chest with a hand as pale as bone, and gave a laugh. "Strength, wisdom, mercy. Yes, this Snowfist possesses them all." He turned his eyes on Walter with a smile. "I find I like you most, little man. *Great* Snowfist. Yes, this is a good name for me. The greatest of the Snowfists. Greater even than my father, Skagar Snowfist, and my grandfather, Svend Snowfist, but who knows...maybe my own son will surpass me?" He thought about that a moment. "Yes, this would make me happy, I think. Our sons...they are a part of us, the most important part, I would say. It is our duty to protect them, and to guide them, and to teach them to be greater than us. Is that not true, Lord of Steel?"

Amron's mind went straight to the son he *couldn't* protect, and the one he *hadn't*. The baby boy lost on the birthing table, and the man grown who fell to the Shadowknight's blade. *My other son,* he thought. *The son I never knew I had. But Aleron...I...I should have told him, warned him. I...I should have done more.* "Our children are what matter most," he finally said. "We do all we can to protect them."

Snowfist smiled, his teeth as white as the rest of him. "You have your own, I can see."

"A son...and a daughter," Amron said.

"And you love them? You would do anything for them?" Amron made to answer, but Snowfist raised a hand. "These were not questions, Lord of Daecar. These are facts. But you, like me, have many more children than that. My son is Svaldar, to be Snowfist when I should fall. He is my only son, but not my only child. I have many children, you see, many hundreds near and far. This is how it is to be a leader. The men and women and little ones of my tribe...they are all my children, from the newborn babes to the crook-back crones. Each looks to me for protection, for that is the job of the Snowfist. Even men who have betrayed us, and wronged us. Even a man like Bragga deserved my protection, until his case was heard. But you, Blacksteel... you took that from me. You took it from all of us when you opened up Bragga's neck and left him there for the wolves. I told you *not* to do this, and you went behind my back, and did it anyway.

"Many...many said I should have killed you for that. Some were even those who liked you. They said there was no choice. That you had cheated us, and needed to follow Bragga to the ice. But what did I do? I told them no. I fought for you, Blacksteel, and showed you mercy. I gave you a chance to live. And now here you are, seeking that same mercy again. Tell me, how can I give it to you, and still be Snowfist? How can I be a strong father to my children, if I cannot protect them?"

"Because you have no choice," Amron told him plainly. "Your stance is admirable, Snowfist, truly, but you have no choice lest you kill us all." He turned to Whitebeard, who stood staring at the dull rock walls. "We came here together and we will leave here together. He is only here on my account and for that, I will share his fate."

"As will I," said Walter faithfully. "But I would advise you consider that carefully, Great Snowfist. Blacksteel is but a ranger. If you kill him, some men may come asking questions. But Lord Daecar? You will bring all of Vandar down upon you if he does not return from this quest. That is not a wrath worth dealing with, for the sake of one man's life."

Snowfist gave that a heavy grunt. "The fat little man likes to threaten, I see. And all with a smile on his face."

"Life is short, Great Snowfist. I confess I prefer to smile than scowl, an expression that Whitebeard has quite perfected."

A bark of sudden laughter blew through Stegra's lips. "Yes, he is a changed man, it's true. He would smile once, when Elurra was living. It was the smile of a young wolf, but a smile all the same. Now..." He regarded the ranger for a long moment. "Now he just looks sad. And old. Blacksteel, you look old, my friend."

"It happens," Whitebeard managed. He gave the chieftain a quick scan. "And you're bigger in the belly than you were."

"And yet I eat less," the tribesman laughed. "Age does funny things to us. Would you not say, Lord of Daecar?"

"There's more hair in unusual places, I find," Amron said. He gestured vaguely toward his ears and nose.

"And less elsewhere," grinned Walter, running a hand through his thinning scraggly dome. "We're all just rotting away really, aren't we? It's what we do before we fall apart completely that matters."

"Yes...yes I like that." Snowfist ran his eyes across them. "But you have not yet told me why you wish to travel to the mountain." There was a suspicion in his cold blue eyes now. "We have not forgotten the days when the steel men would come and go with their horses and carts and misty swords. When the people of these lands were slain in great numbers, and reduced to the bare thousands who remain. For many years your ancestors came here to cut more of your god's body away, and curse your own lands to long years of war. To us, what you have done is an abomination. You have butchered the body of a god and left nothing but darkness and dread and foulness behind." He peered at them, one by one. "Is this your true purpose? Is there more of the godbody in the mountain you seek to carve away, for your wars?"

"Mining the mountain for godsteel is not our intent," Amron said.

"Then what is?"

"*He* is," said Walter. "This man you look upon, Great Snowfist, is a hero across our own lands. A hero who has suffered grave wounds, and needs to be restored. He is the reason why we are here. Amron Daecar, the Crippler of Kings."

"The Crippler of Kings, or the Crippled King?" Snowfist gave Amron a curious look. "I have heard of you, I think. The Crippler....yes, I remember now. Perhaps Blacksteel mentioned you once, many years ago. And now you seek a miracle, do you? You have a new war that you wish to fight in, and need to be healed, is it so?"

"The Last Renewal," Walter said. "The war to end the War Eternal."

"*End*? And what will happen after? There will be no more war? The fire people will chain up their dragons, and the steel people will put down their misty swords? Maybe all the sea people will build big boats, so you might sail together to lands unknown, yes?"

"We'll have peace," Walter told him. "A peace that will never be broken."

"And more lands...this most of all, I think," said Snowfist. "Is that not what war is for where you come from? When we fight other tribes, we do it for hunting grounds, for territory, for survival. You do it for greed. You wish to seize the lands of the fire people, and the sand people and the people of the sun and the moon. And then what will happen? You will just fight among yourselves instead." He folded his arms and shook his head. "War *is* eternal. It will never end."

"Well I suppose it's hard to deny that," said Walter, with a light chuckle. "Men will always fight and quarrel, it's true - that's part of our nature, after all - but never again on a scale to spread a shadow upon all the world. It is that shadow that we fight against, Snowfist. It has come and gone for thousands of years, but this last...it will spread and settle and never recede. We fight to prevent that from happening."

"And one man will make all the difference?" Snowfist was regarding Amron with a new interest. He pumped up his chest. "If that man was named Stegra the Snowfist, I might agree, but he is not. I do not see how this Steel Lord will fight the shadow all on his own."

"He won't. He will be but one piece of the puzzle. But no puzzle can be complete, if even the smallest piece is missing."

"So he's a small piece, is he?"

"That wasn't what I meant."

"No, but I find it funny. A big man, but a small piece." Stegra Snowfist laughed loudly, regarding Amron as he did so. He seemed to read something in his face. His laughter died away. "So...there is doubt in you, Lord of Daecar," he saw. "Doubt that you will be as important as the fat little man hopes, yes? Or is it doubt that your wounds will ever be healed?"

"They *will* be healed," insisted Walter. "By Vandar's blessing, they..."

"He will have no blessing. The way is shut. I have told you this already."

"Then we'll find another."

"There is no other."

"There must be." Walter turned to Amron. Those doubts were etched deep across his face. "We will find the way, Amron. We *must*."

"The fat little man has a faith to him. I like his determination." Snowfist pondered things for a long quiet moment, then said in a more muted voice, "Maybe it would be best for me to show you what you seem not to believe. I do not want this Lord of Daecar dying out here, should the fat man's threats be real. I must think of my children. And they will be best protected, I think, by making sure you do not die." He looked at Amron, his heavy brow wrinkling. "How are your lungs? I am told you cough often."

"I swallowed half the Silver Scar. It has caused some mild irritation."

"The chill can kill," the chieftain said. "Are you better than you were?"

"Yes. Thank you." Amron hated being looked upon like an invalid.

"Good. Yes, this is good." Snowfist continued to contemplate his position, framed by the flickering firelight behind him. He tugged at his beard. There was something new behind his eyes now, some deeper thought he hadn't had before. He nodded, and said, "I will take you to the mountain, and spare Blacksteel's life for a second time, but for this, you must do something for me."

"Anything," Walter said, too keenly.

"What is it you want?" asked Amron, more reserved.

Snowfist smiled at both of them. "Something I should have realised sooner, perhaps," he said. "Something my father spoke of, and his father before him, and his before him, for two hundred years." His face was cast in a new light, as though everything suddenly made sense. "The pieces fit, yes," he whispered, still nodding. "I see that now." Then he laughed, a great bellowing chuckle. "*Great* Snowfist indeed. I have won hunting grounds, defeated my enemies, led my people through the long cold dark. And now *this*. Now the Sea-King's words come true, with *me*, Stegra the Great Snowfist, at the head of my people."

Amron wasn't understanding a word of what the man was saying. Neither Whitebeard, nor even Walter, seemed to be keeping up either. "And...who is this Sea-King?" the Lord of House Daecar asked. "What words, Snowfist?"

"Words that have just returned to me. Words whispered two hundred years ago into my grandfather's grandfather's ear."

"A prophesy?" asked Walter, more interested.

"Yes...yes this is the word. A prophesy." He looked at Amron, then said, "*A lord of steel will come and drive the curse away. One great quest will fail, but one greater will light the way. Steel and snow will meet as enemies, but part as allies and friends. In this the frost shall be taken, and the lands grow clear to tend.*" Snowfist pursed his blue-white lips and shook his head. "Silly words, I have always thought, but perhaps not. My father believed them more than me, and his father more than him. But the years have eroded our faith in the Sea-King's promises, until this day. Now...now perhaps they are restored. You are this lord of steel, I think. The Crippler, Amron of the House Daecar. It seems we were always meant to meet."

"I..." Amron turned to Walter. This was his field, his area of expertise. "Have you heard words like that before?" he asked him. "Is this making any sense to you?"

"I rather wish I had, Amron, but no…I confess this is all brand new."

"Well of course it is. These words are only known to the Snowfist. The Sea-King made sure of it. He spoke them to my grandfather's grandfather, and said, 'these words are for you alone, and the sons to follow in your line. Each father must pass them to his son and heir. Do not let them be forgotten'."

"And this Sea-King is?" Amron asked.

Stegra shrugged. "One of your sea people, I think, from a world away. He sailed here, to the coast north of the mountain through the frozen sea, with some of your steel men with him and their misty swords. They left behind a curse, and said that one day it would be taken away. This…this is your task, Lord of Daecar. You will remove the curse for us."

"And what is this curse?" Amron stood a little taller, sharpening his posture. "Some beast you need slaying?" He gave Whitebeard a quick look. *If there's need to slay a monster, then no doubt Rogen is better placed for that than me,* he thought. It wasn't a notion he much liked, but he'd learned to be more humble since his maiming.

"It may be so, but we are not sure. There is a strange place, a place of dark magic, near where the Sea-King made land. No one dares go there, but those lands…those lands are good. Good lands for living, safe and well protected, if this curse can be cleared. I will have you do it, in exchange for Blacksteel's life, and passage to the mountain. This is the bargain that my people will accept. So, what say you? Do you accept?"

There wasn't much need to think on it. Amron gave a nod. "We do. But the mountain…we *must* go there first." He found Walter Selleck nodding. "We must try to reach the holy chamber."

"Try. Yes…you can try. But you will not succeed. Even if you find a way inside the mountain, there is no way down to its heart. Do not let yourselves be given to hope, my friends. You will only find yourselves disappointed."

Yes, disappointment is something I've grown used to, Amron thought. He stepped forward and reached through the bars with his working right arm. Stegra looked down, as though the gesture was peculiar to him, but knew it all the same. He gripped Amron's cloaked forearm with a white hand the size of a ham, and shook. Up close, he shaded Amron in height and girth both. A wide smile spread upon his milky face. "We leave tomorrow," he said. "You ride with the Snowskins now."

14

Janilah

The throne room rustled loudly with the sound of shuffling feet, leather boots and steel sabatons scraping and scratching on the stone floor. Colours danced between the whitewashed fluted pillars, a blur of standards and sigils from all across the north marked on every tunic and chest.

The silly little King of Rasalan even had his royal banner held high upon a pole, clutched tight in the hands of a youthful standard-bearer with the colours of House Maynard on his cloak. Reprimanding the paper king here in sight of all these lords and ladies would not, however, be appropriate. So Janilah turned to Sir Owen Armdall and said, "Tell the Maynard boy to pull that banner down. We're not on the march to war."

King Janilah Lukar was sitting in his white stone throne, mantled in Tukoran green over a doublet of rich reddish brown. He had on his head his crown, a simple gold ornament without excessive styling. Before him, the gathered throng were accoutred in all manner of garments, from full clad suits of Ilithian Steel plate or mail to unembellished traveller garb, as preferred by some when on the road. All had arrived from their journey across the Stonehills that very morning, some coming from Harrowmoor, others Northgate Castle, others still the City of Thalan. As was custom, Janilah had invited the highborn host to come straight here to greet him, before they might be escorted to their private chambers around the palace, and elsewhere.

As Sir Owen Armdall whispered a quiet word for the Maynard boy to lower his banner, the great bronze doors at the rear groaned shut. The brothers Hunt, Sir Maxwell and Sir Rees, were stationed there. With Ilithor filling with knights and lords of fine skill and repute, the Six had decided to have three of their number in Janilah's company at all times. Janilah didn't object. There was no sense in risking himself at this late stage, with all the men he'd raised to the rank of enemy in recent months.

He counted them out now, running his eyes upon the audience. It didn't take him long to conclude that there were many here who liked him not. *Even my own son has a glare on him,* he thought, finding Rylian pressing forward from the throng. At his sides were Janilah's grandsons, the princes Robbert and Raynald, as dashing as their father in their cloaks of emerald green. Rylian stopped at the foot of the steps and put his head into a deep bow. "Father, you look well."

Janilah looked down at his son, as the room continued to bustle and whisper. He would have a private audience with many here, in the hours and days to come, so speaking of matters of any personal import or sensitivity would be unwise and unnecessary. This was but a short formal affair to welcome the host to his city. "I feel well, Rylian," he told his son. "The winter air rids us of all ills and ailments."

It was a common expression in Ilithor, typical during greetings and reunions. The city had a good record for fending off plagues and other such bouts of disease, and the altitude and pure bracing air was thought to be largely responsible. In truth, it was because the city's sanitation was excellent, and its verticality helped pockets of disease be swiftly confined to the lower levels where the poor resided. *But the air,* Janilah thought sarcastically. *It's all about the air.*

"And Robbert, Raynald," he went on, favouring his grandsons with a smile. "I hear you both fought valiantly during your first campaign." The boys were only eighteen summers into their short lives and newly acquainted with war. Janilah favoured Robbert in particular, being Rylian's heir, though had the good grace not to show that preference in public. "I understand you slew a Suncoat in single combat during the Siege of Shellcrest, Robbert. And Raynald, the reports of your prowess have not evaded me either. Both of you are said to fight much like your father in style and skill; there is no better man to emulate."

"You honour us, Grandfather." Robbert bowed and Raynald followed. Both had Rylian's wavy brown hair, tinted with that rusty red. "It was Sir Manwell Swiftwater, the knight whom I duelled. That *man* was not *well* when I was done with him." He gave a youthful grin.

Janilah offered no reaction to that, but to say, "Very good, Robbert. You can tell me about it later." Sir Manwell was an unfabled Suncoat, but a Suncoat all the same, and the Rasals were proud of their order of Bladeborn knights, fewer in number though their ranks were when compared to the Emerald Guards and Knights of Varin. Sir Manwell's father, Lord Harry Swiftwater, wouldn't take kindly to Prince Robbert's jape should he overhear, nor would the other prominent Rasal lords standing with their sons and knights nearby.

Janilah could see several of note amid the crowd. There was Lord Donal Paramor with the blade-wielding merman of his house on his chest. The ursine Lord Horus Buckland of Northgate and his stag and bear sigil, the two beasts facing one another against a backdrop of black trees. The Oakenlord, Ferry Maynard, and the triple oak tree of his house, to represent his city seat of Oakshore, and the Oakenwood that clothed it to the north and south. All were powerful Rasalanian lords and none had ever called Janilah Lukar friend. He didn't care for that, however.

So long as I have their new king's fealty, that is all that matters, he thought.

The very man stepped forward now, dressed in a grey pitted suit of whaleskin armour with a cloth-of-gold cloak on his back. Janilah had seen that armour before. It was said to have been carved from the carcass of the famed leviathan Galaphan, who'd come ashore at the Rasal holy site of Galaphan's Grounding a thousand years ago. King Hadrin had requested that his wedding to Amilia be staged there among the remains of the whale's great white skeleton, but of course Janilah had summarily dismissed it. More than that, the request had angered him. *To think I'd let my granddaughter be wed between ribs and bones at some pagan site.* He forced his face into a semblance of courtesy, and said, "King Hadrin, welcome to Ilithor. I hope the journey here was pleasant."

The Rasal king dipped his head into a bow. "Most pleasant, yes,

King Janilah," he said in a grating, scratchy voice that was most ill on the ears. "The waters and winds were kind during our voyage south down the Strait, and the trip across Tukor was unburdened by bad weather. A most favourable journey, yes."

That isn't what I heard, Janilah thought. He'd been informed that Hadrin had hosted a feast a week past in the Stonehills, in which the pavilion had near been pulled from its fastenings, such was the fierceness of the gusty wind. "Good," he merely said. "I will look forward to hearing more of it privily. Perhaps we might share audience in my solar later this afternoon?"

"It would be my honour, King Janilah." Hadrin bowed and drew to the side.

The etiquette of the greeting ceremony was thus observed, with the lords stepping before Janilah Lukar in turn, to share short words of salutation. After his own son and heirs, and the foreign king, came the foreign lords by vague order of importance. He decided to appease the Rasals by allowing them to come to him first, so came Lords Paramor and Buckland and Maynard in turn. All were Bladeborn by lineage, and had sons and nephews filling the ranks of the Suncoats.

The Seaborn lords, meanwhile, were typically identifiable by their seafaring sigils. Krakens and whales, crabs and corals, ships and sharks and shells. Janilah had met them all in some capacity before, though several of their names escaped him. He'd never much cared for the Seaborn houses, in truth, nor considered them especially important. Still, the likes of Lord Browlan of Doublebay, Lord Merrymarsh of Calmwater, and Lord Swiftwater of Shellcrest were worth his time. They were some of the most powerful of the Seaborn greatlords and together controlled the bulk of the Rasal navy beneath their king's command. *And that king is me*, Janilah thought, as they came to him one by one. He gave each of them a few kind words, before promising private audiences at another time. Then it was onto the Vandarians.

First to approach from their host was their new Prince and First Blade, Dalton Taynar. He looked a little stiff as he stepped forward in his Varin cloak over full-clad godsteel armour, and was surely displeased to have been made to wait. "Prince Dalton, I must apologise for not seeing you until now," Janilah said. "I had half forgotten you'd been raised to royalty."

He hadn't. This was an intentional snub. Dalton Taynar had one duty to fulfil the Warrior King, and in that he'd already failed. *Vesryn.* The man was still on the loose, and his divine blade unrecovered. Janilah loaded the blame of that entirely at Dalton Taynar's feet.

"That's quite all right, Your Majesty." Dalton's bow was sharply delivered. He looked grim and older than his years, with dark bruises beneath his hollow eyes, and a cold sickly pallor to his cheeks. "When my father arrives, I will hope *he* gets the courtesy of a royal greeting."

Janilah almost smiled to that. *Only if he hands me the Windblade,* he thought, *or perhaps I'll throw him from this balcony too.* He wouldn't, of course, but the thought came to him all the same. Killing Ellis Reynar had been easy, but King Godrik Taynar would be another matter. *Not that I desire it.* He and the new Vandarian king were like-minded enough and had known each other for decades. *We will work well together,* he hoped. *And once I have combined the Blades, none of that shall matter. I shall remove and raise kings as I see fit, and there will be no one to tell me no.* But such a time had not yet come, so he merely said, "I will make sure of it. Your former king's tragic death is still in my thoughts, if that explains my absentmindedness. But seeing you now, you fit the title of prince well, I must say. And First Blade also. All you need now is the blade, to go with the rank."

"It will be retrieved soon," said the grim-faced prince.

"I hope it is, for your sake." Janilah let his eyes darken a moment, before adding, "But of course, this is a Vandarian issue. I am sure you know what you're doing."

When Dalton Taynar stalked away, a younger man of similar face stepped forward from behind him. "You must be Prince Rodmond," Janilah said.

The boy was only about Robbert and Raynald's age, though already had his uncle Dalton's grim and hollow-cheeked look. He'd not developed the man's scowl, though. "I am, Your Majesty." He bowed as low as anyone had that day. Then, standing straight, he seemed to have no idea what to say.

Another one raised to royalty who hardly knows how to wear it, Janilah thought. Though it probably wouldn't last. As soon as Dalton Taynar had a son of his own, this boy would lose his place as heir and be shifted aside. *He looks like he'd want nothing more. Not everyone is born to rule.* "Have you been to Ilithor before, Prince Rodmond? I confess, I do not recall having met you."

"Never, Your Majesty. But I find the place most compelling, so far."

"Your chambers will be also. As prince, we will situate you with fine views through the mountains and valleys. I hope they will be agreeable."

"I am certain they will, great king."

Janilah said no more, giving the boy a chance to step away. When he did, a man about eight times his size took his place. "Lord Kanabar. I am glad you decided to come," Janilah said in a voice empty of enthusiasm. He and Lord Wallis Kanabar had never seen eye-to-eye.

"I'm glad to be here, King Janilah." Kanabar's great red beard looked even thicker than the last he'd seen him, some years ago, flecked now with twisting vines of grey and white. His big nose was all full of broken veins, and his bald head shone bright against the pale morning sunlight, gleaming through the balcony behind Janilah's throne. The Lord of the Riverlands looked that way now. His voice was as blustery and bold as ever. "So this is where Ellis fell, is it? What an unfortunate way to go, so bloody unlucky. Mind if I take a look? I've been most intrigued to see this treacherous balcony that claimed our king's life."

"Of course, my lord. But at a later time. I do not feel it would be appropriate right now."

"Yes, yes, say no more, Janilah. I'm sure I'll have ample time to mosey around up here in the coming weeks. I hear small parts of him are still being found, bits of skull and such lodged between the cobbles. The dowager fairs well, I hope, and Princess Lyriss? You have been treating them kindly, of course?"

I mislike him greatly, Janilah thought. It was typical of the man to be insolent and disrespectful. *King. You will call me king,* he wanted to demand, but he knew that wouldn't be wise. "I have given them every courtesy they could wish for, yes. All guests are given the same." *Even you, you great oaf.* "I will have a tour arranged for you, Wallis," he said as politely as he could. "I'm sure you've forgotten much and more of the city and palace since you were last here."

"At our age, one does become forgetful, as Prince Dalton has just discovered." Kanabar laughed loudly, the sound disturbing several quiet conversations nearby. It seemed as though the burly riverlord had been drinking through the morning, with those great ruddy cheeks of his wobbling as he chuckled. Thankfully, he said no more and lumbered off back into the crowds.

The less I see of him the better, Janilah thought, turning his eyes around the assembly. An ache was starting to develop in his lower back. He much preferred privy audiences where he could speak his mind, and still had to greet his own returning lords, particularly those of the north. Kastor and Gershan, Swallow and Huffort, and the minor vassals beneath them. And there were more Vandarians to get through too. Most of Kanabar's underlings from East Vandar had gone south in defence of the realm, but there were a host of prominent Varin Knights who'd want to come before him, some of them heirs to their houses.

So Elyon Daecar stepped forward.

He seemed to come out of nowhere, having concealed himself amid the throng until now. But suddenly there he was, every inch his father's son, tall, broad at the shoulder, square at the bearded jaw. Black waves of hair fell from his head, neatly arranged, and those eyes of his were cast narrow and firm, a radiant silver-blue. *Daecar features,* Janilah thought, *and the colours of his kingdom*. They had always been a striking family, capturing the very essence of what it was to be Vandarian; grand, noble and supremely gifted with the blade. Janilah had known Elyon's grandfather Gideon well, and much respected his great-grandfather, Balion, too. Both had been First Blades of Vandar prior to Amron, and it was certain that Aleron would have followed that line as well, had events allowed. *And this boy?* It was said Elyon Daecar was every bit as talented as his older brother, he only lacked in dedication. He didn't lack for it now, Janilah had heard.

"Sir Elyon," the king said, as the knight stood still at the foot of the dais in gleaming silver breastplate and Varin cloak. "Welcome to Ilithor. I was just recalling our first meeting, some months ago. Much has passed in that time. I offer you my personal condolences, for the tragic death of your valiant brother."

Elyon Daecar paid obeisance with a neat and noble bow. "Your words are kind and welcome, Your Majesty. Much and more has happened these last months, yes." Most of it bad, his eyes said.

"But you have grown, I can see," Janilah identified. "I have been told you flourish in your brother's stead, unwelcome thought that is. House Daecar has a strong heir to follow its mighty lord, when he should fall."

Elyon had been wide-eyed and green as spring grass when they'd first met. No longer. There was a darkness about the boy now, something cold that could not be unthawed. *He knows a great deal,* Janilah could see. *This one...this one I must watch carefully.*

"I hope so, my lord," he said in an even voice.

A moment passed in silence. The tension between them was subtle, if unmistakable. And if the rumours were true, Elyon had had an altercation with King Hadrin a week past too, sharing terse words with the new Rasal monarch at the feast. *The boy cares not for offending kings, it seems.*

"You sister nears the city with the royal procession from Varinar, I'm told," Janilah went on. "I am sure you are looking forward to seeing her again."

Elyon stared back at him, cold as ice. "I am. And my Auntie Amara too. It will be nice for her to see *you* again, my lord. She has not returned to these halls for many years, I know."

"Too many years, Sir Elyon. I look forward to welcoming her back." *Like hot coals in my eyes*, he thought. Amara Daecar had no love for him, nor he her *And no doubt she will unleash that cutting tongue of hers on all and sundry these coming weeks.* She was a cousin to Janilah, though some twenty years his junior, and had been given to Vesryn for his leal service during the war, and good riddance. That service had involved the tricking of his brother Amron and the stealing of his seed, with the boy Jonik being the creation. *And now both of them hold my blades,* Janilah reflected, a thought sour with irony. *Uncle and half brother to this young man before me. And might he try to foil my plans too?*

"Well, I shouldn't take up too much of your time, my lord." Elyon gave Janilah a final look and then bowed low, before walking rigidly away toward the Varin Knights he favoured. Janilah recognised some of them from the feast in which he'd met the boy. And there was Sir Mallister Monsort too, within the little group. He'd heard that Lady Melany's brother had become fast friends with Elyon, and that might be something he could use.

He drummed his fingers on the arm of his throne, thinking. *I must have Melany keep an eye on him,* he decided. Men told tales in bed, he knew, and he trusted the alluring form of Lady Melany to entice him back beneath the covers. *He may know of Vesryn's whereabouts, no matter what he says.* Elyon had insisted he had no idea where his uncle was, apparently, but who knew whether that was true or not. *Perhaps Melany might extract the truth of it, when she plies him full of wine and takes him between her legs?* If Elyon was going to be vulnerable, it would be in the company of the girl he was said to love. And what a weakness that was; to love. *It makes all men fools, but me.*

The formalities went on for some time longer, as the morning sun wheeled above them, casting shards of golden light through the windows. After getting through the rest of the Vandarians and his own Tukoran nobles, Janilah called proceedings to a close and gestured for the assembly to disperse. "Attendants will show you to your private chambers," he called to them, standing. "And a feast will be held tonight to celebrate your coming to the White City. It will be the first of many these weeks. Enjoy Ilithor, my friends. Let us embrace the high pure air, and the bracing effects of a united north."

They filed out at that, as Janilah dropped back down, letting the false expression of hope and optimism slip from his face. "Not you, Rylian," he said, as his son prepared to step away. The rest left through the large bronze doors, leaving father and son alone. A silence fell as the host rustled off. The brothers Hunt and Sir Owen remained, standing guard at the door.

Rylian gestured to the three sworn swords, as he paced at the bottom of the dais, his royal green cloak draped behind him. "You're taking the threat of Vesryn seriously then, Father?" he said. "Or is there someone else who has you worried?"

"And why should Vesryn Daecar have me worried? There is no reason for him to target me. Nor do I determine the schedule of the Six. With a room full of knights of dubious intent, it's only wise to keep some swords on hand, should they be needed. This is not a time for imprudence, Rylian."

"I suppose so. You have made one or two enemies of late. Though many more friends, I would say, with us all *united* as one." His scorn and sarcasm was clear enough, but Janilah let it pass. "But I do wonder...Lord Huffort's got hundreds of his men searching for Vesryn, I've heard. He even told me himself that the order came from you. Clearly, you're eager to catch him, Father." He continued to pace, side-to-side, looking out toward the three knights at the door. "I just saw these three swords of yours and jumped to the conclusion that you were concerned he might spring from the crowd and strike you down."

He gave Janilah a quick look. "But as you say, you've got nothing to worry about from Vesryn Daecar. You're just searching for him because..." He frowned. "Why, exactly?"

Janilah's patience was being tested already. Rylian's worth was in being dutiful, leading his armies, killing his enemies. If he wanted to be spoken to like this, he'd call upon Cecelia. "You know exactly why, Rylian, but if you need me to spell it out for you, I will. Vesryn Daecar holds the Sword of Varinar. There is no blade more deadly in the world, and we are at war, as you well know. Such a weapon is invaluable at this time. But more than that, the Sword of Varinar and the post of First Blade are sacred..."

"To Vandarians," Rylian cut in. "We're Tukoran, I seem to recall."

"Then you need a lesson in history. House Lukar is Vandarian at its core, like all other Bladeborn greathouses. True Tukorans are Forgeborn...armourers and blacksmiths and metalworkers and builders, and there aren't many of those left. Every Bladeborn house in the north should respect that sword, and that post, no matter which king and kingdom they now pay fealty to. It would seem that Lord Lewyn Huffort agrees with me, even if you do not. He is quite intent on helping track and recover the Sword of Varinar, as every dutiful Bladeborn should be, from the Twinfort to the Crescent Coast." Rylian gave a little smile to that, though stopped short of scoffing. But Janilah could still see it. "You do not believe my words?" he demanded of his son. "You think I have some other motive for hunting down that blade?"

"If you did, would you tell me?" Rylian challenged. He didn't wait for an answer. "It's been rumoured by some that you want the blade for yourself..."

"The Sword of Varinar is an heirloom of Vandar," Janilah protested.

"So are the other blades. But history shows they have found themselves in foreign kingdoms and the halls of foreign lords, at one time or another." Rylian stopped in his pacing and set his eyes upon his father. "People are saying you want them all for yourself, Father. You have the north, now you want the blades..."

"And what do you say?" Janilah asked him. "I care not for rumour. What does my son and heir say to that?"

Rylian thought on it a moment. "I say rumours can be misleading at times, and enlightening at others. You have won the north by political scheming. Why not win those blades by the same? They are the greatest weapons we have, as you say. And you have a habit, Father, of taking, and doing, as you wish."

Those words struck hard at the Warrior King. *He disrespects me openly,* he thought. *He holds me in contempt.* He regarded Rylian firmly. "This is about Amilia," he then said, perceiving the source of his son's ire. Cecilia had been adamant that Rylian had changed, that he was growing weary of being kept outside of Janilah's counsel, and that this wedding would tip him further over the edge. "You curse me for handing your daughter's hand to Hadrin?"

"I don't curse you, no. I understand why you did it. What I *don't* understand is why you didn't consult me." There was a rising in his voice. "She is *my* daughter, Father, and I am your heir. I deserved to be included, for all I've done for you. Too long have you kept me in the cold."

For good reason, he almost said. *You're too noble for your own good.* Duty had its merits, but Rylian had always strayed too close to perfection in matters of honour and chivalry. "I have made Amilia a queen," he told his son. "You swing a sword as well as anyone, that is true, but you're a long way from knowing how to rule. You must be ruthless, Rylian, and even cruel at times. What I have done to secure the north...

"Is what?" Rylian cut in. His hand was on the hilt of his sword, knuckles white. There was a glowing green flame in his eyes. *You're a long way from knowing how to rule.* Those words were as daggers, driven through his ribs. "What have you done to secure the north? Kill a king, perhaps? Or two? I defend you...gods how I have to defend you, from all those who'd question what you do, and this is how you repay me? You say ruthless? You say cruel? I might say *treason*, if these rumours are to be believed. If that's what it takes to win the north then perhaps I want no part in it."

"Then perhaps you'll *have* no part." Janilah threw his eyes to his swords. Three blades sung a steel song as they were drawn from silver sheaths. Sir Owen stepped forward ahead of the brothers Hunt, gifted fighters all, a godsteel mist swirling about them.

But Rylian Lukar only laughed. "You'd have me slain in your own throne room? Your own son?" His laughter went from wall to wall. "Let them try, if you'd like to see a show." He drew his own sword and turned to face them. "Fancy your chances, Sir Owen? I hear you're the best of this bunch?"

Sir Owen Armdall reached for his second blade, smiling. Godsteel scraped and caught the light as it moved to his side, dust motes dancing in the shafts of pale gold light pouring in through the windows. Janilah said nothing for a long moment. An ire bubbled in him such that he'd let all this play out. And then in an instant, his thoughts cleared. "Sheathe your swords, Sir Owen. Hunts, you too." The three sworn swords did as ordered immediately. He looked at his son. "Rylian, enough. I had hoped to find you in better mood, but apparently you're weary from your travels. Go. We will speak again when you've calmed."

The prince plunged his blade back into its scabbard. "You wanted to tell me something," he said, turning. His jaw was set behind his rusty brown beard, green-brown eyes unblinking. It was not the son that Janilah knew, following his commands without question. "You asked I stay behind for a reason, and it wasn't to check how I felt about Amilia. Nor was it to seek my counsel, clearly. What is it?"

"Nothing. It can wait."

"What is it, Father? Something you're afraid to reveal, no doubt. Another wicked scheme of which you know I'll disapprove."

"I care not for your disapproval. Go. We'll speak tomorrow."

"No. I will hear it now, while our tongues are hot. Tell me. *Now*."

Janilah seethed quietly on his throne. "You forget to whom you speak. I am your king, Rylian. There is no one who might command me."

"I will not leave until you tell me." Rylian stared. "Tell me, Father."

"Fine." Janilah shifted in his throne. "It's Robbert. I have arranged a marriage for him also." He checked his son's eyes. Brown and green darkened to black.

"Who?"

"Lyriss Reynar," Janilah said at once. "She is into her fourteenth year now and a good match for Prince Robbert. Nothing has been announced yet; only the girl's mother Elitha and I know of it. I thought you should be the first to hear, before any rumours find their way out."

A smile went to Rylian's lips, glacier slow, and that darkness in his eyes burned like obsidian flame. "Thank you, Father, for doing me this courtesy." His voice was ice. He stared at Janilah for ten long heartbeats, then turned and marched from the room.

Janilah watched him go in silence. The anger in him swirled about a core of regret. Rylian was his son, his heir, his champion, the commander of his armies. There was no one in Tukor more inspirational on the battlefield, no one more loved. *I must resolve this*, he knew, as his son's footsteps echoed away through the antechamber beyond the throne room. No father wanted to make an enemy of their son and Rylian had festered too long outside of his counsel, kept unaware of the more nefarious elements of his plans. *I must extend an olive branch or two.* He thought for a while, tapping his fingers on the cold stone arm of his throne, running them through the coarse brown-grey bristles of his beard. *I will give him the choice,* he decided. *If he wishes to withdraw the wedding offer to Queen Elitha, so be it.* Keeping Rylian in line was more important than pandering to the dowager queen, after all. *But with luck, he'll agree when he's calmed.* The match with Lyriss Reynar was a good one. All Rylian needed was to be the one to arrange it.

"Would you like me to go after him, sire?" asked Sir Owen Armdall, as Rylian disappeared out of sight, down the long wide corridor.

Janilah stood. "That shan't be necessary," he said. "I will retire to my solar. Please send for King Hadrin, once he's had a chance to settle into his chambers. But first, have Lady Monsort brought up to me. I require a word."

To his surprise, he found that Cecilia was not there when he reached his private rooms. He often discovered her at the window seat she favoured near his desk, eager to hear the latest gossip and offer counsel and her own personal brand of wisdom, whether he wanted to hear it or not. When he didn't, he would just dismiss her, and she would go. More oft than not, however, she had something worth hearing. If Rylian had taken Janilah's prowess with the blade and his ability to lead on the field, then Cecilia had all his ability to scheme. She was an asset he had come to value more and more.

Settling behind his desk, he poured himself a cup of hot spiced wine, thick and red as blood, and took a swig. Warmth ran down his throat and through his chest. He thought again of Rylian. His son would be going to greet his lady wife, Clarris Kastor, a woman neither comely in look nor character. *There is no love there*, he knew, *and never was.* When Janilah had arranged Rylian's marriage to her during the war, his son had given no complaint. He understood that Lukars wed for blood not love, and that Clarris Kastor was best suited at the time to secure Tukor throughout a long and turbulent conflict. Even as the entire north was still salivating over Amron Daecar's lady wife Kessia Amadar, Rylian did his duty, and sired three fine children. *So why does he rally against me now?*

He blew a sigh and took another long drink of wine. He knew why, of course. It was about control, and no more. *And I'll give it to him,* he reflected, confirming his choice. *I'll speak to him of Robbert. If he truly wishes to choose someone else for his son, so be it. I'll not refuse him.*

He nodded to that and set thoughts of his son aside. The door knocked a moment later and Sir Owen Armdall announced the arrival of Lady Melany Monsort. The woman was wearing shades of blue, as she favoured, to complement her golden hair and the sparkling sapphires she had for eyes. "You wished to see me, Your Majesty."

Janilah gestured her forward, to stand before his desk. She didn't sit. She knew full well she wouldn't be in his company long. "Elyon Daecar is back in the palace," he said. "I need you to return to his company, as soon as is convenient."

"My duties with Amilia..."

"Will go on. You are her lady-in-waiting and she is to be wed. This is not a time to abandon her. But your nights..."

She understood. "You want me to lie abed with him?"

"Nothing you haven't done a hundred times before."

"To what end, Your Majesty?"

"You know what end."

She gave that a slow nod. The young woman was as fine of face as they came, but knew how to wear a mask. With Elyon she would be demure, inviting, sometimes provocative. With the princess she could offer a firm word, sometimes, and liked to play sarcastic for Amilia's amusement. But with Janilah she was forged of ice, a beautiful sculpture before him, unsmiling and unspeaking for the most part, listening to his orders and carrying them out at his behest. Her father Lord Derwin Monsort, continued to thrive off the back of her efforts, as did her brother Sir Mallister. But their fates were linked to her fealty. Fail him and her family would suffer. Please him and they would prosper.

In the end, she had no choice. *And that, son,* he thought, *is what it means to rule.*

"I will do as you bid, my lord. What do you wish to uncover?"

"Whatever you might find," he said. He scanned her, his eyes running down the gentle curve of her body, visible beneath her silk and satin robes. She was a fine figure of a woman, and no wonder Elyon Daecar could not resist her. "Try to find out if he knows where his uncle is. I imagine he will not, but try all the same. Beyond that, his allegiances, and his loyalties. The boy has changed since you saw him last. His time in Harrowmoor has further hardened him. He may take more time to thaw."

"I will thaw him, my lord."

"I know you will." He smiled.

She did not smile back.

"Good," he said, turning his eyes to the door. "You must be careful who sees you coming here now, Melany. If it were to come to Elyon's attention that you're acting in my service, he will learn to feed you lies. His sister Lillia will also be here soon. I know you got on well with the girl during your time in Varinar. Elyon may tell her something, even if he doesn't tell you. Girls share secrets, I hear. Listen closely for me. I look forward to what you may discover."

"And if I should find out nothing to incriminate Sir Elyon?"

"Then I might have another use for you."

He saw a subtle flinch with those words. "What use, my lord?"

"A girl of your talents has many uses," is all he told her. "Now go."

It was another hour or so before the door opened again and King Hadrin arrived, his coming precipitated by the clank and clamour of armour on stone. Janilah knew that he'd have Sir Munroe Moore with him, the head of his king's guard, as well as a clutch of others. He didn't see them, however, as none were permitted entry save by his leave. Once more, Sir Owen Armdall performed the announcing duties. "His Majesty, King Hadrin of Rasalan," he said, before leaving the two kings alone.

Janilah didn't stand from his seat to greet him. "Take a drink if you want," he said, though he wouldn't pour for the man. He'd never liked Hadrin of House Thala, no more than he had his father. But Godrin was at least a wise king. *An irritation, yes, but a worthy opponent for me over the years. This wretch is but another Ellis Reynar, just older, uglier, and more spiteful.*

"Will you have one, Janilah?" Hadrin asked as he poured himself a cup of wine. Janilah pushed his chalice across his desk. Hadrin filled it, then sat at the chair before him, with plenty of space between his narrow body and the arms of the seat. He'd undressed from his whale-skin armour now and changed into something more comfortable, a tunic of Rasal yellow and blue with that cloth-of-gold cloak he favoured. He looked everywhere but into the king's eyes.

But at least he doesn't shiver so much as king Ellis did, Janilah thought, staring right at him. The late king's feeble fragility had annoyed him greatly. His father Storris and grandfather Horris had been strong men, strong warriors, but Ellis...

He decided not to put any further thought toward the monarch he'd murdered. He was still down in the crypts, rotting away now in a sealed coffin. The acolytes had tried to keep him fresh for as long as possible, so the Vandarians might be able to visit him when they arrived, but the stench had grown too foul, and his body had begun to fall apart.

Janilah took a drink of spiced wine. Ahead of him sat another kingkiller, who'd added patricide to the bargain. Janilah didn't favour the comparison. Even the thought of it triggered his ire. "What were your father's last words before you cut open his throat?" he asked.

The ratty little man almost choked on his wine. A bit of red spittle escaped is lips and ran down his disappearing jaw. "I...I can't recall, Janilah. It was...it was a trying time."

"Then try." Janilah sat back and waited.

King Hadrin frowned, eyes to the side, thinking hard. His lips began to quiver. "He...he told me...he told me it was OK. He told me... to be strong." He pinched the top of his nose, rubbing his eyes with thumb and forefinger. "I apologise, Janilah. It is...it is still fresh."

Tears. Really? Janilah hadn't invited the man here for comforting. "Godrin's death was necessary," was the only succour he'd give him. "His stubbornness would have driven all the north to ruin. Why did he send the Wall away?"

Hadrin let out a wimpish little sniff. "Sir Ralston? He never told me. I heard he was last seen fleeing from Shellcrest. The man's turned craven, as far as I can tell."

Janilah gave the Seaborn king a stiff look. "Sir Ralston Whaleheart was no craven. If he left he left only by his king's command."

"Well...yes. There was a rumour that he boarded a ship with another. A girl, it's thought, by her size. She was cloaked so no one saw who it was, but..."

"I know." Janilah rubbed his bearded chin. Cecilia had speculated that it was the breeder she'd had in her care in Harrowmoor, a girl who called herself Tilda. She'd been taken into the care of Elyon Daecar and disappeared some days later. There was much mystery about all that, though. "Do you think your father might have sent the Wall to protect the girl?"

"He might have done anything in the state he was in. He'd gone half mad those last years, Janilah. He was willing to let all of Rasalan burn, but none would praise me, if they learned how I took his throne. My kingdom will never love me," he moaned.

My kingdom, Janilah thought, *and their love is not what's important.* "Then let them fear you," he told him. "And do not be afraid of being a bad man. Bad men often make the best kings, Hadrin. Good men are rarely able to make the difficult decisions." *Like my son,* he didn't say.

"You are wise, good king."

And you are not. He kept that to himself too. Instead he said, "I heard you had a disagreement with Elyon Daecar. This rumour you *can* clear up for me. What happened?"

Hadrin's teeth were too large for his thin-lipped mouth. A smile did not suit him, but out it came all the same. "I told him his father was dead."

Janilah sat forward a little. "Amron's dead? Where did you hear of this?"

"I didn't hear it, Janilah, I *saw* it." The little Rat King sat proudly in his chair, like a child seeking his father's favour. He ran one hand across a patch of salty grey hair at the side of his head. There was a twin patch opposite and nothing but flaking scalp and wisps of hair in between.

"In the Eye?" Janilah inferred. "You're able to gaze into it?" He found himself surprised. None thought that Hadrin would ever come to master the Eye of Rasalan as his father and more notable forebears had.

"The blood of Thala runs through my veins. I will prove my

doubters wrong." Hadrin sat up a little straighter, defiant, and took a drink. "I have had it only weeks and yet I have seen much, Janilah. In time, I shall master it as Father did."

"And Amron. What did you see?"

"Darkness. He was walking, shambling, limping into the void. I sensed a frosted wind. And a faint light in the distance, silvery white. I took it to mean he is travelling to the Eternal Halls. Elyon didn't much like it when I told him that. He raised his voice and slammed his hands on the table, before storming off. A most enjoyable moment for me, I will say. Those Daecars deserve everything that is coming to them."

"Do they?" Janilah asked firmly. "House Daecar has long served the north with distinction. Do not forget that, just because Kessia Amadar chose Amron over you. It is a choice that every sane woman in the world would have made."

"You..." Hadrin gulped, and up and down went the apple in his pencil neck. "You cannot say that to me. You'd have me withdraw support? Leave your city and..."

"Be quiet, Hadrin. I speak a truth only, and it lays bare your insecurities. Look at yourself. You are ill to look at, ill-loved, and ill-mannered, if what you're saying is true. You would tell Sir Elyon that his father is dead, during a feast? For what? The boy has already lost his brother, and the mother you once loved. Why lay more upon his back, for no other reason than spite? Tell me, *wise* king, what Elyon Daecar has done to earn your hate?"

His lower lip was quivering again. "He...he..."

"He is a *Daecar*," Janilah finished for him. "Apparently that is enough. Now tell me more of Amron."

Janilah gave the man a moment to compose himself. For that he gulped down plenty of wine and refilled his cup, fingers shaking all the while. Finally he spoke. "What else do you want to know?" His voice was curt and hurt. *He will probably weep when he leaves this room,* Janilah thought. *A weak king indeed. Amilia will have no trouble breaking this one, once she learns to stomach him.* "I saw Amron. I saw the darkness and the light. That...that can only mean one thing."

"Death, you have said. But when?"

"When?"

"Yes, when." Janilah blew a breath. "*When* will Amron Daecar die?"

"I...I don't know. The Eye, I..."

"You have had little time to master it," Janilah broke in. "I know."

"Yes, Janilah. It...it takes much time. Months, years even. My father's mastery came through many decades of looking into it, learning it, understanding it. I've had it but weeks."

"So you don't really know what you're looking at? Amron may yet live for decades himself. This light and darkness you see may be something entirely different."

"It...it may."

"Then why are you speaking to me of it?" Janilah found himself frustrated. He'd always respected Amron Daecar and hadn't taken any joy from what he'd done to him. If he'd wished it, he'd have finished him off after the boy Jonik had near-killed him, but he didn't. *I let him live*, he thought, *but perhaps that was unwise*. Cecilia still twittered into his ear that Amron might one day seek vengeance, but in truth it was the boy Elyon who concerned him more. All such thoughts rattled through his mind. He took a breath and silenced them, looking at the Rat King of Rasalan. "Will your proficiency improve, in time? That is all I want to know."

"Of course." Hadrin said those words with little faith or certainty. "I...I know I will."

"Good. Then I will have you search for this vision again. Of Amron. And other matters, if you would."

"I...I don't think it works like that, Janilah. The Eye only shows you what it wants to show. The Eye chooses..."

"I see." Janilah thought a moment. "Well, I'm sure you know best, Son of Thala as you are. Might we get fair warning of attacks, perhaps? I would hope that the Eye can show us when and where the Agarathi may make land, should they sail the Red Sea, or where their dragons may descend."

There had been a fair few attacks already, though those were generally minor. Smaller towns and settlements had been burned and razed along the Black Coast of Vandar and the great fortress at Southwatch had even seen some overtures, as the dragons tested their defences.

"I have seen some such visions already. Fire and burning, ash and smoke. Flashes of dragons in the skies."

"Where?"

"I...I cannot say. The features are often indistinct. The Eye is a window, Janilah. It grows clearer the more you master it, and you can see more of what lies beyond."

"And currently your sight is blurred. I understand. When are you expecting to meet your betrothed?"

The sudden turn in topic confounded the man. He spluttered again and seemed to shrink in his chair. Janilah looked down at him. *This man fears women,* he realised. *No wonder he has never taken a wife. I wonder if he's ever taken a woman to bed at all...*

"I...I would hope to meet her...soon," the paper king said. Sweat was beginning to glisten on his forehead. "Your son...he mislikes me, I feel. It has made me wonder about this marriage, Janilah. Amilia...she might be too...too young for me..."

"You're still of an age to sire children, and Amilia has always wished to be a queen." That was only half true. "You make a perfect match."

"And Rylian?"

"Accepts it, and agrees. I cannot speak for your personal relationship, however. Did he speak ill to you on the road?"

"Not especially, no. He was cordial, for the most part, though he and Dalton Taynar chose to speak past me at my feast. I took umbrage with that, I will say."

"And you're telling me this why? You and my son are both into middle age." *Though you look almost as old as I am,* he thought. "I will not intervene if that is what you're asking. It matters not whether you get along."

"No, of...of course not. I only wanted...well, I had hoped to make a good impression. At the feast, I did what I could with the time I had, but..."

Janilah had heard plenty of this failed feast already. He waved it away. "You did well," he said. "Fear, Hadrin. It is more powerful than love. And with Amilia at your side, you will be formidable." He pulled a piece of parchment from the side. "Now, I have letters to write. We can speak further when we feast. If you do not visit with Amilia before then, you will see her for dinner. I will make sure she looks particularly radiant, just for you."

He looked more frightened than excited by that. "Yes, yes...I will see her then...then." He stood and drained his wine, setting down his cup. "Until later, Janilah. I'll leave you to your correspondence."

Janilah had no urgent need to write letters, but always favoured it as a method of dismissing people. Some he could just grunt at or wave away, but he supposed a king deserved some courtesy. As soon as Hadrin had left the room, he pushed the parchment back aside. Outside, he heard the shuffling of leather boots and the clanging of armour on the stone floor. He slumped back into the chair, weary. The day was hardly half gone and he still had a feast to host, and many such occasions in the coming weeks to attend. It was at times like this that he valued Cecilia most of all. She alone could sit with him and hear his complaints, and help to manage the burden of his schemes. He summoned the Oak of Armdall. "Sir Owen, I would have you find my daughter, and bring..." He trailed off, seeing something in the knight's eyes. "What now?" he asked. "I know that look, Sir Owen." It was the same look he'd had when Janilah had returned from the crypts with Elitha Reynar, and learned from Sir Owen that Vesryn had gone rogue. It was a look that worried him. "Speak."

"Good news, and bad, sire." Sir Owen marched in, hands on the hilts of his blades, triple coloured mantle flowing behind him. "We have just had word from a rider of Sir Kevyn's company. He is but two days from the city, with the Book of Thala safe in his possession. After the difficulty they had through the Redwater Bay, they have made good time overland."

Janilah wasn't seeing the bad news in that. He had expected Sir Kevyn Bolt to return sooner with the book, but he'd been delayed by poor weather and rough seas. The fact that he was now so close was heartening to learn. "And the bad news, Sir Owen?"

Sir Owen Armdall swallowed. "The book has been scoured, sire, during the voyage from Solapia. The scholars are working to decipher the accounts, but..."

"But what? Spit it out."

"There is a page missing, my lord. Within King Godrin's passages. It...it's been ripped out. Recently, it's thought."

A hot hand gripped at Janilah's heart with those words. *No matter how tight my grip becomes, there is always something that slips through my fingers.* "Thank you, Sir Owen," he said, with icy grace. "Please leave me to my thoughts."

Sir Owen Armdall bowed and stepped from the room.

Alone, King Janilah Lukar raged.

15

Saska

Saska woke to the sound of whispered voices. A balmy wind blew over her as she opened her eyes and saw the light of dawn breaking in the east. A shimmer of gold and pink was emerging from the darker purples and reds, blending where sky met sea. The Wall was standing guard nearby to her, his upper body armoured beneath his cloak, yet another long nightly vigil complete. "We're not moving," Saska said, clearing the rust from her throat. Sir Ralston Whaleheart shook his head, inclining it to the side. And there Saska saw it. "Another ship? What's happening?"

"Merchant," boomed the man's deep voice. "They're trading."

"In what?"

"Information."

The second ship had been tied up against the Steel Sister, a trading carrack about the same size as Rikki Bowen's weathered old caravel. Her figurehead was a hawk with outstretched wings and a basket of goods held in its beak. Saska could see crewmen on deck, huddled here and there in the dim light. She perceived no threat from them and if they had ill intentions, those would have quickly wilted at the sight of the Wall.

Both ships had their sails down, their oars stacked, as they bobbed gently on the water with islands dotted to the east and the coast of Aramatia hidden away to the west, not yet visible in the dim dawn light. "Did the ship come from the Telleshi Isles?" Saska asked, looking eastward. The predawn glow made the nearest islands gleam like golden jewels on the black-blue water. There were hundreds of them out there, some havens for pirates, others home to wayfarers and wanderers and those seeking salvation from their sins.

"No. From the south. They speak of tidings from our destination."

"Aram?"

The Wall dipped his head.

Saska got to her feet, stretching like a cat. The nights had become near as warm as the days now, muggy and close, and she'd taken to abandoning the confines of her cabin in the evening. Windowless and small, and just up from the communal quarters where the crew slept, it could be unbearably hot at night, leaving her to toss and turn and sweat, and wake having had little sleep at all. It was more pleasant up here on deck, she'd decided, so she'd taken to sleeping here on occasion when the air below became too stuffy.

She rubbed her eyes, yawning. *But what was I dreaming?* she wondered. It had been a good dream, she faintly recalled. And then it came to her, a heartbeat later, drawing a smile upon her lips. *Elyon.* She'd been back in his tent outside Harrowmoor, and back in his bed too. She dreamt of him sometimes, of those waves of black hair tumbling from his head, neat black beard split into a smile, toned honed body flexing as he took her...

She drew a sharp breath, wondering if the Wall might see some lustful look in her eye at the memory, and turned to look toward the forecastle. The privy conference between captains was going on over there, as they whispered their trade. Saska liked to forge her little nest on the quarterdeck at the rear of the ship, where it tended to be more stable on the waves. She strained to hear what the captains were saying, but could make out nothing from this distance. "Do you know what they're talking about?" she asked the Wall, covering another yawn with the back of her hand.

Sir Ralston was clutching at one of his dual greatswords, ham-like hand wrapped around the whale-pommelled hilt. The man's size wasn't his only merit. His blood-bond gifted him fine hearing and eyesight too, and gods could he move quickly when he needed to. He nodded. "I told you. Tidings from Aram."

'Right. And?"

"Not good," is all he said. "The other captain says we should turn around."

Well that won't do. Saska moved to the gunwale where the Wall stood. The view down the ship was better there. On the main deck, several of the crew of the Steel Sister were watching the conference unfold; those who'd been on night duty or otherwise liked to rise early. Up the steps of the forecastle, Captain Rikki Bowen had his first mate and uncle, Lanky Larry for company. The other captain stood alone, the rest of his crew remaining on their own ship. He was a round-bellied man with a strangely thin face for his size. It made him look like a stuffed bird, porky round the middle but with a narrow beak for a nose. His head was hidden beneath a black leather tricorn hat, his neck bejewelled by multi-coloured shells. It suggested he was Rasalanian, and wealthy.

"So, did you sleep?" she asked Sir Ralston, as she gazed lazily toward the two captains, dimly lit by the pinky-gold dawn.

"No. I was on watch."

"But you'll sleep later? Once we're moving again?"

He gave a reluctant nod. The scars on his face were etched as black lines upon his pale skin in the dim light. She knew them well now, those scars. *If I go to my cabin, I might just be able to draw them from memory,* she thought. She wasn't much of an artist, but had a decent mind for detail, and had taken to scribbling and doodling sometimes when she was bored, using the quill and ink Lancel had given her in Shellcrest. The handsome blond knight had given her a nice woollen scarf too, which she used as a pillow when she slept here on deck. Thus far, the pouch of coins Barnibus gave her when they parted hadn't seen any use, though she was half tempted to hand it to Captain Rikki when she left him for making her feel so welcome.

Captain Rikki and his crew had been good to her and she'd enjoyed her time here more than she could have expected. Some she even considered friends now. Rikki, certainly, and little Billy too. She liked Lanky Larry a great deal and Tanner Twelve Teeth had a way of making her laugh with that deadpan humour of his. She'd even grown to find Bawdy Bron's jokes amusing rather than mildly insulting, and even Kevin the Con's lascivious looks had lessened of late, as he realised she'd never invite him to her bed. There was a comfort to Ralph the Mouth's constant chattering and Pretty Paul Parry had proven himself a delicious singer, quite the rival of Lark among Lady Marian's men.

In all, her time here had been one of laughter and joy after her experience under Lady Cecilia's care. Gone was the threat of being outed as a spy. Gone were the Kastors and their cruelty. The cold and snow had been replaced by sun and sea and even her dark dreams had grown less common. It all conspired to make her wonder about leaving the men at all. A part of her wanted to stay, she knew that much, even though she knew that she couldn't. Because this was but a short break from what lay in wait. *I must get to Aram. I must find the truth of who I am. Part Seaborn I may be, but I don't belong on this ship...*

Her eyes went down to Old Hob with that final thought. As ever, he was sitting on his crate, fiddling with his nets, and taking no interest at all in his grandson's discussion on the forecastle, humming to himself as he liked to do. It was the old man who'd outed her as Seaborn a week ago, pointing from the bow of the ship as she emerged from her first dive, and saying, "She's Seaborn, this one," before tottering back off to his trunk. Three and a half minutes. That's how long she'd gone under for on her first dive and it had seemed like nothing to her at the time. After Old Hob had made his proclamation, they'd taken to testing her to make sure of it.

"See how long you can hold your breath," little Billy Bowen had said excitedly, treading water beside her. "Go on. I'll come down too. I'll hold my breath as long as I can this time. If you can beat me, then you're *definitely* Seaborn. *Definitely*!" He'd taken her hand and dived.

Over five minutes had passed before she'd returned to the surface, and in truth she might have stayed down longer. Twice more she'd dived and twice more she'd extended her time beneath the waves. On her third descent she stayed down for six and a half minutes. By her fourth, she'd stretched herself to just under eight, and felt like she had more to give, if she pushed herself a little further. If there had been any lingering doubt that she had the blood of Thala in her, all that put it out like a candle in a storm. And strong blood too, Rikki Bowen told her. "Not normal to pick it up so swift, Saska," he said, as he sat astride the womanly figurehead of his ship, legs dangling over her shoulders, watching. "I'll wager you've got some greathouse blood in you, and recent too, hey."

If that was true, it can only have been from a couple of generations ago at the earliest, Saska had worked out. She had a good idea who her mother was, and knew her father was some Bladeborn lord. Did one of them have a Seaborn parent? She'd asked the Wall about that, and he'd shown some knowledge of Princess Leila Nemati, her alleged mother. "There's no Seaborn in that line," he'd told her. "House Nemati is a pureblood Lumosi Lightborn House. If there's Seaborn in you it's through your father."

"But my father was an Ilithoran lord," she said. "At least, that's what Ranulf told me. They're hardly known to mix blood with Seaborn houses."

"It isn't common," Sir Ralston Whaleheart agreed. "But it does happen."

If he knew of any such instances, however, he didn't speak of them, and eventually Saska had put it from her mind. But still...Bladeborn, Lightborn, now Seaborn. *I'm a mutt,* she thought, *a mix of this and that.* She wasn't certain how to feel about all that.

She reached into her pocket now as the sun began to peek over the eastern horizon, and drew out a small piece of grey coral. It was unspectacular, really, and entirely forgettable to anyone but her. She turned it between her fingers, running her skin over the rough pitted surface, wondering just what it might say about her future. For a reason she couldn't fathom, the small chunk of coral had called to her when she'd ducked down through the waves for her final dive. The minutes had passed as she'd swum among the fish and turtles, sharks and sea snakes, idly searching through the shells and stones that littered the bed of the sea. There were so many. So many of varied colour and shape and beauty. *Is it this one?* she would wonder, as she picked up a smooth shell that seemed to glow with striations of red and golden light. *Or this one,* she'd think, *it has to be this one,* as she fetched a piece of multicoloured stone that sparkled with opal and topaz, sapphire and emerald all, as though lit from its very core. Yet each one she threw away, each one she let go, until the final minute of her final dive came upon her, and she saw that dull grey hunk of once-living rock and knew...*this is it.*

Why she knew it, she didn't know. It wasn't beautiful or striking or interesting in any way. But, for whatever reason, it demanded she pick it up. So she had, leaving all the other jewels of the deep behind, returning to the ship and stashing the coral away in her pocket as the anchor was pulled and the sails caught the wind.

She turned it over between her fingers again, admiring its lack of beauty. The Wall was watching. "Why do you carry that stone around with you?" he asked her.

She smiled a far-off smile, and gave Old Hob a quick glance. "It's magic," she said. "That's what the men say."

Sir Ralston nodded and offered no further questioning. That was typical of him. He didn't tend to show much interest in the world around him, just the duty he was here to perform. But Saska spoke anyway, answering the question he might have asked. "The men say Old Hob can read your future in the pits and grooves. They say that everyone has a shell or rock or piece of coral that calls to them. If you take it to Hob, he'll tell you where you're going."

"Aram," the Wall grunted. "It doesn't take a bit of rock to tell us that."

"And after?"

The Wall loomed so high above her she had to crane her neck to look into his face. It looked much like the coral itself, Saska decided, craggy and rough and grey. "I don't know. I'm just here to protect you, my lady. I am your Wall now."

She smiled. "So you always tell me." She nodded toward the other boat. "I suppose you were hoping they were corsairs and pirates, ready to leap aboard and slay us all."

He frowned. "Why would I hope for that?"

"Because that's your job. It can't be very fulfilling, standing watching me all day, with nothing to do. Come on, you can admit it. You want something to happen. A part of you does, anyway. You want someone to attack me."

"I don't enjoy killing so much as you seem to think."

"No? But you're so good at it."

He huffed and gave no answer. A silence fell between them, heavy like a wet cloak. Then he moved his eyes down to the grey coral in Saska's hand. "So? Have you spoken to him yet."

"Old Hob?" She shook her head, tossing the coral from hand to hand. "No. I'm too scared, I think. I'll probably just throw it back into the ocean, you know." But she wouldn't, not really. She rather liked having it in her pocket, as a totem if nothing else. Even if she never spoke to the old man again, it would be a reminder of her time here on the Steel Sister, among these crazy Bowens and Hobs.

On the far side of the ship, the conference was coming to an end. Rikki and the foreign captain gripped one another's forearms and then the paunchy man with the hawkish nose and tricorn hat strolled back to the starboard gunwale, climbed up, and hopped the short gap to his own ship. He began calling orders as his men unfastened the lines, and within a few short minutes the vessel was drifting off on the currents. Meanwhile, Captain Rikki and Lanky Larry remained in quiet discussion. Saska thought it about time she joined them.

"What was all that?" she asked, striding across the ship and straight up to the forecastle. Upon the main deck the Steel Sister was coming to life, men emerging from below to get at the rigging and lines. The smell of bacon and eggs came with them, which meant Maid Marlon was cooking up some breakfast. Marlon was neither a Bowen nor a Hob, but had been on the ship for near two decades all the same. They called him maid because he saw to the cooking and cleaning duties. It wasn't the best moniker among the men, Rikki was ready to admit.

Rikki Bowen gave answer to Saska's query. "Merchant captain I know from back home," he said, as the other ship pulled away, and the heavyset merchant gave a final wave from the helm. The sun was rising now in the east, and the skies were clear, promising another blazing hot day. Saska could see dolphins leaping from the water nearby, spinning and flipping as they went. "We call him Rooster for that beak of his, and because he likes to get up early. Anyhow, he's just come out of Aram, and by the skin of his teeth by the sounds of it. Trouble brewing there, Saska. Larry thinks we ought to change course and try to shift our wares elsewhere." He waved to the islands, then back to shore. "There'll be buyers out across the Telleshis, or we can head for Cloaklake, and hope it's calmer there. Or even the Port of Matia. There's a thriving market trade there too, and that'd get you and Sir Ralston closer to Aram, so..."

Saska was shaking her head. "Wait. Just...hang on a minute." Her forehead rumpled into a frown. "We're *going* to Aram, aren't we? You've got buyers, and you promised you'd take us there. There's a whole lot of whiskey and wine down in the hold that's testament to that, Rikki."

"Aye, I'm aware, Saska. And believe me, I'm not one for turning around when the going gets tough. But according to Rooster, it's just not safe there now. Northmen are being attacked all over the south, we hear, and that violence has begun to gobble up Aram too. Started out west in Solas and has spread its way east, all along the Capital Road. Now I don't want to let you down, but I've got my boy Billy to think of, and the rest of the men besides. We can fend for ourselves out here on the seas well enough...this is where we Bowens belong... but pulling into harbour in Aram, with northmen being slaughtered..." He gave a swift shake of the head. "I'm not sure I can take that risk."

Lanky Larry was nodding solemnly, holding a hand to his long pointy chin. His opinion was always worth hearing. "We've seen more ships than usual on the waters, heading north. I had wondered why until now, but clearly they're running from something. Many are heading into the Telleshis to hunker down until the fighting passes. I've half a mind to say we should do the same. I have friends there. We'd be welcomed. But in Aram we won't be, that much is certain. Will we be harmed? Who can tell. I'm sure some of these tales of violence are exaggerated. But even so, trading won't be possible. The best we can do is slip close to harbour and row you in on the skiff. But for that, we'd be taking a risk. And you don't strike me, Saska, as a girl who'd want to put us in danger, if it can be avoided."

Damn you, Larry, she thought, *putting things so rationally.* "No," she had to admit. "Of course not." She turned to the Wall. "Seems you might find yourself needed sooner than we thought, Sir Ralston. Best get to sharpening your blades." *And I'll get to sharpening mine.*

The Wall bowed his head. "I will not let you come to harm, my lady."

Saska looked back to Captain Rikki. "The Port of Matia?" she asked. "Could you get us there at least?"

"Aye," he replied. "Rooster seems to think it's a little safer there, for the time being, anyway. We can run in and drop you off in the skiff, as Larry says."

"And then?" Saska wondered. The plan had been to drop her and the Wall at the harbour in Aram, where Rikki and his men would set about unloading their stocks and selling them to their buyers. That would take a day, perhaps two, and then they'd be setting sail back to Rasalan. Yet now...Saska was thinking of the map down in Rikki's cabin. "Matia's quite a long way from Aram," she recalled. "A couple of hundred miles, as the crow flies..."

"As the eagle flies," squeaked a voice. Little Billy stepped in to join them, yawning, dressed in nought but breeches. His little pot belly and skinny arms were almost copper-coloured from the kiss of the sun. "That's what they say here. As the eagle flies. They love eagles in Aramatia." He looked up at Saska, then his father, then Larry, then the Wall, angling his head higher and higher as he went. The Wall stood almost twice his height. "What's happening? Is that the Rooster's ship out there?" He pointed.

"Aye, son. He's just left. Was aboard a few minutes ago."

"Why?"

Rikki quickly caught his son up on what was happening. The boy didn't like it. "No," he said, after his father had finished. He folded his skinny arms and shifted to stand between Saska and the Wall, looking up at the others. "No, we said we're taking them to Aram, and so we're taking them to Aram. I like having them around, pa. I don't want them to leave yet."

"Nor do any of us, Billy. It's been a pleasure having them both aboard. But this is how it must be, and you'll not go making a fuss, do you hear me? You have to learn to deal with your disappointments better. You'll encounter many in life, believe me." The little lad huffed to that, but said nothing. Rikki turned to Saska. "You were asking about going from Matia to Aram."

She nodded. "I suppose we'll buy horses, or hitch a ride on a wagon or something. It's finding a mount that will take Sir Ralston's weight that's the problem. Southern steeds aren't bred to bear godsteel."

"You'll not find one," said Lanky Larry, with conviction. "A cart'll be your best bet, I'd say. I can't even imagine how heavy you must be, Sir Ralston, fully armoured and armed."

"I may know someone who can help," said Captain Rikki, rubbing a hand along the coarse black stubble of his cheek. Little Billy imitated him. He did that a lot. "I've a contact or two who might be able to arrange transport for you, at a price..."

"I have coin..." Saska started.

"No, this one's on me," Rikki broke in. "I promised I'd get you to

Aram, and I will. If I can't sail you there, I'll see the pair of you carted down the Capital Road instead."

"I'm not sure that's wise," said Larry, thoughtful. "The Capital Road is oft travelled. Better to take the back way and head through the Aramatian Plains. There're many ways and routes through those lands and they'd be less likely to come to harm."

"Harm?" Little Billy gave an amused giggle. "Who's going to try to harm *them*? No one would dare." The boy was still in his phase of thinking Sir Ralston the mightiest man ever to walk the earth.

"Many," suggested his father, darkly. "A big man makes a big target, no matter how strong he is. And there are famed warriors here in the south too, son, as you well know." He turned to the Wall. "Best you keep your cloak and hood on to hide your face. Saska's got that Aramatian skin tone, but not you, Sir Ralston. Be better if you stay hidden, much as you can."

It all seemed settled with that, and sad as she'd be to leave these men, Saska knew they were making the right choice. Once more, she remembered King Godrin's words. *You're exactly where you're meant to be*. Whenever her life took any unexpected turn, she went back to them, and they gave her comfort. *I'm guessing this is my path, then.* She'd still get to Aram, hopefully, it would just take a little longer. The only problem was, she'd be alone with the Wall from now on. And he wasn't much of a conversationalist.

"Right then, let's pull anchor and get some wind in these here sails, hey," said the captain. We'll get into Matia tomorrow night, if luck will allow it and the winds are good." He looked down at Saska, then up and up at the Wall. "How does that sound to you?"

"More than fair, Captain Bowen," said Sir Ralston, with booming grace.

Saska nodded her agreement, but was a little too sad to conjure words. All she could do was smile and curl an arm around little Billy's shoulder, who was looking down at the decks, glum.

And that was that.

As the sun climbed the skies, the Steel Sister cut the waves, changing course for the Port of Matia.

16

Elyon

A brisk wind blew about him as he stood upon a balcony of grey-white marble, looking out over the White City of Ilithor. Beneath the cloud-clogged skies, lights glittered like stars. Some rose high among distant towers set about the mountains and snow-capped peaks. Others lit up the walkways and terraces and white stone courtyards that descended through the levels of the city, down and down into the deep darkness that pooled within the valley below.

Behind him, all was noise and merriment, a great thick blur of voices and laughter and music coalescing into one. Skins skirled and strings strummed and the drums were ever drumming. Elyon cared not for such celebrations right now. The balcony on which he took refuge was small and private, one of many affixed to the sides of the main feast hall in the Palace of Ilithor. The hall was split over three levels. On the first the tables were arranged, a hundred heaving tables full of merrymaking men and women, lords and ladies, landed knights and household knights and hedge knights besides, and the manifold courtiers and companions and cup-bearers in attendance. Above it ran two galleries. The first was wider than the one above it, with several smaller areas and alcoves in which to sit and gather in private groups, away from the feast below. The second terrace, where Elyon had escaped to, was rather more narrow, a red-carpeted walkway encircling the feast hall two levels up, surrounded on all sides by secluded balconies offering ranging views over the city.

And solitude, Elyon thought. He was alone on this third level for now, alone with his company and his thoughts. In truth, these social functions were starting to bore him, and the days to come promised many more. Occasions that the old Elyon would have once relished, but the new iteration did not. Because that foolish boy was dead, he knew, and now stood in his place a man. An heir. And perhaps even a lord...

Amron Daecar...is dead, whispered a cruel ugly voice in his head. Those words were louder than all the voices and laughter and music below, louder than the drums and skins and strings. Those words were embedded deep and dark in his head now, and ever did they come with an image of a foul little rat king sneering from his throne.

He drew a breath and sunk the contents of the goblet he'd brought up here with him. He'd been wise enough to bring a full jug too, and saw fit to filling his cup. *Amron Daecar...is dead,* came King Hadrin's spiteful voice again as he poured. He took another swig, but the voice came again, and again, and again. He flexed his sword hand, and took another drink. The din below was a blur of background noise, but in his head his thoughts were stark as a single black raincloud in a bright blue sky.

Was he telling the truth? Is Father truly gone? He'd wondered that many times over the last week, but had no way of telling for sure. News from the North Downs had dried up like a puddle in summer, and Amara's crows hadn't flown his way in weeks. *Is she doing it to keep the truth from me? Is she intending to tell me of my father's death in person?* He grimaced at that thought. It was plausible, certainly, but so was the idea that Hadrin was just playing a cruel jape. *But his eyes...*He remembered the rat king's beady black eyes. There had been no lie in them, no jest. *But...he cannot be dead. How...why...where...*

"Are you quite well, Sir Elyon? I was told you'd escaped up here, alone."

Elyon Daecar spun. A figure stood at the mouth of the balcony, wreathed in robes of silken blue. Her hair was gold, skin cream, eyes of bright azure. Behind her, firelight shone from a hundred braziers and torches across the three levels of the hall. Flames seemed to dance about her hair. "Mel..." he managed. "I...I didn't hear you coming."

"It's loud, Elyon. Plenty loud enough to hide my dainty steps. Or is this your way of calling me fat? I don't think I've put on so much weight, since last we saw one another, do you?"

She came forward, running her hands down the sides of her svelte body, curved at the hips and bust. *Gods, I'd half forgotten how beautiful she was,* he thought. She moved to kiss him, planting her full lips to his cheek. It seemed for a moment like she'd target his lips, but moved at the last second. A coquettish smile graced her face when she drew back. "So? Is there a reason you're up here all alone?"

A hundred reasons, he might have told her. *A thousand reasons, or just the one. Amron Daecar...is dead.* He cleared his throat and said, "The views are better up here. And I'm not in much of a mood for merry-making, Mel."

"But you are for alliterating, clearly." He missed the smile that clung to her lips, playful, demure, seductive all at once. She took his arm and turned him to look out over the city. "It's good to see you, Elyon. But this isn't the night for taking in the views. It's so dark. The stars and moon are veiled."

"It's beautiful, all the same," he told her. "I have always wanted to visit Ilithor, as you know. For many years it's been high on my list."

"Well here we are. Nice and *high*." She gave the view a cursory look. "Shall we go in, where it's warm? The wind is bitter cold, Elyon."

She nuzzled a little closer to him, stealing the warmth of his body, and before he knew it, she'd tucked herself under his arm. The smell of her hair poured up his nose. A smell to give him comfort. *And she could too,* he thought. *Is it wise to walk that path again?*

"So tell me...how have you been these months, Elyon Daecar. Mallister said the two of you have been getting along well." She gave a shiver, and drew a little closer. "I'm glad to hear it. You're two of my favourite people, you know."

"Your brother is fine company," he said. "He has posited the idea of a marriage between us, on several occasions. Apparently House Monsort is on the up, he tells me. Your father prospers with new lands and mining operations and grows wealthy and influential off the back of it. And he promises, with much enthusiasm, that he will make an excellent brother-in-law too."

Melany gave out a tinkling laugh, more sweet than the singers and strings below. "Don't listen to him, Elyon. Mallister has always liked to tease. It is true my father has thrived of late, but House Monsort is no match for House Daecar. And especially not now that you're heir. Your father made it clear enough that he'd never permit us to wed."

Amron Daecar...is dead, laughed Hadrin's voice. "Times have changed," is all Elyon said. "But that is not something to consider now."

"Of course not. Not now, not ever. We knew that from the start." She shivered again, as a breeze billowed her skirts. "I heard about Vesryn. I must say, I found it hard to believe when I was first told. I always liked him. These last months...they must have been difficult, dealing with the fallout of all that's happened."

"They were." Elyon wasn't willing to speak on Vesryn. *My mother and brother are dead, my uncle is a traitor, my father...who knows.* "Maybe he'll show up sooner or later, maybe not. I hardly care, to be honest."

She gave that a frown, looking up at him from beneath his bearded chin. Blue pools of radiant light sparkled in her eyes. "Did something happen between the two of you?"

"Nothing." He turned to look back into the hall. "Come on, let's go in. You're shivering, Mel."

He took the time to arrange his thoughts as they stepped back onto the second floor gallery, overlooking the elegantly furnished feast ball below. Elyon had promised himself that he'd not fall for Melany Monsort again, nor give in to his desire for her. These last weeks she'd been distant from his thoughts, overtaken by another in his dreams. A girl of silver and blue, with skin like the sun. A girl who joined him as he slept, beguiling and beautiful, mystifying and mysterious all at once. A girl to whom he'd failed in his promise. *Del,* he thought, as he stood at the gallery railing, looking down over the tables below, the serving boys and girls with their trenchers and trays, flagons and flasks. *A boy of sixteen summers...black messy hair...lanky build.* He scanned idly, but saw no one to match the description. And he wouldn't, not here. He'd not found the boy anywhere...

"Elyon, you look troubled." Melany gave a little tug at his arm. "Is there something specific that ails you? Are you...sure you don't want to talk about Vesryn?"

"There's nothing to say."

"Well...if you're certain."

He nodded, silent. There was only one person who knew all his secrets and she was thousands of miles away. He turned his eyes down to the feast once again, looking at the stage at the northern side of the hall. It seemed that King Janilah had departed from the royal table now, though Rylian remained with his sons and daughter, who sat beside her husband-to-be, trying not to bring up the contents of her stomach as he sat small and unsightly beside her.

"How is she?" he asked, looking at Princess Amilia. "She cannot have taken the news of the wedding well."

"She is dutiful," Melany responded. "Hadrin will never make her happy, but she can pretend to be well enough."

That was true. The princess was smiling radiantly under the gaze of the crowd, laughing occasionally as Hadrin spoke. Elyon thought of how she'd done the same with Aleron, at the first feast in which they'd met. That tinkering laughter had made him rather jealous, in truth, though that very night he'd ended up in a dark corner with Melany, hands and lips where they shouldn't be, before getting into a brawl with Sir Mallister over her honour. All that brought a rueful smile to his lips. *Life was so much more simple, back then.*

"Amilia was born for this, Elyon," Melany told him. "She will do what she must, and bear Hadrin an heir. Such is the lot of highborn ladies, married off by their fathers to men they do not love."

"No more than breeders," Elyon grunted. Below, he could see Lady Cecilia Blakewood, off at some side table in the corner, among the less illustrious in attendance. The woman had tried to have Saska raped by Borgin and Sir Griffin. *And if I find myself alone with her...*In his current state of mind, he wasn't certain what he might do. *I could throw her from a balcony as King Ellis was,* he thought. *Or trip her down one of the steep flights of stairs around here. And there are chasms, chasms so deep that no one would ever find her...*Tempting as the thought was, he'd cause no trouble in the White City. His resentments ran deep, but he wasn't so foolish as to unveil them. *No, I will scheme, as they do,* he thought. His eyes went back to Rylian Lukar, sitting beside his father's empty throne. *If only the prince could be made a king, how much better would this world of ours be?*

Elyon felt Lady Melany take his hand, and give a pull as she began to walk away. "Come on, we're leaving."

"What?" He stood his ground. "Where are you going?"

"Away from here. Anywhere. There's too much noise and too much brooding going on in you, Elyon Daecar. I'd rather have you to myself. Come on."

"Mel...we really shouldn't."

"Shouldn't what? Walk around the palace? Take a stroll across the bridges and platforms?" She gave a little laugh. "Not every woman wants to jump straight into bed with you, Elyon, if that's what you're thinking. Believe me, I've been there, I've done it, and I've had quite enough of *that*, thank you very much." Her face and everything about her said otherwise, but Mel did like to tease. "Go, fetch that jug of wine. We can drink as we walk and talk. To help...loosen our tongues."

Elyon looked down to the feast once more, doubtful. "Shouldn't you be here for Amilia? She may wish to call upon you, after Hadrin departs..."

"She won't, Elyon. It was Amilia who told me to come and see you."

That surprised him a little. "Truly?"

"Of course. Amilia cares about you, Elyon, and said you seemed quite...distant, when you saw her earlier. She was adamant I try to cheer you up. So don't you worry about our pretty little princess. She has many others to attend to her, believe me."

Elyon nodded slowly. He'd seen Amilia again upon entering the feast hall, though she'd been sitting beside King Hadrin at the time, and it was all he could do not to slap the look from his ratty face. He'd been seated thereafter at a table second in importance to the royal table atop the stage, with some of the other greatlords and ladies.

Mel tugged at his arm again. "Go on then. The wine, Elyon. We don't have all night."

He did as she bid him, fetching the jug, as she led him along the gallery and through a door out of the hall. Within minutes the bluster of the room was fading behind them leaving nothing but their footsteps behind, as they worked along a torchlit corridor with alcoved balconies to the left. The wind whispered softly through them, causing the firelight to flicker in their sconces and cast capering shadows upon the walls. "So I suppose Prince Dalton is not in need of your protection tonight, then?" Melany asked, taking the jug of wine from him, and enjoying a neat little sip. "I have heard you have spent many nights on duty, guarding his tent from dusk through to dawn."

"Dalton's need for me will lessen here," Elyon explained. "Your king seems certain the city is well protected from intruders, and with all these bowmen about, I'm inclined to agree." There were many, he'd seen, archers and crossbowmen stationed at the gates between levels, watching from the parapets and wall walks with their godsteel-tipped quarrels and arrows ready to be loosed. "If Dalton Taynar continues to be guarded night and day here, it will only paint him as paranoid."

"Janilah has three of his sworn swords on him, always," Melany put in to that. "I rather doubt anyone would ever call the Warrior King paranoid."

"It's rather different for a king, Mel, and let's be clear, Janilah isn't short of enemies."

"Oh? Would you count yourself among them?"

He gave no answer to that. Here, he could never be sure who might be listening.

"Well...I'm glad," Melany went on. "About Dalton, that is. I was worried that your nights would be taken. I rather hope I might have you to myself, for some of them." She clutched his arm with that and drew him into an alcove, shoving him against a wall. There was a look in her eye, hungry and ravenous. *Kiss me,* her face demanded, and when he didn't, she did it herself, pressing her lips into his, warm and wet and smooth.

He pulled back. "I'm...I'm not sure..."

There was flicker of hurt in her eyes. Or was it something else. *Disappointment? Anger?* She covered it all in a smile, but Elyon could see it, behind the veil she wore. "Well I don't know what came over me," she said, waving her hand to fan her face. "The wine. Let's just blame the wine, shall we?"

"You don't need to blame anything, Mel. I just..."

"What?" she asked, her sapphire eyes gleaming in the torchlight. "What is wrong, Elyon? Speak to me. *Tell me.*" She closed in again, setting the wine jug aside on a ledge. Her hands went to his face, running through his hair, down his neck, massaging scalp and skin alike. Already he could feel himself weakening to her, stirring below. He shut his eyes for a split second and felt her lips meet his once more, and this time he couldn't help himself. His hands were upon her body all of a sudden, running up her back, her neck, through her long soft golden hair, and so hers came forward too, reaching down, down, down...

He caught her wrist. "No," he breathed, panted out the word. "No, I promised. I promised I wouldn't, Mel."

"Who?" She squeezed gently down there, massaging. "*Who* did you promise, Elyon Daecar?" Her lips twisted playfully, and her hand twisted too. "There isn't...anyone *else*, is there? Now don't tell me you fell for a camp follower over in Rasalan. It has been known to happen."

Not a follower, no, he thought. *A captive and a spy. A Bladeborn and Lightborn both.*

"Don't be silly, Mel." He pulled her hand away and paced out of the alcove, back into the open corridor.

She followed him, scooping up the wine jug, taking a languid gulp. A little ran over her lips and down the curve of her collarbone, running between her breasts. "Whoops, would you look at that." She wiped the wine across her pale skin, red like blood, and Elyon's mind only went to Aleron. That gush as Jonik opened his neck. The crimson fountain spreading across the sand. "So...who?" Melany pressed. "Or do you not want me anymore?"

He glanced down between his legs. "What does that say?"

"*That*?" she laughed. "It says nothing, Elyon. It takes but a gust of wind to make a man stiff."

He found himself laughing, and gods did he enjoy her still. "Give yourself more credit," he teased. "You're rather more alluring than a breeze, Lady Monsort."

"Well I should hope so. I am not lacking in suitors, you know."

"I am aware."

"Then give me an answer." She folded her arms. "*Who* did you promise? My brother? Has he demanded you keep your hands off me, unless you take me for a wife? Because that won't happen, Elyon. And my brother can keep himself out of it."

"It wasn't Sir Mallister."

"Then who? Your uncle? I know Vesryn didn't approve."

"Vesryn's approval never much mattered to me."

"Well?" She stared at him and then saw. "I see. This is *you*. You promised yourself you'd not weaken again."

"I won't be here long, Mel. I didn't think it would be wise to complicate things again."

"Complicate? There is nothing complicated about two adults copulating. Not the way you do it, at least."

He laughed long and true and took the wine off her, drinking deep. "Your tart tongue remains in good order, I see. I might think my Auntie Amara had already arrived to hear you speak like that."

"Well that would be rather inappropriate, Elyon." A smile fluttered on her lips. "I would hope your auntie has no knowledge of your expertise in the bedroom."

"Everyone seems to have a knowledge of my expertise in the bedroom. Or at least my antics. Everywhere I go this so-called reputation precedes me."

"Oh poor you. To have a reputation for bedding beautiful women, and stealing the hearts of highborn maids. Life is so hard, isn't it Elyon."

His laughter soured a little at that, as Hadrin's voice rasped in his ear. *Amron Daecar...is dead.* He gave a false smile and turned aside.

Melany stepped over a moment later. "You've suffered, I know," she said, more delicately. "That jibe was perhaps inappropriate."

"It's fine. I just have a lot on my mind, that's all."

"Care to share? I'm a good listener, you know."

"I know." She always was, back in Varinar, and during the weeks it took to get there. They'd shared a lot in their time together. *But not so much as I shared with Saska.*

"But you won't tell me," she identified. "That's OK, we needn't talk about anything too distressing, if you don't want to. Let's just walk, Elyon, and catch up on our lives. I want to know how it was in Harrowmoor, how it was to be in a warcamp. I want to know what a siege is like. Will you tell me that, at least? I've been stuck here tending Amilia, while everything happens out there. Take me away, would you? Speak to me of what you've seen."

"What I've seen," he said quietly. "Those are not pleasant tales, Mel."

"Tell me anyway, will you?" She took his hand. "I want to know it all."

Well you can't, he might have said, but in the end he just nodded and set into it, taking her through his time in Rasalan, censoring and holding backing much of it, dodging this truth and that fact, and half of what had actually happened. Melany smiled, nodded, laughed where she felt she should, clutched his arm and swooned at times, but mostly she just listened. And all the while they walked, through the palace and the high elevated levels of the city, across firelit courtyards and thick stone bridges and walkways that swung in the wind, with great deep chasms plunging into the darkness beneath them. At one point as they strolled, they passed beneath the king's throne room, where Elyon had been earlier. Melany pointed up to the balcony, high above them, then down at the stone floor where they stood. "This is where it happened," she said. "King Ellis. This is where he fell."

The drop was longer than Elyon had expected, some fifty or sixty yards, he guessed. There were still some red stains upon the stone, and dark marks in the cracks between the wide flat cobbles, where the blood had trickled in and congealed. Around the square, some figures in white cloaks were shuffling about, picking through the grooves and gaps and searching the flowerbeds and plant pots that bordered the square. "They're searching for pieces of him?" Elyon guessed.

Melany nodded. "They come out each night, when the courtyard is quiet. It's thought a few bits of skull might still be scattered out here."

"Janilah is more thorough than I thought."

"I think it's at Queen Elitha's request. She wants her late husband whole and one when he's returned to Varinar for burial."

Elyon continued to watch the acolytes as they worked, diligently searching inch-by-inch around different parts of the courtyard, fingering at stone and dirt in search of skull. Then he moved to the eastern edge and looked up at the balcony. He'd had a decent view of it from the throne room earlier, when he met the king, but this gave him another vantage. "The balustrade is higher than I thought it would be," he said. "Ellis must have been steaming drunk to have fallen."

"I hear he was leaning over the edge, looking at something in the courtyard. And his footwear...it's said he slipped and went over. It does happen, sometimes, with those unfamiliar with the city."

"Were there any witnesses?" Elyon looked around. There were some other buildings bordering the courtyard, grand white buildings with pillared entrances and high arched doors. "Who lives in these?" They had the look of city residences for some of the greatlords. Melany confirmed as much. "And the witnesses?" Elyon pressed.

"I thought you knew," she said. "There were several knights in the throne room when it happened, even some of King Ellis's Greycloaks. Sir Nathaniel Oloran, Sir Gerald Strand, Sir Alyn Porter,...all where there."

"I know about that," Elyon said. He regarded her a moment. "That sounded awfully rehearsed, Mel. It seems you've learned the party line."

"Party line?"

"I'm jesting." He flicked his wrist to dismiss it. Everyone knew who was there that day. It wasn't just the three Greycloaks, but a pair of Janilah's Six as well, Sir Owen Armdall and Sir Fredrick Ruxmond, and his natural daughter Cecilia Blakewood was said to have been there too. A well selected group, Elyon and others had thought, to conceal the crime of regicide. "But no, I mean witnesses down here, in the square?" he went on, pointing here and there. "I suspect it's a popular enough spot. Surely there were some people here who saw what happened."

"Well...perhaps there were. I don't know, Elyon. You seem to have me pegged as an investigator of some sort, but I only know the same as everyone else. But..." She frowned at him. "You seem to be suggesting something untoward happened. That Ellis didn't fall by accident."

"Rumours, Mel. Warcamps are fertile ground for them, and they spring up all the time. Soldiers need to do something to amuse themselves between battles."

"Isn't that what the camp brothels are typically for? So men don't conjure damaging lies as they sit and drink around cookfires and such? I would say anyone starting a rumour like that ought to have his tongue torn out, so he can tell no more. These sorts of lies can cause much harm."

"And lies they are, I'm sure." Elyon swigged the cold pure air of Ilithor. It tasted sweeter than any he'd ever breathed. "Come on then, let's keep going. I'm starting to feel morbid standing here, watching this lot search for skull and bone."

Mel continued the tour, telling him more of her own experiences as they pushed through the stiffening winds and the night turned dark and darker still. Her time in the palace sounded quite dull, however. "I have largely been trying to keep Amilia's spirits up," she said. "First there was her grief over Aleron, and then she had to contend with the thought of wedding Hadrin. I feel sorry for her, truly. A queen she may be, but she remains a thrall all the same."

"To Janilah?" Elyon gave a laugh to keep things light. "Aren't we all?"

Soon enough the winds began to pick up further, bitter cold and stinging with snow, forcing them back inside. They decided it best to call it a night, so returned to the palace to get warm, and get wine. Melany's own room was within the princess's quarters, in pride of place among the loftier floors, though Elyon's temporary abode was rather lower down. "How many rooms are there here?" he wondered as they went. He found himself putting aside his suspicions and letting the wonder of the grand chambers and halls and staircases embrace him. The Palace of Ilithor was a true marvel, perching atop the Sky City like a great eagle gazing down from its nest. Clothed either side by the high peaks of the Hammersongs, it was the very pinnacle of Ilith's creations, luxurious and spacious and sumptuous in design, running deep into the mountains at the rear.

"Hundreds," was the only answer Melany gave him. "Many hundreds, Elyon. I'll be sure to count them for you, next time."

Elyon's bedchamber was a relatively modest place, compared to many of the great rooms they passed, tucked up in the palace's southern wing. Lady Melany gave a puckish smile as they entered. "Well now, it seems they've put you down in the servant's quarters, Elyon. What a pokey little room this is. How *will* you survive?"

"I'll manage." She was being aggressively sarcastic, but he answered her straight all the same. "Wine?"

"Why else would I be here?"

"I wonder." He poured two glasses.

The room was actually much grander then she was making out. Though not huge in size it remained finely appointed, with a four-poster bed, ornate hearth, lounging sofa, desk and chairs, warm rich rugs and even a golden chamberpot to dirty up when needed. The balcony wasn't looking east through the valleys, as the finest apartments allowed, but southwards instead. From it he could see some of the white towers and building-tops descending into the darkness of the city's southern front, faint firelight marking them here and there amid the thickening grey mists. Beyond, the southern stretches of the Hammersongs rose up high and black and grand. Somewhere further out, the great watchtower of Hammerhigh would be keeping its constant vigil for threats, manned by Bladeborn soldiers with particularly gifted eyesight. "Not much to look at really," came a voice behind him, as he stared out that way. "I rather think you'll prefer *this* view."

He turned, and there she was, nude as her name-day, clutching a chalice of wine between her fingers, smiling. Whatever thoughts were in his head was instantly banished. "Mel..." he managed to splutter. "What...I thought..."

"Shhh now, Elyon. It doesn't matter what you thought."

It was the same as before, the same as the first time. She'd dropped her dress in her room in Keep Daecar and that had been enough for him. *Am I so easy to manipulate? So easy to turn?* He managed to take a short step back as she drew forward, though his body felt stiff as stone. A moment later she was upon him, pulling his hands onto her body, pressing her lips back onto his. What strength he had in him to evade her advances was fast in retreat, washing out like a swift moving tide. Once, twice, trice he considered pulling away, but each time he'd soon succumb. And in his ear she was whispering words that only weakened him further. "Forget your promises, I want you, Elyon. I've missed you...oh how I've missed you." She panted, her breath hot against his ear, and nibbled at his lobe. "Just tonight, just this one. I promise. That's *my* promise, Elyon. Just tonight."

A promise you'll break, just as I'm breaking mine, he knew, as they stepped toward his bed. It was futile to deny her, futile to deny himself. *Just this once,* he said in his head, and then repeated it out loud. "Just the once, Mel."

She agreed between kisses. "Yes...just...just this once...Elyon. Just... just this once."

Lies, he thought, but that wasn't enough to stop him. His clothes joined hers on the floor, and they tumbled onto the bed. *Amron Daecar...is dead,* spat a voice in his head. *Amron Daecar...is dead*...But he ignored it, drowned it out with Melany's moans, sought comfort in her embrace and the joy her company brought him. Yet all the while, there were little flashes in his head. Flashes of another, gold of skin not of hair, honest and confounding and confusing all at once. *Where is she,* he began to wonder, as he lay atop the girl he'd once loved. *Is she safe? Is she free?* Elyon felt his lip bitten, snatching him from his thoughts.

"You're not *here*, Elyon," complained Melany, lying beneath him. "There's a look on your face. Where are you?"

"I'm...I'm here, Mel. Of course...I'm right here."

He went to kiss her again, but she rolled him over, straddling him. The firelight gleamed upon her smooth pale skin, the wind rustling at the balcony, the flames crackling in the hearth. "It's that other girl, isn't it," she said, pressing down on his shoulders, pinning him to the bed. "That one you had in your tent."

Elyon frowned. "You...know about that?"

"Everyone knows about that. She was meant to be a breeder, but you took her for yourself instead. I wonder why. It's said she was very beautiful."

She was, he thought. *More than beautiful, really.* "Nothing happened," he lied. "I was involved in helping lots of Rasal girls escape the Kastor warcamp. That girl was just one of them."

"One you kept in your tent."

Elyon didn't want to talk about this. Not now, not ever. "I didn't take you for the jealous type," he said. "And even so, we're not together, Melany. You've no right to question me on this."

She pressed a little harder at his shoulders. "*Stop* thinking of her, or *anyone* else. I'm right here. Think of me, Elyon. *Me*."

"I...I am." *Gods, she knows what she's doing,* he thought. "How could I not. You're...you're stunning, Melany."

"Then show me. Show me how stunning I am."

"That...sounds...like a challenge," he breathed, as she worked her hips back and forward.

"Then meet it. Let it all out, Elyon. There's too much shadow over you now. Share it with me. Let me help you relax."

There was something about her coaxing that felt a little...off. She'd not been so insistent before, he recalled, and when they'd decided to break off their relationship before leaving Varinar, she'd not attempted to win him back to her bed since. It was he, in fact, who took her to his chambers on their final night together at Eastwatch, before she returned here and Elyon went off to Harrowmoor. *But why now? What is she trying to get from me?*

There was a simple answer to that, of course - pleasure. But all the same, Elyon had grown more suspicious and guarded these last months, and had to wonder if she had another motive. *But what?* A horrible thought went through him, but he didn't give it time to bloom. *No, she's not here for information. She...she wouldn't do that to me. She wouldn't*, he insisted.

Yet still, he came to a decision that night to be careful with his tongue around her. There was only one girl who knew all his secrets, and she was not in this bed, nor this country, this continent. And when they were done, he returned to her in his dreams.

To the girl of silver and blue.

17

Saska

The crew of the Steel Sister spent their final night in celebration, giving Saska and her Wall an impromptu farewell party to send them on their way. Saska went about the crew saying her goodbyes and hearing what words of advice they might offer.

Some even gave her gifts. Bawdy Bron, generous with his ribald jokes, set about writing down as many as he could think of onto a piece of parchment, before folding it and handing it to her. "If you ever feel down, take a read o' these, Sas. Some might just give you a chuckle. There's a few naughty ones in there, but I can see you got a naughty side to you too." She thanked him and tucked the parchment away with her things.

Kevin the Con came to her next. "I'll give you the gift of me, sweetheart," he said in his sleazy voice. "It's your last night here, so let's not waste it. I'll send you off with a big old smile on that pretty face of yours, be sure of that."

A part of her imagined that was true. Kevin had an oily side to him, but he was disarmingly handsome too. But still, she politely declined, as ever.

"Thought you might," he told her, grinning waggishly. "But no matter. I can show you something more practical instead." He set about teaching her a few of his conman tricks, sleight of hand type stuff that might help her pick a pocket or two. "Might come in handy, who knows," he said. "There's a real art to it, swiping something from someone without them knowing. And the rest of the cons I pull; it's not just picking pockets, you know. I'm an artist, sweetheart. And this world is my canvas."

He made it sound so romantic, but Saska could sense a last word coming. She got there before he could. "But it's the bedchamber in which you're most gifted," she said for him. "Right? A true maestro between the sheets."

"Between the legs," he cut in, with that grin. "Mine and yours, sweetheart. We'd fit well together, like pieces of a puzzle. You'd know no pleasure better."

She thought again of her night with Elyon Daecar. "Maybe next time," she said, and walked away.

Another practical gift was given by Tanner Twelve Teeth, who instructed her on several boxing and brawling techniques that she'd not learnt in Thalan. She had a bit of background in certain martial arts, but Tanner's skillset was more suited to the streets. She went away feeling confident in her left hook. "I'd not want to stand in the way of it," Tanner laughed, with that mouth all full of gaps.

The best gift was from little Billy, though. He emerged from below decks, having disappeared for some time, and drew Saska to one side as the men drank to their parting. There was a slightly nervous look on his face. A moment later, she found out why. From behind his back came a necklace of glittering shells and stones and pebbles, multicoloured and marvellous. "I made it for you," he said, chewing his lip, moving his eyes to the side. "I got them that day we dived. When we found out you were Seaborn. I wanted to surprise you later. In Aram. But..."

"I...I don't know what to say. It's beautiful, Billy." It was. There was no lie in that. Tears welled in her eyes from the gesture and she drew him into a hug. "I'll not forget you, Billy Bowen. You know that, right?"

"Aye," the boy croaked. When he pulled back his eyes were glistening. "I'd marry you, you know. One day. Pa says you're too old for me now, but he's just being stupid. You're only eight years older than me. When I'm a hundred, you'll only be a hundred and eight. Then we'll be almost the same age, right?"

"Right," she chuckled, holding the necklace in her hands. "And I'd be lucky to marry you, Billy. Let's just see what happens with the war first. Will you help me put this on?"

He nodded, beaming, and fixed the necklace into place. The shells and pebbles were tied on a string, knocking against one another as she moved and making a light jingling sound. They caught the light of the braziers on deck and gleamed a hundred colours.

"Will you wear it often?" he asked her.

"As often as I can," she promised. "It's the nicest thing anyone's ever given me." It was, for the effort the boy had made. She had the gifts from Lancel and Barnibus, the dagger Sir Ralston had given her from King Godrin, the parchment full of jokes from Bawdy Bron, and now this. Marian had given her a beautiful godsteel blade too, though she didn't have that anymore. She pulled the boy into another hug, and gave him a big wet kiss on the cheek. "You're the sweetest boy in the world, d'you know that?"

He drew back, wiped the wet from his cheek, and grinned. "I know. And I'll be the best sea captain too, when this here becomes my ship. We can sail the seas, man and wife, and have great adventures." He seemed certain all that would happen. "Do you think Giant will come too? I hope he does. I like having him around. He even answered some of my questions earlier. He told me some stories, Saska!"

"You finally wore him down," she laughed. "Did he tell you about the dragon?"

He nodded briskly. "A bit. And other battles in the war. He told me about some of the scars, and how he got them. He's the best, isn't he? I wish I was going with you."

"Now don't you be getting any ideas there, son," said Rikki, stepping over. "This one's like to turn stowaway," he told Saska. "I'm sure there's plenty of hiding spaces under the Wall's cloak he could creep into. Sir Ralston's so big and strong he'd probably never notice." Saska laughed at the image, and the captain grabbed his son's ear, pinching. "Now stop taking up all her time, boy. We're meant to be celebrating. Pretty Paul's about to sing a song."

Sing he did, and sing beautifully, as the stars and moon glittered overhead. They saw a shooting star that night too, and the heavens seemed to burst in colours Saska never knew belonged up there. Some of the wine that the Varin Knights had given them were broken out, and Saska took the opportunity to drink deep. "This is good stuff,"

Kevin the Con proclaimed. "*Such* good stuff. Have a drink, sweetheart...and another...and another. Why not have the whole bottle, in fact."

Little Billy reached up and slapped him. "Shut up, Kevin! I know what you're doing. Trying to get her drunk. She's to be *my* wife, she agreed. I'll have Giant throw you off the ship if you try anything with her again!"

The Wall gave a nod as though happy to oblige. He'd never liked Kevin the Con.

"All right, all right, little man, I'm just having a tease. No need to get violent."

"You deserve it."

"I do. Of course I do." Kevin bowed to the boy. "But many congratulations on your betrothal. I'm sure you'll make one another very happy."

Saska watched on warily. "He's...not serious, is he?" she whispered to the boy's father. "I mean...I wouldn't want to disappoint him or anything, but..."

Rikki Bowen gave a laugh. "He's ten, my lady. Tomorrow he'll be fascinated in something else, don't worry. Though I do declare he'll remember these weeks fondly. We're not accustomed to having guests such as you and Sir Ralston aboard." He smiled and put an arm around her shoulder, giving her a hug. "Now's the night, you know. If ever you were going to speak to my grandfather, this'll be it." He looked over to Old Hob, who was watching from his crate. "He'll not say it, but he's been eager to take a look at that coral you've been carrying around. Why not oblige an old man this fancy, before you step ashore tomorrow eve?"

"I...I don't know, Rikki. What if he tells me I'm going to die in a week's time? Or something else I'd rather not know about?"

"I thought you didn't believe in all that?" He smiled playfully. "It's just a piece of coral, Saska. You don't think it really tells your future, do you?"

"Well...no, I guess. But..." She fingered into her pocket, clutching at the rough hunk of rock. "It did...*call* to me, somehow. I don't know why but this one just stood out, above all the others." She drew it out. "It's dull and grey and ugly, but...I just had to have it. I can't figure out why that is."

"Magic," the captain said. "There's more magic beneath the waves than we know, young lady. And that spot's always been favoured by the Seaborn. Mayhaps that's all it is. Or just a trick of the mind, who knows? Either way, I'll let you decide. I'm sure Old Hob will be discreet, should he read something in that coral you'll not want to hear." He smiled with that, and stepped away.

Saska stood for a moment, mulling it over. The old man was still looking at her, an inviting cast to his eyes. She drew on the cup of wine she was drinking from, then decided to join him. "Mind if I sit?" The old man shuffled a little aside on his crate, and Saska sat down beside him. Some of the men were crooning across the deck, the rest laughing or arguing over this or that, as tended to happen when alcohol was involved. Within all that, she and the old man were alone. "I hear you're eager to fondle my rock." She frowned at her choice of words There was some unpleasant innuendo in there somewhere. "I mean touch my coral. I mean...oh forget it. Here." She handed it over.

Old Hob's hands were as rough and ragged as the rock itself, gouged with deep wrinkles and lines, scarred with a hundred little calluses. Yet he worked them nimbly all the same. "You want to know why I fiddle with these nets all day?" he asked, giving the coral a swift examination. "Keeps my fingers healthy and dexterous for when a moment like this comes along." He began turning the coral more slowly, running his right index finger and thumb upon its surface. His head tilted left and right, and sometimes he closed his eyes a moment, or made a humming sound, or pursed his lips or nodded. Saska watched all the while, her heart thundering.

"You're not going to tell me I'm going to die in a week, are you?" she asked him, a nervous rattle in her voice.

"A week? No." He closed his eyes, and an expression of great and profound concentration came upon him. "No...feels more like two, I'd say."

Saska's eyes flared. Her heart was in her mouth. It made it difficult to speak, but she managed to blurt out, "Two!"

The old man's throat gargled out a chuckle. "Sorry, just a joke I like to play. You set me up, girl. I'd be a fool not to take it."

Suddenly Saska thought this was *all* a joke. She turned her eyes over the deck, expecting to find the entire crew gathered and ready to burst out laughing, as though they played this trick on every newcomer to the ship. But all was as before. The crooning and laughing and arguing was ongoing. She wasn't sure whether to feel relieved or not. *I should never have given it to him,* she thought. *I should have listened to Lanky Larry*. "I suppose it's too late to take it back?" she asked. "Maybe, er...maybe just keep it to yourself, whatever you find. I'm not so sure my nerves can take it."

The old man didn't seem to be listening. He was lost to something, his eyes closed tight, wrinkles wrought deep across his sunbeaten brow. He began nodding to himself, mumbling a few incoherent words. Saska strained to hear what they might be but they were entirely unintelligible. She satisfied herself by trying to read his expression. If he saw something horrible, surely he'd show it on his face? But if he did, there was no great flinch or recoil. The overall impression Saska got was one of confusion. Eventually he opened his eyes and turned to her and said, "Tricky one, you. Very tricky, young lady."

"Why?" She leaned in, regarding him warily. "What does that mean?"

"It means your future is fogged."

"Fogged? As in, you can't see what's in it?"

"Aye, you might say that." He continued to prod and work his fingers at the coral, trying a few new things. If there was a science behind it, Saska wasn't seeing it. "The coral gives a sense," he explained, as though knowing her doubts. "The pits and grooves... when you've examined enough of them, you start to feel patterns, flows, shapes. Some of those will indicate what lies ahead. Once you find them, you go a bit deeper. You look for patterns within the patterns, to gather detail." He smiled a crinkly smile and looked up at her. "After all, I might find a shape or pattern that says you're going to get married one day. But of course, you'd want to know to who and when, wouldn't you?"

Elyon, her head said. It came out of the blue, such that she blinked several times, and blushed red as sunrise. Old Hob watched her all the while. "So there's someone, is there? And not little Billy, I'm guessing." He patted her hand. "You need not tell me, girl, don't worry. Your cheeks are red enough as it is. But you see what I'm saying, don't you? It's easy enough to tell if someone will wed, but to whom and when and where, those are the tricky parts."

"Do you ever get it right?" she asked him. "I mean, exactly right."

"Depends what you mean by exactly." He looked over to Maid Marlon. "When Marlon joined us twenty years back, there was a shell that called to him. I remember it well. A large white shell with jagged blue lines and deep purple grooves. When he brought it to me I told him he was to wed a woman out of the Windwake Isles, from Gustas. Said he'd meet her in the middle of the ocean, by an unlikely happenstance, and they'd be wed within a year."

"And that actually happened?"

"Aye. She was on a carrack on a windless day, stranded out to sea not so far from here. We were nearby, just waiting for the winds to get blowing. To pass the time we got in the skiffs and rowed over to share a drink or ten with the crew." He laughed. "And there she was, out in the middle of the ocean, a girl from the island of Gustas in the Windwakes. And wouldn't you know, they were married by year's end." He gave another wrinkly old smile. "That's how it works, Saska. I don't know names, nor exact dates, but sometimes I can narrow it down a bit. But with you..." He continued running his hands over the coral, frowning. "The details...they aren't there."

"*Nothing*?" A tremor rippled through her chest, and not in a good way. "That sounds...worrying. Is it possible I picked up the wrong coral?"

"Did you?"

"I...I don't know."

Old Hob shook his head. "You didn't. This one called to you, I know. I knew from the moment you brought it aboard."

"How?"

"A sense."

"And your senses aren't telling you anything now? You're saying you can't see *anything* in my future?"

It didn't fill her with much hope, though she had to keep telling herself that this was more hokum than hoodoo. *But he did get it right about Maid Marlon,* she thought, as the old man continued to inspect the coral, searching for shapes and patterns. And she'd heard a few anecdotal accounts bandied about among the men of other faithful foretellings too.

There was a rather unfortunate incident some ten years ago, she'd been told by Larry, about a sailor called Mark Kettle. "The old man foretold his death," Larry had explained to her a week ago. "Said he'd fall to the flame before he reached twenty five summers. The lad was twenty at the time, a foolhardy sort, confident in himself. You know the type. He waved it away as nonsense, did a few seasons on the ship, then went off to try to make his fortune. Later, we heard he'd died in a fire at some sailor's tavern in Doublebay Harbour. He'd fallen on hard times, as it happened, turned to the bottle, and knocked over a candle in his room when he was drunk. The entire place went up like a bonfire, burning him to death right there in his bed." He let out a saddened sigh. "The lad was a dozen days out from his twenty fifth birthday. Tragic it was, and accurate on Old Hob's part. I decided right then and there that my own future was not for telling."

Lanky Larry was always the smart one, Saska thought now. She could only see two things that might be happening here. Either the old man had seen some tragedy in her future and was sparing her from knowing, or he was seeing nothing because she had no future at all. *I'm going to die soon,* was all she could think. *On the road to Aram, maybe. Or when we reach the city. I'll be set upon by bandits or Patriots of Lumara, or Agarathi agents. Eaten by a sunwolf, perhaps? Or maybe the skiff will get gobbled up by some great leviathan when we row to port, and me and the Wall and Captain Rikki will all go down together...*

She found herself laughing to all that, ridiculous as it was. Then King Godrin's words came back to her again. *You're exactly where you're meant to be.* As ever, they proved a comfort, because who was she to believe? A piece of random coral or the Eye of Rasalan? An old man sitting on a crate fiddling with nets, or the great king famed for his foresight and wisdom with the blood of Queen Thala running rich in his veins? It wasn't much of a contest, really. She looked at Old Hob again, and prepared to stand. "Well, you tried," she said, reaching out to take the coral back. "Do you mind if I..."

He shifted away. "No." He huddled over it, eyes shut, caressing a particular section again and again. His finger went up over the bumps and down into the pits, back and forward, back and forward. And then, whispering, he said, "You're...you're Bladeborn. I can see it now... there's...there's a blade in your future...misting...powerful." His words were so hushed she could scarce hear them. "You're going to fight.... the darkness...you're going to fight it, child." She thought of her dream. The shadowed figure, wreathed in flame. The spreading pall of fire and doom. "I see nothing else because...because nothing else matters. All else is shadow and fog. It's the war, child. You're to play a part in the Last Renewal." He opened his eyes and looked at her. For a good long minute he just stared, as though reading something more in her eyes. Then he spoke again. "You're royal," he said, seeing it, *feeling* it. "You've...you've got royal blood in you. Rich and strong and old."

She stared. Throughout her time on this ship, she'd kept these details of her life to herself, but somehow the old man had seen it, somehow he knew. "It's...it's why I'm going to Aram," she confided, leaning forward. "My mother. I was told she was the late Princess Leila Nemati. I'm going to find out the truth of it, Hob. You say I have a part to play in this war? Yes, in helping bring the north and south together. And fighting too, maybe. I'm good, with the blade, though new to it still. It's a lot to take on...it's...it's been a crazy few months." It was all coming out now, gushing from her lips. "That's why I have to get to Aram. My grandmother, she's the Grand Duchess. I have to meet her. I need her to tell me what to do next." She took a breath. The old man was looking at her with a half smile on his face. "What? What are looking at me like that for?"

Old Hob's smile broke off. "I wasn't talking about your mother," he said.

18

Jonik

The seneschal was an old man of seventy, bent of back and hooked of nose with the general appearance of a vulture. He wore robes of white-grey linen to reflect the heat of the sun, and the few wisps of hair that remained on his head were of much the same colour. When he spoke, the loose folds of skin beneath his shaven chin wriggled unpleasantly. "He is not here," he said, in a flowery Solapian timbre. "He has not been in attendance here for some weeks, in fact."

Emeric Manfrey gave little reaction, though this news was disheartening. They had it on good authority that the merchant Vincent Rose had taken up a semi-permanent residence at this estate, just outside the pretty port city of Miren upon the Sunrise Isle. The man was known to have a great many properties, but it was this one he favoured at this time of year, they understood. "Where is he?" the exiled lord asked.

The old man had a small host of household guards with him. They were a motley crew, southern of skin tone, from light tans to deep shades of purply brown. Some held spears, others swords, and all were dressed in lightly coloured leather tunics of cream and pale blue. They looked to Jonik to be the leftovers, unskilled and untrained. If Vincent Rose was absent, he'd have taken his best men with him. But still, their presence gave the seneschal some courage. "I will not tell you," he said. "I do not know who you are, or what you are here for, but I will say this - I have been seneschal here for Master Rose for over ten years and have never once betrayed his trust. I do not intend to start now."

Emeric Manfrey withdrew the eagle-blade of his house. It misted softly against the white pillared entrance of the large estate ahead of them. The guards were standing there. Every single one of them took a step back into the shadows.

The old man stood his ground. "Bladeborn, I see. You believe this will unman me?"

"I only want to know where your master is, good sir. I have no intention of harming him. I mean only to trade."

"Trade," repeated the seneschal.

"Yes, trade. My friends and I are in possession of some items that will be of interest to Master Rose. He will not favour you for denying or delaying us." The man seemed more worried by that than the misting blade before him. "What's your name, sir?" Emeric asked.

"Sechio Arcas, seneschal for the noble and splendid Vincent Rose here at the White Starlight Estate."

"You seem proud of the posting," Emeric said graciously. "And rightly so. You are Solapian by your accent, yes?"

"I am. I have left these shores not once in all my life. I have been proud to serve as seneschal for many noble houses here on the Sunrise Isle."

And now you serve an unscrupulous merchant out of Vandar, Jonik thought. A man with a sizeable chip cleaved into his shoulder, if he'd heard it right. Vincent Rose wasn't born to money or any highborn house of note, but had amassed a personal fortune to surpass even some of the greathouses of the north. It was said he held highborn men in deep disdain, and was happy to undermine them at any given opportunity. But through all that, he'd made contacts all across the south, and that was why they were here. He was in possession of information, Emeric believed, that might help them in their quest.

"I am sure you have served with great distinction," Emeric was turning on the charm quite nicely, a skill he had in abundance. It was a role Jack o' the Marsh also excelled in, but to make them seem less threatening, only Jonik and Emeric had made the walk up from the harbour. "And I am sure you continue to do so, under Master Rose's service. As such, you will of course see the wisdom in unveiling to us his current whereabouts. We will make it worth his while, I promise you."

The vulture-like seneschal nodded, his head bobbing on his long wrinkly neck. "What produce are you selling?" The old man gave Jonik a wary look. "This one...you say you're not going to harm Master Rose, but he's got a look about him. He's killed a lot of men, I can see."

"He's my bodyguard," Emeric lied. "Even Bladeborn need them, sometimes."

"Hmmmm. And these wares?"

"Blades," said Emeric. "Of the godsteel variety. We have...oh, some dozen of them now, I think. I've heard from several sources that Vincent Rose is a collector."

"Yes...a collector. This is true."

It seemed wiser to avoid the suggestion that Vincent Rose procured the blades to then sell to the Patriots of Lumara. Emeric had explained to Jonik that there were some men of mixed blood in their ranks, able to wield godsteel. Rose cared not that he was arming a militarist force that sought to destroy the north, of course. So long as he made a profit off the trade, that was all that mattered.

The old seneschal was thinking, scratching at his wispy white hair. "And just who are you, then? Most northmen are leaving these lands, you may have heard."

"We heard it was safer on the Sunrise Isle," said Emeric. "Safer than the mainland, anyway. The Solapians have a long and proud history of being more welcoming than their neighbours. You are an insouciant people, relaxed and happy. I have always imagined that was largely due to the lifestyle here. The wine estates and flower fields and palm-lined beaches allow for a more pleasant manner of living."

"You seem to know much of our ways."

"I do. I have visited the Sunrise Isle many times." Emeric gave a bow. "My name is Emeric Manfrey, once lord, now exile. I am well known in Lumara, and know your master through mutual acquaintances. Me and my companions have suffered some misfortune of late, however, due to the troubles spreading through the empire. We are in need of coin, and have blades to sell. My mind went straight to Vincent Rose for that. As a man of means and a northman besides, I had trusted that he would understand our plight, and seek to help us."

"My master is most charitable," said Sechio Arcas. "And now that I have heard your name, yes, I know of you, Lord Manfrey." His dark brown eyes shifted to Jonik again. "And you need not tell me who this is. A bodyguard, you say? A *ghost*, say I. A ghost and shadow both. Word has spread of your companion, my lord. It's said you sail with the Shadow of Death."

"And where did you hear that?" Emeric asked, his voice as light as a breeze.

"All ports are places of whispers, my lord," croaked the old man. "Much news comes to us from the mainland, by ship and eagle both." He examined Jonik's swordbelt, but he'd left the Nightblade aboard Invincible Iris to avoid suspicions such as this. But no matter. Jonik could see quite plainly that the man knew who he was. Emeric's vendetta against the Patriots of Lumara had made them infamous in Solas, and many now knew the pair had joined forces. "Now this paints a new picture," the seneschal went on. He seemed untroubled by the realisation, the sort of man who was too old to care much if his time had come. "I cannot in good conscience tell you of my master's location. Not to this man. He is Death Given Flesh, it is said. You will take him to murder Master Rose, for that is what he does."

"Aren't you a little too old to give such credence to rumour, Sechio? A great many falsehoods have risen up about young Jonik here. He is a man of justice, a man of honour. But a man who has his limits as well...as I do. Now, we have been many days at sea, and have a long journey ahead of us still. We would like to resume it as soon as possible. But first we need a location. So I will ask you again. Where is Vincent Rose?"

The vulture shook his head. "I will not tell you."

"I see." Emeric nodded. "Well, that is a shame, truly. But I suspect there are others here who will be more obliging." He walked straight past the old man toward the half dozen household guards standing in the shade of the pillared porch. Clutched in his grasp, the eagle-blade of Manfrey fogged with a silvery green mist. "Where is Vincent Rose?" he asked, as he walked.

"Don't say a word," called the old seneschal. "Do not say one..."

Jonik put his fist into the old man's face. He didn't feel especially good about it, but his tongue was likely to trip up their inquiries. Sechio Arcas collapsed to the side, dropping hard onto the white-paved courtyard. Jonik took a grip of his dagger, listened, and heard a heartbeat. He'd be just fine, in an hour or two.

"Now, where was I?" said Emeric across the yard. "Oh yes. Your master, Vincent Rose. We would dearly like to know of his location." He looked down the line of men as Jonik stepped a little closer to watch. Several of the guards were stiff-lipped, with their chins up and their posture resolute. They might crack, but it would take some work. The death of one of their fellow guards would probably do it, though it would be better if this didn't turn to bloodshed. These were innocent men, after all, and no enemy of theirs. There were a couple of others who looked more amenable, though. The fear was beating hard on their faces. "You," said Emeric, pointing his blade at one of them. He was a hirsute man, with a shaggy head of black hair, thickly bristled cheeks, and tufts of fur emerging from above the top of his tunic. *Piseki*, Jonik knew at once. "Where is your master, my friend?"

The man looked to the others. The stiff-lipped among them gave him a withering stare, and he dropped his eyes and said nothing. Emeric sighed. "Need this turn to violence? You can speak the common tongue, can you not?" *Perhaps they can't,* Jonik thought. Though their eyes suggested otherwise. "OK, one last chance." Emeric added a sabre-sharp edge to his voice. "Your loyalty is admirable, but is it really worth dying for? We truly do only wish to trade with your master. There is no lie in that, my friends."

There was, in fact. They'd not be selling those blades to Vincent Rose no matter what he was willing to pay. No, it was information they wanted.

"I know where he is." The voice rang out from nearby. It was a woman's voice, old and tired and northern, by her accent, somewhere out of Rasalan. Jonik turned to find her working the gardens nearby, pulling weeds. "I'll have no violence here. You look like determined men. You will find him, sooner or later, I can see that plain enough. Master Rose does not care to hide his movements. But I will have something from you first."

She tottered over, just as old as Sechio Arcas if not more so, diminutive and grey-haired, her weatherbeaten face slashed by a thousand wrinkles. Emeric and Jonik both left the guards where they were and joined the woman where the seneschal lay under the sun on the baking white courtyard. "He isn't dead, is he?" she asked, quite nonchalant. "If you have killed him, then..."

"He's just unconscious," Jonik promised her. "I only gave him a little tap on the cheek. He'll come around soon."

"Oh no, young man, you gave him a little more than a tap, but I'll let it pass." She had a smile on her face, as carefree as you like. Not many teeth, though, by the looks of it. It seemed like the loose linen robes she wore weighed more than she did. Beneath them, she was nought but skin and bone and old long fingernails, dirtied from her labour. She pointed with one of them now. "No...don't be stupid. You are no hero, Krabash."

Jonik turned. It seemed one of the stiff-lipped guardsman was preparing to come at them with his spear. *Brave, but foolhardy.* The rest seemed quite aware that any attack would be futile against a pair of infamous Bladeborn men. Krabash grunted and withdrew.

"These silly young men," the old woman laughed. "They have sand in their heads, I think. But I know better, yes I do. So here is my bargain. I will tell you where Master Rose has gone, but first you must give me an oath on that godsteel you carry. I have heard of you, Emeric Manfrey. Honour is important to you. You will not betray an oath made in good faith, not on that blade of your ancestors. What would Sir Oswald think?" She smiled.

Emeric held his blade before him, point down to the pavestones. He reached out with his spare hand for the old crone to take. "State your terms, then, my lady."

The woman let out an echoing cackle. "I have not been a lady for too many years to count. Once I was, perhaps, but no longer. I suppose I am an exile, like you, Emeric. But I'll not bore you with the details of my life. I will just say that Master Rose has been good to me. He has his eccentricities, yes, and likes to pick up waifs and strays like me, but there is a good man in there somewhere, deep down in his bones. A proud man. So my terms are these...*do not harm him.*" She thought a moment, then said, "That is all."

"Done." Emeric took the old woman's claws in his grasp. "We will not harm Vincent Rose, you have my word. By godsteel I promise it. It has never been our intention."

"Good." The little woman withdrew her dirty fingers. "Then I'll return to my weeding. Good day to you both." She began to totter away.

"My lady," Emeric said, halting her. "We still need that location."

She stopped and turned. "Oh yes, of course. Age...it makes you forget things, you will see." She gave a gap-toothed grin. "Master Rose is in Sutrek. He has a manor there, near the waterfront on the Coast of Plenty side. You will find it hard to miss. It's the largest manor on Goldwater Row, with doors painted silver and blue. For Vandar, I've always thought. A little homage for Vincent's home kingdom. He really is a sentimental sort."

"We thank you kindly, my lady. That is most helpful to our cause. But...do you know why Vincent went to Sutrek? And when? It would help us, should we find him absent from his manor."

The old crone thought on that, then said, "He comes and goes all the time on business dealings. And he often visits Sutrek to savour its joys. There's no place more wild and colourful, as you surely know, Emeric. So why he went...for business or pleasure...who can say. I pay little mind to his activities, in truth."

"Right."

"But as to when...I think it was some four or so weeks ago now. He had a friend with him, one of mine from Rasalan, a certain Ranulf Shackton, if you know of him. He'd been with us a good while, since Vincent returned from Thalan, with a few new prizes from his travels." She laughed. "He's such a character. Collecting this and that. Makes a game of life, and isn't that the way? The world is far too stuffy. We need a few more Vincent Roses."

Emeric was digesting that. "I have heard of Ranulf Shackton, yes," he said. "The man's a famed adventurer."

"That he is. And mayhaps that's what they're doing now? You might knock on his manor door and find the pair are out in the desert or climbing some mountain. Though in truth Vincent isn't so drawn to such things as Master Shackton is. Still..." She wiped her hands. A bit of dirt crusted off onto the stone floor. "I've said my piece and will say no more. When I get jabbering I can be too honest and there are some things Master Rose would prefer I didn't say. Now off with you both. And you..." She turned to the guards. "Would you please get poor Sechio inside. He'll wither to a crisp if left to bake under this sun." With that, the woman shuffled back off to continue her weeding.

They left the estate, passing down the sloped pathway and through the outer gate, and then along the private road to the port. It was bordered by olive and fig trees, the world buzzing and chittering with insects. The weather was a lot more bearable here than it had been in Solas. Though the sun beat down hard it wasn't so humid by half, and that made all the difference.

Ahead of them, the city of Miren spread out in whitewashed stone, gleaming beneath the morning light. It was small for a city, low-risen and easy on the eye, and the port was much the same. The wharves and jetties were wooden and well maintained, the expansive harbour walls painted with colourful frescoes. Where other ports teemed with ships all fighting for space, here everything seemed languid and relaxed. Along several of the larger jetties trade cogs and galleys were moored, their wares taken on and off. Among them were many fishing boats, ranging from little rowboats to larger low-slung schooners.

To the south, they spotted Invincible Iris, blue sails furled, bobbing at anchor. Jonik could see the shape of Shade on deck, being taken around the masts by Jack o' the Marsh. They'd stopped for one day in the Islands of the Moon a week ago, and Jonik had had a chance to take Shade out for a gallop while the others gathered some provisions. It had satiated the steed's need to stretch his legs for the time being, and soothed Jonik's guilt besides. But Jack...good old Jack, getting the horse into the open air as often as he could.

"What do you imagine she was keeping from us?" Jonik asked Emeric, as they moved down a set of white stone switchbacks toward the docks, cutting through town. "She turned evasive at the end, don't you think? Something to do with Ranulf Shackton, perhaps?"

Emeric gave a light bob of the shoulders. "Who can say?"

"Vincent Rose, hopefully," said Jonik, "when we finally track him down."

Emeric gave a faint smile. "*If*," he said. "I'm starting to fear we're on a wild goose chase here. If we don't find him in Sutrek, then it might be best to look for men elsewhere. This plan of mine...it has holes, Jonik."

"It's worth a shot," Jonik returned. "I'm sure it's not just Vincent Rose who can point the way. We could also attend the warmoot, after all. Capture some high ranking Patriot and torture what we need out of them? He'll likely be there himself as well, this Pal Palek. Maybe we could interrogate *him*. Who better to know where his stronghold is than the man himself."

"It's an option, I suppose. I imagine the council will gather quite soon, though whether it's necessary anymore is a matter of debate. It seems inevitable now that Empress Valura will bow to the Patriots' demands. But protocol must be observed. And that gives us time."

The skiff was where they'd left it, tied up against a small jetty in the south of the harbour. They'd thought better than to have any of the others come with them, for safety reasons, though the locals here seemed less inclined to violence than on the mainland. Jonik untied the ropes and then joined Emeric at the oars. They pulled against the pale green waters of the harbour, drawing themselves out toward Invincible Iris.

Once aboard, they gathered the crew to update them. Shade joined, standing at Jack's flank. "We're making for Sutrek," Emeric told them. "It seems that Vincent Rose went there a month ago, and has yet to return. As far as I can tell, the voyage will take no more than five or six days. Captain Turner, does that sound about right to you?"

"You know these here waters better than I," said Turner. "But aye, five o' six days sounds about right, so long as the winds and waves behave." He gave the skies and seas a little look. "You'll be wanting to leave right away, lord, or stay here for the night?" That question seemed to be for Jonik. He was likely wondering if the former Shadowknight wanted to take Shade onto land for a ride.

Jonik shared a quick glance with Emeric, then said, "Right away, Captain. It's not yet midday and there's no sense in wasting an afternoon here at anchor."

"Aye. Right away it is, then."

"And you've got an address, have you?" grunted Brown Mouth Braxton, scratching at his bristly, lopsided jaw. "For the merchant."

"We do," said Emeric. "Whether he's in attendance there or not, however, we'll not know until we arrive."

With that, the ship set into action. The anchor was raised, the sails opened, the ship tacking back out of the harbour and toward the open seas. "You want me to take him down?" Jack o' the Marsh asked Jonik, gesturing to Shade.

Jonik shared a look with the horse and knew immediately that he'd prefer to remain on deck for now. He liked to get permission from

Turner for such things, however, so asked him and was told in reply that the seas were idle and there was no need to take Shade down just yet. The horse thus whinnied his appreciation as Jack went off to fetch him some feed and a pail of water, returning from below with young Devin. In the meanwhile, Jonik found himself wondering whether a certain Varin Knight they had in their company had been behaving during his and Emeric's short time on land.

He stepped to Jack o' the Marsh's side for confirmation, as the burly Marshlander fed Shade an apple, which the horse gobbled up with a great toothy smile of satisfaction. "Did he cause any trouble while we were gone?" Jonik asked, gesturing to Sir Borrus Kanabar. The big knight was lying flat on his back, a bottle of rum clutched in his grip, sleeping beneath the shade of the mid-deck starboard gunwale. It was a state in which he spent much of his time, to better endure the unpleasantness of his time at sea.

Jack shook his head in answer. "He's been sleeping all morning."

Good, thought Jonik. He'd wondered whether Sir Borrus might try to get his hands on the Nightblade while he was absent, though it was a concern that bordered on paranoia. In truth the Barrel Knight had shown no great interest in the blade, nor had he been particularly difficult during his time in their company, to Jonik's surprise. A lot of that was due to Jack's minding of the man. They spent much time together, when the Barrel Knight was conscious, and had struck up something of a friendship, such as could exist between a lowborn son of a milkmaid and the middle-aged heir to a greathouse, and war hero. "He didn't try to get his own blade back either?"

"Nope. Like I say, he's just been sleeping. You don't have to worry about him anymore, Ghost. I know you're wary, but you needn't be, leastways not while he's got that life debt hanging over him." He gave Jonik a firm pat on the back. "He'll warm to you sooner or later, never fear. That carefree charm of yours will eventually wear him down." He smiled sarcastically.

"I'm not trying to wear him down," Jonik scowled. It was a stone cold lie, and Jack knew it. He had the good grace not to push the issue, though. Jonik turned to Devin. "Devin, are you ready to train?"

"Always, m'lord. Just so long as Cap has no need of me."

"Go and check. I'll meet you on the forecastle deck."

They set into their daily routine, using the forecastle as their training yard that day. Both Devin and Jack were seeing vast improvements, and once or twice, the Marshlander had snuck through Jonik's defences and landed a firm thwack on the body with the wooden swords they used to spar. It had been Emeric who'd first started their training, some weeks ago, though after Brewilla's death Jonik had taken up the mantle during their time at harbour in Solas. The last ten days had seen Emeric resume his duties, however, and now both he and Jonik took to taking the two men through the various routines they'd devised.

After an hour of sweaty work, Borrus Kanabar stirred from his stupor, and came marching up the forecastle steps. He had in one hand his bottle of rum, and the other a small crate. He set the latter down and took a seat, relaxing under the sun with an easy smile on his face. During his time aboard, his cheeks had begun to thicken back out and he'd gone through something of a physical revival. His scraggly beard was gone, his face had picked up a bit of a tan, and he'd worked hard to restore the great belly he'd once owned, with some small measure of success thus far. "I hope I haven't missed too much," he said. He tended to enjoy watching the fighting, throwing slurs and bantering all the way through. "Are you giving the Shadowknight another thrashing, Jack?"

Jack was unburdened above the waist and showing off an impressively large and sculpted figure. "I think I'm still some way from defeating Jonik, my lord," he said, smiling. He toed the line well, did Jack, though Jonik could tell he enjoyed Sir Borrus Kanabar's favour.

"I'm not so sure, from what I've seen," Kanabar responded, folding one heavy leg over the other. "You're lucky you've got your father's blood, boy," he said to Jonik. "If you weren't Bladeborn, I reckon Jack would have the beating of you soon."

"Being bladeborn counts for little when you're not bearing godsteel," Jonik returned. "It becomes a matter of technique and training."

"In which you're clearly lacking, Shadowknight. I can't imagine your training up there in the mountains is geared toward duelling and battlefield techniques."

"It isn't," agreed Jonik. "We're taught to operate in the shadows, not in the open. For the most part, at least."

"Then I'm inclined to say that perhaps you're not best suited to train these lads?" Borrus Kanabar lurched to his feet, giving Jack a wave. "Come on then, Jack, gimme that wooden sword of yours. I think it's high time I taught the Shadowknight here a thing or two about how a *true* knight wields a blade."

"Are you sure that's wise?" asked Emeric Manfrey, standing with his legs crossed at the ankles, leaning against the bulwark. The wind was breezing though his hair, the ship cutting through the Solapian Channel at a brisk clip. "You still look drunk to my eyes, Borrus."

"Oh don't you worry, Manfrey, I'll be getting to you next. You'll have forgotten half of your Emerald Guard training while exiled down here, I'll bet, and this boy..." He gave Jonik an exaggerated shake of the head. "You're all over the place, truly. There are more rough edges to you than in those mountains where you were raised."

"You seem to be forgetting that Jonik reached the final of the Song of the First Blade," said Emeric. "He had to defeat Dalton Taynar to get there, among others. Is that not worthy of your praise?"

"No doubt he used tricks to win those bouts..."

"And those same tricks allowed him to master the Nightblade too, I suppose?"

That comment seemed to have the Barrel Knight a little stumped. "We're talking about *duelling* here, Manfrey," he came back at the exile, after a pause. "Technique, not talent. I don't doubt the boy is gifted when being godsteel, but he's a long way from the finished article in terms of technical prowess. Now, I've watched you do this little dance daily, and perhaps it's about time I pitched in?" He gave Jonik a little upward nod, his great bald dome gleaming with sweat. "So, what do you say, Shadowknight? If you're training these lads up, then it can't hurt to have the guidance of a true Bladeborn master, can it? Powerform and Rushform, they're my specialties. Of course, I'm a master of Blockform too, but how bloody boring is that? Let's have some fun, shall we?"

Jonik and Emeric shared a look. The exile pursed his lips, shrugged and said, "His expertise would be worthwhile, there's no denying that. Call it your way of paying for passage, Sir Borrus."

"And all that rum you drink," put in Jonik.

Borrus laughed as he lumbered into position, waving both Jack and Devin out of the training circle they'd drawn upon the forecastle deck. "Sounds fair to me," he said, "and I'd best get some practice in before I start slaying Agarathi. Jack, Devin, I'll give you some pointers once I've shown the Shadowknight what's what. Now settle in and enjoy. And you, boy..." He pointed with his wooden blade at Jonik. "Prepare for a lesson you'll not soon forget."

The Barrel Knight, even half sotted and half asleep, was a veritable whirlwind, and by the gods did he refuse to hold back. Without giving Jonik any time to prepare he marauded forward with a furious series of attacks, upslashing here, downcutting there, forcing Jonik right across the deck until his back hit the larboard gunwale and he near toppled over the bulwark into the frothing, shark-infested sea. Jack o' the Marsh and Devin, who'd been standing right there, scattered to either side, as Borrus Kanabar caught Jonik with a heavy cut that knocked right through his defensive parry and slammed right into his upper left arm. "Ha! That's your left shoulder cleaved to the bone," he declared, his breath reeking of rum and wine. "Right where you cut your father. Now where else did you maim him?" There was a sudden bite to his voice.

He surged again, forcing Jonik to duck low and retreat to the centre of the fighting circle. With a further exchange of powerful slashes and cuts and thrusting jabs Borrus Kanabar burst through and caught Jonik with a deep prodding jab to the thigh. Blunt though the wooden swords were, that would leave a nasty bruise, Jonik knew. He gritted his teeth and limped backward. "Your right thigh, never to be the same again," announced Kanabar triumphantly. "And Aleron...I wasn't there, but I know you cut his neck clean through. How about I try the same? Even with this wooden blade I fancy myself to crush your windpipe, boy..."

"Have a care now, Sir Borrus," came Emeric Manfrey's measured voice. "We are here to train only, not cause serious harm."

Borrus Kanabar didn't listen. He was barreling toward Jonik again, swinging his great right arm left and right, up and down. Jonik parried, ducked, stepped back. With one firm swing, the Barrel Knight's blade swished a hair's breadth from Jonik's neck, and he gave out a hearty laugh and bellowed, "Close, gods that one was close, boy!" before surging back into another series of strikes. Yet through all that, there seemed to be less malice in him as the fight went on. Instead of a snarl, a smile began to broaden across his face, as Jonik began to slide forward himself, thrusting, jabbing, seeking to connect with the great target that was the heir of Kanabar. He did, once or twice, striking the man in the right forearm as he parried a thrust, and then whipping a firm hit upon the Barrel Knight's left flank.

"That one would have claimed your life, Sir Borrus," announced Emeric. "I sense the bout is evening up."

"So you'd bloody well say, Manfrey, with your nose half way up this boy's arse." Borrus laughed, though his tone was less quarrelsome and bumptious than normal. Emeric took the jibe well, opening his lips into a fine handsome smile. Borrus raised his sword to Jonik again. "You've got *something*, boy, I'm big enough to admit that."

"Big...aye, you're *big* enough that's for certain." Turner had arrived at that point, and Braxton too. Even Soft Sid had lumbered thoughtlessly up the steps to observe, though didn't seem sure why. Above them, Grim Pete was no doubt peering from his nest.

"Shouldn't someone be at the wheel, Captain?" asked Jack o' the Marsh.

"Fear not, Jack, old Iris takes care o' herself in weather like this. We're cruisin', lad, and this ain't a fight Gill Turner wants to miss."

"The fight won't last much longer," said Emeric. "Not given how heavily this Barrel of ours is breathing."

Borrus laughed again. Sweat was beading upon his bald dome, leaking into his eyes. He gave them a good wipe then unburdened himself of his sweat-stained shirt. His physique wasn't quite the match of Jack o' the Marsh's, but that was no surprise given his age and the troubles he'd endured of late. Still, the shadow of what he was once was clear enough to see. Thick arms, an ample gut, fleshy wide shoulders, and a barrel of a chest from which he'd drawn his name. He was also unexpectedly accoutred in a great deal of body hair, with many war wounds, old and new, latticed across his chest, back, and arms, half of them recently won during his long hard incarceration in Eldurath. "Right then, Shadowknight, you ready for round two?"

Jonik was starting to enjoy himself as well. There was nothing quite like the thrill of the contest. He fixed his stance and said, "Give me your best, Sir Borrus."

"Famous last words, boy," Borrus said, chuckling. "And you, Manfrey, get yourself warmed up. I'll be onto you next."

"That's if you haven't passed out from the exertion," Emeric returned, casual.

Borrus huffed to that. "I've depths in me of the like you've never bloody seen. Jack, be a good lad and fetch me my rum. I find myself thirsty and in need of refreshment."

When Jack brought the bottle, Sir Borrus Kanabar drank long and deep. Then he wiped his mouth, flexed his fleshy build, and put himself into Blockform. "Now boy, let's have to it, shall we? Put me on my back, and I'll stop calling you Shadowknight, how about that?"

It was all the motivation Jonik needed. *Godsteel or not,* he thought defiantly, *I'm going to get this great oaf off his feet.* He firmed himself, sliding into a Strikeform stance, as Kanabar's smile broadened. Jonik couldn't help but smile himself. With the eyes of his men watching, he rushed in.

19

Janilah

Janilah Lukar's personal library within his private quarters was filled with the sound of scratching quills and muttering old men, the rustle of parchment, the scrape of wooden chair legs on stone. A half dozen tables had been brought in and set up for the use of the scholars and their stacks of papers and books, and several more scribes and attendants had been summoned to offer further aid. All were sworn to speak of nothing that transpired here. Each man had a wife, children, family. Janilah had made sure of that to guarantee their cooperation. The threat was, as ever, implicit and unspoken.

"My lord," said Archibald Benton, an old crook-backed scholar who served as senior amongst them. "Our studies these last weeks have discovered a message, written into the book. A code, if you will, through time." He gestured with a liver-spotted hand toward the Book of Thala, laid out grandly upon a central lectern. The other scholars and scribes were coming and going, taking notes or transcribing accounts to then be deciphered and translated. At the book, one man was permanently stationed, his only job to turn the pages with the utmost care. "It began with the Divine Queen Thala herself, we have come to believe. Every so often, an account is unintelligible or otherwise too damaged to read, and these are those that have, we think, been intentionally removed from the record by the king or queen in possession of the book at the time."

Janilah nodded thoughtfully to cut the man off. He needed a moment to think. "A code through time," he repeated. "A code pertaining to what, Archibald?"

"Of that we remain uncertain, sire. These accounts have been destroyed...they are often many dozens, or even hundreds of years apart. From what we can glean from several other unsullied passages, Thala herself issued in her writings orders and instructions to later monarchs of her line, to then be carried out or otherwise passed on. The monarch in question would then destroy the passage, we believe, having fulfilled their orders. As such, whatever secret is being hidden within the code, can be passed from monarch to monarch, through time. And of course, most latterly, that brings us to King Godrin."

"Yes," broke in Janilah, his voice gripped by a cold realisation that this would further disrupt his plans. Or worse, shatter them entirely. "I was told there had been a page ripped from King Godrin's passages. Might this not contain the contents of this code? This secret you speak of."

"It's possible, sire," agreed Archibald Benton. "Godrin's accounts have proven most troublesome to translate. His cipher was quite brilliant, actually, but we managed to break it down eventually. And might I say...the man was truly gifted in his foresight. He demonstrated a quite masterful percipience that few others have ever matched. There are some, of course, but you would have to go all the way back to Thala herself to..."

"The page, Archibald." Janilah knew of the old man's proclivity for going on too long. "You're telling me you have no idea what was on it?"

The old scholar's head went left and right. He had a great big birthmark upon his wrinkled forehead, the colour of wine and shaped almost like a crow's foot. He'd once sported a splendid beard of soft white silk, but the years had stripped some of its thickness away, leaving behind a rather more wispy dangle of threads. "The passages are commonly unrelated to one another," he said. "There is no way of knowing what might have been on the missing page, unfortunately." He could see that answer didn't much please his king. An awkward smile trembled on his lips. "As I say, we are looking for possible links in the chain. So hope is not yet lost, my lord. In time we'll unravel this mystery..."

"You didn't think to send a crow about this, Sir Kevyn?" Janilah asked, turning to Sir Kevyn Bolt. The bull-shouldered sworn sword had been entrusted to bring back the tome in one piece. This missing page was his failure, and the Bull of Bolt knew it. "You had birds aboard your ship, did you not? One might have flown to me sooner with this news."

"I sent two, sire," said Sir Kevyn.

Janilah smelled the lie immediately. "Two?" he repeated, turning to Sir Owen Armdall. "Did any such crows reach us, Sir Owen?"

"No, sire," said the tall noble knight.

"They must have been shot down, or gotten lost," argued Sir Kevyn. "We did...we did send them, my lord. I swear it. Master Archibald will tell you so."

Archibald Benton went to speak in defence of the knight, but Janilah didn't care to hear it. "Why didn't you check the book before you left Miren?" That was by some distance the bigger crime. "I can only assume you failed to do so, Sir Kevyn. If you had, you would have discovered that a page was missing, and taken steps to recover it immediately, before setting sail." The large knight had no answer for that. His dark brown eyes went straight to the floor and stayed there, like a child who knew he'd done wrong. Janilah turned. "Archibald? Care to explain?"

"We...we were seeking to make the tides, sire," the scholar said. "We searched through most of the book in Vincent Rose's library, but... Sir Kevyn, he ordered to leave before our search was complete."

Sir Kevyn's eyes lifted. He gave the old man a fierce snarl. "That isn't true," he protested, angrily. "I gave them all ample time to check through the tome. I was told that all was well..."

"You were busy falling to the charms of the merchant," the scholar returned, unbowed by the bovine knight. "He went off to sample his wines, my lord, and left us to return the book to the ship."

"Where you had plenty of time to check it," Sir Kevyn Bolt came back at him. "You and the lot of them." He waved a hand to the others in the room, scratching and scribbling and pretending not to listen for fear of being drawn into the dispute. "I'll admit, I went to fetch some wine for the return journey, but only to give Archibald and his team time to finish their search of the book. Which you didn't," he said to the old man. His face went from fury to fear as he looked back at Janilah. "I'm not to blame, sire," he said. "If there's a finger to be pointed..."

"Then it's at you," broke in Archibald Benton. "*You* had command and should have been explicit with your orders. We were only following your commands, sir. Do not try to turn this onto us, to save your own..."

"Silence." Janilah had had quite enough of their squabbling. "What's done is done and I'll consider what to do with the both of you later. Now tell me, was this Vincent Rose's doing? Did he steal the page from the book?"

"He must have," said Sir Kevyn, with certainty. "It's why he drew me off with the promises of all that wine. It...it was diversionary, sire."

The scholar nodded more thoughtfully. "Vincent Rose is a known reprobate. He might have stolen the page to ransom it back to you, my lord."

That thought had crossed Janilah's mind, though if Rose was found to have had any part in this then he'd have to sail across the Stormy Sea to lands unknown to escape Janilah's wrath. The risk didn't seem worth it for a businessman as shrewd as Vincent Rose, who'd already tested the limits of his patience by taking the book all the way to Solapia in the first place. He had made his pathetic excuses for that via letter, though Janilah had always suspected the man wanted time to scour the book himself before passing it on. *That* he might just permit. But to steal a page? It seemed too reckless.

"My lord," said Archibald Benton, interrupting the king's thoughts.

Janilah turned to him. "What?"

"There was another you should know of, who may be to blame. A man who was with Vincent Rose when we arrived to take the Book of Thala away. One known to have an interest in all things ancient and arcane..."

"Who?" demanded the king. "Gods, Archibald, stop blabbering. Who?"

The old man shrunk into his sallow skin. "Ranulf Shackton, sire," he croaked. "We...we presume he was recruited by Vincent Rose to help him decipher the tome. It may be that he was the one who stole the page, not the merchant."

"Ranulf Shackton..." Janilah tensed his thickly-bearded jaw. A cold shiver crept up his spine."You're certain of this?"

"Most certain, my lord."

Janilah had to think. He took a step away from them toward the window, looking out over the city. A strong mist was souping among the towers and spires. *I should have killed him when I had the chance,* he thought. Ranulf Shackton had been a guest of his not so long ago, spending several months within his dungeons here in the palace. Janilah had ordered the man captured after his latest adventure summiting the Three Peaks, which loomed loftily to the northeast of the city. He could see them even now, the three mighty tips breaking above the ranges, surging high into the slate grey clouds. When Ranulf Shackton had come down, Janilah's soldiers had been there to apprehend him and escort him straight to the palace dungeons. The war had just broken out between Tukor and Rasalan, and the adventurer seemed to think he was being taken for ransom, but that had never been Janilah Lukar's intention.

No, it was information he sought, which he attempted to extract by placing Ranulf Shackton next to a rather garrulous man who occupied the next cell. That man was a mole by name of Reggie Warren, commissioned by Janilah with the explicit directive of befriending Shackton through their shared troubles, and then gradually introducing topics the Warrior King found of interest, the long-lost location of the Frostblade among them. It was said that Shackton was a scholar of the Blades, and other artefacts besides, and had dedicated much of his adult life to their study. So he sent in Reggie to see what he could find. And in the end, he'd found nothing at all.

And then Ranulf Shackton had escaped, creeping off into the mountains before eventually being caught in the north of Tukor and imprisoned in a cell in Lallymoor. It wasn't until he'd been there for several months that Janilah learned of that, however. Apparently, Shackton had given a false name and been thrown into an oubliette and half forgotten. When Janilah eventually learned of his location, he commanded the man be returned to Ilithor for a more direct form of questioning. Yet by some stroke of misfortune, Shackton was rescued from his prison wagon on the road to Twinbrook, and vanished. Janilah had since given up on finding him again, and had heard nothing of the man since. Until only moments ago, when Archibald Benton spoke of his presence on the Sunrise Isle...

"It was him," he whispered to himself, staring out of the frosted window. The days were growing colder now as the depths of winter set in. "Shackton...I should never have let him live."

"Sire." Janilah turned. Sir Kevyn Bolt had stepped up behind him, cloaked in his triple-coloured mantle. His dual swords were given shape as bull-heads at the pommels. "I will return immediately to Miren, and make certain to track this missing page down. Give me two months, and I'll stand here in delivery of it, and Vincent Rose's head besides."

"It is your head I should take."

Sir Kevyn Bolt recoiled back a step. "My lord?"

"Take him from my sight, Sir Owen. Give him Shackton's cell."

The Bull of Bolt spun as Sir Owen Armdall came forward, Sir Rees Hunt and Sir Fredrick Ruxmond following right behind. "Come, Sir Kevyn. Go easy now," said Sir Owen.

Sir Kevyn looked again at Janilah. In a moment he was on his knees, back bent in supplication. "My king, I beg of you...spare me. I shall not fail you again, I promise it, I'll not!"

Janilah looked down through eyes like sharpened flints. The man's oversight might just have sabotaged his plans, and that set in him a fury he was struggling to contain. *I might just take his head off myself,* he thought, staring down, unblinking. Several of the nearby scholars had retreated to the room's corners. Others were turning away or covering their eyes as though expecting some horrific execution right there. *Do I look so fierce?* Janilah had to wonder. *Good, maybe it'll remind them not to disappoint me.* "Remove him."

The three sworn swords descended, hauling the brawny form of Sir Kevyn Bolt to his feet, marching him from the room. He gave several final pleas, but Janilah ignored every one of them. When the room had silenced of his bleating, Archibald Benton shuffled in, head down, eyes curtained by concern for his own wellbeing. "I would ask, sire, if you have a mind to cage me as well? It would be better for me to hear it now, else my heart might give out from the stress of not knowing." He managed a nervy laugh.

"I need you to continue working," Janilah told him. He said no more than that.

"Of course, sire. I will fetter myself to this room, all day and all night. I am certain we shall find what you're searching for, in time."

"Are you, Archibald? Are you truly? Or are these words just intended to placate me?" He looked around. No one dared make eye contact with him. *Sheep,* he thought. *I am a wolf among sheep.* He gave a grunt and turned to look out of the window once more. His eyes were east, toward the City of Thalan a thousand miles away. The city of the goddess who'd tricked him, through time. "This code of Thala's will not be unravelled lest I learn what was on that page," he said. "It is the key, Archibald. Without it the door will remain locked."

"The door to what, my lord?"

To life everlasting, he thought. *To the winning of the War Eternal. To the fulfilling of King Galin's promise and the granting of my own Table. To divinity, you old fool...that's the door I need to open.* But he merely said, "Victory, Archibald. Victory...and peace." He flung out a hand in irritation. "Return to your work."

The old man drew back. "I will seek you another key, my lord. There may be a spare, hidden herein."

There won't be, Janilah thought, as the scholar shuffled away.

He sunk into his musings once more, cursing his misfortunes. They had been adding up of late, stacked one atop another, threatening to overwhelm all his years of careful planning. *No matter how tight my grip becomes, there is always something that slips through my fingers.* His plans were turning to water, impossible to hold onto. Yet he closed his fingers to a fist all the same, so hard his knuckles went white. *I should have killed him when I had the chance.* He had visited Ranulf Shackton himself in a bid to get a read on the man, though had found himself mostly unimpressed. The man had been a joker, a typical bloody Rasalanian, defiant in the face of his doom. *And now he is having the last laugh. Now he has the information I need.* The irony of that was not lost on him. *He may not have had what I needed while captive here, but now he just might. Only this time he's a world away, and far beyond my reach...*

He festered on that thought until Sir Owen Armdall returned, having delivered Sir Kevyn to the gaolers. "Do you truly mean to kill him, my lord?" the Oak of Armdall asked. "If you will permit my counsel, I would say..."

Janilah raised a hand. "Someone needs to die." *But Sir Kevyn?* he wondered. *Perhaps not.* The man was a valuable member of the Six, and the son of the Old Bull, Lord Brayman Bolt, who was famed for killing a dragon himself once and who'd not take kindly to his son's untimely demise. It was the sort of inconvenience that Janilah need not suffer right now. But still, *someone* needed to die.

"My lord," said Sir Owen carefully. "I would strongly advise against..."

"Do you know of Reggie Warren's current whereabouts?" cut in the king. He stared out of the window as he spoke. *Someone needs to die...*

"The mole? I...I could have him tracked down easily enough, sire. He's known to frequent the bars and brothels of White Shadow."

"Let me know when you have him in custody. And call upon King Hadrin also. He may be able to offer some assistance to Archibald and his team."

"I believe the king is with your granddaughter, my lord."

"I don't care where he is. Send for him. Now."

The Rat King of Rasalan arrived ten minutes later looking perky. There was a flush to his cheeks and a toothy smile on his ugly chinless face. "Amilia is a true dear, Janilah," he announced grandly, as he lurked into the room in his fine cloth-of-gold cloak, embroidered with patterns showing dramatic leviathan hunts. "Goodness, has a finer woman ever been birthed? Beauty and charm and wisdom all in one splendid little package. I feel she shall make me a happy man indeed."

Then you'll be the only one, Janilah thought, but said, "I'm glad she pleases you, my lord."

"Most certainly, yes, she pleases me greatly." Hadrin took a glance around the room. "Oh, I see. So...so this is why you asked for me? I thought you wished to hear of my time with your granddaughter?"

Janilah ignored that. "King Hadrin, meet Archibald Benton and his team. They are scouring the ancestral book of your line."

"Scouring, but not damaging, I should hope." Hadrin had been brought up to speed on Janilah's procurement of the Book of Thala. "I really do insist you take care with it, Janilah, while you perform your studies. I will need it back in one piece, so I might add my own passages to it later."

Which will include what? Janilah wondered. Hadrin's foresight had thus far been limited to sketchy views of dragon attacks and burning buildings and a single image of Amron Daecar limping toward a great white light. It was all meaningless until given context. "We'll take good care of the book, though there is a page missing, you should know."

"Oh?"

"One ripped from your father's accounts. Did he ever speak of a code of Thala's design?"

The Rat King looked befuddled by that. "A code, Janilah?"

"Through time," Janilah said. He waved Archibald over to provide explanation. The scholar duly obliged. When done, Hadrin looked just as confused as ever. "I had hoped you might know something of this," Janilah said, displeased. "Did your father never speak of any of it?"

"No, Janilah, never. Rasal monarchs do not speak of what they write in the book. It's sacred, and not to be shared with anyone."

Until you, he thought. *You worthless cretin.* Janilah so wished to put a dagger through the man's beady black eyes, the mood he was in. "Can you tell me anything of Ranulf Shackton, the adventurer?"

The question came from the blue. Hadrin gave it a quizzical expression and made a confused little huffy sound. "Like what? He's known to have travelled a great deal, and has led solo and group expeditions all around the world. He is widely celebrated in Rasalan for his achievements. I've heard he has an interest in scholarly endeavours too. A smart man, they say, and fond of a story. I met him once some years, though my memory of him is thin. He was more friendly with my father. He spoke of him occasionally."

"Your father did?" Janilah took that on. "In what regard?"

"An affectionate one, I suppose. They only met on a handful of occasions, so far as I know, but my father seemed to hold Ranulf in high esteem. I had a sense he was going to achieve something important in his life. That my father might have seen him in the Eye of Rasalan, perhaps."

Janilah mused on all that. His eyes went to Archibald. "You said King Godrin's accounts were troublesome to translate?"

"Oh yes, most difficult, my lord."

"Yet Ranulf Shackton must have deciphered his code, to have known which page to remove."

"Yes, I suppose he must have. If, of course, it was Ranulf who removed the page."

"It was." Janilah thought some more, rubbing his bearded chin. "Might Godrin have coded a personal instruction to Ranulf, Archibald? As Queen Thala did with the kings and queens of her line."

"It's...possible, given what we have unearthed. But that would assume that King Godrin knew that Ranulf Shackton would come into possession of the book."

"He did. Good King Hadrin here just said so himself, did you not hear? He believes his father saw Ranulf Shackton in the Eye of Rasalan. Godrin must have known Shackton would study the Book of Thala, and more than that, decipher his own code." Janilah looked to the tome, laid out upon the lectern. "And hidden within his own accounts he transcribed a message for the adventurer. We must assume that within that message was the instruction to remove the page, and keep it from falling into foreign hands. *My* hands."

Janilah stepped over to a side table and poured himself a cup of wine. He offered the same to no one else. He drew on it, still thinking. *Even from beyond the grave, Godrin continues to taunt me.* Behind came a shuffling sound of leather on stone. "Janilah, I find myself a little confused," came Hadrin's weaselly voice. "Just what exactly is happening here? What do you imagine that my father has hidden from you? Is this about the Blades of Vandar?" He paused. "You seek them, I know. Had you hoped to find the Frostblade's location in the book, perhaps? Or the Mistblade."

Janilah didn't answer. All the world still thought the Mistblade lost and Hadrin remained among them. He kept his back to the man, and his cup to his lips. He drank long and he drank deep. And all the while, his thoughts turned dark.

"Janilah? I feel I deserve an explanation. This book is mine by birthright. If I should wish it, I could take it..."

"I thank you for your counsel, King Hadrin. You may return to my granddaughter."

"*Return*?" Hadrin's voice was indignant. "You still haven't told me..."

"I will explain to you all that I have learned at a later time. For now I need to be alone. Leave me."

There was a delay before he heard further movement, as Hadrin gave out a huff and stalked his way out of the room. Beyond the door, he heard some vocal complaints issued toward Sir Munroe Moore, the head of Hadrin's guard. Janilah turned once he was certain the Rat King was gone. "Continue the search, Archibald," he said. "If you need me, I shall be in my chambers."

He returned to his solar to spend a short time in private thought. He had yet another dinner engagement that night that he'd rather not attend, and needed a short moment of respite beforehand. Unfortunately, he found Cecilia on her window seat, lips red from wine. "Father, I was waiting for you. How fares the great tome, then? Did fusty old Archibald deliver the news you'd hoped?"

"Not now, Cecilia. I am in no mood for company."

"One of those days, then?"

"Every day is one of those days." Janilah filled a cup and dropped into his wide oaken chair. His bastard daughter had eyes that asked a hundred questions, as usual, and not one of them he was prepared to answer. Instead he asked his own. "How is your brother? Did you speak to him, as I asked?"

"I did," she said, smoothly.

"And?"

Janilah had done as he'd intended, and spoken to Rylian of calling off Prince Robbert's betrothal to Lyriss Reynar. He had hoped it would bring his son around, but he'd remained cold and distant since then. His next move was to send Cecilia to speak to him. He was never quite sure whether that was wise or not.

"Do you really want to know?" she asked, with that mischievous twist to her lips. *Her mother had the same*, Janilah thought. It was what drew him to her in the first place. Cecilia's mother, Lady Jeyne Blakewood, had been a beautiful woman, but that wasn't her only draw. She was clever too, and cunning, and Janilah had bedded her in the hope of siring a daughter of the same. Not a son, no, not from her. It was a daughter he wanted and a daughter he got. She sat before him now, every inch what he'd hoped for.

"He still despises me then?" he asked her.

"No, of course not. I'm just being facetious, father. You know how I get." She slid from the window seat and walked to the table, filling her cup. With her spare hand she curled an errant tress of glossy brown hair behind her ear.

"So? I don't have time for your games, not now. Speak plainly."

"Well in truth there's not much to say." She returned to her seat, perching elegantly on the red velvet cushion, glancing occasionally to take in the view. "It's been only days since he returned, and he is still getting used to that bitch he calls wife. It's no wonder Rylian likes to spend all his time abroad. Clarris seems to grow more spiteful with each passing moon."

"And that explains his foul mood, does it?"

"In part, yes. Who wouldn't be miserable being wedded to that shrivelled old shrew?" She laughed and sipped her wine. "But he'll soon lighten up, and when he does, he'll come to see that you are trying your best to make amends, Father. Rylian only wants control over who his children wed. The die is cast with Amilia, but so long as he can determine whom Robbert and Raynald marry, he'll be satisfied, I'm sure."

Janilah's only response was to give a little grunt. He needed Rylian by his side, perhaps more than ever now, and that irked him greatly. He was still thinking of the missing Blades. *The Frostblade, lost. The Nightblade and Sword of Varinar, stolen. The Windblade on its way,* he hoped. And even that certainty had gone, given what had happened in recent months. He half expected King Godrik Taynar to turn up without the blade he'd promised him, only to tell him it had been stolen too. *And where does that leave my plans?* He had thought about that more and more, as a tide of uncertainty began to rise within him. *If I cannot combine the Blades, or fulfil Galin's promise, what next?* He had control of the north now, but would that be enough to win the War Eternal? Could he defeat the tide of shadow and flame through military might and strategy alone?

More and more he was wondering if that was all he'd have, and if so he'd need his son and heir, the champion of his people, at his side. That meant acceding to him, should he come with any further demands, and the thought alone made Janilah's skin prickle. *But I must,* he knew, *to keep him in line.* He could not let Rylian join his list of enemies. That list was long enough as it was.

He could sense Cecilia watching him as he thought through all that. *Does she smell some vulnerability in me?* He didn't like that notion one bit. "Leave me," he told her. "I have..."

"Letters to write. Yes, I'm sure you do, Father." She slipped from the window seat and stepped toward his desk. "Who do you dine with this evening? Would you like me to attend, for moral support?"

"No," he said, as she put down her cup.

"Still intent on keeping me in the shadows? *The Bastard Bitch of Blakewood.*" She grinned. "Have you heard that one? Some of the Vandarians are calling me that, and no doubt the Rasals too. I have a mind to think it came from Elyon Daecar, you know. That boy knows far too much."

"Lady Melany is working on him. She'll find out what he knows soon enough, she assures me." Janilah pulled a piece of parchment in front of him to make his point.

"OK, I'll go. Though you might want a quill and ink too. Writing letters is hard without them, I find." She grinned with that and left.

Janilah Lukar finally had some peace. In truth he wanted death, to satiate something rageful inside him. *Ranulf Shackton,* he thought again. If the man was still in Miren then it would take weeks to reach him. Sir Kevyn had not been wrong. Two months, he'd said, and he'd return with the missing page and Vincent Rose's head. *Add Shackton's to the bargain, and I might just permit it,* he thought, yet what were the chances of ever finding that page again? Like the Sword of Varinar, it might be lost to him forever, burned or torn into a thousand pieces or crushed and dropped down a well. *Gone*, he thought. *Gone for good.* Try as he might to stay calm, he couldn't help but slam a fist into his desk. *Blood, I need blood.* The thought went around and around, circling through his head like a vulture over a kill. It was still there some two hours later when the door knocked and Sir Owen Armdall stepped in.

"Do you have him?" Janilah asked eagerly, standing.

"I do, sire."

"Show me."

They walked with Sir Rees and Sir Fredrick several steps behind them, moving through the quiet corridors of Janilah's private quarters within the King's Tower to a dark stone chamber set at the bottom of a spiral stair. It was a place of torture and death, grim and dim and stained with blood and worse. Sometimes his Six came here to draw information from his subjects. Sometimes Janilah joined in himself, when his frustrations boiled over and he needed some release. He needed such a release now, and there he was, ready to give it.

"My king," shivered Reggie Warren in his lowborn drawl. The man was a cur, unwashed and unkempt, a mouthy little wretch who was good for sordid jobs. He had but one job now to fulfil. "I...I asked Sir Owen what this was, but...but he wouldn't tell me..." He was tied up in chains against the rear stone wall, dressed in homespun wools. He rattled his fetters in confusion. "Have I done you some disservice, sire? I...I don't understand, I don't...What is it you want from me?"

"Blood." Janilah drew his blade. He stepped forward as the man's tongue went numb, blubbering incoherently. Through it Janilah spoke. "For months you stayed next door to Ranulf Shackton's cell. For months you learned nothing of his intentions. If it wasn't for you he might not have escaped. He tricked you, Reggie. He outsmarted you, and here you are."

"No....no, sire, I...I was only...only tryin' to...to win his...his friendship." His breeches started to darken. The scent of piss washed through the cell. "We spoke...we spoke of ways out, it's true, but I never...I never thought...oh please," he blubbered, as Janilah moved forward. "Please, sire, don't kill me. I can make it up to you. I...I can still serve you, if you'll...." He was weeping profusely. "If you'll let me..."

"You will serve me, Reggie. You'll serve the edge of my blade."

"No...no please, no..."

No was the last word Reggie Warren spoke before Janilah Lukar split open his neck. Blood fountained out in great spurts, raining onto the grey stone floor, running through the cracks where so many others had bled before. Some spattered across Janilah's cloak and beard, wetting his lips. He tasted iron and spat to the side.

He didn't really blame the man for extracting nothing of worth from Ranulf Shackton. Yet he did for helping him escape. There had been no intention in that, of course. As the dying man had said, he'd spoken of escaping the dungeons with Ranulf as a way of winning his trust, so that he might later learn of his secrets, and these last months, Janilah had let all that pass. Yet now...now Ranulf's escape had come back to haunt him. And Reggie...poor wretched Reggie Warren had played his part in that.

He continued to watch the dying man wriggling on the wall, his blood spreading down his chest and pooling across the floor. A long cold quiet took root. Then Sir Fredrick Ruxmond said, "Would you like another, sire?" as though offering him a second cup of wine. But not wine. *Blood.* Janilah's need was not yet quenched, the Ram of Ruxmond could see.

"Another," Janilah repeating, nodding. "Yes...a big one, Sir Fredrick. From the city dungeons." *Lots of blood,* he was thinking. *One with lots of blood.*

"There's a serial raper who'd been prowling the alleys of White

Shadow at night, recently caught. He's a large man, my lord. I shall have him brought up here."

"Two," said Janilah. "Bring me two, Sir Fredrick."

"Very good, sire. Two. I'll see it done."

"Good." Janilah took a last look at Reggie Warren as his cleaved neck threw up a few final gouts of blood. He felt nothing. *Would that it was Ranulf Shackton,* he thought, wiping the blood from the edge of his blade. A grimace passed his lips as he climbed the stair to prepare for his dinner engagement.

I should never have let him live.

20

Lythian

"He has colours much like yours," Sir Pagaloth said, standing at Lythian's side across the rugged mossy hillock where Garlath the Grand and Neyruu were perched. Ulrik Marak and Kin'rar Kroll were busy looking over the multi-seat saddles that had been affixed to their bonded dragons' backs, making sure they were stable for the flight. "The blue and silver of Garlath's scales, they must remind you somewhat of Vandar, Captain?"

Lythian hadn't really thought about that, but come to think of it, Sir Pagaloth was right. Garlath the Grand's rough plate scales were coloured in muted hues of slate grey and blue, glistening from the light rains and damp fog that cloaked the hills and woods of the Western Neck. "Your prince would call that fate," he said, looking over toward Tethian. The Agarathi prince stood with Ashun Klo, the tall fair-headed captain of his guard, and the old bent-backed scholar Sotel Dar, watching as the final preparations were made for their journey. There was a look of great destiny on the prince's face, as his crimson cloak fluttered in the breeze, embroidered with the fiery sigil of Eldur.

Eldur, Lythian thought. *Our quarry*. For today was the day they'd been waiting for. Today was the day they would fly.

"He is a most pious man," Pagaloth said of the prince, "and most merciful too. I will thank him always for sparing my life, though no more than I will thank you, Lythian. It was not a reprieve I deserved."

"It was," Lythian told him. He was garbed in his dark grey woollen cloak, and black boiled leathers beneath. The simple attire was balanced by the presence of Starslayer at his hip, embraced within its scabbard. "How many times do I have to tell you that?"

"The same as always, Lythian," said Pagaloth. "Just the once more."

He gave a good natured smile, and turned his eyes across the hill. The last fortnight had been enough to give Garlath time to heal of his wounds, his flank and wing sufficiently restored to enable the great dragon to convey them to the Wings. That had been the case for several days now, after which it was a simple matter of waiting for the right weather. Across the Western Neck, it was overcast and grey, breezy and cold, and further to the southwest a storm was sweeping in. It would help conceal their flight from watching eyes, and ensure the wild dragons of the Wings were subdued. "Dragons do not like to fly during storms, if they can avoid it," Sotel Dar had told Lythian the day before, as they awaited the right conditions to depart. "They will find dry places to wait out the weather, and that will be our chance to land unseen and unmolested."

There was a nervousness among the group; the more cautious side of excitement. None knew for certain what they would find when they landed upon those fabled islands, nor how the wild dragons would react to the return of Garlath and Neyruu, once free dragons of the Wings themselves before they flew to the Nest to be bonded to their Fireborn riders. Lythian had asked Lord Marak of it, and been told that Garlath would protect them, if any wild drake turned to violence. "He will not like it, but he will shield us from his kin. There will be no dragon on the Wings who can match him, Lythian, not in size nor strength. You needn't worry."

"Do you know that for sure?" Lythian had asked. He had come to find that Fireborn were often prone to puffery when describing their soul-bonded dragons. Kin'rar commonly cited Neyruu as being the fastest dragon in Agarath. 'Nay, the fastest dragon for a thousand years,' he would say. Lythian took it all with a pinch of salt.

"I am as sure as I can be," Marak replied, more soberly. "You saw in the Pits of Kharthar the two most deadly dragons living, Lythian - Garlath and Malathar. Now remind me, who won that fight?"

Lythian had only seen the battle in glimpses, as he and Borrus fought off a score of dragonknights with their tall black spears and dragonsteel blades, but those glimpses had suggested Garlath came away the victor, despite his injuries. He gave that as his answer, and Marak nodded proudly. "The dragons of the Wings will not trouble us. Speak to Master Dar of it, and he will tell you...the bravest and strongest dragons are those that leave those islands to be bonded. And there are none more brave nor strong as Garlath, the greatest dragon of his age."

"That title is commonly given to Vallath," Lythian pointed out.

"In the north, yes. Not so here." Marak's voice was sharp, with subtle hints of scorn. "You northmen exaggerate Vallath's prowess because it makes your own Amron Daecar seem all the greater for defeating him. Yet while Vallath and Prince Dulian were falling to Amron's blade, Garlath and I were killing your king and mighty First Blade both, who held the Sword of Varinar in his grasp. Now ask yourself again, who is the greater dragon?"

"The way you describe it, I would have to say Garlath."

"The way I describe it?" Marak had bristled. "Is there another way of stating the facts?"

Lythian had decided not to get into that particular debate with the man. "No," is all he'd said. "But I just hope you're right, Ulrik, and Garlath frightens the wild dragons away. I rather think that they'll come for me, first of all, should they sniff us out."

"Yes, you may be right. Perhaps it would have been better had Borrus stayed after all. He would have provided ample distraction, I think. And ample meat besides."

"He'd have fed the entire island for a week," Lythian jested. "Leastways before he lost his belly."

"He only lost a part of it. There was still plenty of the man to go around."

Lythian thought of Borrus Kanabar now, as he stood atop the craggy hillock awaiting the call to fly. Life here among these Agarathi outlaws took on a different flavour with the burly Barrel Knight absent, and Lythian often wondered what had become of him. *With luck, he's nearing northern shores by now,* he thought. It had been over three weeks since Kin'rar had flown him to Solas and assuming he found himself a willing captain and ship, he should be deep into his voyage home. *And yet here I am, set to fly the other way.*

Sir Pagaloth seemed to see some shadow of worry in his eyes. "Do you feel nervous, my friend?" he asked, gesturing toward the dragons, as the straps and rigging of their saddles were checked and double-checked, then checked again. "Dragon-flight must be a frightening prospect for a man of your nature. And these conditions will be treacherous. It is highly uncommon for any dragon to fly with more than one rider, you know."

"I have flown before, Pagaloth, if you'll recall. And there was a storm that day too. I am quite prepared for what is to come."

"Of course. You are a noted Son of Varin, and thus a man prepared for anything. And your company will be rather more agreeable this time, I would say."

The dragonknight had a suggestive look on his face. "I take it you're referring to the princess?" Lythian asked him.

"Who else? There are certain men of this company whose company you enjoy, I have seen. Skymaster Kin'rar, certainly, and Sotel Dar, you like discussing scholarly matters with him, that is clear. But none make you smile as Princess Talasha does."

Lythian could hardly deny that. Much as he tried to keep his affections for Talasha private, they crept out more often than he'd like. "She has been very kind to me, since Borrus left," he said.

"Kind, yes, she is most kind, I agree. One of her many virtues, would you not say?"

How long do you have? Lythian wondered. If he was to stand here and list Talasha's virtues, they might be there a while. For weeks now the princess had continued to seek his company, and often they would go on walks together through the woods, gathering kindling for the fires, or searching for mushrooms and herbs to be thrown in with the stew. They had hunted together too, on occasion, taking out bows and arrows and spending hours looking for rabbits and wildfowl, or even deer if they were lucky.

The first time they did so, Lythian had been surprised to see Talasha arrive with a bow to hand and quiver on her back, discarded of her finery and dressed in quilted leather garments suitable for long ranges into the wild. "I didn't realise Agarathi princesses liked to hunt, Talasha," he had remarked upon seeing her.

"There is much you do not know of our ways, Lythian," she'd replied. "In Eldurath it is common for ladies of the court to join the men on hunts, and even participate if they wish it. The lands of the Askar Delta teem with birds and small game. I spent many days of my youth with bow and arrow to hand."

She had proven that when she'd shot a pheasant through the eye from fifty yards. They'd been some miles from camp that day and a storm had soon closed in. Out in the Western Neck, the weather was inclement and prone to rainfall and they'd been forced to shelter beneath an overhang of rock, within the shadow of one of the many rugged hills that broke out beyond the forest. Lythian had taken to forging them a fire for warmth, gathering wood nearby. By the time he returned Talasha had plucked and prepared the bird, her hands all covered in feathers and blood. "Do not look so surprised, noble captain," she had said, with a smile. "The hunt is but the half of it. What use is someone if they can kill a bird, but not know how to cook it?"

They cooked alone and ate alone that night, huddled beneath the overhang, as the storm continued to thicken about them. When the lightning began, Talasha suggested they stay until morning, when the weather would likely clear. "We have our cloaks for warmth, and the fire," she said. "And one another, Lythian. We have that too."

"Princess, we should try to get back," Lythian had protested. "Your cousin will worry where you are. He may think I have stolen you away."

"Maybe you should," she had told him, inching closer. "Would you like that, Lythian? To steal me away?"

"I am no thief, Talasha." His smile turned awkward; the joke was poor. "We are but five miles from camp, by my estimate, much of it covered by the wood. We should not linger here. It may not be safe..."

"I am safe with you." She shifted another inch across the rock on which they sat. "I like being alone with you, Captain Lythian. Alone, we need not worry who is watching." Her hand had reached out, soft and warm upon his cheek, and drawn him into a kiss.

Lythian hadn't slept a wink that night, as he lay down beside her, the arch of her lower back and buttocks pressed right up to his groin. He could only think of her lips, the first lips he'd tasted since his wife Talia, and how he wanted more. For hour upon hour he'd lain there through the long black night, listening to Talasha's soft breathing over the storm, searching through the woodland that spread beyond their refuge in search of wolves and bears and other shadowed threats. It had given him distraction, at least, from his improper thoughts.

I must protect her, he would tell himself. *I must return her safe to camp.* Yet even so, a part of him wished to continue the way they'd been going, to range far and farther still into the depths of the wilderness, to build with her a simple life beyond the shadow of war.

By morning such foolish thoughts had been put aside, withering away with the storm and the rains, as the sun broke out through the thinning clouds, setting upon the world a warm golden glow. Talasha sat up and stretched, looking more beautiful than ever as the pale yellow light caught upon her face, and the trees about them glittered and tinkled as the last of the rainfall drizzled through their leaves. Her glossy jet hair flowed down as though it had been newly styled by her maids. The red in her eyes glimmered, alluring, as the flicker of a flame drawing a moth to its doom. *And I am doomed,* Lythian had thought to look at her. She smiled and the thought came yet stronger once more.

"Good morning, my handsome knight," she'd said, running a hand across his bristled cheek. "You slept well, I hope?"

"Most well, my lady," he'd lied, trying to draw away. "But we best get back, as soon as possible."

"After," she had said, as she reached to pull him toward her. "*After*, Captain."

I am doomed, came that cursed thought again, as she pressed her lips to his. But not long did it linger, as she stripped away her clothes, exposing a shapely body that no man could ever refuse. He'd tried to deny her, of course, as she drew one garment off, and then another, unwrapping the great gift that lay beneath. But even his own words sounded hollow in his ears. "I cannot," he had said. "Talasha, my oaths...my duty...my..."

"Desire?" she'd cut in, pressing a finger to his lips, and pulling his hand to her breast. She smiled a hungry smile. "We both share it, Lythian. Let us not deny ourselves any longer, not while we are out here alone."

"But my oaths," he'd repeated, his words breaking out through his lips, no more than a feeble whisper. "I...I cannot break them..."

"Oaths?" She peeled the last of her clothes away. "What oaths deny you from laying with a woman, Lythian? What oaths deny you your needs?"

None, he might have told her, for the only oaths he was speaking of were those he'd sworn to himself. To never be with another woman. To never sire another child. To never love again. To commit all of himself to the bounds of his duty. To be a Knight of Varin only, a sword and shield for the kingdom he so loved. But he spoke of none of that, for his mind brought up no such thoughts but her, as she bared herself to the rising sun, golden and gleaming, and climbed atop him. *I am doomed,* was all he thought. *Gods, I am doomed.*

When they got back to camp, they made their excuses, and though Marak seemed angry that they'd not tried to return last night, Prince Tethian waved it away. "We cannot control the weather, Ulrik," he'd said. "My cousin and the captain know what they are doing. I trust them both, as should you."

Trust, Lythian had thought to that, feeling a pang of guilt. *I betray my own promises, and now I betray a prince.* Later that same day, he took Talasha aside amid the castle ruins atop the hill. "That cannot happen again, Talasha," he had stressed to her. "We cannot betray your cousin's trust like this."

"Quiet, my handsome knight." She drew him around the safety of a cracked stone pillar, and draped her full lips upon his once more. "Shhhh, we are doing nothing wrong."

Lythian wasn't sure about that. He was a Son of Varin, and she a Daughter of Eldur, a knight and a princess unsuited to such a union. "This is wrong," he said.

"Wrong? No, there is nothing more right, sweet captain. We are just people, are we not? You are a man, and I am a woman. What does it matter where we come from?"

"Your cousin..."

"My cousin cares not for idle fancies such as love and lust. He aspires to greater ambitions, as you know. He will approve, if we ask him."

Lythian frowned. "Ask him what?"

"That we be permitted to wed, of course." Her face had turned so serious that Lythian knew at once it was jest. She had broken out into that glorious laughter of hers, sweet as the sound of morning birdsong.

"You shouldn't joke of such things," he responded. *And I will never wed again,* he'd thought.

Yet despite his reservations and promises and shame, they'd stolen into the woods again since then, thrice more going out under the guise of hunting, only to return empty handed and hot-faced. Each time they came back, a new set of eyes watched them with suspicion. "That was the last time," Lythian would say. "This cannot go on."

And then she would draw him to some private place and convince him otherwise, and his resolve would crumble to dust all over again. "I am a princess, and will have you as I please," she'd tell him. "It takes but your own will to deny me, Lythian. You seem to think that anyone here will care...they will not. But you do, I can see. What is it you're not telling me?"

My dead wife, he thought, but didn't say. *My dead son. The family that I lost and who have haunted me ever since. The family I vowed never to betray.* But all he said was, "Marak suspects us, and Ashun Klo as well. I do not like the shape of his eyes, Talasha. He has the face of a man who will cut your neck as you sleep."

"And risk having his own cut for the trouble," she responded. "You are an honoured guest here, under Tethian's protection. Ashun Klo is a proud and noble man, but no fool. Or is there something else that worries you, sweet captain? Do you believe that Ashun Klo lusts for me too?"

"All the men here lust for you, whether they say it or not. You do not seem to know the power you wield."

"Oh I know. All women are taught to know." She went to kiss him, but for once he resisted.

"Not here, Talasha." His eyes turned through the woods, as men shifted through the trees. "Someone may see."

"Let them."

"Talasha, no..."

She'd laughed as he pushed her away. "Mayhaps I will find Ashun more agreeable, do you think? He covets me, you say? And he is of an ancient house, and a childhood friend of my cousin. A fine match among noble outlaws. Would you turn me to him, Lythian? Would you send me into his arms?"

"Of course not." Her trick was working. He felt a hot flush of jealousy rising upon his cheeks. "I...I feel for you, Talasha. That is what concerns me most."

"How strange, to be so concerned by something so natural."

"Love is more complex than that."

"*Love*? My captain, are you trying to tell me something?"

He didn't rise to the bait. "Just that our courtship can never reach beyond these hills. We live on either side of a great divide, Talasha. You are a princess and I am a knight, and..."

"And you are scared, sweet captain," she broke in. "And making excuses I do not want to hear. For that divide you speak of will come down. And princess? Knight? Out here we are all one and the same, driven toward a higher purpose. These titles are meaningless. What is a princess without her throne? What is a knight without his armour? We have been stripped of all that, Lythian, stripped of the responsibility we once bore. I for one feel liberated for it. I thought you felt the same." She turned with those words, and stormed off.

They hadn't spoken much over the past two days since then, as preparations for their journey were finalised. Lythian had requested that Talasha remain in camp, but Prince Tethian had stated that his cousin would be coming with them. "She wishes to join us, Captain, and I will not deny her. She is descended of Eldur's rich blood, as I am. He will welcome seeing two of his kin upon waking, I think. And could there be a prettier face to look upon, after three thousand years of sleep?"

Not in all the world, Lythian thought. But of course, he'd said nothing.

In the end, his appeals had fallen on deaf ears, and the members of the party had been distilled down to a small group of seven. Neyruu's saddle had been designed to carry three, with the royal cousins Tethian and Talasha set to fly behind Kin'rar. The rest - Marak, Ashun Klo, Sotel Dar, and Lythian himself - would be conveyed to the Wings by Garlath, along with Lythian's godsteel blade, Starslayer, which accounted for several more men in weight. When the group had been finalised, Lythian had wondered, *why not eight?* "The number is sacred to you," he had said to Prince Tethian. "I am sure Garlath can carry another." He had in mind a particular man.

"Sir Pagaloth?" Tethian asked him, reading into his intentions. "You wish for him to join us?"

"He could be of use, Your Highness, should we find ourselves in trouble."

Tethian considered it, then shook his head. "Marak says Garlath can carry no more in his condition, not if we are to bring your blade, which we must. And let us not forget, we shall be returning with another, Captain." He reached out and gripped his shoulder. "The eighth will be the Divine Lord Eldur, my friend."

Now, as Lythian stood amid the morning mists, he turned to Sir Pagaloth with a low word of warning. "You must be careful," he told him. "Once we leave, it will be dangerous for you here, Pagaloth. Ashun Klo's men..."

"Will best be careful themselves," the proud dragonknight said with a stiffening of his trident-bearded jaw. "I have no fear for Ashun Klo's minions, Lythian. If one of them tries to lay a hand on me, they will lose it, this I know."

"That may be just what they want," Lythian said. "To provoke you into defending yourself and then claiming you acted without warrant. They want you dead, I have no doubt. As they do me."

There were three men in question under discussion; Grumlo, Rackar, and Kartheck, each of rough disposition who served under the command of Ashun Klo. Grumlo was a brute, though of a highborn line, Rackar of a middling house and middling frame both, and Kartheck lowborn and a former sellsword, dark of eye and dark of hair with a menacing look about him. They were killers born, all of them, and Kartheck in particular had a dozen tattoos around his eyes, one for every man he'd slain.

"They will not be able to claim anything if they cannot draw breath," Pagaloth responded defiantly. "A part of me wishes for them to try something, Lythian. I am not so enfeebled as when I arrived here."

He'd been with them for some two weeks now, during which time he'd restored his physical strength. The man had near starved to death during his journey from Eldurath in search of Lythian, arriving all skin and bone and sunken cheek, bedraggled and half broken from his travels upon hoof and foot. It was his way of atoning for his betrayal, he had said, and he'd existed on low rations in a bid to mimic, in some small way, the experience Lythian and the others had been through during their captivity. He was back to his old self now, though, tall and leanly muscled, with that triple-pronged beard and greasy jet-black hair, restored by a healthy ration of game meat and root vegetables and what little fruit they would scavenge from the woods.

But strong as he was, he'd be vulnerable all the same. Even now, Lythian could see the fair-headed Ashun Klo glancing over at Pagaloth through his cruel purple eyes. *I wonder if he's given orders to have Pagaloth murdered when we leave?* Lythian thought. He'd seen the captain in privy conversation with his men on many occasions, plotting this or that it looked, though whether it was about Pagaloth, he couldn't rightly say. "Just make sure you sleep among the men at night, and not alone," Lythian said. "Talasha's handmaids have taken a liking to you, she tells me. Remain near them, if you can."

"I do not need to be protected, Lythian." The topic brought out the old Sir Pagaloth Kadosk, short and curt of voice, proud and intractable. "Certainly not by two women."

"They will offer a buffer, is all," Lythian said. "Your stubbornness will get you killed if you let it."

"It will get *them* killed," came back the dragonknight. "I know how to sleep with one eye open, Captain. You do not need to worry for me. It is you who travels to the cradle of dragons and fire, my friend. You; a Son of Varin. I would keep your concern for yourself. You will need every measure of it."

And is that what I'm doing? Lythian had to wonder. *Distracting myself by worrying for Pagaloth?* His duty among the Varin Knights had always required that he think more about his men than himself, after all. And it was in his nature to be selfless besides.

Across the hillside, Kin'rar Kroll was now waving him over as the party gathered around. Talasha came striding up the slope with her maids trailing behind. Cevi had been crying, Lythian could see by the red skin around her eyes. Mirella looked close to tears too, though was of a more stoic persuasion. But clear enough, they feared for their lady. *Not everyone believes we'll be coming back*, he thought. He turned to Pagaloth with a final word. "Tethian put you in my service, so you'll follow my commands, yes?" he asked.

The dragonknight nodded begrudgingly.

"Good. Then you'll sleep close to Cevi and Mirella, as I asked. They may be handmaids, but their presence will offer protection. No arguments, Sir Pagaloth. This is my ruling."

"Then I suppose I must accept." Pagaloth watched the two handmaids a moment, then said, "And when I am awake?"

"Then you'll be awake," Lythian told him, "and quite able to protect yourself, as you have pointed out." He smiled and gripped the man's forearm. "I'll see you in a couple of days, my friend," he said, then marched away across the hill.

The group had assembled now, wrapped up warm for the journey. Tethian was giving a speech, as he liked to do. "The ride will be long, cold, and wet," he said, as Lythian joined. "The Wings are twice as far from here as Eldurath, and the conditions will grow less pleasant through the day. We trust Ulrik and Kin'rar to know if and when we must land. This may be needed, they both tell me, when we reach the southern coast, and before we strike out across the sea."

"Garlath may need a rest," Marak said to that, as though feeling he had to explain. "He has not flown much since healing, and large as he may be, he is not used to carrying four full grown men and a heavy godsteel longsword on his back."

Sotel Dar gave a little coughing laugh. "I am glad I am considered a full grown man, Lord Marak."

"You are twice as old as most of us, Master Dar."

"Yes, and half as heavy. Even Princess Talasha outweighs me, I would say."

"Are you trying to say something, Sotel?" the princess asked.

"Yes," grinned the dark-skinned scholar, leaning on his dragon-head staff. "Simply that I am a shrivelled old man, my princess, who hardly weighs much more than an infant child."

"Then perhaps we should change the seating order?" Talasha proposed. Her eyes shifted momentarily to Lythian. "Might it not be better that I swap with Sotel, and fly with Garlath instead? It would lessen the weight for Neyruu, would it not? Injured Garlath may have been, but he must be ten times Neyruu's weight. Surely it is she who needs to carry the lighter load?"

"Neyruu carried Borrus Kanabar all the way from Eldurath, Princess," said Marak. "You met the man. Even shrunken by his captivity, he will have weighed more than you and Prince Tethian combined, and he had with him his godsteel blade as well. Neyruu will be fine."

"She has another agenda, clearly," put in Ashun Klo in his cold haughty voice. "She wishes to travel with the Varin Knight."

"Or you, Ashun," she said, with a twinkle in her red-brown eyes.

"I rather think not, Princess." Ashun Klo turned from her as quickly as he could. "My prince, we are wasting time. I judge that Skymaster Kin'rar and Skylord Marak know best of their dragons' capabilities. I do not think switching one for another will change anything for such powerful beasts."

"Yes, I'm inclined to agree," said Tethian in his easy way. "We'll keep the seating arrangements as they are. But as I was saying, we will stop en route if deemed necessary by our gallant Fireborn. We all know these are not good conditions in which to fly, but they are essential all the same. The saddles have been tested, and the harnesses will keep us in place. Kin'rar, you have something to say?"

Kin'rar Kroll nodded in his polite manner, grey caped and garbed in his dragonscale armour. "Only that dragon-flight can be an unpleasant experience for the uninitiated." His eyes went across the group. "Ashun, you have yet to have a taste of sky, I understand?"

"I chose not to bond a dragon," the man said, almost defensively. "My gift is the blade." He gave Lythian a bitter look.

"Of course, and gifted you are with dragonsteel to hand. But my point stands. You've never flown a dragon, have you?"

"No."

"Nor you, my prince?"

Tethian shook his head. "Not since I was a young boy, when my father would take me up on Vallath. I do recall the thrill of it fondly, however, riding the skies atop that soaring mountain. I am excited to reach to the clouds again."

"I will take you through them, my prince. Prince Talasha, you seemed to enjoy the experience as well, when I brought you from Eldurath."

"Enormously. Though of course that was a fine dry day. It may be different in this weather."

"You will be fine," Marak said. "Any man or woman of rich Fireborn blood is born to take to the skies." He turned to Lythian. "You threw up, Captain, as I recall? Try to refuse the urge again, if you can."

"I'll try my best, Ulrik." *But if I do, I'll aim it right in Ashun Klo's face,* he thought.

"And Master Dar?" asked Kin'rar. "You've flown dragons several times before, I understand, during your research missions to the Wings?"

"Yes, but I was a much younger man then. I'm not certain how my body will hold up this time."

"We'll take it slow," Marak said, towering above the host. His thick-muscled body was bound in his Body of Karagar armour, and rich red cape, with the Fireblade steaming at his hip. "This is not a day for haste."

"Not so long as the weather holds," said Ashun Klo. He gave Tethian another urging look.

The prince responded with a nod. "Ashun is right. We need the cover of the storm, if we're to land safely upon the islands. This chance may not come again for some weeks, even months. Let us not waste it." He stepped away toward Neyruu, and the rest quickly followed.

Around the hillside, the remainder of the ardent followers of Tethian's cause had gathered to see them off. Lythian could see Talasha's handmaids standing with Pagaloth. Mirella was the more comely of the pair, though both were eyeing the dragonknight with interest. *It seems they are as lustful as their lady,* Lythian thought, as the woman in question appeared at his side, wreathed in warm red robes, and a heavy brown mantle over the top, stitched with the crest of Eldur. "I like your new embroidery," he said, looking at the eight fiery rings around the red dragon's head. "I didn't realise you had taken so fondly to your cousin's cause."

"I am coming with you, am I not? I suppose that means I believe in what we're doing."

"I suppose it does. Your cousin is quite convincing."

"But not enough to bend the mind of the incorrigible Captain Lythian, of course." She smiled that playful smile of hers.

"I am much like Lord Marak. I will be convinced once I look upon Eldur with my own two eyes." *And stab him dead with Starslayer, before he can wake.* He turned from that thought. That was Borrus Kanabar talking, not him.

"A wise course," the princess said. "I did hear, however, that you had asked for me to remain here in camp, sweet captain. Why is that? Do you not wish for my company, down there in the darkness?"

"I wish you safe from that darkness, Princess. I asked that you stay here for your own protection."

"My protection...from who, exactly? The dragons or the demigod? Or you, Lythian? Do you mean to put some distance between us?"

"Distance is inevitable, once I return home to Vandar." *Though I'd sooner keep you near me, always,* he thought.

She smiled as though hearing his mind, and not his words, and reached out to take his hand. "This world of ours is changing, Lythian," she said quietly. "The Vandar you know may not last much longer, nor the Agarath to which I was born. Is that not what Tethian and Master Dar preach? That Eldur will waken, and the heir of Varin will rise, and together they will usher in a new age of peace?"

"I hope that's possible," is all Lythian said.

"*Hope.*" She squeezed his hand. "Hope for that is hope for us, sweet captain. If our kingdoms should unite in peace, then what will there be to stop us?"

She smiled and drifted away, drawing her fingers slowly over his as they parted. *What will there be to stop us?* Lythian wondered. *My oaths, princess. The oaths that have shaped my life, and never once been broken... until you.*

He joined the others at Garlath's towering flank, climbing up onto the dragon's mountainous back by way of the many horns and rugged juts of scale that furnished the beast's hulking mass. The saddles had been designed to seat the men one behind another. At the front sat Marak, then Ashun Klo, then Sotel Dar. Lythian took the seat at the rear, and strapped himself into his harness, making certain that Ashun Klo or his cronies hadn't somehow sabotaged his straps and fastenings. Across from them, Kin'rar, Tethian, and Talasha were doing the same upon Neyruu, lined up in that order. Talasha smiled across at him, looking altogether calm as the heavy wet fog clogged the skies about them. Around the hillside the zealots and outlaws were humming in anticipation, calling out words in their own tongue that Lythian didn't understand.

He understood it when Marak craned his neck back from ahead, and called out, "Are you all secure?"

Ashun Klo and Sotel Dar called words of assent. Lythian gave his saddled seat one final check. He made sure Starslayer was well fastened at his hip, then said, "I feel a great deal more secure than the last time, Ulrik." Then, he'd been dressed in rags, starved and beaten, and had been forced to cling onto Marak's biting scale armour for several long hours of flight. He'd come away with blood streaming from a hundred snicks and cuts on his chest. "I'm ready to go when you are."

Marak gave out something that passed for laughter, a guttural growling sound. He looked over to Kin'rar Kroll, who'd just done his final checks with his own companions. The two Fireborn nodded at one another, Marak turned forward, grunted a command to his dragon, and the beast obeyed.

With a running start, the great grey-blue dragon took flight. Up and up into the thick grey clouds they went.

21

Amron

"My people will go no further," Stegra Snowfist said, as they struck camp that night upon the vast white plains. "They will stay here until we return, Lord of Daecar. I will take you the rest of the way myself."

Around them, the dozen hunters of the Snowskins tribe were unfurling thick hide tents to protect against the cold, hammering them into place, heaping the corners with snow. The winds were calm, the air eerily still, the world all blanketed in darkness. It had been days now since Amron had last seen the sun, peeking ever-so-briefly over the horizon before plunging beneath it for a final time. He shivered within his heaped furs and turned his eyes north. The skies were leaden, the moon and stars veiled, yet through all that the great looming shape of Vandar's Tomb could be seen, rising from the earth. "How far to the foot of the mountain?" Amron asked.

"Several hours ride by greatyak," Stegra said. "We will take one with us to provide shelter, should the weather get worse. The rest will stay here with my men."

They had four greatyaks in the party, each three metres tall at the shoulder, thickly furred and broad of back, with huge curved horns twisting from their skulls. The Snowkins used them when ranging through these vast plains, erecting shelters atop their backs to provide refuge from the winds and cold, and to haul provisions and supplies. Over the centuries, only the Snowkins had managed to tame the beasts, and for the past ten days, Amron had become well acquainted with them, huddled as he'd been atop one or another as they rode northward across the endless white tundra. "You are injured and weak," the Snowfist had told him when they first set off from the honeycomb hill. "If you walk, you will slow us down. Both you and the little fat man will stay in the shelters. Blacksteel will remain on foot."

It had been a form of punishment, forcing Rogen Whitebeard to remain out in the darkness and the storms while Amron and Walter were kept to the portable shelters, but the former First Blade felt envious of him all the same. *I'm an invalid,* he had thought, time and time again, as he sat upon the stinking back of the greatyak, rocking side to side in the shelter, heaped in what felt like a hundred layers of fur. Ever since that first fateful meeting with Stegra Snowfist, the burly white chieftain had taken to treating Amron as a child. "He means only to keep you safe from harm," Walter Selleck told him. "If you're to fulfil this prophesy, then he will need you fighting fit, Amron."

But I'm not fighting fit, Amron thought, *and never will be again if what the Snowfist says is true.* Stegra was convinced the way into the mountain was shut, that all the great chambers and forges and armouries within had collapsed to the point of utter ruin, and not once over the last ten days had he weakened in that stance. "I must remind you, Lord of Daecar," he said now, setting those strange milky-blue eyes on him, "that you will not find what you are looking for. No matter what the fat one says, there is no way into the depths of the mountain, no way to the holy chamber that you seek. That mountain is dead. And good riddance."

Amron gave him a hard look. "We have all heard your views on Vandar's Tomb, Stegra. I do not need to hear them again."

"Perhaps you do. One day I might get through to you."

Amron was tiring of this. Every night when they made camp, he had to listen to the chieftain's censorious views of the holy mountain, to his disrespect and disdain for the gods of Amron's faith. He'd had quite enough of the man's petty superstitions and unending negativity. "You said you'd lead us to the mountain," he said, reaching the edge of his patience. "That was the bargain we struck, Stegra, and it didn't include this constant lecturing."

"I do not lecture, I only tell the truth. Perhaps you misunderstand my purpose, Lord of Daecar. I do not wish to anger you. I only seek to soften your hope, for it will wither and die tomorrow, when you find the way is shut."

"Which I will believe only once I have looked upon the mountain with my own two eyes, and checked for passages that you likely know nothing about. The Godway Door is not the only way in. There are others that may yet be open."

"And if they are, you will find the inside a wreck and ruin. I have told you this too many times to count, but as you wish, I will say it no more. We will leave here once we have rested, and hope that the skies begin to clear. When we reach the mountain, I will give you one day to look. Then we must return. Linger too long, and none of us shall come back. And you have your own side of that bargain to keep, Steel Lord."

The prophesy, Amron thought. The words Snowfist had first spoken ten days past came back to him. *A lord of steel will come and drive the curse away. One great quest will fail, but one greater will light the way. Steel and snow will meet as enemies, but part as allies and friends. In this the frost shall be taken, and the lands grow clear to tend.*

During their time riding atop the greatyaks, he and Walter had spent hours trying to break down the riddle. Some of it was clear enough, other bits and pieces rather more opaque. According to Stegra Snowfist, the 'lord of steel' in question was Amron, and the curse... well, he'd given little information on what it was. Just a place of dark magic, he'd said, that had infected a particularly fertile land that his people had long wished to settle, away near the northern coast of the Icewilds. Out there were wooded hills ripe with game and lakes teeming with fish, secluded hills and valleys with natural defensive features, and a long rugged coastline for the collection of crabs and cockles. It had long been stricken by a curse, allegedly swallowed in a strange darkness and fog since the coming of the Sea-King. Who this Sea-King was was one of the mysteries Amron and Walter had tried to figure out.

"A Rasal, I imagine," Walter had said. "Though whether a king or not, who can say? Stegra said the prophesy was passed onto his ancestor two hundred years ago. Back then, King Kalahan ruled Rasalan, and he wasn't known as much of an adventurer. I find it quite farfetched to believe he'd have sailed a thousand miles west across the frigid northern seas, only to lay down a curse upon a long-forgotten tract of land."

"Might have been a Seaborn lord," Amron said. "This title 'Sea-King' seems to have been conjured by the Snowskins. That could apply to anyone arriving by ship, dressed in fine furs and protected by a cohort of Bladeborn knights."

"A wealthy merchant could masquerade as such easily enough as well," Walter added. "Either way, if these lands truly are accursed, that would require the magic of a mage."

"The Seaborn have always been well stocked with sorcerers," Amron put in. "I wouldn't imagine it would take much to drive off a superstitious tribe."

"True, but to what purpose?" Walter had wondered. Neither man could figure that part out.

The rest of the riddle had been similarly considered. *One great quest will fail, but one greater will light the way.* That part set a sinking feeling to Amron's gut. The great quest that would fail, he had come to think, was his quest to seek deliverance. *The way is shut,* he thought over and over again, growing increasingly convinced by Stegra's insistence. *I'll be crippled and maimed forever.* But what this greater quest was, they weren't sure. Was it just to drive off the darkness left by the Sea-King? To rid the coastal lands of his curse? Or something else? Something grander? Again, neither of them knew.

The rest was easier to unravel. *Steel and snow will meet as enemies, but part as allies and friends.* "We're the steel, they're the snow," Walter had said. "We came together as enemies when they imprisoned us, but have become friends. Or near enough, anyhow."

"I'll call Snowfist friend only once he stops belittling our gods," Amron replied, only half in jest. Beyond that, they agreed on the meaning of that line of the riddle.

The final section also seemed simple enough to decipher. *In this the frost shall be taken, and the lands grow clear to tend.* "We're to take away the curse - this 'frost', I suppose - and clear the lands for them to live on and tend," Amron said.

"Makes sense," agreed Walter, though quite what the purpose of all of this was, neither man could work out.

Nor had Stegra been of any great help. Any enquiries for extra information only led to grunts, shrugs, shakes of the head, and little else. When asked about the last time he or any of the Snowskins had visited these accursed lands, he said, "Not for many years, no. Why would we return? Those lands have been hidden in fog for two hundred years. Even in the long summer, there is a shroud there that cannot be broken."

"And it's lasted ever since the Sea-King arrived?" Walter asked him.

"Yes, since that time. He told us never to go there, never to try, or we would find only death. Some went all the same. Bjorga Bonecrusher. Jonas the Giant. Ronja Ironmaid. All went to find the source of the curse, but none returned. Only Milved of Milkwood came back, but he was half mad when he went and much worse when he got back. Babbled on about giants and ghosts and other foul things until he ran off into the wilds and was never seen again. So I suppose he never came back either, in a way of thinking." He laughed at that. "These are old legends, though, hard to know if true or not. No one has gone there in my time, nor my father or grandfather before me. We had given up on that land until you came to us, Lord of Daecar. But it is you who will break the curse. It is foresaid."

I'm in no fit state to break anything, Amron thought now, as he stared at the shadow of Vandar's Tomb, shrouded by darkness and distance. His lungs still felt heavy from his dip in the chill waters of the Silver Scar, and that was to say nothing of his right limp and lame left arm. Both had grown worse over the past days, as the sun fled and the darkness settled and the cold crawled into his bones, deep and deeper still. Nor did he have godsteel to brace and strengthen him. Until the river he'd had a longsword at one hip and a six inch dagger at the other, and his hands had rarely been far from their hilts. Now he had nothing. No crutch to lean on. No blade with which to defend himself.

And that won't ever change, he thought, dismal. *The way is shut, the way is shut, the way is bloody shut.* He couldn't get Stegra's words out of his head. They'd driven deep into his thoughts like the cold had his bones, icing up his dreams of deliverance.

Yet Walter continued to deny Stegra. "We'll find a way," he would assure Amron, every day and every night, and every morning when they woke. On the last day they saw the sun he'd said it. Through the long cold dark that had followed, he'd repeated those words ten times daily. "We have no choice, we'll find a way. Vandar's light has led us here. He will not have led us astray."

And then Stegra would repeat his own mantra and Amron's fledgling hope would scatter like a flock of birds all over again. Who was he to believe? The man who'd come here a dozen years ago, half crazed from grief and desperation, or the chief of the tribe that lived here and who'd ventured to the mountain only last winter? Amron found himself caught between a rock and a hard place, between Stegra's blasphemy and Walter's faith.

In the end, he'd taken to hearing Whitebeard's counsel. The ranger was pragmatic, realistic, and willing to say it straight. "I believe that Stegra has no reason to lie to you," he had said, when Amron approached him on the issue. "The lands here have become more volatile of late, that much I can say for sure. Earthquakes have grown more common, and felt as far as Northwatch. Enough to bring down the mountain?" he wondered. "To cause cave-ins and collapses? Yes, I would say so. I have come upon rifts and chasms myself, in the foothills of the Weeping Heights, that were not there some years ago. If gouges can be torn so far from Vandar's Tomb, then there is no reason to doubt Stegra when he says the passages into the depths will be blocked."

Stegra's son, Svaldar, had said the same. He was a large boy of only seventeen winters, yet broad of chest and with a short beard of bristly white hair. Stegra had told the Vandarians that Svaldar went with him when he visited the mountain. Amron caught him alone one night, as the boy took a watch at the edge of camp. "You are brave, Svaldar," he'd said, "to have visited Vandar's Tomb with your father. That was a year ago, wasn't it? You probably didn't have that beard of yours then."

"I grew this beard when I was ten, Steel Lord," the young man had said, in a manner much the same as his father's. He'd given his broad chest a pound with his fist. "I am Svaldar, son of Stegra the Snowfist, and do not fear anything. All Snowfists are brave. If not, they will never rule."

"And I'm sure you will rule with distinction, when your time comes." Amron couldn't help but think of Aleron, who'd walked forever in his shadow. Svaldar reminded him of his eldest son, in the way he wished to emulate his father. He'd smiled, then asked, "And what did you find there, when you went? Did you explore the interior?"

Amron knew they had, but wanted to hear Svaldar's account. "Yes, we got inside. There was a way in, near the main door. The Godway Door, you call it, I think? Near there, was a side passage. We went in that way, but did not stay long. My father said it was too dangerous. That the ceiling might come down at any time." He'd given his chest another thump. "*I* wanted to stay, but he said no. We climbed rubble, went into some chambers, but that was all. There was little to see but fallen rock, and darkness...yes, the darkness there was thick, thicker than I have ever seen."

His account had lined up with Stegra's. Amron's only solace was that they'd spent only an hour or two inside, and couldn't possibly have explored the entire place. "And this side-passage you used to get in? Is it still open, Svaldar?"

"My father says no. It was near collapse, and already some of it had fallen down when we went in and out. The mountain has shivered often since then. This way will be blocked, Steel Lord. My father does not think there is a way in anymore."

We shall find out tomorrow, Amron thought now, as he gave the shadow of the mountain a final look, then turned back to camp. He'd spent enough time in quiet rumination and saw no benefit in discussing or thinking about it all any longer. He found Svaldar and Whitebeard digging the pit for the fire, and went to join them. "Hand me that, Rogen, I'll take over."

Whitebeard gave him a frown. "The ice is hard as iron here, my lord. Maybe it's best..."

Amron reached out and tore the pickaxe from his grasp, and started swinging. Like Stegra, Whitebeard had a tendency to think him completely useless, and by the gods it rankled him. "I've slain a dragon, Rogen, I'm sure I can slay a bit of ice," he complained, as he swung hard and fierce, breaking off chunks, which Svaldar then removed with his shovel. It was hard work, but felt good for all that. By the time the ditch was dug, he'd even broken a sweat.

Next, he helped build and light the fire as the communal tent was erected around it. The hide was thick enough that it would shield the light of the flame, and spacious enough for them all to gather inside, to cook, eat, share stories and such at night, before retiring to their own tents with bellies full of food and bodies warmed by the fire.

Kusto Crownbane and Wagga the White saw to the construction of the shelter, ably helped by Walter, who really didn't help at all, but tended to just get in the way. The tribesmen liked him, though, and were often content with being regaled of his stories at night, and his journey to Vandar's Tomb in particular. Whether they believed it or not, Amron couldn't say, but they enjoyed the tale all the same.

Before long the tents were up, the fire was burning, and the salted yak and earthy roots were being passed around for eating. Amron had learned a great deal about the Snowskins' way of life these last ten days, mostly during these nights when they gathered and told of their tales. He'd been less effusive with his own stories, despite regular requests for them. Instead he'd left it to Walter to recount the Echo of Titans and the Siege of Southwatch and Dauntless Daecar and the sundry other stories and songs that featured Amron as a central hero. Of course, the Echo of Titans was the one they liked most, and no surprise there. Walter had taken to singing it nightly, acting out this scene and that, clearing a little stage around which the Snowskins would gather.

One night, Kusto Crowbane had stood up and asked Amron for a duel. The man was an affable sort, and a killer of a hundred Crowmen of the Crag, if his own stories were to be believed. He had a full dozen scars across his face that added some credence to that. "I will challenge the steel lord," he had declared. "Crowbane verses the Crippler of Kings. We will make our own song together, great lord of Vandar."

Men had laughed, and Stega Snowfist said, "The bane of crows against the bane of dragons. I do not think this fight is fair."

"They both fly," Jorgen Half-Eye had laughed, named for his one working eye. The other he kept behind a patch. "That is the only thing they share."

"One and only, yes," chuckled Wagga the White, whose name was ironic, seeing as he was the least pale of all of them, and had a beard of brown and grey. "Do not believe Crowbane's stories, lord of steel. These cuts he has on his face, they are not from blades, no. It was a murder of crows did that to him, scratching with their claws. He is not the fighter he makes out."

"Maybe the steel lord isn't either, then?" Crowbane said. "We listen to the fat man's songs and like them, yes, but are they true? There is only one way to prove it..."

"By fighting you?" scoffed young Svaldar. "Do not be stupid, Kusto, sit down. The Lord of Daecar has come to drive off the curse. Of course his tales are true."

They were, and they weren't, though Amron chose not to say

anything. The songs were always exaggerated to make them seem like myth, though in truth they were usually more prosaic than all that. *And I'm hardly the man who slew Vallath anymore,* he thought, *nor stormed the siege lines at Southwatch, nor cut through those Sunriders when they raided through the marshlands near Mudport.* He'd been two decades younger then, in his prime and decked in godsteel plate, with a fully working body with fully working limbs, and the great godsteel blade of his house at his hip. Now...well, now he was a distant echo of all that. *I was an echo of Varin once, people said, and now I'm an echo of my younger self. Never to be whole again...*

He didn't stay long in the company of the men that night. In the shadow of the feared mountain as they were, a sense of disquiet had consumed the group. Few tales were told. Few songs sung. They sat and ate and spoke little, and what words were shared were those of concern for Stegra and the steel men they had come to know. When the talk turned to the evil of the mountain, Amron took his leave. He couldn't stomach another night of hearing Stegra sermonise on the desecrations the Vandarians had committed by mining godsteel, and leaving only darkness behind.

He fled from all that and took to the privacy of his own tent. The air remained calm, barely a breath of wind disturbing the silence. Stationed to the north and south of camp were a pair of sentries, wrapped up in white fur and well camouflaged against the ice and snow. The tents were much the same. Amron pushed through the flaps, fastened them so that the likes of Walter wouldn't follow, and tried to get comfortable.

The only noise was the gentle murmur of conversation in the communal tent, the occasional snort or snuffle of a greatyak nearby. Amron tucked his furs about himself against the night chill. Even now, the inside of his tent was beginning to glisten with a thin sheen of ice. Sometimes by morning the entire thing would be frozen stiff, and would need to be beaten to loosen up the hide so it could be packed away. Amron's beard would typically be the same, and once his left eye had become sealed shut. Sleep rarely came easily either, on account of the sharp pains running through his right thigh and left shoulder. *Pains I'll live with all my life,* he thought, as he tried to get comfortable. *The way is shut...the way is shut...*

He rolled over, closing his eyes tight, as though that might stop

Stegra's mantra from running through his head. "Shut up," he hissed, as though that might help too, but those words just kept on circling. He tried to think of other things. Of what might be happening back home, but that was hardly much better. *How is Elyon?* he wondered. His last living boy had marched to war months ago. *Is he OK? Injured? Dead? Has he joined Aleron at Varin's Table? And Lillia, sweet Lillia...*He could only pray she was safe in Blackfrost, or back in Varinar, and that the war hadn't yet reached their shores. *And Amara, how is she? How does Vesryn fare in my stead? What of Cousin Gereth, and Killian, and Rikkard? What of the men I once commanded?*

His thoughts tumbled off as he fell into a fitful sleep, as a hundred faces passed across his eyes, coming with a hundred names. But still in the back of his head rang the words that had become his curse. *The way is shut...the way is shut.*

He dreamt that the mountain had Stegra Snowfist's face, with a great sloping valley of snow for a beard. He was laughing, thunder cracking in the skies as the volcano bellowed and boomed. *The way is shut. THE WAY IS SHUT.* Walter was there too, standing at the foot of the mountain, calling out in denial. *We must get in,* he shouted, but his voice was dim and small. *There must be a way, there must, there must...*

But the mountain only laughed more thunderously. Doors opened up within it, yet all of a sudden they came crashing down, snapping shut. *The way is shut...the way is SHUT!* Amron tossed and turned in his sleep. Then he was there at Walter's side, amidst it all, a fierce wind blowing all about him. The mountain loomed high and vast, its face of craggy stone. It had changed to something more ancient, something darker. *The way is shut,* it said, in a voice that rumbled through Amron's very bones. *You should never have come here. The way is shut.* The rumbling came again, and again, and again. Amron could feel the entire world shaking beneath him. *The way is shut.* The mountain began trembling violently, rocks and boulders crashing down its slopes. Amron held up his hands to shield himself as the avalanche came his way. *The way is shut...the way is shut...*

Suddenly he felt a hand gripping him, shaking him awake. The white-bearded face of Stegra Snowfist appeared in the darkness before his eyes. "It is time to go, Lord of Daecar. The mountain shivers. We cannot delay."

But it's still dark, was his first thought, his mind still clogged by the fog of his dreams. Then he remembered where he was. *It's always dark here*. He looked out past the Snowfist. Walter and Whitebeard were waiting behind him, a greatyak saddled for the ride. *The mountain shivers,* Amron thought. He looked into Stegra's eyes, and then he felt it.

Through the earth, came a deep thrumming tremble. "We must go," the chieftain said. "Right now."

22

Lythian

The clouds peeled back to unveil the sight of land. Rugged cliffs rose up from the surging waters, the waves crashing white and wild against the shore. Beyond, the shapes of shadowed mountains thrust up into the leaden skies, disappearing into the thick black pall of thunder-clouds that cloaked the islands.

The storm had grown fierce. Great cracks of thunder split the air, bellowing through the skies about them. *The islands do not want us here,* Lythian thought, as he held fast to the straps of his harness. Some of the lightning looked red to his eyes, fingers of fire reaching down from the heavens. *Agarath watches. The fire god sees all...*

"There," called out the old voice of Sotel Dar, sitting ahead of Lythian in the four-man saddle. He turned his head to the side and pointed for the Varin Knight to see. "I landed there the first time I came here, Captain." His voice could scarce be heard over the storm. Lythian had to grip Starslayer to enhance his hearing. "I was a third of the age I am now, but still I remember. We lost two men during that expedition. One to a chasm. Another to a young dragon. Let us hope we lose no one today, my friend."

Lythian searched through the swamp of clouds and caught sight of Neyruu off to their right. Kin'rar was looking over to them, waving some gesture to Marak. Fireborn dragon-riders had a means of communication through hand signals, Lythian had come to learn, for when they were in flight. "What does he say?" Lythian called out to Sotel Dar.

"He says to fly inland, down the channel between the islands. The door into the mountain is on the other side."

Neyruu gave a sharp right turn, and Garlath followed, cutting between a pair of thick black clouds that roared out their thunderous call. More streaks of red light burst from above them. *Am I dreaming this? Imagining it?* "The lightning is red," Lythian called.

"Sometimes, yes," said Sotel Dar, shouting over the bluster of the storm. "It only happens when the Renewals stir. Below is the Breath of Agarath, cradling the dragons in his glow. Above is his ire. The *Ire of Agarath*, these lightning storms are called. His spirits comes alive as war spreads, Lythian. We must be doubly careful."

Dragons, Lythian thought at once. His eyes scanned for them, hiding in caves and clefts, watching as they passed. He saw none. He'd been taught that they feared the storm, that only dragons soul-bonded to a Fireborn would brave such weather at their rider's command. Yet he searched all the same, as the rumours of their wildness circled his head. The wild dragons of the Wings stirred during times of war, as these storms did. *Let us just hope they do not stir together,* he thought. The risk of lightning striking them was bad enough, without being hunted and hounded by a host of wild drakes.

To the left and right, the twin islands spread as they passed between them. The sea channel below was narrow, no more than three miles at its widest point, and much thinner elsewhere. Black obsidian cliffs broke out from the waves, and he saw few coves and beaches on which a ship might land. It reminded him somewhat of the Sibling Strait between Tukor and Rasalan, and even where the beaches might give passage onto the islands, they rose sharply up into the rugged bluffs, with no easy way through.

There is a strange magic here, he thought, as another shot of lightning lit the skies. This one seemed thicker, brighter in its crimson hue, and lingered for far too long. *Does lightning not come and go in a flash?* he asked himself. *Is that not why they call it a 'flash' of lightning in the first place?* But here the bolts fingered down from the clouds for what seemed like seconds, before withering away into the blackness. *And the patterns...*

Another crack of lighting and thunder came, the jagged red lines branching out in a hundred directions. For a moment Lythian thought he saw the shape of a face, bearded with fire, dragon-like in its features. The face seemed to look right at him, before fading back into the darkness, leaving a faint afterimage behind. A ripple climbed his spine, one disc at a time. *Agarath,* he thought. A dark dread spread to the depths of him. *He is looking at me, watching. How will I ever escape this place? I do not belong here...*

Garlath swung down, taking Lythian by surprise, as the tumult thundered like a great godly drum, relentless. Ahead, Neyruu lead the way, slicing through the low clouds and fog, which swirled and eddied at her passing. Garlath gave pursuit in her slipstream, wearying, Lythian could sense. They hadn't stopped at the coast, as Tethian had said, but had decided to push right on into the storm. Even as they'd flown beyond the mainland and out across Dragonwatch Pass, Lythian had seen the tempest cloaking the world ahead. "It will get worse all day and all night," Sotel Dar had shouted back to him. "Our Fireborn must feel it best we find refuge soon. The next hour or two will be bumpy, Captain."

It had been, and tiring for Garlath in particular, still in recovery as he was. For much of the last hour Neyruu had assumed the lead, cutting the clouds to ease the burden on the great dragon. Yet even so, he was listing a little now to the left and right, wobbling as the winds assaulted him. The squalls were as violent as the lightning and thunder, buffeting them from all sides. *No wonder dragons fear to fly in such conditions.* Though Lythian had flown from Eldurath in a storm, this was another proposition altogether. *Magic,* he thought again. *There is a dark and dreaded magic here. This is not the natural weather of the world.*

They broke beneath the low clouds and into a thick soup of mist. Flying low, Lythian could smell the salt sea crashing beneath them, see the spindrift blowing from the crests of the waves, the great frothing churn as they tumbled toward the cliffs. In places, he saw the occasional shipwreck; old rotting masts breaking from the surf, hulls caught on the rocks. "Who were they?" he called to Sotel Dar, leaning close to the old scholar's ear. He gestured to the wrecks, scattered among the coves.

"Who can say?" the old man replied. "Fishermen. Merchants. Idle travellers caught by the currents and tides. These islands do not like visitors, Son of Varin. Even the seas here defend them."

Aren't the hundreds of dragons enough? Lythian thought, because those were the upper estimates he'd heard. *Hundreds.* He could hardly even compute the thought. A handful of dragons could turn a battle. A score of them could turn a war. What could a hundred do? Or two hundred? Or more? *Shadow and flame,* he shuddered. He had seen it in his dream, the dragons clotting the skies, the world aflame, forests and valleys, cities and forts. Tethian believed that only Eldur could stop that from happening. That only the Father of Fire could command the Bondstone, command the dragons before they flew free of the Wings, and covered all the world in flame and ash and death. The lighting came again, and in its web he saw the face of Agarath, smiling. Another shudder went up Lythian's spine. *This is all wrong*, he thought. *I should never have come.*

But once more the lightning faded, and his fears faded with it. *I am here to document, to observe, to watch,* he knew. *I have to be here. I had no choice but to come.* And then in his head he could hear Borrus Kanabar once more, sounding his words of warning. *Put your sword through him, Lythian,* the Barrel Knight said. *Drive Starslayer through Eldur's cold black heart, if you see him. Do not let that devil rise. He will be the undoing of us all.*

His thoughts melted away into the raging bluster of the storm. Down they went, swooping now over the high rugged cliffs. He saw dark caves cut into their sides, the faint shadow of shapes within. Stars of red light watched as they passed. "Dragons, Sotel," he called out, reaching to the man's wet shoulder, shaking. "Do you see? In the caves..."

"I see," called the old man, his white hair slicked back by the rain and wind. "These are small dragons, Lythian. These ones, you need not fear."

There were other holes and chasms cleaved into the earth, sighted as they flew inland now away from the channel between the islands. Steam rose up from some of them, the suggestion of fires burning deep down below. "Some of these never end, they say," the old scholar told him over the roar of the wind. "They are as your Long Abyss, Lythian. If you fall in you will fall forever, until you die of thirst, or get lucky enough to hit a rocky ledge on the way down."

"And those?" Lythian pointed to one that glowed about its edge with a dull orange flame. Steam belched out from the slit as mist from a godsteel blade. "There is fire down there."

"The Breath of Agarath, yes. Deep down, Lythian, hundreds of metres below. If you fall in one of those, death comes a great deal quicker. There will be many on the paths we will walk, down beneath the earth. Many dangers we must look out for."

Many dangers, many ways to die, and more than many holes and caves and tunnels, that Lythian could see. The Southern Wing was just as mountainous as the island to the north, the ranges honeycombed by an innumerable network of passages. The dragons were as ants, Lythian had been told, gouging their routes through the earth as they built their hideaways and nests. Many of those tunnels were wide and broad, and large enough for the bigger drakes to crawl through. Others were more narrow, dug by smaller varieties of dragons in centuries gone by. Further paths had been fashioned by other natural events; erosion, earthquakes, the movement of subterranean rivers. Sotel Dar's expertise had furnished Lythian with a strong understanding of the islands now, though even the old scholar remained uncertain of the way to Eldur's resting chamber. He knew enough, though, and that gave them a place to start.

"There is an opening, ridged by rocky stalactites and stalagmites that take the shape of teeth," he had told Lythian several days ago. "It is on the northwestern side of the Southern Wing, giving passage into the mountain of Eldur's Shame."

"Eldur's Shame?" Lythian hadn't yet heard the name.

"Yes, so some call it."

"Why?"

"For bringing about the war that set demigod against demigod, that broke the long peace after the gods had fallen. You know this tale, Lythian. That Drulgar, the great calamity of the north, broke from his slumber atop the Nest and wrought vengeance for Agarath's fall. That the dragon turned the south coast of Vandar black, killing thousands of men and women and children, razing cities and fortresses with the divine fires of his breath. That once done, he turned his eyes on Varinar, and to the slaying of Varin himself."

Lythian knew this tale all too well. Every man, woman, and child in the north knew it. "Varin came forth with the Sword of Varinar," he'd said, taking the story up. "He and his son Elin, and daughter Iliva. Elin bore the Frostblade, Iliva the Windblade. Together they rode out and met Drulgar upon the open plains a hundred miles north of the Black Coast. They fought for hours, even days, some say, before Drulgar struck down Elin, and then Iliva, leaving only Varin himself. Enraged by the death of his two eldest children, Varin cut at Drulgar a half dozen times, wounding him gravely, forcing him to retreat back to the shores of Agarath across the Red Sea."

"And after?" asked Sotel Dar.

"Varin sought recompense for what the calamity had done," Lythian said. "He demanded that Eldur kill Drulgar, that he slay his spawn too, as Drulgar had slain Varin's children. He wanted every beast sired of Drulgar's line destroyed, else he would raise his armies in war. Eldur refused. Instead he took Karagar, greatest son of Drulgar, for his bonded dragon and a hundred years of war began."

"The War of Fire and Steel," said Sotel Dar. "A war started by Eldur's inability to control Drulgar, as the others had often beseeched, and his unwillingness to finish off the Lord of Dragons for the horror he brought to your lands. Here in Agarath, Drulgar is often revered and feared in equal measure. Many call him hero for being Agarath's great champion throughout the War Eternal, when the gods fought with men and monsters and armies we cannot even imagine today. This game they played for thousands of years, before they fell, one by one, leaving behind some of the horrors they had created, and Drulgar the Dread was chief among them. It fell to the Five to rebuild the world, to forge it in their image. Eldur, Varin, Ilith, Thala, and Lumo. What wonders they performed together, what magic. It was to be a long age of peace, an eternity of unity, and yet Drulgar changed all that when he laid siege to Varin's kingdom."

Sotel Dar had sighed and shaken his head. "Drulgar sought to return the world to that place of fire and death and destruction that he had always known, beneath his master's whip, yet during his slumber the world had moved on. Some do not blame him for this. Drulgar was devised as the greatest weapon of all, Agarath's greatest calamity. When he woke to find his master fallen, he did only what he was made to do. Yet all the same, his actions sparked back into the world the fires of war that have not yet been quenched. The War of Fire and Steel is considered the First Renewal, as the War Eternal returned to spread its vast shadow across the world. And ever since we have suffered. For three and a half thousand years we have seen war between our kingdoms and continents. Millenia of tragedy. Millenia of shame. For that is where the name of the mountain comes from, Lythian. *Eldur's Shame*. The place where he was said to have gone to rest, after letting the world fall to an eternity of war. And that, now, is where we must go to wake him, so that he might put things right."

Lythian had nodded slowly, thoughtfully, then said, "And Drulgar? What do you believe happened to him, Sotel? There are many conflicting accounts in the north. Many legends that bear his name."

"Many and more, yes, across the north and south. Most believe he returned to the Wings to die. Some even say that Eldur imprisoned him there, in lieu of killing him, to try to satisfy Varin and the others. There are some ancient records that mention this, and those are the ones I have always believed. It has always made sense to me, that Eldur would return to sleep beside Drulgar's bones."

Lythian had heard that too. "And if it wasn't bones he returned to, Sotel? Could the Breath of Agarath not have sustained Drulgar down there? Could it not, in fact, have revived him?"

Sotel Dar's lack of immediate answer was disquieting. "Anything is possible, Captain Lythian," he had said. "We will find out for sure in the days to come."

That conversation played again now in Lythian's mind as they soared across the Southern Wing, passing chasms and clefts, caves and caverns dug into the walls of the mountain. *Eldur's Shame,* Lythian thought, knowing this one must be it. It loomed taller than the rest, swirled in thick bands of red and black mist. The storm seemed to encase it, thundering its violent song, the chaos of crimson lightning flashing through the dark dreaded skies. They had flown almost all through the day, though it was still early enough to be light. Not here. An early dusk had closed in, brought about by this strange unsettling storm, by a dark magic surrounding this mountain, and the island on which it took root.

Ahead, Neyruu was still sweeping forward, Kin'rar and Tethian and Talasha perched upon her back, hunkered low among her scales to reduce drag and the whip of the rain in their faces. *Does he begin to doubt this?* Lythian had to wonder. Prince Tethian had never been to these islands. The only man who had was Sotel Dar, and not for many long years. *Do they all not look upon this place and feel an urge to turn around, as I do? Do they not sense the malice here, the devilry?*

As they drew yet lower to the ground, the air grew thick with the scent of rot and death. Lythian turned his eyes down to the fiery pits below, belching black fumes. Between them he could see bones scattered across the floor, some large and thick and still hanging with ragged lengths of muscle and meat. The dragons here were sustained by the fires of their father, Sotel had told him, yet they liked to feast on fish too. Sharks and whales and other sea-born beasts were all on the menu for the largest of them. And other land-based animals besides, if the reports were to be believed.

They'd heard many tales now of livestock being taken from across Lumara and the southern lands of Agarath. Camel trains and horses had been attacked, men and women and even children killed. There was even a report of a unit of Sunriders being assaulted by a large male dragon of orange and green scales. It had managed to kill three of them, Solasi Lightborn all, and flown off with a great sunwolf in its jaws, having already slain another.

They grow feral, Lythian thought, *and more wild than ever before. And here we are, come to their lair.* Yet for all that he'd seen none but shadows and glowing eyes, none but the small ones, Sotel had said. The storm was keeping them at bay, as hoped, as was the presence of Garlath, grander and greater than any foul beast lurking among these mountains. *But when we enter the depths, what then?* There would be no space for Garlath, no space for Neyruu. The plan was to keep to tight passages, where they could, but some would widen to caverns, they knew, and what then would they find?

Lythian put it from his mind. He even raised a smile. *How odd that I fear to lose the company of Garlath the Grand,* he thought. Through the War of the Continents, all men of the north had feared the beast. No matter what Marak said, Vallath was always the greater terror, yet Garlath ran him a close second. The dragon set the hearts of all men to fear...*yet here I am, riding upon his back, fearing to part with him when the time comes.* He smiled again and even laughed, so absurd was the notion. *This world of ours has turned all askew,* he thought. *Nothing makes sense anymore...*

Garlath banked left around a tower of rock. Beyond, the mountainside rose up in a great vertical wall, so sheer it seemed as though made that way by man. Up and up and up it went, black and gleaming in the rain, disappearing into the swirling red clouds. In places caves had been carved into the stone, and from them Lythian saw more shapes, more eyes, watching as they came. "There," shouted Sotel Dar. "Do you see, Lythian. The door..."

Lythian followed the man's wizened finger and saw it, the passage leading into the mountain. It looked much like the entrance to the Pits of Kharthar, that great open maw, with teeth above and teeth below formed of jutting lengths of sharpened rock. Beyond, a gentle orange glow issued, hissing out a faint wispy steam. "At least it will be warm inside," Lythian jested, to lighten his nerves.

"Warm, oh yes. And warmer still as we descend."

Descend now they did, the two dragons spreading their wings to slow, swinging forward with their taloned feet to land upon the rough rock floor at the base of the towering wall. Spouts of vegetation gave some greenery here and there, though all were coloured dull and dark. Twisted brambles and thorny bushes sat forlorn and alone across the open field. Whatever trees there were were small and stunted, gnarled and leaf-less, dead.

Lythian turned his eyes around as they came to a halt, expecting a sudden assault from the skies, but none came. He quickly unfastened himself from his harness, took a grip of Starslayer to fill his body with strength and light, and leaped deftly to the ground. The others climbed down more carefully. They quickly gathered as one, huddled against the rains. Sotel Dar looked unsteady on his feet, half frozen by the flight. Ashun Klo's tan face had adopted a sallow hue. "The sudden stop in motion can cause nausea," Marak told him. "Throw up, if you must. You will feel the better for it, Ashun."

The proud captain of the prince's guard refused the urge. He gulped several mouthfuls of septic air, suffused with the stench of death and decay, but somehow that seemed to steady him. "I am fine, Skylord Marak. I just needed to take a breath."

"We all do, I think, after that," said Prince Tethian. Despite the dreaded world in which they'd landed, he had on his face a smile. *That same smile,* Lythian thought. *That smile of purpose, and destiny.* "Well here we are, and in one piece. Come, let us get out of these rains." He turned to the passage as carefree and casual as a man preparing to walk through the door of his bedchamber. "Ulrik, Kin'rar, take a moment with your dragons, if you wish. We will see you inside."

Tethian led them on, a queasy Ashun Klo at his side, dragonsteel blade to hand. Sotel Dar tottered after them, clacking with his walking stick. Talasha moved in beside Lythian. She did not share her cousin's expression. "This is a strange place, sweet captain," she said, looking around through hooded eyes. "A dark place, even for a girl like me of Eldur's divine blood. There is something in the air, do you feel it?"

"I do, Princess. Though I cannot tell if it is merely the smell of rotting flesh. I saw a great many bones as we passed."

"You try to spare me," she whispered. "No, there is a magic here, and you know it. Agarath's spirit lingers. He is here, all around us." She moved to his side and took his arm. "You will stay close to me, won't you? You will protect me, my captain, if I should come to harm?"

"I will die for you, if I must," he said. Those words came unbidden, but there was no time for doubting them, not here, not now. He smiled a reassuring smile. "Do not fear, Talasha. I will not let anything happen to you."

That seemed to settle her as they approached the mouth of the tunnel. It had looked smaller from afar, but as they neared it loomed high and wide, plenty large enough even for Garlath to crawl in. To enter, they had to walk between the tall stone teeth that thrust up from the ground like spears. Above, others hung down, longer and sharper, some threatening to fall. Lythian hustled Talasha through, watching the ceiling above them, his hand ever on Starslayer's hilt. Rocks and pebbles were falling with each bellow of thunder, and some larger fangs looked like they might follow. "Come, quickly," he said, leading her on. "The ceiling here is not stable."

The passage continued along its route, almost uniform in its width and height, as though forged by some giant worm. *And might it have been?* Legends spoke of Agarath commanding huge, round-mouth worms during the war between the gods, their insatiable maws ringed with a hundred layers of razor sharp teeth. They would burrow underground, it was said, and appear in the midst of battles, sucking down Vandar's legions before wriggling away out of sight. Lythian had always taken those stories for myths, though. There were a hundred beasts of legend described by the singers and storytellers, bards and balladeers, but not all of them were real. *But this tunnel...*he thought.

Whether dug by dragon or worm, or some other unnatural cause, we best be careful all the same.

They came soon to a wider chamber, giving passage to many separate routes. Lythian counted them out. "There are a half dozen passages out of here," he said. "Which way do we go?"

"Down," said Sotel Dar, leaning on his ruby-eyed staff. All were wet and dripping from the rains, though would soon dry off down here. From half the tunnels came an orange glow, faint but noticeable, and about them little swirls of steam billowed in the air. "Eldur's resting place is said to be many hundreds of metres beneath our feet, at the root of the mountain. Pullio the Wise first saw this in his dreams, a thousand years ago. A great open chamber, cloaked in darkness, with a ceiling so high one cannot see the top. That is the place we seek."

Lythian looked from passage to passage. Some were wider than others. One was especially tight, such that Marak would likely have to duck his head to go through. "That one," he said, pointing. "Do we not plan to keep to the narrower tunnels, Prince Tethian?"

"Such as we can, yes," Tethian replied. "But some paths from here will go up, others down. Others still may go up, and then down. Finding which route will lead us to the core will take time."

"It may become a case of trial and error," added Sotel Dar. "One step back, two steps forward. But to start, I have an idea of the way. That passage you say, Lythian? No, not on this occasion. Narrow it may be, but it ventures away to the left of where we stand, and into an adjoining mountain of the range. Over the centuries, some of these passage have been mapped. Crudely, yes, but mapped all the same. I have in my head that map, though it will only take us so far." He directed their attention across the cavern. "We will go that way, to start."

Lythian looked at the tunnel in question. It was one of the larger ones, glowing a deep shade of amber, and appeared to fall away in a gentle decline, sloping into the depths. Seeing it, the Knight of Mists shed the cloak that he'd worn to keep him warm during the journey, unveiling the beaten leather tunic he wore, studded with points of iron.

Others began doing the same, setting aside their wet-weather garments and exposing their dragon-scale armour beneath. Talasha was garbed similarly as her cousin and Ashun Klo in a protective suit of interlinking scales, shaded black, purple and red. Only Sotel Dar was without such cladding, wrapped in his dark crimson robes, with the stitching of Eldur's crest wreathed upon his back.

It would be hot down there, and for Lythian most of all, a child of the north as he was. He'd learned well enough during his time among the Agarathi that they handled extremes of temperature well. In Eldurath, the flowery Fireborn nobles had often competed over their outlandish dress, donning layers of colourful robes of silk and satin, linen and fine wools, despite the humidity and heat. Lythian would sit sweating in a single light linen shirt, and there they would be, heaped and happy. *I will suffer most here,* he judged. It was another reason not to linger.

A minute or so later, the Fireborn riders appeared. "The dragons will find safe places to await our return," Marak announced.

"They'll be safe?" asked Talasha

"There is no dragon here that can challenge Garlath. They will be safe, Princess, fear not."

Both men were bearing a pair of satchel packs, filled with provisions. One was handed to Ashun Klo, another to Lythian. Marak and Kin'rar kept the other two, leaving Tethian, Talasha, and Sotel Dar unburdened. Lythian checked the contents of his satchel before swinging it over his shoulder. Inside were several skins of water, some cured meat, and a wound length of rope. The other satchels were similarly provisioned.

"Ready?" asked Prince Tethian, looking over his crew. All nodded. "Then let us go. Sotel, do lead us on."

They fell into order, Sotel leading with the bulwark that was Ulrik Marak at his side, bearing the Fireblade on his hip, and the Body of Karagar upon his bulky frame. Behind the leading pair, Tethian followed, with Ashun Klo never more than a foot or two away from him. Talasha and Lythian were behind; Kin'rar brought up the rear.

The first passage took them down a shallow gradient, the air growing warmer, thicker, darker as they went. Marak drew the Fireblade from its sheath to provide a glow. Lythian did the same with Starslayer, which shone and misted with a pale inner light, glittering gold in the darkness. "The mists move strangely," Kin'rar said, a pace or so behind. "I have not seen Starslayer behave as such before."

Lythian had. "The steel detects the dragons," he said. "Godsteel *lives*, Kin'rar. It communicates through the mists."

"The blade is that intuitive?" asked Talasha. "I never knew."

"Godsteel is the body of Vandar, Princess. It has a primal sense to know when its mortal enemy is near."

"But the blade has been near Neyruu and Garlath for weeks."

"True. And in that time it has come to learn that they are not threats, through the blood-bond we share. If I see no threat, nor does Starslayer. But here on this island, they surround us."

On they went, wending down as the tunnel began to snake left and right in a strange serpentine decline. It made Lythian think again of the great worms the singers sang of, though if they were to come upon one of those even the Fireblade and Starslayer might count for nought, gargantuan as they were said to be.

Soon enough, however, the passage came to a second chamber giving access to many more routes. As with the first it was roughly circular in shape, and at its heart was gouged a deep rift, from which a steaming bronze mist poured forth. Sotel Dar tottered toward the edge, and looked down. He nodded to himself, then studied the sundry passages breaking off from the central chamber. "This way," he said, after a short pause to think. "Yes, the second tunnel left of the rift, I recall." He walked around the rip in the rough rock floor as the others followed behind. Lythian dared a look into the fiery depths, yet the chasm seemed to twist away at an angle, blocking his view to the flame far below.

"At least we don't have to leap over it," said Talasha, laughing nervously.

Her words were ill-timed. After a further half an hour they found themselves walking a broad passage where the floor seemed to fall away beneath them at intervals. Some were drops of a dozen metres or so, into tunnels and chambers below. Others showed only darkness; where they ended, none could tell. Another vented that same rusty steam, which came up smelling of sulphur. Most required nothing but little hops to cross, the fissures no more than a metre or so wide. All performed the leap but Sotel Dar, whom Marak lifted and leaped across with. Lythian offered Talasha the same opportunity, which she gamely denied. "I can handle a metre jump, sweet captain."

And then they came to one, some four metres across, perhaps even closer to five. "We cannot all jump this safely," declared Marak. The chamber below was visible, though a good twenty metres down.

Lythian stepped forward. "I can carry you all across," he said. "The leap isn't far with godsteel, nor will your weight greatly burden me." He turned to Ulrik Marak. "Well, yours might, but I imagine you'd rather make the jump yourself."

"You forget I bear the Fireblade, Lythian. It gives power, much like godsteel does." Marak turned to Tethian. "My prince, I will get you safely across. Climb on my back and I will make the leap."

"I rather think I can make the leap on my own, Ulrik," said Tethian. He stepped back to give himself room.

"Prince Tethian, I do not think that is wise."

"I agree, my lord," said Ashun Klo. "Why take the risk?"

"No risk, Ashun. Is my fate not to be the one to awake Eldur from his slumber, as Pullio the Wise predicted? What do I have to fear of a little hole in the ground?" The protestations came, but the prince ignored them. With a languid run and athletic leap he soared across the gap, landing on the other side with mere millimetres to spare. Several loose stones and bits of rock fell into the abyss, kicked up as he landed. He turned with a smile on his face. "Now come, let us not dally. Ashun, Kin'rar, I'm sure the jump won't trouble you. Ulrik, take Sotel. Lythian, if you'd be so kind as to convey my cousin across, we can all be on our way."

So over they went in their singles and pairs, safely reaching the other side. Where Sotel Dar climbed upon Marak's broad back, Talasha chose instead to be held in Lythian's arms. "This is not the most efficient way, Princess," Lythian told her.

"No, but it's the most chivalric. And it makes me feel the most safe."

So be it. He crossed the gap without discernible effort and placed Talasha back onto the ground. No sooner had they all assembled across the rift than a heavy rumble shook through the mountain. It lasted some ten seconds before stilling. Stones and pebbles rained down from the ceiling above them. Most were small, though several rocks as large as a man's fist came loose from somewhere higher up, falling through the honeycomb of passages and tunnels above, crashing all about them. By instinct Lythian tucked Talasha beneath his shoulder, holding Starslayer aloft, eyes up, to defend them. Ashun Klo and Kin'rar raised their own blades upward, flanking the prince.

Marak gave cover to the diminutive Sotel Dar. And then, within moments, it was over.

"The mountain stirs," said the old scholar, as the trembling withered away. "Agarath breathes beneath us. The war is waking his spirit."

As if to illustrate his point, hot orange mists came swirling from below, issuing out of several clefts along their route, forward and behind. A burning dust seemed to fill the air, causing several of them to cough and shield their eyes. "We must hurry," Kin'rar said, covering his mouth as a fierce hot wind blew past them. "Another earthquake like that might bring down the tunnel."

Which tunnel? Lythian wondered. They were innumerable here and many of the routes seemed unstable. Cave-ins were inevitable, he judged. "Are these earthquakes normal, Sotel?" he asked, as the mountain gave another shudder, a light aftershock that lasted no more than a second or two.

"The region is known for them, yes. These islands are volcanic, and temperamental. And more so during times of war."

Like the red storms above, Lythian thought. *Storms above and fires below and dragons and demigods in between.* If there was a hell on earth, this was it. *A fitting resting place for the devil,* came the voice of Borrus Kanabar in his head. *If you find him, Lythian, slay him. You cannot let him rise...*

"Come, we must go." Tethian ushered them on.

An hour seemed to pass, then two, then three, though all that was hard to judge for certain. The winding route took them left, right, sometimes up but mainly down. Lythian lost all sense of his bearings. Some tunnels went straight. Others seemed to turn back on themselves, then back again, then around the other way. Many ended dead, with nought but a wall of rock to greet them. Others still fell steeply down, often too steep for them to risk. Many were torn with ravines and rifts that plunged vertically into the nothingness.

Where they could, they took out their ropes and climbed down to tunnels running beneath them. When this happened, it was left to either Lythian or Marak to stand at the top holding the rope. The rest would then shimmy down the hempen line, bar Sotel Dar who needed to be carried. Sometimes he'd hold onto someone's back. At others, they'd tie the rope about his waist and lower him down in a makeshift harness. Once all were safely at the bottom, the man at the top -

Lythian or Marak - would drop down the rope to be rolled and stored, and then jump down unaided, their bones braced against the fall by the power of the blades they bore. This happened five, six, seven times, speeding their descent. And all the while, the air grew hotter.

Water, Lythian began to think with more regularity. His mind would flash back to his time imprisoned in Eldurath, baking beneath the midday sun, his tongue so swollen from thirst he could hardly even swallow when given a drop. The heat was different here. No sun. Just steam and boiling air, a humidity that saturated his clothes, drenching him to the bone. He stopped regularly to take on liquids, though the rest didn't suffer as he did. "We thought this might happen," Kin'rar told him. "Drink freely, Lythian. We need your strength."

Still, he tempered his need to overdo it with the fear that they might be down here days. They'd discussed the possibility over their meetings in camp, and brought ample provisions just in case. Cave-ins and blockages might delay them, and the threat of getting lost was all too real. For that, they saw to marking their route with scratches and cuts in the stone with their blades, leaving behind a trail that would help lead them out. Lythian spent much time holding out Starslayer against the wall or floor beneath them, slicing a white line as they went. His only fear was making too much noise. "We must be quiet," Marak would commonly warn, whenever any voice rose too high, or someone sneezed or coughed from the dust, the sounds echoing away into the darkness. "We do not want to attract attention. It isn't only dragons that lurk down here."

They saw signs of that too. In places there were nests of brittle old bones built into clefts in the rough rock walls. "*Karocks,*" Sotel Dar called the creatures that forged them. They were giant beetle-like horrors that could grow as large as wolves, their shells of black armour, with razor-sharp pincers that could snip a man in two. "They are creatures of darkness," Sotel said, "and fear the light. So long as we have the glow of the blades and torches, they will not trouble us."

Still, Lythian could see them, shying away as they passed, creeping back from the light of Starslayer and the Fireblade, and the torches that Ashun Klo and Kin'rar carried. When they passed by, the creatures could be heard, scuttling back into the tunnels on their many pointed legs. Other similar beasts lingered here. Further down, crabs and crustaceans were said to live in the molten fires, impervious to its heat. Spiders as large as cats clung to the walls in places, small of body but long of leg, watching with clusters of beady black eyes. Like the karocks, they slipped away into their cracks as the host went by, re-emerging only once they'd passed.

"I do not like it here," Talasha said, when they came upon a chamber filled with webbing. Inside were a hundred spiders, big and small, scuttling across the lines of silk and into the darkness whence they came. "Can we not find another way?"

"We must push on, Cousin," Tethian told her. "Ashun, Ulrik, frighten these foul fiends off."

The two men saw to it, though Marak did much of the work. Swinging the Fireblade through the air, the webbing caught ablaze, fizzling as it burned away. Any spider that hadn't yet retreated fled into the many crevices torn into the rock. Lythian marvelled at how they moved, how they squeezed themselves into such tight spaces. He said as much to Sotel Dar, who replied with, "Yes, these ones can get anywhere. Wherever you go in these mountains, one will always be near."

Another hour went by in a blink. They came upon more spider lairs, more karock nests, and other ancient critters besides. By now Sotel Dar was leading on instinct, the crude map in his head only taking him so far. "Down," he would say, when anyone asked the way. "We must continue down."

Up, Lythian would wish each time, as the heat grew increasingly difficult to endure. "How much further?" he asked, as they stopped to take on water. He seemed to sweat it out as soon as he drank it. "Do you have any idea, Sotel?"

"Some way still, I think," the scholar told him, his white hair slick and wet. "But we are inching ever nearer, Captain. Have faith."

I have no faith, not in this, Lythian thought. The air was cooking him from the inside out, his blood beginning to simmer in his veins. More earthquakes rumbled through the ranges, more steam belched up from below. From some vents it hissed out, hot enough to scald skin. At one point Tethian was looking down one as the steam erupted, only for Ashun Klo to pull him back just in time. On other occasions, the heavy rumbling beneath them caused further rockfalls that they only narrowly avoided.

Once, a great slab of black stone fell right before them, only a metre or two distant from Marak in the lead. *We are at the mountain's mercy,* Lythian thought then, as Talasha flew into his arms. All through the caverns and caves and twisting tunnels of Eldur's Shame, came a din of cracking rock and stone. All it would take would be the ceiling to come down atop them, and their quest would meet its end.

Yet by some fortune, the roof of the passage only fell ahead of where Marak stood. When the rumbling ended and the dust cleared, he called out for Lythian to step forward. "You must cut us through," he said, "and carefully. The Fireblade does not cleave stone as easily as godsteel does."

And this is why I'm truly here, Lythian knew, as he butchered them a path, carving a door through the fallen roof of the tunnel with as much care as he could summon. It was the first cave-in they encountered, but not the last. Twice more he was brought forward to slice narrow tunnels in the stone for them to crawl through, yet all the while the rumblings continued. The peril of collapse was never far away.

An unease began to fester in the group. Every new shudder had them stilling, huddling against the walls, looking up for weak points where they feared the roof might come down. But in truth there was no knowing where that might be. It was random, and varied, and sudden. Every step felt like it might become their last. The tension became almost unbearable.

Yet on they went, through another two hours of nerve-shredding climbing and clambering and crawling. It brought them eventually into a large cavern where many large rocks littered the floor, brought down by the quakes below. It was another place that linked to many others, over a dozen that Lythian could see. Some were broad, others little more than cracks in the stone that might lead to nowhere. There was something familiar about it. "I recognise this place," Kin'rar said, with a troubled look on his face. "Have we not passed this way before?"

Lythian looked around. They'd traversed many such chambers through the long stifling hours down here and many of them looked alike. Then he saw the cut in the stone, the thin white slice left by Starslayer, leading out from one passage and into another. All the others saw it too. A sense of defeat spread through them like a plague.

"We've been going in circles," said Ashun Klo. "How can that be? Have we not been going deeper?"

"It can be hard to tell down here." Sotel Dar was leaning heavily on his staff. He looked weary, bruises darkening beneath his eyes. His breathing had grown strained. "We cannot have passed this way long ago. I recall it now, yes. No more than an hour; that is all we have lost. We must take another passage."

"But which?" asked Talasha. The regret of her coming was written all over her face. Every time they stopped, Lythian could see it. The long dark trek through the trembling mountain was starting to get the better of her. "Maybe we should turn back, before we lose ourselves forever."

Tethian turned on her. Anger flashed across his face, though didn't settle. Still, Lythian saw it in that brief moment. *He doesn't like it when people lose their faith,* he thought. "Calm, dear Cousin," he told her. "We have been down here but hours. This is nothing that wasn't expected."

"We have ample provisions for some days, Princess," Marak told her, in as soft a voice as he could manage. "We needn't consider retreat just yet."

"But the cave-ins, the collapses." She shuddered even to think of them. Her eyes went around the cavern. "These rocks weren't here when last we passed. All have fallen in the past hour. By the time we return, who knows how many more will have come down? Who knows if we'll ever get out."

"Lythian's blade has proven capable of cutting through any obstacles," Tethian said.

"A blade that only he can bear," Talasha came back. "If Lythian gets hurt, or..."

"I won't, Princess," Lythian assured her. He drew her eye. There was no sense in her losing her wits, not now. "The mountain is starting to sleep, I can feel it. We should suffer few more earthquakes from here."

She took that on with a doubtful look, smelling the lie. But before she could respond, Tethian turned to one of the passages and said, "We will go this way. I...I can feel him, below. This is the passage, yes... I know it." A fervency imbued his voice. He drew a breath, nodded with certainty, and turned to the group. "Sotel, are you well enough to go on?"

The old man was looking close to collapse. He nodded all the same. "I can manage, my prince. This passage, you say?" He considered it a moment. "Yes...yes, I agree. It is time for you to follow your fate, Tethian. Your destiny will guide the way."

Your destiny will get us all killed, thought Lythian, though he didn't want to add his own doubts to the party. They moved off, Tethian adamantly striding ahead with Ashun Klo and Marak at his sides. Kin'rar came to Sotel Dar's flank to offer support, should he need it, though the old scholar was made of iron, apparently, and hustled on all the same.

Lythian remained to the rear, a step behind Talasha. She held back a moment as they descended into another endless dark tunnel, hot and suffocating, its black walls glistening with steam. "Is that true, what you said?" she asked, turning back to the Knight of the Vale. "Can you feel the mountain beginning to settle? Tell me you're not lying, sweet captain."

"I'm not," he said, though it was only a half-truth. "Starslayer grants me heightened senses, as you know. The tremors beneath us aren't so violent as they were."

"But they may return? The mountain may just be taking a breath?"

Lythian wasn't going to lie to her. "Yes," he said, "it may." He took her hand for comfort. "But I am here, Talasha. I'll not let anything..."

His words were broken off with a sudden shattering shudder, as the entire world seemed to lurch all at once to the right. Even with Starslayer to hand Lythian was thrown sideward, his shoulder crashing into the rock wall. Talasha stumbled into him, hitting hard, before bouncing off onto the floor of the tunnel as the mountain lurched again.

Then there came a deep rending, a heavy great tearing sound as though the entire world was ripping asunder. In an instant, the floor gave way beneath Talasha's feet, as a chasm opened up to swallow her.

A scream erupted from her throat. Lythian tried to reach down and take her, but her fingers slipped through his flailing grasp. For a moment he saw the terror on her face as she fell into the abyss. Ahead, the others were bracing, shouting, but Lythian didn't delay to hear what they said.

He rushed toward the edge of the fissure and followed the princess in.

23

Amron

Amron gazed upward from the base of the mountain. *It has no face,* he thought. *Not as in my dream.* From where they were stood it looked a mountain, and no more, a colossal surging cone of rock sitting indomitable upon the empty white plains.

A volcano, he knew, and they'd felt its fury over the last few hours. In his dreams he'd felt those shivers, and when Stegra Snowfist had awoken him, he'd felt them too. And many times more the earth had shuddered as they'd crossed the plains under the black-blanketed skies. Now, standing on the ancient winding path that lead to the Godway Door, Amron could feel another.

"Brace," cautioned Stegra Snowfist. "The mountain trembles once more."

A deep rumbling was felt beneath them, and ahead came the distant sound of crashing stone. "Look." Walter Selleck pointed to a tumble of rocks and snow and ice, shifted loose from one of the craggy slopes upon the southern face. They gathered into an avalanche that roared off into the valleys below.

"We must be careful," Whitebeard warned as the avalanche quietened, as the shaking stopped. "One of those could sweep every one of us to our deaths."

They'd heard several over the past hour, that echoing crack and tumble and roar as the mountain shrugged off great heaps of snow and rock. *It's like a dog shaking off fleas,* Amron thought. He couldn't judge whether Vandar's Tomb would consider them as pests or not, to be shaken free and crushed. "We should press on," he said, striding forward with his crutch.

They'd ridden one of the greatyaks to this point, though the beast could go no further. From here the cracked and ancient cobblestone road called the Godway rose steeply up into the low heights of the mountain, where it ended at the Godway Door. Even to stand upon it was a thrill.

To think of all the men who passed this way, he thought. *All the great knights and lords and kings who came here when these lands were not so cursed.*

He wished he could have seen it then, when the road was polished to a shine and the silver-blue banners flew in the breeze. When the trumpets blew out the arrival of the greatlords and kings come to visit. When the wagons and wains went back and forth across the lands, loaded high with Ilithian Steel. When the Godway Door stood grand and tall and ever-open to allow passage inside. When the high fluted pillars stood firm, and the carvings upon the walls were etched in rich detail, displaying the long triumphant history of the Vandarian people. Oh how he longed to see it all as it once was, yet here he stood, looking upon a crumbling ruin. *The way is shut,* he thought, *and soon I'll know for sure.* Amron Daecar put that all from his mind. He strode on up the Godway Road, toward the Godway Door.

The rest came right after him, Stegra leaving the greatyak behind. "Will he not run?" Walter asked. "He won't try to escape?"

"Of course not," said the Snowfist. "The greatyaks are tame and act much as horses do in your lands. There is snow and dead shrubbery here for him to eat. He will be fine. Greatyaks do not fear this place, as the Snowskins do."

And fear it they did. Though several of the tribal hunters had petitioned to come as well, Amron had judged that nothing but a contest of courage. No man wanted to look a coward in front of the others, and so as soon as one announced, "I will come with you," then the rest were compelled to do the same, lest they be called craven. Yet Stegra shut down every request all the same, even that of his son, Svaldar, who'd visited the mountain before. "You will stay here with the men, boy," he'd said. "There must always be a Snowfist at the head of our tribe. If I do not return, lead them on."

Amron could sense Stegra's anxiety now, as he marched up the cracked and broken road, dressed in his white bear-skin cloak. Behind the framing of teeth that bordered his hood, his milky-blue eyes were fixed and fearful, and he'd been less garrulous than usual over the last couple of hours. The route took them around huge banks of rock and up short sets of stairs, cut into the mountain and walled either side. Old stone braziers sat unlit for three hundred years along the path, and there were great iron poles too, rusted and ruined. Once they'd have held banners and flags and been hung with lanterns, but now they sat alone, crumbling away to dust.

"I recall this well," said Walter as they went. He had a smile on his face, but it was a nervous smile. *His faith has been tested,* Amron knew. *He wonders whether Vandar's light has led him astray.* Despite that, the luckiest man in the world remained bullish. "It was brighter then, of course, so I could see a lot more. But these steps. I remember climbing them, wondering which one would end in the door. A long set, I remember. When you rise over the lip, you see it, the way into the mountain."

"It isn't far," Snowfist said, "but that way is blocked. We will look to the side-way, that Svaldar and I took. It may yet be open to you."

It was the only mote of optimism he'd allow. Stegra hadn't told them for certain that they'd not be able to find a way inside, only that if they did, they'd never reach the mountain's heart.

After another ten minutes of short banks of stairs, they came upon a larger one, some two hundred at least cleaved between a pair of cliffs. They rose steeply up, fading from sight into the darkness. Though the skies were clearer and the clouds had thinned, there was little light to guide their way. Snowfist's vision had become adapted to these conditions, and Whitebeard had his godsteel dagger to heighten his senses. Both men gave the steps a scan. "There are many rocks," the wolfish ranger rasped, wrapped in his black furs and frosted cowl. "They must have fallen from the cliffs. We need to be careful."

"Stay close to me," Walter said. "My lord, stay near."

Amron didn't argue. He dragged his heavy frozen frame to Walter's flank as an icy gale sliced right through his clothes, causing him to shiver. No matter how many layers he heaped about himself, the winds here could cut straight through him. "Careful," Stegra warned. "The steps may be iced, and the winds are growing treacherous. It will be easy to slip if you take a wrong step. Use your crutch, Lord of Daecar. I am not having you slipping to your doom here, before you fulfil your oath."

My oath. The prophesy. Amron marched on up the steps beside Walter, as Whitebeard and Stegra Snowfist took position in front and behind. Loose stone was prominent underfoot, and the once fine-carved marble stairs glimmered with black ice in places. Though his faith in ever finding his way to the holy chamber at the mountain's heart had been savaged, Amron still held faithful to Walter's mystical gifts.

He is my only protection now, he thought, as he limped on upward, clacking with his crutch. Even so enfeebled as he was, with godsteel in his grasp he could manage just fine. Indeed he had, during their journey thus far, until that fateful day at the Silver Scar when his blades had been lost, his lungs filled with frigid water, and his ability to defend himself shattered like a broken plate. Now he had nothing at his hip but leather and wool and fur. Several times Whitebeard had offered to hand Amron his godsteel blade to strengthen him, but each time the lord had declined. "You can use it better than I," he told the long-limbed ranger. "I have dragged you all the way out here. I'll not strip you of your blade as well, Rogen."

But at times like this, he wished he had, as the steps rose up high and steep, fading into the gloom. Once, twice, thrice Walter took them around a patch he deemed dangerous. "Not there, my lord, the stone is weak and may crack under your weight," he said at one point. "No, let's go around this section," he said at another. "The ice will have us slipping to the bottom, I don't doubt."

Yet up they went, on they went, until the top of the long stair finally ended. Beyond, the road continued atop a flattened plateau bordered by rugged points and horns of rock. Through the darkness Amron could make out the passage at its end, the huge door, ten metres high and ten metres wide, carved of thickened stone. And crumbled.

The Godway Door was a ruin.

Its left side was shattered and broken, strewn out upon the courtyard beyond. The right side stood askew, cracked in places and missing chunks, but beyond both sides lay a thick blackness. *Rocks,* Amron saw.

The tunnel that led past the door and into the mountain was shut tight by fallen rocks.

"You see now," said Stegra Snowfist. "The Godway Door is shut."

Walter was in thought. He turned to Whitebeard. "Could you not cut us a path through?"

"No," the ranger said without hesitation. "It would take the Sword of Varinar to cut through that."

"This is the sword you once held, is it not?" asked Stegra.

"Once, yes." Amron said. "If I still held it, I would never have come here."

"Then good you lost it," the Snowfist declared. "You are foretold to come, Steel Lord, and take the frost away. These are the words of the Sea-King's prophesy that you have come to fulfil."

Amron didn't want to hear about that right now. He turned his eyes to the left, where an old bridge crossed a chasm. More steps went away into the darkness beyond it, switchbacks that led up and beyond the cliffs and ridges above the Godway Door. "You and Svaldar went in that way," he said. "The side door you spoke of...it was there?"

Stegra nodded. Before he could speak, Amron stepped away.

The bridge was half a ruin, its right wall crushed beneath falling rock. The left flank still stood, though Whitebeard insisted it be tested before anyone try to cross. "The stone may come loose beneath our feet," he said. "I will go."

Rogen Whitebeard reached the other side without issue. He was lighter than Amron and Stegra Snowfist by half in bulk and build, though with his godsteel dagger at his hip likely weighed more than them both. Having crossed he waved the others over. Amron went first, with Walter close by behind him. The winds were picking up, squalls screaming in his ear. White mist surrounded him, but on he pressed on to the other side.

Soon they were all across, though not before a few loose chunks of stone had been dislodged, plunging into the abyss beneath them. They came off a part of the wall, crashing and echoing into the darkness. "The winds were enough to break them free," Stegra announced. "We must hurry, or this whole bridge will be gone by the time we return."

His urgency wasn't without good cause. As they began up the slippery switchbacks, the mountain gave another shiver. Rocks came spinning and clattering down the steps, some large enough to kill. Stegra braced and made himself small, furling his coat about him for protection. Whitebeard stood, godsteel to grasp, slashing.

Amron caught glimpses of the ranger's speed as he hunkered down at Walter's side, shielded in the man's light. Rogen Whitebeard would have made a fine Varin Knight, he judged. He was quick, precise, keen of senses, and dutiful. No he wasn't the best company, but by Amron's verdict the order lost a good recruit when he was sent to Northwatch to don his black and grey cloak. And still he'd not yet heard of the man's true name or lineage. *A strong family sired him, that's all I know,* he thought, as Whitebeard diced up several large rocks, deflecting them aside so they tumbled off harmlessly down the mountain. Within moments, it was all over. The mountain stilled, the stones stopped coming, and Whitebeard waved them on.

Up they went, turning back and forth along the stair. More stanchions lined the way, once holding torches, now rusted and worn and bent out of shape. At each little platform where the stairs turned old statues marked the way. Some were still standing, missing noses and fingers but mostly intact. Others had lost full limbs, or even their upper bodies, standing as legs and little more. "They were once kings," Amron said. "Great kings of the Varin line." Some he recognised, others he didn't. At the top they passed the curly-haired and handsome form that he took for King Ayrin, the youngest son of Varin.

Walter recognised him too. "King Ayrin," he said, for Stegra's benefit. "The one from the song I sing at night."

"Ah yes, I like this one," said Stegra. "*The Song of King Ayrin.*" He looked at the sculpture at length. It was chipped and worn and stained, but otherwise the likeness was good. "It is good to put a face to the name."

"Perhaps one day you'll visit Vandar," Walter offered. "There is a large town in the Heartlands called Ayrin's Cross, a pretty place full of monuments to the great king. There is a great statue of him there that would tower over this one, right at the heart of the main town square. You'd like it, I think."

"Perhaps one day I will come," said Stegra, rubbing his soft white beard. "But I would fear that Blacksteel and his black-cloaked kin would cut me down before I could cross the mountains."

"Not if you were a guest."

"I will never be a guest in your lands." The chieftain stomped on.

Amron reflected for a short time on King Ayrin as they continued up the steps. His song was a sweet, mournful melody, and one well known across the north, often recited at feasts and festivals, weddings and wakes. *And his reign had started in mourning too,* Amron thought. Ayrin had become king after Varin was murdered at the peace parley at Death's Passage to end the War of Fire and Steel, slain by Eldur's treacherous sons Lori and Dor. *A hundred years of war had just ended, and yet those bastards had the final say. It's a wonder Ayrin didn't call his armies back to war, and seek vengeance for his father's fall.*

But then that wasn't Ayrin's way. His older brother and sister, Elin and Iliva, had been the warriors, much alike to their father in spirit, though had been slain by Drulgar a hundred years before. That left only Ayrin to take up his father's crown at his death. He was a gifted fighter, yes, but thoughtful and studious too, and wise enough to see that his kingdom had suffered enough. It was said that Queen Thala of Rasalan spent much time with the young king, mentoring him, teaching him the temperance that his father and older siblings had lacked. For two hundred years Ayrin reigned through a long prosperous period of peace, founding new cities and clearing new lands and ushering in a new age beyond the shadow of war.

Yet Lori and Dor's treachery was never forgotten. When Ayrin died, his oldest son Amron took the crown. He was of a more quarrelsome disposition and soon stirred violence with Agarath once more, striking against the old and dying King Lori who'd succeeded Eldur on the throne. So began a new war, a new Renewal, as Amron son of Ayrin sought vengeance for his grandfather's murder. And so spread the shadow once more.

Amron remembered much and more of all that history, in part because he'd been named for King Ayrin's son. He recalled asking his father Gideon of it once. "Amron, son of Ayrin, grandson of Varin, was a great warrior, as you shall be, my boy," his father had told him. "We Daecars are champions of Vandar now, and we need champions' names. I was named for Gideon the Great, who reigned two thousand years ago and won the War of Wrath. Your grandfather Balion was the same, named for Balion the Brute who claimed the head of the great dragon Larackar with the Windblade in one hand, and the Mistblade in the other. And when you have children, Amron, you'll do the same. The man grows to fit the name, my boy. Always remember that."

Amron had clearly remembered that well, for he'd followed the same tradition with his own sons. Across the years there had been kings and warriors called Aleron and Elyon, and beautiful princesses called Lillia. *The man grows to fit the name,* he thought, as he marched on up the final steps. *Did I get it wrong with Aleron, then, because he doesn't live at all. Did I miss something when I named him? Is Aleron a cursed name, ever destined to die young?*

He pushed through those thoughts as he reached the summit. Aleron had been much on his mind of late. *If I do reach the heart of the mountain, would I not ask for a different blessing?* He'd wondered that more and more. *Why revive myself, an old man who's had his time, when my son might have another chance? Could such a blessing even be granted? Can Vandar's spirit bring men back from the dead?*

When he crossed the level land at the top of the stairs, and saw the passage leading into the mountain, none of those questions seemed to matter. *The way is shut,* he thought. A bitter smile gripped his frosted lips, breaking off bits of ice from his beard. "It seems you weren't lying, Stegra," he said.

They stepped closer all the same, to give the tunnel a closer inspection. Walter scurried off fastest. *He still has faith,* Amron saw, though his own was dead and gone. *Like my son.* "There is a gap," Walter called out, his excitement carrying above the bluster of the wind. "It's small, but looks to open into a wider tunnel beyond. Rogen, come, come. Can you not carve a portion of this stone away, so that we might climb through?"

Amron shambled over. There was a flicker of hope in him, as the light of a candle in a storm, no more. He stood at Stegra's side as Whitebeard moved to the rocks that blocked the passage. "I take no joy in this," the Snowfist said to him. "But it is for the best, Steel Lord. There is nothing but death and darkness in there. You came for a blessing, yes...to me the blessing is that this mountain is sealed."

Amron said nothing. Walter seemed certain they could still get through. "My lord," he said, turning, as Whitebeard hesitated. "He's under your command. Give it, I urge you. He'll not do it without your say."

"I fear the tunnel may collapse," Rogen Whitebeard admitted. "I might be able to cut a wider hole, but there's a risk the passage will come down on us as we pass through."

"A risk worth taking," Walter said. There was a desperation in his eyes now, like nothing Amron had yet seen. "Amron, we *must* try. We have come so far. If we turn back now..."

"I'll regret it forever, I know." Amron had to think for a moment. He had to clear his head. *This is folly,* he thought, *and always was. And if this passage is fallen, what will we find within?* The ruin that Stegra and his son Svaldar had described seemed apt enough right now. No high vaulted ceilings carved in the rock. No great chambers filled with arms and armour. No forges and feast halls, barracks and billets. Only darkness and death and doom...*and the ruin of my dreams.*

Walter seemed to sense his mind. "My lord, we cannot go back," he beseeched. "You have my light and protection. I will not let you come to harm..."

"And them?" Amron gestured to the others. "I'll not have the Snowskins lose their leader on my behalf. I'll not have Whitebeard fall for my folly."

"They won't. We'll stay close together..."

Amron was starting to shake his head. *Do I fear to go in, is that it?* he wondered. *Am I afraid of what I might find?* Whitebeard broke his thoughts. "I can carve an opening at least," he said. "A part of me cannot help but agree with Walter. I will not say that I've endured him all these weeks for nothing. Just...stand back. I will cut a hole, and then we can decide."

Walter was so grateful he near dropped to his knees in thanks. Instead, Whitebeard shooed him away and got to work. By Amron's eye the rocks had fallen in such a way as to leave a hole small enough for a thin child to wriggle through, but no more. Beyond, the tunnel seemed to continue as it had been, collapsed in places but passable. From Amron's memory, this route went for some hundred metres before opening out into the main entrance cavern within, above the Godway Door. There was nothing to say they wouldn't encounter other blockages further in.

Stegra Snowfist said as much. "We may become trapped half way through, if the mountain shivers again."

"I'll go and check the route," Walter told him, as Whitebeard got to his carving. "If I can find a way through, will that satisfy you, Amron?"

"I'd rather you didn't go in there alone, Walter."

"I went in there alone twelve years ago, my lord. I was reborn here, and will die here if I must."

"Such courage for a fat little man," Stegra said, warmly. He turned to Whitebeard. "Blacksteel, best cut a big hole. The fat one is going to wriggle through."

He didn't need to wriggle in the end; Walter was a great deal smaller than Amron and Stegra, after all, even with that paunchy gut. Instead he crawled through the gap that Whitebeard had opened, before a torch was handed through to him, already lit. Whitebeard gave him a few final words. "Make as little sound as possible," he said, "and watch your footing. If you fall and break a leg in there, I'll be damned if I have to come and get you out."

"Encouraging as always, Rogen." Walter smiled and disappeared into the darkness, the light of his torch fading as he turned a corner.

They didn't have to wait too long for him to return, though before he did the mountain gave another shudder and they feared he might have been crushed. Calling out to him wasn't an option, though, nor could Walter risk calling back lest they cause another rockfall. Instead they waited, tense, before the glow of his torch warmed the gelid air again, and Walter Selleck remerged with another smile upon his face. "The passage into the main chamber is open," he said, through the hole in the rocks. "There may yet be a way down."

Stegra didn't like the sound of that. "This is nothing I haven't told you a hundred times. I never said this tunnel would be blocked for certain. But in there? Yes, the way is..."

"*Shut*," finished Amron. "We know." He stepped forward. "But I have to see this for myself."

He pulled himself up onto the shelf of rock with his working right arm, and began clambering through the gap. It wasn't far, only a metre and a half long. Walter reached out and helped drag him. "Gods, you're heavy," he said, heaving. "Are you sure you're not carrying a godsteel blade, Amron?"

If only. Amron landed as quietly as he could, and Whitebeard followed them in. Stegra came last, with a full measure of reluctance. Once assembled, Walter led them on, holding his torch. The air was still and silent as the grave, frosted by their breath as they advanced around one corner, pressing forward down a long narrow corridor. In places they had to clamber over portions of the ceiling that had come down. Elsewhere they had to turn sideways and shift through tightening gaps. The passage seemed to fall in a mild descent. "It opens to a balcony at the end," Walter whispered. "I spied a route down into the chamber, through the rubble."

"And did you spy anything else, little man?" hissed Snowfist. "Did you spy the devil that lurks here? The things that cannot be seen?"

"If they cannot be seen, I cannot be expected to see them."

"They can be *felt*," Stegra said to that. "When the air ices around you, you'll know."

"All the air is icy here," Walter retorted. "These ghouls and gremlins are superstition, nothing more. I met no such resistance when I came here last...not in the way in, or the way out."

"Because you were sick with grief, you said. That sickness blinded you to what was there. Or else you just got lucky."

"Now that doesn't sound too likely," said Whitebeard, deadpan.

The tunnel soon came to its end, opening out into a colossal chamber so large the sides could scarce be seen. Amron thought once again of what it once had been, and what it was now. There were pictures, paintings, and frescoes of the caverns of Vandar's Tomb all over the Steelforge. There were books dedicated to the lore of the mountain, replete with magnificent drawings and diagrams. In the palace of Varinar, there were many such paintings too. In the Halls of the Gods, there were even reliefs etched into the stone walls, carved in spectacular detail. Amron had always looked upon those drawings and carvings and paintings and marvelled at what his ancestors had built in the hollow spaces of the mountain. He'd been assured by those who knew better that they were accurate portrayals of what lay within Vandar's Tomb.

Yet no longer, he thought, looking out. What remained was a desolation of collapsed halls, ceilings, tunnels and walls. Amron turned his eyes around from the half-broken balcony, the light of Walter's torch bringing to life the sad wreckage of what was once here. Beyond was nought but blackness, rock, shadow and dread. No matter what Walter said, there was a darkness to this place that had nothing to do with the absence of light. *Something has settled here,* he thought. *Something ancient. Something evil.*

"We should not linger," said Stegra Snowfist. There was a staring quality to his milky-blue eyes. "Something is here. Something is watching."

Walter gave him a quizzical look. "If this is your way of speeding our departure, I would ask that..."

"Silence," hissed Whitebeard. His godsteel blade was clutched in his grasp, its mists puffing gently from its edge. He cocked his head and listened. "There is something moving down there."

"Falling stones and pebbles," Walter said, unconcerned. "You don't need godsteel to hear that, Rogen. Let's not conjure ghosts and ghouls from the simple sound of falling rocks and dripping ice." He gestured to a descending pile of rubble, down at the edge of the balcony where its edge had been broken away. "There's a way down that way. If you'll look out to the far edge of the chamber, Amron, you'll see a tunnel that leads deeper into the mountain. That is the way to the old forges, I believe. There are ways down from there into the mines. If you'll follow me..."

"It was not falling rocks I was referring to, Walter," Whitebeard told him. "There is something moving below."

"Rats, then, and other such vermin." Walter Selleck's face bunched into a frown. "Here we are, a great tribal chieftain, a fearless ranger, and the most famous hero in all the north, and it's the fat little man from Lakeside who does not quiver in this place."

"Only fools do not fear," the Snowfist said. "Fear is good, sometimes."

"And bad at others. Like *now*, when we are so close to fulfilling our quest. My lord." He turned to Amron. "Come, I will lead you down. If these others wish to stay here, by all means, let them. My light will suffice. But *we* have a destiny to deal, and it's down there in those depths."

Amron hesitated for a moment before following. He could sense something stirring here too, sense the spirits watching from the shadows. *But Walter's right,* he decided. *No matter what may skulk about this place, we cannot stop now. We cannot.* Once he'd made that decision, Whitebeard was compelled to follow. After that, Stegra hesitated, turned back, then grunted and came too. "The fat man will be the death of us all," he was heard to mutter, but he descended with the others all the same.

The way down was simple enough, and Walter took the lead as

their canary in the mines. *But the real mines? Will we make it?* Amron was starting to feel a fledgling hope once more, the embers of a dying fire sparking back to life. But all the while, the men behind were urging caution. "I can feel a restlessness here," Whitebeard whispered. "The tremors aren't done. Another one could trap us all, or crush us if we're lucky, because getting locked in down there..."

"We should go no further than this hall," said Stegra. "The darkness is thicker the deeper you go. That is where *it* lives. It draws strength from the body of your god, I think. This mist from your blades...it feeds it."

"Feeds what, Snowfist?" asked Walter, turning. "You've not said once what lurks here, but for cryptic talk of darkness and dread. There is nothing that feeds on the mists of godsteel, at least not that I've ever heard of."

"All dark and dreaded things feed on the spirt of your god. He created them. All these beasts and monsters to fight in his divine war." Stegra looked around, narrow-eyed, nervous. "You steel men drove all foul things here when you spread out across your lands. They all crept away into the woods and mountains and shadowed places of the world. And darkness doesn't like visitors, especially those who bring the light."

"My light is from Vandar himself," Walter said, tiring of Stegra's protests. "It has protected me for twelve years, and will continue to do so here. Stay within it, and you'll be fine. Stray, my friend, and you may not be so lucky..."

The mountain interrupted him with a sudden violent shake, jerking so fiercely it near knocked them off their feet.

Through the caverns and caves came a sound of crashing rocks, echoing through the tunnels about them. Some fell in the central chamber, appearing from the blackness, plunging into the rubble and rock that littered the floor. "Quick, quick..." Whitebeard hustled them on, as they fled across the cavern into the long dark tunnel opposite. Several boulders tumbled about them, missing by millimetres. To Amron's ears the whole world was coming down. *The sky is falling*, he thought. *This is the doom of all days.*

They bundled into the tunnel and down into the darkness, as a frozen wind followed, and Walter's torch blew out. Suddenly all was black as pitch but for the faint glow of Whitebeard's blade. The mountain quietened, the shaking stilled, and all about them the walls seemed to close in. Yet somehow all four men were still together. Somehow they were all safe and unharmed.

"Your god does *not* want you here," Stegra Snowfist spat. "He makes that clear enough!" He grabbed Amron by the collar, his skin gleaming faintly in the dimness. "We go, and we go *now*. Is it worth it, to rid yourself of that limp?" He threw a hand at Walter. "This man will get us all killed. Damn your light, and damn *you*. We are leaving. Right now."

"But..." Walter started, yet Whitebeard broke him off.

"We must leave," the ranger agreed. He shone his dagger down the passage. "The way is blocked, Walter. And even if it wasn't..." He shook his head. "My lord, I was charged by Lord Borrington to protect you, and will see his orders through. If we go now, we may escape before the rest of this place collapses. We have no choice, and we have no time. This quest has met its end."

One great quest will fail, but one greater will light the way. Amron thought on the words of the prophesy. *Was this always meant to be?*

Ahead, the tunnel that led through into the forges and the mines was thick and dark with fallen stone, impassable. *Might there be another passage, another way?* Walter would urge that, he knew. He would claim that the collapse of the mountain would not harm them, not with his light to shield and protect them. That he would lead them down to the depths and back again, for Amron was to be one of Vandar's champions, and the god would not have led them all astray.

But Amron had never shared Walter's faith. He had been driven on this quest by hope, and that hope had shrivelled and blackened these last days, turning to ash. Now looking at the blocked passage, that hope was dead and cold and done. "I'm done," he said, turning to Walter Selleck. "We're done, Walter. There is no way through." *The way is shut.*

"But my Lord Amron, we...we are so close. Do not lose faith now, I beg you. There are other ways, other routes we might take..."

So predictable, Amron thought. *Still he continues to bang that drum. But I cannot listen to it anymore.* He turned to Whitebeard. "Lead on, Rogen. You have the only light."

"As you wish, my lord."

They turned back the way they'd come, re-entering the main

chamber, as the mountain began to stir once more, and Walter whimpered his petitions to go on. Amron wasn't listening. *Folly. This has always been folly*. Amid the crack and chaos of falling stone he was certain he could hear laughter.

Does Vandar mock us? he wondered. *Has this all been some great trick?* More likely it was a trick of his own mind, the laughter of that side of him that had never believed in any of this. And as they went so Amara's words came back to him, words she'd spoken when he'd first broached the topic of coming here, when he'd sat in the family feast hall in Keep Daecar, and spoken to Amara and Artibus of this quest. "To reach that holy place requires extraordinary courage and sacrifice," she had said. "Vandar only blesses the worthy, and the worthy... they are rare."

He recalled how she'd glanced at him when she'd said those final words. How she'd believed wholeheartedly that he was worthy of that blessing, worthy of deliverance.

But I'm not, Amron thought, as he trudged through the rubble and ruin of the main chamber, as he clambered up toward the balcony, as he squeezed through the passage that had led them all inside. *I'm not worthy, and perhaps I never was.*

And then he thought again of his son, his firstborn who'd died for his crimes. *I sired the creature that killed him,* he thought. *I broke my vows to Kessia, and from that union, came the boy who brought me here, the boy who killed my son, the boy who made me a cripple.* A cripple for life, he now knew, as he climbed through the hole cut into the stone and back out onto the plateau. *And this failure is my penance.*

Stepping back into this icy wind, he looked out over the endless white plains, and filled his lungs with a breath of frozen air. He did not turn back, or give the mountain another look. *The way is shut,* is all he thought, as they began the climb back down. *One great quest will fail, but one greater will light the way*.

He turned to Stegra and said, "I am yours, Snowfist. Take me to these cursed lands, and I will do what I can to help."

24

Lythian

Lythian groped around in the darkness. "Talasha," he whispered. "Princess, where are you?"

It's like my dream, he thought. How many times had he dreamed the same dream? Of Talia and his infant son dancing on the white courtyard, attended by a perimeter of maple trees. Their red leaves seemed to dance and caper as he and his family did sometimes, though not always. The little details were different like that each time; but just the small things, not the big ones. There was always a courtyard, always a dance, always his wife and son. And the black wind that came rushing upon them from nowhere. There was always that too...

"Talasha? Talasha!" His whispers echoed into an open cavern, some way down from where they'd fallen. Hot air wreathed him like robes, suffocating. "Talasha, can you hear me? Please...say something..."

He continued to fumble through the jet black air, as ever he did in his dream. Only then it was his wife and son he was searching for, not the Agarathi princess with whom he was falling in love. What a cruel twist of fate it was. *I have fallen for her and she's been taken away, just as my wife was, just as my son. I closed that door for a reason...I should never have opened it. I should never have let this happen...*

"Sweet captain..."

Lythian's eyes swung to his right. "Talasha!" He quickened his pace. "Talasha, where are you!"

The voice was weak, muddled, thick. "I...I am here, Lythian. Right here, sweet captain."

He scrambled across the cavern toward her, feeling his way around a high bank of stone. Beyond it a gentle light shone, a glimmer of pale gold. *Starslayer*. He'd dropped the blade during his tumble into the abyss, the sword slipping from his grasp as his body was battered on the way down. His sword-hand ached horribly from where it had struck a jutting ledge of rock, and there was a crushing sensation in his chest, but elsewise nothing felt broken. *But her? What of her?* "Princess, I'm coming..."

He found her lying nearby to Starslayer, her face lit by the gentle gold glow of the blade. A glimmer of blood ran from a gash on her forehead, leaking through her thick black eyelashes, meandering down past her nose. She looked dazed, confused, likely concussed. *Please let that be all,* he thought, rushing toward her in a crouch. "What...what happened?" the princess whispered, as he drew to her side. She was flat on her back upon an even section of floor, her limbs all aligned, not twisted terribly as he'd feared. "Where are we?"

"We fell," he told her. "I'm not sure where. Can you feel your legs, Talasha?" His fears were for her spine, her neck. "Can you move?"

She strained, grimacing, but managed to draw her legs up, folding them at the knee. Relief went though him. He went to check her ankles for breaks and sprains, but they seemed in working order. Then she moved her arms, one after another, and sat up. Her left hand went to her forehead where the blood ran slick and dark upon her brow. She wiped and looked and said, "I'm bleeding."

"You have a gash." He moved in to check it. It was half a centimetre wide, two inches long, deep but superficial. It would scar but no more. He ran his hands gently across the back of her head, searching for other wounds, then began pressing at her chest, her stomach, her flanks, searching for signs of internal damage. "You seem OK," he concluded. "You're battered and bruised, but OK. Your armour must have protected you. Can you stand?"

She managed to do so, weakly. The knock to her head made her unsteady on her feet, and there were small cuts and scrapes on her hands, cheeks, and neck. Lythian reached down to take up Starslayer, as a pain went through his chest. The touch of godsteel helped stifle it, but Talasha saw the grimace. "Are you hurt, sweet captain?" she asked, blinking through the dimness.

"Nothing too bad," he said. "A cracked rib or two, I think. I'll be fine."

"Are you sure?"

He nodded. His eyes went up, searching for the way they'd come. It had been a bumpy ride down, but not a straight drop, as it might have been. The chasm that opened to swallow them up had brought them straight into a second passage, spiralling down in a steep descent. *But how far?* He didn't know. It had gone on a while, enough to have sucked them some forty or fifty metres deeper into the mountain, he judged.

Above them, the echoing of voices could be heard. He strained to listen, but the mountain was moaning and rumbling, drowning out the calls of their friends. "We'll not be able to get back to them this way," he assessed. "The fall was too steep." He turned to look into the chamber. "We'll have to find our own way, Talasha. Here, let me clean you up." He tore a length of fabric from his arm and wound it tight around Talasha's head. "This will do for now," he told her. "Stay here a moment and rest. I will search for a way out..."

"*No.*" Her hand squeezed tight to his, slick with blood and sweat. "Do not leave my side, not here." A throb of fear drummed in her voice. He took her into his arms and held her for a long moment, gripping all the while to Starslayer, turning his eyes about the cave. It was smaller than he'd first thought, wriggling away into several other routes. *A maze,* he thought. *This whole mountain is a maze, set across a thousand levels.* "It will be all right, Talasha," he whispered to her. "I told you I'd not let anything happen to you." She nodded into his shoulder. *I followed you down into the depths of hell. And I'm going to get you out.*

Without the Fireblade and the torchlight of the others, the world became a much smaller place, lit about them by no more than a few metres either side. Lythian's eyesight fared better through his bloodbond but even that helped little down here. "Can you walk unaided?" he asked the princess.

"I think so." She tested her footing, as they moved a little way into the cave.

"Do you feel dizzy? Is your eyesight stable?"

She nodded, seeming to come around a little. "I'm OK, Lythian. I...I think I'm OK to go on."

Thank the gods, he thought. He was still wearing his satchel pack, slung across his shoulder, though it seemed to have been torn during the fall. He swung it, opened it up, drew out a deerhide waterskin. Over the many hours here he'd consumed much of what he'd been carrying with him, but one remained full. He gave it to Talasha first to take a drink, then did the same himself. The water was so hot it gave him little relief. "Are you hungry? I have some salted meat..."

She shook her head. Her eyes were looking off across the cavern, a strange quality to them. They looked more red than usual. *A trick of the light,* Lythian told himself. "What is it?"

"The air," Talasha murmured. "It...it grows thicker, do you feel it?"

"Thick enough to cut," he said, with a feeble laugh. "The heat is worse, yes. We need to go up..."

She shook her head. "Not the heat, Lythian." Her eyes were fastened to the mouth of a narrow tunnel ahead. "No. It's different. There is a sorcery here, a power. I...I can sense it."

A thud began to beat in Lythian's chest. He could feel the vein in his neck pulsating. "Where?"

"There." She stared at the tunnel. "Down there. It's coming from down there."

Is she delirious? Disorientated? She began drifting forward, half a step at a time. "Talasha...we need to be going *up*. I have to get you out of here..."

"No..." She drifted forward another step, then another. Her fears seemed suddenly vanished.

She's in a trance, he thought. *She must have hit her head harder than I realised.* He grabbed her arm. "Talasha, stop..."

She turned to him. There was a peculiar look on her face, enough to give him pause. He drew back. "He's this way, Lythian," she whispered. A smile curved her full lips. "I don't know how I know, but I do. We cannot stop now. We...we are so close."

He? Eldur? "Talasha...we have to get out." He swallowed. The air was so close, so hot. He was growing light-headed from it, the very rock at his feet seeming to steam. "We cannot go any deeper. We have to find the others..."

"They'll find us." She stepped away, bleeding into the darkness, drawn by some unseen force. "Tethian will feel this too. He will find the way."

This is wrong, all wrong, he thought, but what else could he do but to follow? Whatever force was calling to her was doing the opposite to him. "This doesn't feel right," he whispered. A primal warning was ringing through his body, saturating his very bones, driving a shiver up his spine. He felt a steady thrum in his right hand, coming from the hilt of his blade. *Starslayer...*The mists were acting strangely, swirling chaotically about the length of the steel. "Talasha, I...I don't know if I can follow. I should never have come. This mountain does not want me here."

But Talasha no longer seemed to be listening. She was several paces ahead of him, moving into the tunnel. The walls closed in, tight and rugged, descending steep down a set of uneven stone steps. It was narrow, barely wide enough for them to walk without their shoulders scraping the sides. Down and down it went, ten metres, twenty, thirty, wending left and right at random, tightening, opening out, tightening again.

Ahead, Lythian could see strange flutters of fiery air blowing up from below. There was a screeching, somewhere far off at the edge of his hearing. *Dragons*. He paused on the steps, frightened, but on Talasha went, down and down, fading from sight around a corner. *Curse this madness.* Starslayer was growing frantic, the mists puffing, heaving, beating a rhythm Lythian had never seen before. *I cannot leave her, I cannot.*

He followed, his legs wobbling beneath him like blades of grass, his clothes drenched wet with sweat. The air grew thick as treacle, every breath a struggle, every step a war. Yet Talasha cut through it without burden, pulled onward as a fish on a line. *She walks to the father of her people. I shy from the enemy of mine*. But he had no choice. On he went.

The steps levelled out into a long corridor of jet-black stone, gleaming and glistening with a million sparks of silver light. An orange tint suffused the air about them, and little rings of red light seemed to dance before Lythian's eyes. *Does she see it too? Is this my imagination?* He wanted to ask her, but his words fell dead on his tongue. *Even my voice is lost in this place. Will I ever get it back? Will I ever speak again?*

An elemental fear enveloped him, as he pressed on into the depths of hell. He tried to catch up, tried to reach out to take Talasha's hand, but she was always one step ahead, one step too far. He reached and reached and reached again, only ever clutching at air.

Talasha, he tried to call, *Talasha, wait,* but not once did she slow or stop or turn to look back. The passage ahead grew narrow and narrower still, ending in a slit of red light. *Stop. No, stop!* He hastened on, as the princess slid through the gap. His shoulders brushed the walls, tightening, tightening, until suddenly he was pressing forward, stumbling from the tunnel and out into a great open space.

He gathered his footing and looked up. Darkness consumed the world above him, and to the left and the right, no wall could be seen. Sotel Dar's words from hours earlier came back to him. *A great open chamber, cloaked in darkness, with a ceiling so high one cannot see the top.*

Talasha stood before him, staring forward, still as a block of stone. The red and black and purple scales of her armour were glittering and gleaming in the darkness. "Princess..." he managed to get out. Even that one word was a struggle. He felt suddenly like he was dying, suffocating. "Talasha..."

She turned. Those eyes of hers, brown slashed with red, were lit now with a bright crimson glow. There was a mad wonder upon her face. "This is it," she whispered, her words coming free from her lips. "He...he is here, Lythian." She reached out and took his hand. "You do not need to be afraid, sweet captain. My cousin was right. Sotel Dar was right. He will be our saviour. Come, you will see..."

She drew him onward, toward the heart of the cavern. But where that heart might be, Lythian couldn't say. His eyes blurred, stripping away his sight, but even clear-eyed and sharp of mind the extremities of this place seemed out of reach.

A place of magic, dark with sorcery. The Breath of Agarath fills the air. He could feel the Fire God's spirit clogging the ether about him, heavy and hot, ancient and evil. He could sense the weight of him, the ageless everlasting terror. All darkness had breathed from him, the northmen said, all the fire and ferocity and devilry in the world. From the flame of his life-force sprung the dragons, the demons, the monsters and madmen that surged out in search of death. *And here he lingers, sustaining his greatest follower.* He searched forward now and could see him. A shadow and shape sitting up against a towering mountain of rock. *Eldur...can it be?*

He squinted. Sweat ran down from his forehead, a sweat of heat and horror all in one. He wiped a hand across his eyes. Starslayer felt heavy in his grasp, so heavy he could hardly go on. The blade seemed to pull backward, but Lythian kept on going, dragging his feet, dragging his blade, dragging his frame on and on. He could feel a faint swirl moving past, left to right and right to left, eddying the air above him. Shadows flashed by. *Dragons.* But he gave them no mind. He was lost to the figure sitting upright ahead. A figure that cleared, little by little, as he grew close.

A man, was his first thought. *Just an old man.* He sat in a stained grey robe, white-bearded, eyes closed, unmoving. His skin looked faded, wrinkled and sallow and dead. A black wooden staff topped with a pale unlit orb lay across his lap. One withered hand clutched to it in an eternal embrace. The other lay at his side, draped against the rough stone floor.

Lythian's every muscle stiffened to look at him. *Can it be? Can this be him?* All the world closed in about him. He stared only at the ancient figure sitting against the rugged hill. Sitting still as stone, fixed in time. Talasha crept on, falling to her knees. Words came from her lips, but Lythian could scarce make them out. All was muddled, blurred, burning. He felt in a dream. *I am,* he thought. *I am dreaming, I must be.* "Talasha..." he said, but he couldn't hear his own voice. *Like my dream, with Talia, and my son.* In the dream, he would call and call and call her name, but he'd never hear the words. *Yes, I must be dreaming.*

Something passed by above, another dragon. He felt the sleeves of his shirt flutter. His eyes went up. *What do I have to fear in a dream?* Shapes clotted the air, black, zigzagging in the endless abyss. Dragons in the skies. *Like my other dream.* He smiled, waiting to wake somewhere far from here. Starslayer was so heavy in his hand. The blade began to slide from his fingers.

He took another look at Talasha, at the old man leaning with his back against the mountain. *A funny mountain,* he thought, as his eyes went up to take it in. It had a shape, one he faintly knew. He squinted through the blurred, burning air, the haze of heat that rose all about them.

A head, he thought. The mountain had a head. And a hulking body, wings, talons, claws, teeth. *Another sculpture of the Dread,* was all he could think. *Like the one hewn into the cliffs of Dragonfall.* He took a short step back to take it all in, marvelling at its magnificence, the fine artful detailing of the Lord of Dragons made stone. *But a dream, that's all this is. Nought but a dream from which I'll soon wake.*

His thoughts were guttering out like a candle, thieving away the last of his wits. He could bear Starslayer's weight no more. The blade slipped from his sweaty fingers, landing on the rock with a dull muted thump. As it left his grasp so fled the last of his strength. A sickness rose up through his stomach, and a heavy pounding echoed hard and harsh in his head. He blinked, staring forward. For a moment he came back around.

This is no dream. He stared at the mountain again, at the demigod sat before him. Drulgar and Eldur, calamities both. A sick fear rose up his throat, and all of a sudden Borrus's warning was in his head. *If you see him, Lythian, slay him. You cannot let him rise...*

An urge took root, deep inside. *I cannot let him rise.* He bent to pick up Starslayer, but the motion was too much. The air boiled and bubbled, and his feet gave way beneath him. He slipped, tumbled, fell. He felt his chest crunch hard on stone, tasted iron on his lips. He struggled to rise but the darkness was closing in.

*I cannot let him rise. I cannot...*He reached feebly for his blade, his fingers brushing the hilt, but no more. His strength was gone, his body cooked. *I'm going to die,* he knew, *this is it.*

The last he saw before his eyes went black, was a pair of red eyes opening.

25

Elyon

Lillia Daecar almost knocked him flat onto his back when she jumped into his arms.

"She missed you, I think," said Amara, stepping in behind her. "How are you, my darling Elyon? My goodness it's good to see you!"

With Lillia still clinging like a limpet to Elyon's chest, Amara moved in and pecked him upon both cheeks. Behind, Jovyn was dragging their luggage into the room with several other attendants. He gave Elyon something of a shy look.

Amara noticed. "Don't be silly, Jovyn, come along, you're part of this family now too."

The boy left the baggage to the servants and shuffled over. He gave a bow. "Sir Elyon, it's...good to see you again."

Elyon laughed. "Now if I've told you once, I've told you a thousand times...drop the 'sir', Jov. Amara's right, you're part of this family too." He shifted out of Lillia's grip and reached out to take Jovyn's hand, shaking firmly, with a big broad smile on his lips. "You've grown," he saw, looking the lad up and down. Jovyn had turned fifteen now and was at that age where a boy could suddenly sprout. And he had, growing longer and leaner, and more handsome with all that.

"Almost three inches," said Lillia proudly. "Isn't that right, Jovy? You'll be as tall as Elyon one day."

"*Jovy*?" repeated Elyon, as the boy shrugged abashedly. "You two are getting on well then?"

"Really well," said the little Lady of Daecar.

Elyon looked to his auntie. "How well?" he asked her.

"Not *that* well," said Amara, smiling. "You father had the same concern."

"What...what do you mean?" Lillia looked at them, one and then the other. "Oh...*that*. Ew...no. Jovy's like my little brother." She grinned and prodded him firmly in the arm.

"He's over a year older than you, Lillia," Elyon told his sister. "And half a foot taller now as well."

The girl shrugged. "He still seems little to me."

"Of course he does," Amara said, with no short order of sarcasm. "Isn't everyone *little* to a Daecar?"

"You sound like King Hadrin," Elyon noted, removing his dark blue winter mantle, and setting it aside. Beneath he was dressed in his Varin attire, fine leathers and cloak, fastened with a brooch wrought into the crest of House Daecar - the knight on horseback, with misting blade held aloft. He took a look around the room. The three had been provided rather more impressive quarters than his own bedchamber in the lower south side of the palace, tucked up near the mountains. They were upon the upper floors, looking east from the sprawling northern wing, with splendid views out through the valley. "Janilah's been very generous with your accommodations, Auntie."

"Well, my cousin did always *adore* me," Amara quipped.

"I thought you hated him?" asked Lillia, taking her seriously. Elyon could hardly stop smiling each time he looked at her. Her effervescence had returned in full force, it seemed, after she'd turned morose following Aleron's death. Much of that was due to Jovyn, he'd heard, and his daily training and tutoring sessions in the use of godsteel. They'd also become fast friends, clearly. *But the boy wants more than that,* Elyon could see. And Lillia was growing more stately and beautiful by the day.

"Well now, I don't hate anyone," Amara told the girl, glancing as the attendants continued to bring up their luggage. "Why would you say that, child?"

"Because it's true and everyone knows it's true. You hate almost everyone."

"Do I?" Amara laughed handsomely, and gave Elyon a funny smile. "Apparently I hate everyone, Elyon. I never knew I was such a loathsome shrew."

"I rather think you take pride in the label, Auntie," Elyon joked.

"Well, there are rather a lot of lackwits and lickspittles in this world, aren't there? Someone needs to be there to tell them so to their face."

"You're tactless, Auntie," insisted Lillia, hands on hips. She arched her pretty blue eyes up toward the tall elegant form of Amara Daecar, wrapped in cerulean robes inlaid with silver patterning. "Now that *I'm* head of this house, it falls upon me to tell you that. So there is it. You're too indelicate with your tongue."

Amara raised a single brow. "*Indelicate with my tongue*?" She pursed her lips as she considered that, then said, "Nicely put. It seems the little Lady of Daecar is learning."

"Yes, but you're not head of this house, Lillia," Elyon was obliged to tell her. "Where did you get that idea?"

"From her," said Lillia, looking at their auntie. "She's the one who calls me it. With Father gone, and you at war, it was me who had to hold court. I did, you know, in Blackfrost *and* Keep Daecar. I dealt with everyone and heard their pleas, and gave out all my rulings. Lords, ladies, highborn and lowborn all. I did well, didn't I, Jovy? I showed tact when dealing with my subjects, but firmness too. Father would have been proud."

Elyon gave a wan smile to all that, as Jovyn nodded politely and agreed with every word the girl said. "I'm sure you did well," Elyon told her. "Though Father always found dealing with his subjects the most tiresome part of the job."

"All lords and kings say the same," Amara declared.

Elyon nodded. *Amron Daecar...is dead.* He drew a breath and searched Amara's eyes. "And Father? How does he fare?"

Amara opened her mouth to give answer, but Lillia got there first. "Who knows," she said, snatching up a pear from a side-table. She had a bite, gave a face, and tossed it to Jovyn, who placed it to one side. "We haven't seen him since he went to Northwatch Castle with that funny looking man. The short one with the homespun clothes and tangly hair. He sends letters, though, sometimes. Just not to me. To Auntie Amara. Where was he the last time he wrote you, Auntie?"

"At the Twinfort," Amara said. Her smile twitched under Elyon's gaze. "He led some of the Borrington and Rothwell banners there, to bolster the southwestern gate. I think he was going to travel to Green Harbour after, to inspect the naval forces. There's a fear that the Agarathi will try to cross the Red Sea and land out in the west where we're weaker, I hear."

Elyon had heard that too. He'd been involved in daily war councils among the Vandarian contingent, led by Lord Kanabar and Prince Dalton, though as yet the gathering of greatlords and kings hadn't materialised. Word was that King Janilah had been waiting for King Godrik Taynar to arrive, before forming his Council of Kings, as it was being called. Well, that day had now come. Weddings and war councils were imminent, Elyon knew.

Still, he wasn't certain what to make of what Amara had said. He had the sense she was lying about his father, for Lillia's sake perhaps, and the gods knew that Amara wielded lies as well as Varin wielded godsteel. She might very well have heard of Amron's death, and kept it from the girl to spare her. *I must find out, and now,* Elyon thought. "Auntie, do you mind if we speak alone?"

"Oh...well of course, Elyon," said Amara. "How about we..."

"No," cut in Lillia angrily. "We've only just got here. I want to hear your stories, El. You'll have so much to tell, I'll bet, from what happened over in Rasalan. I don't even know if you've killed your first man yet. At least...on the battlefield, anyway." She looked aside, awkward.

Elyon knew the reason. "So you heard about Sir Griffin Kastor?" he asked.

"We heard he tried to ambush you in your tent along with some great big thug of his," Lillia said on a breath. "That they tried to *murder* you, and when you killed them in defence, Prince Rylian gave you *ten lashes.*" She snorted and shook her head. "I thought Rylian was nicer than his father? You shouldn't have been punished at all for that. I don't know why..."

"It's a little more complicated than that, Lil," Elyon told her. He thought of Saska. He thought of the bloodied blade in her hand. Of Sir Griffin's disembowelled body at her feet. Of the lashes he'd taken for her, the whip that had cut near to the bone. They were still healing, in truth, though by now he was back in training and swinging his sword each day. The palace had many training yards, and there were plenty more across the lower levels of the city where the gathered knights and lords of the north could hone their skills during their stay. Elyon trained mostly with Lancel and Barnibus, as Aleron used to, though often Sir Mallister would join them, and occasionally Prince Rodmond would come along too.

"How complicated can it be?" Lillia asked. He might have known he'd not get rid of her so easily as that. She had that frown on her face, the one his mother used to possess. Elyon had never been able to lie well to his mother, and his sister was the very same. "What aren't you telling us?"

"A lot, probably," Amara broke in, sparing him. "A warcamp is a dreadful place, Lillia, and you wouldn't want to know half of what goes on there. Believe me, I have seen them, and not the worst parts either. If Elyon wishes to keep certain things from you, let him, that's his right."

"I know what happens in a warcamp," Lillia claimed, indignant.

"You *think* you do, but you don't. Hearing stories and reading tales isn't the same as seeing, child. The true horror of a warcamp comes alive in the experience. Even a man so courageous as Elyon has clearly seen things he'd rather have not. Do not bring to life what he may be trying to forget. If he wants to tell you, he will. You need to learn not to push."

"Asking a question is not pushing. I'm curious. Is that a crime?"

It felt to Elyon like these exchanges between the pair had become more common of late, as Lillia grew into her new role. *The Lady of House Daecar, trained in the ways of the Varin Knights. Gods, what have we done.* "My stories are dull," Elyon said, trying to break the deadlock. "Uncle Rikkard once told me that war sounds fun and exciting in theory, but for the most part, it's a lot of old men talking and not much else. That's been my experience so far."

"Rikkard is wiser than I realised," Amara said. "I've always thought that your mother got the brains and your uncle the brawn. Though it's fair to say they both got the beauty."

"Is he coming for the wedding?" Lillia asked, hopeful.

"He's stationed at Dragon's Bane with the Amadar banners," Elyon told her. "I'll be going there after the wedding to join him."

“Can I come?” Lillia looked at Jovyn. “Jovy can be your squire again, and keep training me on the side.”

“You have duties to attend to now, Lillia,” their auntie reminded her. “Or do you not want to be the Lady of Daecar anymore?”

The thought suddenly seamed to displease the girl. She had always been of a capricious nature, taking up one hobby then growing bored of it just as fast, before moving onto the next. She’d clearly found her passion in the blade, though, which pleased Elyon no end. And worried him too. The intention in training her was to ensure she could protect herself. He was concerned now she’d go looking for trouble.

“I don’t suppose our grandfather came with the host?” Elyon wanted to know. He’d not heard much as to whether the uncompromising form of Lord Brydon Amadar would be attending. He was one of the most powerful men in Vandar, yet didn’t much like to leave his city seat of Ilivar on the eastern coast of Lake Eshina. The last Elyon had seen him was shortly after Aleron’s death. He’d come with Elyon’s grandmother, Lady Lucetia Amadar, to observe Aleron’s expected triumph in the Song of the First Blade, and had departed shortly after they’d laid him to rest in the Steelforge crypts. A short stay, as ever. Lord Brydon misliked having to make the mere hundred mile trip to Varinar. The idea that he’d travel all the way to Ilithor seemed wholly unlikely.

Amara confirmed it in her usual manner. “Of course not. Brydon goes nowhere unless he must. A shame. I would have enjoyed Lucetia’s company during our travels. Your grandmother is a true treasure trove of gossip, you know.”

“We’re aware, Auntie,” tutted Lillia. “The two of you are as bad as each other, badmouthing everyone behind their backs.”

“And don’t you and Princess Lyriss do the same, child? Now come, no one likes a hypocrite.”

“That’s different. We’re young, it’s allowed. But you’re old, and Grandmother even more so. You should know better by now.”

“You see what I’m having to put up with these days?” Amara said, turning to Elyon. She shook her head tiredly. “Now Elyon, you wanted to speak privily? *Please*. Do rescue me from your sister’s tongue.”

“Fine.” Lillia tilted her chin up and took Jovyn’s arm. He was dressed smartly in a blue velvet doublet, and she a pretty sapphire and silver gown, with a grey ermine cloak over the top. She’d grown a little too, Elyon now saw, and was looking more like their mother everyday. "Come on Jovy, we know where we're not wanted." She began leading him away, then turned back to Elyon and said, "Do you know where Lyriss is? I want to go and see her. It's so horrible about her father, isn't it? She needs me, I know it. And I want to see Princess Amilia too. See how she's coping having to marry that ugly Rasal king. And Melany." She nodded. "Yes, I miss Melany. And that beautiful golden hair of hers. Are you still sleeping with her, Elyon?"

"*Lillia Daecar*, that is entirely inappropriate," said Amara. "And you're *not* to go wandering through the palace until I say so, do you hear me?"

"I hear you, Auntie, and happily ignore you." She lifted her little round chin yet higher, clutched tighter at Jovyn's arm, and strode from the room before Amara could say anything more.

"Go with her, Sir Connor," said Elyon, looking to the guards at the door. "And you, Sir Wallace. Make sure she doesn't get into any trouble."

The two men were Daecar household knights and full-trained Bladeborn. They nodded and stepped away. Amara let out a sigh once they were gone. "She has grown bold, Elyon, since your father left us in Blackfrost. She's taken this 'lady' thing very much to heart."

"I can tell." Elyon's smile had gone off the boil. He stepped away as two of Amara's handmaids began unpacking her possessions. "Let's talk on the balcony."

The air was brisk outside, though there was little breeze to speak of. It was a clear crisp day, the views spectacular down through the city and valley, hugged to the north and south by the white-capped Hammersongs. "The views aren't so fine from my quarters," Elyon said. "Janilah...I don't think he likes me very much."

"Janilah doesn't like anyone," Amara told him. There was a bite to her voice, as there ever was when her older cousin was discussed. "And unlike your sister's slanderous accusation against me, that one is quite true. The only person Janilah Lukar has ever truly cared for is himself, and even then, I'm quite certain it's balanced by a healthy dose of self-loathing too."

Elyon's smile crept back out. "I've missed you, Auntie. I'm sorry about what happened with Vesryn."

Amara's face curdled like spoiled milk. "*Vesryn*," she said, part angry, part sad. He could see all that in her face. "He should never have taken up the Sword of Varinar. I said that from the very start."

"You did," Elyon remembered. "Your cousin is behind all this, you know." He knew he could speak plainly with Amara. By his judgement she probably knew almost as much as he did already. "Everything that's happened, I mean."

"Oh yes, that's obvious enough, at least it always has been to me." She gave him a questioning look. "Do you have any proof we might use?"

Proof, Elyon thought. He had the conversation with Vesryn, if that served for proof, though with his uncle gone rogue it couldn't exactly be counted on. Beyond that, much and more of what he knew would fall into the realm of theory. "No," he admitted. "But I think that anyone with half a brain can see that Janilah plotted to take political control of the north."

Amara raised a hand. "I think this conversation calls for wine."

"It's morning, Auntie."

"And I don't care, Nephew."

She returned a moment later with a large jug of sapphire wine and two spiral-fluted chalices. They took to a circular stone table on the balcony, sitting on high-backed cushioned chairs. Vines twirled about the balustrades here, and coated parts of the walls, some with winter flowers of green and pale blue in bloom. "Do you miss this place?" Elyon asked her, taking a sip. The wine was warm and rich, lightly spiced to beat off the cold.

Amara shook her head. "No. Beautiful though it is, it carries with it harmful memories. I've never spoken of my time here, have I? Not to you."

"Not in detail."

"Another time," she said. "Let's just say, living under the roof and rule of Janilah Lukar was never a fond experience. To him, women are nothing but goods to be bartered, as poor Amilia is now discovering. She almost got lucky, marrying your brother. And now look at the creature that awaits her, for her grandfather's political gain."

"Rylian's beginning to turn against him," Elyon said, enjoying the sensation of the wine as it spread through his chest. "I spoke with Queen Elitha, and she gave some indication to me that Lyriss was to be wed as well. I tried to find out who, of course, but she wouldn't say. You know where my mind is going..."

"One of the twins? Oh yes, I can see how that would irk Rylian somewhat, assuming he's being sidelined from such discussions." She grinned like a wolf, taking great pleasure in the thought that the son might turn against the father. "I do hope you've been stoking that particular fire, Elyon?"

"I've fanned the flames a little," he admitted. "I think we'd all be better off if Rylian sat the Tukoran throne."

"Oh, I like this, I do. But be careful. These are treasonous words." She smirked.

"Well why not, Auntie? Half the world seems to be taking up treason as a hobby, so why shouldn't I?"

"Because you're far too sweet." She reached over and pinched his bearded cheek, as she used to when he was a boy. "Treason is a game played by cowards and cretins, and no surprise my dear old cousin plays it so well. But never forget in whose palace we sit and drink. And whose city and whose kingdom. And continent now, I suppose." She glanced around. "The walls and halls have ears, you know. Be careful with whom you share your counsel."

Elyon nodded to her wisdom, though felt certain they weren't being eavesdropped on out here. Amara knew the palace as well as anyone, and wouldn't be speaking like this if she believed their conversation was being overheard. These chambers occupied a large space upon the northern wing of the castle, and they were keeping their voices down. But something in Elyon hardly cared either way. A part of him half wanted to stand up and call Janilah out for what he was. *Amilia's wedding, perhaps?* came a devilish thought. *What better time to do it than with half the north assembled?*

He drank to the notion, but would never carry it out. His father had warned him to keep his own counsel, just as Amara was doing now, and he intended to play a slow, smart game while he could.

"You know what we need," whispered Amara, leaning a little closer. There was a conspiratorial look on her face. "We need a confession from someone who was there that day. Two would be better, from separate sources, but one might just be enough to overthrow him."

"You're referring to King Ellis's death?" Elyon inferred.

"What else? If we could get Sir Nathaniel to admit what happened, well then...we might have what we need."

"I've spoken to him already. He continues to assert that Ellis slipped and fell."

"Well of course he does, but we all know that's a lie. What we need is a pretty young thing to take him into bed. Men are loose with their tongues beneath the sheets, Elyon, as I'm sure you know."

"I tell no secrets in bed, if that's what you're suggesting."

"Well I should hope not." She frowned at him. "*Are* you still sleeping with the Monsort girl, by the way?"

"No," he said on instinct.

"Why lie? You've never been very good at it with me."

"Fine." There was a truth in that. Elyon could never out-lie Amara. "I bedded her once, the night I arrived here."

"*Elyon.*"

"Twice, then." He shut his eyes, vented a sigh. "OK, three times, but that's it, I'm not falling back into that trap. I promised myself I wouldn't."

"Do you know who the easiest person to break a promise to is, Elyon?" asked Amara. "*Yourself.* What you need is someone to keep you honest, someone to be accountable to. Let me be that person. If you're truly intent on ending this tryst with Melany, then tell me now, and I'll be sure to keep you apart."

"How, exactly? By standing guard at my door each night? The woman is insatiable, Amara. I've never met a girl with such appetites."

"And you're complaining? My gods how you've changed."

"I just think it's irresponsible. I plan to leave the morning after the wedding and head south to join Uncle Rikkard, as I said. So long as Prince Dalton permits it, anyway..."

"Oh don't get me started on all that." Amara threw a great gulp of wine down her throat. For a woman of such effortless grace, she could drink like a common sot. "It's been near unbearable travelling among our new king's host. Godrik Taynar must be the single most unlikeable man I have ever met. You would think claiming the throne would make him less surly, but no, all it's done is add to his many layers of moodiness. Three weeks, Elyon, and not once have I seen him crack even the barest hint of a smile. I'll admit I don't know Dalton half so well as his father, but I'm reliably informed he's of much the same ilk. How you serve under him, I don't know. He's not been making life difficult for you, I trust?"

"I have been guarding him most nights," Elyon said, "though that's grown less common of late, thankfully."

"Of course. How else would the insatiable Lady Melany Monsort get the carnal joy she needs?"

"I knew I shouldn't have said anything about that."

"Of course you should, and you had no choice. I'd have gotten it out of you anyway." Another gulp of wine disappeared down her throat. "But that's it? Just a bit of babysitting and night duty? Dalton doesn't have you running unpleasant or embarrassing errands or anything?"

Elyon shook his head. "He's hardly pleasant, or likeable, but I don't think he's especially unfair. He held some suspicions toward me at the start, but they've since faded."

"Because of Vesryn?" She saw the answer in Elyon's eyes. "He expected you might know where he'd run off to?"

"He thought Vesryn might seek vengeance. Still does."

"Because Dalton took his post? Well now, that makes no sense to me. Vesryn was only standing in as First Blade. He always knew he'd have to give the Sword of Varinar up sooner or later. When your father gets back, fully restored, then he'll..." She cut herself off mid-sentence, her wine cup an inch from her lips. There was a shifty look on her face. She took a sip to hide it, but Elyon saw it all the same.

"Then he'll what? What do you mean, Auntie?" And so they returned to the reason Elyon had wanted to speak with her, the reason he wanted to do it without Lillia around. When he'd heard that the host from Varinar had arrived that morning, he'd wasted no time in hunting his family down. He wanted to see them again, of course, but there was something he wanted more. Something he *needed* to know. *Amron Daecar...is dead.* He leaned forward across the small stone table as those words rang out in his head. She'd said his father had gone to the Twinfort and Green Harbour, but he could smell the lie in that. "Where is he, really?" he asked her. "I want the truth, Amara."

His tart-tongued auntie took another long sip of wine, tipped back her head, sighed, and said, "I'd hoped you wouldn't ask, Elyon. Your father didn't want me to tell you."

"Tell me what?"

"You're not going to like it."

"I don't care. Tell me."

She drew a breath and came out with it. "Fine. He's journeyed over the Weeping Heights and across the Icewilds on a quest to Vandar's Tomb. That's why he went to Northwatch. It wasn't to check the western defences as was claimed, but to cross the border in secret, a secret that you now know, along with very few others. Don't worry," she said, seeing the look on Elyon's face, "he has company. The best company he could hope for, in fact. That funny little man Lillia mentioned? His name's Walter, and he'll keep your father quite safe, I assure you."

Elyon was utterly dumbstruck. "What...what in Varin's name are you talking about? The Icewilds? Vandar's Tomb? What would possess him to..."

"Oh don't be silly, Elyon. You know just what. Think of the tale of Sir Oswald Manfrey, and you'll have your answer."

Elyon loved that tale. Sir Oswald had been a swordsman of meagre skill who'd travelled to Vandar's Tomb in search of a miracle four centuries ago. He'd reached the depths of the mountain, communed with Vandar's spirit, and returned a knight of unmatched brilliance, becoming First Blade, defeating not one, but *two* dragons in single honour-bound combat, and winning himself a lordship. *But that was just a story, wasn't it?* "He's gone to seek a blessing?" he said. *Restored. She'd said restored.* "To...to heal himself?"

"Well aren't you a smart boy. Well done."

"And Walter is...?"

"Walter Selleck. *The luckiest man in the world*. A fine title, wouldn't you say?" She smiled and supped her sapphire wine. "He's an old friend, and was kind enough to provide Amron escort. He knows the way, fear not."

"He...he's been there before?"

"Of course."

"*Of course*," Elyon repeated. "Why bloody 'of course', Amara? You seem to be treating this as a game."

"I am not. I'm treating this entirely seriously. Your father *will* return to us restored and reborn, as though Varin risen again. He will help win us this war as he helped win us the last one, and once he's done that, he'll win us my cousin's head."

“Right, so this is about vengeance?” Elyon said, his brows drawing over his silver-blue eyes. He couldn’t believe what he was hearing. “You’ve sent him off on this mad errand so you might have your vengeance against Janilah. For how he once treated you.”

“So we *all* might have our vengeance, for how he’s treated us *all*,” Amara told him. “Your father is the only one...”

“My father is dead.”

A chill wind started blowing from down in the valley, sweeping through the vines. Amara’s greying blonde hair danced upon the breeze, before settling. “Why would you say that?” she asked. “If this is some cruel jape, then...”

“It’s no jape of mine. Hadrin’s maybe, but not mine. He told me, Amara. He said he’d seen Father in the Eye of Rasalan, limping into the darkness.” He stopped and in an instant it all made sense. “Into the darkness,” he repeated, his voice shrinking to a whisper. “Hadrin...he must have seen him in the dark of the Icewilds. *That’s* what he saw.”

“So the Kingkiller King has some foresight, then,” Amara said, sitting back. “Gods, Elyon, you frightened me. No, your father isn’t dead, he’s just a good long way from here. Hadrin must have been mistaken, or more likely, just trying to get a rise out of you. He was always a petty little creature.”

Elyon was still thinking. *Couldn’t both be true?* The Weeping Heights were treacherous enough, but the Icewilds? *And at this time of year.* “I can’t believe you let him go,” he said quietly, shaking his head. “You put this madness in his head, no doubt. Why, Amara? No one goes into the Icewilds and comes out alive, no one...”

“Walter did. He went there alone, a dozen years ago. On foot, with no mule to carry his belongings, barely any belongings at all. *Alone*, Elyon. He walked there alone, found his way to the holy chamber alone, and got the blessing he’d earned alone...”

“So you say. And what was this man’s blessing, exactly?”

“I told you. He’s the luckiest man in the world. Vandar’s light follows him wherever he goes, and beats away the darkness. He saved my life once, and I’ve heard a hundred other tales of the same.” She paused, judging his reaction. “I knew you’d be like this. One has to meet Walter to see it. That’s why I never mentioned him to your father, until we reached Blackfrost. I knew he’d not believe me if I told him, just as you’re not believing me now. But you know what, Elyon? Your father did meet Walter, and he did understand, and he did decide to travel north beyond the Heights. I had a letter from Lord Borrington of Northwatch, sent on your father's request. Coded, of course, should it fall into the wrong hands, but not hard for me to figure out. It turns out, the finest ranger under Borrington's command went with them. So you see, it isn't just your father and Walter out there. They have a seasoned hand to help guide them too, and a fiercely gifted one at that..."

"Oh well that's OK then, I can relax. Thank you, Auntie, for putting my worries to rest. So long as Father has a *ranger* with him, he'll be absolutely fine."

Amara's serene blue eyes deadened. "Spare me the sarcasm, Elyon. It doesn't suit you."

"But it serves to make my point. *One* ranger, Amara? One bloody ranger? I'd have sent a full score of Varin Knights with him, and still feel thankful if half of them returned."

"You're exaggerating. And being dramatic, I might add. Men fear what they don't know. Those lands beyond our borders have become lost to memory, forgotten since the last of the wagons came back stacked high with Ilithian Steel. So we fear them, because we no longer understand them. But this ranger does, and so does Walter. They'll get your father safe to the mountain, Elyon. And once he's fully restored, *he'll* get them safely back."

Elyon knocked back his wine. He didn't like any of that. Nor did he believe it. *Your father...is dead.* Until he saw him again, a part of him would always think that Hadrin was telling the truth. "You put too much faith in him," he said eventually, refilling his cup.

"Walter or the ranger?"

"Father. Even if he returns renewed and restored, he may not make the difference you suppose. He's just one man, Amara. You expect too much of him."

"Perhaps. Or perhaps I was just sick of seeing him moping around the halls of Keep Daecar, pining over days gone by, and cursing himself for his part in Aleron's death."

That caught Elyon's attention. "His part? What do you mean?"

Elyon knew what part of course, but did she? Elyon and Amron had both known whom Aleron was up against, known who the man posing as Fitzroy Ludlum truly was. *The Shadowknight. My brother.*

Jonik, he thought. *Jonik.* He closed a fist. He'd beseeched his father to warn Aleron, to tell him who Ludlum was, but Amron Daecar preferred to thrust his head into the sand and keep it there instead. So Aleron never knew. And Aleron died.

As all that went through Elyon's head he regarded his auntie closely. It didn't take long for him to see that she knew much and more of all that too. "You know?" he asked her, before she might have a chance to answer. "You know who the Shadowknight is?"

"Your half-brother, yes."

Elyon stared at her, though was hardly surprised. What confused him was why she'd never spoken of it. "But....you never said anything. Back in Varinar, you never mentioned..."

"It took me a little while to figure it out, I'll confess, and in truth you're giving me the confirmation I've needed right now. Before today it was more of a suspicion, a feeling deep down in my gut. But here you are, with your honest face, verifying all my fears." She paused a moment in sadness. "I'd hoped I was wrong, these last weeks. But alas, it all makes a great deal of sense."

"How did you figure it out?" Elyon asked her. "Jonik has my look. Daecar features. Was that it?"

"I always knew your father had sired an illegitimate child, Elyon," she explained. "But *Jonik*...that's his name?"

Elyon nodded. "Vesryn told me."

"Vesryn...of course. Foolish sweet Vesryn, whose past transgressions have finally caught up with him." She paused and looked into Elyon's eyes. She could see he needed a proper explanation. A sip of sapphire wine went down her throat, then she went into it. "After the war, when Janilah gave my hand to Vesryn, the curious side of me had to wonder why. I may not have been adored like your mother, but I was something of a beauty myself back then. I had many suitors lining up to wed me, even a few greatlords here and there. I do believe that Hadrin himself was once an option, and I thank the gods every day that that never came to pass."

She placed down her cup, leaned forward. "But then, suddenly, I was put on a carriage and shipped off to Varinar and told it would be Vesryn Daecar whose bed I'd be warming from now on. Now don't get me wrong, he was a fine and handsome young man, a respected knight and warrior, and had fought admirably during the war. But he wasn't a greatlord, and he wasn't an heir. When your grandfather Gideon died at the Burning Rock, that made your father Lord of House Daecar, and Aleron his heir, then you. Vesryn was shifted aside, as ever happens with subsidiary sons. And in this cruel social world of ours, he became overnight of lesser importance. Yet Janilah gave me to him anyway."

"A gift," Elyon said. He remembered what Vesryn told him that night his uncle had disappeared, that night the white flags went up around Harrowmoor, that night when they learned that both King Godrin and King Ellis were dead. *The night Janilah took the north.* He looked his auntie in the eye. "He told me. He said that you were given to him...for his service to Janilah. For helping..." He wasn't sure he should say it. *But she knows,* he realised. *She already knows.*

"For helping trick Amron into siring a bastard son," she finished for him. "Yes, I know. I got all that out of Vesryn one night soon after we were first wed. He was drunk, ravaged by guilt. It all came out, though of course he doesn't remember. I might have slipped a little tonic into his drink, to help loosen his tongue and soften his mind so nothing he said returned to him the next day." She looked at him. "We all need our tricks, Elyon. Poisons and tonics are a woman's weapon, I'm sure you've heard that before."

His mind went to Lady Cecilia. The Bastard Bitch of Blakewood, some of the men had been calling her. No doubt Amara had her own thoughts about her too. "You know who Jonik's mother is?" he asked.

"Cecilia Blakewood, yes. A comely woman, with a snake for a tongue. I hear she's risen to a station beside her father. That Janilah has come to enjoy her counsel." She huffed. "They're as treacherous as one another. Any woman who can birth a child and then hand him over to be raised as an assassin, in a tower of torture and torment, must have a heart as black as the Long Abyss. I would sooner lay down my life for one day with a child of my own. Just one day, Elyon, to feel that joy. To look into that baby's bright little eyes and know...I made this. This one is mine." Tears were welling in her eyes. Elyon reached out, but she sniffed, wiped her face, filled her glass, and smiled. "Ignore me. I'm just being silly."

It had been her curse, to never have a child of her own. Some women were robbed of life on the birthing table, but Elyon knew that Amara would kill for that chance sooner than live her life barren. "This is all Vesryn's fault," he said, a fury rising in him. "It was *his* treachery that cursed you never to have children together. Maybe... maybe he's the one who's infertile, Auntie? Perhaps you might still..."

"That ship has sailed, Elyon. I've grown old, and have long accepted my fate. And I have you, and Lillia. You have both been as children to me, even though you're not of my blood. I've been blessed in that, at least. I couldn't have hoped to have a niece and nephew as dear to me as you."

Elyon couldn't help himself then. He rose, moved to her, lifted her to her feet, and hugged her tight. "I love you too, Auntie. I always have and always will."

He'd never seen her so vulnerable, though of course Amara Daecar didn't let it last. When they sat back down, she wiped her eyes again, drew on her wine, and filled her lungs. A smile returned to her face. "Nothing like a good cry," she said, putting a positive spin on it all. "And it's good to get things into the open, Elyon. All this treachery is like a weight on our backs. Shared, the load is lightened. We all need to vent, from time to time."

Elyon turned his eyes over the ranging view. Some clouds were beginning to close in from the east, and over the mountains, a fine snow seemed to be falling. Snowflakes came their way, blown on the breeze, dancing as they drifted down and gusted about on the air.

"I don't suppose you know where Vesryn might have gone?" he asked. "He didn't speak of anywhere he might find sanctuary, or..."

"Never. I've heard my sweet husband has fallen to the Sword of Varinar's will, so who can say where he might be."

"There are many theories going around."

"I'm sure. Soldiers like their theories. It passes the time between battles. But if the blade is driving your uncle, Elyon, it will surely be blood he seeks. Those blades seek war, especially during these Renewals. We'll see Vesryn again, one day or another. And his golden blade will likely be red when we do."

"But whose blood will be on it? Dalton fears vengeance. So does Janilah, I suspect. It's clear enough that both are concerned he might come here..."

"He won't. Vesryn isn't so reckless as that."

"Perhaps not, when in his right mind. He isn't, Amara. He's grown obsessed with that blade and told me himself he might seek to take

Janilah's head for controlling him." He looked at her. "You know about that as well, I suppose? That Janilah seeks to gather the blades?"

"Don't we all? But so far as I see it, it's the Daecars who continue to hold them. A bastard assassin and a traitorous turncoat they may be, but..." She gave Elyon a look. "Perhaps it's time the noble heir of House Daecar takes up a Blade of Vandar of his own? Your half brother has one. Your uncle has one. So...why not you?"

"I can think of a few reasons," he said. "The Mistblade and Frostblade are lost, for starters. And the Windblade..." He stopped, seeing the twist of Amara's lips. "It's *here*?" he saw. "King Godrik brought it with him?"

She waved a hand. "Of course. How else would he have paid for his crown?"

Elyon had to laugh. *She's too clever for her own good.*

"That blade is an heirloom of Vandar, Elyon," Amara went on. Her face had lost its smile. "Only a Vandarian should ever possess it."

Elyon caught her meaning, but wasn't much sure he liked it. "You think I should try to thieve it?" He wouldn't give that any thought. *Too reckless,* he thought. *Too wild.* "I can't. How can we be sure it's even here?"

"It's here, believe me. And there wouldn't be any thievery involved, just the righteous return of a blade to its proper keepers. Janilah has bought that blade with the blood of a king and he has no right to wield it. There is no lord in Vandar who will ever claim otherwise, and should the Taynars and their banners try to do so, it'll only out them as treacherous themselves and weaken their claim to the throne. A throne, lest we forget, that *should* have gone to your father."

Elyon couldn't disagree with any of that, but he knew infighting wouldn't serve anyone at a time like this. "This isn't a time for civil war, Amara. We can't afford that."

"I'm not saying we should. When your father returns and this war is won we can consider making a claim for the throne. But that's a concern for another day. Right now, we're talking about the Windblade, and the rights of the Vandarian people. At times of war the Blades of Vandar have been known to be taken up by chosen warriors, champions to fight in the vanguard, to lead and inspire our men. Can Janilah, this foreign king, deny us that? Can our own king do the same? I say no, but my voice carries no weight. Yours does, Elyon. And I hear there's a Council of Kings coming up."

He caught her meaning. "You think I should bring the topic up when we gather?" He gave a huff. "I'd have to be invited first. Janilah may yet keep his council small."

"You're the heir of the greatest Vandarian house, royal or not. And I'm sure Janilah wants to keep an eye on you. Of course you'll be included."

"And if I am, and I make a claim for the Windblade..." He shook his head. "That won't lead anywhere, Amara. King Godrik will just say it's safely stored back in the Steelforge vaults."

"Oh yes, I know. But you'll know otherwise. And to hear our king lie like that? To know that he gifted it in secret to a foreign monarch?" She tutted, shook her head, supped her wine. "Such scandal. Any good and noble knight of Vandar would be compelled, in such a situation, to retrieve the blade..."

"Amara, please stop putting these thoughts in my head."

"They're tempting, are they not?"

"Of course they are." The thought of defying both Janilah and Godrik Taynar in one fell swoop was more enticing than he cared to admit. *But no, I can't,* he thought. *Too reckless. Too wild. Too much like my uncle,* his detractors would likely say. Still, he thought on it for a long moment, as a breeze brushed through his hair, and the snowflakes capered about him. *Imagine soaring the skies with that blade...imagine the thrill...*He blew out a breath and shook his head. "How can you be sure it's even here?"

"Because I glimpsed it on the road," Amara had a smile on her face, as though she could see how much the idea allured him. "Godrik thought he had it all under lock and key, but a soft word here, and a sultry smile there, and perhaps a little drop of sleeping tonic into a night guard's drink, and a woman can perform wonders." She smiled, shrugged, sipped her wine. "It's just a thought, anyway. I doubt there's anyone in this city who'd master the Windblade as well as you, Elyon. Nor anyone more worthy to hold it." She squeezed his hand. "Just have a think, OK? And if you want my help, do let me know. Remember, I know this palace about as well as anyone. And I understand there's a wedding in the offing, when all eyes will be on a certain king and his pretty little princess. Could one ask for a better diversion?"

She smiled and sipped her wine once more, and left it all at that.

26

Janilah

He greeted the new king of Vandar without pomp and ceremony. Godrik Taynar was not a man for it. *And neither am I. It credits us both.* "Godrik, I'm glad you could finally join us."

Godrik Taynar was of an age with Janilah, though not of a build. He wasn't tall, nor broad, nor youthful for his years. His seamed face was hollow and gaunt, skin sallow, hair deeply receded beyond the forehead, once black, now grey with wisps of white. He had a thin nose, pointed jaw, and eyes as empty and expressionless as a corpse. *His face could do with a beard to thicken it*, Janilah thought, but Godrik Taynar had never favoured facial hair.

"Janilah." The word was an icy breath. Taynar stalked forward with the shade of a limp in his left leg from an old war wound, dressed in dull silver and earthen brown, with a bit of Vandarian blue colouring the hems and sleeves of his robes. His shoulder clasps were in the form of steel-clad knights, thrusting their blades downward into the ground, the crest of House Taynar.

He stood from his throne to greet the new king. This man was not Ellis Reynar, nor Hadrin of House Thala. Godrik Taynar was of a very different sort, not the sort that Janilah could bully. He moved down the steps and joined him between the fluted white pillars of his throne room. They nodded to one another in unison, a sort of exchange of bows that served as a hand-shake between men of their high station.

Behind the Vandarian king came a small host of Greycloaks and other attendants. Sir Nathaniel Oloran led them, having now left the service of Queen Elitha Reynar. His underlings who'd been there the day Janilah murdered King Ellis were also present at his side, as ever; Sir Gerald Strand and Sir Alyn Porter, Taynar men both. And of course Janilah had the welcome presence of Sir Owen Armdall and Sir Fredrick Ruxmond with him, who'd also borne witness to the regicide. The sworn swords were exchanging glances with the Greycloaks, and didn't much like one another, it seemed. *We are bound by treachery,* Janilah thought, *and these men don't like it.* Still, it was all a means to an end. Ellis's death had paved the way for this meeting. It was one Janilah had been relishing for weeks.

"Come, Godrik, let us drink to our alliance."

Wine was brought forward, and handed to the two kings. Godrik looked long into his cup. "I don't like to drink until evening."

Janilah felt something shrivel inside him at the man's voice. Godrik Taynar had that effect. "A sip to seal it, is all I ask." He had to be tactful with this man. He raised his own cup, hoping Taynar would follow. He did, though with reluctance. "To your crown, and the winning of this war," Janilah said.

Taynar only grunted, took a perfunctory sip, and then handed the wine back over to an attendant. *There are too many unknown faces here to talk plainly,* Janilah thought. "Let us speak on the balcony," he said, opening his arm to guide the king that way.

Taynar held his tongue until the two men had climbed the steps and ventured out into the brisk wintry air beyond the throne. A light snow had started to come down, though the skies were mostly clear, the city gleaming resplendently beneath the late morning sun. The sworn swords and Greycloaks knew better than to follow. Instead, they began ushering most of the excess bodies from the hall. Before long the two northern kings were alone, save for a handful of loyal knights and guards, standing far out of earshot within the throne room.

King Godrik Taynar looked over the edge of the balcony, the white stone balustrade topped with a fine coat of snow. "Are you planning to throw me from here too, Janilah?" he said.

Was that a jest? The Warrior King had been accused of being humourless himself, but this gaunt and shrunken king from the Ironmoors had mastered the art, it seemed. He decided to ignore the quip, if that's what it was. "I had hoped you'd have a trunk for me," he said. He gestured vaguely backward. "I didn't see one among your host."

Godrik Taynar got his meaning. "The Windblade is safely kept," he said, staring out over the city enclosed amid the mountains. His head moved left, moved right, slowly, taking in the sights. His expression remained unreadable all the while, unchanging. "I wondered if I might give it to my son."

Janilah frowned. *Now that surely is a jest.* "Your son?" He regarded the man, as a burning sensation began to spread through his chest. It had come on more often lately, with all these setbacks he'd suffered. *Stress*, his physician had told him was the cause. He'd supplied him with tonics and balms to soothe the burning, though Janilah knew they'd give him little succour. *No, the fulfilling of my ambitions will do that,* he knew. *The fulfilling of King Galin's promise.* He looked down at the hollow-cheeked king. "Tell me you're joking, Godrik."

"I would be lying if I did so, Janilah. My son is First Blade of Vandar now, and needs suitable steel to accompany the role." He glanced over. "I hear you've been unable to track down Vesryn Daecar."

"That duty does *not* fall to me. It was your son who let him slip the net."

"Perhaps. But that warcamp was Tukoran. Your sentries failed to track his escape."

"For which you blame me? I wasn't there. It was my son's warcamp, and Lord Kastor's..."

"Then our sons are both useless. Or more likely, you drove Vesryn to defy you through your demands, and he escaped with the Sword of Varinar for that reason. Either way, a First Blade must carry a Blade of Vandar. Dalton can do much good with it in the war, if given time to master it."

Janilah could scarce believe what he was hearing. *The impudence of the man.* "You forget yourself, Godrik. Must I remind you how your predecessor died?"

Godrik Taynar's line-for-a-mouth cracked open, twisting up at the corners. *So he can smile, after all.* "Is that the Warrior King's answer to everything? Murder everyone who displeases him?" The smile vanished. His eyes turned back to city and sky. "You have half of

Vandar wishing you dead, Janilah. Don't make the other half your enemy too. You don't seem to see what a thin edge you're walking on."

Oh I see, Janilah thought, furious. *I see more than you know, Taynar.* That burning continued to fizz through his chest. He gripped the stone top of the balustrade, freezing cold to the touch, to steady himself.

Godrik Taynar didn't miss it. "You seem unwell, Janilah," he noted. "I had been told you were in fine health. Do the crows caw lies, old friend?"

Friend. You call me friend at a time like this. Janilah held his fury and said, "My health is fine. The spices in the wine can bring on a burning sensation sometimes, is all."

"I'm sure. So I suppose you would think Rylian best to wield the Windblade, would you?"

No, me. Only me. Janilah said nothing.

"That cannot happen, you must know," the Corpse King went on. "Your son is much loved and respected, but the Five Blades are not for Tukorans to claim."

"Then why did you agree to this bargain?" barked Janilah. "I gave you a crown, and you'll give me that blade. I need it, Godrik."

"Why? To wield. *You*? No, I think not. You're old, and in ill health, it would appear. A Tukoran will not bear that blade."

"Then a Taynar will not bear a crown. I gave it to you, I can take it away."

"You cannot. Doing so would make all of Vandar your foe. How long, then, do you think it would take for Rylian to oust you from that white stone throne of yours, should you lose our backing? I have heard mutterings already of his displeasure toward you, and I've been here but an hour. There are shadows all around you, Janilah. Add to them, and you'll soon find yourself in total darkness."

I am the shadow, Janilah almost said. He had cast it over his son, his subjects, his kin and kingdom for decades, yet was finding it couldn't cover all the north. He had come to learn that already. Tukor was small. The north was big. *I need my son at my side,* he thought, as he had many times before, but Rylian was still cold to him. *And now this corpse of a king comes and puts it plain. Perhaps that's what I need, to be spoken to straight?* He thought on that a moment, giving himself time to consider his next words. Many passed his head that would only make matters worse, and Godrik Taynar was not a man to alienate. *How to convince him I need the Windblade? The truth, perhaps? The full and absolute truth...*

He looked down at the old Lord of the Ironmoors, judging him, wondering, and deciding...*no.* The man had made plain his mind, and despite his treasons, Godrik Taynar kept loyal to the traditions of his kingdom. He had accepted that Amron Daecar needed to be removed to allow them to unite the north. He had accepted that King Ellis was too weak a monarch to rule during war. Those treacheries were necessary to bring them to this point where they might win this Last Renewal together, but letting Janilah claim the Blades of Vandar, the heart of his god, had never been part of the bargain. *He tricked me with his promises,* he thought, as another fiery pulse raged through his chest. *No matter how tight my grip becomes, there is always something that slips through my fingers...*

"There's a rumour," King Godrik murmured, when he saw that Janilah's tongue had failed him. "It says you want the Five Blades to give to your sworn swords. Another has whispered into my ear that you'll hand them out to your greatest champions. Your son, Cedrik Kastor, one or another of your Six. Or perhaps your grandsons, Robbert and Raynald...they are much as their father, it's said. Maybe that's your plan, to keep the Five Blades in the family, make them heirlooms of your house and kingdom?" He stood still, straight, small, looking out into the whitening skies. The snow was falling thicker, the winds blowing harder. A heavy grey cloud had come in to block the sun, casting a shadow over the city. "All whispers, all rumours, and all gross miscalculations," Taynar went on, "no matter which one might be true. I deceived you, Janilah, I know. And for that I take no pleasure or pride. But I have said it already and I'll say it again. The Blades of Vandar are for Vandarians only. Your house gave up any right to them when Galin Lukar sieged this city three hundred years ago."

How little you know, Janilah thought. Even now, the Mistblade was no more than a stone's throw away, hidden away in the secret chamber within his private office. *All the world thinks it lost, but here it is, right under their noses.* Janilah's mastery of the Mistblade was as complete as any of the great kings of the past, and its unique properties made it well suited to certain tasks. *I will have the Windblade, whether you like it or not, old king. If you'll not willingly give, then I'll be forced to take it.* That thought brought a smile to his lips, well hidden in the thick tangles of his grey-brown beard. He kept it private, of course, and instead simply said, "You owe me, Godrik. You promised you'd deliver me the Windblade. You promised you'd convince your son to hand me the Sword of Varinar, should he retrieve it. Those are not oaths to be broken on a whim. You smear your own honour with this betrayal."

"Perhaps. But I'd sooner betray you than betray the traditions of my kin and kingdom. You are right, however, I do owe you, and shall make this right. I have brought from the Steelforge a score of fine new godsteel blades; shortswords, longswords, greatswords, bastard swords and daggers. These are my gift to you, in lieu of the others."

"An insult. A score of common Ilithian Steel swords bears no comparison to a Blade of Vandar."

"Quite so. I have with me some shields as well, suits of full plate armour, gold and jewels and other fineries. All yours."

"All an insult. I have shields, armour, gold, jewels, and as much finery as I could ever need or want. Do you take me for a man of such pleasures? I have known you for five decades, Godrik. Even as a boy you know I had no interest in *finery*."

"Then what is it you want? I can be amenable, Janilah. Tell me and I will make it so."

"The Windblade. And the Sword of Varinar. As promised."

"Must I tell you 'no' again? Why pine for what you'll never have? And the Sword of Varinar is gone, perhaps for good if what I've heard is true." He looked out through the valley. Far down in the depths of the city, beyond the outer walls and great white gates, the main road from Ilithor twisted away through the foothills and out onto the open plains. "Life on the road is dull. I like to pass the time by reading. Books, scrolls, letters. Yes, I've had many letters brought to me by wing and rider that tell of Vesryn's disappearance. I know you have Lord Huffort searching high and low for him. I know it is not only my son who seeks to find the turncoat Daecar. But will he, or you, or anyone? I'm not so sure. Some men who go rogue go wild...others, well, they go away, and are never seen again. I know Vesryn Daecar. He holds his honour in high regard, as his brother does, as his father did, and this rash move will haunt him. He'll not come back, no. He will run, hide, disappear. The Sword of Varinar is gone."

Janilah didn't want to further this conversation. There was no merit in speculating over what Vesryn Daecar might or might not do. Over the last weeks, a few sightings had been reported, though when fully investigated, they all turned out to be hoaxes and lies. A man who lived in the hills near Stormhold in Rasalan had spoken of a cloaked warrior bearing a golden blade, getting on a ship heading for the Windwake Isles. His report turned out to be false and his tongue had been taken in turn. Another had spotted Vesryn Daecar rowing down the Sibling Straight, he'd said, hiding in the little coves and bays. Lord Huffort's hunters had interrogated him and unearthed another hoax. The liar lost an eye for his efforts.

As ever when a reward was being offered for information, men of dubious intent sought to profit. Any found lying ended up losing a great deal more than they gained. Tongues, eyes, fingers, toes, and other parts had been removed. The only problem was, word of all that soon spread, and now people were disinclined to come forward. Even true accounts were like to remain privy from now on.

Janilah returned to the throne room, escaping the winds as they began to pick up. In the chamber's corners, beyond the inner pillars, stone braziers set a warmth to the air. Godrik Taynar followed. "We can speak further at the feast this evening, to welcome you and your host to the city," Janilah told him, by way of dismissal. "I will be convening war council meetings in the Black Tower, in the coming days, now that you have arrived. There is much to be decided, as to how we might move forward in this war."

"Indeed. Until later, Janilah."

Godrik Taynar said nothing more. He turned and walked away, Sir Nathaniel and the remaining Greycloaks trailing behind him, sabayons clacking on the white stone floor.

Once they were gone, only Sir Owen and Sir Fredrick remained. Both knights stood quietly either side of the door. On its opposite side, Sir Maxwell Hunt was stationed, completing the three of his Six always on guard. "Have Sir Kevyn released from his cell," Janilah said to the pair of sworn swords. "I require a word with him."

The disgraced knight arrived some quarter hour later, flanked by a pair of gaolers who handed him into Sir Owen's care. The Oak of Armdall led him to the foot of Janilah's steps, where the king sat in his polished throne, hands perched upon its broad stone arms. Sir Kevyn Bolt looked less a knight and more a beggar right now, without the triple-coloured garb of the Six and his dual bull-pommel blades.

Instead he was clad in poor leather and wool, with coarse stubble covering his cheeks and chin and a few prickly hairs sprouting from his usually bald head. His eyes were hollow, dark. Sleep clearly hadn't come easily in the cold dark dungeon he'd inhabited these last days.

"Your penance is served, Sir Kevyn," Janilah told him, as the Bull of Bolt stood before him, head down, wide shoulders pulled in, fearing the very worst. "I have need of you, and you're wasted in a cell. Do you remember what you said to me?"

The broad-shouldered knight looked up. "I...I said I'd return to Miren, to track down the missing page, sire. That I'd return with it and Vincent Rose's head both. I will. I'll leave today, with a score of killers at my heel. We'll ride hard and sail swift, my lord. I'll make it up to you, I will."

Janilah raised a hand. "I have dispatched men to that effect already." He'd done that the same day he'd had the Bull of Bolt locked away. That was less than a week ago, and not something he wanted to wait on.

"Sire? You...didn't want me to go?"

"A man like you would only have attracted attention. The waters south of the Horn of Aramatia are growing more treacherous by the day, and the southlands even more so. A man so obviously *northern* as you would be make a tempting target for half the men in the empire. No, this job calls for sellswords and spies, not knights clad in silver steel. I need men who'll go unnoticed. Men who might blend in."

"The Bloody Traders?" Sir Kevyn guessed, and rightly.

Janilah nodded. The *Bloody Traders* were a sellsword company of mixed colouring gathered from a multitude of kingdoms, nations, islands and cities, north and south, east and west. They had some two thousand members, all told, with men to fit whatever assignment they were hired for, and a strong reputation for getting the job done. They had no political leanings, no care for colour, creed, or gender, and were best suited to seek out Vincent Rose, Ranulf Shackton, and the missing page from the Book of Thala.

"*The Surgeon* is out near Eagle's Perch as we speak," Janilah said. The man's real name was Pete Brown, a Bladeborn bastard whose mother had been a southern healer, legend said. He had his tan skin from her, and had grown up learning every tongue in the south; with his father's Varin blood it made him well adapted to life as a sellsword captain south of the Red sea. "I've sent him instructions to take twenty of his best and track down Rose, Shackton, and anyone else who might prove of aid. He's weeks ahead of you, and better for this sort of job, Sir Kevyn. No, I have another use for you."

Sir Kevyn Bolt dropped to a knee. "Anything, sire."

Good. His time in shackles hasn't dimmed his sense of duty. As Janilah had hoped, it had instead served to reinvigorate it. "I need you to find out where the Windblade is being kept for me," he said. "You are a ghost in this city, and know this palace like few others. Godrik Taynar will have taken steps to keep the blade well hidden; you will uncover its location, determine how well it is being guarded, and report back to me what you find."

The Bull of Bolt looked mildly confused by the assignment. "I thought King Godrik had promised to trade you the blade for his crown, sire?"

"An oath he has just broken, and not one I'll fast forget. But there are other means by which the Windblade can be retrieved. Find its location for me, and I will see to the rest. As yet, your return to this city has not been noticed, so dress accordingly, cloak and cowl, and make sure you're not seen. Use whatever resources you must. I need a location, and soon."

"I will see it done, my king." Sir Kevyn Bolt rose. He looked little like the man who typically plodded the halls of this palace; another benefit of his time locked away. "Do I have leave to use force, sire, if the occasion calls for it?"

"Use your judgement. But no killing, Sir Kevyn. If I should hear that some of Godrik Taynar's guards have turned up dead, I'll not be happy. We can ill afford any friction between our kingdoms and houses at this time."

"I understand, sire. I know how to be discreet, when needed."

He did, and had proved it so in the past. Despite his size, the Bull of Bolt was swift, light on his feet, silent as a shadow. Janilah hadn't chosen his Six without making sure they could serve his needs. He stood from his throne. "Go. Report to me when you know more."

The unkempt form of Sir Kevyn Bolt left the room to see to his duty.

27

Saska

Saska had never been so hot in all her life.

It was a sticky, humid, suffocating sort of heat that put the conditions she'd endured in her cabin on the Steel Sister to shame.

At least then she'd been able to escape onto the deck at night to sleep, where the sea breeze kissed her skin and helped to keep her cool. Here in this creaking old carriage there was no escape. Not from the heat. Not from the constant rattling and bumping of the road. Not from the reek that now filled every breath she took. And it wasn't just her gigantic companion who was emitting a foul odour. Half the stink was down to her, she wasn't ashamed to admit.

"I need to wash," she moaned, for the hundredth time. "Mellio, do you hear me. *I need to wash*. There's got to be a well or watering hole somewhere."

The last one they passed was dried up, and that had been two days ago. The two before that were too busy with other travellers watering their horses and filling their skins and Mellio had judged it safer not to stop, with them still close to Matia. They were trying to go unseen, after all. And that meant staying here behind the thick dark drapes of this carriage, cooking to death, day after day, and filling the air with this eye-watering, unwashed reek.

A voice came from the driver's seat. "Soon, girl, soon. We will have another chance soon, yes."

"What does that mean?" she returned. Mellio had a habit of giving half answers. "How soon? When! You know this road, Mellio. You know these lands. For goodness sake, speak plainly."

"Soon. Yes, soon. Maybe later we will pass one. Maybe tonight, when it is dark. Yes, tonight. There will be one tonight. Maybe."

Saska grunted, shook her head, and looked at the Wall, a hulking mass of scarred muscle and godsteel armour, filling the wooden bench across from her. It said a lot about the unbearable heat that even Sir Ralston Whaleheart had relinquished most of his plate. All he wore now was his breastplate, with sleeveless linen undershirt beneath and lightweight breeches for his legs. Both were a dirty creamy colour, stained from sweat and filth. His enormous arms were unburdened, great bulging boulders of hairy muscle gleaming with perspiration, day and night. "Doesn't he drive you mad, Rolly?" Saska asked the giant. "The way he speaks. Never a straight bloody answer."

"I can hear you, you know." Mellio had a chirpy voice to match his chirpy face. He was never not smiling, though half the time that just annoyed Saska even more. He pulled back the curtain that blocked him off from them, as he sat on the driver's seat beside Pig, his young helper. "You seem to think that the curtain stops words, girl. No, that is not the case. I can hear everything you say. Yes, everything. You should remember that."

"I know. I meant for you to hear."

"OK then." He smiled broadly and let the curtain fall away.

Saska grumbled. Mellio was an associate of Captain Rikki, and apparently trustworthy, but there was something about that ever-present smile that made him seem so false. Still, Rikki had paid the man well enough to escort them to Aram, so if nothing else, she could trust that. A man like Mellio relied on his reputation for work. Smugglers were like that. Fail too many contracts and business would begin to dry up.

The Wall was looking at Saska sternly. "You know I don't like it when you call me that," he said.

Her lips cracked into a grin. "What? *Rolly*?" She knew it irritated him, and that was half the point. Not much else passed for entertainment around here. "Don't blame me. I didn't think it up."

The Wall scowled. "Who did? The boy?"

Saska sighed. She missed little Billy most of all from her time on the Steel Sister, and still smiled to think of him and the necklace he'd given her on her last night on the ship. She didn't wear it often - in truth, the corals and shells and stones were quite uncomfortable against the skin of her neck, and heavy besides - but she always kept it right beside her on the bench, along with the godsteel blade Sir Ralston had given her from King Godrin, the pouch of coins from Barnibus and quill and ink pot from Lancel, and that wonderful parchment full of jokes that Bawdy Bron had been so kind as to write out for her.

And my coral, she thought. The coral that called to her. The coral that Old Hob had read with his gnarled, callused fingers that last night on the ship. "I wasn't talking about your mother," he'd said to her. He'd somehow known she was Bladeborn from what he read in the pits and grooves, that she would help fight the shadow, help play a part in the war. *And he saw that I had royal blood,* she reflected. *Rich and strong and old, he'd said.* She'd thought that meant her late mother, the Princess Leila Nemati, but Old Hob had seen otherwise.

I wasn't talking about your mother, she thought again, picking up the little chunk of pitted grey coral from the bench. She turned it over in her fingers as she had a thousand times. If the old man was right, that meant her father was royal as well. Royal, northern, Bladeborn, and powerful, and that didn't leave too many options, so far as she could see.

She turned from that, setting the coral back to the side, as the carriage rattled on down the road at the slow ponderous pace they'd been keeping for a week. It was entering the hottest part of the day, that part when every pore of her body wept like a wailing child, drenching her from top to toe in a slick sticky coating of sweat. She'd chosen to wear a simple shift dress of white linen, as lightweight and airy a garment as she could hope to have, but most of the time, even that was too much. If it wasn't for the Wall, she had often mused, she might well have gone naked, but hadn't yet lost all her sense of impropriety.

She gave answer to him now. "It wasn't Billy," she told him. "He just called you Giant. One of the crew thought of the name Rolly." She thought a moment. "Kevin the Con, I think. It suits you, Sir Ralston. You look a bit like a 'Rolly' to me." She grinned to see his annoyance at the subject. "What do you reckon, Mellio?"

"Oh yes, suits you, yes, very much," called the smuggler from the front.

"I disagree," boomed the gigantic knight. "And that sleazy conman should guard his tongue better. I never liked how he disrespected you, my lady."

Saska shrugged. Kevin had made some salacious remarks to her, but nothing too insulting. "I've lived with worse," she said. "Kevin was harmless, really, just a talker. I know how to deal with men like that."

"By encouraging them?" he accused.

"By ignoring them," she said.

The Wall scoffed. "As long as you're sure. I am sworn to protect you, and that includes from tongues. His I'd happily have ripped from his mouth."

Saska called out to their escort again. "You hear that, Mellio? You'd best be careful how you speak to me, or Rolly will rip your tongue out."

"Oh yes, he could. Very strong man. Very big. But I am always respectful, yes. Very respectful, all the time."

"You'd be more respectful if you gave us a straight answer for once," Saska complained. "Honestly, I am dying to get out of this carriage. Can we not stop for a bit? Or open these curtains at least? We need fresh air in here. It's *stifling* today."

And worse than ever, she judged, though that could have been because they hadn't washed in a week, and their skin was coated in a layer of grime that made them all the more hot. Or, more likely, it was because they were headed further inland and through an arid region of high jutting rocks and stumpy hills that hadn't seen rainfall in a hundred years, to look at them. All was dusty and orange and red, and there was no wind or breeze to speak of. But that was the price they paid to travel this route. The Capital Road was said to be well paved, lined with towns and fish markets and never more than a mile from the coast, bursting with flowers and greenery and colours. The coastal route afforded it a generous southeasterly breeze in this region that was said to be quite refreshing. But inland there was none of that. A few tented habitations dotted the lands, and they'd seen goat and cattle farmers around, but mostly the Aramatian Plains west of the Port of Matia were dry, rocky, and less than pleasant to travel.

But the heat. The heat was the worst of it.

Mellio gave answer, peeking back through the curtain again and shaking his smiling face. "No, oh no, it would not be wise to stop during daylight, girl, no. Many travellers moving around. Horses come by from nowhere, and you could be seen. Not good for you or the big man, or Mellio. Especially Mellio." He laughed. "Captain Rikki didn't pay me enough to die."

But he did pay enough to *risk* dying, Saska knew. That was the whole point with such men as this. If caught smuggling illegal goods they risked a great deal, depending on the cargo. A minor offence might get them a fine. A larger one might lose them a hand or foot or both. The most egregious offences would lead to execution, Saska had heard. She wasn't certain where she and the Wall ranked as forbidden cargo, but either way, Mellio had clearly judged the risk worthwhile, when Rikki led them to his little storehouse in the Port of Matia a week ago.

"Just these two?" the grinning smuggler had asked, as he sat behind a small desk, feasting off a bowl of dark dried dates. "To Aram, you say?" He'd pondered it, tapping the deep cleft in his copper-coloured, clean-shaven chin. Mellio was not a handsome man, with a heavy belly, skinny arms and legs, and lank strips of black hair oiled back over his head. He had no facial hair except a pair of sideburns that went down to his soft chin, linking where jaw met neck. It was a curious type of beard, Saska thought, eye-catching if hardly arresting.

She'd watched the exchange carefully, her instinct to mistrust him. If it wasn't for Rikki's assurances that Mellio was discreet she'd have likely gone looking elsewhere for transport.

"Aram, aye, and down the safest road," Rikki Bowen had confirmed, counting out his coins as he spoke. "Through the plains will be best, I would think, given what we've been hearing."

"Oh yes, dark words reach me daily," Mellio had chimed, nodding warily. "The plains will be much safer than the Capital Road, yes. But much longer. Two weeks, at least, if we make good time." He'd regarded Saska and her giant protector. "It will take strong horses to pull you, I think. You are Bladeborn, yes?"

The Wall loomed above him like a cliff. "I am."

Mellio leaned back as though a great gust of wind had blown him to the back of his seat. "His voice is like a storm!" He'd laughed to himself for a good full minute, then scanned Sir Ralston once more.

"Godsteel armour, godsteel blades, and a giant as big as a moonbear. This is the cargo? And this girl here? I do not think she will add much weight."

Saska didn't mention that she carried a godsteel blade too. It was only a small dagger and didn't seem necessary with the huge great weight that the Wall brought with him.

"Do you have a suitable cart or carriage for them?" Rikki had asked.

"Yes, I think so, yes. If we go slow, my horses can manage. But these two will need to stay hidden. The big one especially. I can take them to the outskirts of Aram, but not inside, no. If I am caught smuggling in a giant Bladeborn knight, it will not go well for me." He frowned at Sir Ralston. "I hope you have no intention of killing anyone important there? I do not wish to transport an assassin."

"I am not an assassin," boomed the giant. The tone of his voice brooked no argument on the topic.

Mellio nodded, smiled. "Good. Then that is settled. Now let us talk prices, my friend."

He'd engaged in a short exchange with Rikki, though the haggling hadn't lasted long. They'd left the Port of Matia that very night, and had been on the road for seven long days and nights since.

And those days went on forever, it felt. The carriage was not comfortable, even when not accounting for the heat and the reek. The benches were hard as teak, the noise constant, the caravan a rickety mess. Saska had wondered whether it might fall apart during their first day on the road, once they'd left Matia behind and ventured forth onto the bumpy dirt tracks that spread away into the arid plains. With all the weight they were carrying, it seemed inevitable, but Mellio had put those fears to bed.

"No no, girl, no, it is all a part of the illusion. I have built the carriage to make lots of noise, yes, to *look* like it might fall apart. But really it is strong. Strong as your giant here."

Saska wasn't understanding. "Why?"

"Bandits and thieves and other dangerous men," Mellio told her. "They will be less interested in a rotting old coach like this, yes. Nothing to steal, they will think."

That made some sense, and in truth Sir Ralston's armour - the parts and pieces that he wasn't currently wearing - had been safely stowed and stored in secret compartments that were admittedly hard to find, along with their other luggage. He kept only one of his greatswords with him, often lying it across his lap as he ran a whetstone down its misting edge again and again, hour after hour, to keep himself busy. Saska wasn't sure that godsteel needed such attention - she'd always thought it stayed sharp of its own mystical accord - but made no mention of that. Instead she tried to entertain her companion by reading out some of Bawdy Bron's jokes. They hadn't gone down well, though Mellio loved them, and so did Pig, the smuggler's mute helper, who'd been born without the ability to speak, she'd learned, but could still make a snorting sound when roused to amusement.

Saska had asked Mellio where the young man got his name. "It's for his nose," he'd told her, laughing in a way she found more cruel than playful. "Look, it is so short! Like a snout. Is that the word you use? Snout?"

"Yes. Snout. But why pig? That's the common tongue of the north. Why not call him 'pig' in Aramatian?"

"Why would I? I am not Aramatian. I was born on the South Sun. You know this place?"

Saska remembered it from Rikki's maps. The Twin Suns were islands between Pisek and Solapia, she recalled. "I didn't realise you had your own language there. I thought you just spoke one of the main southern tongues."

"We do. All are spoken well by many of us. And we also have several dialects of our own, yes. But the word for 'pig' is too long in all of them. So I just call him *Pig* in your common tongue. It is a funny word, I think. And Pig is a funny man. Aren't you, Pig? Make that snorting noise you make."

Pig had snorted, Mellio had laughed, and Saska had discovered then, if not before, that she didn't really like this man.

And right now she was liking him less than ever. "We're stopping at the next well or river we pass," she said now, peeking through the drape along the left side of the carriage. Outside she could see nothing but a high wall of rock from one of the large blocky mountains here, the colour of rust, filling her view. She went to the other side, pulled back the drape, and took in a more ranging view away to the north. Amid the stumpy hills out that way she could see the distant shadow of trees, clumped at their base. That was a good sign. Trees didn't grow unless there was some water about. "I don't care if there are other travellers and local people waiting to fill their buckets, we're stopping. If we have to wait for them to leave, we will."

Mellio's smile turned servile. "As you say, my lady. We will pass a well soon, I hope. Pig will look out for one ahead. Sometimes they are off the road, and harder to see. But Pig has good eyes. Don't you, Pig?"

Pig made his snorting sound. Mellio laughed. The Wall scowled and Saska huffed and on they went along the bumpy road.

Several more hours went by before the heat of the day began to recede. It was barely perceptible. Just a minor leeching of the intolerable humidity as the sun faded down into the west, and a crimson dusk filled all the land. This was the best part of the day, Saska had come to find, when the colours changed and the reds and golds exploded among the low clouds, and a vidid beauty that made it all worthwhile swelled radiant upon the horizon. Then all too soon it would darken to night, and she'd have to suffer another evening lying on this back-breaking bench with nary a breeze to cool them.

But that time was not yet come. The skies were drenched gold, lilac and lavender, with the first streaks of vermillion kissing the clouds, when Pig made an excited noise. Mellio drew the curtain aside. "There's a well and small river ahead," he said, translating the young man's incoherent mumblings. "It seems quiet, we are lucky. The settlements here are far, and people do not like to walk at night. They come in the day instead."

"How many are at the well?" Saska asked, almost delirious at the news.

"Not many, no, not many. Half a dozen, it looks. They must live nearby and will leave soon, to beat the darkness. There are wild starcats out here, and other beasts besides, so the people do not like to linger."

Saska took that in. "And travellers?"

"None. No horses or wagons or carts or carriages. Only the local people, and they are a simple folk. You should be safe to wash in the river here."

Saska sat back, smiling stupidly. It was how she used to do it with Del and Llana in Willow's Rise, unless Master Orryn gave her a treat and permitted her use of his bathtub. But she preferred the river anyway. The cool flowing water, the stones and sands beneath her feet.

She'd washed too many lords and ladies and their kin to ever feel at home in a bathtub. And she'd killed the last one too.

"The river is not large," Mellio informed them. "A stream is a better word, yes. But it should be good enough for bathing. Pig and I will fill our skins and water the horses, while you and the big man wash."

"I don't need to wash," Sir Ralston said.

Mellio laughed. "Pig cannot speak and the big man cannot smell, it seems."

"I think he's trying to tell you that you stink, Rolly," Saska said, hiding her own laughter. "And I say that with full acknowledgement that I do too, just so we're clear."

"Yes, this is true." Mellio was still chuckling. "The girl smells just as bad. There is just less of her." Pig snorted, his fleshy shoulders bobbing. "You see. Even Pig agrees!"

Sir Ralston continued to sit sternly, aggressively running his whetstone along the length of his enormous blade. "Fine," he relented. "If I must."

"You must," Saska said, gracing him with a smirk. She reached down and pulled open the little drawer built into her bench, where she stored a spare shift dress, this one dyed a pale blue. There were some bars of soap in there too, made from wood ash and mutton fat, bundled into rough linen rags. She tossed one to the Wall, who put aside his whetstone and caught it, grumbling. "You might want to leave your breastplate here," she suggested.

The giant gave a grunt, then began unfixing the links and intricate chains that held the breastplate in place. Saska came forward to help him. "It'll be quicker if you let me," she said, when he made to complain. "Elyon used to let me help him out of his armour at Harrowmoor. I know what I'm doing. Don't moan."

"And who is this Elyon?" asked Mellio curiously, as the carriage clattered on down the road. "Father? Brother? A *boyfriend,* perhaps?"

"Never you mind." She'd learned that the smuggler, as poor as he was at giving straight answers, loved to ask straight questions. She'd decided it best to give crooked responses.

The carriage soon began to slow, as Saska drew aside the curtain and peeked out over the dusk-drenched lands. It was growing darker now, the purples emerging where once they'd been pinks, the radiant reds deepening into deep crimsons the colour of winter wine. A little off to the right of the track, Saska could see a few local people still at the well, pulling up the pails and filling their buckets and skins with fresh water. There were a couple of dogs with them, ears up, sniffing for trouble. They looked the sort to give pre warning of any lurking threat. Both seemed relaxed enough.

The carriage came to a juddering halt along the side of the road, the horses snorting their relief to get a short rest. "Wait here, just a moment," Mellio told them in a hushed voice. "I will make sure it is safe."

"It is," Saska said, unwilling to wait any longer for fear Mellio would change his mind. She took up her spare shift dress, soap, and washing rag and slipped right out onto the rough rocky earth.

The river could scarce be heard it was running so quietly, drifting down from some taller hills that hooded the northern horizon. The water reflected the light of the sunset, rippling in colours of maroon and amber. It looked cleaner than Saska had expected, its edges bordered by dark reeds that burst from rounded stones along its banks.

She paced quickly toward it, finding a spot some thirty metres from the carriage, perhaps forty from the well. There was little privacy here, though the dusky twilight would help shade her. Even so, Saska found she didn't much care. The southerners were less prudish, she'd come to see, and thought little of baring themselves in full view of others. At every well, river and water hole they'd passed, she'd glimpsed naked men and women outside, caring not to conceal their privy parts as they washed their bodies and clothes. She'd seen people walking like that too, women baring their breasts as they wandered down the road, men wearing breechclouts that left little to the imagination, children capering about fully exposed to the harsh burning glare of the sun. It just seemed the way here. *And I'm half Aramatian too,* she thought, *so why not join them?*

Saska pulled off her fetid dress, exposing her naked body to the evening air. It took a little work, peeling the sticky soiled linen from her skin, but once off she felt immediately better. Nude, she glanced back to the well, but no one seemed to be taking any notice of her. It made a pleasant change from the lurid looks she'd dealt with all her life.

She smiled a smile of deep relief as she waded out into the knee deep water, flowing slowly down from the north. Though tepid and warmer than she'd like, it was still much cooler than the air around her. A sigh slipped through her lips as she stood there a moment, then went down to her haunches, letting the water wash over her legs, her stomach, her chest, splashing it over her shoulders and arms and soaking it through her hair. Reaching out, she plucked a few rough reeds from the bank, unfurled the soap from its linen wrapping, and began scrubbing at her skin with soap and reeds and rag all, scraping off the many long days of filth that lacquered her body.

An awkward cough came from behind her. "My lady, I...I didn't realise you would..."

"Bathe naked?" she finished for him. She stood and turned, making a half-hearted attempt to cover her modesty. The Wall stood near the bank, averting his eyes to the side.

"Yes. I thought you would wash...in your clothes."

"Then you thought wrong. This is how they do it here, Sir Ralston, and I'm past the point of caring." She continued to wash, in full view of him.

The man shuffled uncomfortably on his huge sandalled feet.

"If you're that awkward, you can go and bathe upriver," she told him, scrubbing at her belly. She pointed to where the river bled out of sight behind some rocks. "There. It'll be private up there behind those boulders."

He didn't move. "I...I am sworn to protect you, my lady. There may be dangers here. I should not let you from my sight."

Saska saw then that he had his sword with him. He was never likely to come out here without it. "Then by all means wash here with me." She looked westward, to where Mellio and Pig were now working the winch and pulling up water from the well. Only three of the local people remained, the rest having shuffled off into the hills to the north. Mellio appeared to be making light conversation with them, though they were too far away to be heard. A dog remained as well. It was looking to the east, the way they'd come, ears up. "See. No one is watching," she said. "No one cares. And it's dark anyway. I can hardly see you." She shrugged and soaked her rag, running the soapy fabric along her right arm.

"It's...not appropriate," the giant murmured, in that voice that seemed to shake the ground. He continued to look aside, resolutely away from her. "A knight should not see his mistress in…this state. "

"Then go further upriver, if you must." She was growing weary of it. Saska was not one for casual nudity most of the time, but right now she didn't care. The Wall was pretty much asexual in her estimations. *Walls don't care for that sort of thing,* she thought, amused.

She saw her guardian dip his head into a nod, as though addressing a nearby shrub. "I will," he decided. "You should wash in private, my lady. I would not want to embarrass you."

She laughed to that. "I think you've got that turned around, Rolly. I can see the blush on your cheeks from here."

"You said you could hardly see me," he came back. "And I do not blush."

She grinned at his affront and then bent down to begin scrubbing at her inner left thigh. That was far too much for Sir Ralston, who looked mortified. The giant took that as his immediate cue to leave. He marched away into the gathering darkness and beyond the rocks upriver.

Saska returned to her cleansing, enjoying the sensation of the stones beneath her bare feet, the gentle caress of the lukewarm water as it ran past her legs, the cooling effect it had as it began to dry and evaporate off her skin. Even the mild pain of scouring herself with the reeds felt good. Soon enough her thighs were red and raw, her midriff the same, her rear looking as though it had seen a stern beating from the cane. Then she got to work on her upper body; arms, chest, shoulders, neck, and hair, before attacking her filthy clothes with gusto, massaging in the soap and scrubbing hard with a pair of rough stones to leech out as much dirt as she could.

That was when the dog first barked.

She looked over to the well, peering through the dimness. The others were glancing down the track they'd travelled. The dog's barking had alerted them to something. Its owner, a tall thin man wrapped in a simple white tunic, gave a whistle, but the dog didn't move. It stared, ears pricked high, then barked again, louder. The owner called out to the hound in words Saska didn't understand. The dog ignored him. He barked again. His owner shouted firmly, whistled shrilly, and that finally got the beast's attention, which spun and bolted back to the well, tongue lolling from his mouth.

By now the tall man was hastily gathering up his waterskins, slinging them over his shoulders on straps, along with the two companions he had with him. They picked up buckets sloshing with water and began moving off into the hills. A moment later Saska knew why. From the east, she could hear the thunder of hooves on packed dirt, galloping up the track. She turned to look at Mellio, some forty metres away at the well. A chill ran up her spine as he heard him calling out, "Girl, get dressed! Men...they come. Men are coming! Get dressed and out of sight!"

Saska reacted right away, tossing her sopping clothes aside, rushing for the dry blue dress she'd laid out on a nearby rock. Her skin was dripping wet, hair soaked, body glimmering beneath a sudden burst of moonlight. She was still wading through toward the riverbank when a coarse voice barked from behind her. She startled, almost falling over, but managed to keep her footing. The moon shone down upon a man on horseback, looming on the opposite bank. His almond eyes stared across at her beneath a heavy beetled brow, cut with white scars. Both his hair and beard were black and oily, twisted into braids.

A scout, she knew at once. The others were still a way off. The man looked Piseki to her eyes, with that thick black hair and light brown skin. He wore leather armour and old rusted mail, with a sheathed shortsword on one hip and a khopesh hanging on the other. A mace poked out from his saddlebag, and she thought she saw a few dirks and daggers there as well, one with a red ruby in the pommel. Stolen, no doubt. The man had all the hallmarks of a brigand. *Or worse,* she thought. *A Patriot...*

She began backing away toward her clothes, covering herself with her hands under the menacing eyes of this man. They reminded her of many others she'd seen in the past as they ran her up and down, greedy. She reached the rock and grabbed her shift, holding it to her chest to cover herself. The man reacted poorly to that, grunting angrily as he vaulted down off his horse. He stepped forward.

Behind her, Saska could hear Mellio rushing over, calling out in one of many southern tongues he knew. The bandit gave him a passing look, then withdrew his cruel-looking khopesh sword, dull grey and worn. He waded forward through the shallow water in old leather boots, bearing in on her. Rough words ran off his tongue as he pointed the blade in her direction.

She drew away, moving backward to the riverbank, her bare wet feet slipping in the reeds. She tumbled onto her back. The Piseki's eyes seemed to glow in delight to see her sprawled before him, trying to cover herself. He grinned an unpleasant yellow grin and reached to undo his belt. Mellio was still some twenty metres away, it sounded. The man ignored him completely, judging the short paunchy smuggler no threat.

He didn't ignore the Wall.

"Step back."

The bandit turned. The shape of the figure before him caused his delight to curdle into horror.

Greatsword in hand, dressed only in his breeks, Sir Ralston Whaleheart looked a titan. No man was so large, so muscled, so fearsome to look upon, a figure as haunting to his enemies as he was heroic to his allies. In the dim wash of moonlight his face was craggy as a cliff, gouged with deep ruts and scars, soaring eight feet from the earth. The bandit stumbled backward, cursing in fright. He slipped on a stone, splashing into the slow-flowing river, and scrambled right back to his feet. His khopesh sword pointed forward, and from his leather sheath scraped the dinted shortsword he carried.

The Wall just stood, watching, enormous misting greatsword glowing a soft gold-blue in his grasp. "Leave," he said. "Now."

The bandit didn't seem to understand. His upper lip pulled back into a defensive snarl. Mellio came rushing in, panting. He came right up to Saska's side as she stood and drew on her pale blue dress, as hastily as she could. Down the track, the thunder of hooves was growing louder with each passing heartbeat. She glanced that way and saw the shadow of a mounted host charging from the darkness toward them, leaving the track now as they spotted the standoff. Saska judged there to be at least eight of them, all armoured in patchworks of mail, leather, and rusted plate, with an array of weapons fastened to their hips and backs.

Saska's eyes went back to the Wall, as Mellio called out in a bid to restore calm. Somewhere behind, Pig was snorting in alarm. *He's unarmored,* Saska thought. Even a man so mighty as Sir Ralston Whaleheart might be vulnerable against ten men should they all attack at once. Without his armour a good bolt to the neck or heart might be enough to take him down, and by the looks of things a brace of the raiders had crossbows slung across their backs.

I need to help him, Saska knew at once. She didn't give that any more thought. In a flash she was gone, sprinting back to the carriage, barefoot and dripping and dressed in pale blue.

A moment later she was at the coach, pushing through the drapes, reaching to take up her godsteel dagger. She'd kept it hidden during her time on the Steel Sister, keeping the truth of her Bladeborn side from the men to avoid any unnecessary questions. Only at night did she take it to grasp, inspecting the beautiful, intricate design. Sir Ralston had handed it to her on her first day on the ship. "A gift from King Godrin," he had said. She wondered now if it was for times like this. Whether the wise old prophet king had seen this in the Eye of Rasalan.

As ever his words came back to her. *You're exactly where you're meant to be.* She took heart from them as she always did, the slim, six inch dagger catching the moonlight in a glow of soft pale blue. The symbols intricately inlaid into the hilt and pommel were lit a deep silver. *Silver and blue,* she thought. Elyon had said that a few times about her. She smiled to think of him, as she let her blood-bond fill her with an old and ancient power. And over at the river, she heard a piercing scream.

She turned, blade to hand, and ran. By the time she got back, the bandits had arrived, charging in on their mounts, launching themselves to the hard stone earth in athletic, practiced leaps. Sir Ralston was standing over the body of the Piseki scout. The man had been hewn in half at the chest, his separate parts lying beside one another in the river, which flowed and eddied around him. Blood ran out into the water, thick and black, spreading downstream.

Mellio was still calling out for calm, such as she could tell by the wild gesticulations of his arms. His efforts were proving futile. The brigands were closing in.

"Rolly, watch out! Crossbow!"

Saska's warning came just in time.

A man on horseback was circling around with crossbow to hand, taking aim at the Wall's wide chest. A deep *thwump* sounded as the string cracked back into place, loosing the quarrel. The giant turned and sidestepped as the bolt went flying past his shoulder and out into the night. His movement was unnaturally quick for a brute of such size. It didn't seem to put the raiders off, or perhaps they didn't notice, because at once they all charged in, screaming.

Saska made to follow. Then she spotted a second man, hunkered behind a rock, loading a crossbow. He was setting the bolt in place and turning the crank to load. She sped for him before he could fire and put her beautiful blue knife through his neck. His crossbow tumbled to the rocks with a clatter, eyes blinking in confusion as he looked at her, wondering where on earth she'd come from. She drew the knife across his windpipe as though it were made of water, and left him there to die.

The other men were engaging the Wall, closing in like a pack of hounds, heedless.

The bandit on horseback was reloading.

Saska left her guardian to deal with the others and sped for the mounted man, ghosting through the darkened plains toward him. He spotted her coming, spurred his steed, which reared and whinnied in alarm, kicking. Saska drew back. The bandit raised his crossbow, already cranked and loaded, took aim and fired. The bolt whooshed past her and cracked into the rocky floor, bouncing harmlessly away.

Grunting, the bandit dismounted in a leap, pulling out a scimitar sword. He seemed to notice then whom he was duelling, this young girl with the short wet hair and fluttery blue dress. He laughed and pressed forward, swinging, as the clash of steel echoed out down at the river. Mellio's voice was still shouting over all that. Somewhere, Pig was snorting in terror.

Saska only had eyes for her prey. She ducked his first swing, arched her back and limboed the second, then thrust forward with her own assault. It was too easy. Her knife went through mail and leather, flesh and bone like butter, puncturing the place where she'd been taught the heart to be. Her opponent dropped like a stone, legs giving away beneath him, bundling on the floor like some discarded garment.

"Girl!" came a shout. "Behind you!"

She spun, expecting to see a man approaching her, but something altogether more dark and elegant was bounding her way across the moonlit plains. Its fur was sleek and dark as ink, dotted with a thousand silver spots that shone like starlight against a black night sky. Saska knew at once what it was, long-limbed and rangy, broader at the chest and slimmer at the hips, with wide padded feet and claws as sharp as godsteel. Eyes of silver gleamed from the shadows of its face, its shoulders rippling as it ran, rhythmic and beautiful.

She watched on in wonder. Despite the danger, the clatter and clang of conflict about her, Saska grinned like a goon to watch the starcat approach, gracefully leaping over rocks and boulders, scenting the blood of battle.

"Watch out!" Mellio called. "Run! It will kill you!"

Saska didn't move. She could scarce take her eyes off the creature. It seemed to be coming right for her, but at the last moment it swerved, changing direction, pouncing to her left. Saska ducked, turned to watch. A man had been rushing in behind her, blade brandished to strike. He had time enough to let out a scream as the starcat emerged from the shadows and pressed him to the ground, claws digging deep into his shoulders, fangs ripping at his throat. It gave a deep low growl and pulled its jaws back, ripping the man's windpipe from his throat, a ruin of raw flesh and sinew. Blood gushed out onto the rock, seeking cracks into which to drain.

Saska took a step back. It had all happened right next to her, no more than a metre or two away. Up close the starcat looked monstrous, five feet tall at the shoulder, its body long and lithe and elongated, adapted for speed and agility and strength when climbing. It stared down at the dead man beneath it with those silver lights for eyes, growling, a long tongue rolling across its four-inch fangs, turning them red to white.

"Get away from it!" she heard Mellio cry. "Away! Away! Away!"

Another voice echoed the sentiment. "Get back!" bellowed the Wall. "Get back you foul beast!"

The giant charged toward them from the water, his blade coated red and dripping, blood splashed across his chest and arms. Down in the river bodies were piled high, every man of the raiding company dead, limbs and body parts scattered all over. The starcat turned to face the knight, claws flashing from between the pads of its feet. It crouched as though ready to pounce. Sir Ralston blazoned forward, unafraid, greatsword brandished before him. "Me, monster! Fight me!"

No, Saska thought, strangely. *No, don't hurt it.* She uprooted her feet and rushed past the starcat as the Wall marauded across the plains.

"No, stop, it's not going to hurt us!" She put herself between man and beast, hands outstretched to her sides. "Stop!"

The Wall came to a thundering halt, death in his eyes, blood on his face. "Move, Saska!" be roared. "Get out of my way. NOW!"

That last word near knocked her from her feet it was so forceful, but she stood her ground all the same. "No." She turned. The starcat's polished silver eyes were staring, narrow, every muscle primed to pounce. Saska had no idea who might win that fight, who'd be quicker, the cat or the knight, but she knew she didn't want to find out. "Calm." Her voice was suddenly quiet, suddenly soft. "Calm," she told the creature. "It's OK. Be calm."

The cat glanced at her. She saw intelligence in those gleaming grey eyes. A soft low rumble sounded from its chest. Saska felt she understood. "He isn't going to hurt you," she said. Without looking back, she dropped her voice and whispered, "Rolly, lower your blade..."

"What? No, I'll..."

"Do it. That's an order."

She could hear Mellio scoffing in confusion. Somewhere, Pig was snorting in panic.

The Wall sounded perplexed. "My lady, I must..."

"Drop the blade, Sir Ralston. This creature means us no harm." Saska turned directly to face the cat, blocking its view to the giant, bare-chested brute. She drew eye contact, and smiled to placate it, studying its features. The cat was a female, she judged, by the sleek fur about its neck and shoulders, the smaller shape of the head. Males had short manes, she'd read somewhere, and larger heads. "It's OK, he isn't so scary as he looks." The cat tried to look past her shoulder but Saska shifted again, hand outstretched. "Look at me, girl," she whispered. "Just ignore him. He's a softie once you get to know him." She smiled.

The Wall made no further attempt to dissuade her of whatever the hell she was doing. Whatever it was, it felt right. *I am Lumosi Lightborn,* she thought, *born to bond with creatures like this.* "He's putting down his sword," she whispered, "and I'm going to put down my knife." She leaned to the side, placed her dagger on the ground, and glanced back to make sure the Wall was doing the same. Against his better judgement he was. She stood and smiled again, her voice as soft as a kiss. "Now put yours away," she coaxed, glancing to the cat's extended claws. She understood. Her claws slowly slid back beneath her fur, retracting, and the snarl on her face relaxed, hiding her four-inch fangs. "Good. Isn't that better?"

The cat drew slowly forward, padding a half pace closer. It neared Saska's outstretched hand, bloodied from the men she'd killed, broad nostrils flaring. She heard the Wall shifting behind her, as though worried the beast was about to bite, and raised her spare hand to stop him. She could sense his dismay but he said nothing. She smiled again as the starcat hesitated. "It's OK. We're all calm now. All of us...nice and calm."

The cat crept on, her nostrils opening in another long sniff. Then, from between her lips, a long tongue slipped out, purple as the dawn, licking the blood from Saska's skin. It was course as sandpaper, but somehow gentle, scraping across her palm and between her fingers, ticklish.

Saska let out a giggle. The starcat drew back, skittish. "No, no, it's OK." She stepped forward, reaching out. "I didn't mean to scare you."

All was silent. All was still. Slowly, surely, the big black cat moved in once more. When she started licking at Saska's face, she heard that it was purring.

28

Jonik

"This must be it," said Emeric Manfrey. "The doors painted silver and blue, the old woman said."

"For Vandar," added Jonik, nodding. The manor was also the largest one they could find on Goldwater Row, standing that much taller and broader than the rest along the harbourside. "Let's hope he's here."

Emeric nodded. Jack nodded. Sir Borrus Kanabar gave a yawn. The rest were still on the ship at anchor, though Kanabar had insisted on coming along so he might stretch his legs. Having the extra sword with them might come in handy too. Given his good behaviour, the burly Varin Knight had been returned his godsteel blade, with the watery flow to the cross-guard and the small emeralds and sapphires encrusted in the hilt that made reference to the Riverlands where House Kanabar stood supreme.

Borrus called the blade Red Wrath, for the reddish light that sometimes caught the steel at certain angles and in certain lights. "That can happen when a blade cuts a dragon's hide," he'd explained during their voyage from the Sunrise Isle. "I got a few good deep slashes on Malathar the Mighty when I fought him and Vargo Ven during the war. Before then many of my ancestors used Red Wrath to fend of those foul fiends in this Renewal or that Renewal, going back centuries. Red Wrath has drunk its share of dragon's blood, believe me. Though none so much as that black blade of yours, I'll wager."

Jonik didn't doubt it. Though the Blades of Vandar had often found themselves scattered and lost across the centuries, they'd once been stored within the Steelforge, one and all, to be handed out to Vandarian champions during times of war. Each knew the taste of dragon blood well.

As Emeric began knocking loudly on the door, Jonik turned his eyes around the waterfront, wary of watching eyes. Though busy, Goldwater Row was nothing like the other ports in the city of Sutrek. Further down to the west, either side of the narrow band of land that led out into Lumara's Teardrop, were huge noisy harbours cut with a hundred great wharfs and jetties, fruit markets and fish markets and meat markets, markets that sold silks and spices, furnitures and fineries, jewellery, perfume, oils and horses and goats and camels and animals exotic and rare.

And that was just the harbourfront. Beyond, within the city proper, the bazaars and brothels, shops and show-stages, plazas and palaces and taverns and temples were more manifold than any other place in the world, a frenzied maze of distractions and diversions that could consume a man if he wasn't careful.

But here, less so. Goldwater Row was further east, a waterfront lined with lofty manors that rubbed up, shoulder to shoulder, as though trying to appear taller and grander than the rest. Each had a private jetty, moored with pleasure ships and other such vessels, and when the sun came down in the west, the waters gleamed with a golden glow. Jonik suspected that's where the name had come from.

He turned back to face the door painted silver and blue as he heard the bolts go. A moment later it opened a crack, and a copper-skinned steward appeared at the threshold, peering through the gap. He was a short man, young, a third of the age of the seneschal, Sechio Arcas, whom they'd encountered at Vincent Rose's Solapian estate. "Yes? What do you want?" Behind him Jonik saw a brace of large guardsmen, armed to the teeth with massive halberds and bound up in rich scale-mail armour.

Emeric Manfrey did the talking. "We're here to see Vincent Rose."

"He isn't here," the young steward said, curtly. He had suspicious eyes. "Good day."

When he went to shut the door, Sir Borrus Kanabar planted down a heavy boot to prevent it from closing. "Now that wasn't very courteous, friend. Why don't you try again?"

The steward's brazen behaviour soon wilted when he saw the glitter of godsteel mist rising from Kanabar's sheath. The big Varin Knight had lifted Red Wrath an inch to let the steel breathe, for effect. "Who are you?" the small man asked, looking from one intruder to the next. "If you are here to kill my master, then..."

"We're not." Emeric drew the man's eyes with his measured voice. "We mean to trade."

"Trade?" That surprised him. "Trade what?"

"That is for your master to hear. Is he inside? Answer truly, now. We have no time for games."

The steward's lips pinched closed.

"If you're worried we're here to kill him, then do you really think that a man such as yourself will stop us?" Emeric asked, all friendly. He had that warm smile on his black-bearded face. Jack was smiling too. That always appeared to calm people.

"I have guards." The Steward gestured behind him, though neither of the soldiers looked eager for a fight, not now they'd seen that swirling mist. "There are many...many guards here. Dozens." He glanced at Kanabar's blade. "Master Rose has Bladeborn too."

"Oh he does?" laughed the Barrel Knight. "Well good for him. Now come, boy, step out of the way. It's bloody hot out here and I've got no patience for any of this." He began pushing forward.

Jonik and Emeric had been worried about this; they preferred a more tactful approach, but perhaps Sir Borrus's bluntness was just what they needed. And it *was* hot here, much hotter than it had been in Solapia. The shade beyond looked welcoming.

The steward didn't seem to know what do to. With an easy swipe of his paw, Borrus pushed through the door and moved the man aside, drawing out his blade as he went to deter an attack from the guards. "Don't even think about it," he said to them, as they tensed with their huge great halberds. The others shrugged, exchanged partly amused glances, and followed in behind.

"I must protest," the steward was squeaking. "You...you cannot go through there..."

“Oh quiet down,” Kanabar said. “I’ve got a roaring headache and that squealing isn’t helping. Now where is he?”

The steward glanced around, panicking. “I...you must let me announce you, at least,” he exclaimed. “Master Rose, he has...he has expectations of his staff. I must fulfil my duties. I insist that you wait here, while I...”

“Insist all you like,” Borrus said loudly. “If we wait here, that’ll only give Rose a chance to slither off through some crack like the snake he’s said to be.”

The young man looked aghast. “He would never. Vincent Rose is a man of courage, of honour. He...”

“So you admit now that he’s here?” asked Emeric. There was a bit more bite to his voice. “We’ve come a long way and are weary of the hunt. No more arguments. Lead us to your master.”

The skittish steward considered that briefly, but seemed to see no other way out. Resigned to his fate, he led them through the manor.

It was a large place, even larger than it looked from the outside, with colourful walls in the Sutreki style, mosaics on the ceilings, fine drapes on the walls embroidered with dramatic battles and leviathan hunts and scenes of a more erotic nature.

Jack fell in beside Jonik, taking them in with a bemused look. “Take a look at that one,” he said, gesturing to a large tapestry dominating an entire wall. It showed a divine orgy of sorts, gods and sprites, nymphs and faeries all embraced in some twisting tangle of limbs upon a mountaintop, beneath the gleaming shine of the sun. Amid it all there was a single human figure, laughing as he lounged in an outlandish throne, drinking wine and being tended by a brace of naked naiads with hair like flowing kelp and necklaces of shining shells about their necks. “This Rose thinks a lot of himself,” Jack went on, guessing at who that man might be. “He’s not afraid of disrespecting the gods, is he?”

“Emeric says he’s hardly known for his piety.”

“But he is his hubris, clearly. It’s a brave man who mocks the gods, Ghost.”

“It hasn’t done him much harm so far. The man’s amassed a personal fortune to match half the noble houses in the north.”

“Pride comes before the fall,” Jack o’ the Marsh intoned gravely. “I am most intrigued to meet this man. It’s been a long time coming.”

It had. Weeks, in fact. First came the voyage from Solas to Solapia, and Rose's sprawling estate outside Miren. Then there was the short trip across the Solapian Channel and westward down the Coast of Plenty to Sutrek. That portion had taken five days, as Captain Turner had said it would, the winds easy and breezy, the waters well-behaved, and they'd had few run-ins with any of the empire's warships that were now prowling about the coasts in preparation for war.

Many were gathered at the southern tip of Lumara's Teardrop, word was, with the celestial sun and moon and star lords of the south converging for the long-awaited warmoot. What little word they'd had on that suggested it was in full flow and not likely to last long. A formality, Emeric had called it. A custom they had to observe for fear of insulting their gods. But all the same, preparations were being made all across the south for war, with the conclusion of the warmoot foregone. And if the whispers they'd heard were true, King Tavash Taan of Agarath had already begun sending dragons to raze towns and villages along the Vandarian coast.

Things were beginning to escalate, Jonik knew, and soon enough an invasion proper would be commanded by south or north or both at once. *But I have a war of my own*, he thought. And that's why they were here.

They found their quarry in an inner courtyard, sitting at a shaded marble table, white with veins of grey, out of the glare of the sun. The courtyard was bordered by high stone pillars and open to the skies above, with flowers dressing the walls and birds chirping among the branches and vines.

Vincent Rose was on his feet as soon as he saw them march in through the arched entranceway. He wasn't much to look at. Shortish, with a soft belly, thinning hair, and a plain face, this man they'd heard so much about cut a disappointing figure, dressed in a plain white tunic that hung loose from his sloping shoulders. He was said to wear extravagant clothing, a brand new outfit everyday, with silks and satins, velvets and jewels, to add to his eccentricities, but apparently not today. *Perhaps he only dresses like that in public, or when he's expecting company,* Jonik thought. They had rather barged in, to be fair to the man.

"What is the meaning of this?" the master of the manor called out. He shot the young steward a deadly glare. "Tizan, who are these men?"

The steward scuttled forward, bowing as he went. "I am, sorry, my master, I...I couldn't stop them. They are well armed with godsteel. Bladeborn, my lord..."

"*Bladeborn*?" Vincent Rose's voice leaped in alarm at the word. He stepped back so quickly he almost stumbled to the floor. "Who...who are you? Janilah's men? I will pay you twice what he is. Ten times. *Twenty*. Anything you want. Just...just don't hurt me. Guards!"

From the many passageways leading from the courtyard, armed men came swarming like bees from a hive. Some were armed much as the pair who'd escorted them and Tizan through the mansion, with huge silver halberds; others held forge-made swords of fine workmanship, with daggers and dirks thrust into many sheaths about their swordbelts. To a man they wore that expensive scale mail armour that glittered wonderfully when it caught the sunlight, with soft silken capes of gold clasped at the tops of their shoulders. They were very unlike the rag-tag group of guards that Rose had left behind at his White Starlight Estate, Jonik thought. These men had the bearing of experienced soldiers and sellswords, hired from one of the many companies that plied their trade in these parts. Within moments the group were surrounded by some dozen men, blades drawn and directed at them.

Sir Borrus went to draw Red Wrath, but Emeric held a hand up to him, then stepped forward a single pace, calm as a windless sky. "We mean you no harm, Master Rose," he said, "and are in no way affiliated with Janilah Lukar. Quite the opposite, in fact." He glanced around at the soldiers surrounding them, as several more arrived from the shadows, their numbers swelling all the while. "You may relax. All of you. We have not come here to stir violence."

"Relax?" Rose had black bags beneath his eyes that spoke of a man who'd not been sleeping. A sour smell was coming off him. Evidently, he'd not been washing properly either. This was not the man they'd expected. "You intrude on my home unannounced, and tell me to relax? And four Bladeborn, no less."

"Three," Jack put in, cheerfully. "I'm lowborn, my lord. Son of a milkmaid and preacher."

Vincent Rose studied him. "So it seems." He looked to the others, the mask of fear slowly dissolving from his face. "And who are you?"

"Friends," said Emeric.

"I have enough of those already. *Who* are you?"

"He wants our names," came Sir Borrus's blustery voice. "Fair enough; we're in his home after all." He turned to face the merchant, hand ever on the hilt of his blade. "My name is Sir Borrus Kanabar, Varin Knight and heir to the Lord of the Riverlands. You've heard of me, of course. No doubt you've heard of the others as well." He gestured to Emeric, then Jonik. "Emeric Manfrey, of Sir Oswald's own blood, exiled by Lord Modrik Kastor some...what was it, a dozen years ago now?" Emeric gave a nod. Kanabar continued. "And this sullen bastard in black? You've likely heard of him too. The boy's become quite notorious these lasts months, and picked up a name or two along the way."

A few of those names ran through Jonik's mind. Hadrin's Horror. Shadow of Death. Nightstalker. Death Made Flesh. There were a few others he'd heard as well, but of course Ghost of the Shadowfort was most popular. *That is what they will call you now, but it is only one...one of a hundred names you'll have,* the Nightblade had whispered to Jonik once. He didn't have a hundred yet, but he was well on the way.

Vincent Rose was staring at him in disbelief. "I...I thought you'd be...older," he said, breathily. "And...more frightening. You're just a boy."

"Looks can be deceiving," said Kanabar. "This boy's a killer, make no mistake."

"A killer and a crippler," the merchant said to that, his disbelief quickly moving into curiosity. "I understand that you're near as kin to Lord Daecar, Sir Borrus. The man this boy maimed and mutilated, the rumours say. And his son Aleron..."

"Water under the bridge," Emeric cut in. He gave Borrus an uneasy look.

"For now," Borrus agreed. "The Shadowknight was deceived, and only doing his duty, dark and despicable though it was." He spoke stiffly.

Jonik turned to look at him. "You're not allowed to call me that anymore, Sir Borrus," he rasped. "I won the wager, no matter what you say."

Kanabar gave a bitter laugh. The two were never going to be close friends, but they tolerated one another now, at least. The last five days at sea had seen them turn something of a corner, though who knew when Borrus might spin and come charging back around it, sword in hand and murder in his eyes. Still, they'd passed the hours sparring often on deck these last days, Borrus handing down the long wisdom of his years among the Knights of Varin, helping Jonik grasp a few of the finer points of battlefield swordsmanship and Emeric hone the skills that had grown dull during his time as an exile.

"I only landed on my side," the heir of Kanabar came back at him. "I promised to stop calling you Shadowknight if you put me on my back, you will recall. The flank doesn't count. I can still call you whatever I bloody well like."

That had been the wager they'd made when they set off from the port of Miren five mornings gone. "*Put me on my back, and I'll stop calling you Shadowknight, how about that?*" Borrus Kanabar had said. With the big knight drunk and tiring, Jonik had done just that, but Kanabar had since argued he'd turned at the last minute, rendering the wager moot.

"Oathbreaker," Jonik grumbled to him.

Kanabar laughed. "Speaking of which, can I kill one of these guards here and call it my life debt to you done? I might be able to find a ship down at port to take me home. Be free of your gloomy company for good."

"No," Jonik said.

"Thought you'd say that."

Rose was watching them quizzically, taking it all in. He turned his eyes to Emeric Manfrey. "The exile," he said. "How is it that we've never met?"

"We've heard of one another," said Emeric. "That's a good start. Perhaps you've heard of my reputation as well? If I say we're not here to bestir violence, I mean it. Please, ask your guards to lower their swords. This is no way to stage a discussion, my lord."

"No...no, you're right, Lord Manfrey." The merchant turned to one of the guards - their captain, Jonik guessed - and gave a nod. Halberds were drawn back to flanks and swords slid into scabbards, as each man took several steps back until they fell back into the shadows.

Emeric watched. "I recognise the raiment," he said. "These are men of the Sunshine Swords."

"Good eye, my lord," said the merchant, dipping his chin. "I often hire them to offer me protection during times of hardship. They are expensive, but come well armed and armoured, as you can tell. Of course, against such as you, they wouldn't stand a chance." He gave a tittering laugh, eyes passing briefly over Jonik as he did so. "But I do wonder...how was it that you came to know I was here?" There was still a shadow of doubt in Rose's beady eyes. "I have been sure to keep my presence here secret. Coin buys many things, including the spread of rumour. I've paid many a tongue to tell of my presence on the Sunrise Isle."

And they'd fallen for those whispers. It was what had driven them to sail to Solapia in the first place.

"We went there first," Emeric admitted. "Your network of sneaks and whisperers is clearly in good order."

"Not good enough. You found me, Lord Manfrey. I'm asking *how*."

"There was an old Rasal woman at your White Starlight Estate. She told us."

Rose shook his head, weary and bemused. "Greta should better guard her tongue. I left Seshio in charge with strict orders to protect my whereabouts. Why was she speaking to you at all?"

"The seneschal proved uncooperative. Greta was more accommodating. She made me swear by godsteel oath that you would not be harmed, if that helps her cause. I'd not see her punished for speaking the truth; she did it to prevent bloodshed."

"And was there any? I would not take kindly to hear that poor Seshio was killed or injured. He has been as leal a steward as I could hope for." He turned a pair of darkening eyes on Tizan. "You have much to learn on that front, boy." The young steward nodded to the stones of the courtyard at his feet. His master glared at him for added effect, then looked up again at Emeric, waiting for his answer.

"Sechio was left with a sore jaw, but nothing worse than that."

"You struck him? A man of seventy summers?"

"I did." Jonik moved forward, a half pace.

"You?" Rose judged him for a long moment. "Well, from what I've heard of you, striking an old man ranks low on your list of violences." His eyes moved to the folds of Jonik's airy black cloak. "Do you have it on you now? This Nightblade. I would dearly like to see it."

"Another time," Emeric said. "We have a hasty need of you."

"I see. And what is it you want?"

"Information."

Vincent Rose's lips awoke in a sneering sort of smile. He had an oily way about him that Jonik didn't like. "What information?"

Borrus Kanabar groaned. "Before you get into the particulars, how about you be a good host and offer us some refreshment, Rose. I'm parched. And you're a wine merchant, such as I hear it. I take it you have some good vintages here?"

"The best. I trade in wine as well as many other things. Information among them." Rose clapped his hands together and servants emerged as if from nowhere, carrying silver cups and flagons upon ornate golden trays. "Come, do join me." He retook his seat upon the finely carved marble table as the wine and refreshments were laid out. Food followed, sweetened breads with honeys and jams, fruits of all shapes and varieties, olives and trays of meats. "Help yourselves, please. Sir Borrus, try the sapphire, it's one of my favourites."

The drinks were poured and Borrus Kanabar seemed a happy man, supping greedily as Jack took a seat beside him, sampling the fruits and breads. Neither Jonik nor Emeric partook. "We were told you came here with Ranulf Shackton," Emeric said, as a server poured him a cup of water upon request. "Is he here?"

The smile that had taken hold on Vincent Rose's face soured. It all seemed false to Jonik's eyes, every expression of his a mask. "No, I regret to say. Ranulf is...elsewhere, at this time."

"On some adventure is he?" asked Kanabar, noisily chewing on a leg of ham, gulping his sapphire wine between bites. He raised his cup. "Good stuff indeed, Rose. I'll keep you in mind next time we get a shipment brought to the Riverlands."

"I'm glad you like it, sir." He avoided the question about Ranulf, tellingly.

Emeric was watching him with a careful look, putting things together. "I'm intrigued, Vincent, as to what has put you in fear of Janilah Lukar. These sellswords of yours...and your attempts to keep your presence here hidden...what is it that stokes the king's ire?"

Vincent Rose drank a sip of pale red wine, hiding a moment behind the rim of his cup. "A trade went a little awry, I regret to say. I cannot know for sure, of course, but have a mind to think he will send men in retribution."

"And you think these men will protect you? The Sunshine Swords are known as gifted warriors, but are no much for the power of a king.

Your steward mentioned you have Bladeborn in your household? I confess I do not see them."

"I have one or two."

"You could have five or ten. Twenty, even. If Janilah Lukar wants you dead, you're dead. What madness would provoke you to cheat him?"

Rose looked aghast. *Another mask,* Jonik thought. "Do I have a reputation for such things? What makes you think I cheated him?"

"Logic," said the exiled lord. "If Janilah cheated you, what reason would he have to come after you?"

The merchant accepted that with a ponderous nod. "If you must know, it was Ranulf Shackton who stirred the hornet's nest, not I. He... he stole something of value, that I am quite sure the Warrior King will want back. I have put all this in a letter to Janilah, but at times of war, who knows whether the message will reach him. Or whether he will believe me if it should. I did stretch the boundaries of our bargain somewhat. Rarely do I regret things, but...well, the breadth of my ambition may have gotten me in trouble this time."

"So Shackton stole something that you were meant to give to Janilah, then ran off?" asked Borrus, chomping loudly on his ham. "Is that the way of it?"

"That about sums it up, yes." Rose took another sip of his drink. He had a cunning look in his eye, as though sensing some opportunity. "This information you seek? What is it?"

Emeric shared a look with Jonik. The exile had outlined his plan some weeks ago as they'd set sail from Solas. It was somewhat speculative, but worth the chance, seeing as they were sailing eastward anyway. "A location," Emeric told the merchant. "For the Moonlord Pal Palek. We understand that he is a high ranking member of the Patriots of Lumara, with whom you've done business. We wish to know where his stronghold is."

Vincent Rose was trying to hide his smile, and failing. "The Patriots have gathered for the warmoot, I'm sure you know. Pal Palek is likely to be there too."

"It is not Pal Palek whom we wish to deal with."

"Oh? Then who?"

Emeric sipped his water. "It's said Pal Palek has a hatred for northmen rare even among his own people. That he has dungeons filled with men and women he has captured across the years, those he subjects to extreme acts of cruelty and debasement. Some of these are Bladeborn, the rumours say. This is the reason we are here."

Vincent Rose tried to look appalled, but it was as obvious as a broadback in a brothel that he knew all about Pal Palek. "And...if I should lead you to this place? What do I get in return?"

Emeric leaned back in his chair. "What would you like?"

Rose popped a grape into his mouth, cheeks bunching as he ate. "Protection," he said. "I dare say a trio of swords as capable as you will be better than what I currently have."

"Our swords are not for selling," Emeric said.

Kanabar took it one step further. He flew to his feet, chair flying away behind him. "I'm heir to House Kanabar, you squalid little knave, not some bloody bodyguard. You mind your tongue or I'll have it out."

Vincent Rose opened his hands. "I meant not offence, my lord. Please, do sit."

Borrus Kanabar grunted and retook his seat, as a servant scurried in to pick it up. He gulped down his wine and waved for it to be filled, a thick vein of scorn pulsing in the side of his head. "The shit I've had to put up with these last months..." he grumbled, shaking his head. "I've already had to lower myself to the service of this bloody bastard, I'm not going to add a snake like you to the list, Rose." He took another gulp of his wine.

Jack o' the Marsh found air to speak. "My lord has endured much of late, Master Rose," he explained with delicate courtesy. "He only wishes to return to his homeland."

"Not one of us can stay here, Vincent," Emeric added bluntly. "What else can we offer you?"

"Well, if I may...and without wanting to reignite Sir Borrus's ire, I will say again...*protection.*" Borrus stirred, but Vincent Rose was swift to add, "But not here, no no. That is not what I'm saying."

"Then what?" asked Emeric. "We have a quest to fulfil and will not deviate from it. The only way we can protect you from Janilah is if you remain within our company."

Vincent Rose smiled broadly. "A quest? Well why didn't you say so? I love adventures."

"You'd come with us?" Emeric said, frowning. He turned his eyes around at the guards, then looked at Jonik directly. Jonik knew what he was thinking. Rose would likely bring along these sellswords, perhaps even a bladeborn or two, as he claimed. There were dangers in that, but benefits too. They needed men, after all, men who knew how to fight. That was the entire point of their coming here.

"There will be dangers," Jonik said, drawing the merchant's sly gaze. "We mean to head north, back to our lands. Your safety cannot be guaranteed."

"When can it ever?" Rose announced, too happy with this twist in his fortunes. "But better that I stay on the move than linger here, I think." He plucked another grape, popped it into his mouth, chewed. "Oh, I should say...Ranulf Shackton, you may find him among Pal Palek's menagerie of prisoners. I take no pride in confessing that I led him there myself. A short-term punishment, for crossing me and getting me into all this trouble with Janilah, but one I rather regret. Ranulf is a dear friend to me still." He grinned, sipped on his wine. "You will see him safely from there, I hope?"

"So long as he's still alive, we shall free him with all the rest," Emeric said.

"Excellent. I'm sure you will find him hale and hearty. He hasn't been there too long."

Jonik didn't like this man, not one bit. He called Ranulf Shackton friend and yet sent him into the desert to be tortured and terrorised. It was nothing that they hadn't already heard about him, though. Word spoke of a man as merciless as he was mirthful, a man whose smile could shift from kind to a cruel in a heartbeat. He leaned forward, his eyes gleaming like steel. "What did he steal, this Shackton?"

The merchant's sleazy smile slithered out again. "Information," he said. "I trade in it, as I say, and hired Ranulf to unearth some for me. It wasn't just his failure that vexed me, but his lies and deceits. Look at me as a monster all you like, boy, but Ranulf Shackton earned his time down in those cells."

"Your rift with Ranulf Shackton is not our business," Emeric said. He levelled a firm look at the man. "Where is this stronghold?"

Rose sat back in his chair, all smiles. "A few hours on camelback from here, northwest into the desert. We can leave on the morrow."

"We can leave now," said Jonik.

"No, we cannot. It is entering the heat of the day and you do not want to be on the sands when the sun is right above you. You do not strike me as a man who takes to the sun well, Shadowknight."

Jonik rose sharply to his feet. The Nightblade came out in a blur of black fog, smoke pouring wildly from its edges. He pointed it across the table at Rose's fleshy throat. "Never call me that again," he hissed.

Vincent Rose's fear did not make a reappearance. The frightened man they'd first encountered only minutes ago was gone. "My thanks, my lord, for showing me the blade as I'd asked." His eyes ran along it, tip to hilt to pommel, a greedy look all over his face. "And what a wondrous weapon it is. Tell me, does it whisper to you? I have heard..."

"No," Jonik lied. He sheathed the blade as fast as he'd revealed it. The whispers were hissing softly in his head, controllable, even welcome, but dark and dangerous when his temper was up. He had found it best to convene with the blade only when calm. Elsewise he had learned to ignore it, as he had been advised, lest it begin to take a hold of him.

The puffy look on Rose's face wasn't going anywhere. He opened up his hands in apology. "You'll forgive me, I'm a most curious man by nature and am a keen collector of the weird and wonderful. I have in this very manor a great many items of interest. Perhaps you would like to see them?"

Jack looked interested. "I would," he said. "There was a tapestry, as we arrived, in one of the entrance halls. An orgy, it looked. I'd love to hear about it."

"I know the one," Rose said. "That was a commission I had made, no more than a passing fancy on my part. A bit gaudy, I should say, but it never fails to amuse me." He laughed. "No no, there are other items and artefacts both ancient and arcane herein, my friends. I should arrange a tour, and you may stay here the night, should you wish it? We can set off for the desert before sunrise to beat the heat."

Kanabar seemed immediately keen on that. "Your treasures have little appeal to me, Rose, but your wine does. And the air is chill here, unlike on the ship. I vote we stay."

"This isn't a vote, Sir Borrus," Emeric said.

The big knight snorted. "You think because the boy has a life debt hanging over me I'll follow his every command? Bugger off, Manfrey. I'm staying here tonight, whether you like it or not. Go back to that stinking ship if you like, I'll meet you at dawn for the ride."

Emeric sighed. "I might have known that would be your response."

"He does have a point, my lord," said Jack, diplomatically. "It would make a nice relief to spend a night off the boat."

Jonik couldn't deny that. He'd spent so long at sea these last months that it felt oddly queer to have stable earth beneath his feet. Yet welcome. He considered it a moment and then gave Emeric a nod, and with that, it was sealed.

"We have a few others, on the ship," Emeric told the merchant. "I'd ask that they join us."

"Of course. The more the merrier. I have plenty of room here, as you can tell."

And so the day unfolded. Borrus remained at the table, drinking, while Jack went on his tour with Rose and Emeric and Jonik returned to the ship to fetch the others. After a brief conference on the deck of Invincible Iris it was decided that all would come save Soft Sid and Grim Pete, who as ever would remain to guard the ship. Grim, Jonik had come to realise, never liked to set foot on land if he could avoid it. "Dry land feels unnatural beneath my feet, m'lord," he had told him before. "When you spend all your life at sea, tis strange when the world don't move beneath you."

Jonik understood. He'd spent much of the last few months at sea, and by now was used to the constant motion of life aboard ship. Even returning to land today took a little getting used to.

They soon returned to the manor to find Borrus still lounging in the courtyard, working through his second flagon of sapphire, and Jack o' the Marsh away with their host, taking in the treasures of the house. "Fancy place this," grinned Brown Mouth Braxton, gazing about as they arrived. "How does your castle compare, m'lord?" he asked Borrus. "Can't be much bigger or better."

Borrus Kanabar's pompous laughter rang through every corridor, hall, and room in the manor. "This place is a piss-pot compared to my keep, Brown. I've got ten of these across the Riverlands."

"And our host has a hundred, so we hear it," put in Turner, grinning through the tangles of his unruly flaxen beard. "You sniff out some booze there, Sir Borrus? Any good?"

"Bloody good, Turner. Here, come join. Brown, you too. Did you bring the dice?"

"I did, m'lord."

"Great. How about you, boy?" He'd spotted Devin, who was stuck staring at a tapestry in the hallway outside. He seemed transfixed. "Boy! Are you playing or not?"

"Oh, sorry, milord." The young man spun, and scuttled over, smirking. "There are so many nudes here, on the walls. I might have to go for a wander later."

"Well don't wander too far, or else you'll get lost," said Turner, settling into a seat. The servants came forward to fill their cups, half of them looking bemused by their master's guests, though saying nothing. As the four set into their games, Jonik and Emeric moved to a side table for a privy discussion.

"Do you trust him?" Jonik asked the exile.

Emeric didn't need to be asked who. "Not so far as I could throw him, no. But his anxiety was honest enough. The man has been living in fear here, Jonik. He'll be all too happy to come under our wing."

"So you don't think he's setting us up for a trap?" Jonik didn't like any of this, he was coming to realise. Rose was too oily and too cunning by half. "The man's slippery as an eel, everyone says. Maybe we should just sell him the godsteel blades and be done with it. Forget all of this. We can hire sellswords in the north with the money he pays us, use them to...."

"No." Emeric said the word more bluntly than he typically would. Jonik knew why. "We know full well who Rose would sell those blades to, Jonik, and I'm not going to help arm the Patriots of Lumara. Not after what they did. Not after Brewilla. We're here now, so let's see this through. If he crosses us like he did Janilah, he'll have only added to his enemies."

"If you're sure."

"As sure as I can be." Emeric reached out and gripped Jonik's shoulder, a fatherly look on his face. "But we'll keep a close eye on him, just in case," he promised. "If we smell something untoward, we can leave him here when we return to Invincible Iris."

Jonik frowned to that. "You'd break your oath?"

"For you, son, yes I would. And there are no oaths between serpents and men."

29

Elyon

Elyon received word at the training yard that the Prince of Tukor wished to see him. He had been sparring with Lancel, Barnibus, and Sir Mallister, the four engaged in a bout of two-on-two when the messenger boy brought the letter. Elyon took to the side of the yard, broke the seal, read the words, and then turned to the others. "I'd best be off," he said. "I have a private audience to attend."

He didn't tell them where, or with whom, and that made them guess of a certain young lady with hair as bright as polished gold and eyes of sapphire blue. "Isn't it a little early for such a summons, El?" called out Lancel, blond of hair himself, though it was darkened with sweat right now. "I thought the Lady Melany only liked to come to you by night?"

Barnibus made a lewd joke to that, which Sir Mallister didn't much like. "You forget you talk of my sweet sister, sirs. Must I insist we swap these training swords for something with a bit more bite?"

They used blunt steel swords when training half the time, rather than their own godsteel blades. The latter required that they garb themselves in godsteel armour too, and the effort wasn't always worth it.

"Feel free, Mallister," said Barnibus. "Either Lance or I will still best you."

"You think so? Well I rather think not. Word is there may be a vacancy in Janilah's Six, you know. I'm being talked up as a possibility."

Apparently, Sir Kevyn Bolt hadn't been seen for many long weeks now, leaving the duties of Janilah's sworn swords up to the other five. Elyon had seen Sir Owen Armdall, Sir Fredrick Ruxmond, Sir Edwyn Huffort, and the two Hunt brothers regularly around the palace, though not the Bull of Bolt. *No doubt Janilah has him off on some scheme*, he thought. "You're too nice to join the Six, Mallister," he called across the yard, as he wiped down his brow, and donned his Varin cloak. "A man as honest as you wouldn't suit the role."

"The Six are just babysitters, just as the Greycloaks are," chimed in Lancel. "How dull to stand guard over a king all day and night. Would you want to spend the entire war stationed in Ilithor, Monsort? There are dragons to kill out there, I hear."

Lancel flew back into action at that, engaging Sir Mallister in a stirring attack that had the Emerald Guard swift on the back foot. They were rather well matched in skill, speed, and look besides, both tall and blond, lean and comely. Barnibus might well have been the best of them with a blade, but that's where the similarities ended for the chubby cheeked man. He walked over to Elyon, a cup of water to hand. "So, what's the summons, then? Must be important, to have the heir of Daecar off and running from the yard."

"Rylian," Elyon told him. "He wants me up in his solar before the council meeting."

"Ah yes, that long awaited Council of Kings. Rather a misnomer though, I'd say, seeing as certain lords and knights have been invited too. But then I suppose the Council of Kings and Lords and Knights and Such doesn't slide so well off the tongue." He smiled and clapped Elyon on the shoulder. "We'll drink your share between us," he assured him. "I feel a thirst coming on that only the fine establishments of White Shadow can quench."

The training yard they liked to use was some way down into the city, on the border of the district of White Shadow, a twisting warren of streets beneath the shadow of the white mountains to the south, hence the name. Most days, after they trained, they would head to a tavern or two to escape the stuffy confines of the palace. There were many shadowed corners there that were good for discussing illicit topics, of which Elyon, Lancel, and Barnibus liked to indulge.

Mallister too, sometimes, though they were more careful with what they said around him, being Tukoran, as they were with Prince Rodmond when he came to train with them. But there was no time for all that today.

Elyon bid his companions goodbye and began up through the city levels, climbing steep banks of stairs, crossing over bridges and beneath archways, passing under tunnels and through the guarded gates that gave access to the upper tiers.

The city was clutched by the mountains on either side and had half a dozen walls dividing its separate districts, each one built of solid stone and set with heavy iron gates. Up in the high battlements and towers on every level, great ballistas and scorpions sat watching the skies, attended by expert Bladeborn archers and engineers with stacks of huge godsteel-tipped bolts. It was the same with every major city, fortress and castle in the north, though the capitals were particularly well defended. Any one of those bolts catching a dragon in the right spot could send it spiralling to the ground, dead.

They have fire, we have godsteel, Elyon thought, as he climbed. Above him, far back at the rear of the palace, the Black Tower rose, sparkling obsidian against the frigid blue skies. It was where the Council of Kings was to take place, Elyon had heard, where all Tukoran kings presided over matters of war, unless absent from the city. A part of him relished it, another part felt queasy at the thought of sharing a room with the likes of Janilah and Hadrin and Cedrik Kastor.

And still, Amara's words was ringing in his ears. *Might I bring up the subject of the Windblade?* he wondered. He might just, only to study the look on the faces of Janilah and Godrik Taynar as he did so. A sick feeling rose up his throat. *If our new king has handed that blade over...* The more he'd thought about it, the more angry he became. *Perhaps Amara's right. Perhaps it's my solemn duty to take it back into the hands of a Vandarian...*

His thoughts on that twisted back and forth as they had for some days as he made his way to Rylian's private quarters in the Prince's Tower, thrusting upward from the north of the palace. He found a household knight ready and waiting for him, one of Rylian's men. "I'm here to meet the prince," Elyon said.

"This way, Sir Elyon." The guard led him into Rylian's solar among his chambers. He knocked on the dark oakwood door, heard a voice saying 'come in' and opened it to allow Elyon to pass. "Sir Elyon Daecar, my prince," the knight announced.

"Thank you, Sir Roger. You may leave us."

Elyon stepped inside as the knight shut the door. The solar was cosier than he'd expected, dim-lit but comfortable. There was a single window, bordered with frost and piled with a coat of snow on the sill. Rylian sat there, dressed in a simple tunic of brown, with dark green breeches, and high leather boots. There was a chair opposite him, and a small table with wine and a tray of cheese, fruit, and breads between. "Join me, Elyon. You look like you need to sit down." He smiled through his rusty red beard, trimmed neat to his chiselled jaw. "How was your training? I could find you a better match than Sir Lancel and Sir Barnibus, if you'd like?"

Elyon found himself laughing as he sat. "Aleron used to fight them both at once," he said. "Even then they were no match for him."

"Not many were." Rylian poured the drinks, handed Elyon a cup. "To Aleron," he said, raising his. "Taken too soon."

"Too soon," Elyon echoed. He drank to his late brother, and cradled the mulled wine in his hands as he sat back, crossing his legs. "How did you know where I was?"

"You're in my city, Elyon. I like to keep tabs on my friends when they're here."

From someone else that might sound sinister. Elyon pointed out as such, then said, "And what of your enemies, my lord?"

"Those too." Rylian drew on his wine, thoughtful. "Perhaps I'll come and spar with you myself, one day. I haven't swung a sword in weeks, and that itch needs scratching. I'd be keen to see what you're made of, Elyon."

"You've seen me fight before in tourneys, I recall."

"Not since you grew up."

Elyon frowned. "I fought Aleron only last summer, at your warcamp near Tukor's Pass. I seem to remember he humiliated me in front of half of your men."

"You've improved since then, and not only with the blade. You have grown into your role as heir, Elyon, a part that suits you well. Besides, you fought with skill and flair that day and only lost in part because your mind was elsewhere. You spent half of the bout glancing over to see if my daughter was watching, if memory serves."

"And she was," Elyon said. "Only it was Aleron she had eyes for."

"Rightly so. I'd told her already that Aleron was to become her betrothed, so long as they consented. I'd discussed that many times with your father in the past. Even when the two were children, it seemed fated they would wed. And now...well, we know what's to happen now. Amilia's to become a Rasal queen, her children to be half Seaborn. They'll never be great warriors, as I once had hoped."

Elyon observed the prince, as he sipped on his warm mulled wine. "You still have Robbert and Raynald," he said. "I've heard one of them is set to wed Princess Lyriss. A Lukar-Reynar match would be plenty to sire great warriors, my lord."

Rylian looked up with half a smile. "And where did you hear that?"

"I spoke with Queen Elitha. She let something slip out about there being 'another wedding' soon enough and I put two and two together."

"I imagine you know more than that, Elyon." Rylian leaned in, a note of conspiracy about him. "You know that my father arranged that betrothal too, without my input or approval. You know how much that vexes me. And you know just what you're doing, bringing it up." Elyon went to speak, but Rylian cut him off. "What you don't know, is that my father is trying to heal the rift that has opened up between us. He is not a man to concede much, so you can imagine my surprise. Yet it betrays his vulnerabilities. This union he has forged in the north is precarious, and there are many unsavoury rumours surrounding him. We are bound by our mutual foes, but beneath that thin veneer of unity, there are many fissures and fractures between the kings and lords of this land. When the war with the south is done and won, those fractures will widen and deepen, and all the north will shatter like a clay plate. We have gone from war with Rasalan, to war with Agarath, to war with all the south, but when all that is over, there will be war in the north instead...I can feel it in my bones."

He stopped for a moment and looked out of the window. "House Reynar was never the match I wanted," he went on. "I wanted a union with the Daecars, as your father and I tried to deliver. Had my king father not bought the Rasal crown with Amilia's hand, I may have given her to you..."

"I'd have refused..." Elyon started.

"I know you would. To loyalty to your brother, to love for Lady Melany, call it what you will. That is your right, of course. But I have two sons. And you have a sister, very much her mother's daughter. That is the union I propose."

Elyon wasn't sure how to respond. Lillia was not yet fourteen summers, a child still, to his eyes. She was maturing fast yes, but marriage? "That's not for me to decide," he said. "My father..."

"Isn't here."

"No, but..."

"Believe me, Elyon, your father will be most happy with the match. I had hoped you would be too."

"I will be so long as my sister is. I've heard it say that Lukars wed for blood not love, but I've never conformed to that myself, my lord. Lillia will wed who she wishes, if I have my way."

"Within reason," said the prince. "You can say that all you want, Elyon, but there are realities to which we must adhere. My father arranged Amilia's marriage to Hadrin without my consent, without my leave, and there is not much I can do about that now. But Robbert and Raynald are different. My job, and your job in your father's absence, is to present options to those who fall within our realm of responsibility. Robbert is a prince and heir to a kingdom, Lillia a lady of pure blood and birth, and a rare beauty. The match is perfect."

"And Lyriss?"

"Was my father's choice, not mine."

"So this is in defiance of him?" Elyon wasn't certain why he was even questioning this. Denying Janilah this match with House Reynar would weaken him further, and drive that wedge deeper between him and his son. *Isn't that what I want?* Elyon asked himself. This was another step toward Rylian taking his father's throne. But in the end, he wanted Lillia to be happy more. "I'd have to talk to my sister," he said, before Rylian might answer. "But..." He thought about it some more. She'd talked often about Prince Rylian's dashing sons in the past, he remembered, and likely wouldn't object. "I think she may be amenable."

"I would hope so."

"And Robbert? Have you spoken to him?"

"I have. Given the choice between Lyriss Reynar and Lillia Daecar, there really isn't much to ponder. That is no slight against Lyriss, more a tribute to your sister. She is young, yes, but will soon be of an age to marry. Robbert and Lillia will be very much what Aleron and Amilia might have been. This is my way of making that right."

And defying your father, Elyon knew, though he didn't offer that accusation again. It seemed that the prince had grown to know more of his father's treacheries, though, whether confirmed or merely suspected. In that, all the north seemed to be growing wise, and every day a new rumour of the Warrior King's transgressions began to circulate among highborn and baseborn both. Elyon and his friends had heard much of that when in White Shadow, sampling the taverns cloaked against the chill and absent their Varin cloaks to better go unknown and unnoticed. Among the local population of stoneworkers and labourers, stablemen and artisans, dark rumour about Janilah was rife. It seemed he wasn't much loved, even in his own city, leastways not by all. "His ambition will drive us to victory," Elyon had heard one old whitebeard say, "but what then? What's the use in beatin' the south if only to win enemies with half the north in the meanwhile?"

It was much as Rylian had put it just now. *Fissures and fractures, and war in the north, on the back of Janilah's scheming.* From lowborn to high the sentiment was shared, it seemed, and Elyon had to wonder how long it would take for the Warrior King to crack. *Sooner or later, he'll make a mistake,* he thought. *He'll trip and fall and show some weakness, and then the scavengers will strike.*

Prince Rylian stood from his seat. "I would have you bring this to Lillia, but keep it between yourselves for now. I have not yet told my father and would like the pleasure of informing him myself, not having him hear it from another source."

Elyon finished his wine, and stood to join him. "We'll be discreet."

"Good." Rylian took a pace toward the door. Before he could take another, it opened, and a woman silhouetted the frame dressed in wrappings of grey and green. Her hair was unkempt, uncut, unwashed, leeched of all its colour. Her skin looked much the same, bloodless and sickly, with a yellowy-grey undertone. Rylian's posture grew taught at the presence of his lady wife, Clarris of House Kastor. "I was just leaving, Clarris," he said. "If you're here for another quarrel..."

"What's *he* doing here?" The woman pointed a shivering finger in Elyon's direction, the nail chipped and stained and long like a claw. There was a slightly maddened look in her eye. "I want him out, Rylian. Out...*now*!"

"We were just leaving, as I say."

"Why did you bring him here in the first place?" She rolled her lips as though she was about to spit. Elyon could just about see the faintest shadow of Amilia in her, something in the shape of the nose and jawline, but that was all. The woman was otherwise a shrivelled shrew, a known recluse, and an ungodly harridan who'd whiled away the last three years of her life mourning the death of her father, Lord Modrik, after he'd cracked his head open on the hearth. She didn't come to feasts, she didn't come to court, and getting her garbed and garnished for her daughter's wedding was likely to be an almighty task. But besides all that, Elyon knew of the woman's reason for hating him. *She believes I killed her nephew, Sir Griffin,* he thought. *Just like everyone else.*

"I had business to attend with Elyon, now complete," Rylian told her. "We'll leave you to your embroideries."

"What business? With *him*? Do you not recall he *murdered* your nephew, Rylian. And you invite him into our home?"

"*Your* nephew, Clarris. Griffin was never my blood."

Spittle glistened on her grey wrinkled lips. "You speak ill of him? Of dear sweet Griff. He was such a good boy, so kind-hearted. How can you say that? How!"

"I do not have time for this. We have a war council to attend with my father."

"I don't want you ever to come back here!" The woman was shaking so hard she looked like she might topple over. "Never, do you hear! *Never*!"

"I'll not trouble you again, Lady Clarris," Elyon said. He stopped as he passed her. "But for what it's worth, I'm sorry about what happened with your nephew." His mind was on Saska, and Saska alone. "I'm sorry about a lot of things that happened that night."

"Sorry won't bring him back." She spat in his face, then stormed away down the corridor.

Rylian went to march after her, his face filling with fury. "Clarris! Clarris, don't you walk away..."

Elyon reached out to stop him, using his spare hand to wipe the spittle away. "She barely caught me," he lied. "It isn't worth it, my lord. She's grieving, and not in her right mind."

"She's been grieving for almost four bloody years! It's high time she made good with her threats and threw herself from one of these windows."

"You don't mean that..."

"Perhaps I do...the state she gets herself into. Perhaps we'd all be better with her gone." Rylian blasted out a breath, refilled his lungs, calmed. "I'm sorry, Elyon, for that. I ought to have her lashed at the least. You're the heir to a greathouse and don't deserve to be treated as such." He turned. Sir Roger was standing nearby, watching quietly. "See that she doesn't do anything stupid, Sir Roger," Rylian ordered. "And call for her physician. She may be low on her tonics. They keep her calm, mostly," he added, for Elyon. "But sometimes...sometimes she gets like this. It's that Kastor blood, there's a sickness to it as you know. Sir Griffin..." He shook his head. "The boy was a cur, cruel to his bones, and sure to get a knife in his neck eventually. I told her what happened, how he ambushed you in your tent, but she..."

Elyon raised a hand. "It's really quite all right, my lord, you don't have to explain." If anything, he was glad for the introduction. He'd heard a great deal about Clarris Kastor, but hadn't yet had the displeasure of a meeting. It was nice to see just how wrong a marriage could go, when love was left out of the equation. *And that isn't a mistake I'm going to make. Not with Lillia. And not with me.*

"If you're sure." Rylian looked like a man who'd dealt with this for far too long, but duty had bound him to this woman, so he continued to suffer her all the same. "Well then, we should get going. The Black Tower awaits."

THE PRINCE LED the way down corridors and sets of stairs, across courtyards heaped with snow, beneath arches clinging with icicles and monuments to the gods, towering here and there. There was much of the palace Elyon hadn't yet discovered, and the Black Tower was one such place. It was accessed across a cloistered bridge at the rear of the palace, lined either side with lanterns burning dim. At the far edge a white stone courtyard opened out giving access to the tall black roundtower, its summit reaching ten tall storeys from the floor.

Outside, they found the big-bellied and big-bearded form of Lord Kanabar approaching the entrance, with the rather more modestly proportioned Lord Paramor at his side. Ahead, the bear-like Lord Buckland and the Oakenlord, Ferry Maynard, were already reaching the bottom steps, which circled upward through the heart of the roundtower toward the council chambers at the top. "Elyon, I half expected you to sit this one out," Wallis Kanabar exclaimed upon seeing him.

"Why would that be?" Donal Paramor wanted to know. The smaller man had a necklace of corals and beads and shells about his neck, in a thousand different hues, and a fine gold and blue mantle over a quilted cerulean doublet. "I would think that Sir Elyon would relish meetings such as this, no?"

"You weren't there at our siege camp outside Harrowmoor, Donal," Lord Kanabar told him. He was dressed as he often was in a huge pale blue cloak slashed with silver and green, and with the regal elk of his house, with its great bladed antlers, emblazoned proudly upon his back. As always, much of what he wore was hidden by his huge red beard. "Elyon looked like he wanted to be anywhere but the war council, most days we met."

Elyon could hardly deny that. "I never saw the Rasals as our enemy," he explained. "It was hard to be enthusiastic, hearing of Lord Kastor's plans to win the fort."

"You and me both, Elyon," grunted Kanabar. He'd been drinking, Elyon could tell, by the red in his eyes, the broken veins in his nose.

"We have a common cause to fight against now," Rylian put in. "My lords, let us not freeze to death out here. The chambers above will be plenty warm to beat off the chill."

The stairs spiralled around through the core of the Black Tower, all the way up to the top, ten levels above the snowy yard. They ended within a small antechamber that gave access to the council chambers. Elyon drew a breath to steady himself before entering, taking to Lord Paramor's side as Rylian, then Kanabar marched within. All were seasoned commanders, veterans of the last war, as would be the rest of those included. It was no wonder Elyon felt out of his depth at such meetings.

Aleron had been bred to attend them, not me, he thought. It was always his brother who'd spent his twilight hours with his nose in books on siege strategy and warfare, preparing to one day lead. *House Daecar was to be his, and the Sword of Varinar too, most thought.* Now Elyon had to take up that mantle and fast-track his own education, which he'd been doing for some months. Besides his greater focus on his training, he read each night as well. Histories on warfare and tomes on tactics and strategy had become his bedfellows. *And they give a pleasure of their own*, he thought. Not the sort he was used to beneath the sheets, of course, but a different pleasure; a pleasure of betterment and learning, of the growth of a second son into a first, a playboy into an heir.

He walked into the council chambers, head high, and looked around. The room was circular, with a dozen windows about its circumference, a high domed roof, and a large rectangular table at its heart, white marble streaked with blue, its surface etched with an engraving of a map that comprised all the known world. At its head, King Janilah Lukar sat unsmiling. The other end had been taken up by King Godrik Taynar. The two men were glancing at one another in a manner that wasn't particularly friendly. Prince Dalton sat at his father's right side; Rylian would take the same position beside Janilah, Elyon imagined. Others were arranged here and there, at seats of their own choosing. Lord Kastor and his cruel pale face, with old stoop-backed Lord Gershan, Master of the Moorlands, to one side, and Sir Gavin Trent, Kastor's lead commander, at his other. Lord Huffort of Rockfall was present too, as was Lord Swallow of Blackhearth; both had served beneath Lord Kastor during the siege of Harrowmoor.

The Rasal Seaborn lords with their crab and kraken sigils sat side-by-side; Lord Swiftwater, Lord Merrymarsh, and Lord Browlan. The Oakenlord was settling in next to them, as Lord Horus Buckland bulled his way right for the side table to pour himself wine. Lord Kanabar followed to join him. At most feasts they made sure they sat together, and rarely a night went past when they didn't get sotted, competing over their drinking prowess and the great sizes of their beards and bellies both. Elyon was offered a cup but declined, seating himself at Kanabar's side.

The room was replete with half the greatlords of the north, though many still were absent. Elyon could have done with his father here, or his grandfather Lord Amadar. Lord Oloran, Sir Killian's father, hadn't made the journey from Elinar, nor had Lord Porus Pentar from Redhelm. The same was true of many others, though there were more than enough men here already, Elyon thought, and not a woman in sight. It was said that few women had ever graced this room, and no surprise; Janilah didn't think much of the fairer sex, after all.

The young princes Robbert, Raynald, and Rodmond Taynar hadn't been included either, it seemed. As far as Elyon could tell, he was by a distance the youngest member of the council, by far the least experienced, and the only one who hadn't been involved in the erstwhile war. *My being here is a courtesy,* he realised. *Perhaps Rylian even demanded it of his father, to ensure there was a Daecar presence.*

He put the thought aside as Lord Paramor asked, "Where's our good king? I hope your daughter isn't keeping him, Prince Rylian."

Rylian took his seat at Janilah's right, as anticipated. "Who can say, my lord." He looked around, as though to take charge. "Shall we begin without him?"

"No," said Janilah, at once. "We will wait."

They didn't have to wait too long. King Hadrin could soon be heard puffing and panting as he climbed the stairs, the clank of armour accompanying him. He arrived in his cloth-of-gold cloak with Sir Munroe Moore, commander of his guard, at his side. "Oh, no guards?" he saw, moving his eyes around the room.

"Sir Munroe can wait downstairs," Janilah told him.

"I see. I had thought he might offer good counsel. But...as you wish, Janilah. Join the others below, Sir Munroe. I shall see you after."

The rest were downstairs too. Greycloaks and sworn swords and sundry other knights of the various houses. *A lot of testosterone...a lot of tension...a lot of blades,* Elyon thought. *Down there, and up here both.*

"So, I'll...well, I'll just sit here then, I suppose." The Rat King of Rasalan looked displeased that the two heads of the table were taken, but he had to be realistic, he was the lesser of the three by some distance. Lord Paramor kindly stood and drew back a chair to sit beside him. That put him right across from Elyon, unfortunately. *Amron Daecar...is dead,* came the king's scratchy voice in his head. Elyon swallowed the thought and tried to keep his eyes from the ugly little man, as Janilah's voice filled the chamber.

"My lords, thank you for coming. We all know why we're here and I'll not waste our time with a long preamble. First, let's hear tidings." He looked around the room, an invite for anyone to speak.

Lord Wallis Kanabar took up the request. "I had word from Dragon's Bane just this morning, so it happens," he announced, putting down his cup of wine. "From your uncle Rikkard, Elyon. He told me he fought off an Agarathi sally not two days past. They're probing for weak points through the Bloodmarsh Isles, it seems."

"As they ever do," said Cedrik Kastor in his clean clipped voice, also across from Elyon. *Why did I sit here, facing these two bloody men?* he had to wonder. "Crossing the Bloodmarshes is the surest way to reach Vandar with an army afoot. There are a hundred ways through those isles that can be passable when the waters are low, and the thick fogs and mists work as cloaks to hide them. History tells us that many a southern army has appeared from the fogs without warning, to lay siege to Dragon's Bane, or the smaller forts nearby. That is a concern. If they can march an army to take Dragon's Bane, they'll have..."

"A strong foothold in the north, yes," broke in Kanabar. "We don't need a lesson on history, Kastor, certainly not from a man of North Tukor. I've been charged with defending the southern border around Dragon's Bane for decades, and know the Bloodmarshes better than you ever will. These probes happen all the time, but sneaking into Vandar with a few dozen men is very different from marching any army across Death's Passage, which is more rare than you're suggesting. We have that tract of land well sealed and well watched. Sir Rikkard has with him five thousand Amadar men, and Sir Killian the same with the Olorans. Lord Rammas has thousands more Marshlanders in camp outside, with Lakelanders and my own Riverlanders too under the command of Lords Shorton and Fullerton. In all, that's some thirty thousand fighting men in or around the fortress, watching the passage south. If King Tavash wants to send an army that way, let him."

"He won't, not until he has support from the Lumarans," said Prince Dalton, wrapped in a sleek grey tunic that brought out the deathly pallor of his skin.

His king father agreed in his frosty, toneless voice. "These sallies and probes are overtures only," he said. "King Tavash will do nothing until he has the full backing of the sun and sand empire. It would be folly for him to engage until he has the Lightborn to bolster his ranks."

"It's said they've gathered for their warmoot," came Lord Buckland's big growly voice. He filled his seat, huge black beard seated happily atop his belly, tightly bound up in dark brown leathers. "That suggests to me that the Lumarans aren't yet sure what they're going to do."

Janilah Lukar shook his head. "The warmoot is a formality, required of their faith. Their participation is not in doubt."

"The Patriots of Lumara have made sure of it," put in Lord Browlan of Doublebay Harbour. He was in his early forties, mild of face and manner, clear of voice, and powerful. His force of ships was said to be vast, his wealth similarly well stocked. It gave him a measure of pomposity, such as Elyon could judge. "I hear many tidings from Doublebay, via my sons and subjects, from sailors and merchants newly returned from the south. I suppose I don't need to share them; we all know well enough that northmen are being exiled from their lands all across the Lumaran Empire, harried and harassed by the Patriots and their supporters, who've committed innumerable atrocities these last months. They've made Empress Valura's position untenable. She has no choice but to agree to go to war, else she'll have a civil one to deal with instead."

A murmur of agreement went around, though all knew it would take time for the Lumarans to assemble. When they did, they'd have legions of Starriders and Sunriders to add to the Agarathi ranks, let alone the tens, even hundreds of thousands of trained soldiers at their disposal. And Moonriders? No one seemed to know how many of those there might be. Lord Kanabar put forward the question, looking to the Seaborn lords. "Do you hear tidings of Moonriders among those reports, Lord Browlan?" he asked him. "We all know how calamitous one of those can be."

"Nothing that we could consider fact," said Browlan.

Lord Swiftwater of Shellcrest nodded along. He was a jovial chap, short and chubby and always smiling, with thinning salty hair, cheeks the colour of beet, and a clean-shaved face that unveiled the full account of his chins. Elyon counted at least three, though occasionally a fourth seemed to emerge from the folds of his collar as well. With all that his Seaborn blood was as pure as anyone's; rumour was he could swim a full forty minutes underwater on a breath, and dive as deep as Daarl's Domain. "I lean toward them having a half dozen," he said in a tuneful voice, the very antithesis of frost-tongued King Godrik Taynar. "About the same as last time. The moonbears are proud creatures, near impossible to tame, and there aren't many left. They're not swarming like the dragons, as we're hearing."

"And are we hearing any more on that?" asked Rylian. He glanced around. "Do we have any idea on numbers?"

"Over a dozen have been sighted, all different," said Lord Kanabar. "I get word often from Lord Pentar down in Redhelm. Every time there's a new dragon attack anywhere along the coast, he sends men to hear reports from those who got a good look at them. By now there have been thirteen distinct sightings, though it's hard to be sure with some of them."

"That doesn't tell us much, Wallis," said King Godrik, in a whisper to chill the bones. When he spoke the very firelight in the room seemed to flicker and die.

"It tells us that we'll have to slay a dozen dragons at least," Kanabar came back. "We can safely assume they've got two, even three times that number."

"Or that they have only those," returned Godrik. "This new Agarathi king is shrewd and cunning, they say. He's shown us these dragons for a reason. This isn't just about testing our defences and charring a few coastal towns. It might be that he's trying to inflate his numbers, put the fear into us, to prevent an early invasion."

"He might. He might not. We cannot know." Janilah shook his head. "In this I agree with Lord Kanabar. We've heard for many months that the Wings teem like never before. Thirteen? No, Tavash commands many more."

"But not Garlath, nor Lord Marak, if these rumours are true," said Sir Gavin Trent, scarred of face and broad of chest, with the blustery voice of a seasoned battle commander. "Apparently Marak no longer lords over the Nest; that post has gone to Vargo Ven."

"Vargo Ven, who my son near-slew," grunted Kanabar. "He and that brutish dragon of his both. What was its name again?"

"Malathar," said Elyon. "The Mighty."

"Right, yes of course. Stubby nosed one, that. Borrus caught him with a few good shots that would've opened up another dragon. A shame they'll not get a second round."

"We don't know that for sure, Wallis," said Lord Paramor, across the table. "These rumours of a breakout at the Pits of Kharthar... Borrus may yet be living."

And Lythian, Elyon thought. He wasn't going to give that much hope, though. Those rumours and whispers might be nothing but sailors stories, warped in taverns from a hundred tellings, and entirely untrue.

Lord Kanabar seemed of much the same mind. "Until Borrus marches though my door, I'll keep thinking him at Varin's Table," he said, to a round of nods to suggest others agreed.

The conversation moved on. A lot of it remained the subject of half-heard whispers and tidings that couldn't be counted on. King Godrik informed the council that the Tidelands were a matter of concern. "The tides are receding yet further," he said, "and unusually so for this time of year. As they go out, they're opening up paths between the islands that the southlanders might cross. They've been known to do this before, in Renewals past, when the waters drop low, travelling north by foot and hoof right up into the west of Vandar. I have given orders for searches to be conducted to ascertain the truth of this. A half dozen galleys are sailing back and forth, checking for bridges that were once submerged. The Twinfort and Green Harbour are also being fortified with more men, should the Agarathi venture that way. Most of these are from Daecar lands. Sir Elyon, I'd hear your voice on this."

Elyon cleared his throat. He had little to say, in truth, but for what Amara had told him. "My lord father has provisioned both with men from Houses Borrington and Rothwell, as well as many of our own Daecar men. I believe Lady Crawfield is also sending soldiers beneath her banners."

"Is Amron there now?" asked Prince Dalton.

No, he's somewhere in the Icewilds, he thought, *likely dead.* "So far as my auntie Amara tells me," he said instead.

King Hadrin's lips twitched at that, as though involved in his private joke. *Not so private. I know what you're thinking, Rat King.* So did Janilah, by the look of him. He gave the Rasal king a withering look, then said. "We could hope for none better than Lord Daecar to hold the western passage."

A silence blew through the room. Many here now suspected with some conviction that Janilah was behind Amron's maiming, Aleron's death, and a great deal else. Kanabar said that with something of a huff, though held his tongue. Elsewise none spoke or made a sound, but for an awkward cough that escaped Lord Huffort's throat, and a sneering lick of the lips from nasty old Lord Gershan, with his hooked nose and sinister eyes.

"A Red Sea crossing is the typical form of invasion," Prince Dalton finally said, to break the silence. "We have our naval forces massing at our harbours along the coast, but we can't watch all the sea. Our ships are most vulnerable to dragon attack as well, as we know, some of us from bitter experience. A naval invasion supported by dragons will be their most likely course."

"As ever, yes," said Janilah. "That is why King Hadrin has kindly offered to bolster our naval forces there."

Hadrin nodded, looking at Swiftwater, Merrymarsh, Browlan. "My noble lords will send warships through the Bloodmarshes, into the Red Sea," he declared, proudly. "These are not your normal ships, but great war galleons built to withstand dragon attack, and bring them down from the skies. My Seaborn mages have been working hard in their alchemies, producing fireproof oils and balms in great quantity. These we aim to share, of course."

"Of course," echoed Janilah. "You have our thanks, Hadrin. I doubt your father would have been so generous."

"No, perhaps not," agreed the Rasal king, stiffly.

Another short silence took root. Men exchanged glances, others looked off elsewhere. Hadrin's personal hand in his father's death was another rumour that wasn't going away. *Has there ever been a council so treacherous as this?* Elyon had to wonder, looking around. Hadrin the kin and kingkiller, who'd slain his own father for a crown. Cedrik Kastor, whose cruel behaviours and abuses with his southern slaves was well known. Godrik Taynar, who'd plotted to overthrow his own liege lord, and his son who'd driven Vesryn to the point of despair. *If Vesryn was here, he'd have his own treasons to answer for,* Elyon had to admit, and there were others too. Lord Gershan was a bitter old recreant who was known to have killed several of his mistresses, and sired a hundred bastards. Sir Gavin Trent, Kastor's loyal commander, had murdered children at his lord's behest, people said. The Rasal lords weren't perfect either. Lord Merrymarsh had merry in his name yet was anything but. Lord Swiftwater, jolly as he seemed, was greedy and covetous and had swindled and cheated a great many people in assembling his great wealth and power.

And then there was Janilah, the man behind it all. A man who bred Bladeborn to be turned into swords and assassins, who stole a babe from his own daughter's breast to be raised a ghost and a killer. A man who lied, cheated, deceived his way to controlling the north. A man who had maimed their greatest hero, ordered for his son to be slain, ravaged a house he professed, so commonly, to admire and respect. *A man whose comeuppance will come,* Elyon thought, staring at him. *Oh it'll come, Warrior King. One day soon, you'll answer for your crimes.*

For a heartbeat, and no more, Janilah's eyes linked with Elyon's. They were hard as flint, displeased with everything and everyone, but watching everything and everyone too. "Let's move on," he said, shifting his gaze to his next target. "Lord Paramor, you have a question?"

Donal Paramor nodded, stroking his short white beard. His blue-gold eyes went to Prince Dalton, then Lord Lewyn Huffort of Rockfall. "I was curious as to whether there was any progress in the hunt for Vesryn Daecar, my lords?"

"It's vengeance you want against the man, is it?" queried King Godrik to that. "I'm told Vesryn killed your son, Sir Brendan, when the parley turned to violence at Harrowmoor."

"Yes, and we all know who sparked it," said Lord Kanabar. He stood from his chair and lumbered over to the drinks table, filled his cup, and returned with a flagon, so Lord Buckland might do the same.

"This is not a feast," Janilah said, displeased by that as well.

"No, it's more like a wake, how morose we all are. I'll lighten it with wine, if you don't mind, Janilah." Kanabar drew on his drink, turned his eyes to Cedrik Kastor, and then said, "I'm referring to you, Kastor. Just to be clear."

"Of course you are, my lord."

"A matter for the gods to judge," said old King Godrik, tunelessly. He looked again to Lord Paramor. "So, my lord? Is it retribution you seek against our short-lived former First Blade?"

"By no means," Lord Paramor said, quite sincerely. "My son died a knight. He died fighting, with sword in hand."

"He died with a the Sword of Varinar through his back," Prince Dalton hissed. "There was no honour in his death, not on Vesryn's part, certainly. He has since unveiled his true colours, turning his cloak and running off with that blade. Many are coming to believe that he will join the south against us. There have been reports that a man of his build and framing boarded a ship near Stormhold."

"A report proven false," said Janilah. "The man who spoke it has had his tongue removed."

Lord Huffort confirmed. "We've had to part many tongues from mouths these last weeks." He arranged his face into a stiff smile, lengthening his lantern jaw. "As well as other body parts."

"Unwise," Lord Buckland declared. "You cut off tongues and soon none will be talking. These are Rasals you're maiming and mutilating, men who only recently were having their lands invaded by you and yours, Lord Huffort. If anything, they'll be more inclined to shelter Vesryn than expose him. We're a defiant people, you know."

"Any man or woman known to have aided Vesryn will have more than their tongue removed, Lord Buckland," said King Hadrin. "We are all friends now, and cannot be known to be harbouring traitors."

Lord Kanabar began laughing to that, and loudly.

"Something amusing, my lord?" the Rat King asked him.

"A private joke just came to me. And a bloody funny one too."

"Care to share?"

"Not particularly. I'm not sure that would be so wise, in present company."

"Yes, we can all imagine what you're thinking," said Janilah, entirely unamused. "But to answer your question, Lord Paramor, no, there has been no progress in the hunt for Vesryn."

"If you haven't caught him yet, you won't," Lord Kanabar said, gulping down wine. "I suppose that's why you brought the Windblade with you is it, Godrik?" He wiped his mouth with the back of his hand. "You're planning to give it to Dalton, are you?"

Elyon watched intently. He'd not spoken to Lord Kanabar of the Windblade being here, though it was possible Amara had mentioned it to him. It was like her to stir things, even when absent. *She probably thought I'd not have the nerve to mention it*, Elyon thought. *Wallis Kanabar, on the other hand, can always be counted on for that.*

Godrik Taynar didn't stiffen. He was stiff as stone already. He merely turned his icy deadened eyes on Kanabar and nodded, just once. "A First Blade needs to hold a Blade of Vandar. I brought the Windblade from the Steelforge, should the Sword of Varinar not be recovered."

"And if it is?"

"Then perhaps another might take it."

"Elyon," said Kanabar immediately. He gave the heir of Daecar a swift wink. "There's none better."

"None better?" sneered Cedrik Kastor. "You must be half mad, Kanabar. He'd only run off with it like his uncle did."

"You mean *fly* off, my lord?" japed Swiftwater, chuckling.

"Run, fly, it makes no matter. The Daecars are a spent force. Vandar has better and more deserving men."

King Godrik nodded to that. His cold dark eyes were on Elyon. "Sir Elyon will never hold the Windblade. If it should not go to Dalton, it will be given to a champion of my choosing. Elyon is unproven."

Elyon bristled silently at the insult, but showed nothing on his face. Kanabar did the talking for him. "Unproven? Well, we could arrange for that to be sorted. Line up your finest champions and we'll see who wields the blade best. I'd wager all the wealth of my house that Elyon would win that contest."

Godrik Taynar was not for convincing. "No."

"No?" Kanabar laughed scornfully. "You stole his father's crown, Taynar. The least you can bloody well do is hand him that blade."

Prince Dalton was fast on his feet, blade singing from its sheath. "You'll not speak to your king..."

"*My* king?" Lord Kanabar cut in. "We'll see about that when this war is won." He sat back in his chair, as relaxed as if he were reclining by the hearth in his solar.

"That sounds awfully like a threat." Dalton was still standing, seething. "You'd call your banners to rebellion, to civil war? You're talking treason, my lord."

"*Treason*?" That was too much for Wallis Kanabar to bear. His laughter came louder than ever. "Well that's a little rich, don't you think? There are so many snakes in this patch of grass, I truly don't know where to tread."

Dalton made to answer but his father cut him off. "Take a seat, Dalton. Let him conjure his fantasies. There's no sense in rising to them."

"He's a known sot, and clearly drunk," said Cedrik Kastor as Dalton sat. He turned to Janilah. "Perhaps it would be best to clear the tables of wine next time, my king?"

Janilah Lukar gave no answer. Through all that, Elyon had half forgotten him, but looking at him now, he saw him glowering, his eyes locked on the table in private thought. *So Godrik never gave him the Windblade, as promised,* Elyon realised. He wasn't sure what to make of that. Thieving the Windblade back from Janilah was one thing. That would be just. But taking it from his own king? *No, not* my *king,* he thought. *That would be my father, by rights. Godrik Taynar will never be a true king of mine, never...*

He turned his gaze on the icy old man once more, staring into those black emotionless eyes. *Sir Elyon will never hold the Windblade.* Those words circled his head, an insult, yet another insult, to him and his house to bear. Beneath the table, Elyon Daecar flexed his sword hand. *Well, we'll see about that,* he thought. *There is only so much offence one family can take. You'd do well to remember that, Godrik.*

House Daecar still has teeth.

30

Janilah

Rylian remained behind when the others filed out. "I'd like a word, Father."

The council had been as chaotic as expected, in large part due to Wallis Kanabar and his constant loudmouthed heckling. *That great oaf needs his tongue out too,* Janilah thought, as he watched him lurch away beside the burly black-bearded Horus Buckland, the redoubtable Lord of Northgate. Near every night he had to stand the two laughing and drinking at the feasts, their great shouty voices carrying across the hall. *Can I afford to kill another greatlord, or two?* he wondered. Much as he'd like to take Kanabar's tongue and head both, he knew it wouldn't be wise. His position was too precarious for such recklessness. He'd have to suffer the Lord of the Riverlands for now.

Janilah Lukar looked at his son as the room cleared. "What is it?"

Rylian remained seated at Janilah's side. "Robbert," he said.

"I see." Janilah had been expecting this at some point. "I trust you've decided to permit his union with Lyriss Reynar." Something in his son's eyes said no. He duly delivered that very word.

"No," the prince told him. "I have a better fit for him."

It wasn't a word Janilah often heard - no. *I must be humble,* he thought. *Don't react too sternly.* "Might I ask who?"

"Need you, Father? You can probably guess."

"Lillia Daecar," the Warrior King said, without pause. He could see it in Rylian's eyes, that defiance he'd been exhibiting lately. *This is a choice to wound me,* he knew, but even so he managed to say, "A good choice, Rylian," with as much grace as he could summon. *Swallow it. Swallow your scorn.* "I'm sure Robbert will be most happy."

"He is. I have asked Elyon to speak to his sister of the proposal. He doesn't doubt she'll accept."

Accept. Janilah had to swallow that too. What did a girl of thirteen have to say on the matter? Marriage was a game played by one's elders, by those who knew better, not children. Lillia Daecar ought to have no voice in it. *And no doubt Elyon had his hand in that.* The boy had been studying him during the council meeting, barely saying a word, trying to hide his grin every time the great lout Kanabar made another boorish jape. *He is behind this,* Janilah decided. *He and that lance-tongued auntie of his.* "Was there anything else?"

Rylian stood and moved over to the drinks table, casting his eyes through one of the high windows. A light snow was coming down. There had been talk lately of a storm. "I thought you'd put up more of a fight, Father. It's not like you to lay down so meekly."

"The match is good, as I say."

"But not one you'd have chosen."

"No," Janilah admitted. "Lyriss Reynar is a princess..."

"*Was* a princess." Rylian picked up a flagon of warm spiced wine, and began pouring a cup. "House Reynar is old, strong, noble, that's all true, but its line of kings is now broken. House Daecar was always the better fit for us. Once this war is won, a strong Lukar-Daecar union will help heal the north." He poured a second cup. "Would you like one?"

Janilah nodded idly, thinking. *He's setting up his own alliances, for when I'm gone.* Rylian always looked up to Amron Daecar, always wanted their children to wed. *And if they do, no doubt he'll put his support behind the Daecars should they try to take back the Vandarian throne.*

Rylian returned to the table, placed down Janilah's cup, then moved to the seat at the far end. *There is something in that gesture,* Janilah thought. *We sit at opposite ends of the table now.* "So, Eagle's Perch," Rylian said, looking at the map carved into the white stone surface. He ran his fingers along the rugged coast depicting the Horn of Aramatia. "A bold move, Father."

"I'll want you leading the siege, as soon as Amilia's wed."

"I suspected you would. And the Trident?"

"Godrik will assign his commanders to that task. I imagine he'll want Dalton leading the van."

Rylian nodded, thoughtful. The plan was simple, enumerated by Janilah during the meeting. With the Lumarans busying themselves with the absurd formality of their warmoot, and with these whispers of infighting among the Fireborn ranks, there was never a better time than now to take the initiative. Janilah had laid it out as plainly as he could, and seen little dissent, even from Lord Kanabar. A pestilence though the man was, he was a storied battle commander and warrior, and loved nothing more than a good true fight with the Agarathi and their southern allies. By taking Eagle's Perch in the northeastern tip of Aramatia, and the great fortress of the Trident along the northwestern coast of Agarath, they would have two strong footholds, two staging points from which they might further their invasion plans, tighten the noose from east to west. *I can no longer wait for the Five Blades to be gathered and combined,* Janilah had come to realise. *I'll win this war through military might alone, if I must.*

He watched his son tracing his fingers along the Aramatian coast, sipping his wine in thought. *Good, he is sold on this plan.* Rylian was never better than when given a target, and this one he truly believed in. He'd never been fully invested in the war with Rasalan, Janilah always knew, but this...this was different. *I have my champion back.* "How many men will you need?"

"A lot." Rylian's lips quickened into a smile, a light glinting in his brown-green eyes. "I'll take Kastor too. He's cruel, but a killer born, and his men are seasoned warriors. I'll speak with him, arrange it."

"Good."

"You don't want to come as well, Father? There was a time you'd lead such a campaign yourself."

Janilah took a sip of warm spiced wine. "My place is here, for now. I have much I need to arrange."

Something passed Rylian's face. *He doesn't trust me still,* Janilah did not fail to see. *These rumours that cloak me aren't going away. Mayhaps that trust will never return.* "What Lord Kanabar said about the Windblade, about Elyon having it," Rylian started.

Janilah's eyes narrowed. "Yes?"

"We should support that."

No, we shouldn't. "The blade will go to Dalton. You heard his father."

"Elyon would wield it better, as Lord Kanabar said. The boy is much loved by the East Vandarians, and those in his own lands to the northwest too. It would serve to build a bridge to them if you should support Elyon's claim. Wallis wasn't lying when he said that Taynar took his father's crown. Amron should be king, Elyon prince and heir. The Taynars don't need the Windblade too."

"I have no voice in that discussion." Janilah's meeting on his balcony with Godrik Taynar was still sour in his mind. "The Blades of Vandar are a Vandarian concern..."

"Says the man who's got Lord Huffort's men out there taking tongues, toes, teeth, and worse, in a bid to track down the Sword of Varinar." Rylian was seeing through all of it. "Godrik was meant to give it to you, wasn't he? The Windblade. That's why he brought it here."

Janilah thought it best to say nothing.

"It's hardly a secret anymore, Father. The way you looked at Taynar..." He shook his head, blew through his lips. "If looks could kill, and all that. You'll soldier on to keep the peace, but you're regretting putting him on the throne, that's clear enough. You had your reasons, I know. And Ellis?" His demeanour darkened. "Your minions can lie all they want; I know what happened that day. I'll not say I approve, but I know in your heart you're only trying to win this war. *Bad men make good kings,* I've heard you say more than once. You live up to that well. Perhaps that's your excuse?"

"I don't need a humbling from you, Rylian. I have cursed my honour, cursed my reputation, I know. But all for a greater purpose."

"And that greater purpose will be further served by putting the Windblade into Elyon Daecar's hands. The boy can become an inspiration for the north. The son of Amron Daecar, soaring the skies. He'll do more good with it than Dalton."

"Perhaps." Janilah ground his teeth. "But I've told you; I have no say in that."

"Of course." Rylian's scorn was creeping back out. "Or rather you choose not to."

"I choose to keep out of business that isn't my own. Godrik made it clear to me it is a Vandarian issue. You heard him, Rylian. The Windblade will go to his son, until the Sword of Varinar is recovered. If that happens, he'll choose another champion, as is his right as king. Sir Brontus Oloran, I would imagine. It is hard to dispute that he is next in line."

"And what a sorry affair that is. Sir Brontus is a gifted knight, but he was taken apart by Aleron during the Song of the First Blade, every report says. Elyon would do the same, I do not doubt, to Oloran, Taynar, all of them." He drank his wine, moved to the drinks table, and set down his cup. "But I can see your mind is not for turning. Perhaps you have other plans at hand? It wouldn't surprise me, given your recent record." He refilled his cup, took another sip. A frost seemed to fill the air. "Hadrin's ramblings," he then said. "Do you believe them?"

"The dragon sightings? Of course." Janilah was happy for the change in topic. The Rat King of Rasalan had regaled the council of his latest sightings in the Eye of Rasalan, when queried on it by King Godrik. He'd spoken of a great dragon, black and red, wreathed in flame, bringing death on a calamitous level. *A shadow over all the world,* he termed it, dramatically. Well they all knew that. You didn't go to war with Agarath without knowing you might have to slay a dragon or two. And fire and shadow and ash, all that came with the territory. "Hadrin will never master the Eye like his father did. We cannot rely on him to give any forewarning of attacks."

Rylian nodded pensively. "He seemed sincere, I'll say that for the man. I even spotted a bead of sweat on his brow as he spoke. He seems to think some catastrophe is approaching."

"And he's right. All the world is on the verge of total war. Hundreds, even thousands have already been lost to the early sallies and assaults. There have been over a dozen small towns razed to the ground by dragonfire along the Black Coast of Vandar, and these reports from the south...hundreds of northmen have been murdered in Solas, Lumos, Sutrek, Aram, and every great city and town in between, perhaps many more than that. Yet this is but the calm that precedes the storm. There is no insight in Hadrin seeing the approach of some catastrophe; all war is such, is it not?"

"It depends whether you win or not."

"In part, yes. But lines are fine in war, as you know. One side can suffer more loss of life, but gain more land. Who then is the victor?"

"Both. Neither." Rylian waved a hand, dismissive. "War is fickle, Father, and this one we've been fighting for over three thousand years.

The ascendency is always shifting. A thousand years ago the Agarathi held lands all across the north. During the time of Rufus Taynar and Oswald Manfrey four centuries past *we* ruled the lands east of the Ashmount, and had forts and garrisons through much of Aramatia. There are examples like this throughout our history. Lands change hands. Hundreds of thousands die. And here we still are, ready to do it all again."

"For the last time," said Janilah. "Perspective is important, Rylian. To some insects, a day is a lifetime. To men they are fleeting, one of tens of thousands we suffer and see. War is much the same. Each battle, each war, each Renewal...they all blur into one eventually. It's a game, son, played by gods. And that game is coming to an end."

"So people say." Rylian took a final sip of wine, placed down his cup, and moved to the door. "The Last Renewal...or perhaps just the *next one*." He shrugged. "It makes no matter in the end. We'll try to win it all the same." With that, he strolled away, disappearing down the spiral steps.

Janilah considered his son's words as he made his way back to his chambers, trailed by Sir Owen, Sir Maxwell, and Sir Edwyn today. *He is more thoughtful than he once was, more cynical. This last year has tested him.* Not long ago, Rylian was the model son Janilah wanted, an inspirational and astute commander, fearsome champion, loyal to his liege and unwavering in his support. *I have driven much of that out of him,* Janilah had to concede. *But the champion remains, the commander, the hero. Does it matter that he no longer trusts me? He will still fight to win this war all the same.*

Rylian was still in his thoughts when he reached his solar to find Cecilia there. *My bastard daughter, who serves me still.* "You're wondering how it went?" he said.

"Why else would I be here?"

"Only the gods know that." Janilah poured himself a cup of hot wine, for his chest. His physician had given him a special brew to add to it. He tipped a bit of the tonic in, swirled.

Behind him, Cecilia tittered. "Now what's that? Some new flavour for your wine?"

"Yes," he lied. He took to the seat behind his broad oak desk; Cecilia was perched by the window, as ever. Outside, the snows were coming down thicker, hiding the world in white. It had come on quickly; when he'd crossed through the yard from the Black Tower the fall had still been light. "Storm's coming," he said.

"It'll last days, the augurs say," Cecilia sighed. "Master Bagly says five, Master Cerwyn over a week. Others claim it'll last ten days or more. Seems we'll be locked in tight up here throughout the wedding festivities. What joy." She drew a breath, smiling, ever in her happy little world. Outwardly, anyway. *There's a great darkness in her too,* he knew. "So, tell me...how did it go?"

"Well enough."

"That's all you're going to give me?" She frowned, playful. "I didn't climb all these steps to hear 'well enough', Father. Go on, you can elaborate."

Something cracked in him. "You forget yourself," he barked at her. "Don't ever demand words of me again."

She shrunk back a little. "I was only..."

"Joking, I know. Half of what you say is a joke. I'm in no mood for it."

You never are, or never were, her eyes said. He knew that full well, but he'd taken out his displeasure on her more often of late. That was her job, though. She was deep in his counsel, a sounding board to whom he could vent. That was the bargain. For the payment of his secrets, his anger was the price. "I'll speak to you of it later. Go."

She began to slide from her seat, then stopped. "This must be Rylian," she said, a little stiff. "You always grow rageful when you speak to him these days."

"Rylian is my son and heir. You are my bastard daughter." He set two dark eyes on her. *My son turns from me, and leaves me with this harlot. You made that bed yourself,* a voice inside him said to that. *You sired her to be your schemer, Rylian your champion. But why couldn't Rylian be both? Why couldn't he understand?*

"Your bastard daughter who keeps your *closest* counsel," Cecilia said.

A threat, Janilah saw. "You threaten to unveil me?"

"Of course not. Who would believe the Bastard Bitch of Blakewood? And what is there to unveil anyway? The whole city whispers of your treacheries, Father."

"Let them..." he started.

"Let them," she agreed, her voice a purr. "Whatever they think of you, they still stand in line. Let the sheep bleat. Why should livestock concern a lion like you?"

He liked the sentiment well enough, but it wasn't just sheep who were bleating. "Rylian wants Robbert to wed the Daecar girl," he said. *Her counsel will be worth hearing on that,* he decided. In matters of war Cecilia was worthless, but her wits were valuable elsewhere. "I sense Elyon Daecar's hand in it. He was with Rylian in the Prince's Tower, I'm told, prior to the council meeting. I have to give him credit...the boy is sharper than I knew. He seeks to drive distance between me and my son, and furnish more support for his own house and claim. Rylian likes the boy; he sees him as a young Amron, no doubt. He'll seek to raise the Daecars to the crown, when this is all done. Elyon knows this, and he's using it. He's shrewd, as I say."

"And dangerous," Cecilia said. "Dangerous and growing in support. That Daecar name has a power to it, a power Elyon is better learning to wield." She set her sultry brown eyes on him. "You should remove him from the picture."

Janilah sat back, frowned. "Kill him? I can't. I'd bring half of Vandar down on me."

"That depends on how you do it."

Janilah didn't want to hear it. "Elyon can scheme as he likes. Rylian will soon be sailing to Aramatia to take Eagle's Perch, his thoughts on blood and conquest."

"And Elyon?"

"Isn't for me to command."

"You should kill him, Father." Cecilia had some twisted look in her eye. "Elyon denied me my prize, that Tilda girl. Let me punish him for that."

"Your prize is of no consequence. If Elyon should come to harm..."

"I know a way." That caught his interest, just the way she said it. "A way that would keep your hands quite free of blood, I assure you. Though, you'd have to risk one of your *pets* for it...I'm sure that won't trouble you too much, to be rid of the Daecar boy's interferences."

Janilah drew on his wine. *I've bred a spider,* he thought, *weaving her wicked web.* "I didn't realise you hated him so much."

"He tricked me, he and that Aramatian bitch. I don't forget, Father."

You get that from me, he might have said. Instead, he'd heard enough. "Let me consider it. You can bring me details on this plan of yours later. I weary of this scheming for one day. Leave me."

She left without another word.

He had no engagement that night, no privy audience, no celebratory feast. A rare bit of respite awaited, though not from his thoughts... those were unsleeping, a constant noise in his head. He took his wine to the balcony, though the snows were coming down too heavily, blowing in from under the stone roof and settling upon the terrace floor. Still, he stood there for a while and looked to the skies.

I should have owned those by now too, he thought. Any Blade of Vandar took time to master, but a man with powerful enough blood could quickly grow strong in the basics. *If Taynar had given me the Windblade as promised, I might be out there now, soaring.* That had been his plan, to have time to learn the ways of each blade, one after another, to train with them, master them, so that when they were eventually combined, he might know better how to wield the united Heart of Vandar. Yet that hope seemed lost now. *Vesryn, Jonik...*Those names had become curses to him, creatures of betrayal. *And Rylian asks me to help another Daecar claim one of my Blades?* He scoffed at the thought. *No, never. Those Blades are mine, mine by rights no matter what Godrik or anyone else might say. They were forged here in Ilithor, and will be remade here too. I have sought them out all my life. I have held the torch, I have lit the way...*

When he returned to the warmth of his solar, the hearth had burned down to cinders, and the place turned dull and dim. He took a seat behind his desk, filling himself another cup of wine, adding the tonic to soothe the burning in his chest.

Sitting in the gloom, he fell back into his musings. *The Windblade... where does he hide it?* It was close, so close, yet seemed so far away. Last night, Sir Kevyn Bolt had come to him with his latest report, slipping through the parts of the palace only his Six and a few others knew of. The Bull had arrived dressed in his cloak and cowl, only pulling back the hood when he stepped before the king. The light had been much the same as it was now, the candles guttering out, the hearth a feeble thing, a foreboding gloom filling the air. And Sir Kevyn's report had suited it; it had not been as Janilah had hoped.

"You haven't found it," he'd seen immediately.

The sworn sword shook his head. The coarse black stubble on his face had grown thicker, creeping high on his cheeks, low on his neck. There were heavy black bags hanging beneath his eyes. "I've been watching night and day, sire," he'd told his king, in a gruff voice. "Taynar keeps the chambers you gave him well guarded, but last night, I saw a chance, and managed to climb in through one of the balconies. I was careful, of course, to not be seen. Inside, I found several chests and trunks, all the same it seemed to me, all locked and fastened with godsteel chains. I searched where I could, but some rooms were occupied. He may have many more."

"He was said to have arrived with much luggage."

"Aye, he was, sire. But there's more. He's got guardsmen elsewhere in the city too, watching here and there. They work in shifts, all night and day. At least a dozen places, from the Marble Steps down to White Shadow."

"What places?"

"Three are storehouses, that I've seen. There are a few taverns too; I'm guessing he's using one or another of the rooms inside for storage, though which one, I couldn't say. The guards are always outside, never in. Might be that there's nothing there. It all stinks of diversion."

"Then he knows I'm going to try to steal it."

"I'd say that's likely, sire. There's another too, a private home. A stately place on the Marble Steps. I looked into it...seems the house is owned by a merchant called Rich Dick Mallory. He travels to Vandar a lot, apparently, wealthy as they come. Does a lot of dealings about the Ironmoors, so I'm guessing he's a friend of King Godrik's. Might have hidden the Windblade there."

"Can you get in?"

Sir Kevyn's big bald head bobbed right and left. "Hard to say. There are guards outside, I've seen, but might be a few ways I could get in to have a root around. Trouble is, this Dick Mallory's got a big family. Wife, litter of kids, a pair of mistresses too, if the rumours are to be believed, and a few bastards from them besides. Hard to sneak around with that lot infesting the place."

"No. This man sounds a cur."

"Rich and unscrupulous," nodded Sir Kevyn. "There are a few other rumours about him too. Nasty man, so I'm told. I was thinking... maybe I could stage a break-in. Or hire a few lowlifes for the job, see what they report back."

Janilah shook his head. "It would only alert Taynar if we go barging into one of his dens. I told you to be discreet, Sir Kevyn. I want you to remain unseen."

"Of course, my lord. As you say."

Janilah studied him. "But?"

"But...I'm not sure that's possible, sire, if you'll permit me saying so. You'd need the Nightblade for that." He laughed, uncomfortable.

Janilah didn't. "We don't have it, Sir Kevyn."

"No, sire, of course not." The Bull of Bolt shifted on his feet. "There is the other, though. The...the..."

"The Mistblade."

"Yes, sire. The Mistblade. You could use it, to..." He looked up. "To infiltrate..."

"I have no time to infiltrate, Sir Kevyn. I have council meetings, feasts, audiences, court to hold, my granddaughter's wedding to host, and more besides. Creeping through the inns of White Shadow is not high on my agenda."

"Then might I..."

"No. You couldn't wield it, not with your blood."

"No, sire. I wasn't meaning..."

"The Mistblade is *mine*, Sir Kevyn." Janilah's voice darkened. "Never ask me again to use it."

Gerrin had done the same, the last Janilah had seen him. It was the day the Shadowmaster had informed his king that the boy Jonik had stolen the Nightblade, all those long months ago. "I could use the other," Gerrin had told him. "It would make killing the boy easier..." Janilah had told him no, without pause, just as he did Sir Kevyn Bolt. *He might lose it, fall to it, try to take it from me as Vesryn did, as Jonik did. No, none will hold the Mistblade but me.*

And he didn't want to think about Gerrin either. The former sworn sword was a world away now, on Jonik's tail, though how well he was doing, Janilah couldn't say. *Might he have the Nightblade back by now? It was possible, though felt unlikely.* With all these disappointments, a part of Janilah had come to think that Gerrin was likely dead, caught up in all this trouble in the south.

Sir Kevyn had interrupted his thoughts. "I would never," the Bull of Bolt assured him. "Truly, sire, I wasn't meaning that. To hold the Mistablade...no, I know I couldn't master it, not as you have, my lord.

What I meant to say was...I might arrange to have all the locations searched at once. We would have to use force, yes, but it would be the best way to ensure we recover the blade. Taynar would have no time to move it, even if he got wind of..."

"Too direct," Janilah cut in. "I will not have you drawing Taynar blood, Sir Kevyn." The man was a bull, being direct was all he knew, but this needed more tact. "Nor do I want Godrik tying me to the theft when he finds the Windblade gone."

"But, he'll know..."

"Of course he will. But without proof, that matters not." *The man deserves it, for his betrayal.* Janilah had refused the gifts that Godrik had brought him, the swords and shields and spears, spices and silks and jewels. *That mightn't have been wise,* he realised after. It made it clearer than ever that he would seek to take what was owed him, sooner or later, and no doubt that had driven Taynar to arrange for all these decoys and diversions. But still..."I need a location, Sir Kevyn," he had commanded. "Go out and find me one."

He'll be out there now, Janilah thought, as he moved to the window in his solar, taking the window seat on which Cecilia liked to lounge. It smelled of her, so often was she here. He looked through the darkening snowy skies, down through the city. The Marble Steps was the finest district in Ilithor, perched beneath the palace and temple of Ilith, a network of staircases and bridges and glorious white walkways, with many sumptuous and stately homes erected among the peaks and prominences.

Below was the Sentinels, where soldiers made their home, with barracks and stables and yards for training, and beneath that, separated by a further wall and gate, stood Many Markets, whose name was self explanatory. After that came White Shadow, the city's most populous district, home to lowborn mostly, though many were skilled workers. It was the draw of Ilithor for most, with shops, taverns, shows, and everything in between to kindle one's fancy. From his high lofty nest atop the King's Tower, Janilah could see a portion of the Marble Steps only. The rest was hidden behind a white wall of falling snow, concealing all before him.

Once, he'd have taken Sir Kevyn's advice. He'd have returned to his throne room, taken the Mistblade from its secret chamber, donned a heavy fur cloak, and melted off into the streets and squares below to conduct his own search for the Windblade. But now, the mere thought of it was exhausting. He felt weary to his bones, and old. He'd seen sixty five summers, but had never felt the weight of those years on his back. Now he did. The years, the secrets, the lies, the treacheries. The burden had grown crushing.

But I can bear it, I must bear it, I will bear it yet longer. He returned to his desk, refilled his wine once more, added the tonic, and drank. It gave him some relief, fortifying him against his bitter thoughts. *I must feel young again,* he thought, *if only for a time. I must take action, as I once did.*

Age was a curse upon all mankind, one that all men had to bear. *Even kings,* he thought, *with Varin blood so rich as mine.* Once that hadn't been the case. When the gods fell, and their followers lost the power of immortality, they still lived for many hundreds of years. Their sons and daughters did too, lest they be slain prematurely, but each generation that power waned, dimming as the light of a star at the break of day.

And now here we are, cursed to endure regular lifespans. Even the late King Godrin, direct of the line of Thala, had grown withered and rotten before his death. He'd been some way north of ninety, but wouldn't have lived much longer, even if Hadrin hadn't cut open his throat. *We are mortal men,* Janilah thought, *the magic in our blood failing.* To hold a Blade of Vandar made one feel part-divine. But what would it be like to hold two? To hold three? To hold all of them combined? Janilah's hope of ever knowing was guttering out like the candles about him. *My hope has cooled and darkened, like the last embers in the hearth.*

He drained his wine, and drained another, to calm the pain in his chest, in his head. *How to blow that blaze alight again?* he wondered. *How to reignite my hope?* Finding the Windblade would be a start. Vesryn, Jonik, Ranulf Shackton and Vincent Rose and the missing page in the Book of Thala...all were being hunted. *But the Windblade, that is here. It is here right now, somewhere in this city, and that is something I can take care of myself.*

He rose, a little unsteady on his feet. The wine was thick in his blood. *I must feel young again, if only for a time. I must clutch a part of a god in my grasp. I must remember what it is to feel divine.*

He didn't question his decision. Donning his thick fur cloak, Janilah Lukar rolled back the years. He ventured out through the private passages in his palace, dismissing Sir Owen and the others when they tried to follow. *No, I will go alone*. He came to his throne room, moved into his office, passed through the hidden door and into the hidden chamber. There it lay, alone in its groove on the carved stone table, four others sitting empty beside it. The Mistblade, glowing a soft cobalt blue.

Janilah stepped toward it, took it to his grasp, and let his form dematerialise. A smile warmed his face; he felt young again, stronger, fiercer. A whisper fluttered through his head, the echo of a god, but he ignored it as he always did, as he'd learned to do, as he *had* to do.

Turning, he slid the blade into the sheath hidden beneath his cloak, pulled up his cowl, and bled out into the night.

31

Jonik

"We'll take them with us," said Emeric Manfrey, gesturing to Vincent Rose's armed guards. A half dozen of the Sunshine Swords had accompanied them from the merchant's manor that morning, each wearing a fine suit of silver scale mail armour and lightweight golden cloaks, armed with their gilded swords.

There were two Bladeborn with them too - on that the merchant had told no lie - though neither was of true blood. One was a gruff old mercenary from the Ironmoors of Vandar, gaunt of face and grey of hair, with cold pale skin the colour of pitted stone. He was a bastard born of a lesser branch of House Strand, some distant relation of Lord Styron the Strong, he said, and went by the name Harden. The second was Kazil, younger and bigger than the first, a broad-chested figure of mixed heritage, with thick black hair on his arms and cheeks that told of his Piseki ancestry. "My mother was Piseki," he'd told them, in a guttural growl, "my father of the north, somewhere. He bedded her in the war. She's dead. Him, who knows? Left me with some Varin blood, though. I can hold godsteel well enough."

Along with the half dozen Sunshine Swords, the two Bladeborn mercenaries made up the merchant's personal guard. Vincent Rose looked at Emeric, balking. "*All* of them? You want to take...all of them? What if someone should come by while you're gone? I'd be left undefended."

"No one will come by, Vincent," said Emeric, coolly. "We're in the middle of the desert. Who would trouble themselves to come this way?"

"Pal Palek's men," the merchant said, shrugging. He'd accoutred himself in simple silken attire that day, a pale yellow for camouflaging against the light golden hue of the sand. "They come and go occasionally. If one should..."

"You'll be nicely hidden among that copse of cacti and well out of sight," Emeric said, pointing to a spread of trees and shrubs nearby. "And you'll have Braxton with you too, should you need protecting."

Rose saw straight through that. "So now I see why he came," he said, looking into Braxton's horrifying grin. "He's your insurance. To kill me if I betray you?"

The man had it right. "You're a snake, Rose, everyone knows it," declared Borrus. "Brown will stay with you until we get back. If we don't, well..." He ran a finger across his neck. "Best speak up now if you've arranged some trap."

Vincent Rose just looked indignant. "A trap? Why on earth would I want to try to trap you? Did you not hear the bargain we struck yesterday? I want your protection, not your lives."

"A snake's hisses can be hard to trust." Borrus slapped the man on the back with a meaty paw. "We'll see you soon, with a few more men in tow, hopefully."

They left him at that, a round dozen in number, the six sellswords and brace of Bladeborn mercenaries accompanied by Jonik, Emeric, Borrus, and Jack, who had insisted on coming to get a taste of battle. "My training's been going well, and I'll need to draw my sword for you eventually, Ghost," he'd said the night before. "If not now, when?"

Never, Jonik had thought, though didn't say the word for fear of offending him. It didn't matter how skilled Jack became with the blade, he wasn't Bladeborn and never would be. Among such a troop he would always be out of his depth. "Stay close to Emeric," he told him instead. "I'll ask him to keep an eye on you."

Jack had seemed happy enough with that, though when young Devin asked for the same treatment, Jonik told him a straight 'no'. "You're too young, Dev, and we don't know what we're going to face. I can't be having both you and Jack along with us. We'll take you next time, OK?"

Devin grumbled some agreement, but seemed none too happy about it. Such was the curse of leadership, Jonik had come to learn. It was impossible to please everyone.

Though only a few short hours past dawn, the sun was already growing hot as it rose up swiftly in the east. A shimmer of heat was beginning to dance upon the sands. According to Rose, the sandstone fortress of the Moonlord Pal Palek was a mere half mile ahead, though there would be watch-posts and sentries hidden about its border, erected upon the hills and dunes. "I'll have to deal with them myself," Jonik said to Emeric, as they led from the front. "If they see us coming, they'll alert the rest of the guards. Best if we can creep up on them unseen."

"Unseen," repeated Sir Borrus Kanabar, joining them. "Hard to go unseen in broad daylight, boy, even with the Nightblade."

"*I* can," Jonik said, with a note of pride.

Borrus raised a single eyebrow "Truly?"

"Near enough," Jonik told him. "There might be a black wisp or two, but not something you'd see unless you were really looking for it."

Borrus pursed his lips. He seemed like he was about to praise him, but decided it better not to. "Well, I'll believe it when I see it," he said instead, churlishly.

The walk took a further ten minutes at a slow pace, before they came in behind a shallow sand dune that gave them shelter from the lands ahead. They'd travelled from Sutrek on camelback, great Piseki camels bigger even than destriers and strong enough to bear godsteel, but had left them with Rose and Braxton so as to approach the fort afoot. "It's right up there," old Harden said. He was wearing a worn grey cloak to shield against the glare of the sun, hood up. Beneath he had boiled leathers and rusted mail that had seen much use by its look.

"You've been here before?" Borrus asked him.

"Once, years ago. Wouldn't have known the way from Sutrek but recognise the area now."

Jonik had no idea how. The entire desert looked the same to him, endless and featureless but for the occasional sprout of rocks and dried up desert shrubs.

"Do you know where the sentries will be?" Emeric asked.

The old man shook his head. "High up," is all he said. "Where the views are best."

"The greybeard is wise," Kazil gave a grin, his face wide and more thickly bristled than any Jonik had ever seen. He had a sarcastic way about him. Harden just looked stern and humourless, a common feature of men of the Ironmoors.

"Wait for my signal," Jonik told them. "Once I've cleared a path, you come running." He turned to Sir Borrus Kanabar as he drew out the Nightblade. "Night night, Borrus." He disappeared from sight, to an audible round of gasps.

Smiling, Jonik paced off, his feet leaving impressions in the sand as he went. That might be a problem. He moved swiftly around the sandbank, staying as low as he could, keeping to what shadows there were as the sun continued its leisurely climb. Ahead, he could see the vague shape of walls amidst the dunes, low slung towers further on. Vincent Rose had explained to them last night that the stronghold had been erected within a valley of sorts, well concealed by the gentle rise of the lands about it. Some of those summits were solid hills of stone, others heaps of sand that were constantly shifting over time like waves on the ocean, slowed to a glacial crawl. Jonik imagined any permanent sentry posts would be erected upon solid foundations.

He found firm footing and began moving up, wisps of black smoke occasionally stirring about him. Those annoyed him. His mastery was not yet complete. When he reached the top of the nearest rise he scanned and saw a well camouflaged shelter looking away to the east, hidden amidst a jut of rocks. He went in for a closer inspection, but found that it was unmanned. The next he saw was the same, and the next. *Curious*, he thought. Perhaps Pal Palek only ordered for a sentry guard to stand vigil when he was present. Or perhaps the guards he left here simply abandoned that duty when their master was gone. Either way, it made things a little easier.

Jonik turned and unveiled himself, appearing upon the top of the nearest hill in a puff of black smoke. He lifted his blade and waved. A moment later, they came running.

Jonik rushed on down the hillside to join them. "No sentries," he said.

"Blast," grunted Borrus. "There better be *some* Patriots inside. It's high time I rid myself of that life debt, boy. I'm sick of having it hanging over my head."

"You'll get your chance."

A life for a life, that had been the bargain. Borrus needed only to slay a single foe and his oath would be discharged, his service complete, the Barrel Knight free to make his way home, with or without them. Rude and truculent and boorish though he was, a part of Jonik had learned to like having the man around. He didn't much care to see him fulfil that oath just yet.

Borrus didn't miss the smile. "What's that look, Shadowboy? I've never seen you look so devious."

"Shadowboy's better than Shadowknight, I suppose."

"That doesn't answer my question..."

"Quiet now, Borrus." Jonik gave him a smile. "We wouldn't want to alert the enemy, would we?"

The Varin Knight grumbled something, but by then they were rushing toward the fortress's arched opening, accessed down a narrow ridge where the rock rose higher on either side. Beyond lay a broad dusty courtyard, the cobbles covered in a coat of sand, with a large sandstone structure further on, three storeys of thick yellow stone with squat towers at its corners.

To the right Jonik spotted a stable, a well, a training yard, several storehouses. Left was a pair of single storey barracks, a tall watchtower that looked half in ruin, and all about them were many gardens and enclosures filled with rich green vegetation that contrasted starkly against the dust and sand and chipped flaxen stone of the buildings within the compound. No sooner had they sped onto the courtyard than the roars and bellows and hisses and caws filled the air, a cacophony of noise clattering from left and right, high and low as the animals of Pal Palek's famed menagerie called out in greeting at their arrival.

"They will bring every guard down on us," grim-faced Harden said.

"Good," declared Borrus Kanabar, drawing Red Wrath.

"Palek may have given orders to kill the prisoners if his defences are breached," worried Emeric. "I'll go, make them safe. "Harden, Kazil, with me."

"And you, Jack," Jonik ordered. "Go with them."

Jack had paled a little. "Yes...um, right."

They set to it, Emeric rushing for the central mansion, following the directions Vincent Rose had given them. That left Jonik behind with Borrus and the Sunshine Swords. Their captain was a man called Sansullio, a clean-shaven Lumaran with deep dark skin and piercing purply-black eyes who had some noble blood in him, Jonik did not doubt. The Company of the Sunshine Sword was old, he'd learned last night, and attractive to men seeking adventure, often luring into its web of rogues lesser sons of greater sires. Many had Lightborn ties, and some had even bonded sunwolves and starcats, it was said, with the rest only selected after rigorous vetting. To a man they were skilled with sword and spear and quite able to stand toe-to-toe with weaker Bladeborn, Sansullio had claimed with pride. He drew his gilded steel blade now, and pointed it across the yard. "They come."

A host of men were emerging from a barracks there, rushing through the stone exit in a cloud of orange dust. The typical patchwork armour and assorted blades, blunts, spears and swords of the Patriots of Lumara were on full show. War cries rang out as they saw the armed intruders and came charging forward.

At that very same moment, Jonik caught a glimpse of movement on the other side of the courtyard. Two sunwolves were creeping out of the stables, yawning and stretching. They were several times the size of regular northern wolves, near big as horses and gold all over, with thicker fur about their necks and shoulders and deep amber eyes ringed in black. As soon as they spotted the host their languid posture took on an altogether different frame. Both snarled and tensed and began prowling forward menacingly, forming a pincer with the guards coming from the left.

"I suppose we'll deal with those," Borrus Kanabar said casually, gesturing to the wolves with his ancestral blade.

"I think that would be best," agreed Sansullio. He was of a height with Borrus, splitting six and seven feet, with long arms and a slim body wonderfully adapted to swordsmanship. There was a grace to him common among those who'd trained in the fluid fighting styles of the south. "Come, men, let us dance." He led his soldiers into the fray.

The clash and clangour of combat soon filled the yard as the kiss of steel rang out. Borrus was already fast on the move, marauding toward the incoming sunwolves, their claws ripping chips from the stone cobbles as they ran. Jonik gave chase, blinking out of sight. As Borrus reached the first beast and swung upward at its throat, Jonik deftly put his own sword in the way, blocking the shot. The sunwolf growled and made to bite down on the big knight, but he was too swift and spun away, perplexed. "Shadowboy, was that you!" He looked around. "Show yourself you blasted sneak!"

Jonik grinned. The Nightblade was laughing. *We are one,* he thought.

"There you are...I...I can see you! Ha!" Borrus was looking entirely the wrong way, judging a wisp of dust to be Jonik. "Seems you haven't mastered the blade after all, boy!"

"I'm behind you, Borrus."

The man almost keeled over in fright, but their games had to end there; there were two gigantic wolves to deal with. As Borrus spun, Jonik took off, rushing at the nearest beast, upswinging through its golden mane and jaw, which split asunder in a shower of blood and teeth and bone. The wolf's front legs gave way beneath it, body sliding bloodily to the floor. A plaintive whimper broke out from the ruin of its throat, and Jonik would not see it suffer. He thrust the Nightblade through its skull and into its brain to end the beast's pain. Not a moment of that felt good to him. But the Nightblade, it was purring.

"Ah, so there are you!" Borrus exclaimed behind him. "Yes, I see you. Don't think I don't, boy."

Jonik removed his cloak and let his form breathe back into the burning daylight. "You saw the wolf die. You didn't see *me*."

Borrus laughed. The second wolf was charging him. "Excuse me while I deal with this foul beast." He turned to face the sunwolf, but Jonik wasn't going to allow that. He puffed out of sight again in a breath of black smoke and slipped in to intercept the creature, driving the Nightblade through its neck before it could get within five yards of Red Wrath. The wolf went down in an instant, its throat severed, blood gushing to the cobbles. "Blast you, that one was mine!" Borrus bellowed.

Jonik reappeared again. "Oh I'm sorry, Sir Borrus. The Nightblade compelled me." He grinned a mocking grin and set off.

Sansullio was doing his dance across the yard, skipping from foot to foot as he pirouetted and parried, deflecting the attentions of a pair of Patriots with a deftness rare seen. When one got frustrated and rushed at him, his purple eyes lit up and he went to one knee, slashing right through the man's gut. His innards squirmed out onto the baking pavestones, hot and steaming. The second man judged it better to dance with someone else.

No matter which partner they chose, they'd not last long, Jonik could see. He held back to watch, letting the Sunshine Swords show their skills, and goodness were they good. Each moved well and in rhythm, often pairing with another, moving in and out in unison, covering defence and attack as though of one and the same mind. Half a dozen Patriots were already dead or mortally wounded, moaning on the floor, and only a small handful remained. Only one of the sellswords looked to have suffered an injury, cradling a bloody arm as he drew back from the fighting.

"Right, let's be done with this," Borrus Kanabar said impatiently. "I didn't come to watch a dance. This isn't how war is done." He tramped toward the nearest enemy, barging away one of the sellswords as he went, but just as he was about to swing, Jonik darted in and killed the Patriot first.

Borrus Kanabar was incandescent. "WHAT ARE YOU DOING, DAMN YOU!" A shade of purple had climbed all the way up his neck and into his flabby cheeks. He stared at him in bewilderment. "That's the second time you've taken my kill. Don't you *ever* get in the way of Red Wrath again, do you hear me! Never!"

"I thought he had you, Sir Borrus. I was only trying to protect you."

"Protect...protect me? *Me*? Are you mad, boy! Has that blade driven you round the bend?" He blasted a breath, turned his eyes around. Only one man was left standing. He set off toward him, but made it a mere pace before one of the Sunshine Swords swung through his neck and opened his gullet. Borrus Kanabar let out a roar as though he was the one who was dying.

The sellswords, led by their gallant captain Sansullio, joined the cry. Up went their gilded blades, catching the light, as they roared out their victory. And all about them, the beasts of Palek's menagerie were singing along with them.

"You truly are a bastard," Borrus said in a low growl. "I know your game. You want to hang that life debt around my neck like an anchor, until you have proper need of me." He shook his head, though something in Borrus Kanabar seemed proud of him for that. "You bloody bastard," he said again, though this time there was a smile creeping onto his face. "That's just the sort of thing Elyon would do. Seems you've got more in common with him than you might think."

Jonik held his innocence. "You think too much of me, Sir Borrus. I have no mind for such tricks."

"Yes, well...you can't kill everyone, Shadowboy. I'm wise to you now. Next time we find ourselves in a spot of bother, I'll clear that debt and be gone."

"Well, you might need to clear it a few times," Jonik said, with a dry smile. "I did save your life a couple of times just now. That's two more debts you owe me, sir."

"Don't push it." Kanabar's mirth was gone. "Do *not* push me, boy."

Sansullio stepped in. "What are your orders?" The question was addressed at Jonik, which didn't much help Kanabar's mood.

"Um...clear the compound, Sansullio," Jonik said. "Make sure there's no one else here. Borrus and I are going to head to the dungeons."

"Very good." Sansullio nodded and set off.

They knew where the dungeons were by the directions that Vincent Rose had outlined, yet didn't need them. The trails of blood and dead bodies were enough, and the lower they got, the thicker the reek of foul air became. "It stinks of death and rot and shit all in one," Borrus complained, as they descended a steep stone stair, moving into the putrid darkness.

"Don't forget the piss," Jonik added. That was most pronounced of all to him.

At the bottom of those steps, and down a short corridor, they came upon a long dark cavern of ancient stone, the cracked walls spotted with lichen, a central walkway spreading into the darkness left and right, punctuated by the occasional glow of torchlight. Either side of that walkway were deep pits topped by iron grates, cells for the doomed and the damned, and from them came voices, mumbling and groaning and calling out for help. Harden was awaiting them. "Ah, it's you," he said, his worn godsteel blade misting softly in the dimness. "How is it above? I thought I heard the sounds of battle."

"You heard right," Borrus told him, his voice a little choked by the stink and the sounds. "How many are there?"

"Prisoners?" The gaunt Ironmoorer shrugged. "The others are

trying to figure that out now. They've been going up and down, counting. Seems a lot, though, by the voices."

Jonik could perceive many dozens of them, calling out from their pits. "Your master sold this short," he said, with a bite of anger in his words. "This place is inhuman."

"You'll not find me disagreeing with that, lad," said the surly old mercenary. "I'm not much fond of hearing Vincent Rose called my master, though. Suppose he is, if you want to get technical, but sounds sour on the ear, I'll tell you."

"The man's a perfumed upstart," Borrus said, "with not a scruple to his name. I've met merchants like him before; they gather up a bit of coin and think they're worthy of a seat at the table. They're not and never will be. But they'll keep scrambling all the same."

And you're the other side of that coin, Jonik thought, though decided it wiser not to say. Borrus was pompous and superior and talked down to about everyone around him. But at least he was honest, a quality Vincent Rose seemed to lack, he of the many masks and sly little smirks. Vincent Rose had that quality of smiling with his lips and not his eyes and those sorts of men Jonik could never take into his confidence. Borrus was just a boor, impolite but authentic. He didn't have it in him to scheme.

"We'll need provisions for these men," Jonik said. "I'd not counted on there being so many."

"There are women here too," Harden said. "Listen careful and you can hear them. Some crazed wench was screaming hard down that way, before the others went down there. I've seen others too, in the pits. Gods know what they've been subjected to here." The old man shuddered.

This is going to take more work than I thought, Jonik realised. They'd come to find a few fighting men, hopefully Bladeborn, to join their cause, but most likely the majority here would be good for little, judging by the conditions they'd been kept in. Could they just pluck out those they wanted, and leave the rest? The thought passed through his mind but didn't linger. Of course they couldn't. They had a duty now to free them, every man and every woman, and see their health restored.

He stepped away, leaving the others where they were, and moved down that central walkway between the pits and cells. Voices called out to him, begging for food and freedom. Hands reached to the air, clutching wildly for the bars beyond their grasp. Some of the prisoners seemed in adequate health, others stick-thin and skeletal, with barely enough energy to lift their heads as he passed. Others still were dead or near-enough, already starting to rot. Then there were the mutterers and madmen, the weepers and wailers, men pacing side to side or sitting in place, swaying. The hollow eyes were everywhere, staring from the shadows. And that stink...that suffocating stench that suffused the air was all encompassing, pervasive, truly inescapable.

He found his friends at the far end, buried in the deepest darkest recesses of the dungeons, standing over a pit only a couple away from the wall. Emeric was talking to the man inside, Kazil standing beside him, trying his best not to retch. Jack drew away as he saw Jonik appear. "Ghost, you're safe...good." There was a flutter in his voice, a strange sort of excitement mixed with horror. Blood was spattered across his face. Jonik saw a rip in his cloak, the studded leather jerkin he was wearing beneath it slashed red on his right flank.

He stepped in. "You're injured."

"A scratch," said Jack 'o the Marsh. "Emeric's checked it out and I'm fine. A few stitches will sort me out." He looked down the long dark tunnel. "Are the others OK? Borrus? Sansullio?"

Everyone seemed to like Sansullio. "They're fine. One of the Sunshine Swords took a wound to the arm, but that's it, last I saw. They're checking the rest of the compound. How many guards were there here? We must have passed a half dozen bodies on the way down."

"Sounds about right. I got one myself." He didn't grin, not here. Jack o' the Marsh fancied himself a warrior of promise and wasn't going to gloat over his first kill.

Still, Jonik was proud. "You can tell me about it later. Who's Emeric talking to?"

"Ranulf Shackton," Jack said at once. "Rose had him taken right down here with the crazies, it sounds. He doesn't seem to know how long he's been here."

"A month or so. Rose told us."

"I know. But time runs differently when you're locked away in the darkness. He says it feels like it's been much longer."

"Is he hurt?"

"Seems OK. Apparently the man's been imprisoned before, and for longer periods of time than this. Says there's a girl somewhere, called Leshie. A Bladeborn. He's not sure where she is but seems desperate that we find her. Kazil and I are going to search. You coming?"

Jonik shook his head. "Take Borrus as well, just in case. There might be more guards about." Suddenly he cared not if the Barrel Knight found a foe to complete his life debt. Jack's safety was more important.

"Right. Be well, Ghost. This...all this..." He gulped.

"I know." Jonik clasped his shoulder in brotherhood. Then off the Marshman went with Kazil, bleeding into the shadows.

Jonik drew a breath and stepped up to Emeric Manfrey's side. Beyond the iron bars of his cell sat a short man in dirtied rags, his hair matted and filthy, beard scraggly and wild, the flesh of his cheeks withered to the bone. His back was against the rear wall, one leg outstretched, the other propped up to his chest with his hands resting on his knee. It was an altogether too casual pose for a place such as this. The man turned his eyes to Jonik and smiled. "And this must be the famous Ghost of the Shadowfort. A pleasure to meet you, my friend."

"Ranulf Shackton," Jonik said. "I'm happy to find you in working order."

Down the passage, in the nearby pits, a man was clucking loudly like a hen. Ranulf smiled fondly. "Lord Cluck," he said. "You wouldn't believe he was a real lord once. Between clucks he can become quite talkative, you know." A woman began laughing hysterically in another pit, cackling like a crone. "The Moaning Maid," Ranulf told them. "And that man you hear mumbling incessantly is Sir Torvyn of the Riverlands, son of Lord Blackshaw. He was thought killed during the war but it seems he found his way down here instead. There are others like him too. Varin Knights. Emerald Guards, Suncoats. Seaborn and Forgeborn as well. Pal Palek was more than happy to boast of his greatest prizes."

He stood to his feet, glancing down at the skeleton that shared his cell. Jonik had only just noticed it, the body dressed in shrivelled ribbons of grey papery skin and tattered rags, the black sunken holes in the skull staring out vacantly. "He, I've not had the pleasure of a proper introduction with just yet," Ranulf said. "I have found him a fine cellmate all the same, a good listener, it's so." He looked at the bundle of bones with an almost sad expression. "I shall miss our conversations, my friend, even if they were a little...one-sided."

Emeric turned to Jonik. "We should get him out of here at once."

"And the rest," Jonik agreed. "There are Bladeborn here, then, as we'd hoped."

"Many, it sounds. And some names we'll likely know. Sir Torvyn Blackshaw was a gifted Varin Knight, and will have served with Sir Borrus during the war. The Blackshaws are bannermen of the Kanabars. Perhaps Borrus might help bring him around."

Jonik felt a stirring. His personal quest aside, this was important. "I'll cut the lock," he said, stepping forward, drawing the Nightblade. Ranulf watched on as he struck the lock free and pulled open the hatch in the grate. The drop was some ten feet deep. "Can you jump up and grab my hand?" Jonik asked. "I can pull you up."

Ranulf's eyes went to the side. "There should be a ladder on the far wall."

Jonik spotted it, dashed over, pulled it off its hooks. He returned to the cell and lowered it down. "Can you climb? You look a little underfed."

"I've been worse than underfed before, my friend. I can manage."

He did, climbing up the ladder a little shakily, but easily enough in the end. The stench of the man was almost overpowering up close. He was as small as he'd seemed from above, only five feet six or seven if Jonik judged it right, narrow at the shoulders and slender of frame, even accounting for his starvation. "My eternal thanks, gentlemen," he said, with courtesy. "Might I ask how you come to be here?"

"We came to liberate you and the others," Emeric said. "Your friend, Vincent Rose, was kind enough to lead us here."

"Ah yes, *my friend Vincent*. I trust he told you he brought me here himself, under false pretences no less."

"He told us you stole something of value."

"Steal would be the wrong word. But yes, I can see why he would think that. In truth I bear him little ill will for this, strange as that may sound. He had his reasons, as I had mine." He looked at Jonik with a curious expression. "And there is some fate here, I feel. I had faith that someone would come, I just...I didn't expect it to be you."

"That faith has been rewarded, Ranulf," said Emeric, seeming eager to shift things along. "But know that we did not come here for you. We seek warriors for a great quest. It seems we may have found some."

"A great quest, you say?" Ranulf smiled an honest smile. "You know, I have one of my own, or did before Vincent brought me here. So I say again, there is fate in your coming. You have liberated your warriors for yours, and liberated me for mine." He gave out a laugh, and turned his eyes to the pits. "Now, what can I do to help? I do believe I owe you a debt."

32

Saska

"I don't like that cat," grumbled Sir Ralston Whaleheart. "It's unnatural. When is it going to go away?"

Saska was looking through the drapes of the carriage, watching with a smile as the starcat loped along casually a little off the track, following them. "She's beautiful, don't you think? Have you ever seen a more elegant creature?"

"I have," Mellio said from the driver's seat. He could always be relied upon to join their conversations. He leaned back, smiling as usual. The only time Saska had seen that expression slip away was during the attack a few nights ago. He looked her in the eye. "You, my lady. The way you moved with that blade of yours...very elegant, yes. Very graceful."

Compliments from this man never felt quite sincere. Still, she smiled in thanks, and then asked, "And Rolly? Was he graceful with his greatsword, Mellio?"

"No." Mellio shook his head in an abrupt motion. His voice went more blunt than usual. Even his smile soured. "No, graceful is not the word I would use for Sir Ralston. I have never..." He gulped. "Such brutality, no, no, I...I do not have the stomach for it, or the words. The way you killed those men at the river...."

"They'd have killed us all if he hadn't," Saska said. "You and Pig included."

"This I know, yes. And for that I am thankful." The smuggler inclined his head to the Wall. "But...it makes sense, now. I did wonder who you were, given your size. Not many men as big as you, no, no. But Sir Ralston...the King's Wall. Yes, we know this name here in the south. You are said to have killed a dragon, during the last war. This is true, yes?"

"It was only a small one." Sir Ralston continued to polish the whale-head pommel of his blade with an oiled cloth.

"But this is where you got these burn scars, yes? I did think. You have many old wounds, but those burns...they looked like dragon-fire to me, when I saw you undressed at the river. Much of your flesh is covered in them."

The Wall's eyes were suddenly hard as flint. He gave Mellio a look to curdle milk.

"Yes, of...of course. You do not like to speak of this, I see. I will not press you further." The smuggler withdrew.

The carriage was rattling as loudly as ever, bumping along a narrow track just large enough to accommodate its width. Out front the horses were plodding along stoutly, used now to the presence of the deadly cat who'd decided to join them. Saska continued to watch her as she paced lazily under the sun some dozen or so metres away atop a shallow bank. She'd done that a lot over these last days, finding the cat's rhythmic movement entrancing, watching her for hours on end by day, letting her come near at night so she might lick her hands and face as she had when they'd first met, purring that rumbling purr all the while that lit a glow in Saska's heart the like she'd never felt before.

Last night, when Mellio had found a secluded spot to stop for the night where they might sleep outside of the carriage, Saska had even awoken to find the giant spotted cat sleeping beside her, that long lithe body stretched out upon the soil, dark as jet and peaceful. She'd smiled, savouring the moment as she watched the cat's smooth fur coat shimmer and sparkle like starlight, before the Wall noticed from his nightly vigil and called out to shoo the beast away.

The cat had quickly bolted, but not for long. By dawn she was back, watching them break their fast on heels of bread and hard old cheese and some figs that Pig had found growing along a riverbank nearby. And when they'd set off, the starcat had followed them once more, as she had for some four days, languidly loping in that idiosyncratic flow, looking for all the world like she could go on and on forever if she wanted.

And still, there she was. Happily escorting them on their way.

Saska grinned again, fully and hopelessly enamoured. "What do you think we should call her?"

"You shouldn't," the Wall grunted at once. "If you name her you'll want to keep her."

"*Keep* her," echoed Mellio, chuckling. "She is not a pet, sir. No no. The cat is bonded to the girl now. That is why she follows."

"Then stop this carriage and let me *sever* that bond." Sir Ralston gripped the hilt of his greatsword menacingly. "Northerners should not bond with southern beasts."

"But the girl is not northern, clearly." Mellio turned back again, drew the curtain aside, and slipped into the carriage to sit with them, uninvited, leaving Pig to take the reins. He shuffled into position next to Saska on the bench; there wasn't much space to sit beside the Wall. "I've been wanting to ask," he said to her. "About who you are. I knew this Wall of yours was Bladeborn all along, even if I didn't know who he was, exactly, but you...no, girl, no no, I did not think you would be Bladeborn, not with that colouring. But now it seems that you are Lightborn too. This is most curious to me. A most rare and unusual mix."

"And what of it?" broke in the Wall. "Your point, smuggler?"

"My point is that I am smuggling you into Aram, and..."

"You're not smuggling us anywhere," the Wall countered, not letting him finish. He'd been particularly peevish ever since the starcat had joined the company. To him she was a beast to be slain, no more.

"Oh? And what is all this, then?" Mellio asked, rising to his accusation. "I am a smuggler, and you are my hidden cargo. What is this if not smuggling?"

"*Transporting*," the giant grunted. "If you were smuggling us, you'd get us *inside* the city walls. But you're not. You're planning to leave us outside."

"This is true," Mellio admitted. "But wherever I take you in these lands, I will be smuggling you. You are not meant to be here, no. And already ten men are dead for it. Ten bad men, yes, and this is good that they are gone, but still...I am taking a risk. Without my horses and my carriage, how would you get to Aram?"

The Wall had no answer to that.

Mellio's smile grew victorious. "So..." He turned to Saska again. "Am I correct in assuming that you have some important errand to complete, yes? That perhaps you are more precious cargo than I thought, to be delivered to someone for an important purpose? You must be, for that starcat to have come to save you. You must have very strong Lightborn blood, yes, very strong. It is not common for that to happen, you know. Most Lightborn must go and find their beasts to bond. They do not usually come to them."

The Wall swung out his huge greatsword, until its point was directed right at Mellio's chest. "You talk too much, smuggler. Enough with these questions."

The man quelled, drawing back. "Yes, yes, if you insist. But please, do not point that blade at me. It...it makes me very nervous." He eyed the swirling mists with profound trepidation.

Saska agreed with the man. "He's just doing what he was paid to do, Rolly. You don't need to threaten him for being curious."

The Wall's massive blade swung back. He laid it across his lap. "It's my duty to keep you safe, my lady. I told you before, that includes from wagging tongues such as his. And this man asks too many questions."

"Curiosity is not a crime here in the south," Mellio said, laughing nervously. "You think I would betray you? After seeing what you both can do? Oh no, you know where I live. I will go to the stars never speaking a word of any of this. Why do you think I chose Pig to come with us? Mute men make trustworthy workers, yes." At the front, Pig snorted.

Saska glanced outside again. The lands here were much the same as those they'd passed for the last ten days; arid, hot, mostly barren, but with patches of grassland beginning to appear amid the rugged red tundra. The humidity wasn't quite so stifling as before either, which made for a refreshing relief. Mellio explained that it was to do with the higher elevation, and true enough, they'd been moving steadily uphill for some days, where the air was a little lighter and not so intolerably dense.

Saska scanned idly. The starcat wasn't where she'd been a few moments ago. She pulled the curtain back a little more, and stood to get a better look. The cat was nowhere to be seen. A spike of worry went through her. "She's gone. The cat. I can't see her." She strained to look, but could see nothing of the beautiful black feline. "Check your side, Rolly. See if she's out there."

The Wall reacted lazily to that, though poked his head out of the curtain to check. "Nothing," he said. "Maybe she's given up on you?" There was far too much hope in his voice for Saska's liking.

"She wouldn't."

"She might. Animals get bored. Perhaps the novelty of trailing us around has worn off."

Saska didn't like his tone. "And what do you know about it?"

"Enough." He continued polishing his blade.

Saska wasn't having it. "Enough? What does that mean?"

The giant shrugged. "Those animals are dangerous. Who knows when she might turn on you and take out your throat, like she did that bandit. I can't take that risk. I'm sworn to protect you..."

"She'll protect me too." Saska had gotten that sense about the cat. Their bond was new, yes, but strong and growing stronger. She turned again to look over the plains, worried the Wall might be right. Worried her beauty was gone.

"Do not fear so," Mellio offered, in sympathetic tones. "She has done this before, when other travellers pass by on the road. Starcats are skittish creatures, especially when they are newly bonded. It takes time for any wild animal to grow used to the presence of men."

Saska had noticed that before too. The cat did disappear occasionally when they passed carts and wagons and horses on the road, but so far as she could see, there weren't any nearby. She stood again and looked out, scanning up and down the path, taking the hilt of her dagger to enhance her vision. The view was good both ways. No wagons, wains, carts and carriages were visible upon the dusty track. No horses. No people. Not so far as she could see. "There's no one ahead or behind us. Not for miles."

"Then maybe she has gone to hunt?" Mellio suggested, showing a more delicate side. "Her own territory is a long way gone now, my lady. She does not know these lands, no, and might not have eaten for days. This is common with these creatures. She will hunt and eat and find us again. Their senses are excellent, and so are their instincts. She will return to you when she is ready, you'll see."

She didn't. Not that night, when they found a copse of trees in which to spend the evening, nor by morning when they continued back onto the road.

Saska's concerns mounted unreasonably. "I feel like I've lost someone important to me," she said, despondent, as Mellio ushered her into the carriage beneath a blood-red dawn. Overnight he'd been sympathetic where the Wall had just been silently smug and gloating, or so it seemed to her.

"It's much as you say," Mellio told her, that ever-present smile turned down in condolence. "You only had days with her, yes, but still, that is enough to secure a bond. It hurts when that is broken."

Sir Ralston looked like he wanted to say something, but decided to bite his tongue. Saska just collapsed onto the bench and glowered at him until the morning passed into afternoon and still, there was no sign.

When dusk fell that evening she'd all but given up hope. *It's a good thing really*, she reasoned, trying her best to rationalise something that she didn't truly understand. She had enough on her plate without having to worry about a giant black cat following her around day and night.

But still...it stung.

It stung more than she could say.

She'd read about the bond between man and beast in the south, but never truly appreciated it until now. The Fireborn said that when a bonded dragon died, a part of their soul died with them, a loss more profound than any northman could ever truly comprehend. It was worse than losing a loved one, they said, worse even than losing a child. It was losing yourself, darkening a part of you that would never again reach the light. The same was true among the Lightborn, some believed. Many great Sunriders and Starriders had been known to take themselves off into the wilderness and never return after their sunwolves and starcats died during the war. Others fell into long dark depressions, turning to the bottle and the brothels and other vices to overcome their agony, if only for a time. Others still had taken their own lives, committing that gravest of sins in a bid to escape their torment.

Strange as it was, Saska understood that better now. Her loss was but a fraction of such despair, a taste of it, no more. But all the same, she could see it, see the sacrifice that such men and women made when they bonded to a beast. To kill one was to kill the other too. There was no mercy in sparing half a soul, half a life. It was cruelty, Saska now knew, to leave a man so cursed.

That night they stopped beside a grassy knoll, with a brook babbling softly not far away. The air was cooler than it had been in weeks, scented sweet and pure, and Mellio permitted them to sleep outside under the stars. As they rolled out lengths of padded fabric on which to sleep, the Wall took himself away to the top of the hillock to stand sentinel overnight. By day he could doze within the carriage, knowing there were other eyes on watch, but the long quiet hours between dusk and dawn were when he was most vigilant.

Saska couldn't sleep that night. She felt restless and ill at ease, despite the bright twinkling stars above her, the soft whisper of the grasses bending in the breeze, the gentle trickling of the river nearby. She watched the moon wheeling overhead. She watched the stars twinkle and gleam. She listened to the calls of the wild, of the chirping of insects and deep rumblings of distant beasts, and wondered whether her starcat might be out there somewhere, searching for her, wondering where she was.

She rose. It was doing her little good to lie in thought. Mellio and Pig were snoring softly beside the carriage, the horses munching gratefully on the grasses at the base of the hill. Saska turned her gaze up, to where the shadow of Sir Ralston sat, looking out upon the silent plains. She scrambled up the hillside to join him beneath the bright golden glow of the moon.

"It's beautiful here," she said, moving to sit beside her giant guardian. He wore his cloak over his breastplate and leathers, his tree-trunk legs folded before him in a pose Saska didn't imagine a man his size could achieve. Cool as the air was, it wasn't cold enough for wool. "Why the cloak?" she asked him.

"It hides the gleam of my armour," he answered. "It can catch the moonlight on nights like this."

She smiled. *My noble guardian. Thinking of everything, as usual.*

"Are you not tired, my lady?"

"Can't sleep," she said, looking over the darkened plains. The vantage here from the summit of the hill gave a panoramic view of the lands around them. She looked back the way they'd come. The Wall must have seen some sadness in her eyes.

"I am sorry about the cat."

She nodded, mustering a solemn smile. "It's for the best. I've always tried to keep my guard up with people, to avoid getting hurt when they leave me or die. I just didn't expect that to happen with a wild starcat, out here on the Aramatian Plains."

"The bond is strong," the giant intoned. She couldn't judge whether it was a statement or a question. She answered as though the latter.

"Stronger than I'd expected."

"It's the Lightborn in you, the magic of Lumo in your blood." He thought for a moment. "I should not have been so callous. Any Bladeborn like me should understand the importance of a bond. If I were without my godsteel blades..." He shook his head in self-rebuke. "I spoke out of turn, and unfairly. I only hope you will forgive me."

"Already done." She reached out, gripped his hard, callused hand, her fingers wrapping around his like an infant's around an adult's. "You're sworn to protect me, Sir Ralston. You were only doing your duty."

"No. I was being selfish. I know that cat would never have harmed you. But me? Well, perhaps that is a different story." He smiled, a rare thing. There was a kindness to Sir Ralston's features, despite all those pits and scars, when his eyes sparkled in that way. His face was like a gnarled old tree, ugly and grim and leafless, but so fond to the children who climbed it.

And she had grown fond of this man, grunts and grumbles all. "It's in your blood to mistrust a creature like her. I don't blame you for that. But she'd never have tried to harm you. I'd have made sure of it."

She filled her lungs with a breath of clean air, idly turning her eyes over the plains once more. Each time she hoped to see a black shape in the night, running her way, lean and long-limbed and beautiful. She hid her disappointment. It would pass, she knew. "I was thinking earlier about Amron Daecar," she said, breaking the short silence.

The Wall raised an eyebrow, slashed with an old scar.

"You beat him once, didn't you? In a duel at one of the tourneys, back before the war."

"Only once. He defeated me on several other occasions. I never faced a more formidable opponent." He frowned at her. "You're wondering if he will recover from his wounds?"

She hadn't been thinking that at all. "I was wondering about his blade," she said.

"The Sword of Varinar?"

She shook her head. "The other one. His ancestral blade. The one he used to kill Vallath."

"Vallath's Ruin," the Wall said. He seemed confused. "You didn't know the name?"

"I knew," Saska said softly. Everyone knew. "I just wanted to hear you say it. I wondered which one you'd chose."

"I do not understand, my lady. I might just have easily have said the Mercyblade."

"But you didn't. I find that telling. Everyone has their preference when naming that blade. I used to think of it as the Mercyblade. I liked the thought, that he showed Prince Dulian mercy, and that mercy helped end a war. I've always thought there was something noble and poetic about that, something that fits in the stories and songs." She shrugged. "Vallath's Ruin implies death and defeat. I understand why people like it, but I never did."

"It's heroic," the Wall put in. "There is no fight more true than between Bladeborn knight and dragon with a Fireborn rider atop its back. Vallath's Ruin speaks to that instinct we all share. It tells a story in itself. That of our greatest champion defeating theirs in single combat. That is why the name is so loved."

Saska smiled wanly. She understood all that. She understood the merits of both names. But now the one she'd favoured - the Mercyblade - had soured on her tongue. "They might have called it the *Crueltyblade*," she found herself mumbling. Her eyes passed the plains again. A melancholy echoed inside her.

"My lady?"

She drew a sharp breath. "Ignore me. I'm being morose."

"I think I understand," the Wall said. His voice was deep as distant thunder. "What Amron did seemed a mercy to us, yes, but perhaps not to Dulian. I know how lost a man can became after the death of his bonded dragon. Many believe that the madness that took root in Dulian when he was king started that day at the Burning Rock."

"Were you there?" Saska asked suddenly. "I don't think I've ever asked you."

The giant's massive head swung left and right. "I had not yet recovered of my injuries. It is one of my great regrets that I wasn't present." He sounded ashamed.

"Well I for one am glad for it. Elsewise you might not be here now."

The Wall stared out. He hardly seemed to hear her. "I was absent from the greatest battle in centuries, perhaps a thousand years. All those who were there get to wear that badge of honour. I do not." He sighed deeply, and gripped the hilt of his greatsword. "Ever since then I have stood as a guardian, first to a king, and now to a princess. That duty has been the pride of my life. King Godrin, now you. You are more important than battles and blades and duels with dragons, my lady. I failed to be there at the Burning Rock, but I will not fail you, I swear it." He shifted all of a sudden to one knee. "I hope you believe me, Lady Saska. I hope and pray you do."

"With all my heart and soul, I do," Saska said on a breath. Her eyes were glistening with tears. She'd never seen the Wall so open, so doubtful. "You blame yourself for the river?" she asked him. "What happened that night..."

"I was almost too late. I should not have let you from my sight. I should have been there..."

"You were there. You were a few dozen metres upriver, and got there in good time. That isn't your fault, Rolly, it's not. Don't be so hard on yourself. I ordered you to leave me."

"I was embarrassed," he came back. "You were right. I have... women, they...my life has been one of service, my lady. I do not feel comfortable when..."

She put a hand to his once more. "I know. You don't have to explain. But I'm fine. I'm safe, Sir Ralston..."

"Because of your cat." He shifted back to sit down beside her. "It was the cat that leaped to save you when that brigand rushed in behind. That should have been me. I should never have let that happen."

"I had my blade with me," Saska countered. "If that was anyone's fault, it was mine. I was staring at her as she raced toward me. That's why the man came in behind me. Otherwise I'd have dealt with him myself. I got distracted, and almost died for it. That's *my* fault, Rolly, not yours. Mine."

He was already shaking his head, as though unable to accept that she could be at fault. "I should have insisted with the ship captain," he then said. "He was under obligation to take us directly to Aram. I should have held him to that oath."

"How? With a blade to Rikki's neck? No, that was my call too. I wasn't going to put them in danger. And we'll reach Aram soon. We're only a few days away now, Mellio says."

"And getting in?"

Saska wasn't sure about that yet. "We'll figure that out when we get there."

The Wall gave out a signature grunt then. "The king should have told me more," he said, showing a rare disapproval for the man he's served so loyally for almost two decades. "Godrin...he was always so cryptic. He might have made our task clearer. I do not think he expected us to come this way."

Saska had little idea what the late king did and didn't expect, in truth, nor what he had and hadn't foreseen. Yet she heard his words in her head all the same, words she continued to lean on. *You're exactly where you're meant to be.*

In the silence that followed, she found her hand rooting around in the small pockets of her dress, fetching out that little piece of pitted grey coral that had come to mean so much to her. It was the totem that reflected her Seaborn side, a side she often forgot about, for where she could fight with godsteel and bond with a southern beast, what use was it for her to hold her breath for twenty minutes or dive down deep beneath the waves?

She turned the rock between her fingers. Her conversation with Old Hob came back to mind once more, a conversation she'd not yet shared with her guardian. But now felt like the right time. "Old Hob said I have royal blood," she whispered, drawing the giant's dark eyes. She could see the confusion in them, gleaming in the moonlight. He knew already who her mother was thought to be. "On my father's side," she added.

The Wall considered that quietly, his brow rutted all the while. "You'd do well not to trust that old fortune teller," he told her, with a stern edge. "A piece of coral cannot tell your future, my lady."

She imagined that would be his response. It was the reason she'd not spoken of it yet. "But...if it could? Just humour me, Rolly. Do you know if any northern king or prince went south at that time? Ranulf always said that my father was an Ilithoran lord, but maybe that wasn't true. Maybe he was Ilithoran royalty instead."

The Wall understood her concern. "King Janilah never went south that I know of, if that worries you," he assured her. He despised the Tukoran king as much as anyone, Saska had come to see, and the tidings they'd been hearing from the north had only deepened that ire. Rumours that Mellio had learned at the fish markets of Matia. Rumours that spoke of Janilah's hand in King Godrin's death, and the killing of King Ellis Reynar too, of the Warrior King's steel grip closing around all the north. He had full and total control now, those whispers said. And for those in the south, that was worrisome indeed. A united north under the lead of a man like Janilah Lukar would not take long to strike in force.

And yes, that *had* worried her. The idea of being spawned by that man was abhorrent. "Are you sure?" she asked.

"No," he admitted. "But I am sure enough. Janilah spent much time in Ilithor during the war, and when on campaign, never ventured so far south as here. His son would be more likely. Prince Rylian was very active during the war and oft on the move. He would have been a more appealing prospect for your mother too, I would say. Have you met him before?"

"Prince Rylian Lukar? Oh yes, many times. He's a close friend, actually."

The Wall scowled. "I am trying to point out that he is a comely man, heroic, and charming. I would not put it past him to engage in a secret tryst with a beautiful southern princess."

"But you don't believe he ever sailed down here?"

"No," the giant admitted. "But I do not believe in reading one's future in coral either, as I have said. Those Bowens and Hobs were half mad, my lady. Do not lend this any credence."

"I asked you to humour me."

"And I am."

"Then continue to do so, please." She smiled a big smile to keep him engaged. "I suppose it could have been one of the Reynars instead? King Storris. Did he ever..."

"King Storris was a fine warrior, ruler, and war leader," Sir Ralston cut in. "But not a man to engage in forbidden love affairs. If you are to take this seriously, then consider more distant royal relatives. Royalty is not limited to kings and the sons they sire. Brothers and nephews and cousins can be princes too, as can men who wed themselves to princesses, who are just as common. Take Amron Daecar. He is cousin to Ellis Reynar, nephew to King Storris, grandson to King Horris. By rights he should be King of Vandar now that Ellis Reynar is dead, as his son Elyon should be prince." He paused, raised a brow. "You know him, of course."

"Elyon? Yeah...a bit."

"Well, I wonder what this piece of coral would say about them? Are they royal in its estimations? During the war, Gideon Daecar held the office of First Blade and Lord of House Daecar both, before Amron took them on at his father's death. Gideon might just as easily have been called prince as well, being married to Princess Nadiya, King Storris's sister. The Daecars have always been royalty, my lady, whether they sit the throne or not. So if you want to believe this eccentric old fortune teller, perhaps look no further than them."

Saska had never heard the Wall speak so much. She wasn't so glad that she had, not now. "Amron Daecar can't be my father," she said, not thinking beyond that small but troubling possibility. Her mind was of course on Elyon. *My brother, who took my maidenhead. No, it couldn't be.* "He wouldn't have dishonoured his wife..." She said those words before thinking. Because she knew from Elyon that he had. Not knowingly, of course, but this notorious Ghost of the Shadowfort had sprouted from Amron's loins. "He...he never came this far," she went on. "Amron Daecar was too busy with dragons and Agarathi hordes to waste time sailing down here."

She was making excuses to herself; who knew if that was true? But the Wall nodded his head in agreement, and suddenly she could breathe again. "Amron spent much of the war either side of the Red Sea where the fighting was fiercest," he said. "And Gideon famously led the siege of Eagle's Perch, before being driven back to the coast by the great Moonrider Justo Nemati. I do not believe he travelled any further south than that..."

"Justo *Nemati*?" Saska broke in.

The Wall smiled his rare craggy smile. "Yes, your great uncle. I suppose it is no wonder that starcat came to you so eagerly, with blood as rich as Lord Justo's coursing through your veins."

Saska had heard the name once or twice before, she realised, but so long ago as to be a faded memory. To think this great Moonrider she'd heard tell of at the hearthside during her youth was her relation, the brother of the grandmother she was here to find. Revelations like that still made little sense to her. *I am just a serving girl from North Tukor,* she thought. *A scullery wench and washerwoman and housemaid. How can I be related to such as these? Princesses and Grand Duchesses and famous Moonriders who'd fought valiantly in the war.*

It hardly even mattered who her father was all of a sudden. Her mind was back on the starcat who'd abandoned her, a soft dull pain that still felt fresh, a bond that made such sense. She knew House Nemati were of rich and ancient blood, but a Moonrider? They were rarest of the rare, great and gallant men and women who lost their lives, more oft than not, when trying to bond those great silver beasts.

And yet she left me, Saska thought, her sadness swelling anew. *Is it because my blood is not pure enough? Because I'm only part Lightborn, part Bladeborn, and part Seaborn too?* A mutt, that's what she called herself, and now she thought that again. *Better to be a whole of one than two halves of two,* she thought. *I'll never be a great Bladeborn, as I'll never be a great Lightborn.* Her thoughts turned dark as the night around her, before suddenly Sir Ralston Whaleheart spoke.

"It seems we have a visitor."

Saska lifted her eyes.

She caught sight of movement on the plains.

Suddenly the darkness in her was gone, and a light as bright as dawn erupted in her heart. A smile leaped to her lips, brisk and hopeful. Across the grasslands a black shape was bounding, long and lithe and graceful, glittering with silver light. She was on her feet in an instant, and the cat was approaching the hill, rising up and up and up at such speed as Saska had never seen before.

When she reached the summit, the starcat pounced, and the Wall just sat aside, smiling and shaking his head. Saska felt the full weight of the beast push her down to the floor, the stink of hot breath as her mouth opened wide, and out came a long purple tongue, licking.

Saska giggled like a girl, as that rough tongue flapped around her face like a hound, hoisting herself up to wrap her arms about the star-cat's sleek and shining coat of black fur, sparkling with ten thousand tiny silver spots. It was a joy she'd rare felt, a moment she'd remember forever, and in that moment, she thought of a name.

"Joy," she cried out, gleeful, "I'm going to call her *Joy*!"

33

Ranulf

Ranulf Shackton stood washed and cleaned and dressed in smooth soft silk, his beard removed by razor, his hair neatened and cut. His sleep had been patchy, and there was a deep weariness in his bones that would take time to leech. *How many times,* he had to wonder, turning his eyes down upon his shrivelled frame. *How many times will I find myself imprisoned and starved and stolen of my strength?*

He shook the thought away and looked to the guard at the door. He was one of the Sunshine Swords, in glittery scale mail armour and golden cape, with a gilded sword sheathed at his hip. It was rich raiment for sellswords, but these ones didn't come cheap. "How is she?" he asked, in the common tongue. Ranulf could speak a dozen languages with varying proficiency, but knew these sellswords were well trained in mind as well as body.

"Resting, my lord. I have not heard her stir." The guard spoke with a soft Aramatian lilt, and had the look as well. Olive skin, hazelly-green eyes, flowing hair of a deep chestnut brown. A good jawline seemed to be a prerequisite for joining the Sunshine Swords as well, if the rest of the company were anything to go by.

"Might I enter? I would very much like to see her."

The soldier gave a nod and stepped aside. "Of course."

"My thanks." Ranulf stepped forward, opened the door a crack, and peered into the darkness beyond. The heavy drapes of the bedchamber had been drawn shut, though the sun still crept through slim cracks between them, cutting several narrow shards of light across the room. One of them ran right across the four-poster bed where Leshie sat, knees curled to her chest, staring at the door. "You're awake, good." Ranulf whispered. He smiled and made to step in, then stopped. "Do you mind if I..."

"Come in, Ranulf." There was a rough texture to her voice, a hoarseness borne from dehydration. Ranulf knew the feeling. His water rations had been limited these last weeks, his food even more so. Beyond that he had been lucky enough to suffer no physical ill treatment. But her? He had come to find out.

He stepped inside, shut the door, walked to the nearest window. When he made to draw the drapes aside Leshie said, "No. I'm still getting used to the light."

He understood that too. After a month in darkness, one had to be weaned back onto light as much as they did water and food. He looked at the girl, his eyes gradually adjusting. When they'd found her in the dungeons, she'd been passed out and too weak to talk. Under the command of Emeric Manfrey, their troop of saviours had worked tirelessly to liberate every man and woman within the compound, and have them ferried to Sutrek and the manor of Vincent Rose. The man did not take kindly to that, of course, when the Ghost of the Shadowfort, who's real name he'd learned was Jonik, told him that would be the case. "Your punishment," he'd hissed at the merchant, "for affiliating yourself with a man like Pal Palek. You're lucky I don't cut your neck right here and now."

Vincent had of course relented, and over the remainder of the day and through much of the night, the great Piseki camels had gone back and forth, their humped backs fixed with multi-seat saddles to convey the prisoners to his sprawling manor on the waterfront known as Goldwater Row. The manor had dozens of rooms, plenty of space for all of them, and one of the main halls had been turned into a temporary infirmary to cater to the patients most in need of constant care. From what Ranulf had seen, the majority would be counted in that number. Some had been so starved as to be little more than living skeletons. Others were more full of body but stricken of mind, driven to madness by the darkness and dread of their never-ending torment.

Some might come around, but others would be too lost to ever return to the light.

He wondered now, as he studied the diminutive girl sitting on the bed, where she existed upon that spectrum. He could see that she'd grown thinner, and older besides. Leshie had always looked much younger than her seventeen years, with that youthful face with the small nose and chin, the freckles and strawberry hair, but no longer. She looked to have aged a decade. It wasn't just the taut skin and sunken cheeks, the ashen pallor of her flesh, the dulled colour of her hair, but the trauma behind her eyes...those scars that weren't so visible. She had always been such an ebullient girl, quick to temper and unpredictable. Was that still in there, somewhere? He hoped and prayed it was so.

"Did they hurt you?" His words were whispered, but he needed to get right to it. Vincent had told him he'd try to make sure she wasn't abused, when he'd led him down into his cell a month ago, but who knew if that was true. "Did they..."

"No," she said, brusquely. "One tried...a guard. He ripped at my clothes, and I ripped at his skin. Got him good in the eye, Ranulf." She lifted her thumb, the nail bitten and sharpened to a point. "Without my blade I had to improvise a weapon. He didn't try again."

He smiled. She had some life in her yet, then. "You were always fierce, even without godsteel." He looked around the room. "Did they bring you your armour back? They said they would..."

"I don't want it. *He* gave it to me. I want nothing from him." Her voice was a snarl.

"I know." Ranulf moved forward and took a perch on the side of the bed. He angled his scrawny body to face her. "I wanted to say... what I did, I...I am so sorry, Leshie. I never expected any of that to happen."

"You don't have to apologise, Ranulf, not one bit. It's *Vincent*. It's *him*. *He* led us there. *He* tricked us. If you were keeping something from him, something you found in the book, I guessed it must be important. I trust you, Ranulf. I trust you to do the right thing."

There was something in her words there, something in her face. "The right thing?" he asked.

"I want you to help me kill him," she said at once. "I said I would, when they took me away. I said I'd kill him, Ranulf. I will. He deserves it." She closed a fist and snarled and said it again. "*I will.*"

Right then and there he didn't doubt her, but hoped her anger would simmer down sooner or later. *Perhaps it's better that they've not given her back her blades and armour just yet,* he thought. Vincent had plenty of protectors here, yet he had no doubt that Leshie could get to him with godsteel to grasp, if she really wanted to. The girl was quick and nimble, swift and silent as a shadow, and all it would take would be one good slash and Vincent Rose would be no more.

Ranulf would hardly miss the man, not after these last months, but he didn't imagine Emeric Manfrey, the honourable exiled lord, would care for their host to have his throat cut, having struck a bargain with the man. He made a note to himself to warn them to keep a good eye on the girl. She was weak now, but would soon recover. He didn't want her to do anything rash.

As he pondered all that, Leshie's ire was already beginning to settle. She turned to the shard of light cutting through the curtains. It was another hot day out there, but cool in here beyond the thick brick walls, and the gentle murmur of voices and movement could be heard outside on the waterfront. "How long will we stay here?" she asked. "You wanted to go to Aram, didn't you? That was a month ago. They said that's how long we were down there. A month." She shook her head. "It felt like a lifetime."

"It's over now," Ranulf told her softly, reaching to squeeze her hand. He'd suffered long stretches in cells and pits before, though truly, they always felt longer than they were. "I'd hope to leave soon," he then said. "It seems that Lord Manfrey and his companions wish to make haste as soon as they can. They're trying to determine who might go with them. It appears they're seeking warriors for a quest, Bladeborn preferably. They will ask you to join them, I'm sure."

"I don't care if they ask me. I want to stay with you. I want to go to Aram."

Ranulf smiled fondly to hear her speak like that. He'd feared she might hate him, blame him, curse him for subjecting her to all that, but she'd been more understanding than he'd dare let himself believe. "You don't even know why I want to go there, child."

"Saska," Leshie said, without delay. "It's about Saska, I know it."

Ranulf gave her a quizzical look. "We left Saska in Thalan," he said.

"She was to go with Lady Marian south, into the clutches of war. What makes you think she'll be in Aram, Leshie?"

She shrugged. "I didn't say she'd *be* there. But she's half Aramatian, isn't she? I thought maybe you wanted to go there to find out who her mother was? Or..." she peered at him. "Or maybe you already know?"

Ranulf said nothing. Leshie didn't know about Saska's royal parentage, as far as he remembered, and certainly he'd never discussed it with the girl.

Leshie shifted in her bed, leaning forward, studying him. "You *do* know," she saw. "You do, I can tell. Who is she, Ranulf? Someone important, I'll bet. Someone *beautiful*."

Ranulf's smile was faint and fond. "Beautiful, yes, and important... once." He considered it a moment and then decided she'd earned the right to know. After all she'd suffered, she'd earned it.. "Saska's mother is dead, Leshie. She died a noble death, bringing her only daughter into this world. Before then she was a princess, a princess of rich Lightborn blood. Leila Nemati, perhaps you've heard the name? Her mother is Safina Nemati, the Grand Duchess of Aramatia. I was hoping to secure an audience with her to find out the truth of all that. That's why I wanted to go to Aram at first."

Leshie would once have reacted spiritedly to all that, grinning in awe, asking a hundred breathless questions. Now she just gave out a gentle huff of disbelief, smiling a strange sort of wistful smile and said, "The daughter of a princess, granddaughter of a Grand Duchess. Yeah, that sounds like Saska to me. She always seemed special."

"I thought so too. That's why I dug into her past."

"And her father?"

Ranulf shook his head. "That I don't know. My inquiries pointed toward a powerful Ilithoran lord, but there are strands to the story that I've not yet pulled together. As I say, my intention was to find out from the horse's mouth, so to speak. I have spent time in Aram before and have friends there among certain circles. I'd hoped that might help me seek a conference with Safina Nemati. Though now...with all that's been happening here, and the warmoot, who can say."

Leshie had a small frown on her face, a single crease upon her brow. "You said at first. That finding out the truth of Saska's mother was why you wanted to go to Aram...*at first*." She looked at him. "Is there a second reason?"

Yes, he thought, *the instruction of a dead king. The command written in a coded message within the Book of Thala, on a page that I ripped out and burned to protect its secrets.* Among those instructions and secrets had been one that told him to visit the Grand Duchess. *'Go to Aram, and seek the counsel of Safina Nemati,'* King Godrin had written in a passage scribed many long years ago. *'She will help you fill in the gaps, my friend. You are two pieces of the same puzzle. You must find her. No matter what, you must.'*

Those had been the final words he'd written, a last command that had rung out in the head of Ranulf Shackton for four long weeks as he sat in that festering pit, wondering if he would ever get out. Whether it involved Saska or not, he wasn't sure, though he wasn't going to rule it out. The fact that Safina Nemati held another piece of the puzzle, and was probably Saska's grandmother too, was rather too convenient to ignore.

Yet still, he didn't feel it right to tell Leshie of all that yet. The girl had always been a capricious sort and might just change her mind and decide to set sail with Emeric Manfrey and his crew once she had time to properly meet them. Theirs was a fascinating troop, after all, and had enticements for a girl like her, not least the roguish young men of the company, of which there were several he'd seen. It would only take one to turn her head and, well, her desire to remain at Ranulf's side might wilt like a weed in winter.

Thankfully, a knock at the door interrupted her from furthering her questioning, and the Sunshine Sword posted outside spoke in a muffled voice, "Master Shackton, you are needed."

Ranulf turned to the door. "I'll be out in a moment." Then he looked at Leshie. "I'll come back soon," he promised her. "Rest up, Leshie, and recover your strength. Is there anything you need? I can ask..."

"I'm fine," she cut in, defiant. "I'll be on my feet in no time. Just... don't say anything about what I said. About Vincent, and everything. I'm not sure about...well, I need to rest, as you say. Killing him, I mean...maybe he's not worth it. Just this talk of Saska and everything. I want to see her again, and Marian, and even Astrid, one day. I want to hear about their adventures and have more of my own. If I kill him, then all that might be gone. It would be murder, I guess. Justice. But still murder."

He was more glad than he could say to hear her speak like that, though a part of him worried whether it might be a trick. Leshie was more cunning than she made out and might sense that he'd not allow her to be so reckless. *Perhaps this is her way of putting me off my guard?* he wondered. He decided to take her words sincerely. "I'm happy to hear you say it," he told her, standing. "Vincent Rose is not worth risking or ruining your life over. He'll get his comeuppance one day, Leshie. Men like him always do." He smiled with those words, and slipped out of the room.

He found Emeric Manfrey waiting outside. "How is she?" the exile asked.

"Better than I could have hoped." Ranulf glanced back to make sure the door was shut, then lowered his voice. "Her armour and weapons..."

"Are downstairs," Manfrey said. "We found them in a storehouse within the compound, late last night. Very nice, I must say, the red leather. The detailing is quite intricate. They were gifted her by our patron, I assume?"

Ranulf nodded. He'd explained who Leshie was to them the previous day.

"I can have them brought up to her, if you would like?"

"Best not, just yet," Ranulf told him. He wasn't going to betray the girl's trust anymore than that, but Emeric was shrewd enough to understand. "She can be somewhat...impulsive," was all he said. "Best give her time to recover before she takes godsteel to grasp once more. And...keep an eye on her, if you would be so kind. She is quite important to me."

"After what you've been through, I can quite imagine. I will speak to Sansullio. He will make sure there is a man at her door at all times. Vincent will not object."

"Thank you, my lord. I will say your presence here gives me great succour. Life beneath the roof of Vincent Rose is never truly comfortable. But with you and your companions here, we can all sleep a little easier at night."

"Of course. We do not intend to stay long, however, as I have told you. You will be welcome to join us when we leave. You and Leshie both."

"We would be much obliged."

"Wonderful." Emeric Manfrey had a good natured smile, framed by a neat black beard. His hair was black too, well groomed, and his golden eyes seemed to miss nothing. They were honest and kind, and in line with what Ranulf had heard about the man. There were of course some scurrilous rumours about how he came to be exiled, but those had been borne from Kastor lips and no more than another of their abuses.

The truth was quite different and greatly more romantic. Ranulf had heard tell his true tale last night from the lips of a young man they called Jack o' the Marsh, who seemed to share his own passion for storytelling, as they'd ridden alongside one another through the desert. The Marshlander was one of the men who'd be likely to turn Leshie's eye, Ranulf had judged, while listening to him. Tall, strong, with fire in his hair, he had a smile as welcome as the dawn and music in his laughter that would send Leshie weak at the knees. The old Leshie, anyway. He still didn't know what form she'd take when she emerged from her convalescence.

"Walk with me, Ranulf," Emeric said now, and they began moving down a tiled stone corridor beneath a roof of colourful frescoes. Tapestries and oil paintings lined the way on either side, one in every two of them either erotic in nature or otherwise grotesque. In between were a random assortment of fine portraits, beautiful and expressive battle scenes, and obscure and unusual artworks that were not easy to understand or interpret at a glance. Some were simply painted a single colour, black or rich red or deep dark gold; others were abstract and bizarre in a manner not seen in the north, with humans and animals queerly distorted and inanimate objects come alive.

"Your friend Vincent has unusual tastes," Emeric said, glancing at each one as they passed. "Is it real?"

"His eccentricity?" Ranulf asked.

"Yes. Some men like to wear a mask. They hide behind quirky clothes and odd mannerisms and peculiarities such as these, all to confound and confuse people, when really they have no liking for them at all."

"A good read, Emeric," Ranulf said, nodding appreciatively. "I have always thought much the same of Vincent. He plays a part, or many parts, you might say, depending upon whom he's trying to impress or intimidate or cheat or charm. I have often wondered who he really is, but I'm not even sure he knows anymore."

"He strikes me as typical of the hopelessly ambitious. No matter how much wealth he gathers, he will always want more."

Ranulf nodded briskly. "A man like Vincent Rose takes pleasure in the pursuit, not the prize. By now the prize has becoming irrelevant. It's the chase that matters."

"And this chase he's run with you? Is the prize worth it?" The exile turned those keen golden eyes on him.

Ranulf's instincts told him he could trust this man, but even so, he wasn't going to reveal what he'd found in the Book of Thala. His late king had commanded he keep those secrets to himself, until the time was right. That time was not now. "There is no prize more important," was all he was willing to say. He trusted another thing of Emeric Manfrey. He trusted that he'd not push for an answer, when Ranulf didn't want to give one. "Much rests upon it, my lord, but I am sworn to an oath of secrecy. Vincent did not take kindly to that. He is a child, wanting a toy he cannot have."

"And as soon as he gets it," the exile said, "he will grow bored and toss it aside." He nodded. "I understand."

They came to a grand, high-ceilinged gallery, shaped in a half-moon, it's flattened side descending in a broad, white-stone staircase down onto the ground floor below. Beyond that lay a larger central hall where beds had been set up for the ill and infirm. Ranulf could hear the bustle of activity as servants and maids tended them.

They stopped upon the top of the stair for a moment, the surrounding gallery filled with more artwork, with busts and statues set here and there on small ornamental tables, and a sparkling diamond chandelier glittering at the heart of the ceiling above them. Ranulf found it inelegant and cluttered, as though Vincent had gathered more art and artefacts than he knew what to do with. There was a look in Emeric Manfrey's eyes that said he wasn't done on the topic of the man.

"I want to hear of King Janilah's involvement in all this," he said. "You needn't break your oath of secrecy, Ranulf, but I would hear the broader tale. Thus far Vincent has been evasive on the subject, but it's clear enough how much he fears a violent reprisal from the king. So much so that he wishes to remain within our company as protection, as I have told you. But if he is to sail with us, and so are you, I would have the air cleared first." He stopped and waited for an answer.

It took a few long heartbeats for Ranulf to contemplate his next words. As with Leshie learning of Saska's mother, Emeric and his men had earned the right to hear some of his own tale. They had rescued him, after all, and in doing so, played a hand in a great deal more than they knew. So he told Emeric the story of the attack on the Palace of Thalan, of the theft of the Book of Thala, of the day he arrived aboard Vincent Rose's ship in the harbour of Bleakrock to discover that it had been the merchant, in fact, who'd arranged the theft by order of a certain Warrior King.

"He was meant to deliver it straight to Ilithor," Ranulf finished, "but instead sailed south to his estate outside Miren, taking the Book of Thala with him. He had brought me aboard so that I might decipher its secrets, find something of value that he could sell or use to blackmail someone of riches and noble birth. Vincent has never cared for the high nobility, Emeric. Sometimes I wonder how his arm stays attached to his body, such is the depth of the chip on his shoulder, and it came to me that he wanted to take down a greathouse or two by unearthing some great scandal."

"And did you?" Emeric asked, listening intently. "You found something that might ruin a greathouse and determined to keep it from him?"

"Not quite, no. I had my own task at hand; that of finding out just what it was King Janilah Lukar was looking for, so that I might serve my country and king. What was the reason he'd commissioned the book be stolen in the first place? What was he expecting to find? Those were the questions that drove me, though I never spoke of them to Vincent. He grew vexed and suspicious, of course, and unpleasant to live with. He has a way about him. One moment he will smile and tell you how dear you are to him, the next that smile will slip away, and you'll see that deadened look in his eye. I am not typically unmanned by a look, but there is a manner to Vincent Rose that unsettles me, at times."

"I can imagine. But you will not tell me what it is you found?"

"I cannot, no."

"Very well. I will not ask you again. Your business is your own, Ranulf, but I have a duty of care to the men under my charge." He checked himself then, and said, "Lord Jonik's charge, I should say. In truth this is his crew, though I have the honour of standing beside him, and lending him the experience of my years. You know his story, of course?"

"I have heard tell of it, yes. Young Jack was kind enough to recount much of what you've been through yestereve as we rode across the desert."

"Jack is most loyal, and would have only told you what he felt Jonik would permit. Let me tell you something he may not have mentioned." Those golden eyes shaded darker. "Janilah Lukar is hunting us already. The Shadow Order whom Jonik betrayed were working by his commission and command, and are on our trail as we speak, we do not doubt, trying to retrieve the Nightblade. Jonik...well, he has an attachment to the blade, as you can surely imagine. I have heard you are a scholar of them, the Blades of Vandar. You have studied their histories at length, have you not?"

"I have, among other artefacts both magical and mysterious. They are a passion of mine. I have devoted much of my life these last years to understanding them, and to see one up close...it gives me quite a thrill. The boy seems to have mastered the Nightblade, to watch him. He seems very comfortable bearing it, unlike many others in the past. It was always said you could see in a man's eyes the degree of his obsession. Those who grew fixated upon the whispers, the divine power...they would show it in their eyes, and in their behaviours, often growing short-tempered or quick to violence, losing themselves to their thoughts for long moments at a time. I have known the boy but a day, but have seen little of that in him." Ranulf looked Emeric Manfrey in the eye. "Do I have that right, my lord?"

The exile gave a thoughtful nod. "You do...mostly," he said. "There have been times when I have seen that hidden rage, the ghost of something dangerous lurking behind his eyes, but they have been few and far between, and less now than when I first met him. I have tried to counsel him against listening to the whispers, though I sense my advice is wearing thin. Who am I to speak on the matter, after all? I have a famous name, yes, but not for any deeds I myself have done. I am but a faint shadow of Sir Oswald, I feel no shame in saying, and have no true idea of what it means to bond a Blade of Vandar. For all that, I hope I have helped, in some small way, but I wondered..." He thought for a second. "I wondered if perhaps you might offer your own wisdom, from a scholarly perspective, if you get a chance?"

"I would be honoured, should Jonik be willing to listen."

"I trust he will. The boy is most eager to learn, and does not shy away from those who try to help him, so long as he sees no threat in their interest. He has grown enormously, even in the short time I've known him. I have come to see that serving and supporting him is my true purpose now. Too long have I lingered down here, in hiding. At Jonik's side, many ills will be healed."

Ranulf had not yet inquired as to the true nature of their quest. All he knew was they were gathering warriors to head north. "It's said that every exile has his demons that he needs to exorcise," he said. "This army you're assembling. Do you mean to march them on Ethior?"

Emeric was quick to shake his head. "I will gain no peace in seeing House Kastor fall, Ranulf. Lord Modrik was the man who cast me out and he is already dead. I cannot lay the blame of his cruelties at the door of those who still walk the halls of his house." He shook his head again, and firmly. "No, this is about the boy. About something greater." He gestured down the stairs, to the infirmary set up in the hall beyond. "We have become liberators earlier than anticipated," he declared. "As we have broken the chains of these northmen, we will do the same for those fettered as Jonik once was. The boy means to free his brethren of the shackles that have bound them. He means to take the Shadowfort for his own, to strike down the masters and all others who oppose him."

Ranulf was too weary to be stunned. "That is...quite an undertaking," he said, tiredly. "I have studied the Shadowfort too. There is a malice there that will not yield easily."

"My grandmother used to speak of it by the hearthside," Emeric said, with a reminiscing smile. "My lands were in the shadow of the Hammersongs in North Tukor. I have heard whispers of this malice. The *black storm that never ends*, some call it. Jonik has spoken to me of a Shadow King, though briefly. He seems to know little of it himself. I wonder, once more, whether we can make use of your insights, Master Shackton. Perhaps you have uncovered something in those ancient scrolls you're said to like so much?" He gave a smile, then. The conversation was growing too dark.

"I'll have a think," Ranulf said, to blow air on the embers of that levity. "But I should say, Emeric, that I do not plan on remaining with you long. My own task will take me to Aram. I would be much obliged if you could drop me off there, as you pass by."

Emeric Manfrey's eyes drew in, frowning. "It will not be safe for you alone, Ranulf. You've heard of what's been happening to northmen here. There had been terrible atrocities all across the south. My own estate, my own staff. My friends, and...and my..." He turned his eyes aside. Ranulf had heard of how the man had suffered already. "I would advise you remain with us," he said, regathering himself. "Ours is a perilous trip, yes, but you would be among friends, among fighters, among Bladeborn. Alone, you'll surely..."

"I have no choice," Ranulf cut in. "Would that I did, but I don't. Something of vast importance compels me."

Emeric studied him. "This has to do with what you found in the Book of Thala?" He smiled. "I can see you'd rather not say. Very well."

Ranulf was grateful for his tact. "I hope that Leshie will accompany me," he said, after a pause. "She says she will, but...she has a habit of changing her mind. Men like Jack and Jonik and that other boy, Devin is he called? Well, they may turn her head. And even you, my lord... she enjoys the company of men, shall we say."

"The girl is young enough to be my daughter."

Ranulf Shackton laughed. The exiled lord was into the latter part of his thirties, though Vincent Rose was a shade older and that hadn't stopped Leshie from spending half her time in his bed. When he wasn't being entertained by the Lumaran twins, of course. "Leshie likes a slightly older man, in my experience," was all he said. "But besides that, she is drawn to adventure as well. Yours is just the sort that will sweep her off her feet."

"I see." Emeric stroked his short beard pensively. "I might try to put her off. Or deny her outright, if you wish."

"No," Ranulf said at once. "She must be allowed to make her own choice. If her decision is to join you, or sail back north and return to her own lands, or anywhere else of her choosing, I cannot stand in her way."

"Well, no matter whether she goes with you or not, Aram will hold many dangers, I am sure you know."

"I am aware. Thankfully, I have a friend or two there who might be willing to help me, should I be able to reach them. I have been to the city several times before and know it well, as I do the southern tongues. I have faith that all will be well."

"Faith," Emeric repeated, smiling. "As you had faith someone would liberate you from Pal Palek's pits?"

"The very same."

Their privy discussion ended there, as Emeric opened out his arm in a gesture for Ranulf to begin moving down the steps. "The guard called through the door that I was needed," Ranulf said, as they descended. "Was it to discuss these great quests of ours, Emeric, or do you have a more practical requirement of me?"

"Both," the exile said. "But now that we've covered the former, let us move to the latter. I'd like your help in working with the patients. Some of them you know. Others you may help bring around, given your shared experience of living in those pits."

"Of course," Ranulf told him. "I will do whatever I can."

Together, they descended the stair, and moved into the hall beyond.

34

Jonik

Jonik judged the shrivelled old man sleeping on the pallet bed, trying to comprehend the depths of the suffering he'd endured. He knew much of suffering himself, but nothing quite like this. "Over twenty years," he said, shaking his head. "Can you imagine, Jack? More than two decades locked away in the darkness, living off gruel and dirty water, surrounded by all that shrieking and howling, never knowing when the next beating might come."

"It's unthinkable," Jack o' the Marsh intoned sombrely. "I'm amazed he's still alive."

"He's strong," Jonik said. "Ranulf says he was a lord once." The old man had a long grey beard, tangled and matted. Twisting strands of filthy hair fell away from the sides and back of his head, stripped of all colour, his pate bald on top. He was a pitiful thing to look at, and hadn't yet had the attention of a razor. For now they were letting him sleep, tending him as gently as they could with small rations of soft food and water and tonics to keep him calm. He was one of the worst of them. *Lord Cluck,* Ranulf had called him, though it wasn't his real name.

"Lord Leyton Greymont," said Jack. He looked over. "Ranulf told me," the Marshlander explained. "He said he managed to learn a few things about him when he wasn't clucking. Greymont's not a greathouse, but not far down the ladder, he says. Lord Leyton was lost during the war, shipwrecked off the coast of Pisek when his forces got scattered during a storm. Everyone thought him dead. Seems he clung to some piece of driftwood and made it to shore, only to be taken prisoner, then turned a slave, then bought by Pal Palek and added to his menagerie. All that clucking comes from years spent living with chickens and hens in a coop. Eventually he started to think he was one, I guess."

It seemed a bit cruel, after hearing all that, to refer to him as Lord Cluck. "A sad tale," was all Jonik could summon.

Jack nodded. "Sir Borrus knew him. And his son, Giles Greymont. He became lord of his house when Lord Leyton here went missing. His grandson's a Varin Knight, Sir Borrus said. Sir Lancel."

Jonik knew the name. "He was one of Aleron Daecar's best friends," he said, stiffly. A memory took him, unbidden. A memory of the day he'd cut through Aleron's neck on the sands of the stadium in Varinar. Of the gale of horror that erupted in the crowds as their favourite son was slain. He'd looked up into the stands where the Daecars sat with their allies. Sir Lancel had been there, alongside Sir Barnibus, Aleron's two closest friends. He had no doubt that either would try to kill him should they ever encounter him again. "I want to take him home," he said, looking down at the old man. "We can have him delivered back to his lands and family once we reach safe harbour in the north. Make a note of it, Jack. I'm not willing to leave Lord Greymont behind."

"As you wish, my lord," Jack said.

He followed Jonik as he turned, moving to another of the patients. He'd spent the morning as such, judging their strength, both mental and physical, and whether they might be able and willing to join them when they sailed. It was tough going. Many had spent years in that nightmarish dungeon and the burden of all that darkness and doom had told. Those physically frail would recover, in time, and with a long journey north, time was on their side, but the mental scars were different. Those would not be so easily tended and many would be too far gone to ever fully heal.

They reached a man sitting up on his bed, looking to the side with a hollow, thousand-yard stare. A healer was attempting to feed him water, but most of it was dribbling though his open lips. How he'd managed to survive without help in those pits was beyond Jonik's comprehension. "Has he spoken?" he asked the woman.

She was young, small, with round kind eyes and a soft smile. She reminded him of the pretty girls of the Golden Isles, and perhaps that's where she came from. "Not a word," she said, with only a hint of an accent. "I think the change in conditions has broken him. The light. The movement. The space. I don't know. I will keep working with him, my lord."

Jonik dipped his chin. "Inform me or one of my men is there's any change."

He stepped to another, this one a woman. Jonik remembered the name Ranulf had given her when they'd found him in the pits; the Moaning Maid. She looked of early middle age, though her years in the dungeons had aged her prematurely, latticing the skin around her eyes and mouth with a thousand tiny wrinkles, blanching her hair a pure white. She lay on her back, blankets covering her wasted frame, jaw a jut of bone protruding from a quill-thin neck. Even sleeping she looked in anguish. "Did Ranulf speak to you of her?" he asked Jack.

His friend nodded. Jack had ridden with Ranulf when they'd returned to Sutrek last night, sharing stories and learning of the poor stricken souls who'd inhabited the cells nearby to him. "Her name's Katheryn Merrymarsh, sister to Lord Humphrey Merrymarsh of Calmwater. He's one of the most powerful Seaborn lords in Rasalan, Ranulf says. The Moaning Maid...Lady Kathryn, I should say...she went missing on a voyage over a dozen years ago. She was unmarried, a maiden still. It's said that Lord Humphrey was once a fit for his name, merry by nature, always smiling. His smile slipped away and never returned when his beloved younger sister went missing."

"We shall return it," Jonik declared, looking down at the sleeping woman. "We'll return Lady Kathryn and restore Lord Humphrey's smile, make him merry again. Take a note, Jack. Lady Kathryn Merrymarsh is to come with us as well."

"Very well, my lord." Jack lifted the board and parchment he held, and gave a scribble with his pen.

Jonik turned his eyes around the hall. It was large, quite able to accommodate several dozen patients with ease. It was thought best to have most of them in the same chamber to make it easier to watch over them, with the entrances and exits guarded day and night by Sansullio and his men. Some others were in private rooms; those thought in good enough health to forgo constant supervision, or otherwise less afflicted by mental trauma. The girl Ranulf Shackton had been desperate for them to find was among that number, a small Bladeborn girl who'd been trained as a spy in Thalan, Jonik had heard, and who'd travelled with Ranulf all the way from Rasalan.

The others were mostly the more recent additions to the pits. There was a massive Bladeborn cutthroat of mixed heritage out of the Tidelands called Maurice who'd been there a few months, he'd said. Though as with Shackton, he couldn't be sure. He was missing his right ear and a portion of his right cheek from a morning star he'd taken to the face once, a blow that should have killed him, by rights, but Maurice, or Big Mo, as he called himself, wasn't so easy to slay. That boded well, seeing as he'd sworn them his sword.

Another was Cabel, a lean Tukoran youth with dark hair and dark eyes who had been personal bodyguard to a Rasal fur trader. He'd been in the dungeons a year, he judged, but was too stubborn to let it unman him. "Bladeborn?" Jonik had asked on meeting him.

"Fling me that dagger of yours, and we'll see."

Jonik shrugged and did so. The man caught it with surprising deft. "Bugger me, feels good to touch godsteel again," he'd whistled. "Never thought I would."

"You'll get a blade of your own if you join us," Jonik told him. They had a number of them, collected from various skirmishes, to be handed to any Bladeborn willing to swear them their loyalty.

"Join you in what?" Before Jonik could answer, Cabel had laughed and said. "Ah, who cares. I'm in. You saved my life, I figure. Give me a sword and tell me who to kill and I'll kill 'em, yes I will."

That made two.

There were over a dozen others in private rooms, though few of them were fighters. One was hideously fat, to their surprise. Where others had been starved, he'd been force fed for Pal Palek's vile enjoyment, required to dance and perform for him tricks. Another was a woman so tall her legs reached over the end of her bed, and there was a man so small he could barely climb onto the mattress. There were two women who'd been pleasure girls, kept fit and healthy but terribly abused. A woman with a beard, a man with a second head, small and deformed, growing from his neck, and a hybrid wolf boy had all been captured and imprisoned together. They'd been part of a grotesquerie touring the southern cities and states when Pal Palek had spotted them and added them to his own. Jonik had promised each and every one of them that they would return home safe and soon. If not on Invisible Iris, he told them, Vincent Rose would arrange for them to travel on one of his own ships.

But it was the men who'd once been Varin Knights, Emerald Guards, and Suncoats who interested Jonik most of all. Those most in need of constant supervision were kept in the hall; others were given private rooms under guard by one of the Sunshine Swords, or Jonik's own men, with Turner, Braxton, and Devin all standing sentry about the manor.

So far, most were being kept asleep with tonics and brews, their ails and ills inspected and nursed. What Jonik had learned of their experiences had come in fits and starts from the likes of Maurice and Cabel, and the others who still had their voices. They spoke of the humiliations and beatings, the shows that were staged, the fights with animals and each other. It wasn't always darkness. Sometimes they were brought up into the light to perform or dance or duel for the pleasure of Palek and his guests. It seemed that other high ranking members of the Patriots of Lumara liked to visit as well, to savour the debased and debauched entertainments that Palek put on.

As if we needed more reason to want every last one of them dead, Jonik had thought. Every story he'd heard deepened his anger. He had wondered if they might go back to the compound and await Pal Palek's return, so that he might answer for his crimes. He'd even thought about capturing him, bringing him north, subjecting him to the same horrors he'd inflicted on others. Emeric had advised against it. "Palek can wait," he'd said earlier that morning. "The longer we linger, the more dangerous these lands and waters will become. We must make haste to the north."

As he stood now in the hall, amidst all those traumatised men and women, he saw Emeric and Ranulf Shackton arriving from the antechamber beyond. He went to join them. "Master Shackton, how is your friend?" he asked. "The girl? Does she fare well?"

The adventurer smiled and nodded. "She'll be on her feet soon, she tells me."

Good, Jonik thought. The girl was healthy, well trained - if a shade callow - and gifted. She might make a good recruit. "I'm glad. We were hoping that you might help us. I suppose Emeric has filled you in?"

"He has. I'm willing to do all I can. Where would you like me to start?"

"Jack," said Jonik. "Where do we currently stand?"

Jack stepped in, parchment to hand. It contained many notes and scribblings, names and numbers, listing each patient's aches and ailments, their mental state, former employment, and suitability to join their crew. "So far only Maurice and Cabel are pledged to accompany us," he told them. "Assuming you honour your oath to Vincent Rose and take him with us, my lord," he said to Emeric, "then we'll get Harden, Kazil, and with luck Sansullio and his Sunshine Swords as well."

Emeric nodded. "It's a good start. But we'll need more." He looked around. "Where is Sir Borrus?"

"With Sir Torvyn Blackshaw," said Jack o' the Marsh. "He's been with him for a while. Apparently he's making some progress."

Sir Torvyn had been put in a private room by Borrus's request. The two had been good friends once, and the Barrel Knight was working devotedly to bring him around.

"Sir Torvyn won't join us," Jonik said. Much as it pained him, it was the truth. "Even if he does come around, Borrus will take him back to the Riverlands when we return north. He's not going to let him come on our quest."

"That will be for Sir Torvyn to decide," Emeric countered. "Each and every one of these men owes us a life debt, and a Varin Knight like Sir Torvyn would be honour-bound to repay it."

Jonik shook his head. "I'll not demand a life-debt from any of these men or women, Emeric. If they wish to join us, that is their choice, but I'll not compel them on their honour. They've suffered enough."

Jack nodded to that, Ranulf smiled, and Emeric merely said, "I agree. But that doest not extend to Borrus Kanabar, who still owes you a life. He told me all about the trick you played yesterday, Jonik, denying him a kill. Very crafty, I will say."

Jonik felt a bit cheap and dirty about that now, in truth. "If Borrus wishes to go when we make land in the north I will let him," he said. "I cheated him yesterday; his debt is paid."

Eyes were raised at that.

"Your honour does you a service, Jonik," Ranulf Shackton was first to say. "All this time spent with the noble Lord Manfrey has evidently rubbed off on you."

"Perhaps too much," Emeric said, with the softest of smiles. "It seems my own honour has betrayed me on this front. I would gladly play a trick to make sure Borrus Kanabar remained in the company. The man is worth a small army in himself."

Jonik wasn't sure whether he was joking or not. Either way, he'd made his decision on the matter. For all his bluster and boorish behaviour, he had to remember that Borrus Kanabar had suffered too during his time as a captive in Eldurath, and had the right to go home, if he so wished it. He looked at Jack o' the Marsh. "Who else is there, Jack?"

The Marshlander referred to his notes. "So far as I can tell, we have seven Bladeborn knights here, besides Sir Torvyn; two further Varin Knights, three Emerald Guards, and two Suncoats. The best candidate is Sir Lenard Borrington. He's weak right now, but will recover, I believe. Unlike the others, he's quite young, barely older than I am. I think he'll join us, once he recovers."

Ranulf had a thoughtful look on his face. "He's a son of Lord Randall Borrington, I believe," he said. "His third or fourth, if memory serves. I recall his story. He was said to have gone missing from his post in Green Harbour several years ago. He was last seen in a brothel, I seem to remember."

Jack nodded. "I've not got much out of him, but he did mention a brothel, and falling asleep in a bed, and then waking up in darkness. He doesn't seem to recall what happened in the interim. My guess is he was poisoned and abducted, then thrown on a ship and brought down here to Palek's pits. The ordeal has half broken him, but I think he can be put back together, in time."

"Good," said Emeric. "Who else?"

"Sir Corbray Walsh," said Ranulf. "He was near enough to me, and we shared a word or two whilst I was there. I got his name from him, anyway, and enough to gauge that he still has some of his wits about him."

Emeric looked around the room. "Do you know which one he is?"

"Well, that's the thing about being kept alone in a subterranean pit in pitch darkness, my lord, you don't get much face-to-face time." Ranulf gave a weak smile.

"So you don't know what he looks like?"

"No, but I'll track him down."

"And you're certain he's a Varin Knight? He told you as such?"

Ranulf thought for a moment. "I'm not entirely sure. He may have been a Bladeborn household knight or hedge knight. I do know that Walsh is a minor Bladeborn house out of Vandar, but whether he was a Varin Knight...I can't say for certain."

"Borrus will probably know," said Jonik.

Jack o' the Marsh nodded. "I can ask him." He made a note. "There's also a Suncoat who seems eager to join. I went to see him with Kazil, to confirm he's Bladeborn, and sure enough, he could carry Kazil's godsteel blade well enough."

"Who?" asked Jonik, frowning. "You've not mentioned him before. What's his name?"

"I don't know. It's all been a bit hectic, really, people coming and going, so I'd not had time to tell you. He's in reasonable health, and seems of sound mind, mostly."

"And you said he's eager to join?" asked Emeric. "How can he tell you that, but not know his name?"

"He can't speak, my lord," Jack said. "Had his tongue out, not sure when, probably by Pal Palek. He's sleeping now but I'll get some parchment in front of him when he wakes and find out more details. But as for joining us, I told him some vague details of our plan, and he nodded without hesitation. He seems committed to serving us for saving his life. He has...intense eyes, that one."

"OK, good." Emeric thought for a moment. "So that's Sir Lenard Borrington, Sir Corbray Walsh, once we find out which one he is, and his state of health, and the Silent Suncoat. Added to the others, we're getting somewhere." He turned to Ranulf. "You mentioned a relation of Janilah, Ranulf. An old Emerald Guard. What of him?"

"Too old," Ranulf said. He gestured to a tiny, ancient man lying on his side beneath a blanket, his lips trembling as he slept. But for the quiver of those lips, one would be sure he was already dead to look at him. "Must be an older cousin of Janilah's or something, I'm not sure. Pal Palek spoke of him when he led me down there, so I remember how he looked, but otherwise, we never spoke."

"Perhaps we should send him back to Ilithor," Jonik offered.

"He'd die on the voyage," Emeric said. "At that age, a long trip can be a killer."

"*Can*," said Jonik, "but not for certain. Jack, make a note to keep the old man in mind. If there's space, we'll try to take him."

"As you wish, my lord."

"We'll have to consult Captain Turner over this, Jonik," Emeric said. "Let us not forget that it is his ship. He will not want it overburdened."

"It won't be," Jonik came back. There was the first little tang of tension in the air. "Those who cannot travel with us will be conveyed home by Vincent Rose."

"So I hear," came a voice. They all turned. Vincent Rose came striding through the centre of the hall, plumply dressed in gold and crimson silk. It was as though he was trying to make a point, draping himself in finery as men lay withered and weakened around him. Jonik held his snarl. "Apparently I'm not only to host all these men in my manor, but arrange passage home for one and all as well. I think the boundaries of our arrangement are being stretched a little, do you not, Lord Manfrey?"

"Call it a gesture of good will," said Emeric, before Jonik might speak. "You have the riches and the means to patch up a little of your honour, Vincent. An act of kindness every once in a while does wonders for the soul."

"Oh I know. I give to charitable causes often, my lord." He was trying to wear his mask of charm today, Jonik didn't fail to miss. "And in this I am happy to help, of course. My only question is how. I understand you intend to leave in a matter of days, and as per our arrangement, I will be aboard Captain Turner's fine ship when you do. How then will I manage the revival of these patients, when I am away, let alone the hiring of sailors and deckhands to bring them all home?"

"You'll leave instructions for your steward to arrange it," Jonik told him fiercely. "And if you do no trust him to do the job, send for Seshio Arcas, or another of your underlings. Or simply let them convalesce here until you return. You will *not* be in our company long, if I have my way."

"Goodness, what spite. I fail to see what I've done to earn it?"

"Don't play the fool, Vincent," Ranulf's voice came in. "You are party to Pal Palek's cruelties by association with the man."

"Am I? You don't think what he's done to these poor people appals me just as much as it does you?"

Jonik drew forward. Jack put a hand on his shoulder, shaking his head.

"I am a businessman," Vincent Rose went on. "I obtain goods of value and sell them for a profit. Yes, I have sold arms to the Patriots of Lumara before, Pal Palek among them. That is the limit of my association with the evil he perpetrated in those pits."

"You sent *him* to those pits," Jonik snarled, gesturing to Ranulf. "You did to a friend what few would do to their worst enemy. You're beyond contempt, Rose. Borrus has been asking for your head and I've half a mind to let him take it."

"Sir Borrus?" Rose said, feigning confusion. "Why would he wish such a thing?"

"Because of Sir Torvyn Blackshaw," Emeric informed him, maintaining his sense of calm. "He is dear to Sir Borrus and spent many long years suffering in those dungeons."

"And how am I to have known that? I have never heard of Sir Torvyn Blackshaw before."

"That makes no matter. You knew northmen were being imprisoned and tortured and did nothing to help them."

"What could I have done?" Rose's voice pitched a little higher. He looked around, surrounded by enemies. Even the Sunshine Swords were regarding him angrily and Jonik had seen how old Harden of the Ironmoors held him in contempt. "I will say again, I am a businessman. I have no power to challenge a man like Pal Palek."

"You could have told someone," Emeric said. "You travel often to the north. Why did you not report this to the authorities? You might have done so during your time in Thalan; you were there only months ago." Rose went to speak but Emeric cut him off. "You said nothing because you did not care, tell it true. You preferred to keep in Pal Palek's good graces so that you might continue to profit off your trades with him and his allies. What were a few imprisoned northmen to a man like you?"

"I..."

"I don't need an answer from you, Vincent. That wasn't a question.

We all know how much value you put on any human life that isn't your own." He shook his head at the man, pityingly. "I wonder what it was that made you into this?" His hand went up. "No, you needn't answer that either. I'm sure you'll summon some story to try to explain yourself, but I sense it will fall upon deaf ears. What we need from you is your patronage and your promise that you will see these men and women fully restored and returned home. That is your penance and price for the suffering you've helped cause."

Vincent Rose was trying to hide his rage, but Jonik could see well enough the shade of purple rising up his neck. He bowed his head and said through his teeth, "I consider myself truly humbled, my lord. A long overdue chastisement, I'm sure." The smile on his face was as forced as any Jonik had ever seen. "I will of course do as you say, to cleanse my soul of the filth I have layered atop it. But might I make a suggestion?"

Emeric regarded him coolly. "By all means."

The merchant gestured to the old and infirm, the emaciated and the maddened. "I judge it better to have every last one of these poor souls taken north as soon as possible. Some are very old, yes, and may not survive a long voyage at sea, but I consider the risk worthwhile. These are men and women of the north, and none will be safe here once I have left. My political power here has protected me, as a northman, during these difficult times, but I cannot protect these people if I am not present. And should Pal Palek discover that they are here... well, I shudder to think what he will do."

"You're trying to save your own skin," Jonik bit at him. "You're afraid Palek will find them here and then come after you. You're afraid of burning that bridge."

"It's a part of my motivation, I am not too proud to admit. But no matter what you think of me, I do not want to see these people suffer further than they already have. If they can be taken back to their homelands now, why wait?"

"We don't have the space," Emeric said. "Invincible Iris is likely to be overburdened as it is."

"Yes, I am sure. But by the grace of the gods I have been fortunate enough to possess a vessel or two of my own. Those rather more suitably outfitted, one might say, for the conveyance of these poor patients, who will need good clean beds and comfortable linens and healers to tend them during the voyage. I can provide all of that in a fashion that Invincible Iris, you'll forgive me for saying, cannot."

Jonik found he couldn't deny a word of that, whether he wanted to or not. Having another strong seafaring vessel alongside Iris would make matters a great deal easier. And if they could return these people home under their own protection, wasn't that for the best? It seemed the others agreed, by their nods and murmurings.

"We'd need to disperse our men sensibly," Emeric said, thinking forward. "For one, I would call it inadvisable to have Sir Borrus travel with you, Vincent, and I'm sure the same could be said of others." He gave Jonik a brief look, though Ranulf and the girl Leshie would also be best kept away from the man, for what he'd put them through. "I will talk to Captain Turner and see what he thinks. Ranulf, I understand you are a fine seaman yourself?"

"As good as any," Vincent Rose said for him. "Ranulf Shackton's adventures are a thing of legend, my lord. Many of them have been under sail; famed leviathan hunts and such that would make a lesser man quiver to hear of them."

"You're too kind, Vincent." Ranulf said, his voice dull with courtesy. "Though I doubt these men will quiver at their telling. So far as Jack tells me, they had a run-in with a particularly quarrelsome kraken only months ago, while sailing the Tidelands."

"Goodness," said Vincent Rose, looking to Jack. "Perhaps you'd regale me with the same tale, my friend?"

"It's one I never tire of, Master Rose," Jack told him.

"Later," said Emeric Manfrey, thinking. "We'll need more men if we're to crew two ships. We have gotten by with the remains of Captain Turner's crew until now, but that won't be sufficient to man two vessels."

"I can find men at the docks," Rose said, waving a bangled hand. "Many of them have worked for me before, at one time or another. It shan't be hard to..."

"I'd rather find men who *haven't* yet worked for you," Jonik said to him. "We can find men ourselves, Emeric."

Rose gave out a laugh. "One little transgression and suddenly everything I do is dismissed out of hand. How silly. You show your age, my lord." He turned. "Lord Manfrey, perhaps we might discuss this privily. There are too many snapping maws here to engage in a sensible discussion."

"Have a care, Vincent," Emeric warned him. "You are on thin ice here and would do well to remember that."

"How could I forget? Everywhere I go I am accosted by ugly stares. And in my own home, no less. I would hope to be treated more respectfully for my patronage."

"Respect is earned, Vincent," Ranulf Shackton said. "For all your wealth it cannot be bought."

The merchant laughed. "How droll. I have missed you, my friend, truly. Though I'm sure you'll not say the same, after what I put you through. And for that, of course, I beg your forgiveness. Yours and Leshie's both. I only meant to loosen your tongue so that you might spare us both a most unpleasant fate. You do understand that, don't you? This thing with Janilah..."

"You needn't worry," Ranulf broke in. "If Janilah has cause to blame anyone it will be me. You are quite safe, Vincent."

"Yes, well, you'll forgive me if I don't take your word for it."

"I have much to forgive you for, it would seem," said Ranulf.

"Oh, much and more, you and everyone else, for all the horridness I have caused." Rose's mask was slipping, and he didn't even care to reposition it. A man so utterly vain as he found it hard to be publicly chastened like this. "I think...I think I had best retire," he said. "There are a pair of Lumaran twins awaiting me who will not judge me for every little action I take, every word that falls from my lips. If you need anything, anything at all, please do not hesitate to come to me." That was for Emeric most of all. And with those words, he spun and walked away in a stream of flowing silk.

Jonik watched him go with a hatred deep in his bones. "I'll travel on Iris," he said in a dissatisfied grunt. "Ranulf, you as well, and Leshie. Emeric, it might be best for you to accompany him; you seem able to hold your composure in his presence better than me."

Emeric nodded. "That might be for the best, yes. Turner will want to stay with Iris, but perhaps he'll permit some of his own men to crew Vincent's vessel. It would be better that way, to have men keeping an eye on him."

Jonik agreed. "Braxton can help. Devin as well. Maybe you, Jack."

Jack nodded dutifully. "I'll go where I'm needed," he said.

"We can figure it out later," Emeric said. "Either way, we'll need more crewmen. I'll speak with Captain Turner, get his thoughts. Do you know where he's stationed?"

Jack referred to his board, as though it had all the answers. "I think he's standing guard at the Silent Suncoat's room. It's on the third floor, west wing."

"Right. Ranulf, perhaps you can take this opportunity to help us track down Sir Corbray Walsh?"

"Yes, good idea."

"Jack, go help him," Jonik said, noticing a small disturbance in the adjoining hallway, leading away to the front door. "I'll see what this trouble is."

They parted at that, as Jonik strode across the hall and through the open archway beyond, where he spotted Sansullio in conversation with a trio of ragged men, dressed in sweat-stained cloaks and worn boiled leather, with rusted old scabbards at their hips. The tall dark sellsword captain seemed to be subjecting them to a short interrogation, checking their weapons, as the young steward Tizan stood aside.

Jonik marched forward. "Sansullio, who are these men?"

"Northmen, my lord. They say they are soldiers, seeking passage home to your lands."

"Aye, it's true," said the oldest of the men. Several of his teeth were missing, the rest yellow and brown, his nose so badly bent out of shape it must have been broken a half dozen times. Even Brown Mouth Braxton's lopsided jaw looked straight as an arrow next to that zigzag of a nose. "We been here for weeks seekin' a way north, but no ship will take us, m'lord. We even thought about stealin' some camels and trying to cross the desert. Madness, I know. But that's what we've been driven to."

The biggest of them gave a ponderous nod. He was a man of round shoulders and round head, with barely a hair to speak of. His small black eyes had a piggish quality, hidden in all that facial fat. "It's not been easy, m'lord," he said, in a thick Tukoran drawl. "We were working for a merchant who got himself killed in the riots. When he died so did our journey home. Been stuck here ever since, trying to stay low."

The youngest and smallest had a jittery way to him, his eyes always darting and looking around, never still. "We had others with us too, at first," he said in a nervous voice. He sounded Rasal to Jonik's ears, like the older man. "Were seven of us, but they're all dead now. We're all that's left."

"And your names?" Jonik asked.

The old man did the talking. "The whelp's Trigger. Big one's Mugs. They call me Sir Ben mostly. Not a knight of course, but the name stuck. Elsewise I go by Benjy, m'lord."

"I see." Jonik looked at their steel, wondering. "Are any of you Bladeborn?"

The question didn't seem necessary. The men's laughter was their answer.

"If we were Bladeborn, you think we'd still be here?" cackled old Benjy with the bent nose and missing teeth. "No, we'd be on some ship by now, demanding they take us home at the point of godsteel." He shook his rusted sheath. "Can't do much with old rotten blades like this."

"No, I suppose not." Jonik paused, judging them. They were soldiers, at least, and the big man looked like he could probably fight well enough. Benjy maybe too. Old men often seemed unthreatening to look at, but any sword for hire who'd lived as long as him had to be doing something right. "You're soldiers, you say. Can you sail as well?"

"We can, m'lord," said Benjy. "We all worked the decks headin' down here with Master Frogmoor. That were the merchant we served, before his untimely passing. A shame too. He were a good man, and true. But such are the times, I s'pose. Either way, if you're looking for deckhands or sailors or sellswords, we're your men. We'd be happy to serve in exchange for passage."

The others nodded eagerly. There was a desperation to them that tugged at Jonik's compassion. He continued to judge them. They'd not exactly put the fear into a Shadowknight, but they'd be bodies in a battle at least. More to the point, they could help crew Invincible Iris assuming the likes of Brown, Devin, Emeric and possibly Jack sailed on Rose's vessel. "Where are you trying to get to?" he asked them.

"*Where*? Anywhere but here!" laughed the big one called Mugs.

The small one gave a jittery nod. "Anywhere, m'lord. Anywhere north. Rasalan would be best."

"We'd be passing Rasalan," Jonik said, not giving too much away. He scanned them. Each man seemed sincere enough in their trials, and looked like they'd been here a good while too by judge of their clothing. The stink wasn't pleasant, either. "How did you find us here?"

"We been keepin' a lookout down at the docks," old Benjy said. "One of us here around Goldwater, the others further west at the busier ports. Twas Trigger stationed here. He saw some northmen comin' and goin' over the last day or so, and thought it might be worthwhile us seeing what it was all about. We hoped...well, we hoped you were gathering northerners to sail home, m'lord. Some rescue mission or such. And if so, that you'd have space for three more willing hands. As I say, we can do anything you need. Swing a sword, scrub a deck, clean out the chamberpots, whatever you like." He glanced through into the main hall. "Seems you've got a few ill to tend as well. I got some experience as a healer, back on Rasalan. Might be that I can help there too."

They had that well enough in order, in truth, but another set of healing hands couldn't hurt. "I'll have to think about it," Jonik told them. "Come back tomorrow, and I'll have my answer."

"Tomorrow, aye." The old man drew a breath, nodded. Big Mugs dropped his eyes. Young Trigger looked anxious about spending another evening out on the docks or in the city. Jonik could quite understand why, with the threat of discovery and death never too far away. "Well then, we'll um...we'll be back tomorrow, m'lord. Much thanks for your consideration, anyhow." He seemed resigned to being left behind.

Jonik had a sudden change of heart to look at the men's frightened faces, the young one in particular. He was barely older than Devin, it looked, a youth still in his teens, his chin mustering only the sparsest spouting of hair. There seemed no need to send them away with all the spare rooms they had. "We have space here," he told them, just as they were about to turn. "I'll have a room prepared for you, so you might rest here tonight in peace. Tomorrow, you'll have my decision." Their faces brightened, one and all. "In the meanwhile, perhaps you can prove yourself, Benjy? Rasals are known as skilled healers. Please, show me what you can do."

"Aye, my lord, I'd be most honoured."

"Good." Jonik turned and led them through.

If nothing else, he'd deny Rose filling the decks with any of his own creatures. And that was good enough for him.

35

Elyon

She lay naked upon the bed, the light of the fire glistening off her smooth sweaty skin.

"This is the last time, Mel. It cannot happen again."

He said that every time, every damn time, and not once had he followed through. He filled two cups of wine, his body garbed in nought but a pair of short linen breeks. The shutters were clattering gently in their holdings, the wind blowing fierce outside as the storm continued to rage. He turned, walked to the bed, handed her a cup.

She took it, still sprawled out in all her lustful splendour, propping herself up on one elbow as she drew a sip. *One cup,* Elyon had just told her, *and then you must go.* She'd try to stay longer, of course, and typically she would. Elyon always tried to get rid of her, but sure enough, she was always there by morning. *But not tonight,* he knew. *Tonight, I have business to attend to.*

"It'll last for some days more, they say." Melany gestured to the balcony, the door leading to the terrace shut tight. Still, the occasional draught came in, creeping through the cracks and causing the candles to flicker, stirring shadows on the walls. *And on her body,* he thought, cast golden by the firelight. *Her skin looks almost alike to Saska's in this light...*

He cleared his throat, cleared his head of that thought. The girl who'd shared his secrets and bed still lingered in his mind more oft than he'd like. He'd even continued to ask anyone he could if they knew a 'boy of sixteen summers, lanky, with a mop of messy black hair. Name of Del'. He did that for her, the girl of silver and blue, the girl with the blood of Varin and Lumo both. *I wonder where she is? I wonder how she's doing? I wonder, I wonder, I wonder...*

"Elyon, you're drifting again."

He blinked back into the room, smiled, and settled into a seat by the hearth. Melany rolled onto her belly, exposing her pert rear, the smooth curve that ran up the small of her back to her shoulders. Her skin was unblemished, soft and perfect. Saska's was scarred, Elyon remembered. *Cut by the lash...just like mine.* He took a sip of wine. "I'm just thinking of our war plans, is all. They have a habit of occupying my thoughts. I'll soon be at the heart of it, Mel." He looked at her, lying there upon the rumpled silk sheets. "This...all this...it has to stop."

"It will. When you're gone." She smiled, turned again to lie on her side. Elyon still lost half a breath to look at her in such a state. *And she knows it. She knows my weakness.* "You haven't spoken of what those plans are. Won't you tell me where they're sending you, my noble knight?"

"I shouldn't," he told her. "They are matters for the council..."

"And not a girl like me?" She grinned, ran her fingers through her golden hair. "You forget I know how to wield godsteel too, Elyon. I'm not your normal lady of the court."

"You're anything but," he had to admit.

"In a good way, I hope." She smiled and sipped her wine. "Lillia's growing to be quite the skilled little fighter too, it would seem. She was kind enough to show me during one of your many long meetings. She caught Jovyn out once or twice as they sparred, though the boy seemed admittedly distracted. He was rather more sullen than I've seen before. Do you know why that is?"

"I shouldn't say."

She rolled her eyes, tutted, and slipped her feet onto the floor. "Now Elyon, you say that about everything. Why do you have to be such a bore?"

Because men shouldn't share secrets in bed, he thought. *And you've started to give me reason to doubt you.*

When he said nothing, she stood and walked over to him, sliding her legs back and forward in a sultry gait. "Is there space on that seat for two?"

"There's a spare chair right there, Melany." He gestured to a chair opposite.

"I want to sit with you." She drew forward and straddled him, linking her fingers behind his neck. The feel of her atop him stirred him below. "So, care to try again, Elyon? What has sweet young Jovyn got to be so broody about, I wonder?"

"I...I couldn't say."

"You *shouldn't* say. You *couldn't* say. What's next? You *wouldn't* say?" She leaned in to kiss him before he could speak, gently gyrating her hips as her lips pressed to his. *Gods, woman, why can't I resist you?* When she drew back, she took Elyon's wine from him, drank deep, then said, "Fine, don't tell me. I already know what's got Jovyn down anyway."

He frowned. "You do?"

"Of course I do. You might keep your secrets, but Lillia's more open. She told me all about the betrothal to Prince Robbert."

That didn't please him. "She shouldn't have. That news is not yet for sharing."

"Don't worry, it won't go past my lips. I know you'll be saving the announcement until after the wedding."

"Then why..."

"Why did she tell me? Oh, let me think...because she's excited, and wants someone to share the news with, perhaps? Jovyn is hardly well suited for that role now, is he? Seeing as he loves her, and all."

Elyon regarded her a moment. "So why did you even ask me about Jovyn's sour mood, if you already knew the cause?"

"Why? Because I wanted to see if you'd trust me to know." She leaned back, her smile slipping away. "You don't share things with me like you once did. I've begun to think that you're just using me to forget."

He wasn't sure her meaning. "Forget what?"

"Forget *what*?" She laughed, slid her legs back off him, and walked to the bed, taking up her wine. "What do you think? I was told you'd gone cold in Harrowmoor, that you don't trust anyone anymore. What happened to your father, to Aleron...it's only natural that you might close up like a clam. But I thought I meant more to you than that. I thought we were close enough to share our secrets and fears, but apparently not." She sat down, folded her legs, her breasts gleaming in the firelight. "That's all fine, Elyon, if that's all I am to you. But be honest about that at least. I don't like to be used..."

"Used? It's *you* who comes to *me*, and near every night, Mel. I think that says something, doesn't it?"

"It says you're a man, with needs that require tending. You use me, Elyon, don't deny it, and don't care for me as you once did. You *never* let me in."

"And yet you try to get in, every single time you come here." He stared at her. "Why? Why do you want to know *everything*, Melany? Don't think I don't see it. You're subtle, yes, and too damn smart for me half the time, but I still see what you're doing..."

"And what is that?" she challenged. "Just what do you think I'm doing, Elyon?"

"I...I don't know. Asking a lot of questions. Listening to everything I say."

She pressed a hand to her mouth in false horror. "Oh my, what a villain I must be! How onerous for you to have me show an interest in your life, and actually listen when you speak. Women don't grow up with the same courtesy, you know." She stood and stepped over to where her clothes had been tossed to the floor, and began dressing.

"Mel..."

She ignored him, pulling on her undergarments, gown and girdle, stockings and gloves.

He tried again. "Mel, I didn't mean..."

"You meant every word," she came back at him. "As I say, you don't trust me. That's fine. You don't trust anyone, so I'm told. That's your right. Enjoy being alone."

"Mel..." He had to chuckle. "You're being dramatic. Come on, don't go."

"Don't go?" She blew out a sigh, exasperated. "One cup, you said. Well my cup's empty, so I'm going. I won't come again, don't worry, or burden you with all my cruel questions." She made for the door. "Good luck wherever they send you. I hope you live through the war..."

Elyon was still laughing. "Mel, I'll see you at the wedding, at least."

It was only two days from now. Hopefully she'd have calmed down by then.

She stopped at the door. "I'll be sure to avoid you, then," she told him. "And this room..." She looked around, sneered at the place as though a chamber of horrors. "I'll not be coming back *here*, that's for certain. We're finished, Elyon Daecar." She wiped her hands. "Done. Good luck in the south. I pray you become less of a bastard one day." She slipped through the door and slammed it shut.

Elyon was still seated in his chair. That will have angered her more, he judged, that he didn't stand to calm her. *She'll probably expect me to go after her too, drag her back here, cuddle her close and pour my heart out.* Well, that wasn't going to happen. Elyon liked Melany Monsort a great deal, still loved her in part, but knew this was right. Whether he trusted her or not didn't really matter. He'd promised himself he'd end their tryst and had failed himself over and over again. *That ends now,* he thought. *I've let myself down enough.*

He stood, dressed, and drew on his dark grey winter cloak, lined about the collar with fine vair fur. The halls of the palace could be frigid in sections where the torches were rare, and especially so at night. *And this storm.* It had been going on for days, and had many more to go, if the rumours were true. It had locked all of Ilithor in its cold embrace, and parts of the city were said to be heaped so high in snow that men could get lost in the drifts. *A palace full of treacherous snakes, and we're all locked in here together,* he thought, as he made for the door. He gave a slightly ironic laugh. What he was planning would be considered a treachery in itself, but he'd made his peace with that. Godrik Taynar's insult still stung. Sir Elyon will never hold the Windblade, he'd said.

We'll see about that, old king

~

He arrived at the far side of the palace fifteen minutes later, knocked, and entered the apartments of Amara Daecar. It was his auntie who greeted him. "Elyon, good, I was starting to wonder if you'd come." She pecked him on each cheek and stepped back, shutting the door as he passed.

"Your handmaids aren't here?" he asked. "It's not like you to open your own door, Auntie."

"I thought it best they be absent tonight."

He nodded, and they made their way into the communal living chamber. Sir Lancel and Sir Barnibus were already waiting. "You look out of breath, Elyon," said Lancel. "It's tiring coming all the way up from the servant's quarters, I'll wager."

Elyon gave that the laugh it deserved. It was a running joke that he'd been situated further down on the southern side of the palace, in chambers of lesser grandeur. "I'm higher up than you, Lance. I suppose that must put you in the dungeons."

"Where he belongs, the things he gets up to," quipped Barnibus. Both were drinking wine, lounging happily in a pair of cushioned armchairs. Amara moved in and closed the double doors behind them. She filled Elyon a silver cup of wine and handed it over, then took a seat, as Elyon did the same, so they were all positioned around a central table.

"You've been with Melany," Amara said. "I can smell her on you."

"I wish you could smell her on *me*," grinned Lancel. He noted Elyon's eyes. "Sorry, that was in poor taste."

"But no lie," Amara said, and quite correctly. "What man wouldn't want the perfumed aroma of the Lady Melany Monsort on his person?"

"I'm sure many have had that aroma on them in the past," Elyon said. "I can say with some certainty that Melany was no maid when I met her. Now, shall we get down to business? Amara, what do you have for me?"

"It seems someone is seeking to avoid the topic," Lancel said, folding one leg over the other.

"No, I'm merely trying to get to the reason we're here. It's late, and I'm sure we're all ready for our beds. To *sleep*," he said, seeing the jape brewing in Lancel's eyes. "And nothing more. Now, Amara. Your report. I hope you have something good for me?"

"Of course I do. When have I ever let you down, sweet boy?"

When you sent my father into the bloody Icewilds, he thought, but didn't say. He wasn't afraid of keeping anything much from Lancel and Barnibus, but that was a rabbit hole he didn't want to fall back down. "So? Do you know where he's hiding it?"

"Alas no," she admitted. "But I think we've narrowed it down to either Godrik's private apartments, or Prince Dalton's. If our jolly new king has decided to hand the Windblade to his son, as he keeps on suggesting he will, why would he wait? It would serve for Dalton to have it in his possession as soon as possible, so that he might learn to master it."

"It would," Elyon agreed. "Though if Dalton does have it, he's said nothing to confirm that fact."

"He wouldn't. Clearly, Godrik's trying to obfuscate the entire thing, and keep the Windblade's location uncertain. He's even proven himself wise enough to create a healthy number of diversions and decoys, no doubt to fool my dear sweet cousin Janilah." She smirked happily at a thought. "Oh, what a joy it will be to deny him that blade. And when Godrik finds it missing? I wonder who he'll blame..." She grinned fiendishly.

"Janilah will be his first thought, certainly," said Barnibus, "but it won't take long for him to realise Elyon has it. And when he does, he'll be sure to demand it back. How are we going to tackle that particular problem?"

"We're going to do absolutely nothing," Amara declared.

Barnibus frowned, looked around at the others. "And you think King Godrik will just allow Elyon to keep it, my lady?"

Amara spun the stem of her chalice, seated upright and elegant in her chair. "Elyon will have the backing of half of Vandar," she said. "Kanabar, Pentar, Amadar...all greathouses, all behind him. And that's to say nothing of the Daecars and their banners. That's plenty enough to keep the Windblade in his grasp."

"They took my father's crown," Elyon said, "so I'll take that blade. I've had enough of these insults and offences. Taynar has this coming."

"And Janilah?" asked Barnibus. "What if he gets it first?" He glanced over at Lancel, a troubled look on his face. "There's been talk of murders going on in the city...they're being talked about as robberies and break-ins, but I'm not so sure that's true. Did you hear about that merchant killed in his home on the Marble Steps?"

Elyon nodded vaguely. "A failed burglary, I heard. The guy stumbled upon the thieves and they killed him out of shock."

Barnibus shook his head. "That's what they're saying, but it's not true. Lance and I looked into it. The merchant who was killed was called Rich Dick Mallory, a friend of King Godrik's, allegedly. It seems he'd been tortured when they found him. Fingers cut off, skin flayed, all sorts, as though whoever broke in was trying to get information out of him. And his wife, his mistresses, all dead. Even some of his kids, the older ones, they were killed as well. Only the nippers were left, locked away in some room. They bawled about a ghost. A blue ghost, they said." He looked at Elyon. "A *ghost*, El. You don't think..."

Elyon got his meaning immediately. "It isn't the Shadowknight, if that's what you're thinking."

"But...how can we be sure? He was working for Janilah, wasn't he, this Ghost of the Shadowfort? Maybe he's come back to serve him again?"

"He abandoned his order. It wasn't him."

"We don't know that. Maybe he returned?"

"He didn't," Elyon said, coldly.

Amara agreed. "Jonik's a world away, and has no love for Janilah. If he ever comes back here, it'll be to slay him, not serve him."

Lancel and Barnibus traded a glance. "*Jonik*?" said the latter. "That's his name? How...how do you..."

"He's Elyon's brother," Amara told them.

Elyon's eyes shot to her angrily. "Amara, for goodness sake..."

"Oh come on, we have no secrets here. They deserve to know the full truth of it, Elyon." She ignored the look on her nephew's face and went straight into it. "The Shadowknight is his *half*-brother, I should say," she told the pair. "The bastard son of Amron Daecar, sired during the war without his knowledge, then taken to the Shadowfort to be raised a weapon and a killer." She thought a second. "What else? Oh yes, Lady Cecilia Blakewood is Jonik's mother. Janilah's bastard daughter. So, Jonik's the bastard of a bastard, really, a double-bastard, if you will. Sired of House Daecar *and* House Lukar, if that explains how worryingly gifted he is. And a villain, of course, but...well, sort of not a villain too..."

"He murdered Aleron," Barnibus gaped.

"He did. Or, well, he killed him in a contest, but that's by the by. He was under orders, under coercions. You heard about that Whisperer killed in the town of Russet Ridge, with a dozen Bladeborn sellswords?"

"Of course. Everyone heard about that."

"Well that was Jonik, breaking free of his shackles. Now I'm not saying he's a saint, by no means, but he's not quite the sinner he's thought to be either. Like any thrall, he was being governed by others, and not acting of his own free will. There's no denying the things he did, but they can at least be understood in that context."

"He killed Aleron," said Barnibus again. This time his voice was more of a growl. "I don't care who was controlling him, I don't care about any of that...he *killed* Aleron. His own half-brother. And...he maimed his own father. You've got to be wicked to your bones to do that."

"Or under coercions and controls," Amara said, lightly. "But of course, you're right, to a point. I'm sure his life experience has made him somewhat wicked. But anyway, that's not important now."

"No," said Lancel.

"It's not," agreed Elyon, wanting to move on.

"It might be," said Barnibus, frowning. "Maybe Janilah had him tracked down? Put him under the controls of another Whisperer, or..." He turned to Elyon. "He could be in the city right now, El."

"He isn't, Barny," Elyon assured him. "This talk of a ghost...they were terrified children. That can't be counted on."

Barnibus nodded to that, a haunted cast to his eyes. Deep ruts were cleaved into his brow. "I just...I can't believe he's your brother..."

"Nor can I." The door kicked open. Lillia Daecar stood there in her silken nightgown, hands to hips, furious tears in her eyes. "When were you going to tell me! *When*, Elyon!"

Elyon pushed to his feet. "Lil..."

"How long have you been out there?" demanded Amara.

"Long enough." She sniffed, wiped her eyes, stamped forward. "He's our brother, Elyon? That *monster*? He killed Aleron. He crippled Father? He...he..." She was trying and failing to compose herself. Her face coiled in anguish, voice weakening. "Father, he...he betrayed our mother? He had a son with...with someone else?"

"The Bastard Bitch of Blakewood," said Lancel. He coughed. "Um, Lady Cecilia, I should say."

"No, you needn't spare her, Lancel," Amara told him. "Bastard Bitch is putting it quite lightly; that woman deserves a whole lot worse. And *you*..." Her eyes spun to Lillia. "You have a lot of explaining to do, young lady..."

"*I* have a lot of explaining to do? *Me*? How can...how can you... you're actually serious? You're being serious right now?"

"It's rude to eavesdrop."

"It's rude to *lie*," Lillia spat back. "How...how could you keep this from me? *I'm* the lady of this house, not you! You have no right..."

"To spare you from knowing something horrific? That isn't a right, it's a responsibility. But you're here now, so you might as well come in and shut the door. I suppose you know what else we've been talking about as well?"

"The Windblade," muttered Jovyn, following in, looking sheepish. He'd remained beyond the door until now, cloaked in shadow, but as ever he was at Lillia's side. "We...we could help, you know. If...if you need any."

"You're bored are you lad?" asked Lancel, with a big wolfish grin. "I suppose playing babysitter to the little lady here must get tiresome after a while. You're itching for some proper action, I'll bet."

"*Excuse* me?" Lillia marched over to him, indignant. She folded her skinny arms and stared down into his pale green eyes with a fury in her own. "What did you say to me?"

"To you? Nothing, my lady," Lancel said, all innocence. "I was speaking to your *Jovy*, I do believe."

Lillia's chin went up, as it ever did when she tried to look important. "I could have you whipped for your insolence."

"You couldn't," Elyon told her, his tone as dry as dust. "Lancel is heir to House Greymont, and a Knight of Varin's Order. You sound ridiculous speaking like that. Now sit down."

Lillia seemed ready to shout a reply to that, but seeing the stern look in her brother's eye, decided to swallow it. Instead she smiled and put on a sweet little voice. "Only because you asked so nicely, *my lord*." She finished with an exaggerated curtsey, and then flopped down onto a chair. It was big enough to hold two. She patted the space beside her and Jovyn took his seat, looking glum, after a short hesitation. "What are you so miserable about?" Lillia frowned at him, annoyed by his delay. "*I'm* the one who's just found out her father cheated on her mother, sired a bastard, and that bastard went on to murder her brother and cripple said cheating bastard of a father."

"Well put," Amara said, "but inaccurate. You father never knowingly betrayed your mother."

Lillia shrugged, huffed, and placed a pillow on her lap to cuddle. Suddenly she was a little girl again.

Elyon looked around. "Enough talk of Jonik," he said. "His time will come. And we can talk about that later, Lil, OK?" She nodded and bit her lip, then fell sideward into Jovyn's shoulder. *Poor boy,* Elyon thought, seeing him turn rigid at her touch. He was too young to hide the fact that he was so obviously infatuated with her. "Right then." He cleared his throat, took a drink of wine. "Where were we?"

"We were talking about the murders of Dick Mallory and his family," said Barnibus.

"Right."

"There's more to that," the ruddy cheeked knight went on. "More killings, I should say."

"At the merchant's house?"

"No, a tavern in White Shadow. One we've been to, actually. Happened the same night as Mallory's place became a morgue." He frowned. "It was the same night as the storm started, come to think of it, that day you had to run off for the inaugural war council meeting."

"The night you told me about Prince Robbert," said Lillia. That thought brought a fleeting smile back to her face. "Do you know about that, you two? I'm to wed the prince."

"*Lillia.*" Elyon gave her another stern look. "You're *not* meant to be sharing that."

"Oh go away, Elyon. We can't all keep secrets so well as you."

Elyon sighed. *I probably deserved that.* "Which tavern was it, Barny?"

"One of the ones we go to after training. The Dead Dragon."

"Dead Dragon?" Lillia bunched her lips. "What sort of name is that?"

"An aspirational one," Elyon said. He looked to Barnibus. "What happened?"

"Well, this one's being talked about as a failed robbery too," the Varin Knight said. "Some thief managed to break into the tavern after the landlord had locked up. I spoke to him about it myself. He said that he'd locked all the doors, and there were no signs of a break in. Couldn't think how the guy got in. But anyhow, it was late when it happened, dead of night kind of late. Seems the thief startled a soldier while rummaging through his room. They quarrelled for a moment, then the thief put a length of steel through his heart. Still, the short commotion was loud enough to wake a few others nearby - there are some soldiers staying there as you know, some of the Kastor lot - and they came barging out of their bedchambers to grab the guy...but he cut them all up, easy as that, and escaped."

"A Bladeborn, then," Elyon said. "How many were there?"

"Thieves? Just the one."

Elyon shook his head. "How many were killed?"

"Oh. Five, I think."

"And did anyone get a good look at the killer?"

"Not really. A couple of them caught a glimpse of him, though only from behind. All they saw was him rushing off across the landing, cloaked and cowled, and down the steps into the main tavern below. Both followed, but by the time they reached the bottom of the steps, the thief had disappeared."

"Disappeared?" Lillia crinkled her brow. "How did he get out? Through the main door?"

"Well that's just it. There were no signs of a break-in, like I say. According to the landlord, the locks were still fastened when the thief was gone. No windows broken, nothing. He thought he was hiding in the cellar or elsewhere, so gathered up a few of the other Kastor soldiers and tried looking for him, but still....nothing. It was like he'd vanished." He shrugged. "Just made me think of the Nightblade, is all. That maybe he hid somewhere until the doors were opened and then slipped out? It was all that made sense to me. But, as you say Elyon... he's somewhere south, your brother, so it couldn't have been him."

"*Half*-brother. And no true kin of mine. So where does this lead us? You think these killings were Janilah's doing? That these are his creatures and cutthroats, creeping about in search of the Windblade?"

"Just that. The Dead Dragon was likely one of King Godrik's decoys, same as Dick Mallory's place. Janilah found out, sent in his goons, and they came out with nothing but blood on their blades."

"So nothing was stolen from the Dead Dragon?"

"Nothing."

"Or Dick Mallory's?"

"Seems not. And clearly Janilah's willing to turn to violence to get his hands on the blade. That should worry us. Who knows when he might storm Godrik and Dalton's own quarters and try to find it?"

"He can't," Elyon said. "The home of a merchant and a tavern in White Shadow are very different from the king and prince of Vandar's privy chambers. He can't risk shedding royal blood in his own palace; tensions are too high for that."

"I agree, "Amara said, spinning the flute of her glass between her long nimble fingers, her nails painted a deep dark blue. "My kingly cousin is not so reckless as to have his killers barge in on Godrik or Dalton's chambers, but that's not to say he won't find another way in. Any move he makes will carry great risk, however, and Godrik will know this. *We* are not so constrained, and have the element of surprise on our side. Let them play their little game, while we plot to steal the prize."

"When?" asked Lancel.

"The wedding," Amara replied. "There will be no better opportunity, with the palace so distracted."

"Which Godrik will know," Elyon told her. "He'll have the Windblade well guarded."

"Of course he will," she said, "but I'm sure we'll figure out a way around them." She had a devious look in her eye, though didn't elaborate. Instead she supped her drink and said, "Let me think on it some more. I know this palace, and I know my king cousin, and these rumours of a blue ghost, well..." She paused, pensive, but said no more. Amara could be vexing in this sort of mood. After a few moments she went on. "Lillia, Jovyn, since you're here, perhaps we can find a task for you as well in all this. You in particular, Jovyn. You're hardly well known around here, it's no insult to say, so when you're absent from proceedings, I doubt anyone will notice. That will serve us...so long as you're willing to participate, of course?"

Jovyn had a dutiful look on his face. "It would be my honour, my lady," he said. "I...I've missed being your squire, Sir Elyon."

"Just Elyon,' Elyon told him, for the thousandth time. "Goodness, Jov, you do have a short memory, don't you?"

"Um, sorry, Sir...um, Elyon. It's just been so long since I served you. I forget, is all."

"It's a force of habit, I know." Elyon gave the boy a smile. "I was the same when I squired for Captain Lythian. Took a while for me to drop the 'sir' even when he asked me to." He paused a moment in reflection. Those days squiring for Lythian had been some of his fondest. No boy could ever hope to serve a better knight, and Elyon had always tried to emulate that bond with Jovyn. But this? Did he really want to include him in something as dark and devious as this? He looked his squire in his round brown eyes, as open and honest as ever, and said, "This is hardly squirely work, Jov, it's best we be clear on that. We'll be stealing a Blade of Vandar, a crime that carries with it the charge of execution. You have to be certain you want to be involved. If we're caught..."

"You won't get caught," Amara told them. Her certainty was somewhat comforting, it had to be said. *But then, she did send my father out into the Icewilds to die...*

Lillia took umbrage with that, though. "How do you know?" she demanded, looking more worried all of a sudden. "I don't want Elyon or Jovy to die on account of that sword. Is all of this even worth it? I'm starting to wonder....I mean, look what the Sword of Varinar did to Uncle Vesryn. It drove him mad, everyone's saying. Even if Elyon does steal the blade, I don't want him to go mad." She looked at him. "I don't want that, Elyon. Maybe this isn't a good idea after all."

"Spare no thought for your uncle," Amara told her. "He is another matter entirely, and you'd do well to leave all that wondering to your elders, little bear. Elyon and I have considered all of this at length and feel we must take a stand. For your brother, your father, the honour of this house, we must. It's high time we sought some justice for the wounds this family has suffered."

Lillia remained unmoved. "*We*," she said. "You keep saying 'we', Auntie, but as far as I see it, Elyon's taking all the risk. It makes me wonder what exactly *you'll* be doing during the wedding."

Amara raised her chalice. "I'll be doing what I do best, child. Drinking, and hoping all goes well."

Lillia rolled her eyes, but Elyon knew full well that Amara would play a much larger role than that. She was the architect of this little scheme, and more central to their plot than she was making out. Still, he'd heard enough for now. "Then it's decided," he said, standing from his chair. "We have two days to forge a plan from this, but right now, unless there's anything more to report, I'm going to bed." He looked around, saw nothing. "Good. Lil, we can talk about our half-brother tomorrow, if you want. I'll explain everything, I promise."

She nodded quietly. "Fine." The word was a whisper, soft as a spider's step. "Tomorrow, then."

"Tomorrow," he said, already dreading it. Not once had he wanted Lillia finding out about Jonik, nor everything else that accompanied the reveal, but alas she deserved to know. There was no helping that now. "And nothing we've spoken of tonight leaves this room."

He left them there, walking back through the apartment, and out of the front door. The corridor beyond was silent as death, lit by lamplight ensconced at intervals along the white-stone walls, with deep pools of shadow in between.

He thought he caught a flash of movement to his right, turned, and saw nothing. *A trick,* he thought. *A trick of the light.* But all the same he stopped in place, took a grip of his godsteel dagger, and listened. His ears perceived something...the lightest patter of feet, far off at the edge of his hearing. He turned that way, frowned, drawing a full breath through his nostrils, *smelling*. His heart fell into a steady, plodding beat, his sword hand flexed, and a shadow of suspicion fell upon his face.

For in the air swirled a sweet scent he knew well.

The scent of Lady Melany Monsort.

36

Lythian

"What are they discussing?" Lythian whispered weakly.

Talasha dabbed at his head with a cool wet cloth. "Do not trouble yourself to know, sweet captain." He detected worry in her voice. She smiled uneasily.

"They mean to kill me?" Lythian croaked, glancing blearily through the trees. The discussion below sounded heated, murmured voices blowing hot in the brisk morning air.

She put a soft hand to his cheek, leaned in, kissed his burning forehead. "I'd never let them," she promised him. "*Never.* Now sleep, my sweet knight. You need to rest. The fever is still with you."

It had been with him for over a week, a fever deep down in his bones, a fever they feared would kill him. And if not the fever, it would be Ashun Klo and his thugs, he knew, Grumlo and Kartheck and Rackar. Lythian wasn't blind to what they were arguing about down the hill. He knew what it was that they wanted. *My blood,* he thought dismally. *Every last drop of my blood...*

Lythian faded off into another dark and fevered sleep. He was back on that courtyard of cracked white stone, dancing with his dead wife Talia and his unnamed infant son. Around them, the maple trees were standing attendance, only instead of red leaves they had dark red eyes hanging from their branches, a thousand of them, a thousand thousand, all watching him unblinking. He turned from them, turned from them all, and looked into Talia's eyes instead. But they were red too, and so were his son's, manic and wild and staring. *Those eyes,* he thought, in terror, recoiling. *Those haunting red eyes...ancient...evil...*

He woke again to a bloody sunset, the clouds drenched in vermillion and maroon, a cold damp chill in the air. He shivered beneath his blankets, turning his eyes through the broken ruins of the old castle, up to the plateau beyond the bailey where the forested hills and valleys of the Western Neck rolled away into the mists. He could see Talasha up there, with her cousin Prince Tethian, standing beneath the dusk. She looked to be pleading. And Kin'rar was there too, in his silky grey cape, and the diminutive old figure of the scholar Sotel Dar, leaning on his dragon-head cane, thoughtful.

"You wake," said a deep voice.

Lythian turned his head to find Lord Ulrik Marak seated beside him on the perch Talasha had made her own. The princess had been ever at his side during the long dark days of his fever, nursing him as best she could with the help of her handmaidens Cevi and Mirella, tending him day and night as Sir Pagaloth stood ever faithful on guard.

Lythian cleared his throat. It was rusty, burned from the inside out, like the rest of him. The depths of Eldur's Shame had been too much for a man of the north to bear, a man with the blood of Varin coursing through his veins. He was not meant to be there. And the mountain had let him know it.

"Ulrik." He managed to shift up a little on his raised pallet bed of feather-stuffed pelts and furs. "I heard...I heard you conferring earlier." He searched through the growing gloom of the ruins, down the slope into the woods where the outlaws made their camp. "Ashun, he..."

"Wants you dead," Marak told him plainly. His salt and pepper hair was coarse and cropped short, jaw broad and tightly clenched. "He believes you will try to kill Eldur when your strength returns."

Lythian frowned. "Kill him? I thought...I thought Ashun believed my blood would *revive* him."

"Sotel Dar has mused long and hard on that and decided otherwise. There is nothing in the record to suggest the blood of Varin will wake him. They are...desperate, Lythian. Nothing has worked so far."

Lythian knew only bits and pieces, in-and-out on consciousness as he'd been. In truth his memory of all that had happened that day at the Wings was fractured, and everything since even more so. He recalled the flight to the islands upon the back of Garlath the Grand, the fiery red lightning storm that Sotel Dar called the Ire of Agarath. He remembered parts of the journey into the mountain of Eldur's Shame, the tunnels and passages, the strange creatures that lurked there, the heat, yes he recalled the heat most of all, that stifling unbearable heat that had cooked his bones and blood.

He remembered with clarity following Talasha down that chasm, the tumble into the depths, the eerie expression that had come upon her face. She had gone into some sort of trance, leading him down and down into the depths, and then...then all was muddled but for glimpses. A great black cavern. A heat so fierce he thought he would die, air so thick he could scarcely move, dragons...dragons wheeling above him, and a great stone mountain in the shape of Drulgar the Dread, with an old white-haired man, wrapped in a robe with a staff across his lap, sleeping up against it. Sleeping as he had been for near three and half thousand years.

And sleeping still, he knew.

The last he could remember before he passed out in that cavern was seeing Eldur open his eyes, red and wild, before his own world went black as tar. He had to hear the rest of what had happened from Talasha. Hear of how the others had found their way down to join them, how Eldur had only awoken for a few fleeting moments, before his eyes flickered shut again. How he'd been carried out upon Lord Marak's own back. How Ashun Klo had told them right there and then to leave Lythian to his fate, yet Talasha and Kin'rar had argued otherwise, and Prince Tethian had agreed, ordering Ashun himself to help Kin'rar carry him.

He'd been saved, but not Starslayer. There were none among the host who could wield its metal, so his ancestral blade, to his deep aching sadness, had been left behind, left there in hell amidst the heat and the horror, the dread and the dragons.

The thought sent cold fingers of despair reaching through him. He felt naked now without his blade, and more anguished than he could say to have left it behind. The divine mists of godsteel were said to be Vandar's very soul leaking from the metal, and Lythian could remember how those mists had twisted and writhed in a rhythm he'd never seen before. *And now they will lie there in that twisting terror forever,* he thought, miserable and ashamed.

He'd spent the days since here in this bed, hearing the latest reports from Talasha and Kin'rar and Pagaloth whenever he briefly woke. They had tried everything to awaken Eldur, he was told, unearthing arcane rituals and rites, rubbing balms and oils into his body, fanning him with flames to try to stir him back to life. Nothing had worked. Not when Neyruu and Garlath were brought before him, roaring to wake him, breathing their fiery breath. Not when they'd poured potions through his lips. Not when Ashun Klo had marched through to where Lythian was being nursed, slashed his knife across his arm as he slept, returned to Eldur and flicked the blood onto the demigod's face. Ashun had claimed to see Eldur stir, spotting some flicker in his eyes, and that had spurned him to suggest they empty Lythian of all his blood, spill every last drop atop their Fire Father and watch him awake in a bloody red glory.

But he'd been denied. Sotel Dar had proclaimed it wouldn't work, Marak was telling him. But the rest? That Lythian would somehow rise from his fever, rise from his bed, take up the blade he no longer had, get past every one of Ashun Klo's guards and strike down the demigod where he lay.

He shook his head and scoffed. "I'm in no fit state to kill anyone, Ulrik," he said, "let alone Eldur. What would make Ashun think such a thing?"

"He has believed all along that you wished Eldur dead. That your very reason for staying with us when Borrus left was to see him killed. He is not a trusting man, Lythian. He has never wanted you here."

Nor have his men, Lythian thought. And perhaps they had me right all along. He'd not gone down into those tunnels to kill Eldur, no, but when he saw him, when he felt the ageless dread about him, and the dragons, and saw the mountainous form of Drulgar calcified to stone, something had come over him, a sudden urge to strike him through and stop him from ever rising. Borrus had warned of it. And Lythian had sought to act on it, driven by an ancient compulsion, a deep-seated fear written in his very blood and bones. But before he could, he'd collapsed. And he'd awoken right here on this bed.

He turned again to look up the hill as the sunset faded darker. "Do they discuss me?" he asked, in a voice both brittle and broken. "The princess...she entreats her cousin to spare me?"

"She does. As do Kin'rar and Sotel. None believe you will seek to slay our Fire Father. Nor do I, Lythian. I will not let you come to harm."

Lythian turned back to him. Marak's lips held the closest thing there was to a smile. "But if Tethian should will it?"

"Then he will lose me and Garlath from this company. You have only sought to help us thus far and have sacrificed much for this cause." He paused a moment. "I am sorry about your blade, Lythian. I tried to lift it, but the metal, the magic, it is different to the Fireblade. I had not the strength. I am sorry."

"Don't be. I'm grateful that you tried."

Marak nodded then filled a cup of water. He reached out. "Drink. The princess gave me instructions, should you wake. She says you must take on more liquids."

Lythian took the cup and drank long and deep. The water was cool and refreshing and the chill air helped soothe him. He felt a little better than he had the last couple of days. It felt like the fever was breaking.

"There is more," Marak went on, as Lythian drew on the water. "Our discussion earlier was not solely about you, Lythian. Sotel Dar has spoken of another way in which Eldur might be revived. A final way, that he believes will work." He glanced up the hill. "I suspect they are discussing it now."

Lythian got the sense that Marak wanted to rejoin them. "You can go, if you want. I'll be OK on my own."

"I do not think Talasha would approve. She asked me personally to sit with you while Sir Pagaloth goes hunting."

"So that's where he is," Lythian said. "I'd wondered." Mostly, when he woke, he found Talasha at his side and Sir Pagaloth standing sentry, only sleeping or eating or hunting when he knew that there were others nearby to watch over him. The one time Ashun Klo had managed to get through to cut him, Pagaloth had been taking a moment to relieve himself behind a tree, he'd later heard. The dragonknight was mortified to have let Ashun get to him, and had been doubly dedicated in his duty since. Lythian shifted up a little more on his bed. He felt stronger. Well enough to stand and walk, he judged.

"Perhaps I could join you then?" he asked. "I'd be interested to hear what Sotel has in mind."

Marak considered it. "Your counsel is always worth hearing. I do not believe Prince Tethian will object. Can you stand?"

"I would think so. Eight days is plenty long enough to lie here idle."

With some effort, Lythian Lindar emerged from the furs and blankets and took unsteadily to his feet. From down the slope the cookfires were burning, meat being roasted, vegetables boiled for soups and stews. The smell of it filled his nose and made his stomach churn. His appetite was returning. That was another good sign.

The pair turned and moved up the hillside, beyond the broken towers and walls, to where the others gathered on the shelf of mossy rock that looked out over the foothills. The twilight was deepening now, the hills and misted valleys drawn beneath the pall of night. The smell of pine and wildflowers and the damp must of rotting leaves filled the air, earthy and strong.

The group was in strained discussion, all frowns and fraught voices. "...it's a trap, and will not work," Talasha was telling them. "We cannot put him in such jeopardy. Eldur is father to us all. We should not risk him until we know for sure that..." She broke off as she noticed Lythian approach, a swift smile meeting her lips. "My captain, you're up."

"I thought it about time," Lythian said. He gave her a secret smile, though the bond they'd built was hardly a secret anymore. Lythian, noble and naive as he was, still hoped they were viewed as no more than friends, though Talasha hardly cared. To her they were all outlaws here, all brothers and sister under a single banner, and could do as they pleased. Lythian didn't imagine everyone felt the same. He had not missed how Ashun Klo looked at the princess during his time here. *And perhaps that's another reason why he wants me dead*, he thought.

Kin'rar stepped forward, grey-caped and slim, smiling. "It warms my heart to see you risen, Captain. We have missed your wisdom these last days. You had us all worried."

"You did," agreed Sotel Dar. "But it would seem that this Son of Varin is made of stronger stuff." He tottered forward with his walking stick and gripped Lythian's upper arm. "I will look forward to furthering our discussions by the fire, my friend. There is much we still need to talk about."

About the heir of Varin, the old scholar might have said. He seemed sure that Lythian would help them unravel the mystery of just who, and where, this fabled figure was.

Lythian smiled back at the scholar and turned to the prince, who regarded him with a weary and wary look. He'd scarcely come to his bedside over the last week, perhaps finding it easier to put distance between them as he pondered his fate. Tethian was a man of conviction, not easily swayed by others, but it was clear that his captain and childhood friend had gotten into his head. That showed on his face, and in his uncertain smile. "I am glad to see you risen, Captain Lythian," he said. There was something tired in his eyes, something desperate. He smiled faintly. "I know that you are aware of the discussions we have had about you. Talasha, my dear cousin...she has made it clear her mind, and others..." He looked at Kin'rar, Sotel Dar, Marak. "I have listened to their counsel and wisdom and been guided to a better course. I hope you understand...any thought I had to take your life was only in pursuit of something greater. There was nothing personal in it. You...you do see that, don't you?"

"I do," Lythian said, no lie in his words. "This cause has been your life, Prince Tethian, and yet you are stumbling at the last hurdle. Any man would do whatever they could to vault it, and see their task complete."

Tethian brightened. "I am glad to hear you say so. This matter of your blood...that is one thing, but Ashun worries you will try to slay our Divine Father now that you are back on your feet." He paused to judge his reaction, then smiled, looking relieved. "I can see that you will not. Ashun was always a worrier, even in our youth. And these times have grown tense, since we returned from the Wings. Everything we have tried has failed and each day we sense he grows weaker. The Breath of Agarath was sustaining him, but now..." He shook his head. "Now we find ourselves at an impasse, with but one true choice ahead of us." He turned to Sotel Dar.

"The Bondstone," the old man explained. "If Eldur was being kept alive by the fires beneath his tomb, then the very Soul of Agarath will surely awaken him. I have come to realise that this is the only way. But, it is fraught with risk."

"Much risk," nodded Talasha fervently. "If we travel there, my brother could kill or capture us all, the Fire Father included. Tavash will see this as a trap, I am sure, and as soon as he spots you, Tethian, he will think you're there to take his throne."

"I will tell him otherwise, Cousin. I'll tell him the throne interests me not. And even should he kill me, it makes no matter. My life is inconsequential, so long as Eldur lives."

"Tavash might kill Eldur too. He will not know who he is, and see only an old man. Why should he believe us when we tell him the truth of it? He took his throne by treason, Tethian. A man like that sees darkness around every corner."

Kin'rar turned to Lythian with a full explanation. "I have made contact with King Tavash and Vargo Ven," he said, with that cool composure of his. "A parley is being arranged at the Nest, three days hence. We plan to fly Neyruu and Garlath there, expose Eldur to the Bondstone, and see him restored. Once this is done Tavash will yield. He will have no choice, in the face of a god."

"You do not know my brother like I do," Talasha came back. "This parley will go ill, I know it. If we have need of the Bondstone, we should steal it. We have strength enough to stage a heist, and with Lythian back on his feet, perhaps..."

"Lythian cannot help us any more. He no longer has his blade." Tethian's words were enough to silence her. He shook his head firmly, his crimson cloak spotted with stains and bits of dirt. Even the sigil of Eldur was beginning to fray, Lythian didn't fail to note. "We have no time to make plans to infiltrate the Nest. Ulrik will tell you, Cousin; the fortress is not easy to enter and so far as Kin'rar reports, Vargo Ven has the place well guarded. Half a dozen of his best Fireborn are there, and several others of a lesser repute. If you say there is risk in the parley, then there is greatly more risk in a heist, and should we fail, we will not get another chance." He took a breath, and went on. "No, there is only one way, one solution to this riddle. If we wait any longer Eldur will surely wilt and perish and all we have done will be for nothing. We must take a chance, and be bold, my sweet. Everything relies on this. Everything."

"*I know.*" Talasha looked suddenly close to tears. "I just...the risks... I had thought it would be easier. When I saw him...when I saw him there in the cave...when he opened his eyes, I thought, I thought that was it, but it was nothing but a false dawn..." She shook her head, cringing.

"That dawn will soon brighten, dear Cousin," Tethian assured her. "And when it does, it will be the fairest dawn we shall ever see. A radiant dawn of change. The start of something great. We shall soon forget these difficulties we have faced, when Eldur stands before us, restored and renewed. Keep that thought in your heart, Talasha. This plan will work. It is foretold that it will."

Talasha nodded quietly to that, her worries subdued. In the quiet that followed, Lythian wondered who would be going. "Will it be the same group as last time?" he asked.

"No," Tethian said at once. "You will not be coming with us, Captain. You are too weak, and after what happened between you and Tavash..."

"I understand," Lythian broke in. He didn't need to be reminded of his time in King Tavash's care. Nor would he be much worth without Starslayer in his grasp. He turned his eyes to Talasha. She was his chief concern.

She saw the question and concern in his eyes. "I will be going, yes," she said. "Tavash is my brother. He may listen to me, if I speak to him."

"Tavash killed your mother," Lythian reminded her. "He killed the woman who brought him into this world to make himself heir. And he killed his own uncle to make himself king. Who's to say he won't kill you too, Talasha, if he detects a threat to his crown."

"No one is to say," Tethian came in. There was a shallow spike of anger in his voice. "This is the way, Lythian. There is no sense in worrying about the whats and the whys, not now. You care for my cousin, I know, and beyond what many would consider correct for a man such as you, yet your concerns are not relevant here. Talasha *must* come. She will be at no greater risk than the rest of us, but once Eldur has risen, Tavash will kneel, and Vargo Ven and all the rest will go to their knees alongside him. All of this is prophesied. I will hear no more of this despairing." With that, he spun and marched away, more animated than Lythian had yet seen.

Once the prince was gone, Kin'rar gave an apologetic smile. "He has been most tense, these last days," he explained delicately. "But I will stand at the princess's side, Lythian, as will Lord Marak. She will be well defended."

"She will, but unnecessarily," croaked Sotel Dar. "A parley is considered sacred here as it is in the north. Tavash will accurse himself should he break it."

"He has already done that, Sotel." Lythian gave a weary sigh. "A man who can murder his own mother is beyond salvation in the eyes of gods and men."

"With this I agree," the old man said. "And the gods will judge Tavash when he falls. Or before." He gave a crinkly smile. "I trust that Eldur will condemn the king himself when he rises. He and all those who have colluded in his treacheries will pay the dearest price."

But how many might be dead by then? Lythian had to wonder. He'd experienced Tavash's treacheries first hand and knew how the man liked to plot. Drawing them into a parley to kill or capture them all would free him of any other claimant to his throne, ripping them all out root and stem. Tethian was by rights the lawful King of Agarath and he in particular would be under threat. And Eldur? Who could say whether this latest bid to wake him would work, or fail like all the rest. Lythian shuddered to think of it all. He wasn't sure what disquieted him more; Tavash's plotting or the prospect of Eldur's fated rise and renewal.

Those eyes, he thought again, *those fiery red eyes.* It had been only a flash, only a glimpse, but he could not get them out of his head. He turned his gaze down the hillside and through the ruins. Lights were flickering in the camp as the dusk ebbed into a bloody black darkness. "I'd...like to see him," he said, all of a sudden. "Your Fire Father. I've not seen him since the Wings. I would like to look upon him again, if I may."

The group traded looks. "I see no reason why you cannot," said Lord Marak. "But you will need an escort. Ashun's men will see a warning in your coming."

"I don't mean to get close," Lythian said. "I just...want to look at him." *I need to,* he thought, *to banish my nightmares.*

Talasha smiled and stepped forward, taking his arm. "Come, sweet captain, I will take you." She glanced to the side. "Kin'rar, if you would be so kind as to shadow us."

"As you will, princess."

They descended the hill and passed once more through the ruins, moving at a gentle pace. Lythian felt his heart beating faster with every step. Talasha seemed to sense his unease. "You fear him, don't you?" she asked him softly. "You do not rejoice as we do to have him here with us."

"It's not in my nature to, Talasha. I...I try to believe everything your cousin and Sotel Dar say, but it's difficult. This balance they speak of. I know of no heir of Varin. And Eldur has always been a figure to fear in the north. As Varin has to the Agarathi." He swallowed to moisten his throat. It still felt parched and dry. "I cannot truly express how it feels to know he still lives. If Tethian and Sotel are wrong..."

"They're not wrong, sweet captain." Talasha's smile was comforting, as she pulled a little tighter on his arm. "I saw the goodness in him when I looked into his eyes. It was brief, yes, but I saw his mind, I feel. Eldur has no intent to cause harm or hurt. He wishes to atone for the darkness he brought. It is why he went to that mountain to sleep. He knew he would rise one day. He knew he would become a saviour."

Or conqueror, Lythian thought, for when he'd seen that glimpse into Eldur's eyes, he'd felt something quite different. But what could he do? Kill the demigod? He might as well sprout wings and fly home. Speak of his doubts and try to turn Tethian to another path? That would be even more futile. In the end he was impotent here, and in truth he didn't even know what he felt. His fear of Eldur was etched deep in his bones, much the same as Talasha's awe and admiration was, and he had to admit, that clouded his judgement somewhat.

The Father of Fire was being kept away from the main camp, in another part of the old castle ruins that once acted as a temple. The wall was still standing to shoulder height in most places, the stone floor cracked and overgrown with weeds. In one corner a larch tree had burst forth through the paving, and all over the stone was spotted with lichen and moss, with several rusted iron braziers burning softly around the sides. Sentries stood guard at the entrance, a brace of them, with several others around the circumference should someone try to climb what remained of the walls. Ashun Klo always kept one of his lead thugs on duty at the front. Today it was the deadly cutthroat Kartheck, with those mirthless ink-black eyes and the thin sneering smile. His lips peeled back as he saw Lythian approach. "What is *he* doing here?"

"Step aside, Kartheck," Kin'rar told him. "We wish to enter."

"My orders come from Lord Ashun."

"I am a Skymaster of Agarath. You will do as I command. Or must I call upon Neyruu to settle matters?" Kin'rar gave an easy smile.

Kartheck grunted and nodded at the other guard, then stepped side. "I will be behind you," he warned Lythian. "If I see you move, I will put my sword through your back."

Lythian would usually give a mocking response to that, but all he said was, "I don't intend to get too close," as his heart hammered hard in his chest.

He drew a painful breath into his lungs and stepped inside. Kartheck followed behind, as promised, his hand clutched at the black leather grip of his ferocious kilij sword, gently curved and deadly sharp, with a wooden pommel carved into the face of a screaming man. "Stay several paces back," he told him. "Do not approach the bier."

Lythian was unarmed, enfeebled, and feeling as weakened as he had in Eldurath. *What does he think I'm going to do?* He had no time to contemplate that question. Ahead lay his quarry, lying swaddled in fur upon a bed of grey stone, looking for all the world like he was dead. The Knight of the Vale looked upon the ancient figure of Eldur - the long white beard, the sallow papery skin, the deep-etched ruts and wrinkles - and saw nothing but an old man, sleeping peacefully in his bed. His chest was moving up and down, though slowly, and rarely, almost imperceptibly to Lythian's eyes. It was the only sign that he still lived.

This is he who once led Agarath's armies to war, he reminded himself. *He who rode upon the back of Drulgar the Dread, who fought and died seven times for his master during the War of the Gods. He who battled Varin at the Battle of Ashmount in the greatest duel of all. Who found a kingdom, spawned a race, erected wonders in his name, birthed the Fireborn from his blood.*

To anyone passing by, he looked like nothing but a feeble old man, white-bearded and wrinkled, softly taking his final breaths. Yet Lythian had seen the truth in those red eyes. He'd seen all his deeds and darkness. Seen the thousands of years he'd lived. It had been the briefest of moments only, but he'd seen it. *The truth is behind those lids,* he thought. *This old husk is only a deception. The true terror likes within.*

He drew a step back, then turned away, as his heart raced on, thudding beat after thunderous beat. He felt lightheaded again, his skin burning, brow beading with sweat.

"That's it?" Talasha asked him. "You have barely given him a glance." She sounded almost offended.

"A glance is all I needed." He continued to withdraw.

Talasha followed. "I do not follow, sweet captain. Does this ease your fears to see him? He is benevolent, can you not feel it? A great aura of goodness surrounds him."

Lythian nodded as he hastened out of the ruins of the old temple, back into the cold bracing air. "Yes," he lied, "I feel it too, Princess." He smiled for her to hide his fears.

For all he felt was shadow, and death.

37

Amron

"This is not a normal fog," said Amron Daecar, looking down from the top of the rise. "It soups strangely. I've never seen a mist so thick and..." He was trying to think of the right word. "Static," he finished.

"It is magic," intoned Stegra Snowfist. "I have told you this a hundred times, Lord of Daecar. The Sea-King did this, when he came here two hundred years ago. He left the lands accursed with this ugly grey mist. Now you see for yourself...I have not been lying, as you thought. Any man who enters the fog does not come back. Except you. *You* will return to us."

Amron nodded solemnly. He'd heard tell of the tales. Bjorga Bonecrusher, who was so big he could crush a man's skull in his fist, had ventured here over a century ago and never returned. Jonas the Giant was even bigger, and carried an axe so large no other man could lift it, but that hadn't much helped since he'd not come back either. Nor had Ronja Ironmaid, who had some dashes of fire in her milky white hair, and was as skilled as any of the Snowskins with blade and bone spear. Or Iceheart, the legendary hunter, Eivar the Earless, Jonna Jormund the Snow-Bear-Bane, or several others Amron had heard about. All were heroes worthy of song who'd thought themselves capable of breaking the curse. None had. Every one of them had been swallowed by the fogs and never been seen again.

The only one who had returned, Stegra had told him, was Milved of Milkwood, who some of the other men called Milved the Madman. It was said he was mad before he left, and madder still when he returned. He preached manically about ghosts and giants and spiders big as greatyaks, but no one had much listened to him. "If he saw all those things, he would have died like the rest of them," Jorgen Half-Eye had claimed one night. "Milved the Madman was no great warrior, not like Bjorga Bonecrusher and Ronja Ironmaid. Those tales he told are lies."

Amron certainly hoped so. He didn't much like the idea of facing off against a spider as big as a greatyak, and wasn't so sure about duelling a giant or ghost either. The former would tear him limb from limb without his armour, he did not doubt, and the latter...well, how did you even fight a ghost? That was mage work, and not the realm of a warrior.

"The land is vast," Amron said. He scanned the horizon. The mists seemed never ending, blanketing a great tract of land that went on beyond the boundaries of his sight. He could see the faint shadows of hills and short stubby mountain ranges breaking above the fog, but nothing else. The coastline was out there somewhere, he knew, but how far he couldn't say. "How would I even know where to start?"

Stegra gave a shrug. "I have told you the words of the prophesy many times, Lord of Daecar. This is all I know."

"That's not very helpful," grunted Walter Selleck. He had a glum look about him, one he'd worn since Vandar's Tomb nearly ten days ago. "Every curse has a source. It could take weeks, even months, to find it."

Stegra Snowfist looked down at him with those strange milky eyes. "You should cheer up, Walter. We have made it here at least, that is a good start. I miss how you were, always singing at night, always smiling. It has been many days now since you sung the Echo of Titans or the Song of King Ayrin. You call yourself the luckiest man in the world...you might want to change that to the *unhappiest*." Stegra smiled.

Walter didn't. "You denied Lord Amron a chance to heal," he complained. "He should have been restored by Vandar's light by now, but your fears got the better of you. You as well, Rogen. And now you expect him to defeat some curse, Stegra? It seems to me that you've cut off your nose to spite your face. How do you expect him to defeat anything in his state?"

Amron bristled at that. Walter was not usually so dismissive of his capabilities. "Careful, Walter, and remember who you're talking about. If you have cause to complain then aim it at me, not Stegra or Rogen. *I* gave the command to abandon the mountain. It was coming down. If we'd not have left when we did every one of us would still be trapped in there. Or dead, more likely."

Somehow Walter was still insisting the opposite. "My light would have protected..."

"*Enough* about your light," Rogen Whitebeard cut in. He gave Walter a lupine snarl, a dark look in his amber eyes. "We nearly died just climbing back down the stairs, if you'll remember. No light of yours would have protected us in there, when the ceilings and caverns collapsed."

It had been a close call, getting back down the mountain. No sooner had they climbed back through the tunnel and into the frigid wintry air as the volcano began to shake and shudder again. Their descent had been treacherous, and more than once one or another of them had almost taken a tumble and gone over into an abyss. Whether Walter's light and luck had something to do with their survival, Amron couldn't say for sure, though he suspected it might have. Still, it wouldn't have saved them inside, no, not from what he'd heard. It sounded like the entire mountain was caving in on itself, collapsing under its own great weight. It felt like Vandar himself was stirring.

Walter judged it better to move on from the topic. "What's done is done," he said. "Now we're onto this *next great quest*, I suppose."

One great quest will fail, but one greater will light the way, Amron thought. In truth he'd not fully believed that this prophesy could be true, but seeing this strange grey fog, this unmoving mist...it had him part convinced.

"We should rest before we leave," Whitebeard said. Below them, in the shadows of the ridge, the rest of the Snowskins were setting up camp, erecting their tents and shelters, digging firepits, tending the greatyaks. "We can set off at first light."

They'd come fractionally south now, from where they'd been at Vandar's tomb, and well over a hundred miles east. They got a peek of the sun again, as a result, though it hardly showed its face for more than a half hour each day before disappearing back below the horizon. Still, that time was precious. It would feel less ominous to enter those mists with the sun risen, Amron supposed.

But Stegra Snowfist shook his head. "No," he said.

Whitebeard wasn't understanding. "You suggest we leave now?"

"No," the huge chieftain repeated. The bear-head hood of his cloak hung behind his head, looking like it had been snapped grotesquely backward. "I suggest *we* do not leave at all. This quest is for the Lord of Daecar. He will go alone."

Whitebeard reacted at once to that. "Over my dead body."

"That can be arranged," returned Snowfist. "Do not forget about Bragga Burnside, Blacksteel."

Whitebeard ignored the threat. "I am charged with protecting Lord Daecar and will not leave his side."

"You will," Stegra claimed, angrily. "I have made it clear that Lord Amron will go alone."

"Have you?"queried Walter. His red cheeks bunched incredulously, brittle bits of ice breaking from his scraggly brown beard. "I confess I've not heard you say that before. It sounds like you're making it up."

"The Snowfist does not make things up. He may omit things, or forget things, but he does not make things up." He looked at Amron, ignoring the others. "This is how it must be. I think you knew all along, Steel Lord."

"I had a feeling," Amron admitted.

"No, my lord," said Rogen Whitebeard. "If one must go, let it be me. My life is worthless next to yours."

Amron smiled a craggy tired smile at the man. "By no means is that true, Rogen. You're a better man than you know. One day, perhaps, you'll tell me who you really are."

"I'm a ranger sworn to guard and guide you. My life before I came to Northwatch is of no consequence." He turned his eyes over the expanse before them, choked in fog and darkness. "You *cannot* go out there alone. Please, let me take your place."

"You cannot," Stegra told him. "You are *only* a ranger, Blacksteel. The prophesy tells of a steel lord. It can only be the Lord of Daecar."

"I know the prophesy, Stegra," Whitebeard came back. "You've spoken of it enough. And nowhere does it say that Lord Amron must go alone."

The Snowfist laughed. "I told you, I forget things and omit things. But always this task has been for the Lord of Steel alone. We will go no further, and await his return here in camp. If you like, you can watch from this ridge, Blacksteel. Perhaps those orange eyes of yours will be good enough to keep watch from afar?"

"Spare me your jests," Rogen spat back. "We're talking about a man's life here. You've heard enough stories to know how important Lord Daecar is to the northern kingdoms. And yet you'll send him away to his death, and based on what? Some words spoken to your grandfather's grandfather two hundred years ago!"

"Yes," said Stegra, quite plainly. He turned his eyes down over the ridge. Some of the Snowskins were looking up, such was the force of Whitebeard's voice. "Fear not, my friends, Blacksteel is just getting stroppy."

Kusto Crowbone and Wagga the White both laughed. Svaldar, the Snowfist's son, beckoned them back to their work.

"Your sense of duty is something to commend, Blacksteel," Stegra allowed, turning back to face the ranger. But for their voices, and the scuff and crunch of the men working in the snows below, all was eerily quiet. There was barely a breath of wind in the air. No birds or beasts drew near this strange place. "But this is how it must be. The Sea-King declared it so when he and his steel men put a curse on this land. He also said the lands will clear when the curse is lifted. So this is what we shall watch out for. When the Lord of Daecar has found the source and defeated the malice then we shall know. The fog will fade and the mist will burn and we join him in his triumph."

Rogen Whitebeard gave Stegra a displeased glare, then drew out his godsteel blade. "You'll take this at least, Lord Amron. Let it brace you against the darkness, and whatever else you face out there."

Amron hadn't felt the touch of godsteel since he'd lost his own blades in the Silver Scar. He'd spent most of those long weeks either imprisoned in that honeycomb hill or riding upon the back of a greatyak, sheltered from the icy winds. But going into those mists alone would be different. He would need godsteel out there, as he'd need his courage and his wits. He took Whitebeard's blade gratefully and said, "I will give it back to you when I return."

"Yes," exclaimed Stegra. "Yes, this is good. The Lord of Daecar has confidence, and faith." He looked rebukingly at Whitebeard. "Why cannot you have the same, Blacksteel? You fret like an old woman. And you, Walter...you are very quiet. That is unusual. Even sour-faced as you have been of late, you still have much to say, even if it is just to moan. But not on this? Do you not have any complaints?"

"Would you care if I did?"

"No."

"Then what use would it serve for me to say anything at all? The only one who matters here is Amron, and his mind is made up, I can see."

"Yes, so can I." The Snowfist smiled broadly. "Then let us not stand here forever. You were right about one thing, Blacksteel. It would be better for the Lord of Daecar to rest and leave in the light. That gives us time to drink." He grinned happily and marched away.

Amron's last supper was had in the communal shelter, a stew of greatyack meat and turnips, with old stale heels of bread on the side, that softened when dipped in the soup. It was mostly tasteless, but Amron didn't care. He could scarce eat a mouthful anyway.

He was nervous. Nervous to the point of being deeply afraid. He sat quietly as the others slurped and supped, passing around the sour milky grog that passed as wine among the tribe. Stories were shared, as always, and the tribesmen sang songs of their own, and songs for Amron too, crooning Dauntless Daecar and the Echo of Titans and getting the words mostly right. Still, Walter *tsked* and tutted, shaking his head at each mistake. "They're butchering the verses, my lord," he grumbled. "Are the lyrics truly that complicated?"

"Why don't you join in, Walter?" Amron suggested. "You've been morose for far too long. Anyone would think it was you who'd be stuck as a cripple for the rest of his life."

Walter gave a quiet and shameful nod. "I've been selfish and unthinking," he admitted dourly. "I suppose...well it's no excuse, not really, but I suppose returning to that mountain, it stirred feelings in me, from a past long forgotten. I feel the shadow of who I was creeping closer behind me, my lord." He sighed deeply, shook his head, and said, "I feel my light fading, somehow. Like a star dimming in the night sky, its beauty and brightness dulled. My purpose was always to lead you to your salvation, Amron, yet now...with this failure, I sense my gift is being taken away. It's as though Vandar is displeased with me, for not doing my duty to restore you."

"You're not to blame, Walter," Amron assured him. "You put too much stock in your faith. This talk of Last Renewals and champions and blessings...perhaps you were just wrong." The sour milky wine they called *sickmilk* reached him as he spoke, named for all those who threw up after indulging. He took the skin, took a swig, and recoiled. It was truly unpleasant stuff.

"I suppose I could have been," Walter said. It was the closest he'd get to admitting it. He took the skin and had a sip, wincing. "But a champion takes many forms, Amron. They don't all fell dragons and lead the van. You still have an important part to play in this, of that I have no doubt."

Amron wasn't so sure. *No one returns from those mists,* he thought. Walter had been wrong about him reaching the heart of Vandar's Tomb, so wasn't it possible that Stegra was wrong about this prophesy too? Fear blew through him like an ice cold wind, driving a shiver up his spine. He took the skin back and swallowed a generous gulp. As ever, the second wasn't so bad.

"Do not hog the sickmilk, Steel Lord," called Kusto Crowbane. "Come, come, I have a thirst."

Amron begrudgingly handed it over.

The singing went on, loud enough to drown out any hope of conversation. Amron receded back into his thoughts, waiting for the sickmilk to come back around to him, as one of the tribe's own songs, Iceheart and Elenor, was chanted to a raucous beat. Iceheart was a famously cold and closed off man, yet a woman named Elenor eventually managed to thaw him. To have him prove his love for her, she asked that he travel into the Land of Mists and drive away the curse that had blighted the lands, so that they might be settled once more, as in days gone by. Amron knew how that ended. Iceheart never came back, and Elenor was left to rue the task she'd set him. The Snowkins had many songs and stories like that, tales of valour and heroism, love and loss and tragedy, and many ended the same way too, with their heroes venturing into those fogs, never to be seen again.

One would think they'd learn eventually, Amron thought, as a chill air came rushing into the large communal tent, and Whitebeard stepped inside. His beard and cowl were frosted, his eyes glancing around, intense. He found Amron across the fire, circled the tent, and crouched down beside him. "I have a plan, my lord," he hissed into his ear, giving Stegra a glance to make sure he wasn't watching. "There's a break in the ridge, a little to the east. It's the best way through into the fogs. I'll meet you there, before dawn. If we leave before Stegra realises, he'll have no way to stop us."

Amron started shaking his head. He wasn't sure exactly why. Would it not be better for Rogen Whitebeard to come too? And Walter? No matter what the man said, Amron felt sure his light and luck was still in good order. Yet all the same, he was shaking his head. It didn't take him long to realise why. "No one will be coming with me, Rogen," he said. "This task I must do alone."

"Why?" demanded Whitebeard. "Because Stegra said so?"

"Yes. I gave him my oath to see this quest fulfilled. If he says I must go alone, I must. To go behind his back would be dishonourable."

"*Dishonourable*?" Whitebeard said the word like it was a curse. "Pardon me, my lord, but to hell with your honour. It serves you well east of the Weeping Heights, I'm sure, but out here it's all shadows and ice, dread and death and honour has no place. It'll get you killed if you let it."

"Then I'll die as I have lived. I am not breaking my word."

Whitebeard spat out a breath. "And what of my word? What of my oath? I swore to Lord Borrington I would do all I can to protect you."

"I know. And you have. But this I must do alone, Rogen." He turned away, telling the ranger in no uncertain terms that he wasn't going to be moved on it. No matter his fears and trepidations, he'd made a promise, and was going to follow through. *I am Amron Daecar,* he thought, *Slayer of Vallath, Crippler of Kings. I am not going to let myself be unmanned by a bit of mist.*

"And what shall I report back when I see Lord Borrington again?" Whitebeard pressed. "What shall I tell him to put in the letter they send to your daughter, my lord?"

Amron's will wilted, just a moment, to think of Lillia. "The truth," was all he could think of. "Tell Robert the bloody truth, Rogen."

"The truth will not paint you well, Lord Daecar. You say you will die as you lived. I never thought you lived as a fool." He stood at that and marched away, back out into the cold.

Amron might have struck him if he'd stayed. He watched him lurk away angrily. "He forgets who he speaks to," he grunted.

"He worries, is all," Walter said. "Say what you like about Rogen

Whitebeard, but he is unwavering in his duty. It wounds him that he won't be at your side, Amron, as it wounds me that I failed to lead you to the holy chamber. I'd not put it past him to follow you regardless."

"If he does then he'll only secure his death. Either he'll die out there with me, or Stegra will kill him for an oathbreaker when he gets back. Either way, Rogen Whitebeard will be dead. I trust he's smart enough to work that out."

"I'm sure he already has, but that won't much matter to him. You've seen him, Amron. He hardly cares whether he lives or dies. If he has a choice between your life and his, I have a good idea of which he'll choose."

"Then I'll speak to Stegra of his intentions, and make sure the man is under guard until I'm long gone from this place. I will not have him dying with me, if that should be my fate."

Another two hours of singing and drinking passed before Amron returned to his own tent to rest. He spent that time speaking with a few of the tribesmen to better understand where he might go. Few were much help, in truth, though they tried to offer him guidance all the same. Jorgen Half-Eye suggested he strike north toward the coast, and search for the place where the Sea-King was said to have landed on his great ship with blue and yellow sails. Wagga the White told him to remain near higher ground, where possible, so that he might break out above the fog and help orient himself. "You will need the stars to navigate, Lord of Daecar," he said. "Use the hills and high points as markers. Go from one to the next, as best you can."

He got other tidbits, some more obvious than others, as he went around each man in turn and sought whatever counsel they might give him. Secretly he was hoping to get words of encouragement as well, which he did for the most part, though some still looked at him doubtfully all the same. *They don't see a great warrior in me, but a cripple,* he knew. He could see that they didn't all share Stegra's faith in the prophesy either. Kusto Crowbane was a lively and cheerful sort, but wasn't afraid to speak his mind. "How will you defeat the malice if you find it?" he asked, quite straight. "You have spent weeks atop the greatyak, and cannot move quickly with that leg. I do not see you as a great fighter. Perhaps you were once, but now...I do not see it."

Amron took no insult from the man. "I have a powerful blood-bond to godsteel," he explained. "It will help brace my limp and give me strength, speed, and power."

"But enough to defeat the malice?"

Amron didn't know how to answer that. No one was in agreement of what this malice was. "I don't know, Crowbane. *Malice* could cover all manner of things."

"No," said Kusto Crowbane. "I know what the malice is. It is a giant man...no, a giant *woman* with the head of a greatyak, with horns and hoofed feet, and two huge bone-spears for arms, ten feet long. This is the malice you will face."

Amron had to laugh. He'd heard a few peculiar accounts like that though none had any base in fact. This was nothing but a figment of Kusto's energetic imagination. "I do hope not," is all he said.

"If you find this thing," Kusto went on, as though not hearing him, "go for the legs. Cut those and it will fall, so you may finish it. Then you can take its greatyak head, and clear the fogs. But the legs, Lord of the Easterlands. Always remember. Go for the legs."

Amron thanked him for his wise counsel and went on his way, soaking up the wisdom of the tribe for all the good it would do him. All the while those eyes watched him shamble from man to man, those querying, pitying eyes that he'd come to know so well. *They fortify me like godsteel does*, he thought, defiant. *They light a fire in me to prove them wrong*. These men knew him from the stories, but had never seen him in his pomp and prime. They'd never seen him decked in lobstered godsteel plate with the Sword of Varinar to hand, fogging gold against the skies. They could hear Walter warble all day long about his deeds, but seeing was believing, and all they saw was a bearded old cripple in a big black cloak, living on past glories. *But when I return, they'll see different,* he decided. *They will see the man from the songs appear through those thinning mists. They'll see the legend come alive.*

But where to go? He still didn't know. To the coast? To the nearest ranges? There would be lakes and valleys and forests out there, hidden amid the mists, and his quarry could be anywhere. The most spiritual answer came from young Svaldar when he said, "Follow your heart, Lord of Daecar, and it will show you the way."

It was as good an option as any, Amron supposed. Stegra thought so too, judging by his pursed lips and nodding head. "My son is wise," he agreed. "The Sea-King foretold of your coming, Steel Lord, and will guide you where you need to go." He tapped a finger to Amron's chest and then his forehead, saying, "Follow this, and not this. Magic is in the heart, not the head, and you have a strong heart, Lord of Daecar. Let go of your doubts and do not worry. It will lead you true."

It will lead you true, Amron thought now, as he lay there in his tent, heaped beneath the pelts and furs. It was not something he was accustomed to, following the whims of his heart, yet he told himself to trust it all the same. He didn't have much choice. *I have my instincts, and they'll help guide me,* he decided. *Perhaps that's what Stegra and Svaldar meant?*

He couldn't say when he fell asleep, but it felt like he'd lain there in thought forever. Yet when he opened his eyes once, and saw the thin film of light glowing beyond the flaps of his tent, he knew that it was time. He donned his quilted leathers and furs, boots and gloves and cloak, and massaged the feeling back into his right thigh. His swordbelt came next, fixed with Whitebeard's godsteel dagger and sheath, then he hauled on the pack he'd filled with provisions, drew aside the flaps, and looked upon the tribe.

There they stood, lined up in camp, each and every one of them risen early to see him off. Kusto Crowbane with the many scars on his face. Wagga the White with his light brownish hair. Jorgen Half-Eye and the patch on his left eye. Svaldar, young and strong and fearless. Stegra the Snowfist, huge smile on his face and something that resembled a mist in his eyes.

The rest were there too, Arnel Hammerhand and Sigurt Seven-Sons and Niklas and Verner and Briggor the Big, who was only five foot three. Walter and Whitebeard stood together beside them, one short and paunchy, the other tall and grim. All were smiling, every one of them but the ranger, who merely scowled and looked in no way happy to see Amron set off alone.

"My friend," said Stegra the Snowfist, stepping forward in his huge white snowbear cloak. "You do a great thing for us this day. So we stand here to honour you, and send with you our prayers and wishes, our hopes and our dreams. And when you return, you will have our thanks. You will always be welcome among the Snowskin tribe."

The men nodded. Some looked as teary as Stegra. To them this day was momentous, whether they truly believed Amron would break the curse or not. *It means the world to them,* he saw, more touched by the gesture of their gathering than he could say.

"We will escort you to the ridge, Lord of Daecar," announced Svaldar son of Stegra. "Come, join us. The fogs await."

They fell into step around him, in some sort of ceremony Amron didn't know. Stegra took the front, Svaldar the back, with the rest flanking him either side. Neither Walter nor Whitebeard were permitted within the circle. Both walked alongside them instead. Amron could hear Whitebeard muttering his complaints, and Walter shushing to shut him up.

There was a breach in the ridge, the one Whitebeard had spoken of Amron guessed, where a narrow channel gave access through the hills. These lands were well protected with natural defences, Stegra had told him, with many such hills and prominences, and secluded valleys teeming with woods and lakes for fishing and hunting and trapping. It was why the land was so desirable to them, yet what the Sea-King's motivation for covering it with this shroud was, none could say. It was a puzzle Amron and Walter had been unable to figure out; who the Sea-King was and why he'd done what he'd done. In truth Amron hadn't believed it, as Stegra had rightly said, yet seeing the mists, feeling the air in this place, that strange eerie aura, the unnatural quietness...now he was beginning to believe. And a part of him, the part that wasn't afraid, was eager to unravel the riddle.

"We leave you here," boomed Stegra, as they reached the end of the opening where it broke out into the plains. Ahead of them, some twenty metres away, the grey mists eddied ever so gently, swirling languidly at the edge of the blight. Beyond, they looked thick and still, pervasive and uninviting. "Go straight, Lord of Daecar. I know at least that the valley here goes on for a way, until you reach the hills beyond." He pointed. "You can see them, shadowed in the distance. Make for those, climb them, and that will be a good start."

"And follow your heart," added Svaldar, joining them as the men broke formation, lining up once more. "The Sea-King will call to you, Amron son of Gideon. You will hear him in your heart. Follow his voice, and you will meet the malice." He stepped in and took Amron's arm. "Good luck."

Amron smiled at the boy. "My thanks, Svaldar son of Stegra. I'll not let you down."

In that moment, something in him believed it. *This feels strangely like fate,* he thought, as he looked at the Snowfist and his son, at the tribesmen and huntsmen lined up behind them, at Walter and White-beard standing nearby, the shorter man looking on with an expression of great hope and expectation, the taller one still grumbling silently of this folly, yet somehow, Amron saw, somehow caught up in the moment all the same. *Even Rogen Whitebeard sees something in this,* he realised. And that, if nothing else, was the push that he needed.

He turned to face the mists. "I will see you all soon."

With those words, he wrapped the fingers of his right hand around the hilt of Whitebeard's godsteel blade, braced his right leg so that he might walk without a limp, and stepped away into the fog beneath the gleam of a rare risen sun.

38

Jonik

"How is he?" Jonik asked, peering through the half open door.

"Weak," said Sir Borrus, humourlessly, "but he's getting stronger by the day, in mind as well as body. I've had him talking plenty enough this afternoon, remembering the olden days. He's still in there, I can tell. A bush that needs trimming, that's all. And I'll keep working with my shears."

Jonik smiled at the analogy. Sir Torvyn Blackshaw had once been a brawny knight, to hear Borrus tell it, with a shock of dirty blond hair and a smile never far from his face. It was hard to reconcile the image with the brittle grey-haired man lying in the cabin bed, so slight beneath the blankets and muttering occasionally in his sleep. "Do you need a break, Sir Borrus?" Jonik asked. "I could ask one of the maids to watch him, or Benjy? He's always willing."

"It's fine, I'll stay for now. He'll stir in an hour or two and it'll be best if I'm here when he does." Borrus gave him a sincere smile. His bluster and bolshiness had been entirely absent since that day in the desert. "But thank you, Jonik. I can tell you care about Torvyn, and the rest of these men. What you're doing here..." He shook his head, and gave a tired laugh. "I'm not great with words, not of this sort, anyway. Let's just say...you've proven me wrong, lad. You're not the man I thought you were."

Jonik was touched. He had no idea what to say to that, so he just bowed in thanks and drew the door shut again, only unleashing his smile once he'd stepped down the corridor and back up onto the deck. Sad though it was, Borrus Kanabar's approval meant a lot to him, for the fondness and friendship the man felt for his father. He let the smile linger a moment as he walked over to give Shade a brush, the horse enjoying the cover of the mainsail as he stood as stoic as ever, looking out over the glittering waters.

"See anything of interest out there?" Jonik asked him, taking up the grooming brush and running the thick bristles over his glossy jet flank.

Shade's chestnut eyes moved to Vincent Rose's grand caravel sailing a hundred metres off to port. It was called *One World*, Ranulf had told him, for the variety of sailors and seafarers the merchant liked to hire, plucked from all across the world, north and south, east and west. Another of his eccentricities, Jonik imagined, rather than some noble desire to make all men equal beneath his sails.

"You miss Jack?" Jonik guessed, looking at Shade. "And the others?" Jack, Emeric, Braxton and Devin were all aboard Rose's grander vessel, enjoying her spacious cabins and clean wide decks and the naked woman she had as her figurehead, Jonik did not doubt. Well, Devin would anyway. The boy had spent any spare moment he had in Rose's manor ogling the nude portraits and paintings on the walls. And when he wasn't, he was ogling those beguiling Lumaran twins that the merchant liked to keep around.

Shade gave his version of a shrug.

"I know how you feel. I got used to having them all around too. Strange with only Turner, Sid, and Pete here, isn't it?"

It certainly felt strange to Jonik. The three were the only ones left of the original crew who'd sailed from Green Harbour all those months ago. Aside from Borrus Kanabar, Ranulf Shackton and his young companion Leshie were with them aboard Invincible Iris, as were the three sellswords whom Jonik had taken on as sailors, old Benjy and big Mugs and the nervous young one, Trigger.

They had a few of Rose's Sunshine Swords too, to help with the patients they had aboard - though not Sansullio, regrettably, who Rose insisted remain with him on his own ship - as well as a few healers and maids. Captain Turner hadn't much liked having women aboard - it was bad luck, he said - but he'd made no more of it than a passing grumble. Then there was Maurice, the scar-faced Bladeborn cutthroat, who Jonik had since learned had once been a member of the Bloody Traders, and Cabel, the dark-eyed youth, both of whom had seen a fast and furious recovery from their imprisonment in the pits and were helping as deckhands under Turner's charge.

But still, it was odd not having the others with them, Jack and Emeric mostly. Jonik had come to rely on both of them as his right and left hand men and felt strangely exposed without them at his side.

"We'll be back in the north soon," he said more brightly, moving around to brush Shade's other flank. "How about that? A month or so, and you'll never have to come south again. I'll even let you run free, if you want, up in the Highplains where you belong." He tried to get the horse to look at him. "Would you like that, boy? To run free up there with your kin?"

A cough sounded behind him. Jonik turned to find old bent-nosed Benjy standing there with mop and bucket. "Sorry, m'lord, didn't mean to disturb you. You, er, you seemed to be havin' a profound conversation there. With this fine horse of yours." He smiled, showing that mouthful of cracked yellow teeth.

"I like to talk to him, from time to time," Jonik said, a little defensively. "It calms him."

"And you too, I'll wager. Nothin' like chatting to a horse to ease your troubles. Had one myself, back north. Not such a fine thoroughbred as this, but a good strong horse all the same. Used to love to ride him, just for the joy of it, out into the Lowplains west of Stormwall, Lord Tandrick Payne's seat. I worked the stables there once, in the castle. But that's another story." He laughed, then frowned, as though losing his train of thought. "Anyhow, one day he got crocked, my horse, broke his leg fording a river and I had no choice but to put him down right there and then." He looked at Jonik. "Sometimes that's the way, is it not? When a horse goes lame or a hound goes wild, you have no choice but to put it out of its misery."

"I suppose."

"Aye, well that's my experience anyhow." The old man smiled. Shade was giving him an unsure look. "Not sure he likes me, you know. Perhaps I talk too much? Or perhaps it's my smile." He reached out, as though to inspect Shade's teeth, but the horse gave a snort and pulled away. "Meanin' no harm, boy, just want to see those fine teeth of yours. Your smile's a shade better than mine, I'd wager. *Shade*!" he repeated, grinning lightheartedly. “Good name for you that, with that colouring. Bet it took a few tries, m’lord? Rasal thoroughbreds are real picky with their names, I know.”

Jonik nodded absently. “Yes, a few tries, certainly.” He frowned. “Was there something you wanted, Benjy?”

“No, m’lord, nothin’ specific. Was just washing the deck here and wondered if you might have a better use for me?”

Jonik thought a moment. “I may, a little later. Captain Turner says we’ll be in Aram by this evening and I’m going to be rowing Ranulf onto shore. I might need another man on the oars, or to watch the skiff if I go ashore with him.”

The old man went into a bow, his stained linen shirt flapping in the breeze. “Course, m’lord, whatever you need. I’m honoured you’d think of me.”

“You’ve proven yourself reliable,” Jonik told him. “And half my crew are absent.”

“Well I’m happy playing second fiddle, m’lord. Anything to repay your kindness.”

“You already are,” Jonik said, with grace. “You and your companions are all proving yourselves worthy seamen, as you’d promised. And you’ve done much to help tend the ails of the patients. You have my thanks, Benjy.”

The man bowed again. “Just happy to be of service.” There was something in his gruff tones that rang a distant bell.

Jonik turned to the stairs that led below decks. “If you’re looking for your next duty, refer to Captain Turner. He’s in his cabin, I believe, catching a few hours rest. I’ll come for you later if I need you on the oars.”

“As you say, m’lord.” Benjy picked up his mop and bucket and hustled off to the stairs.

Jonik didn’t fail to notice Shade watching the man go. “You don’t like him, do you?” he asked. The horse had his favourites and those he didn’t care for. Benjy seemed to have fallen into the latter category, for reasons Jonik couldn’t fathom. “Not everyone can be like Jack o’ the Marsh or Ranulf Shackton, you know. Benjy seems a good sort to me. You shouldn’t be so haughty just because he’s lowborn.”

Shade whickered and flicked his mane. The comment had clearly annoyed him. Jonik smiled. The horse had been grumpy ever since they'd left Sutrek five days ago, no doubt because Jonik had ordered Jack to travel on the other ship. At least that was his read. "Stare all you like at that ship, Shade, you're not going to magic Jack back over here," he told him, getting a dangerous look for his trouble. "Well, I can see you're not looking for company right now." Jonik left him there to sulk.

He found the small studious figure of Ranulf Shackton at the wheel, manning the helm in Gill Turner's absence. The affable adventurer had thickened out nicely over the last week, restoring much of his health for his imminent dance with death. "You're sure about leaving us this evening?" Jonik asked him, as he climbed the steps to the quarterdeck, his black cloak pulling in the wind. "I don't suppose there's any way I can convince you to stay?"

"None, but I'm grateful you'd consider trying." Shackton looked the part commanding the ship, much as a good king looked the part sitting a throne. It wasn't any man that Turner would permit at the wheel, but Ranulf Shackton had swiftly won him over, as he had the rest of them.

"Will the girl be going with you?"

"You had a mind to have her join your quest?" Ranulf grinned amiably. "I'm to ask her later, for the final time. With Leshie, you might pose the same question a hundred times and get a hundred different answers. And when it comes down to a yes or no choice, well, she'll give fifty yeses and fifty nos and you'll be left to wonder what she actually wants. So, that leaves me here, waiting until the final hour to find out where her thoughts truly lie."

Jonik wasn't buying it. "I'm sure she's made up her mind," he said. "She seems loyal to you, such as I've seen. I've no doubt she'll go with you."

"Yes, you're probably right," he sighed. "Though whether that's for better or worse, I cannot decide."

"You seem as indecisive as she is, Ranulf."

He favoured Jonik with a smile. "It's so. In this case, at least. Leshie's company and support will be welcome, of course, but her safety is my highest priority."

"I'm not sure she'll be safe wherever she goes," Jonik said. "Certainly not if she were to decide to come with us. You know where we intend to go, Ranulf. Aram may be the safer course."

Ranulf nodded thoughtfully. "Yes, and this journey of yours..." He paused and turned his eyes down at the black scabbard fixed at Jonik's swordbelt. "Are you sure you're ready for what's to come? I cannot confess to know as much as you about the Shadowfort, of course, but I know enough. I cannot imagine taking it will be easy."

"It won't be," Jonik had to admit. "That's why I've been building this army, Ranulf." The adventurer's eyes were still on his scabbard, staring with an unblinking interest. By instinct Jonik shifted his weight, so that his airy black cloak covered the Nightblade's sheath.

Ranulf didn't miss it. He looked up with a faint smile. "You are protective of it, the Nightblade," he asserted. "Is that fair to say?"

"As anyone would be with a priceless blade," Jonik said in a stiff voice. "Sir Borrus is the same with Red Wrath."

Both men knew that wasn't true.

Ranulf considered his words carefully, then said, "The topic makes you uncomfortable. You would prefer not to talk about it." When Jonik didn't answer, Ranulf smiled and went on. "You'll forgive me if I'm being too forward. As a scholar of the Five Blades, I cannot help but be hopelessly intrigued by having one so near. Regular godsteel is fascinating enough, but the unique magic of the Blades of Vandar, their history and creation, the whispers people speak of..." He smiled. "Each has a riveting tale of itself to tell. The kings and lords and knights and champions who have bonded them. The dragons and monsters they have slain. The places they have gone and deeds they have done. They've been used to start wars and end them, to win kingdoms and countries, cities and forts, to fetter people in chains and liberate them from their shackles, to inspire wonder and awe, dread and despair in equal measure."

He watched Jonik all the while as he spoke, reading him, the former Shadowknight could tell. "I am no Bladeborn, just a humble man of common blood who counts the accumulation of knowledge as my greatest gift and joy. I could never hope to know what it's like to bond a Blade of Vandar, to feel that link to a long fallen god, to hear the echoing whispers of his spirit. I have read so many books and tomes on the topic, accounts from kings and First Blades and knights raised to champion during Renewals and wars, yet all that is but a reflection of an experience, words written onto paper and parchment for one's imagination to bring to life." He gave a laugh. "I have as good an imagination as any, Jonik, but not good enough to truly understand what you're going through, no matter how many accounts I read. I trust no one can, but for those who have walked that path before you. And at such a time as this, with war spreading its shadow, with all this dread and darkness filling the realms...well, I can only imagine how strong you must be, to keep of a sound mind, and not fall to its lure."

"You know who my father is," Jonik broke in. He watched the man closely. Ranulf Shackton was far too clever to have failed to work it out. "Did Emeric tell you?"

"No. I have come to see it for myself. You have the Daecar look, Jonik. And you have the Daecar strength. That goes a long way to explaining how you've been able to master the blade so well."

"It's not been easy." Jonik's voice was a little dull, a little faraway. "I had a master in the Shadowfort, Gerrin, who helped me learn its ways. Back then I would only wield it in training, for short bursts. To have it at my hip, night and day, for months...I am afraid it will start to take a stronger hold," he admitted. "The whispers were more insistent before. They grew quieter when I came further south, and when Emeric joined me. He's helped me more than he'll ever know. And Jack too, in his support, and the others. But when we go north again, when we get closer to the Shadowfort...I worry those whispers will grow louder."

"What is it they say?"

Jonik drew a sharp breath. He could hear them now, hissing softly. A welcome comfort to him, when all else was quiet and still. A companion he knew he could no longer live without. "Nothing bad," he said, considering it. "They speak of me becoming a champion in the Last Renewal. Of the names I'll have. Of the men I'll lead. They speak of taking the Shadowfort."

The ship lurched gently as it rose over a shallow swell. Ranulf glanced up and idly spun the wheel a half turn to starboard, judging the waters. His eyes were back on Jonik a heartbeat later. "Is that why you want to return there?"

"No," Jonik said at once, though he wasn't sure anymore. "We...we both want it," he explained, after a short pause. "We are one. We..." He didn't like how that sounded, not when speaking it out loud. He cringed. "Does that make me sound mad?"

Ranulf's smile was reassuring. "By no means. It's common for bearers of a Blade of Vandar to think and speak as such, and many have written as such too in the accounts I have read. I am sure your father thought the very same during his long years with the Sword of Varinar. What is more important, *far* more important, is how righteous one feels, how justified in their claim and intentions. Men who doubt their strength or worth or ownership of a Blade of Vandar will often be drawn down a darker path. Perhaps this explains why the whispers were stronger before, when you first escaped the yoke of your order? When you had no noble claim or reason to possess the blade. When, perhaps, your reasons for taking it were more selfish?" He let Jonik ponder that a moment. "But ever since then, you have come to see a greater purpose in your possession of it, an important need. You are becoming an emancipator and liberator, a hero to many, a saviour. All of this secures the bond, Jonik. It helps you remain stable, where others might stumble and fall."

Jonik nodded to that. He liked it, and...it all made sense, didn't it? The more certain he'd become of his course, the more comfortable he'd felt having the Nightblade at his hip, on show for all to see. He didn't try to hide it in the same way as he used to. He had come to care little for his notoriety. All of that, perhaps, came from this noble quest he was on. From having honourable Emeric Manfrey staunch at his side, and Jack too, bringing the light where once Jonik had only seen darkness, and the others, all the others, who'd supported him every step of the way. Even Borrus had come to appreciate him and what he was trying to do. That said a lot, didn't it? Didn't that say it all?

A gust of wind crossed the quarterdeck, pulling his cloak aside. He reached down and drew the Nightblade from its sheath on a whim. "They're always there," he said, in a soft reflective voice. "The whispers. Mostly, they're quiet, barely loud enough to hear. It's when I grow angry or short of temper that they become louder, more aggressive, more...*dangerous*. When my thoughts turn to darker emotions, anger or hate or vengeance. It's why I needed to be on a different ship to Rose. I cannot abide that man, Ranulf. If we'd only taken Iris home, I might have been forced to leave him behind, lest I do something I regret."

"Would that you had," Ranulf said, chuckling. "Vincent Rose is a spoilt child, really, a boy in a man's body, gathering houses and horses, property and people as though they're nothing but toys. But inside he's a deeply dissatisfied man. Have some pity on him for that, Jonik. He will never know what it is to be part of something greater than himself. He will never understand a cause like yours."

"Or yours," Jonik said, shifting the attention on him. "There must be something important driving you to go to Aram at a time like this, Ranulf."

"Ah, there is. A duty most profound."

"And secretive," Jonik added. "You won't tell me what it is? I feel this exchange will be slightly unfair if you don't."

"Much as I would like to, I cannot." His eyes shifted to the Nightblade, with those swirling black mists, the tiny wisps and curls that faded as they rose into the briny afternoon air. He looked like he wanted to say something, but didn't. His eyes returned fore, gazing down the ship. For a long moment the two men stood in silence.

Jonik returned the Nightblade to its sheath. "There is much of the mystery about you, Ranulf Shackton. But I suppose Emeric didn't push you on your purpose, so I won't either."

"I fear you will come to know of it, in time," the small man said, curiously. "Our paths may be more linked than you realise, Jonik."

Jonik gave him a questioning look. "And yet you still won't speak to me of it?"

"The time is not yet now. I will only ask you...what do you plan to do after?"

"After? You're talking about the Shadowfort."

"I'm talking about the man you want to be, for I'm sure you're still trying to figure that out. I'm talking about that blade you carry. I'm talking about the difficulty you may have letting go of it, when the time comes."

Jonik wasn't understanding. "What time? I have no plans to give up the Nightblade, Ranulf, not yet." He stiffened.

"Nor should you." Ranulf Shackton smiled unreadably. "But...there may come a time when you must."

"*Must*? Why must I?" Once more, the adventurer refused to yield an answer. Jonik stared at him, his indignation spiking. "You can be quite vexing, you know. Gods forgive me, but I'm starting to understand why Vincent Rose grew so frustrated with you."

"A charge commonly directed at me, I regret to say. It's why I find myself so regularly imprisoned." Ranulf laughed, though it was slightly more awkward than before. The man had mined for information but now he was closing up.

Jonik decided it best to leave him there. *Must*, he thought. *Why must I ever give up the blade? Has he not listened to a word I've said? We are one, the Nightblade and I. My father held the Sword of Varinar for almost twenty years and there's no reason why I cannot do the same...* "I'll row you to shore later," he said brusquely. In the west, the sun was starting to make its slow descent. "We'll be under cover of night. You're certain this is what you want?"

"Want has nothing to do with it," the man said, in that mysterious way of his. Jonik had heard that the late King Godrin often spoke in riddles, and this Rasalanian seemed to be stricken with the same affliction.

"Well I imagine you have preparations to make." Jonik took a step toward the stairs down to the main deck. "I'll fetch Captain Turner back to the helm. He's had plenty of rest by now, I'm sure."

"I'll not forget what you've done for me, Jonik," Ranulf said suddenly. There was a great sincerity in his eyes, a probity Jonik could trust. "The Nightblade elects you champion, and I cannot disagree. Sometimes the noblest of us come from the harshest of beginnings. You are living proof of that, young man. And you'll do the right thing, when the time comes. I know in my heart you will."

With his face twisted halfway between a frown and a smile, Jonik moved down the steps. *You'll do the right thing, when the time comes.* Was he talking about giving up the Nightblade? Jonik was considering that when he reached the main deck and found old Benjy mopping the floors, pushing tirelessly back and forward at the stairs beneath the quarterdeck. "I think it's clean enough, Benjy," he said.

The old man startled, looking up. "Oh, I, er, I didn't see you there, m'lord. I tend to lose myself when I get into a task. Bit absentminded like that, see."

"Right. Did you speak with Captain Turner?"

"No, m'lord. Gave a knock and got no answer. When I peeked inside I saw that he was having a little kip, so left him be. Thought I'd just get back to my moppin'. 'A deck can never be too clean,' I always like to say."

"I suppose not." Jonik thought that he might want to apply the same mantra to his general state of appearance, which was best described as shabby, but imagined it would be impolite to point out. "Well, keep at it, Benjy. We'll be able to see our reflections in the wood soon."

"Aye, m'lord, that's the goal. Gotta get old Iris lookin' as sleek as One World out there."

Jonik looked to the patched sails, the little chips and cracks in the masts, the rot that had set in here and there. "I'm not sure a mop's going to be quite enough."

Benjy laughed, guttural and gruff. "Not enough by half, m'lord, but I'll keep trying all the same."

How can Shade not like this man? Jonik wondered as he turned and descended the stair that led below decks. He paced the corridor and knocked on the captain's cabin. Hearing no answer, he opened the door and looked inside. The drapes were drawn in the small dim space, Turner lying on his bed. He groaned and cracked open an eye. "It's stuffy in here, Captain. You might want to let some fresh air in."

"Aye." The word sounded a little off. Turner sat up queasily. "Not feelin' my best, I'll admit," he said. "You have need o' me, lord?"

"Nothing urgent. I sense we'll be nearing Aram soon enough and thought it best you return to the helm, so Ranulf might arrange his things."

"Aye." Turner nodded wearily, shifted himself to his feet, and pulled his leather coat over his tan shirt and breeches. "Bit o' fresh air. Aye, that's what I need."

"If you're sure? Was it something you ate, do you think?" Jonik might have wondered if the empty bottles of rum scattered across his desk might have something to do with it. But then, Gill Turner could drink like a fish. He *was* part Seaborn, after all.

"Not sure, lord. My gut doesn't give in easy, not to rough seas or rum or rotten food, even. Guessin' I caught a bug over in Sutrek. Can happen, when visitin' queer places."

"Right." Jonik didn't mention that they'd been five days gone from Sutrek, and if Turner caught a bug there, he'd have felt it long before now. More likely it was something he'd eaten, and if so, others would be coming down with the same trouble soon, Jonik reasoned. That was the last thing he needed, half the crew turning up sick when he was shorthanded and had ill patients in every cabin to worry about. "I'll lead you up."

When they reached the wheel, Turner swapped over with Ranulf so that he might see to his preparations. The fresh air seemed to have some effect, though it could just as well have been Turner putting on a brave face. Behind his heavy flaxen beard his skin looked a little pale, eyes a little glassy. He hid it all as best he could, though, drinking in the salty sea air as the light began to fade. "Shame that Ranulf Shackton is leavin'," he said. "If I go down, we'll have no one to run the ship. Meanin' no offence, lord."

"None taken. I'm no sea captain, Gill."

"Aye, a captain o' swords but not o' sailors." He smiled grimly. "S'pose we'd have to link up with One World and have Brown or Lord Manfrey hop back over. Else you can think o' someone here?"

Jonik scanned the deck. Of the Sunshine Swords and other sellswords aboard, old Benjy seemed best placed to take the wheel. He said as much and Turner gave a reluctant nod. "Aye, he's Rasal and knows the waves well enough. I'd trust him to take command so long as the weather's not too grim. Sailing should be easy enough this time o' year. North is where the worst of the storms are."

"It's enemy ships that I'm more worried about," Jonik said.

"Those Sunshine Swords are useful for that, and that big Piseki cutthroat. What's his name again?"

"Maurice. Or Big Mo."

Turner managed a throaty laugh. "Aye. *Big Mo*. Good sort o' name for sailors and sellswords that."

"He was once a Bloody Trader. Do you know much about them?"

"Bits n' bobs. Sellsword company, mixed colour and creed and such. Lots o' members, hundreds maybe thousands far as I know. Useful havin' him aboard, though. He and those sunshine boys can do the talkin' if we come across southern ships. Might do enough to stop us gettin' boarded. And if they do...well, guess that's when the likes o' you and the Barrel Knight come in."

"Let's hope it doesn't come to that."

"Aye, hope all's well and good, but best to be prepared as well." He gave a sudden wretch, heaving to the side, though somehow kept from vomiting.

"You OK there, Captain?" Jonik asked. "Wouldn't it be better to just let it out?"

Turner righted himself, putting his hands back on the wheel. "Aye, perhaps, but I've never once emptied my guts on this here ship and I don't intend to start now." He swallowed. Jonik could only imagine what.

Soon the light was leeching out of the world, a deep red dusk setting in. Down on the decks, the crew started to gather to watch as the distant lights of Aram began to flicker on the northern horizon. Jonik could see Big Mo and Soft Sid standing side by side on the forecastle deck, giving him a chance to judge their respective heights for the first time. Sid edged him, but only just. The former Bloody Trader was a true brute of a man, just shy of seven feet tall and fearsome to look at with that gruesome scarring across the right side of his face. Elsewhere, Mugs and Trigger stood in privy conversation, bickering about something or other, and Cabel was there, crouched upon the starboard gunwale in that casual way of his, picking at his teeth with a knife.

And then there was old Benjy, working tirelessly at the decks. As everyone else stood and watched the lights grow brighter, he just scrubbed on and on, back and forward, never once looking up. "He works as a man possessed," Turner noted, seeing him too. "Sir Ben!" he called down. "Take a break, enjoy the view. Old Iris ain't never gonna be a looker, no matter how hard you scrub at her."

The old man looked up, nodded, put aside his mob and bucket, and joined his friends at the bow.

And all the while, Shade was watching him.

39

Saska

"Are you sure this is wise, my lady?" asked Sir Ralston, bedecked in godsteel plate from heel to helm beneath his black woollen cloak. "This could very well go wrong. You heard Mellio. He urged caution. And these sewers. Perhaps we might..."

"I am not entering Aram through a tunnel full of shit, Rolly," Saska said firmly. "I have my dignity. And besides, I doubt you'd fit. Those tunnels aren't built for men of your size to squirm through, you know. When they get blocked they send in children to clean them out. An eight foot tall giant all dressed in steel isn't what they had in mind. Nor a starcat." She gave Joy a stroke of the head, as the great black feline loped along beside her.

The Wall nodded heavily. "Fine. Then we find a quiet part of the city walls and try to cut our way through."

"Unseen?" Saska had to laugh. The perimeter of Aram was well watched and the coastal road swung around its inland side, right along those walls. As soon as anyone came past by saddle or sandal they'd be spotted. "And do you have any idea how thick the walls are? Fifteen feet, Mellio says. Even with godsteel it'll take an age to cut through."

They were walking the final stretch of their journey, travelling a well worn track that wended down from the hills north of Aram, passing little villages and cattle farms in the hinterlands beyond the city. Mellio had left them up in those dusty hills, unwilling as he was to be spotted escorting the pair into the city. Saska didn't blame him for that, though the Wall continued to claim that he wasn't a proper smuggler unless he got them past the city gates. He'd tried to goad Mellio with that accusation, though the smuggler hadn't been having any of it. "I prefer to keep my head on my shoulders, yes," he'd said, with that ever-present smile. "I do hope yours stay where they are too. Yours especially, my lady. It would be such a shame, yes, such a shame to part such a pretty head from such a pretty set of shoulders."

The Wall gave him a withering stare. "Enough talk of parting heads from shoulders," he'd warned. "You will put a hex on us."

"That is the last thing I'd want to do. No, I bid you the best of luck. You are brave, yes, very brave, and fortune favours such as you, I have heard." He grinned and dipped his head at Saska. "My hopes go with you, my lady. I hope you find who you are looking for." With that, he'd given the reins a shake and the horses had gone trundling off down the track, eastward back to Matia, with Pig snorting his farewells.

That had been about an hour ago, when the sun was wheeling over toward the western hills through a cloudless azure sky. By now a deep red dusk had set in, the immense city walls ahead bathed in shadow as the last of the city-comers were admitted through the gates. Saska had thought this the best time to arrive, when the crowds were thinner and the gate-guards weary after a long day on watch. It might make them more compliant, she hoped, and the last thing she wanted was an audience.

"It's going to work," she said quietly, bracing herself as they drew nearer. "Just stay quiet and let me do the talking. Stick to the plan, and we'll be fine."

The Wall gave out one of his many grunts, this one to show his displeasure, but said not a word as they continued forward to the back of the queue, joining the country folk and costermongers waiting to get inside. Already the massive gilded gates had been drawn mostly shut, though there remained space enough between the doors for the wagons and wains to wobble through, heaped with the wares they'd been selling in nearby villages during the day. There were travellers among them too, a pair of carriages ahead being subjected to a formal inspection. Saska watched from the rear with interest. *Formal* was a stretch, really. The guards seemed tired and disinterested at this hour, giving the interior a glance and then waving them on by.

The Wall didn't fail to notice that either. "Mellio lied," he said, leaning down to her. "They scarcely even looked inside."

"He wasn't to know."

"He lied," the Wall repeated angrily, before standing tall again and sealing his lips.

People were starting to notice them now, though not for their whispering or the presence of the starcat, but the size of the giant at Saska's side. Sir Ralston was a hard man to miss, and up on the wall walk and gate towers to the left and right, soldiers were looking down, gathering in their twos and threes, gesturing and pointing in their direction.

"I knew this was a bad idea." Saska could sense Sir Ralston's unease. He slipped a hand into his coat, gripping the hilt of one of his greatswords.

"No," she told him, careful to keep her voice as low as possible. "Just stay calm, Rolly. It'll all be fine. I promise."

The queue was moving forward, a wain loaded with apples and oranges rolling on through, heading down for the dawn markets, no doubt. Behind followed a pair on horseback, then a huddle of villagers who had the look of a family, dressed in poor cloth and seeming nervous beneath the great looming walls and huge curved bastions jutting out from the stone along its outer side. Each was permitted entry without much questioning, ushered through into the open yard beyond. Above the gates, the soldiers were watching, black shadows with tall spears thrusting up from their sides, standing between the merlons and crenels where many mounted crossbows were fixed. A couple of soldiers idly moved to those crossbows. They didn't go so far as to aim, but the threat was plain enough. *Just stay calm,* Saska told herself for a dozenth time. *Everything's going to be fine.*

A voice barked at her in Aramatian. She turned her eyes back to the gate where a pair of city soldiers were marching toward them, gesticulating.

Curse my poor linguistic skills, she thought. For all her feeble attempts to learn a bit of Aramatian aboard the Steel Sister, she'd barely picked up a word. The two guardsmen pressed through the gentle wash of twilight, dressed in shirts of copper mail, each little scale overlapping intricately over the next. They wore brass halfhelms on their heads, shaped at the top into an eagle's beak, with scimitar swords on one hip, curved dagger on the other. It was the standard garb of the Aram city guard, she knew, with lightweight bronze capes, fashioned into the image of folded eagle wings, hanging from their shoulders.

The lead man spoke again, a jumble of words that Saska couldn't hope to comprehend. She picked out one, perhaps two, this time. One of them was '*Aram*'; easy enough. The other she thought was *city*. He was probably asking her what she was doing in the city of Aram. It didn't take a genius to work that out.

"I am sorry," she said, in her own tongue and accent both. "Unfortunately, I do not speak Aramatian."

Both men stopped short, frowning. Ahead, the rest of the city arrivals were being hastily led through the gates. Saska didn't fail to note that the two men on the mounted crossbows above were now loading them, swivelling them down in their direction. She could almost hear the Wall's pronouncements of 'I told you so' already, as he shifted uneasily behind her. *But we still have Joy,* she thought. *None of these men will attack us so long as we have Joy.*

"Northern?" asked the first guard. He had hair the colour of dark honey beneath his eagle halfhelm, falling in tight curling waves. "But... you are not. You cannot be." His eyes were on Joy, her secret weapon. "This is *your* starcat?"

"She is," Saska said, giving an easy smile.

The guard was still frowning. He shared a glance with the other man, who looked similarly bewildered. "Why do you speak northern? You are Lightborn, and your skin tone..."

"I was raised in Tukor," she told him. "But I am Aramatian by blood. I have come to speak with the Grand Duchess Safina Nemati. Please, let us through. Our business is urgent."

The man had no idea how to react to that. A few scoffing laughs could be heard above on the wall walk. At the gate, other soldiers in that interlinking copper scale mail were looking over. Whether they understood everything she was saying, or merely heard mention of their ruler, Saska couldn't know. Either way, she had their attention, for better or for worse.

The guard with the honey hair turned his eyes to the Wall. They narrowed. "Who is this man?"

"This is Sir Ralston Whaleheart," Saska said. "An anointed knight of Rasalan and long time guard and protecter of the late King Godrin, direct of the Blood of Thala. You may know him as the King's Wall. He has turned his cloak, and comes here as my protector now, in support of your city and ruler." She paused to gauge their reactions. Through the dusky light she could see the shock on their faces. "Now, I ask that you escort us through the city to the Grand Duchess, so that our arrival might be announced. She will be expecting us."

A silence followed her words. She could feel Sir Ralston's eyes glaring out to the shadows above them, manning the high parapet. She was running on instinct and guesswork, and hoping all went well. Was the Grand Duchess expecting them? Did she even know who Saska was? She couldn't be sure, but something told her this was what King Godrin had intended when he'd sent Sir Ralston to protect her. She had to trust that impulse, and she had to find the truth.

Eventually, the lead soldier found his voice. "The Grand Duchess isn't here," he said. "She left for the warmoot some weeks ago, and hasn't yet returned."

Saska had half expected that. "That's OK. We don't mind waiting. If you could show us to a good inn or rest-house where we might stay until she returns, we'd be happy to..."

"No." The guard was shaking his head. "This man cannot enter the city. I know who he is. No. He cannot be trusted."

"He is my protector."

"He is a killer."

Saska could hardly deny that. Sir Ralston's reputation went before him, unfortunately, and sneaking into the city with a man of his size was never going to work. No, she needed to be up front about who they were and why they were here. If she didn't, they'd be set upon, she knew, sooner or later, and everything they'd been through would have been for nothing.

"What if he were to give up his arms?" she asked, trying to figure a way out. She heard the giant grunt his dismay, but went on all the same. "Without godsteel Sir Ralston is just a big man." Saska looked up at him, saw his smouldering fury. "A *very* big man," she corrected, "but a man all the same. He means no harm, and nor do I, and we will both be willing to swear it by oath. You have heard of godsteel oaths, I take it? They are unbreakable, sealed by an ancient magic. To break a godsteel oath is not only to die a horrible and painful death; but worse, to sully one's honour in the eyes of the gods."

The guard gave a short nod, then whispered a few words to his companion. "We have heard of these oaths, yes." He looked at Saska quizzically. "You are Bladeborn too? Bladeborn *and* Lightborn?"

She was taking a chance here, and she knew it. These men might consider her some sort of aberration, though even so, what could they do? Send her to a cell to await judgement? Spark violence with a man like the King's Wall at her side, who'd be sure to bring untold carnage to their lines before they could get close to stopping him. No, they'd do neither. They would do what any good gate-guard did when encountering an unusual or eminent arrival like this and refer it up the chain of command. Sooner or later, the Grand Duchess would hear of their coming, and all would be well. She hoped.

So out came her godsteel blade, the one King Godrin had given her via Sir Ralston, lit silver against the red dusk above and gleaming with those ancient glyphs. "I am," she declared, speaking in noble tones. "And by godsteel oath I swear to you that we are not here to cause trouble."

The guard turned again to the soldier at his side, and gave him a nod. The man dashed off in a glitter of copper scales toward the gate, disappearing beyond. "This is not a decision I can make," the lead guard told them. You will wait here, both of you. Do not come any closer. Stand where you are, and wait. Someone will be with you soon." He looked nervously at the blade in Saska's grasp and backed away, returning to the other men watching from the gate. A few words were shared and then all of them retreated beyond the great golden doors, which began groaning shut with a heavy resounding thud that echoed off over the plains.

Silence fell. Above them, Saska saw more soldiers now, more figures shadowed against the dusk, half a dozen of them standing at the mounted crossbows, locked and loaded and pointed right at them.

"I don't like this," the Wall said. He slid a hand beneath his cloak, eyes scanning from man to man. "I fear they mean to leave us out here while they gather their strength. We should go, my lady. There will be many Sunriders and Starriders in the city. Many more than I could ever handle alone."

"We have one out here," Saska said, giving Joy a stroke of the head. The big cat started purring that big rumbly purr of hers. Saska smiled.

When Joy purred everything in the world just felt right. "I'm a Starrider too. They're not going to attack one of their own."

"You rode her a half dozen times, for a half dozen metres. That does *not* make you a Starrider."

"It's a start," Saska came back. "It's not easy when I've got a godsteel blade at my hip. Starcats aren't exactly used to that. It makes me heavy."

"Then take it off."

"No, I have to train her." She had to get used to the weight, so far as Saska saw it. "I'm Bladeborn *and* Lightborn, Rolly. It's no good being both if I can only use one at a time."

"Well why don't you take the cat swimming too, so you can indulge your Seaborn side." Sir Ralston was still glaring at the soldiers atop the ramparts. Saska could count at least two dozen of them now, probably more, all poised to attack.

"Cats don't like the water," she pointed out.

"Some do."

"Most don't."

The Wall moved his eyes to the starcat. "If they attack," he whispered, "get on her back and ride. As hard and fast as you can, my lady. I will hold them here. Run back to the hills and catch up with Mellio. He will help hide you."

"Nothing's going to happen." Saska gave him a comforting pat on his armour-plated arm. "At worst they'll take us to some tower cell and keep an eye on us, until my grandmother returns. I trust her, Rolly, and I trust King Godrin. He intended for us to come here, I know it. We have to have faith in that."

Sir Ralston Whaleheart did not seem sure. "As you say, my lady," was all he managed. "I sincerely hope you're right."

A groaning sound gave out once more as the great gilded doors opened up again. Saska's protectors stiffened, both of them; Sir Ralston on her right and Joy on her left, the starcat's purring fading off fast as she watched the city guards reappear. With them this time was an older man with white in his whiskers and a stern disposition, and another, a more flowery nobleman who came riding out atop a magnificent old sunwolf with streaks of silver in its golden mane.

That stern man spoke first. His voice matched his appearance, gruff and short, like his cropped grey hair. He wore no helm, holding it instead under his arm, and his mail armour was mixed in colour, the scales copper and gold and silver, showing his rank as commander of the gate. "You are here to see the Grand Duchess," he said. "Why? Who are you? This big one we know, but who are you, my lady? You must be brave or foolish or both to have come. You know what has been happening here."

Saska dipped her head to him. "We know, yes, but have made the journey despite the dangers. It is of the utmost importance that we visit with the Grand Duchess as soon as she returns."

"Yes, I have been told. But you are not answering my question. Who are you?"

"Who I am is not important."

"Not important? You are a girl of mixed blood, born during the last war at your age. Bladeborn and Lightborn, I am told. Not often do we have arrivals at this gate bearing godsteel in one hand, and the collar of a starcat in the other. And with the King's Wall at your side." He narrowed his eyes. "Who are you?"

"I don't know," she admitted, and there was a lot of truth in that. "I could tell the story of my life, but you'd only disbelieve me..."

"Try," said the flowery man, sitting on the sunwolf. He was bound up in silken robes of silver and gold, though for all that his great girth was clear enough. Saska felt a little sorry for the sunwolf to have to bear such a weight. He gave a good natured smile, speaking in a polished, singsong lilt. "I would like to hear this story, I think. Cross-breeding among the north and south isn't unheard of, but every such tale is worth a telling. And that starcat. Very beautiful, and newly bonded, it seems to me. She does not seem so sure among our company," he observed. "And the way she is looking at Taro, very menacing." He gave his wolf a stroke. The beast seemed perfectly calm, though true enough, Joy was tight and taut and in flight or fight mode to look at her. "What is her name?"

"Joy," Saska said, a little sheepish.

"Joy?" the Sunrider repeated. A couple of the guards laughed. The man turned to them. "I do not see the joke. Is Joy a funny name to you?" The guards swallowed their chuckling. "This name has meaning to you, I can tell," the perfumed nobleman went on, turning back to her. "That is good, and common. It helps secure the bond. Taro means *honour* in the tongue of the Islands of the Moon, from where I hail.

Perhaps you can see, the animal comes to fit the name." He gave his wolf a stroke of the mane once more, running his fingers through the faded golden fur. "He is old now, but was always a noble beast. And Joy...she brings you happiness, yes? This is why you named her such?"

Saska gave a silent nod. She wasn't liking how well this man was reading her.

He trotted forward a step, smiling broadly. He was bald of head and face, with thin eyebrows above a pair of keen hazel eyes. "Let me introduce myself. I am Sunrider Mar Malaan, leal servant of the great Sunlord Elio Krator, who will be glad to take you and your companion into his noble custody, to await the return of Her Serenity, the Grand Duchess Safina Nemati." He shifted a leg over from the saddle and slid lightly to the ground, despite his weight. Mar Malaan stepped toward them, still smiling pleasantly, his sandalled feet scraping against the rough earthen floor. "I was told you would be willing to swear by godsteel oath your intentions? Is this true?"

Saska nodded. "Our intent is to cause no harm, only to visit with the Grand Duchess."

"In time." Something twinkled in the man's hazel eyes that Saska didn't like. "First, you'll have the honour of Lord Krator's company. He is newly returned from the warmoot himself." He grinned and reached out his hand. "This is how it works, yes?"

Saska reached forward, gripped his pudgy wrist. He wore several rings encrusted with precious stones, rubies and emeralds and a sparkling diamond that shimmered as it caught the red twilight.

"And now?" he asked, seeming amused by the entire experience.

"Now I take out my blade," Saska said, doing just that, "and...make my oath."

"And I get to choose it?" asked Mal Malaan. His hand slipped from hers. "You understand my concern, if I lead you to my lord master? I would not do so unless I have your assurance that you mean him no ill will."

"Lord Krator?" Saska asked. The name rang a distant bell to her, but she couldn't place it. "Of course we don't. Why would we?"

"Because he's a senior member of the Patriots of Lumara," said Sir Ralston Whaleheart, stiffly. He gave her a glance that sounded a warning, but they were in too deep now to turn back.

"Yes," nodded Mar Malaan. "He has supported the Patriots in the past, but that aside, we are now at war. A man like Elio Krator must be protected from the threat of assassins."

"We're not assassins."

"Oh I know. No assassin would walk so brazenly to our gates like this, I do not think." He laughed, his chins wobbling. "But of course, we can never be *too* careful. So I will have your oaths, and then I will have your blades. These will be kept safe until the time comes that you prove your innocence, and your intent. I hope these terms are fair to you?"

"Most fair," said Saska, concealing her disquiet. Her confidence was her shield, she knew. She had to stand by her convictions.

The Wall gave a less than satisfied grunt. "No Bladeborn likes to be without his blades," was all he said.

Mar Malaan craned his neck up at him, grinning. "I understand. It will only be temporary, of course." Without looking back, he waved a hand, and a sturdy cart came rattling through the gates. "So, oaths first, then blades. Once this is done, you will be permitted entry into the city."

With a great deal of reluctance, the oaths were made and blades unsheathed, to be placed upon the cart and transported into Aram. The wood complained loudly as Sir Ralston laid down the two greatswords he carried, the wheels pressing into the earth and gouging shallow ruts as the powerful oxen hauled the wagon inside.

Mar Malaan followed atop Taro, with the gruff gate commander at his side. Saska and the Wall went after, attended by some two dozen guards. She could tell her guardian was liking this not at all. In truth her own concerns were mounting, but it wouldn't serve to show them. "Don't look so worried," she whispered up at him. "This is all going to plan. Sort of."

"Elio Krator was not a part of that plan," the Wall came back at her, tense. "You have not heard the stories, my lady. The man's a Patriot of Lumara, and an influential one at that. You know as well as I how much they detest men like me. You may be safe, but I will not." He watched on forlornly as his blades were taken away.

She gripped his hand. "You will, I promise. Trust me, Rolly, I'll not let them separate us. You me, Joy, we're all staying together, I'll make sure of it."

Her promises were soon proven false. When they reached the palatial residence of Lord Elio Krator some twenty minutes later, Saska and Sir Ralston were immediately drawn apart. Her anxious complaints fell on deaf ears as Mar Malaan assured her he'd be fine. "We cannot have such a brute as he beyond the confines of a cell, no," said the heavyset Sunrider, trotting proudly along on his wolf. "He will be well treated, but must be caged until we are sure..."

"Sure of what?"

The man ignored the question. "You will stay in the residence, however, along with your beautiful Joy. It will give her time to get used to the presence of other starcats and sunwolves, of which there are many who come and go."

Saska was watching her protector taken off by half a dozen strong men, though even the tallest of them only reached as high as his shoulders. He made no struggle to escape their grasp, knowing it would be futile.

"When is the Grand Duchess expected back?" she asked, looking again at Mar Malaan. "You said Lord Krator has just returned from the warmoot. Why isn't she with him?"

"Her Serene Highness rules Aram by the authority of Empress Valura, my lady. She was required to stay longer, and sent Lord Krator back in her stead to manage affairs in the city."

"But...how long will she be?"

"Who can say? A day or two? A week? Perhaps more. I do not know."

He led her through the gated residence of pristine white stone, through colourful outer gardens crossed with paved paths and past a tall carved fountain showing an eagle surging from the pool with water running off its wings. The estate was near the heart of the city upon a series of shallow hills clothed with other manors and residences, overlooking the Amedda River which ran down from the Scales far to the west, splitting Aram in two and emptying into the bay. Out there Saska spotted a sprawling harbour, teeming with ships large and small, with many more shapes and shadows spotting the calm waters of the Solapian Channel in the distance.

Between the low hills where these princely residences were found and the flatlands of the port lay a city of order and harmony, the streets planned around circular city courtyards and squares, branching off as spokes on a wheel. Across the river it was the same, and on those wide waters more boats were sailing up and down stream, bringing soldiers and supplies from Starcat Keep over a hundred miles upriver, where most of the Empire's Sunriders were officially sworn in and trained.

Spanning the river were many bridges, some thin and narrow and no wider than two men abreast, others broad and busy, with stores and markets built into their parapets. Beyond sat an immensity that could only have been the palace; a three tiered pyramid of bronze, silver, and gold rising imperiously above all the buildings clustered around it. Even from this distance a mile away, it loomed like the single thrusting peak of a mountain above its smaller foothills, banners fluttering from its balconies and the many poles that jerked out from its towering facades. To Saska, they gave a resemblance of feathers, as though the pyramid itself were set to unfurl its great wings and take flight.

"The symbol of the eagle is important to Aramatians," Mar Malaan told her, as they stopped in the gardens and took in that view. She rested a hand upon Joy's head for comfort, felt the deep rumbling as she breathed. "The goddess who gave us our name used to have her own eagle, a great eagle called Calacan, with feathers of gold and silver and bronze, and eyes like the brightest emeralds you will ever see. But this you know, of course."

She did. Little Billy used to talk about it often. "Is Lord Krator inside?" she asked, a shudder moving through her.

"No, he is away this evening on important business, but will return tomorrow. I will lead you to your room."

Her bedchamber was spacious and comfortable and airy, the ceiling high and walls creamy white, with plush red carpets and cushions to add colour and warmth. It was more than large enough to accommodate Sir Ralston as well, but her requests to have him brought to her were ignored out of hand. "No, but Joy will be with you." The Sunrider gestured to a bed, clearly designed to fit an animal as big as a starcat. "Most rooms in residences like this are fitted with places for starcats and sunwolves to sleep." He smiled. "They are members of our households as much as the riders who mount them. I will have food and wine brought to you, and meat for the cat. Does she have a preference?"

"I...well, I'm not..."

"You do not know yet, of course. I will have meat and fish brought. And fruit and breads and olives for you as well. Please, relax. You may wander, if you like, but not beyond the bounds of the residence. I will check in on you in the morning." With that, he withdrew.

Saska took to the window seat, high up above the gardens, with views over the river beyond, and the palace and city and harbour. A cool salty breeze was blowing in from the coast. She sat there with Joy at her side, wondering what she'd gotten herself into. The Wall's warning about Elio Krator rang through her ears. The name was enough to make her anxious, close as it was to another house she'd served.

Sitting there, she couldn't help but think of the Kastors, Lord Modrik and Lord Cedrik and Sir Griffin who'd all left their mark on her. *But I got two of them,* she thought, grimly. Sir Griffin she'd disembowelled in Elyon's tent, and Lord Modrik she'd struck with a candleholder, knocking him off his feet as his head split open on the hearth. She'd only been a girl of fifteen then, old enough for the drunken lord to finally claim her. For years she'd lived in his service, and for years she'd been abused, but that night something was different. He had a look in his eyes, behind the stupor of whiskey and wine, that said it all, a lust he could no longer contain. She could still remember that look as she could the feel of his rough old hands groping at her clothes, trying to rip them free, the grunts and heavy moans as he'd tried to press her down onto the bed, the fear that had coursed through her veins as she wriggled and squirmed and attempted to fight him off, the flicker of rage that passed his face as she'd denied him. "You're a slave," he'd slurred angrily. "*Property*. Be thankful I've not done this yet. Be thankful I've waited this long. Now lie still!"

She had lain still, but only for a moment. When he reached out and tore open her shirt, she'd fetched that silver candlestick from the bedside table and swung with all her force, striking hard at his temple. He'd recoiled, stuttered, his eyes going glassy, and slipped on the cold stone floor. The sound his head made as it cracked against the hearth had been sickening, the stink of piss as his bladder emptied so pungent she'd had to gag.

Thinking about it all now, her heart began to race, as the panic she'd felt then came back to her. She was sure that was it, that she'd be caught and killed, but by some grace and good fortune, she'd managed to slip back to her own chambers without being seen, creep into her bed, and hide until the Lord of Ethior was found.

By morning the castle and city beyond were falling to rumour of how he'd died. Most believed he'd slipped and fell, drunk as he so often was back then, and it was no more than an accident. That rumour still persisted to this day. Yet all the same, Saska had always wondered whether Lord Modrik's wife, Lady Cordelia, knew different. The Lady of Ethior had never liked her husband's infatuation with her, and wasted no time in having Saska sent away in the company of slavers, to be sold to an abusive new master, she did not doubt.

Perhaps she thought that fate would be worse than death? Saska had often wondered. Yet if that was the case, Lady Cordelia's plan had failed when those slavers were attacked by bandits, and Saska escaped in the ensuing chaos, rushing away into the wilds and eventually finding herself in that barley field outside Willow's Rise, owned by Master Orryn.

The food was brought to her chamber. She ate little, preferring to calm herself with wine, as Joy sampled the fish and fine cuts of meat the servants placed down before her in bowls. Saska watched with a smile, thinking now of Orryn, of Llana and Del, of Marian, Leshie, Astrid, Ranulf, Roark and Quilter and Braddin and Lark, Elyon...she thought of Elyon often, and Lancel and Barnibus, and Rikki and Billy and Lanky Larry and Old Hob and all the others on the Steel Sister who'd shown her what a normal life could be, if only for a time.

These last three years had been so different from those that had come before, and these last months even more so. Yes she'd slain Lord Quintan after he'd tried to force himself on her as Modrik Kastor had, yes she'd failed to kill Modrik's son Cedrik and instead thrust a blade through his nephew Griffin's groin, yes she'd had to endure the menace of Lady Cecilia Blakewood, with all her smiling threats, but for all those wicked souls she'd had to suffer, she'd grown to know and care about, even love, a great many more.

That thought brought a smile to her face, broad and true. *And now I have Rolly and Joy, and I'll not let either of them come to harm. Soon my grandmother will return and we'll be drawn under her wing. She'll take us in and tell me the truth of who I am, of what I am, and what I have to do next.*

She nodded to that as she gazed out of the window, over the twinkling lights of the city and harbour of Aram, the deep black waters of the bay beyond. She could sense the hum and noise below, the buzzing streets, the bustling port. Joy hopped up to sit beside her, purring and licking her lips with that long purple tongue. She smiled. Her long journey here was at an end, and what came next, she couldn't say for sure, but Joy helped brace her, and so did the words that she'd leaned on every day since she'd heard them. The words of a wise old king, watching from the Eternal Halls.

You're exactly where you're meant to me.

40

Ranulf

Ranulf held the parchment to the candle and let the flame take its edge. It took well, quickly devouring the words he'd hastily scribbled with quill and ink. The paper blackened and curled and fell to the floor as ash. Ranulf was halfway through stamping out the embers when he heard the door behind him open with a woody creak.

He turned. "Leshie..." She wore her red leather armour, her short, strawberry blonde hair slicked back and mean. At one hip was her godsteel shortsword, a dagger at the other, a light black cloak over all of that, fastened at her neck with a simple iron brooch. "I thought you said you'd never wear that armour again," he said.

"I changed my mind." She looked to the blackened parchment under his foot. "What were you doing? You shouldn't be burning things on a ship, Ranulf. It's made of wood if you hadn't noticed."

"So it is." He smiled, twisting his booted heel left and right to make sure the paper was destroyed.

"So? What was it? I don't like it when you hide things from me."

Well, she's back to her old self again, there's no denying that, he thought, as the girl stood there in the doorway, hands on hips, tutting. "It's nothing," he lied. "Just a silly drawing. I like to draw, sometimes, to relax, though never was much of an artist. This one was particularly poor. It earned the honour of the flame, I assure you."

The girl was shaking her head, rolling her eyes. "You'll never change, will you? But keep your secrets, if they're so important to you. I'll find out sooner or later." She took her hands from her hips, folded them at her chest. "Now are we doing this or what?"

Ranulf frowned. "Doing..."

"Going to Aram, *obviously*. They're waiting for us up top. That Jonik boy told me, the one with the Nightblade." She stamped her foot. "Come on, Ranulf, hurry up. You're getting slow in your old age." She grinned and withdrew.

Ranulf gathered up his small sack of belongings and followed her out, making sure, one final time, that the parchment had truly burned through before he left the cabin. It had, thankfully. And once again, the secrets King Godrin had passed onto him in the Book of Thala resided, once more, only in the mind of Ranulf Shackton.

He stepped out into the corridor, as Leshie sauntered toward the stairs leading to the decks. "So you're coming then?" he called forward to her. "I was going to ask you one last time, just to be sure."

"Of course I'm coming. Haven't I made that obvious?"

"Not at all."

She scoffed. "You're really not so insightful as you think, Ranulf. I'll bet you really thought I wanted to murder Vincent too?" She glanced back, a devious grin warping the softening contours of her face. Her sunken cheeks had taken on a bit more flesh since their rescue, though she'd never look quite so cherubic and young as she had before her imprisonment. "Well, a part of me does, I will admit," she said. "But... next time. I'll kill him *next time* I see him. Now isn't really convenient, you know, with this profound calling of yours, which you *still* refuse to tell me about." Her grin moved into a snarl, then a glare. The girl was just as capricious as ever, it seemed.

They found Jonik on the main deck with Captain Gill Turner and the old bent-nosed man called Benjy, whose smile was almost as rotten as the one they nicknamed Brown Mouth. And he liked to smile a lot, much to Leshie's displeasure. "Do you mind closing your mouth," she said to him. "I've just eaten."

Gill Turner gave out a bark of laughter so sudden he looked like he might throw up.

"Leshie. That was horribly impolite." Ranulf shook his head at her. "You can't say things like that to people."

"Why not? It's the truth. I'm sure he knows it too."

"Aye, I do," said Benjy, smiling gamely. "The gods cursed me good, I say, making me such a smiley sort and givin' me these awful teeth."

"They cursed *us*, more like," Leshie said. "We're the ones who have to look at you." She turned her eyes over to the north, where the twinkling lights of Aram blazoned bright along the coast. "So are we rowing from here? We're quite a long way out."

"Captain Turner thought it best that we not get too close," said Jonik in a quiet voice.

"Scaredy cat," Leshie grinned at him, then nudged him in the side. "You've got a Blade of Vandar at your hip. What on earth could scare a man like you?"

"I didn't say I was afraid." Jonik seemed unsure of how to behave around her, and that was no great surprise. There were no women in the Shadowfort, Ranulf knew, and none among Jonik's new crew either. The young man's eyes slid aside, and he mumbled, "You're very antagonistic, you know."

Leshie laughed. "Yup, I know. You see the truth in people when they're put under stress. And you're shy. You try not to be, but you are. The *Shy Shadowknight*." She smirked as though it was the cleverest name in the world.

"He, er, don't much like that name, young-un," Turner said.

"Shy Shadowknight? What, someone's already thought of it?" She looked confused.

"Just the second part," Ranulf told her. "Now come on, let's not waste their time, I'm sure they want to pull anchor and be on their way." He leaned in. "Another word from you and they'll be like to throw us to the sharks. *Stop it*, Leshie. Know when enough's enough."

The skiff had already been lowered into the water off to port, some of the crew gathering around the main deck above to say their farewells. Leshie had a name for all of them. Maurice she liked to call 'Scarface', Soft Sid was 'The Plodder', Grim Pete had earned the name 'The Ugly Crow' for his days spent in the crow's nest and his rather unsightly appearance, while old Benjy's friends, Mugs and Trigger she'd renamed as 'Bull' and 'Nerves' for the former's broad shoulders and the latter's stuttering disposition.

She had names for the rest as well. Borrus Kanabar was 'Baldie', Captain Turner was 'The Pirate' for some reason, and the dark, dangerous looking youth called Cabel she'd merely named 'Slick' for the way he greased his black hair. Ranulf wondered now if she'd done the same to hers to mimic him. She had spent time with Cabel these last days, he'd seen, and he was one of the reasons he thought she might stay. But alas no, she was coming too, so they said their goodbyes and climbed the ladder to the skiff, joining Jonik and old Benjy as they sat at the oars.

"Oh great, *you* again," Leshie said grumpily, seating herself opposite the old man. "Do I have to look at you smiling the whole way to shore?"

Ranulf was spotting the first signs of displeasure in the old man's eyes, though he did enough to hide it. "I'm afraid so, girl. I'll try my best not to smile too much. Just for you."

"Good."

Jonik began calling the stroke, pulling hard at the oars as they cut the black waters. He seemed eager to get this done. With a half dozen good strong strokes Invincible Iris began bleeding into the darkness, a soupy mist embracing her hull low on the water. Above them, a cloak of clouds had gathered, blotting the moon and the stars. It made spotting other ships and rowboats more difficult, which often emerged from the pall of blackness suddenly and menacingly as they cut the calm waters of the bay, looming high to the left and right, ghostly and forbidding.

"Straight to the harbour then, is it?" asked old Benjy, unsmiling.

Jonik looked to Ranulf for an answer. "If you wouldn't mind," he confirmed.

"That wise, m'lord?" Benjy wondered. "Aram's not near as chaotic as Sutrek, I know. There you can hide like me n' Mugs n' Trigger did, but not in Aram so I hear it. It's more formal, like. More guards and custom officers and such at them docks checking everyone comin' in and out."

He wasn't entirely wrong. Aram was distinct from many of its southern neighbours in its uniformity and structured design, though in some ways that was just a veneer, covering a more tumultuous underbelly. Much of that was down to what happened three hundred years ago when Aramatia went to war with Pisek over land rights along their border. The fighting had been savage before the Lumarans stepped in to wrest them apart, and both Sutrek and Aram had been brutally sieged.

In the subsequent rebuild, the Aramatians decided to refresh and update the city structure, carving wider streets and grander squares, with straight, paved roads favoured over the narrow twisting warrens of sandstone alleys more common among the major metropolises. There were now a dozen districts beyond the harbour, with circular plazas branching off into one another, creating a series of interlinking webs of sorts. Ranulf had always enjoyed the symmetry and beauty of it, though the original inspiration had been function, the wide streets and easily traversable routes enabling their soldiers and Sunriders and Starriders to move more quickly to where they might be needed most, should the city come under attack.

"My hope is that they'll be busier with the bigger ships," Ranulf said in answer to Benjy's question. "Aram has always had a teeming port and there's no reason why a little skiff like this should be noticed, so long as we choose a quiet jetty."

"Quiet or no, you'll have trouble hiding that pale skin of yours," Benjy said gruffly. "Believe me, I know. We had to have our hoods and cloaks on all day and night to keep ourselves hidden in Sutrek, me n' the lads. And in this heat? Horrible."

"No wonder you smell so bad," Leshie said.

"Do I now?" The old man pulled an arm from his oar a moment, sniffed his armpit long and deep. "Aye, seems you're right, girl. Anythin' else you want to poke n' prod at me about? My hair's thin, wouldn't you say? And you've not made mention of my smashed up nose yet..."

"I was going to get to that. It's hideous. You look like you've been trampled by a broadback." Leshie leaned back on her bench, dangling an arm over the side, letting a finger cut the water. "How'd that happen, anyway? Pick a fight with the wrong person, did you? Maybe it was that big friend of yours, Bull. He looked mean. I didn't like his piggish eyes."

"Seems you don't like anyone."

"I like Ranulf. And Jonik. He's quiet, but sweet beneath all that brooding. It's not his fault he's shy."

"I'm not shy," Jonik said, shyly.

Ranulf had to smile. The boy was a different person with Leshie around, glancing at her as though she was some strange foreign creature whom he simply couldn't figure out. "You *are*," she said, grinning at him. She pulled her hand from the bay and flicked seawater into his face with her fingers. "If I was staying on the ship, I'd help lighten you up. Guess you don't have much experience of girls, do you?"

"I..." Jonik didn't know how to answer. He seemed abashed. "I didn't...I didn't grow up around girls."

"I can tell. Even if I didn't know you were that Ghost guy, I'd be able to tell *that*. Maybe you should come with us, for tonight at least. You can return to your ship in the morning. You'll be a *proper* man by then, I promise."

"I am a proper man."

"Don't rise to it, lad," put in Benjy, as the two began to lose the flow of their stroke. "I've known her sort before, all provocative like. She just wants to get a rise outta you."

"A *rise*? Oh yes, that's *exactly* what I want." She smirked and looked suggestively at Jonik's groin. Not for the first time, Ranulf Shackton saw that Leshie's time in captivity hadn't changed her one bit.

"Leshie, that's enough now," he said in a firming voice. "Is this any way to repay Jonik for his kindness, taunting him like this?"

"I'm *trying* to repay him for his kindness. Show him what he's been missing out on." Her eyes flicked between Jonik and old Benjy, who's face was beginning to glower. "What, you jealous old man?"

"Leshie! Enough!"

"Ah, it's all right, Master Shackton, she's just bein' playful, is all. We're all friends here." Benjy's tightening jaw said otherwise. His mouth gave a twitch and he looked out over the water, fuming.

Ranulf was about to apologise for Leshie's behaviour when they rowed around the side of a huge great galleon and the harbour appeared beyond in a blaze of bustle and light.

"Quiet now," Jonik commanded. "We're getting close. Ranulf, tell us where you want to land."

Ranulf began searching through the blur of light. Suddenly there seemed to be ships all around them, great galleons and galleys, four masted and grand, slimmer caravels and wide carracks and trading cogs burdened with crates and barrels. They were still far enough away to give Ranulf time to consider where to go. The obvious choice would be the edge of the docks where it was quieter.

He gestured to his left, where a couple of cogs were being unloaded at a pair of wooden wharves. The officials there were checking the cargo, backed up by a brace of city guards with their eagle-crested halfhelms and glittery copper mail, and those feather-shaped cloaks that hung stiff at their backs. Beyond that was a much quieter pier where a small two-masted carrack was moored. There looked to be a few sailors on deck, drinking and smoking and playing dice. If they could land on the other side of it, they should be able to sneak ashore unseen.

Jonik saw immediately where Ranulf was pointing, and in tune with Benjy, they began weaving the rowboat between the anchored ships, cutting quietly and calmly through the waters. A light fog souped about them, swirling as they passed. Drawing nearer, Ranulf spotted an old disused shipyard just beyond the wharves, fronting a set of storehouses. It was an older part of the harbour, he judged, that hadn't been part of the renovation, clustered beneath the city's outer curtain wall. It looked largely deserted. *Perfect*, he thought.

After a few tense minutes they were approaching the jetty, rowing silently past those cogs and beyond the moored carrack with the sailors and deckhands aboard. Keeping close to their hulls, they remained out of sight of the soldiers and officials until they'd rounded to the far side of the carrack and come in quietly against the pier.

"I'd rather not wait here long," Jonik whispered. "Do you have all your things?"

The skiff ran alongside the quay as Ranulf reached out to snatch at a mooring post, steadying it against the dock. The boat bobbed lightly in the water. To their right, a couple of the sailors on the carrack glanced over, shrugged, and returned to their dice and drinking. "We do," Ranulf answered. "I thank you again for your kindness, Jonik. Remember what I told you. Attachment is good, but always be ready to let go. *That* is true strength."

"I...will remember, Ranulf. Be safe."

"He's got me with him," Leshie said. "He'll be fine." She leaped from the rowboat and landed on the dock, as Ranulf followed her out. "Thanks for rescuing us from those pits, Ghost of the Shadowfort. I won't forget it." She looked down at Benjy and sniffed. "I hope I forget *you*, though, but something tells me I won't. That smile of yours will haunt my dreams for a good long while, I'd say."

The old man's lips ripped back into a snarl. "Be gone and good riddance to you," he spat. "I hope the Patriots find you, harlot."

Ranulf was taken aback. "Now Benjy, that was a little much, don't you think? She was only joking." He gave Leshie a glance. "I think."

The sellsword blasted a breath. "I'm...I'm sorry, m'lord. It's just, the girl, she..." He looked to Jonik, eyes dipping. "That were improper of me, I know. She just riles me, is all. All those insults...there's only so much a man can take."

Jonik gave no reply to that. He merely looked at the old man with those steely silver eyes then said, "We need to go. Ranulf, give us a push."

Ranulf obliged, kneeling and thrusting the skiff from the pier. It floated off on the inky waters, giving their oars room to work. And work them Jonik did, turning the boat swiftly about and putting his back into a firm stroke. Old Benjy kept up, despite his age. He seemed durable and sprightly for a man of his years.

Leshie was smirking as she watched the boat bleed away into the mists. Ranulf glanced up to make sure the sailors on the carrack weren't watching, grabbed her arm, and led her quickly and quietly into the shadows of the old shipyard a little further inland from the pier. Once they were safely inside he turned on her fiercely. "Now what on earth was all that about!" he demanded in a harsh whisper. "I mean there's being playful and there's being downright unpleasant. You crossed a line, Leshie. Goodness, what has gotten into you?"

She began tutting. "Oh Ranulf, Ranulf, you just don't see, do you? I was *trying* to get a rise out of him. I said back on the ship, that's how you see someone for how they truly are. And that old man...I don't trust him. He's hiding something, I can smell it."

Ranulf blew out a breath, shaking his head. "Old Benjy? The man's harmless. What could he be hiding?"

She shrugged. "Dunno. Something."

He raised his eyes. "*Something*? Well isn't that useful."

"Shut up." She gave his arm a firm jab. "I don't know, maybe he's working for Vincent. Him and Bull and Nerves, all of them."

Ranulf sighed. "Ah. So this is about Vincent Rose," he said. "Of course it is. I might have known."

"Isn't *everything* about Vincent Rose? Doesn't the whole world revolve around him?" She spat to the side, demeanour darkening. "I'm just saying, there's something off about that old man. That's all I was trying to do, get him to react. And he did, at the end there. He called me a harlot! That's like a whore, isn't it? And said he hoped the Patriots would get me! What sort of man would say that."

A man at the end of his tether, Ranulf thought, though he merely said, "It was a bit unseemly, but you did push him into it, Leshie. I'm not sure you can read much into a person simply by goading them and hoping they react. Most men would do the same in that situation."

"I made him show his true colours," she came back, as though not hearing him. "I knew all that smiling and bowing and boot-licking was fake. He's just trying to ingratiate himself with the Ghost, I know it. Spying for Vincent, most likely. He probably wants the Nightblade. He's probably still working for Janilah."

A rustle of noise came from outside, footsteps and voices as several men walked by, muttering in Aramatian. Ranulf drew Leshie further into the shadows and put his finger to his lips. The men passed on by without detecting them, though the interruption was enough to shift his mind to more pressing needs. "OK, enough about all that. We don't have time for it now." He looked to the little sack on her back. "Do you have the lotion?"

She frowned. "What lotion?"

"*The* lotion. The lotion you said you'd make. Gods, Leshie, tell me you brought it."

She grinned. "Course I did. I'm not stupid, Ranulf." She dug into her bag and drew out a little pot. Leshie had more uses than swinging a godsteel shortsword; her training in Thalan had given her the skills to disguise herself to a basic degree as well. In this case, make a balm to rub into and darken their skin, so they might move about the city undisturbed. It required a few unusual ingredients, but that hadn't been a problem. Their host's manor on Goldwater Row had a very well stocked pantry and apothecary, after all.

Leshie reached out with the pot. She'd made enough for them both. "Here, you first."

Ranulf took it hesitantly. "Why me?"

"*Because*. I might have gotten it wrong, the blend. Who knows, maybe you'll come out in a horrible rash or something."

Ranulf exhaled tiredly. "So I'm your canary in the mines, is that it?"

She frowned. "I don't know what that means, Ranulf. What's a canary got to do with it?"

"It doesn't matter." He twisted the cap off the pot, dipped his finger into the creamy ointment. *No burning sensation.* That was a good start. "Right, well here goes." He stopped, looked at her, hoping to see a smirk or smile or something to say she'd been joking. "You're really not sure if this will work, are you?"

"I will be in a second." She grinned.

"Fine. Here goes..." He scooped a fingerful of the brownish cream and began rubbing it into his face.

As he did, Leshie laughed. "You might have started with your hands, but oh well..."

In the end, it turned out fine, Leshie's doubts proving unnecessary as Ranulf Shackton's pallid sunless skin began to deepen and darken into a rich shade of olive brown. Leshie watched, pleasantly surprised by her efforts, then took her turn, lathering the balm into her face, neck, and arms as he had. Once that was done, she drew out a different pot for their hair. It was much the same, if a little more oily. As Ranulf rubbed it into his hair and eyebrows, he realised that Leshie had already seen to that part. "I wondered why your hair was so greasy," he said. "Thought you were trying to copy Cabel."

"Who's Cabel?"

"You called him Slick."

A dreamy look came upon her newly tanned face. "Ah, Slick. Now there's a boy who *isn't* shy around girls, let me tell you."

"Please don't."

She laughed as they completed their camouflage, before the pots were shoved back into her bag to be used at a later time, if necessary. Ranulf hoped that wouldn't be the case. He could speak Aramatian well and so long as Leshie didn't open her mouth, they'd not be spotted as northern, he hoped.

"So where now?" the girl asked, readying herself to step back out of the shipyard. "You said you had a friend here who would help us, didn't you?"

"I have several who *might*," he said, "though whether they're here and willing, well, that's another matter. Harbouring northerners is dangerous business right now, Leshie."

"Yeah, but we don't look northern anymore. Near as makes no matter, anyhow."

That was true enough. Leshie still had her big blue eyes, but that wasn't completely unheard of down here, especially in Aramatia.

Shades of blue and green and gold were common, and with her strawberry hair darkened to black and that olive skin tone she should blend in well enough.

He looked out into the docks. Getting in through the portside-gate might still be a challenge, and at this time of night, it might well have been shut. The harbour was something of a city-within-a-city itself, however, self sufficient and bustling with sailor taverns and merchant houses for those who had no intention of entering the city proper, and only wished to stop over at the port for a day or two at a time. Those would be less inclined to ask questions so long as Ranulf had coin, which he did. Vincent had been kind enough to give him a full pouch as reparation for his imprisonment, though in truth it wasn't from kindness at all, but by demand from the boy Jonik. The young man had demanded the same for the other patients too. For a man like Vincent Rose the constant chastisement and humbling would begin to tell. And Jonik, Emeric, Borrus Kanabar...none of them knew Vincent Rose as he did. They did not realise how dangerous he could be.

For a moment he reflected on Leshie's concerns. Might Vincent have struck a deal in secret with Janilah? Might he have sent Benjy and the others to keep watch on Jonik? Might they be leading him north, and directly into the Warrior King's grasp?

If any of that was true, well, there was little and less Ranulf Shackton could do about it now. One day soon enough the Nightblade would have to be given up, whether it was Jonik or Janilah or anyone else who held it. And the same, Ranulf knew, was true of all the others. Whoever held them, wherever they were, the Blades of Vandar were destined for something greater.

Leshie's voice snapped him out of it. "Well, where are we going, Ranulf? Don't tell me you're getting cold feet now that we're here."

He cleared his throat. "We'll find a tavern for the night," he said. "Let me do the talking, and play along. We can think about getting into the city tomorrow."

"Fine. Lead the way."

Cloaks furled about them, they crept out into the darkness of the shipyard, and ventured to the light beyond.

41

Janilah

Janilah Lukar stood at the balcony of his throne room where he'd murdered King Ellis Reynar. "Will Raynald appease you?" he asked, stiffly, staring out at the pale blue skies. The storm had finally passed overnight after a long cold week of heavy snows, the gales calming, the air sweetening with the sight of sun and sound of birdsong once more.

The dowager queen gave a curt nod. Elitha Reynar was not a comely woman, with rather too much of the sow about her, though if she had a handsome feature it was her smile. It didn't appear. "I suppose he will have to, Janilah," she said. "Why the change of heart?"

"Rylian," he told her bluntly. "He was not privy to my discussions with Hadrin over Amilia's hand. He took that poorly. I thought it best to include him on matters concerning the betrothal of his son and heir."

The dowager queen looked out, unreadable. "So Rylian means to give Robbert's hand to another. Pray tell who, good king."

Janilah's mouth twitched to even speak the name. "Lillia Daecar. Rylian has always favoured the girl's house, Elitha."

"I know." The queen said nothing for a long moment, garbed in rich wools and a fine cloak of fox-fur against the chill air of the morning. It was early yet, the sun barely risen, the day young. It was set to be a long one, with the wedding to unfold. *And more else besides,* Janilah thought, flexing his fingers. Finally, Elitha spoke again. "And Rylian is happy for Lyriss to wed Raynald, is he? I would not want to be disappointed again, Janilah."

Janilah held his tongue on that. The woman was pushing her luck. *As everyone does around me now.* "He is," he told her. "He would not want to alienate such an ancient house as yours."

"No, I can see that." Her eyes glanced over the edge of the balcony to where her late husband's body had shattered on the stone courtyard below, clothed in a pristine blanket of unspoilt snow, sparkling beneath the sun. It was a far cry from how it had looked not long ago, coated in blood and bone and shards of skull, strewn about the marble flagstones. "As long as I continue to have the support of House Lukar, I am happy," Elitha went on. She allowed a smile to break onto her lips. It was a forced smile, Janilah did not fail to miss, but he'd already come to see that Elitha Reynar's one and only concern was securing strong support for her daughter. Robbert, Raynald, it made no matter really, so long as she had the backing of House Lukar.

"You will have our support," Janilah confirmed, telling her what she needed to hear. When he saw the signs of satisfaction in her piggish face, he said, "Now, if you will excuse me, I have other business to take care of, before the ceremony starts..."

"Say no more." Elitha turned to move away, then stopped. "I imagine you will want to wait to make this announcement until a later date?"

"There is no rush," he said.

"No, of course. But I would have the agreement signed and settled this time, after the wedding is done. It would make me feel more comfortable to sit and talk terms with yourself and Rylian, as soon as is convenient for you both. The prince will be leaving Ilithor shortly, I have heard. Might we seek to discuss this on the morrow, once the wedding is completed?"

"I will talk to Rylian about it," Janilah said.

That was enough to please her. "Good. Then I will see you later, for the ceremony and celebrations." She glanced to the clear sunny skies. "A good omen," she declared. "Six days and nights of snow and they end on this fateful day. It would seem the gods bless this union, Janilah. I do pray it is a fruitful one."

With those parting words, she strode away, passing Sir Owen who stood guard at the heart of the throne room. The Oak of Armdall bowed as she passed. Sir Rees Hunt and Sir Fredrick Ruxmond were manning the double doors, where King Hadrin waited, having just arrived. Elitha stopped a moment to share words with the Rasal King, before moving down the corridor with her small retinue of personal guards and household knights. Then Hadrin entered, leaving Sir Munroe Moore outside with several other members of his royal guard. Janilah took to his throne. The double doors were shut. "Are you nervous, Hadrin?" His voice echoed through the capacious white chamber.

The Rat King hustled forward, dressed in his ostentatious raiment; cloth-of-gold cloak, blue and yellow velvet tunic beneath, beads and shells and other aquatic jewels sparkling about his wrists and neck. The golden crown seated atop his head was decorated with more multi-coloured treasures of the deep. Yet for all that finery his face was still thin and ugly, his jaw feeble and receding, his nose narrow and long, mouth bulging with overlarge teeth. Even Janilah had to feel some sympathy for his granddaughter having to wed this creature. *But he has proven himself loyal, at least,* he thought, *unlike Godrik Taynar.*

"I will not lie, good king, I am a fraction anxious, yes." His apprehension was clear enough in his jittery voice and the mask of tension in his wonky-toothed smile. "But excited all the same, of course."

"Common emotions on the day of one's wedding," Janilah said. *And the day one beds a woman for the first time,* he didn't. Rumours about Hadrin's virility and experience in the bedchamber were rife and ungenerous. Many were of the belief he'd never once lain with a woman, not least several of the more talkative Rasal lords whom Janilah had dined with these past weeks.

Janilah stood from his throne and guided Hadrin to a table at the side of the hall. Sunshine came bursting in through the high arched windows, setting a pale warm glow to the room. "A fine day on which to wed," he declared. He filled two small cups of spiced wine, handing one to the smaller man, who took it between trembling fingers. "It will give you courage," Janilah told him. "Just make sure not to overindulge, so that you might perform tonight. A wedding isn't sealed until consummated in Tukor." *And I need my granddaughter with child, to secure my hold on your kingdom,* he thought.

"It is the same in Rasalan." Hadrin's voice pitched suddenly high as he spoke, as a boy struggling through puberty. He took a sip, smiling awkwardly. "I have...I have heard some troubling rumours, Janilah. About Amilia and...*Aleron*." Even speaking of a dead man he'd never met, he couldn't hold back his sneer. "I was told your granddaughter was a maiden, but...well, some are saying that she took Aleron to bed, during their courtship in Varinar."

Janilah waved a hand in dismissal. "Give those rumours no mind. They are false, I assure you."

"You're certain?"

"Of course." Janilah was the opposite, in actual fact, and knew full well that Amilia had bedded Aleron Daecar during their long weeks at Keep Daecar. She'd bedded others too, he knew from Lady Melany, though his granddaughter's chastity had never been of concern to him. He decided to move things on lest the Rat King dwell on it too long. "Now, how are your visions coming along, Hadrin? Have you taken the time to do what I asked of you?"

Hadrin sipped his wine, slid his tongue over his oversized teeth. "I have."

"And?"

"And there's not much to report, I'm afraid to say. I told you before, the Eye of Rasalan doesn't show you what you wish to see. I have tried to search for the missing blades' locations, of course, but have seen nothing of that kind. It is the dragon that most concerns me..."

"We're at war with Agarath. Of course there are dragons."

"Yes, I...I know that, Janilah, but...it comes to me more regularly, this vision. The great dragon, the shadow, the fire and ash. I sense a shadow over all the world, as I've said. It may be somewhat symbolic or...or allegorical, I don't know, but..." He blew a worried sigh, shook his head, shuffled his feet. "I sense some doom coming," he finished, in a tremulous voice. "This dragon, this shadow and shape...it represents a great calamity."

"It represents *war*," Janilah said to that, as he had to Rylian a week ago. "Now the blades..." He set his grey flinty eyes on the little king. "You're sure you've seen nothing."

"Nothing, no."

"Perhaps you've heard something, then? About the Windblade's location." Loathe as Janilah was to seek Hadrin's help on the matter, he'd asked him to keep an ear out from his subjects, should any rumours surface about the Windblade's whereabouts.

"I have been making enquiries, yes," Hadrin confirmed. "Tactfully, of course. I know you want to do this in secret."

"I do. Have you discovered anything?"

"Well yes, I think I have. The Windblade is being stored in Prince Dalton's chambers, as far as I can figure. It would be logical, after everything Godrik has said about the First Blade needing to hold a Blade of Vandar..." He shrugged his narrow shoulders, sipped his wine, wiped his long ratty nose.

Janilah had come to the same understanding. "Do you have proof?" he asked.

"Well, not proof, exactly, but something close enough. Apparently, there have been some unusual sounds coming through the ceiling of Lord Swiftwater's chambers, a rumour that Sir Munroe came upon during a security brief with some of Swiftwater's household guards. These sounds include grunting and clunking, and occur late at night, I'm told. And Swiftwater's chambers..."

"Are right beneath Dalton Taynar's," Janilah finished. "I know." It was a happy happenstance, really, and not something he'd arranged. He'd expected the Windblade to have been handed to him willingly, after all. Not once did he anticipate having to steal it. He stroked his grey-brown beard in thought and asked, "So you think Dalton is training at night with the blade?"

Hadrin gave an energetic nod, delighted to have been of service. "I do, Janilah, yes. I would imagine a Blade of Vandar would make quite a thud if dropped, even through a carpet and thick stone floor, and would require some exertion when training with it for the first time. Lord Swiftwater has posited that Dalton is merely an aggressive lover, but I rather think that untrue." He chuckled awkwardly, a shade of blush rising up his thin wrinkly neck. "I am no Bladeborn, but I know how heavy godsteel is, and the Blades of Vandar especially. I'll wager these are Dalton's attempts to train with the blade, at night, as you say. I can't think what else they might be."

Janilah agreed. "The Windblade is the lightest of the Five Blades," he said, "but heavy all the same for any man not yet bonded to it." He thought some more. It wasn't quite cast-iron evidence, but better than Sir Kevyn Bolt had managed to bring him. "That is helpful, Hadrin. You have my thanks."

"A pleasure, as always." The Rat King shuffled his feet.

Janilah regarded him. "Was there something else? I'd not want to keep you from your preparations."

Hadrin gave another uncomfortable little bob of the head. "There was...well, I did want to ask, while I have you alone, how long you expect to hold the Book of Thala for? I had hoped to have it back by now, I will admit, so that I might scribe my own accounts. These foresights I'm having, in the Eye...the...the dragon...they ought to be documented, Janilah. It is my holy duty as Rasalanian king."

Janilah drank the rest of his wine, set down his cup, refilled it. "Ask me again in a day or two," he said. "Archibald and his team are still labouring to translate the final passages."

Hadrin bowed, happy enough with that. "Have they found anything of interest?"

Much and more, in terms of historical scandal and insight, Janilah thought, but little that helped light his own way. "They hope to have something for me soon," is all he said. Thinking too deeply on that topic tended to flare the pain in his chest, for the entire episode had proven a failure. *If there's a location for the Frostblade, it's on the page that bastard Shackton stole*, he knew. He'd harboured a vague hope that Hadrin might spot a location in the Eye of Rasalan too, but that had also proven hopeless. All the man ever seemed to see was dragons, fire, ash, and shadow, all of which a blind lackwit could perceive with all the world at war. *No, I cannot rely on Hadrin to offer me anything of worth.* He had commissioned a band of ruthless sellswords from the Bloody Traders, led by the Surgeon, Pete Brown, to hunt down Shackton, and had to hope that would bear fruit. How much progress they'd made in the last two weeks, however, Janilah didn't know. As with Shadowmaster Gerrin, communicating with his creatures and cutthroats that far south was notoriously unreliable, especially during war.

Hadrin seemed to identify that Janilah had seen enough of him. "Well then..." He sipped the last of his wine and placed down his cup on the polished stone table, with a gentle *clack*. "I will see you at the temple, Janilah." The small measure of wine appeared to have done little for his courage. He wiped his brow, drew a full bracing breath, and expressed an uncomfortable smile. "Enjoy the rest of your morning, good king." Awkward smile holding, he stepped away.

When the Rat King of Rasalan had scuttled from his presence, and the double bronze doors closed, Sir Owen Armdall stepped over to fill the breach. Sir Rees and Sir Fredrick remained at the doors. "My king, Sir Kevyn is ready for you," said the Oak.

Janilah nodded. "Send him in."

The Bull of Bolt arrived from a private side door that few used or even knew was there, carved into the shadows of the throne room in its northwestern corner. Janilah observed Sir Kevyn as he arrived, cloaked and cowled, bringing an unwashed reek with him. His cheeks were yet thinner than before, stubble yet longer, eyes descending into dark pits in his skull. The man had slept no more than an hour or two a night this last week, Janilah judged. "Sire." He bowed.

Janilah regarded him coldly. "I have just spoken with King Hadrin. He has given me something resembling confirmation that the Windblade resides with Prince Dalton, in his privy chambers."

"Aye, sire." Sir Kevyn looked out through his cowl, nervous. "It...it makes much sense. I have thought for some days now that it was there. But, getting in..."

"Is difficult, I know." Dalton's chambers were even harder to access than his king father's, and no doubt he kept the blade close to hand at night when sleeping. During the day, there were guards within and without at all times. *But today, with the wedding...*

"Do you wish for me to take it, sire?" Sir Kevyn went on. "The palace will be quiet beyond the feast hall. There would be no better time than now." He bowed low, his broad back spreading beneath his cloak. "Sire."

Sir Owen remained standing tall. His nostrils flared as he took in Sir Kevyn's putrid reek. "I will help him, my lord," he put in proudly. "Sir Rees, Sir Fredrick, and Sir Maxwell will be standing guard for you at the feast. The people have grown used to seeing three of us with you at all times. My absence will not be considered unusual. If I garb myself in cloak and cowl like Sir Kevyn, we will be able to get in, get the blade, and get out, unseen," He lifted his chiselled chin, tall and gallant with a flavour of arrogance. "*I* can wield it, sire. You can trust me to see it done."

The Bull of Bolt side-eyed the taller, younger, and greatly more handsome knight. There had always been a streak of healthy rivalry among the Six, as was common with fighting men and knights, and each man liked to think himself the best of them. It had grown clear enough in recent months that Sir Owen thought that most loudly. Sir

Kevyn was not impressed. "I need no help, sire," he said, turning back to Janilah. "I can retrieve the blade myself."

"Like you have so far," asked Sir Owen, snidely.

"I have done all that has been asked of me," the Bull said in defence. "Sire, I have worked tirelessly to check each location, even through the storm, as per your command. The snows...they have made it difficult. And you ordered me not to use force."

"An order you ignored," said Sir Owen. "You killed five men at the Dead Dragon, Sir Kevyn, and how many more at the merchant's house? Women, even children..."

"That wasn't me." Sir Kevyn's dark brown eyes swept beneath his heavy brow. "I had nothing to do with that."

"Then who was it?" Sir Owen demanded.

"I don't know. Thieves and robbers, they say."

"Enough," Janilah said. He appreciated them refusing to admit it, but he had no time to do this dance. "You both know it was me." He regarded them, and saw that clear enough. "I take no pride in that. As you say, Sir Owen. There were women, children..."

"Whores and bastards," Sir Owen told him, swift to change his tune. "None to be missed, my lord."

"Aye," agreed Sir Kevyn, subservient. "Rich Dick Mallory...he was a known knave, sire, and deserved all he got. And those soldiers at the Dead Dragon were Kastor brutes, worth less than the shit on my boots."

Janilah wasn't interested in their unctuous pandering. "You were ready to curse Sir Kevyn for killing women and children, Sir Owen. Pray tell, why not me?"

Sir Owen's mouth opened and closed, giving no immediate answer.

It came to Sir Kevyn to answer for him. "You're...you're our king, sire." He bowed low again. "You can do with your subjects as you please."

"Whores and bastards, as I say," added Sir Owen, rediscovering words. He smiled, not so handsome or arrogant this time. Just servile. *Too servile,* Janilah thought. *I have surrounded myself with sheep, none to tell me true.*

"You condone the murder of innocent women and children?" he asked both men, with a flare of fire in his eyes.

"Of course...of course not, my lord," said Sir Owen, backtracking. "But, you had no choice. You..."

Janilah didn't want to hear it. He raised a hand to silence him. *Rylian would say it true to me, he'd tell me what I've become,* he thought. *But this? If he heard of this? No...if he knew I was murdering innocent women and children he'd be sure to abandon me entirely, take my crown and throne and deny me my divinity all at once. No, I cannot allow that. I must fulfil King Galin's promise. I must win the War Eternal. That is my purpose. That is my task. I will see it done, or die trying. No one will stand in my way. No woman. No child. No son or heir or prince or king. No one. No one. No one...*

"Sire?"

Janilah drew back into the room. His face had coiled into a maddened scowl, his eyes staring wide and wild into empty space. He blinked all that away and looked Sir Kevyn Bolt in the eye.

"You...you went quiet, sire," the Bull continued, chin low. Even through the dirt on his face, the black shadows beneath his eyes, Janilah could see his disquiet.

They think me mad. Driven to despair by all these setbacks. And might I be? Might I be losing myself, as my plans unravel? He had to put all that aside, to stay calm and in control. There had been mad kings through history and every one of them had been reviled and feared, their record sullied, their name spoken amid cautionary tales of pride and greed and their crazed lusts for power. *I cannot let my own legacy be so tarnished. I cannot...I will not...be remembered as a tyrant.*

"Your Majesty," said Sir Owen. "Your orders, my lord?"

Janilah nodded quietly, thinking. His intention had been to retrieve the Windblade himself. To have Sir Kevyn confirm its location and then infiltrate using the Mistblade. Walls were no barrier to him, yet the chance of being spotted was. He could do that out in the city and the snows, do that at night when the skies were blotted and black, but the palace? With all the north assembled?

He shook his head to himself. *No, I cannot risk it.* He'd made the merchant's mansion a morgue, but he couldn't let that happen here. *The Mistblade...it whispers more loudly than ever,* he thought. They came alive during war, the Five Blades, record and rumour said. Baying for blood. Speaking to a man's deepest desires. *And what are mine? To win the war, claim a divine Table of my own, a spot in the pantheon of gods, to be remembered and revered for all eternity.* A piece of Vandar's spirit was urging him onto that. Even now, he could hear his voice, whispering in the dark places of his mind. *Claim the blades...kill if you must...win the war...win it for me...*

Janilah shut his eyes, drew long and deep on his wine. The voice faded. The sounds in the room came back to him. Birdsong outside. The gentle scuff of feet across the room as Sir Rees Hunt shifted his stance. Sir Kevyn's heavy breathing. The flex of a leather glove as Sir Owen gripped the hilt of his blade, standing tall and noble before him. Janilah had learned to control the whispers, the voice, ignore them these long years. But they were growing stronger, louder, more insistent. *And if I take up the Mistblade again? If I take it up on a day like this...*

Two nights ago, he'd almost done just that. He'd been here in his throne room late at night when Lady Melany Monsort had come to him with her latest report. "My king," she had said, bowing before him. Her scent filled his nose, the hot smell of wine and perfume and sweat, the stink of copulation.

"You have come from Elyon's bed," he'd known at once. "Has he told you anything yet?

She shook her head, as she did every time. "He doesn't trust me, that has become clear. But I followed him, to Amara's room...after. I fear they may be planning something. Lillia...she admitted to me that she's to wed Prince Robbert. I may get more from her, my lord. The girl is more honest than her brother."

What plot can the boy be cooking up this time? Janilah had wondered. *And does this golden haired girl tell me true?* Cecilia doubted the Lady Melany, Janilah knew. She called her his pet, said that the girl was in love with Elyon Daecar still, protecting the boy and his plots and schemes. *And perhaps my bastard daughter is right. The spider always knows when a fly rattles its web, and Cecilia's silk spreads far.*

"When will you next visit with the girl?" Janilah had asked.

"I cannot say, my lord. I will hope to spend time with her during the wedding two days hence. She will likely be permitted a drink or two by your lady cousin. Mayhaps that will get her talking."

But of what? Elyon had already conspired to twist Rylian's mind, Janilah had no doubt. But for the boy's interferences, Prince Robbert's betrothal to Lyriss Reynar might have been signed and sealed by now. "He conspires to put Rylian on your throne," Cecilia had whispered to him, night after night when he found her in his solar, perched upon that window seat she favoured. "You must eliminate him, Father. Elyon has the power to undo all you've worked to build."

And perhaps this latest plot will further my fall? Perhaps the spider I sired is right? He had looked Melany Monsort in those bright sapphire eyes, ever detached and unreadable, yet lit with a cold blue flame of displeasure, he saw. *He has spurned her, and cast her from his bed,* he realised. *She cares for Elyon,* as Cecilia says. *She cares for him deeply, and for all that, she has failed me.* "You continue to disappoint me, Melany," he had told her. "Go."

She bowed low. "My king. I will bring you something better next time."

You won't, he knew, *but you have another use to me now.*

It was then, two nights ago, as the girl had fled his throne room, that Janilah had gone to the secret chamber in his office and stood above the Mistblade. Its cobalt mists swirled, enticing, and so those whispers came. *Elyon stands in your way. Slay him. Slay him. Cut his throat as he sleeps...*

He had been close to doing just that, close to taking the hilt to his grasp and bleeding through the walls and corridors, through the dark places of the palace to Elyon's room to see his head from his shoulders, yet had strength enough to repel the urge.

But if I take up the blade today? If I let those whispers in? He feared what would happen if he did, with all the north assembled. A white day would become a red one. The peace he'd sewn in the north would be shattered. The southlanders would swarm with their dragons and their golden wolves and their legions, and take the north for their own. *I will lose the War Eternal,* he knew. *I will fail to fulfil King Galin's promise. That I cannot allow. No, no, I cannot...*

He broke from those thoughts, turned to the two knights before him. "I will trust you to see it done," he told them. "I will be on show all day, all evening, but you..." He nodded. It was the only way. "Cowls and cloaks," he went on, "and don't be seen. I would have you avoid violence, if you can."

The sworn swords traded a look. "There will be guards at Prince Dalton's door, sire," said burly Sir Kevyn Bolt. "There always are when he isn't there, a good few of them. Half the time Sir Taegon's there, and that man's near big as the Wall."

"Big men have further to fall," Sir Owen said to that.

The Bull looked set to respond, but Janilah shook his head. "Sir Taegon Cargill will be at the feast. He is the highest ranking Cargill here, with his lord uncle and cousins absent, and will need to be present to represent his house."

"Aye," Sir Kevyn agreed. "Might be so, sire. Dalton likes to keep Sir Brontus Oloran around as well. He's lesser ranked than his cousin Nathaniel, who'll be there to watch King Godrik. Might be that Dalton will leave Sir Brontus in charge of his rooms."

Sir Owen didn't think so. "Dalton Taynar is turning craven, they say, and paranoid of Vesryn's vengeance. He'll keep his best men nearby."

"Mayhaps," grunted the Bull, "but it makes no matter if we can't use force." He turned. "If I may, sire, we'll have no trouble cutting through a few lesser knights, I'll wager. We'll be cloaked, cowled, as you say...no one will know who's done it..."

"My granddaughter is marrying a king today, Sir Kevyn," Janilah cut in. "I want no blood, lest there be no other choice."

"The balcony..." started Sir Owen.

"Impossible," the Bull of Bolt cut in. "The climb's too treacherous, godsteel or no, and visible from a full dozen other balconies on the opposite wing. We're likely to be spotted on the way up."

"Through a wall, then?" Sir Owen Armdall offered. "We could cut through from an adjoining passage..."

Sir Kevyn had an answer for that too. "The corridors will be guarded, and Dalton's got a whole level of the Ghost Tower to himself. Soon as we climb up those steps and are spotted..." The knight looked to Janilah in one final beseech. "Sire, if we were only to injure the guards there..."

Janilah raised a hand. He turned to Sir Owen Armdall. "You overheard my conversation with King Hadrin?" he asked. The Oak of Armdall gave a nod. "Then you will know that Lord Swiftwater occupies the chambers directly beneath Prince Dalton's rooms." *Unplanned,* thought Janilah, *but most welcome.*

Sir Owen's lips showed a smile. "Yes, my lord. I understand."

"Good. Then see it done," Janilah commanded. *And if there must be blood,* came a thought, came a whisper, *so be it.*

42

Elyon

The ceremony had been a difficult spectacle for Elyon Daecar to observe. *It should have been Aleron,* was all he could think, as he watched Princess Amilia move up onto the dais within the Temple of Ilith, her simple silken emerald gown swirling about her legs as she walked. Atop it she wore a mantle of fine sable clasped by a brooch bearing the crest of Tukor, her slender hands hidden behind supple brown leather, her feet slippered in the same.

Her new husband was smaller than her, shorter by an inch even in boots made to enhance his height. His crown gleamed magnificently against the pale late morning light, drawing the eye from the unpleasant features of his face, but when he spoke his vows, there was no hiding from *that* voice. A snivelling, scratchy, ugly thing, it echoed unpleasantly through the vast open hall, and yet all Elyon could hear were those words the Rat King had said to him weeks ago in the Stonehills.

Amron Daecar...is dead.

Amron Daecar...is dead.

He focused on Amilia instead, and when the princess said the vows that would make her a queen, her voice rang out as pure and practiced as the smile upon her face. A false smile, everyone knew, but not one you'd know to look at it. "She looks radiant," Lillia whispered at Elyon's side, clutching her hands together. "Will I ever be as beautiful as her, Elyon? When I marry Robbert...will I stun as she does? Say I will."

"Of course you will, Lil. More so," he promised.

She beamed, and Elyon was glad that Jovyn wasn't there with them, lest his heart break all over again. Instead they had Amara for company, with a host of the Vandarians filling the benches about them. Elyon and Amara had, by mutual consent and intention, chosen to sit a little further back than their station merited. Elyon was heir to House Daecar, Lillia to wed Amilia's brother and become her sister by law, and Amara a close blood relation of the bride. By all that they should have been seated at the very front. Instead they were clustered amid the crowds, wishing for it all to be done.

It didn't last long, thankfully. The High Priest of Ilith took them through a fairly perfunctory service, reading a few solemn scriptures, expressing some touching sentiments, asking for the bride and groom, princess and king, to recite their vows and share their words and swear their oaths before the nobles of the north. It wasn't how it would have been done in Rasalan. They were a more pious people, all told, more prone to long-winded prayers and songs for their many gods of sea and storm, to rituals and customs that were not permitted here. Janilah had made this an exclusively Tukoran wedding, it seemed, and Hadrin, so oily as he was, had bent his back and accepted.

Elyon was glad for that. The Tukorans liked to feast, and the drinking had already started for some. By noon some would be deep into their cups. By mid-afternoon and early evening, half the feast hall would be sotted. *But not me,* he knew. *Today I keep my wits about me. Today I join the game.*

When the High Priest had completed his droning, and the vows had been shared, the temple emptied out into the late morning sunlight. The courtyard beyond had been swept clean of snow, the drifts piled up high, a dirty white, on every side. All gathered to form a tunnel, smiling and cheering and tossing multi-coloured flower petals as husband and wife stepped out, beaming.

"All hail King Hadrin and his beautiful bride, Amilia Lukar, Queen of Rasalan," called out one of the Rasal knights, to a round of stamping and clapping from their side. Elyon didn't join in. He stood to the rear, watching as the short procession moved between the crowds and up toward the palace to take their place at the feast. After Hadrin and

Amilia came King Janilah, alone, then Prince Rylian and his dreadful wife Clarris, whose spit still felt hot and wet on Elyon's cheek, then the twin princes Robbert and Raynald, dashing with their curly auburn locks, and the rich green raiment they wore.

"I should be walking beside him," Lillia said, watching as Prince Robbert passed. "He's to be *my* husband. I should be there."

Amara hushed her. "Be quiet, little bear. All in good time. You'll have your prince, fear not."

The rest passed by, notable relatives of the new queen consort - bar Amara, of course - and an even more notable *lack* of relatives for the unpopular Rasal king. "Does Hadrin not have any close relations?" Lillia wondered, as the loftiest nobles filtered through behind, and the crowds began to follow up into the palace in a stream of colours and cloaks.

"I do believe that Hadrin is an only child," Amara answered. "Godrin had several siblings from his father, King Astan, I know." She counted on her fingers. "Godrin was firstborn, of course, then came Tayrin, Nula, and Atia. All are dead now, though Princess Atia was the first to go. The rest lived much longer."

"How did they die?" Lillia asked.

"Well let me think," Amara said, tapping her chin. "Tayrin and Nula...old age, I do believe, or some associated ailment. Both were into their eighties when they died, oh, a decade or so ago, just a year or two apart. Godrin went on much longer, of course, some say in part because of the purity of his blood. The firstborn of any line has the purest blood, we all know." She smirked at them. "I'm sure you're both happy to hear that, second and third born as you are."

"I'm the firstborn *girl*," Lillia claimed. "So it's different for me."

"It's nonsense," Elyon said, "all of it. Many famed kings, lords, knights, scholars and all else in between have been second, third, fourth and lower born in their family lines and gone on to achieve great things. You only have to look at King Ayrin to see what wonders can be achieved by subordinate sons."

"He would be a good example, yes," Amara agreed. "There have been few monarchs so wise and humble. He may just be the finest king Vandar ever had."

"*After* Varin," said Lillia, in that I'm-always-right voice of hers. "Ayrin's father was greater."

"Some say yes, some say no, sweet bear," Amara said, all light and airy. "Varin lived through the time of gods, through hundreds, even thousands of years of war and death and rebirth. Once he lost his immortality after the fall of the gods, and became a mere man, he did much good, that's true, but he also helped spark the War of Fire and Steel..."

Lillia's frown deepened. "Drulgar the Dread did that," she said, indignant. "And Eldur. Varin was only seeking justice for the death of his children."

"Yes, and that justice brought the world to its knees, and sparked the First Renewal. A hundred years of war followed, a war that Ayrin, in his wisdom, chose not to restart when Varin himself was murdered at the parley by those spiders and snakes that Eldur sired." She smiled handsomely, as they passed along the frosted colonnades, the skies bright, the snows glistening, not a breath of wind in the air. "Perhaps we should revisit this later, sweetling? I do love a good historical debate."

Lillia wouldn't stand a chance in that, Elyon knew, but she'd try to win it all the same. "Fine...later," she said, marching along. "But you still haven't told me about how Princess Atia died."

"That's true, I haven't." Amara thought for a moment. "Tuberculosis, I recall, when she was only a teen. A tragic loss. She was said to be more beautiful than you'd expect, to look at the family. None have ever been famed for their looks."

"And Hadrin least of it," Elyon muttered, as they followed along with the crowds, their voices hidden amid the din of footfall and conversation.

Lillia screwed up her face. "He's the ugliest man I've ever seen, I think, even in that golden cloak and crown. He looks half a corpse, in the wrong light. How old *is* he?"

Elyon gave a shallow laugh. "Fifty, or fifty one, I think."

"So..." Lillia turned her eyes around. "He doesn't have any relations at all? What about cousins? Surely his uncle and auntie had some children of their own? And they'd be his age, wouldn't they? So they'd have children too."

"He has cousins," Amara confirmed. "His uncle Tayrin had several children. So did his auntie Nula."

"And where are they?"

"Not here," Amara said. She looked down, lowered her voice. "Haven't you heard, little bear? Hadrin's a kin and kingkiller. His family want no part in this farce, believe me."

The banquet hall had become a familiar venue these last long weeks, with the incessant feasts that had taken place in the build-up to the wedding. Elyon had learned to hate them, where once he'd rejoiced in such settings. Today none of that mattered. There was no joy, no hate, no resentment, no emotion at all. *Just duty,* he thought. *Just justice. Just a man in a mask, playing a part.*

His seat was in a place of high esteem. Though the invitees to the temple and ceremony were permitted to sit where they wished, the feast would start with a more formal arrangement, before devolving as the hours fled by, as was the Tukoran way. Elyon bid his Auntie Amara goodbye, put a kiss on Lillia's forehead, and pulled back their chairs when they reached their table. Both were to sit elsewhere from Elyon, though together; Lillia was too young yet to be here without a chaperone.

"Act well, sweet Elyon," Amara told him, her eyelid waving a wink. "You've had years of experience of getting yourself blind drunk at these things. It shouldn't be so hard for you to pretend, should it?"

Elyon smiled, turned, moved off through the crowds to his own table, and took his seat. It was situated near the far left edge of the rectangular royal table - the rest were circular - and out of the direct eyeline of the trio of treacherous kings at its heart. *Thank the gods for that,* he thought, seating himself in his place, which afforded a generous view of the entire feast hall, with its many hearths and galleries and huge great banners hanging on the walls.

No sooner had Elyon settled himself into his chair than a cup came down onto the table before him, its brim sloshing with wine, deep red and smelling of spice. "What a day. What a wonderful day." Lord Wallis Kanabar gave him an earthy smile, planting his enormous frame upon a groaning seat beside him. He had in his own hand a full cup. "Down it goes then, heir of Daecar. Down down down!" He threw the drink down his neck, wiped his lips with his sleeve, and slapped Elyon on the back. "Well, if you won't, I will." The overflowing cup of wine he'd just placed in front of Elyon followed the first into his ample gut. Elyon imagined it would be in good company.

He frowned, looking over the place-names for the table. The

folded piece of parchment beside him was written with the name of Humphrey Merrymarsh, Lord of Calmwater. "I do believe that seat is meant for someone else, my lord," he said.

"Ah, so it is." Wallis Kanabar grabbed the piece of parchment, screwed it up, and tossed it over his brawny, blue cloaked shoulder onto the floor. "Don't worry, lad," he said, noting Elyon's quizzical reaction, "it's all been cleared. Merrymarsh is taking my seat, over yonder." He thumbed toward a nearby table, where Lord Merrymarsh was taking his seat.

"Are you sure?" Elyon had to ask. "He looks rather grumpy, Wallis."

"When doesn't he? He's merry in name only, as you know."

Elyon looked at the big, red-bearded lord with a smile. "My thanks, Wallis. I'd much rather spend the evening with you." *Though feigning getting drunk mightn't be so easy,* he realised. Elyon had already noticed that Horus Buckland was to be seated at the table too, and the two brawny lords did like to share a drink. "I take it you want to resume your nightly contest with Lord Buckland?" he asked him.

"Oh of course," the Lord of the Riverlands laughed. "Janilah can try all he likes to break us up, but I won't be having it, oh no." He waved over a serving boy, who filled their cups halfway. "Do I look like half a man, boy? Give me a full bloody measure."

The stripling did as ordered. As he poured, Elyon considered asking him if he knew a boy of sixteen summers, lanky, with messy hair, name of Del, but refused the urge. *That race is run,* he knew. *All I'm doing is chasing ghosts.*

When their cups were refilled, Kanabar raised his goblet for a toast. Before he could speak, however, Lord Harry Swiftwater arrived. "This is me, I think," he said, pulling out a chair next to Lord Kanabar. "I thought I was to sit with Merrymarsh, but Wallis, you're much better company."

"Buckland is here with us too," Lord Kanabar told him, with a greedy smile. "We're planning to make this evening as wonderfully uncomfortable for sour old Janilah as possible."

"No change from any night, then," Swiftwater jested, his many chins jiggling as he laughed. "What were you toasting? I hope I'm not interrupting?"

"By no means." Kanabar hoisted his cup higher. "To your king and his beautiful new queen. Let's start with that."

They drank, and Elyon joined, though he took only a small sip. By that time others were pulling chairs, sitting, the feast hall filling with laughter and music. The Oakenlord, Ferry Maynard, was with them too, as was his second son Sir Francis. Sir Wallis Paramor, son of Lord Donal, took the seat on Elyon's left. "Well, a fine bunch," he said, smiling mildly. "Elyon, I'm delighted to spend the evening with you."

"And I you, Sir Wallis." The man was his father's spit in manners and look, just half his age, slim, plain of face, thin of hair, and decent to his core. He wore gold and blue, and the merman of his house, rather than the typical raiment of the Suncoats. "Your father graces the royal table, I see."

Sir Wallis nodded, and took a neat sip of his wine. "I do declare my king a less than popular man," he said in jest. "You may have noticed no relations of his have come. Well, my father steps into the breach, to lessen his embarrassment. As with Lord Browlan, as you can see."

"I feel sorry for them both." Elyon raised his cup. "Much more fun down here."

"Oh yes, very much so."

Elyon took a small drink, only to wet his lips, then set his cup back down. His intention was to be seen to be drinking, but in actual fact, drink very little at all. He glanced around his table. But for Lord Kanabar's sudden intrusion, he seemed to have been placed among Rasal highlords and knights exclusively. *Is there some meaning in that?* He couldn't be sure. What he did know was there would be eyes on him tonight, and for that, he'd have to bide his time.

He looked around to note the location of his allies and co-conspirators. Lancel and Barnibus were seated separately at tables near the heart of the hall, both placed with an assortment of middling lords and ladies, knights and heirs from the three northern kingdoms, deemed within their social strata. Jovyn was absent, working in the shadows of the palace in preparation for later. Amara and Lillia were, of course, seated side-by-side at a table nearby. As his eyes passed them by, he saw his auntie looking at him. She gave him a secret smile through the shuffling bodies as other guests arrived to take their seats, and servers hustled about with trenchers and trays. Her eyes seemed to glance at the unmissable form of Lord Kanabar for a moment, and in that moment, Elyon felt her hand in his abrupt arrival. It was fleeting, but telling. He turned his attention to the Lord of the Riverlands, leaned across to him, and asked. "Have you spoken with my auntie recently, my lord?"

Kanabar had a secret smile of his own, hidden in the foliage of his flaming orange beard. "As often as I possibly can, Elyon. Your auntie is a delight. Any woman who can drink me under the table is worthy company, and if that woman has a deep seething hatred for Janilah Lukar, well...that's even better." He grinned a wine-stained grin. "Why ask?"

Elyon spared a glance at his auntie again, then put his eyes back on Wallis Kanabar. Both still wore those knowing little smirks. "I feel I'm being left out of something," he said.

Kanabar lowered his voice. "To the contrary, Elyon, I do believe you're centrally involved in what will transpire tonight."

Elyon frowned, checked no one was listening, then said, "So you know? She told you, about..." He left the rest unsaid.

Kanabar nodded, his big bushy beard perched upon his thick girth. "She came to me the very night she arrived in the city," he confessed. "Mentioned to me that she'd travelled with a certain Blade of Vandar, kept out of sight in a gilded chest within one of Godrik's luggage carts. I'd hoped our void-of-charisma-of-a-king would have consented to give it to you willingly, as champion, but it was only a fools hope really. A Taynar giving a Daecar a leg-up? You could go a thousand years without that happening."

"Rodmond might disagree with you, Wallis," Elyon countered. "We get along well."

"Rodmond's of a lesser line, born of Godrik's second son. It doesn't count."

"Doesn't it? He's second in line to the throne now. At least until Dalton has a son of his own."

"He can't. The man's infertile, far as I know, I think he's bored all his seed to death. But no matter, the Taynars won't hold the crown for long, my boy. We'll get all that corrected soon enough, and put your father on the throne where he belongs, but later...for now we're talking about payback, glorious bloody payback, and I'm in, Elyon, you've got my backing all the way."

A hopeful smile simmered on Elyon's lips. "I...I had hoped I would, my lord."

"Then you should have come to me sooner, like your auntie did."

He raised a hand. "I know, I know, perhaps you didn't want to get me embroiled in it all, but by Varin, Elyon, embroil to your heart's content." He gave a thundering laugh, which probably wasn't wise, as half a hundred people looked over. "Oh, let them look," Kanabar went on, uncaring. "I'm just playing to my reputation. Lord Buckland and I are going to make a raucous old racket tonight, get the whole feast hall sotted to their souls. Songs, Elyon, there are going to be songs. Songs so loud they'll ring all through the palace, down every corridor and up every tower."

He grinned, dimming his voice. "Mayhaps even to the Ghost Tower? Do you think we can get them singing over there as well?" Kanabar twirled the thick hairs of his maple moustache. "There are guards posted there, outside Prince Dalton's chambers, you know. Eight of them, I hear, with that serpent Sir Gerald Strand in charge. Now I wonder why a highborn Greycloak knight like Sir Gerald would be loitering over there, away in that cold haunted tower, with his king here at the feast? He's heir to his house as well, you know, firstborn son of Lord Styron. He should be here among the guests, wouldn't you say?"

Elyon absorbed all that. He had Jovyn out there now, checking the passages around Dalton and Godrik's chambers, to ascertain how many guards would be stationed at their doors. He'd not expected this, though. "So the Windblade's there," he said. "In Dalton's rooms." They'd thought as much, but been unable to confirm it for sure. Even Amara, queen of gossip as she was, hadn't been able to get absolute confirmation. *At least, as far as I know,* Elyon thought. It seemed Amara had kept a few parts of her plan secret from him until now.

"It's there," Kanabar said. "Godless Godrik gave Dreary Dalton the blade some days ago, as far as I understand. He's been training with it nightly since, so he might make use of it when he sieges the Trident."

Elyon shifted his eyes about them to make sure their conversation was private. The hall was noisy, the rest of the table chatting cheerfully among themselves. Those nearby were the same. There were a multitude of guards posted about the perimeter, but none so close as to hear them, even with godsteel to grasp.

Above them, on the stage, those upon the royal wedding table were sharing courteous words with those seated to their sides. At the centre, on high backed wooden thrones painted in the colours of their kingdoms, were the three perfidious kings, Janilah flanked by Godrik and Hadrin. *Unity*, the trio said, looking imperiously down upon their host. Elyon scowled to look at them. *Unity bought by blood and treachery. A unity that will not last.*

He turned back to Lord Kanabar, satisfied they weren't to be overheard. "How do you know?" he asked him. "Has someone seen him with it?"

"Seen, no. But *heard*...well, that's another matter."

"Who? Sir Taegon? Sir Brontus?" Dalton tended to use one of the two when guarding his door at night; recently, Elyon's own duties to that end had been withdrawn. *And perhaps there's something in that? Perhaps he didn't want me listening?*

"No," Lord Kanabar said. "Me." He smiled.

"You?"

"Yes, me." The huge old man inched closer, conspiratorial. "It just so happens that Happy Harry Swiftwater here has chambers right beneath Dour Dalton's." He gestured to the chubby Seaborn lord sat beside him, who was turned away in conversation with Sir Francis Maynard and oblivious to their discussion. "I was over there a few nights ago, hearing the latest fisherman's tales. We got into our cups, nice and deep...you know how I like to get." Kanabar grinned, slurped his wine for illustration. "Well, Happy Harry just couldn't keep up. Passed out on his chair, snoring like a broadback, and wouldn't you know, I heard something rather interesting going on in the rooms above. Heavy breathing, grunting, cursing, all sorts of strange things. It piqued my interest, naturally, so I took out my godsteel dagger, put my ear to the wall, and listened. Now my hearing isn't what it was, nor my blood-bond I regret to say, but it's good enough to know when a man's training with a new blade. And having trouble, it seemed to me. Dalton did not sound a happy man."

"When does he ever?" Elyon asked, forcing a smile to his face. He judged that anyone looking at the pair would expect them to be smiling, and drinking too, so he raised his cup, took a sip, and Kanabar did the same. "So...Dalton's chambers, then. You say Sir Gerald is guarding the passages?"

Kanabar nodded. "With eight Taynar men for company."

Elyon turned his eyes across to his auntie. "And just how much of our plan did Amara tell you, my lord?"

"All of it," Lord Kanabar said at once. "And I added in my own spice as well, you should know. You're going to act drunk, take off with some lovely lady, as your reputation would expect, then creep away to thieve the Windblade once you're free of the hall." His eyes crinkled. "So here I am to help."

"Help? How, exactly?"

"By making sure you are seen to get absolutely sotted with the rest of us." He put down his cup, right next to Elyon's. "I may be big and old and drunk, but I'm not so clumsy with all that. I can switch our cups around easily enough, my boy, make sure yours is seen to be filled often, should anyone be watching." He demonstrated just that, reaching out, using the folds of his big cloak to conceal the switch.

Elyon smiled. "It seems it isn't just my auntie who has her tricks, my lord."

"Tricks, yes, we all have our tricks, Elyon." He flicked his eyes toward Janilah, sitting grim at the heart of the top table. "The only question is...will Janilah's creatures have cooked up a few tricks of their own tonight? I rather think they will. But you know that already, don't you?"

"Of course," Elyon said. "Their plan is part of ours, Wallis." *We just have to hope they follow through,* he thought, *or else we'll be moving onto plan B...*

"Indeed." Lord Kanabar was enjoying all this, Elyon could tell. He drank another liberal swig of wine, skilfully swapped cups with Elyon, and waved over the serving boy. "Boy, my young friend here has an appetite," he said loudly, so others might hear. "Fill him up, right to the brim. And don't stray too far. We plan to get legless tonight."

"Yes, m'lord, of course, m'lord." The boy did his duty and stepped away. Kanabar swapped the cups back around, drank, wiped his mouth.

"This'll be a night to remember, young Elyon," he said, sitting back, folding one huge leg over the other. "Though in all truth, I don't expect to remember a thing."

Kanabar drank deep. Elyon pretended to do the same.

The hall was beginning to grow hot and loud.

Let the games begin, Elyon thought.

43

Janilah

I really do hate that man, Janilah seethed, as the great Oafenlord Wallis Kanabar sat belly-laughing at his table, slapping a meaty paw on his thigh. *No, not* his *table. I put him elsewhere on purpose.*

The man had defied him, though, just as Godrik had, and his own son had, and the Daecar whelp had, and how many others besides? Even over the music and the voices of the hundreds of guests, and the singing and the merrymaking and the clangs and clacks of cups and plates, Janilah could hear Kanabar's laughter. *I will kill him one day,* he promised himself. *I will cut out that tongue and nail it to his sweaty forehead. We'll see how he laughs when he's choking on his own blood.*

The evening had been as painful as anticipated. *I have been cursed by kings,* he thought. He'd been a rival of King Godrin of House Thala for years, hated the wise old prophet to his marrow, and yet his son was somehow worse. Spiritless, fawning, and tittering like a lovestruck teen with his new bride, Hadrin had tested Janilah's patience to its very limits, whispering endless compliments into Amilia's ear, grinning that impossibly ugly grin of his as he sat in his sparkling crown.

And the other flank wasn't much better. Godrik, the Corpse King of Vandar, perched still as stone, pale as ice, with eyes as dead as his predecessor, unspeaking, un-eating, only occasionally sipping at his wine in measures a kitten lapping up milk would be ashamed of. The only words he did utter were tidings about the war. "Save it for the council," Janilah had been forced to tell him, more than once. Sat next to King Godrik, he felt the cheeriest man in the world. "This is meant to be a wedding, not a funeral." Somehow, Godrik Taynar made every room he entered feel like a crypt.

I should have kept Ellis alive, Janilah had reflected, again and again as the night wore on, and the speeches were made, the dozens of courses brought forth, the barrels of beer and wine emptying with a haste rarely seen in this hall, mostly due to Kanabar, Buckland, Elyon Daecar and all the rest. Janilah Lukar was not a man prone to regret, but that one - killing Ellis, putting Taynar on the throne - was starting to weigh on him. Ellis Reynar had been a fool, but a harmless fool, and pliable as soft leather, the son of a king and man whom Janilah had respected. He'd thrown him from the balcony for a reason, but that reason had proven a lie, the deceit of a greedy old man, hungry for a throne.

Janilah blew out a breath. The place was growing hot, hot to the point of stifling. Banners of blue and green, brown and gold were hanging everywhere, trapping in the heat that blazed from a hundred hearths. And the bodies. There were hundreds, laughing and shouting and drinking and singing, their voices rising up and over the music, which only played louder to be heard, forcing the voices to rise louder still, and the music to follow, and on, and on, until there was nothing but a wall of noise.

Janilah sighed. *I should have let Ellis live,* he thought again, for the dozenth time. *Is this guilt I'm feeling? Remorse?* It wasn't, he knew, just regret for this inconvenience. *But tonight I'll correct some of that, at least. Soon I'll hear word from Sir Owen and Sir Kevyn. Soon I'll have my justice. Soon I'll have my prize. Soon soon soon...*

Janilah drew a breath. He'd been drinking too much. Too much wine to soothe the pain in his chest, the ache in his ears from Hadrin's tittering and Kanabar's barking, and Godrik's deathly silence and the constant accusations in those cold black eyes. *Does he know I will try to take it tonight? Has he planned for it, to catch me out? Is he trying to put Rylian on my throne too, like the Daecar boy and his scheming bitch of an auntie.*

Amara. He turned to look at her now, sitting amidst the sea of tables, sleek in grey and blue. *Vandarian colours. Daecar colours. She is no Lukar, no kin of mine.* All night she'd been giving him the eye, some wicked little grin on her face. *She hates me, I know, for who I am, for what I am, but is this something more?* Melany had said Elyon met Amara two nights past, said they were plotting something, planning something, but what? *What!* It had crossed his mind that they aimed to take the Windblade too, but that felt more like paranoia. *Is that what I am? Paranoid? Is that what I've become?* Would Elyon steal such an heirloom from his own king? Would he dare be so reckless, so bold?

His uncle was, Janilah reflected. *Oh he defied me too. And the boy Jonik, Daecars both.* There would be a cruel irony to it, should Elyon seek to claim a Blade of Vandar too. Yet if he planned such a thing, it seemed less than likely tonight. The boy had been in no fit state for it, by judge of the raucous laughter and drunken tomfoolery at his table, and every time Janilah had glanced over, Elyon had been holding a cup, or having it refilled, drinking as heavily as Kanabar and Buckland.

He wasn't there any longer, though. The last Janilah had seen of the Daecar heir, he'd been ensconced in some shadowed corner with a pretty red-headed girl, their hands all over one another in ebrious embrace. He had a reputation for that, and Melany had said Elyon had begun to lose interest in her; this seemed a natural next step, to find some slattern with whom to spend the night. *Yet still...*

Janilah took a breath. The noise was an insult to his ears, incessant and unforgiving, those drums and skins and pipes, and the blur of voices filling the spaces in between. He'd never liked feasts, nor functions where he had to sit on ceremony, bandy courtly words with foreign lords and ladies, most of them inert and unambitious and unctuous in his presence, unworthy to share the air he breathed. Yet for all that they could be revealing. Plots and schemes could be hatched among the whispered words and wine-drinking, and Janilah had learned to keep watch. *And Elyon...was all that a trick?* he had to wonder. *All that drunken roistering with Kanabar? That redhead's fond attentions?*

Through the fog of noise, smoke, and hot febrile air, he saw the triple-mantled figure of Sir Fredrick Ruxmond returning to the hall, appearing from a side-door at the rear. *Good, I'll find out soon.* "You'll excuse me," he said, though no one seemed to be listening. He stepped back from the table and to the side of the hall. The host had lost all sense of formality now, the tables bleeding into one another, colours swirling, nobles and knights swapping seats. Janilah had hoped that would finally break Kanabar and Buckland up, but to the contrary, they were now stood side by side, arms draped over one another's shoulders, swaying and singing and getting everyone around them to chant an ungodly version of the Echo of Titans.

He reached the sworn sword. "Sir Fredrick."

Heavy browed, with too-close eyes, small teeth, and pockmarked skin from a bad bout of pox when he was a boy, the Ram of Ruxmond was not a handsome man. But he wasn't a member of the Six for his looks. "I followed the boy," he said immediately. "As ordered, sire."

Janilah studied him. "And?"

"And nothing, my lord. He and that redhead went stumbling off back to his room, down in the south wing. Nothing untoward; lad's just having some fun, is all. I've got a boy there, watching from the corridor outside, should he come out, but..." He shrugged. "Seems unlikely, with that one. Elyon Daecar's known for going all night, the gossips say."

Janilah considered that. *Paranoid,* he told himself. *You're just being paranoid.* "Good. And the others. Do you have an update for me, Sir Fredrick?"

"Not as of yet, sire. There were some of Swiftwater's men not invited to the feast in his rooms, Sir Owen told me. They were waiting for them to leave before they went in."

"And have they?"

"Left?" Sir Fredrick nodded. "Last I heard, aye. Think they drank Swiftwater's rooms dry and went looking for more ale elsewhere. Seems to be lots of drinking out there, sire, as well as in here. Even guards on duty are sharing a cup or two about the palace. You know how it gets with these things. They smell all the fun and want a piece of their own."

"Is Sir Gerald indulging?"

Sir Fredrick shook his head. "He refused the wine brought up to him, and commanded his men to keep their beaks dry too." He snarled, spat to the side. Sir Fredrick was the oldest of the Six, the longest serving, the most embittered, and considered good manners optional. "I know you don't want blood shed, sire, but I'd go join Sir Owen and Sir Kevyn if I could and see to Sir Gerald Strand myself. I've been itching to open his neck, as you know. The man's scum." He spat again.

"Mind that here, Sir Fredrick," Janilah told him. They were away in a corner, but still, this wasn't the place to be boorish.

"Apologies, my lord. I just...I take my oaths to protect you seriously. I know you bought those Greycloaks' silence, but I'd sooner die than betray you like they did King Ellis."

And what does that make me? Janilah wanted to ask. *For murdering a king, the son of a man I once called friend?* He knew what Sir Fredrick would say to that. He'd tell him it was necessary to secure the north, and to gather the Five Blades, though recent events had proven otherwise. Instead he merely said, "My thanks, Sir Fredrick. There are none more leal in their service than you."

"I live to serve you, sire." Sir Fredrick bowed low, then moved his close-set eyes through the hall. "It's loud tonight," he identified. "The noise can be heard as far off as the Ghost Tower, even. That's good. It'll help cloak Sir Owen and Sir Kevyn when they cut through Swiftwater's ceiling."

Janilah had hoped as much. The great racket Kanabar and his cronies were producing was grating, yes, but it served a purpose too. This feast was always like to be loud, but the Oafenlord had contrived to amplify the clamour. *The fool knows not that he aids me tonight*, Janilah thought. *Mayhaps I'll thank him later.* "Anything else?"

The Ram shook his head. "Not as yet, sire. I'll hear from Sir Owen soon, I hope. Once he has the Windblade safe from the prince's chambers, I'll let you know, right away."

Janilah nodded, returned to his table, and retook his high-backed wooden throne. A frosty breath signalled the voice of King Godrik Taynar. "Problem?"

Janilah gave the man a cursory glance. "None. A security update; nothing to trouble you, Godrik."

Taynar gave no reply to that, though his emotionless black eyes continued to simmer with suspicion. He studied Janilah a moment and then returned his gaze to the feast, the tension between them thick and dark as pitch. The singing was louder now, a competition of sorts unravelling as men of the three northern kingdoms bellowed out their favourite songs. Janilah saw his grandsons Robbert and Raynald in the midst of it. The pair grew boisterous during feasts like this and liked to provoke brawls, though that wasn't something Janilah would permit this night. *Too much tension. Too many blades.* If mens' blood got up and something sparked, fists could turn to steel easily enough, bruises to blood, and that wouldn't do. *We must preserve this peace,* he knew. *If it should break, all the north will suffer for it.*

Godrik Taynar watched on, dull-eyed and dissatisfied. "Well," he said. "I do believe I've seen enough." He began to ease from his chair. "I have no taste for brawling. It's time I took my leave. Dalton."

Prince Dalton had been sitting beside his father all night long, as dour and untalkative as his sire. He couldn't stand quick enough when his father called his name. "I shall accompany you back to your rooms, Father, then retire. The air is too hot in here for my tastes."

No, thought Janilah, *that will not do, not yet.* "There is much entertainment to come," he told them. He waved over his master of ceremonies, a flowery perfumed man named Costus, who came hustling over twirling a cane; the man doubled as a performer himself. "Costus, tell them what we have left."

"It would be my pleasure, great king." He bowed and set into it, describing the jugglers, fire-eaters, dwarven men to joust on dogs, tumblers and singers and snake-charmers and sundry other performers yet to emerge. Many and more had been entertaining the crowds through the feast, though not all had lasted long, booed off stage as soon as they bored their audience.

Godrik Taynar looked colourful Costus dead in the eye. "I have no appetite for theatrics or asinine amusements, and it seems the guests have long lost interest in them too." He gestured to the merrymaking. "My ears grow weary of it all. It is the quiet of my bed that I want."

"We don't care for this sort of thing in the Ironmoors," Dalton told the perfumed man, harshly. "These base amusements grow quickly tiresome." He paused, looked to the corridor leading toward the Ghost Tower. "And I have other matters to see to, before the night is done."

Training with the Windblade, Janilah thought. *But will you find it gone when you return, or in the process of being stolen?* The latter could turn ugly. "The night is yet young," he said, still seated. "We can forgo Costus's entertainments, if it would please you both. And give no mind to my grandsons, Godrik, there will be no brawling here tonight. I have forbidden it."

"Be that as it may. I am old, and need to rest. But by all means, enjoy the rest of the feast."

Janilah gave Hadrin a look as Godrik turned to move away. The

Rat King was quick enough to understand his need. He stood from his throne, its back carved into a speared leviathan, painted yellow and blue for his kingdom. "I would have you wait until I take my new bride from the feast hall, good king," he called out. "Is it not custom that we should be first to depart on the night of our wedding?"

Godrik Taynar turned slowly. He regarded Hadrin for a long moment, then said, "How you haven't already left this hall astounds me, I confess, with such a beautiful bride to take to bed."

"I wouldn't want to deny my queen the joys of her wedding feast," Hadrin came back.

Godrik smiled his icy smile. "Of course. Or perhaps it is nerves that stays your hand."

Amilia drew quickly to her feet before Hadrin might answer, clutching at her husband's scrawny left arm. "My husband speaks true, good king," she said. "I am a Lukar, a Tukoran, and these feasts are in my blood, loud and lively as they are." She smiled a glittery white smile. "I wish to stay a little longer, if I may. Perhaps you might wait until then, before you take to your rooms?"

Godrik looked unmoved. "I would not want to insult you, of course, Queen Amilia. All I ask is that you do me a courtesy of your own, and let an old man take to his bed. I am of a quietly spoken disposition, and to even be heard with all this noise...it is taxing. I feel my presence here will not be missed."

"I am sure that isn't true, my lord," Amilia said.

"It is," said Godrik. "But I thank you for your courtesy." He turned to leave.

Amilia gave Janilah a glance then said, "Perhaps your son can stay, at least, in lieu of you? It would be a shame to lose you both so early into the evening."

"I leave that for my son to decide." Godrik Taynar continued on his way.

Dalton bowed stiffly. "I am sorry, Queen Amilia. I am to leave soon for war, and need my rest. Enjoy the rest of your evening." He followed behind his father.

Janilah had no more cards to play. If he tried to stop them, they would smell a rat. *I need to give Sir Owen and Sir Kevyn more time.* He stood from his throne, thinking. If Dalton discovered two of his Six in the act of taking the Windblade, there would be blood. *This wedding will turn red,* he knew.

He opened his mouth to speak, still unsure of what he would say. And just then, Amara Daecar strode up onto the dais.

Her arrival was so sudden it had them all turning to look at her in surprise, Godrik Taynar included, who stopped in his step as he shuffled off, turning to face her with a frown.

"Leaving so soon, Your Majesty?" she said.

The king gave a small cough. "That is the intention, Lady Amara, yes. I am oft early to bed, as you know."

Amara placed a hand to her mouth, and laughed. "Goodness, my lord, you'll get people talking. Now why should *I* know of your bedtime routine?"

"Because we travelled together here for some weeks," Godrik said, without mirth, "and dined together most nights. Now if you'll excuse me."

"Of course, my lord." Amara bowed. "I did think you might want to remain, however, for the announcement."

That stopped the old Corpse King. Janilah looked at his scheming cousin with a frown. Rylian, a few places down the table, had already been disturbed from his conversation with Lord Paramor. Both were looking their way. Amara smiled as only she could smile, smugly delighted with herself. "Oh look, I have your attention. Aren't words a powerful thing. What is that old phrase? The pen is mightier than the sword? Well so is the tongue, I should say, to see you all so absorbed."

"Had you drawn a sword, you'd have gotten a similar reaction, Cousin," Amilia pointed out.

"Quite so, pretty queen," Amara returned. "And I'd have a host of armed guards surrounding me by now as well, I would think." She laughed again, her white teeth stained with spots of red from the wine. *Drunk,* Janilah could see plain enough. *The loathsome woman is drunk again.* Her eyes went to him as though sensing his thoughts. "King Cousin, we've not yet spoken this fine evening, and so little since I returned home. I do declare I have missed you so. Yet you seem to be avoiding me."

Godrik spared him having to give answer to that goad. "You made mention of an announcement, Lady Amara. What is it?"

Janilah had wondered that too, though by now he was starting to put the pieces of the puzzle together. The little figure of Lillia Daecar hovering at the bottom of the stage was a clue that was hard to miss. "It is one I think we all should hear." Amara turned to look at Amilia. "Sweet Cousin, I'd hate to steal any of your thunder on your wedding day, but do you mind? Do you mind awfully? There's no better occasion than now."

Amilia looked vexed. "Mind what, Amara?"

Amara's attention went straight to Rylian. "Would this not be a good time, Cousin Rylian?" She glanced to Lillia, waved her onto the stage to join them. "She's been dying to let all the world know."

Lillia Daecar was not a timid girl, not like the donkey-faced Lyriss Reynar. Nor did she share the former princess's distinct lack of beauty; to the contrary, all the world believed she would grow up as beautiful as her late mother, Kessia, and the resemblance was already strong.

Rylian was frowning and shaking his head. "This mightn't be the best time, Amara," he said. "I had planned to announce it later, in a day or two, once..."

"Once you've already left for war?" Amara laughed, as though it was all a game. "No no, Rylian, better to do it now, so long as Amilia doesn't mind, of course."

Amilia continued to look confused. "Amara, I confess myself perplexed. Lillia, what is she referring to, child?"

The little Lady of Daecar went down into a perfect curtsy. "My betrothal to your brother Robbert, Your Majesty." She beamed. "We're to be sisters. Isn't that wonderful!"

Amilia's eyes didn't say so. "You're to wed Robbert?" Her voice was dull.

"I am. It's all been agreed." Lillia's beaming smile slipped away at the expression on Amilia's face. "It...does that not please you, A-Amilia?" she asked, a flutter of disappointment in her voice. "I thought...I thought..."

Amilia was practiced in courtesy and courtly behaviours, so warmed her face with a smile. "Of course. I am delighted for you, Lillia, truly."

Janilah knew the source of her distaste; a simple matter of envy. Robbert was to Lillia what Aleron would have been too Amilia, only more. A prince, young and handsome and gallant, with his first taste of war behind him. The sort of match any young woman would kill for, and yet Amilia had just signed her life away to an overgrown rodent king two and half times her age and widely despised. The marriage had made her a queen, yes, but of Rasalan, a land of seafarers and pirates and privateers, whereas Lillia would be Queen of Tukor one day when Robbert became king, outranking her. *And she doesn't like it,* Janilah saw. *No more than I do.*

"Well, I confess this is...interesting news," said King Godrik Taynar. He looked at Janilah with a frown frozen on his deeply wrinkled brow. "I had heard a rumour that Princess Lyriss would wed the prince."

Janilah had no chance to answer. Rylian stepped in. "A falsity," he declared. "It was always my intention to wed my son to Lillia."

"But not yours, Janilah," said Godrik. "You do not seem to have had everything your way, old friend."

It was all Janilah could do not to strike him. "The match is good," he judged it best to say. "It is my son's right to decide whom his children will wed."

Amara laughed at that. "I do believe my King Cousin just made a joke," she said. "You'll excuse me, King Hadrin, but I do not believe you were Rylian's first choice for his daughter's hand."

"Nor his bloody hundredth," came a barrelling voice nearby. The great boor Kanabar stood at the bottom of the stage, ruddy faced, sweating, wine soaked into his beard, with a huge drunken grin on his lips. Hadrin seethed, but Kanabar cared not. He lumbered up to stand beside Amara, with little Lillia Daecar in between. "Sorry for butting in, but I couldn't help but overhear. A wedding, you say, between Lillia and Prince Robbert? Gods be good, what a match you'll make." He dropped to a bow before the girl, who giggled as the huge old lord took her hand. "You'll be a great queen, child, every bit as beloved as your mother." He flicked his eyes at Janilah. "You can set these dastardly Lukars to order...though I doubt that'll be necessary, once the incumbent king is gone."

Janilah Lukar stared, a fury in his face. "Another word, Kanabar, and I'll have you gutted like the pig you are," he growled.

"*Treason,*" the man came back at once, standing straight, turning. His huge barrel chest looked enormous beneath that forest of a beard. "How about that for a word, Janilah? It's one of your favourites, I hear."

Eyes were beginning to turn to the commotion about the royal table. The music started to stutter as musicians lost their rhythm, staring down from the galleries where they perched and played. The songs trailed off, the laughter died. The great roar began to leech away into a deadened hum. Through all that, the soft ring of steel could be heard as swords drew from scabbards. Janilah knew on instinct that Sir Rees and Sir Maxwell Hunt would be in the shadows at his back, waiting. So would others. Sir Munroe Moore and the men of Hadrin's guard, Sir Nathaniel Oloran and his Greycloaks; all would be hovering near.

No one seemed to know what to say. Janilah took several deep breaths to compose himself. Cedrik Kastor was watching on with a devious look in his eye. He brought blood to the parley at Harrowmoor, it was said. His face said he wanted the same to happen here. *But no,* Janilah knew. *I cannot rise to this boar.* It was what the man wanted, he could see clearly, and he'd not give him the satisfaction of being goaded.

In the end, it was his cunning cousin who broke the deadlock. She did so with a musical giggle, and a playful little prod at Kanabar's broad shoulder. "Oh, you boys. Still quarrelling after fifty years. Now come, let's not let this descend into bloodshed. This is a wedding, a time of joy, not suffering. There's no sense in coming to blows, is there?"

"None at all, Amara," said Rylian, firmly. His fingers were clutched at his sheathed dagger. "Wallis, they were ill-judged words. Do you mean to spark violence here tonight?"

Kanabar waved a hand. "By no means. Me and your father are just having a little chat, is all. As Amara says, we've not seen eye-to-eye since I battered him at the tourney here in Ilithor almost five decades ago, when I was but a bright-eyed knight and Janilah here a prince, no older than your twins. We were friends before then, Janilah, if you'll recall? Or did I knock all memory of that out of you when I put you on your arse for all the north to see?"

Janilah remembered that day well enough. Kanabar had been a monstrous fighter in his youth, there was no lie there, much as his son Sir Borrus was. It had been a long tourney, a long contest, and that day Wallis Kanabar and Janilah Lukar reached the final bout, beating out the princes and heirs of their age in the process, to come face-to-face across the field. A hot summer's day, they'd fought for a full twenty minutes before Kanabar eventually breached Janilah's defences, exploding forth in his favoured Powerform and knocking him onto his back. They'd been eighteen, he recalled. *A lifetime ago*. It was almost enough to bring a smile to his face. Those days had been a great deal simpler, before Janilah Lukar took up the torch of his house...before he fell captive to his lifelong obsession.

A silence had fallen around them. He turned his eyes about the hall. Half the north were looking on, just as they had that day in Ilithor. *You'll not put me on my back again, Kanabar,* he thought, *not here.* He removed the scowl from his face and said, "I got my vengeance in Eastwatch, a mere moon's turn after that day, Wallis. I trust you recall it? Or is your memory more selective than all that."

"A man of East Vandar recalls his victories more fondly than his failures, I'll not deny. That's just our way, but true enough, you bested me on my own lands, and were bloody good that day too. But you didn't put me on my backside like I did you." Kanabar gave a laugh. "We were well matched back then, though. You, me, Storris, Gideon, Brydon, Donal, even you Godrik..." He turned on his king. "You triumphed occasionally, as I recall. But you were better in the lists, more skilful on horseback with lance to grasp than when swinging a sword. I much preferred to keep the mud beneath my feet."

"My brother Patrik was always the better swordsman," Godrik said.

"Patrik was better than most. I was there the day he defeated Raythal the Red at the Battle of Short Claw, and what a sight that was. Now *there's* a true test of a man; killing a dragon. And you have me there, Janilah, I'll grant you. Never did kill a dragon in single combat myself."

"Not many have."

"No, too true. And yet you did, and Rylian besides. Now that's rare as breasts on a broadback, a father and son both slaying a dragon in single, honour-coded combat. I can think of another pair that did, though. Gideon and Amron Daecar, and who knows, perhaps Elyon will yet add to that list. Or maybe Aleron would have, if..." The big man didn't further that thought, but his silence said it all anyway. He paused, then smiled again. "And maybe your boys will do the same, Rylian? Robbert's already killing Suncoats, I hear, so why not dragons?

And Raynald even, let's not forget him." The twins were both watching now with the rest of the crowd. "What rotten luck for Raynald to always be forgotten, which he always seems to be. How long was it between their births? A minute? Two? That's a fine margin between being heir to the throne and not." He laughed to himself and looked down the table at Clarris Kastor, sitting stiff and stern beside her brother, lips pinched in anger. "Are you sure you didn't get them mixed up on the birthing table, my lady? Now wouldn't that be a scandal, twins fighting for the right to rule."

Rylian stepped over to the man and put a hand on his arm. "My lord, enough. All the hall is watching."

"Good." Kanabar drew away. "That's why you came up here, is it not, Amara? To announce Prince Robbert's betrothal to Lillia?"

"That had been my intention, yes," Amara said, enjoying every second of all this. "I do feel you have somewhat hijacked things, however, Wallis."

"For which I apologise. It's too hot in here, and there's too much wine in there." He slapped his massive belly, laughed, then looked at Rylian. "I'll shut up now, and let you do the honours. Forgive me if I've overstepped, good prince."

Rylian looked less than impressed with the brawny bearded lord, but had no real choice but to agree. Half the crowd had likely heard already, with Kanabar's loudmouthed prattling. He turned, raised a hand. The murmuring that remained in the hall faded off until all was quiet and still. "I have an announcement," he called. "One I had hoped to make in the days to come so as not to draw attention from my daughter on her wedding day, but alas...my hand has be forced."

He gave Kanabar and Amara a sharp look, then called for Robbert to join him. The boy lurched forward from the crowd, a shade drunken, and took to his father's side. Lillia Daecar went to Rylian's other, looking all the world at home beneath the dazzling gaze of the northern nobility. "We have a betrothal, a union of greathouses," Rylian proclaimed. "My firstborn son, Robbert of House Lukar, Prince of Tukor and second in line to the throne, is to wed the Lady Lillia of House Daecar, only born daughter of Amron Daecar, the Crippler of Kings and former First Blade of Vandar, a union that will sire warriors, kings, champions all." His pride came bursting forth now, unrestrained. "Long have I wished to see our families unite, to see what sons and daughters such a union will birth. Now we shall. Now we shall know. Robbert, will you seal it with a kiss?"

"It...it would be my honour, Father," said Prince Robbert, in a slight slur. He righted himself all the same, turned, and took Lillia's dainty hand in his. "I promise to make you the finest husband, my lady, when our time comes to wed. I declare it my solemn oath, before the nobles of the north, of Vandar, Tukor, and Rasalan, to love, serve, and protect you, always."

He kissed the back of her palm, smiling a handsome, if loose-lipped smile, as Lillia held her poise, and said, "I will make you a fine wife, my prince, a fine queen when you are king, and a fine mother to our children when they come. I will do this, and love you, honour you, be faithful to you, always. This is my solemn oath, before all the nobles of the north."

The cheering began a moment after, as Rylian started the clapping, proclaimed the marriage pact witnessed and ratified, and ushered the pair down into the crowds to be toasted and praised, as though the wedding was suddenly theirs. Amilia was quietly seething at all that, though said nothing, and nor did her mother Clarris appear pleased by the look of that snarl on her withered old face. Hadrin looked like he'd been entirely forgotten, which he had; there was some small mercy there, at least. Rylian was too content with Robbert's match to spare much of a thought for his daughter, or his wife, or his second son, and Godrik Taynar...well, it was hard to say what he made of it. The union would only strengthen the Daecar claim on the Steel Throne, should they fight to take it, and by that smile on Rylian's face, it was clear enough to all and sundry which of the Vandarian greathouses he favoured.

But it was Amara and the Oafenlord Kanabar whom Janilah observed most keenly.

There they stood side by side, watching things unfold, smiling those conspiratorial little smiles. Amara's intervention had seemed fortunate, delaying the Taynars' departure, but the woman could scheme as well as Cecilia, and she'd had that look in her eye all night. A feeling of unease came upon the king to look at her, at that little smirk gripping at her lips. And Kanabar, the great boorish brute, looked too happy with himself by half.

Janilah turned and locked eyes with Sir Rees. The older of the two Hunt brothers came marching over. “Sire.”

The king leaned in and spoke over the rapture and applause. “Fetch Sir Fredrick, and find out what’s happening in the Ghost Tower,” he commanded. “I have a feeling I’ve been tricked.”

44

Elyon

"Quickly now, quickly, this way," said Carly Flame Mane, leading them on. Her fiery hair bobbed against the back of her neck as she jogged down the dim stone corridor.

"Slow down," Elyon breathed. "I can...hardly...keep up." Though Lancel, Barnibus, and Jovyn were all on hand to help him, if needed, the Windblade was still a damn heavy sword.

"You're a Daecar," said Carly with that devious smile, glancing back. "It's in your blood and bones to be able to hold a blade like that. Stop complaining."

Elyon might have responded if he'd had the breath in his lungs. *And this the lightest of the Blades of Vandar. No wonder Vesryn had to drag the Sword of Varinar through Keep Daecar when he first claimed it.*

"Didn't your father ever let you hold that big golden sword of his?" Carly Flame Mane asked, bounding along.

"No," Elyon spluttered. "Not....not once."

"More's the pity. He might have prepared you better." The girl was as carefree as she was pretty, and as pretty as she was deadly. Beneath her slim black woollen cloak she wore a leather swordbelt and twin scabbard, each sheath bearing a short godsteel blade. She hadn't worn them at the feast, of course. Then she'd been dressed in her finery, a sleek jade dress and silken gloves to mark her as a noble-lady, though in truth she was anything but. She was a sellsword, a spy, a Bladeborn mercenary under Amara's employ, and had several gruesome scars to match the profession. He'd seen them when she'd changed her clothes in his bedchamber, flinging silk and satin aside and donning leather and wool in its place.

"Not many girls get naked in front of you without wanting a little more, I'll wager," she'd said, grinning that puckish grin. She'd turned to him, nude as a newborn, her slim nubile frame lit by the hearth-light, confident as anything. "Shame we don't have more time, Daecar. I'd sit you down on that bed there and show you the time of your fancy young life. You know I bloody would."

He didn't doubt it. "Next time," was all he'd said, though those scars on her body - especially the half dozen that ran diagonally across her back; whip-wounds, he knew, and deep ones too - had made him think of Saska.

"Yeah, next time." She'd pulled on her swordbelt, blades, black traveller cloak, boots. "I'm going to hold you to that, Daecar."

Now there she was, out front, leading them on through the bowels of the palace, down and down and down some more, to places rare trodden, judging by the cobwebs and dust, the lack of lanterns on the walls, the cold that crept into his bones.

"How far are we going?" panted Lancel, breath frosting the air. "Amara never said it would be so far."

"Ladies love to lie," Carly came back. "Or hide truths, which isn't much different." Her laughter rang down the corridor. "It's not so far, just a little further on. We'll get that blade safely out of here, don't worry. I'll make sure of that."

The plan had gone as well as hoped so far. After changing their clothes in Elyon's bedchamber, they'd left by way of the balcony, climbing up two floors into a quiet corridor above should anyone outside be watching. After that it was a simple matter of creeping through the quiet places of the palace to the Ghost Tower to meet Jovyn, and lie in wait. The boy had been in the designated spot, awaiting them in some darkened store-room. "How's it looking, Jov?" Elyon had asked him when they arrived.

"Good, Sir...er, Elyon. You got here just on time. I think they're about to steal it."

"How many?" asked Carly Flame Mane, who they'd first met the night before. She was Amara's secret weapon, and had been prowling about the city for some days, watching, waiting, feeding her lady master all manner of juicy treats and tidings. One such treat was juicer then all the rest. Sir Kevyn Bolt, she'd reported, was alive and well and in the city, cloaked and cowled, searching for something. They all knew what that something was.

"Two, that I saw," Jovyn told them. He was cloaked too, using his speed and fleetness of foot to scuttle about unseen. "One was tall, the other wide. Both wore cowls and cloaks."

"The wide one is the Bull of Bolt, there's no doubt there," Flame Mane said.

"And the tall one?" Elyon asked. "Another of Janilah's Six, I'm guessing?"

"Well aren't you a clever cookie." She grinned. "The Oak of Armdall, I'll bet. The Ram and those Hunt brothers were at the feast and Janilah's not gonna trust anyone but his Six to see this job done. That leaves Sir Owen and Sir Edwyn. I know who I'd choose." Carly knew much and more about the Six, Elyon had discovered, and just as much about Ilithor and the palace too, with all its secret passages and ways. She'd grown up here, the daughter of a whore down in White Shadow, who'd taken so many lords and knights to bed that her father might have been one of a hundred highborn men. "But Sir Owen, Sir Edwyn, it makes no matter," she went on. "What matters is it's happening, and just as your auntie Amara hoped." She gestured beyond the storeroom door. "They're going to have to come back down this corridor, assuming the theft goes well. It'll be heavy, and they'll be slow. If we're quick this should go easy."

It had gone easy, and even more so than expected. They'd waited no more than a few short minutes before they heard puffing and panting outside, and the scuff of feet shuffling along the stone corridor. As soon as it had passed, they'd burst out, hoods up, bludgeons to hand.

Sir Kevyn Bolt spun in shock though went down quickly enough, Carly leaping at him like an alley cat and connecting with a swift swinging thump to the head. Sir Owen Armdall was a different proposition. Quicker to react, speedy in defence, he slid straight back from their first flurry of blows, drawing out a godsteel longsword in a clean, quick motion, as a blue-green mist glittered the air.

"Thieves!" he bellowed, in a moment of wondrous irony. Yet before he could strike, Lancel and Barnibus flew in from behind him, arriving from their own secret hiding place, swinging. The first blow wasn't quite enough to fell the tall knight, Lancel connecting with a glancing strike that bounced right off his hooded head. Sir Owen turned, swung, slashed, and Lancel shot away. By the good grace of the gods he did so in time, the Oak's blade leaving nought but a gash through Lancel's black cloak. As all that was happening, Elyon saw his chance, rushing forward and catching Sir Owen flush on the temple with a clean strike. The knight went toppling immediately sideward from the contact, felled like a tree. He landed with a soft thump on the stone floor.

"Right, let's be quick about this," Elyon said, moving forward.

The two sworn swords had been carrying the Windblade in a gilded chest, which Elyon struck open with his dagger, flinging open the lid. Light spilled out, a blinding silver, and swirling mists puffed forth, thick as fog. It seemed to Elyon's ears as though a song of storms came with it, a howling gale blowing through the hall, and within those winds a voice was heard to whisper, speaking distant words he couldn't make out. And then all at once, the winds died and the mists settled and the blinding silver light receded, and all was quiet and calm again. Elyon took a short sharp breath, leaning down, reaching to the ornate hilt of the blade. He was acutely aware of the eyes of the others, watching, waiting, wondering what might happen. *Will he lift it? Will he fail? How strong is he really, how worthy?*

A shard of Vandar's Heart, was Elyon's only thought. All his life he'd been within touching distance of the Sword of Varinar, but had never held it, never felt its weight and power. This...this was different. This was about him, not his father. *My test. My fate. My chance to make a difference.*

His fingers grasped the blade.

The hilt felt strangely warm to his touch, thrumming with a deep distant power. That song of storms rustled through his head once more, though quieter this time, the sound of far off winds. He drew inside himself, mustered his full force of will, tightened his fist about the haft...and hauled the Windblade from its fixings.

"Well look at that, he did it," came the insouciant voice of Carly Flame Mane, watching on. "You must be a Daecar after all." The others were staring at the blade in wonderment as Elyon heaved it from the chest, planting the tip to the ground with a dull heavy thud. "Well come on, what are you waiting for?" Carly clapped her hands. "Let's get to work! Go go go!"

That roused them. The hallway was put back to order as swift as they could, Lancel and Barnibus dragging the two unconscious knights into the storeroom, Jovyn removing the chest. Carly just stood against the wall, arms crossed, legs crossing, waiting. A moment later, Jovyn returned with the Windblade's sheath. "It was in the chest, Sir Elyon....er, Elyon."

"Hold it up, Jov." The boy did, and Elyon hauled the blade up and in, slipping it inside with a grunt. He went to a knee. "Help me get it onto my shoulder. It'll be easier to carry like that."

Once that was done, Lancel and Barnibus took to his left and right, Jovyn his rear, and off they went to their extraction point, Carly leading from the front.

She knew the palace well. Apparently, Carly Flame Mane would sneak through these halls and high passes as a child, testing her mettle against the guards, making a game of how far she could get before being spotted and caught. It was a dangerous game, but to her that seemed the point. *She has the soul of a sellsword all right,* Elyon thought. Few of her ilk felt alive unless there was a bit of danger about the bend.

They went down halls, past balconies and terraces, descended steps. A half dozen staircases brought them into the lower places of the palace. The air grew colder, the walls spotted with lichen, the sconces fixed upon them empty of lanterns and light, dusted with rust. Once or twice they heard the echoing footfall of guards on their rounds, and Carly would hold up a hand, grip her dagger, wait and listen until they'd passed.

No blood, Elyon thought. *No witnesses. No traces.* So far all had gone without a hitch. Amara's confidence that Janilah would stage a robbery tonight had proven true. Why she hadn't told him earlier about Lord Kanabar's involvement, or that she knew Dalton had the blade in his rooms, he couldn't rightly say, but in truth it didn't matter now. Her plan had been to watch, to wait, and to let her king cousin's creatures do all the work. To lay the bait, set the trap, and take the spoils for their own.

And it had worked.

Yet Elyon wasn't going to get ahead of himself; much remained to be done. It wouldn't take long for the Oak and Bull to wake or be found, for the empty chest to be discovered, for the thievery to be unearthed. When that happened, Lancel and Barnibus needed to be back at the feast, Elyon back in his room, Jovyn the same. Carly Flame Mane, on the other hand, would see no rest tonight. She was a sell-sword, a spy, the bastard daughter of a White Shadow whore. And she was about to become the guardian of one of the most powerful weapons in the world.

"We're here," she said.

They'd come to a thick wooden door at the end of a long musty corridor, lined with old rusted suits of armour, way down deep beyond the forgotten places of the palace. A draught was seeping beneath the threshold, breathing between wood and stone, cold. Elyon could see flakes of snow amid the breeze, hear the wind blowing hard outside. The calm weather earlier hadn't lasted long, a heavy churn of grey cloud curdling the air, dropping a light snow. Elyon had spied that on the balconies earlier as they'd ventured for his room from the feast. *More luck.* Dark cloudy skies were well suited to this sort of business. "Open it," he said.

Carly Flame Mane moved forward, threw the bolts, gripped the handle, and pulled. A great groan gave out, of whining wood and screaming metal as the rusted hinges turned. With it came the wind, the sight of rock and drifts of snow, broken stone walls and ancient ruins.

"What is this place?" asked Barnibus.

"A part of the city never rebuilt after Galin Lukar's siege three centuries ago," Carly said. "A part long forgotten." There was a tower, Elyon could see, crumbled to piles of loose stone and choked by snow and weeds, looking over the hills beyond. Out there, a track led away from Ilithor and into the wilds. "These passes lead south and west, down through the hills and into the southern ranges of the Mistwood," Carly continued. "There are few who know of it, but we of the Flame Mane travel it often."

"Vandar," Elyon said, looking out through the shadows of the foothills. "The Mistwood marks the border to Vandar."

Carly smiled, flakes of snow capering across her flaming hair. "And leads into the Heartlands, no more than a week from here. When we pass beyond the Mistwood we'll be greeted by hoof and carriage and a host of men from the Riverlands. Lord Kanabar told you earlier that he'd added his own spice to this plan, did he not? Well that spice awaits us below; leal men of his house and lands, ready to take guardianship of the Windblade, to transport it wherever you wish." She turned and gave a whistle, and shadowed figures began to appear among the ruins of the tower. "My men," she told them. "Men of the Flame Mane. We'll make sure the blade reaches Kanabar's men, by oath to Lady Amara."

The sellswords advanced forward, their black cloaks trimmed with red at the collars and sleeves. They'd gone so far as to take on their own sigil, a laughing black skull with a flaming head of hair, sewn as badges on their chests. All had red hair too, dyed or otherwise it was hard to tell, with boiled leather dotted with crimson studs beneath their cloaks. A few swirls of mist rising from the occasional scabbard called Elyon's eyes to godsteel. "How will you carry it?" he asked, still holding the Windblade upon his shoulder. His legs felt close to buckling, in truth, but he didn't want to lose face now. "How many of your men are Bladeborn?"

"Enough," said Carly. "We have sturdy garrons for the work, sure-footed and strong, and several Bladeborn with enough Varin blood to heft the blade when they must." She raised a hand, whistled again, and called out, "Crowfoot, Will Red, Sally Scarlet, come."

The three came forward. Elyon could tell easily enough which was which by those names. Crowfoot was old, hunched, with a shock of grey hair on his head, and deep wrinkles seared about his eyes in a pattern resembling crowfeet. Will Red was young, no more than a boy of sixteen, but tall as a tower. He had long orange hair tumbling about his neck, and the early signs of an amber beard emerging from his pointy chin. Sally Scarlet was a burly woman, homely as they came, with a huge bust, legs thick as tree trunks, and one half of her head shaven to the scalp. The other half gathered into a twisting red braid that went all the way down to her hip.

Carly Flame Mane looked upon them proudly. How she'd come to lead this band was a tale Elyon hadn't yet heard, though was eager to. *But not now*, he thought. Time was pressing and every minute counted.

"A fine host," is all he said, with grace.

"The finest," Carly smiled. She turned to him. "You can put the blade down now, Daecar. We'll take it from here."

Lancel and Barnibus came forward to help him shift it to the floor, as the trio of Flame Manes stepped in. "You're, er, sure they can take the weight?" Lancel asked, doubtful.

It was the big woman Sally Scarlet who gave answer. "Just watch, pretty boy," she grunted, reaching to take the hilt. The other two followed in, tall Will Red and crookbacked Crowfoot, grappling with the length of the blade, grunting and huffing and puffing loudly as they laboured it from the ground as a three. Eventually they had it lying across their arms as they stood side-by-side, cradling it like a babe, panting. Elyon could hardly watch. Something about all of this felt wrong to him. He'd stolen the Windblade from his First Blade and prince and given it to a band of sellswords. It wasn't as simple as all that, of course, but still...

He put all that aside. *It's done,* he thought. *No turning back now.* "Make for Dragon's Bane," he said to Carly Flame Mane. "That's where I expect to be within the coming weeks."

"I'll report as such to Kanabar's men," the sellsword said. "If you think up a change of destination, send a crow or rider."

"I will."

"Then we'll be away." She drew forward, right up in front of him, and planted her mouth direct to his in a kiss. A tongue ran across her red lips as she pulled back, purring. "Next time, Daecar," she promised. "The time of your life, I told you. You better believe I'll follow through."

"I don't doubt that, my lady."

"Lady? *Please.*" She laughed, spun, and was gone.

***

THEY WASTED no time in returning to the palace, though a few words of doubt were shared among the Varin Knights as they rushed along, retracing their steps. "Are we sure we can trust her?" Barnibus asked. "I know she said she swore an oath to your auntie, but that means nothing coming from a sellsword. Those oaths are only good as long as you're the highest bidder. Soon as someone with more coin comes along..."

“We can trust her,” Elyon said. He didn’t want to believe otherwise and saw no profit in doing so now. “Amara wouldn’t have hired her if she didn’t. And she’s not shy of coin, believe me.”

“How does she know her anyway?” asked Lancel.

“Who can say. My auntie has a social network beyond my comprehension. You’d be amazed at the sorts of people she rubs shoulders with back in Varinar.”

They hastened on, sparing little time on talk, parting when their paths diverged. Elyon clasped hands with each of his allies, in turn. “Suspicion will fall on Janilah first,” he said. “We speak nothing of this to anyone, not a single word. Not Mallister, not Rodmond. No lord or knight you consider friend. This stays between us, and us alone. Understand?”

They nodded.

“Good. Then Lance, Barny, back to the feast. It’s early enough yet that you’ll be able to slip back in without arousing suspicion. Jov, head to your room. Try not to be seen. You know what to do.” He gave the boy a smile. “I’ll see you all in the morning. We’ll be questioned, no doubt, but just play dumb, stick to our stories, and we’ll be fine. Dalton’s already given us the go ahead to join my Uncle Rikkard at Dragon’s Bane, so there’s no reason why we can’t leave from here within the next day or two.” There was nothing more to say. He nodded at them. “Until tomorrow.”

“Tomorrow,” said Barnibus.

“Tomorrow,” repeated Lancel.

Jovyn answered in a nod of his own, and the four parted there and then.

Elyon made for his room, face hidden in the shadows of his hood. He was still wearing his quilted silver-blue doublet and padded breeches from the wedding, but had overlaid all that with a dark cowled cloak for concealment. All had done the same, should they be spotted, yet the palace was huge, the guards disinterested, and with Carly leading them on, they hadn’t lacked for guile.

Alone, now, Elyon had to be careful. When he and Carly had stumbled drunkenly from the feast hall, playing at their pretence, he was certain they were being tailed. Carly had thought the same. “We’ve got company,” she’d whispered between her false giggles and drunken hiccups, and when they’d reached Elyon’s room and bolted the doors, she added, "They'll have someone stationed outside, watching the door. We'll have to use the balcony."

We used it to get out, and I'm going to have to use it to get back in, Elyon thought now, as he reached the terrace two floors up onto which they'd climbed. He drew out his godsteel dagger to sharpen his speed, strength, and senses, and threw a leg over the top of the stone railing. The balcony jutted out from the palace facade, leaving a perilous drop below into the mists and snows. His black cloak pulled hard by the winds, he swung his other leg over and began the short descent.

The climb was harder going down than it had been going up, but a palace as old and ornate as this great monstrosity had plenty of carvings, crevices, sills and shelfs to usher him back into his room. Dropping from the short ledge above his own private balcony, he landed with a soft thud, moved to the fluttering curtains, and pulled them back. Relief went through him. The inside was as he'd left it, Carly Flame Mane's discarded clothes still flung about the floor, Elyon's Varin cloak hanging on a hook by the door. The hearth had burned down a little, but fire still licked from the coals. He turned to the door; it was still locked and bolted. No one had entered. *Good.*

He stepped inside, shut the balcony door, drew the curtains back across it. Gathering up Carly's clothes he tossed them into the hearth to feed the flames. Then he removed his own garb; cloak, doublet, breeches, boots, until he stood in nought but breeks. He judged that they'd have indulged in more wine during their night of passion, so stepped to the table, poured two full cups, and sent them both down his throat. A smile embraced his lips. *Done and done,* he thought. *As easy as that.*

But...too easy? he did have to wonder. That was only natural when a thing went so well. *We've suffered setbacks, this is our recompense,* he thought. *It's about time something went right.*

He satisfied himself with that, poured more wine, drank more wine. He wasn't going to leave anything to chance, and he'd be expected to be bleary-eyed and hungover come the morrow. With four full cups of rich spicy red swimming in his gut, he took up the flagon and went to the bed, set it down on a side table, and began mussing up the sheets and covers. Carly had been good enough to give him a little vial of perfume. "My scent," she'd called it, handing it to him with a sultry smile. "In case anyone comes sniffing around. Sweetest thing you'll ever smell."

He pulled the cork and took a sniff. It smelled of pine, somehow earthy, somehow deadly, but of her. With a few flicks of the wrist, he sent the contents of the vial spraying across the bedsheets and blankets, then went back to the window, opened the shutters, and threw the vial out into the mists. A cold wind blew in, snowflakes capering, firelight flickering. Chill air wrapped about his undressed flesh, causing him to shudder. He fastened the shutters once more, went to the bed, and sat up against the headboard. Picking up the flagon, he drank long and deep, an intense feeling of warmth reaching to the corners of his chest. Beyond the room, he perceived no discernible sound, far from the feast hall as his chambers were. The silence was strangely discomforting,

Maybe I should return to the merrymaking? he wondered. He'd done that often in the past when running the social circuit of Varinar, absconding for an hour or two with a willing young lady before returning for a second round, often to cheers, always to a great deal of singing and drinking. *But no, not tonight.* If he returned now, it would look odd unless Carly was with him. If asked about her in the morning, he could make his excuses easily enough. "I woke to find her gone," he would say. "Can't remember a damn thing."

He shifted a little lower onto the bed, so that he was lying nearly flat, pulling a warm woollen blanket over his legs. Sleep wouldn't come easily, he knew, with the adrenaline coursing through his veins. *Did we tie up every loose end? Did we cover all our tracks?* He found himself mulling on just how Sir Owen and Sir Kevyn stole the blade without being heard. Most likely they cut up through Swiftwater's ceiling, found the right chest, and transported it back down the same way, but to do all that without making a sound...

Or maybe they did make a sound? Elyon thought. *Maybe Sir Gerald Strand heard them, barged in, and sparked an affray? Maybe that turncoat's blood is staining the rushes red as we speak.* It seemed unlikely, in truth, but he could hope all the same. Sir Gerald would pay for his treachery one day, like Sir Alyn Porter and Sir Nathaniel Oloran. They'd been witness to their own king's murder, and continued to spread the lie that Ellis had fallen, a lie that few were buying anymore. Godrik and Dalton were embroiled in all that too, though, winning the rule of

Vandar the day that King Ellis fell. *All will get their due,* Elyon thought, *and that has started here tonight.* If ever he began to doubt what he'd done, he need merely think of that.

He shifted yet lower on his bed, his thoughts beginning to drift. By now Lancel and Barnibus would be back among the guests, singing, drinking, toasting their triumph with Kanabar and Amara. Jovyn would be safe in his room, fretting no doubt, for that was the boy's nature. *Perhaps I'll take him with me to Dragon's Bane,* he mused. He missed having Jovyn at his side, and loathe as he was to deny his sister the boy's company, perhaps that was for the best. After tonight, Lillia would be Robbert's betrothed, protected by oath and untouchable. Amara had told him about that. How she planned to make the announcement herself, if she must, declare their union before all the north as witness. "It will guarantee her protection," she'd said. "You'll be at war, Lancel and Barnibus the same, but Lillia...Janilah might use her to get to you, and we can't let that happen. As soon as the world knows she's bound to the prince, that will be one less thing to worry about."

He didn't disagree, though all the same, he'd asked that Amara take Lillia to Ilivar immediately after the wedding. Amara hadn't questioned why. Ilivar was the great city seat of his grandfather Brydon Amadar, and would give Lillia all the protection she needed, should Godrik Taynar seek some vengeance of his own. The old king was far too cautious to raise Lord Amadar's wrath. He ruled Ilivar as his own city-state, sitting all-powerful behind its thick stone walls. It was smaller than Varinar, but no less well protected from the threat that Agarath might pose, founded almost three and a half thousand years ago by Iliva, Varin's firstborn daughter. *A good place to wait out the war,* Elyon knew. *Lillia and Amara will be safe there, beneath my grandfather's roof.*

Another ten minutes passed, then another ten came and went, and all the while the wine did its work, relaxing him, calming the swift beat in his heart. Shutting his eyes, he felt the first pull of sleep tugging at him. Those tugs came harder, more insistent. Before he knew it he'd fallen away into his dreams.

He wasn't sure how long he'd been asleep then he awoke to the sound of thumping at the door, a fist pounding on wood. A voice came with it. "Elyon...Elyon, are you in there? Elyon...wake up!"

He blinked the echoes of sleep and dreams away, sat up in his bed. *Her voice,* he knew at once. *Melany. What has she come for now?* He said nothing for a long moment, thinking it best to ignore her, hoping she would go away.

She called again. "Elyon! Wake up, now! I know you're in there! Let me in!"

He flexed his fingers, drew a long breath, grunted, stood, and stumbled toward the door. The wine was having the desired effect. He reached the bolt and slid it right, drawing the door open with a groan. He didn't need to fake being drunk anymore. "What do you want, Mel? I was sleeping..."

She pushed in, looked around. "Where is she?"

He shut the door behind her. "Who?"

"You know who? That girl you took here from the feast? The redheaded slut...where is she!"

He regarded her carefully. *This isn't real. She's pretending, lying, acting, as usual.* Still, he had to keep to his story. "I don't know. She left, I guess." He shrugged, took up the jug of wine, supped.

She slapped the flagon from his hand. It cracked upon the stone floor, rich red liquid seeping into the carpet. Elyon only laughed. That got him a slap too, a stinging swipe to his cheek. "Bastard! How could you do that to me...in front of everyone...how could you?"

"Easily enough. We met the same way, as you recall." She slapped him again. He laughed again, though sourly this time. "If you want to tickle me, you might have brought a feather."

"Who is she?" She stood staring at him, eyes wide and manic. *Gods she's good.* He had to give her that. She missed her calling as an actress. "Who, Elyon!"

He took a step back. Her slaps were more fierce than he was making out, no matter how he japed. "Beats me. Some slut, you said. I didn't get her name. That wasn't what I wanted from her tongue..."

Her eyes were fire and fury, though she didn't make to strike him again. Instead her hand hovered on the sheath of a small godsteel blade, hidden within the folds of her coat. His eyes looked down at the swordbelt, the scabbard. *Is that why she's here? Has Janilah ordered her to kill me?* If so, she was going about it the wrong way. Those slaps had put him on guard now, and if she wanted to slip a knife in his neck, it would have been wise to keep him relaxed.

He stepped back another pace, her hand hovering over her dagger. She was trained to use godsteel, he knew, and trained well. "I hate you," she seethed. But that wasn't what her eyes said. "I...I can't believe you'd do this to me. In...in front of all the nobles, the lords and ladies, my friends, my *brother*...and on Amilia's wedding day! I hate you, Elyon!"

Elyon drew another step away. "You said it yourself, Melany, we're over. I can do as I please. You're overreacting."

She'd been drinking, that was plain to see. He'd spotted her at the feast a few times, even saw her speaking with Lillia once. That had angered him, but he couldn't show it then. He had to be seen to be drinking with Lord Kanabar, singing and laughing at the entertainers and performers, the troupers and tumblers. But he wanted to do it then. He wanted to march over to her, grab her shoulder, spin her around, and tell it right to her face. *I know,* Melany, he'd wanted to say. *I know you've been spying on me.*

That wouldn't have been wise before, not when he had such work to do, but now? Why not now? He had her alone. He had his chance. Why not let it all come out? He did. "How long have you been working for Janilah?" he asked, the question running sudden off his tongue. He stared into her cool blue eyes, and saw something pass her face. A shadow, a cold white shadow, turning her features icy and stiff. And in that instant, he saw that it was true. "Why, Melany?" he asked, frowning. "What does he want from me?"

"Your life."

He drew back. *She admits it freely?* He flashed his eyes on her dagger again, but it remained sheathed at her hip, her arms to her side. He glanced beyond her; his own dagger was across the room, sitting on the table beside his bed. *I can reach it if I'm quick,* he thought. *If I strike suddenly, strike fast, I can get to it...*

"I'm not going to kill you, Elyon," she said. "That isn't why I'm here."

His eyes were back on her, narrow, mistrusting. *Those words... they're intended to lure me in, relax me, then she'll strike.* "I don't believe you," he told her.

Her lungs puffed out a huff. "You never have, not since you arrived here." She spoke calmly now, her face a mask of stone, expressionless. "I told him that. Told him you'd not let me in again. You did once, though. I got past your defences back in Varinar, do you remember? I saw my duty done *then*."

Elyon frowned. Something dark and dangerous simmered inside him. He thought back to the day of Aleron's death. He'd heard shouting from Melany's room in Keep Daecar, found his father there, drunk and grieving, Sword of Varinar to hand. He was accusing her of poisoning Aleron's water jug, an accusation she denied. He'd believed her then, but now? Now he knew different. "It was you."

She stared. There was no smile on her face, no shame, no fear. Nothing at all. Just an admittance of the truth in those eyes of hers, those eyes he once loved, those eyes he now hated. "It was my duty to weaken him before his bout with the Shadowknight," she said. "Jonik would never have won otherwise, everyone knows that. So I poisoned him, Elyon. *I* made that happen. *Me*. It was me who killed your brother."

His right hand was around her throat in a heartbeat, his left grabbing at her wrist. He lifted her from the floor, squeezing. Red. All he saw was red. Red for Aleron's blood that day as it gushed out onto the sands. Red for the rage within him, deep and dark. Red for the colour of Melany's face as she struggled in his grip, but only feebly. *Feebly. She wants this,* he realised. *She isn't trying to stop me. She wants it.*

He threw her to the floor.

She landed in a heavy heap, her lungs pulling hard and harsh in a series of ragged, spluttery breaths. Elyon marched to take up his dagger from the side table, drew it from his sheath, flung the scabbard aside. He stood over her, looking down. "Get out," he said, quiet and cold. "Get out, Melany. Now."

She gathered herself, breathing deep, swallowing. Her neck was marked by the outline of his fingers, black and blue and bruised. On tremulous legs she stood to face him, the mists from his dagger swirling about the air between them, a glitter of silver and blue. *The colours of my kingdom. The colours of my house. The colours Aleron would have worn proudly, as First Blade of Vandar. As champion.* "GET OUT!"

His roar caused her to flinch back, but she shook her head, stood her ground, drew a breath and said, "No."

"No?" he repeated, disbelieving, almost laughing. "No!"

She shook her head. "No, Elyon. You should kill me for what I did...I deserve it. Go ahead. Kill me for killing your brother." She stepped forward, grabbed his wrist, turned the blade to her belly. "Kill me, Elyon. Go on. Kill me!"

He pulled away in disgust and confusion. "No, I'll not..."

"Kill me!" She pulled hard at his hand again, made to drive it into her chest. "I killed your brother, Elyon. *I* poisoned him. *I* weakened him. He died because of me. Because of me, Elyon. *KILL ME*!"

She was strong, stronger than she had any right to be. The blade bit at her skin, scratching through the silken fabric of her dress, drawing blood. He hauled his hand back with a sudden jolt, but she continued to cling on, eyes mad with tears. "Kill me," she called, she pleaded. "I murdered your brother! He was destined for greatness and I took that away from him. I should die for that. I'm meant to die for that." Her eyes were wide and wild and red. "You have to kill me, Elyon! Kill me, kill me, *kill me*!"

Have to? You have to kill me? That mask of cold stone was cracked and broken now, tears running from her eyes, steaming down her cheeks. Real tears, he saw this time. *Is this the first time I've seen the real Melany Monsort? Does she even know who that is?* "No," he said firmly. "I'm not going to kill you, Mel."

"You have to! You have to! They'll die if you don't! You have to!"

She tugged at his wrist again, but he pulled right back, keeping the tip of the blade away from her belly. Strong as she was, he was a great deal stronger. "I'm *not* going to kill you, Mel!" he shouted, ripping free of her, withdrawing several steps across the room. He was digesting what she'd said. *Have to. You have to kill me. They'll die if you don't.* "What does Janilah have over you?" he demanded. "Who's going to die, Mel?"

"Everything," she sobbed. "*Everyone.* My brother, my father, my family, *everyone*! He gives with one hand and takes with the other. I never wanted to poison Aleron. I never wanted any of this. I know you've been planning to steel the Windblade, Elyon. I know about that...but I never told him so. I did that because...because I love you. I do, I love you, that's true." She stepped forward. "I'm sorry for what I've done. I'm so sorry about Aleron, but if it wasn't me, it would have been someone else. I've had to live with that. I've had to go to sleep with that, wake with that, and I'll die with that now too." She looked at him, tear-stained and pleading. "Kill me, Elyon. Kill me, else my brother will die. And my father. My family. Everyone I know and care about will die. Kill me, Elyon. Kill me, *please*."

No, he could only think. "I can't," he said, backing away.

She cringed, weeping. "Then you've cursed Mallister to death. He's your friend, and you've cursed him."

"Flee," he told her. "Go. Just go, now, run. I'll find Mallister, I'll tell him. You can send a crow to your..."

"My father will be dead by morning. My brother will be too. My service...Janilah...I've always done it for them, always. And this..." She looked at the knife in his hand. "This is my last duty. I have no choice in that now." She lunged.

Elyon drew his blade back and away, threw it across the room, and grappled her into his arms. "Stop, Melany, stop!" She began wriggling, thrashing, screaming loudly for him to let go. *No, I can't, I can't let this happen.* She jerked left and right, kicking at him with her feet, scratching with her nails. "Mel...Melany, stop, stop!" She spat, snarled, clamped her teeth down on his left hand, biting hard through skin and flesh. He gave out a roar as blood seeped from the punctures, and in that moment, lost his grip.

She wriggled free, darted away across the floor. Her eyes were red and raw from weeping, voice ragged as she spoke. "I'm so sorry for this, Elyon," she panted, despairing. "For everything, I'm sorry for everything."

A glint of silver caught the firelight. Mist rose from the edge of the blade. She drew it up to her neck. Elyon leaned forward, reached forward. *No...*

"I'm sorry," she sobbed, a final time. Then she drove the knife through her throat.

Blood gushed from the wound, flowing between her fingers. She stumbled back as she pressed the blade deeper, sawing. Elyon lurched forward. Melany dropped to her knees. "Melany, no...no!" He caught her before she could fall, the blood pouring out in great thick spurts, spraying across his chest, his face, rich and wet and warm. "Help! I...I need help!"

He didn't hear the door open. Just the plod of heavy footsteps, boots thumping on stone, then carpet. He looked up. Guards were surging in, grabbing him, hauling him to his feet. Melany was still gargling, the knife lodged in her throat, bubbles of blood frothing from the wound. "She's not dead!" Elyon bellowed. "Someone...someone help her, she's not yet dead!"

No one helped her. No one cared. Her job was done.

And so am I.

That was the last thought that passed through Elyon Daecar's head as the cudgel came across and struck him on the back of the skull. But not before he caught sight of a shapely figure standing beyond the door, wrapped in wools and furs of brown. There was a smile on her face, a cruel smile, a smile of vengeance and triumph. It was the smile of a serpent and a snake and a bastard.

It was the smile of Lady Cecilia Blakewood.

45

Saska

He came to her in the gardens, dressed in a cloak of golden feathers. He moved in a smooth gait, his skin a deep olive, seamed and lined from the sun. There was a smile on his lips, but not in his eyes. "I heard we had a guest," he said, in a deep and sonorous voice. "I am sorry I could not be here last night to greet you, my lady."

Saska watched Elio Krator approach warily. She dipped her eyes. "I am grateful for the hospitality of your house, my lord." She wore white silk, smooth against her skin. Her hair had been washed and dried and styled, her body scrubbed clean. Mar Malaan had insisted that she look presentable and beautiful for his master, not giving her much choice when the servants arrived to bathe her and dress her and rub ointments and balms into her skin. Somehow she felt *too* clean now, *too* soft and pretty and fresh. *And all for him,* she realised, as Elio Krator strode toward her. There was something in that thought that unsettled her.

"My house is yours," said the sunlord. He was in his mid forties, she judged, and slim, with a flat stomach and hairless vascular forearms corded with muscle. There was a warmth in his words, but not in his voice. "Mar did the right thing bringing you here. What do you make of the view?"

She'd been awaiting him on a terrace giving a view of the river down the hillside, with the pyramid palace of Aram erected grandly beyond in its feathery banners of gold, silver, and bronze. They were the Aramatian colours, commonly worn by the city soldiers and nobles and even some of the staff she'd seen about the residence. The goddess Aramatia's great eagle, Calacan, had feathers of gold, silver, and bronze too, so she supposed that was the inspiration for those banners fluttering from the palace balconies and walls.

"It's beautiful," she said. "I could stand here for hours, my lord, and never grow weary of it."

"I come here often," said Elio Krator. He drew to her side, took her hand, kissed the back of her palm. His touch sent a shiver crawling up her spine. Even his skin felt cold. "You've never visited, I've been told."

She shook her head. "Never."

He turned to her, half a head taller. The sun washed across his face, catching in his rich golden eyes. His hair had streaks of gold in it too, amid short waves of deeper brown, not a single strand yet greying or losing its colour. There was an elegance to him, with those fine golden feathers in his cloak, a cold composure in the way he turned his eyes over the city, then back at her, studying the form and features of her face without so much as saying a word. His gaze lingered long enough to make her uncomfortable. She shuffled her slippered feet, smiled awkwardly, looked aside. But still she could sense those golden eyes boring in. For a long time, *too* long, he just stood there, and stared.

Eventually, he spoke. "You have come to meet the Grand Duchess, Mar Malaan tells me." His eyes finally moved away, turning to look at the palace across the Amedda River. "Do you think she will have the answers you are looking for, Saska?"

She started. "How...how do you know my name? I don't remember telling anyone..."

"Your friend told me."

Sir Ralston, she thought, alarmed. Had he visited her giant guardian already that morning? So far she'd not given her name to Mar Malaan or any of the servants. She'd given them nothing, in fact. Not her name or who she was or why she was truly here. But this man. This sunlord...*Does he know something about me already? Is that why Mar Malaan was so happy to accommodate me last night?*

She put those thoughts aside. "I'd like to see him," she said, thinking of Sir Ralston. She had Joy here with her, lounging on the cream pavestones nearby, but not Rolly. She wanted him back with her. She wanted to make sure he was safe and unharmed. "Mar Malaan told me he would be taken to a cell. He means no harm, Lord Krator. I would feel greatly more relaxed if he could be here with me in the residence."

She hoped to appeal to his sense of good manners but could already see that the man was unmoved. "I will consider it," he merely said, in a voice that told her he wouldn't consider it at all.

"Please do," Saska pressed. "He swore by godsteel oath he would deal no harm here, and his blades have been taken away. He would be little threat to you even if..."

Elio Krator raised a hand. "Enough of Sir Ralston. I haven't yet had a moment to speak to him personally. When I do I will judge him myself. Until that time he will remain caged."

Saska's brow quickened into a frown. "You haven't spoken to him yet? Then how did you know..."

"You name? I have said. Your friend told me. Well, the one who can speak, anyway. The other one is mute, I understand."

Mute. Pig! Saska felt a sudden wave of worry wash over her. "Mellio," she said. "He...he came to you?" Her mind was full of betrayal. Sir Ralston had warned her of being too trusting of the smuggler. But what could Mellio have gained from coming to him? She'd handed herself over to his care willingly, after all, a decision that she was fast coming to regret.

Yet Elio Krator only shook his head, quick and curt, and said, "No. My men came to *him,* child. They found him heading east into the plains shortly after your arrival at the gate."

She wasn't fully understanding. "But, how did you know..."

"That you had help crossing the Aramatian Plains?" he cut in. "Logic, Saska. There is no mount in the south capable of carrying a man like Sir Ralston, not armoured and armed with godsteel as he was. Mar Malaan knew this. He sent riders to search for this helper of yours, and they soon tracked him down on the road."

"Where are they?" Saska blurted out in demand. She'd tolerated Mellio mostly, but Pig...the boy was innocent. She didn't want to see either of them punished.

"I have them," Lord Krator said. "When I have a moment, I will muse on their fate, but as I'm sure you know, the punishment for smuggling can be...severe."

“He didn’t smuggle us. He only...*transported* us.” Those were Rolly’s words, coming back to her. “He never tried to sneak us into the city. We arrived willingly. We’re not spies or assassins. We have no ill intent.”

“Yes. You wish to visit with Safina Nemati, you have said. But Her Serenity is not here, and in her place, *I* stand as ruler.” He seemed to take great pleasure in that fact. For the first time she saw something resembling joy in his golden eyes. “That gives me the power to act in judgement of crimes brought before me. You may wonder where I was last night when you arrived?” He gestured to the palace across the river. “I sat in court, hearing pleas and petitions, until past midnight. Your friend Mellio will have his chance to stand before me, and explain himself. If I deem it just, I will bestow upon him a lesser punishment.”

“And Pig? He was just working for Mellio. He doesn’t deserve to be punished.”

Elio Krator laughed; a short, abrupt sound. “Being mute does not make one immune. The boy’s fate will be the same as his master’s.”

“*No*,” Saska said, standing her ground. “No, that isn’t fair. How can you punish either of them for bringing me here if you’re not going to punish me too?”

“Who says I’m not going to punish you?”

The air stilled. Her pulse quickened, her heart rising up into her throat. She felt suddenly exposed and somehow Joy seemed to sense it too. The starcat was on her feet, prowling to her side. A low growl rumbled from her chest. Saska put a hand onto the cat’s head to still her. And still herself. “You can’t,” she said eventually, finding her courage. “I’m here under your protection, by your honour. Mar Malaan promised that I would not be harmed. That I’d be taken to visit with the Grand Duchess when she returns.”

Elio Krator had eyes that never seemed to blink. “A lot can happen between now and then,” he said. “Perhaps Her Serenity will never return at all? She is old and the road is treacherous. There is much that might befall her.”

Saska drew back. She could scarce believe what she was hearing. This man was speaking treason. “You mean to kill her?” The thought sent daggers of dread through her chest. What had she gotten herself into? She’d come all this way to meet her grandmother and now....now *this*?

Elio Krator's laugh was mirthless. "No, of course not," he said. "I am not like your king Janilah Lukar. I would never lower myself to such treachery, no."

She didn't believe him. Not a word. "Janilah Lukar is *not* my king," she argued.

"No? But you are Tukoran, clearly. Your accent gives it away."

"I'm not Tukoran," Saska told him, as firmly as she could. "I just grew up there."

"Of course."

He studied her again for a drawn out moment, those unblinking eyes taking in the contours of her face. Once more it grew unbearable. Saska turned away to look elsewhere, anywhere, and found her eyes upon the three-tiered pyramid where her grandmother had ruled for so long. Her doubts were mounting, heavy and hot inside her gut.

"I thought you'd gotten what you wanted," she said, to break the silence. She glanced up at him. "The Patriots. I know...I know you're one of their leaders."

"You say it so fearfully. Why?"

"Because you hate northerners. You hate how they abuse the natural world, how they hunt and kill for sport." She looked at his cloak of golden feathers, and the banners upon the palace, and elsewhere among the city where the sigil of Aramatia - the soaring eagle with an armoured knight crushed in its talons - was displayed so widely and proudly.

"And why should that worry you? You told me you are not Tukoran, after all."

"I'm *half* Tukoran. Or...half northern. I'm not exactly sure where."

He smiled coldly. "So I've been told. But you say I've gotten what I wanted? What did you mean by that?"

"War," Saska said, looking over the harbour. There were so many warships out there she could hardly count them all, great four-masted galleasses and galleons, sturdy carracks and swift caravels outfitted with slings and scorpions and fire-breathing spouts. "The Patriots want war with the north, always. That's why you sparked rioting all across the south...to force Empress Valura into the warmoot."

Elio Krator gave a stiff nod. "Yes, this is correct. The Lumaran Empire was built upon tenets of peace, a foundation that my order has never agreed with. When King Tavash took the Agarathi crown we sensed an opportunity we could not miss. These last months have shown just how widespread the support for our cause is." He gave a scornful grunt. "Empress Valura, in her great hubris, seemed to think that we were few in number, that near enough all her subjects were bound to her peaceable ways, but that was never true. For two decades we have grown in strength and numbers and now we have stepped forth from the shadows, powerful enough to force her hand."

"But that's not enough," Saska realised. Now it was her turn to study him, see the truth behind his eyes. "You want to *break up* the Empire, make Aramatia independent again. You...you want to rule."

Lord Krator gave her a thin smile. "I was *always* meant to rule, child," he said, turning to look at the palace. "There was a princess here once, young and beautiful. She looked...very much like *you*, in fact. Perhaps you have heard of her? The late Leila Nemati, daughter of Her Serenity Safina. She died almost two decades ago, a death most tragic. A death mired in mystery and rumour, but a man like me would always know the truth. She was...dear to me, once, before she was taken so cruelly. What a wife she would have made, sitting at my side."

Wife. Cold fingers gripped her heart. "You...you were to marry her?" she whispered.

"We were betrothed from a young age," he nodded. "It was a long engagement, made longer by the war. We decided to wait until it was over before we said our vows and settled down. In the end, we never had our chance. Her death robbed me of much, Saska. Of a wife and a throne, and the promise of...children."

Saska felt a sickness curdling in her gut, a palpable fear beginning to bubble and brew inside her. She dared not look at him, though could sense his eyes on her again, staring hard and cold and cruel. Then all of a sudden he turned away and looked upon the palace once more.

"Leila's mother is a strong woman," he went on. "A woman of resolve, stout and determined. I admire Safina in many ways, though we have rarely seen eye to eye on everything. How could we? She is a firm follower of our empress, a proponent of peace, whereas I bow only to war. We have locked horns many times over many things in the past, but there is one thing...one matter that has always vexed me most of all." He turned to look at her with those unblinking golden eyes. "*You.*"

Saska felt a powerful and sudden urge to run. By instinct her eyes moved around the gardens, seeking a way out. The shadows of sunwolves and starcats and soldiers seemed to have appeared from nowhere, blocking every exit, every path. She turned back to him, smiling anxiously. "Me, my lord? I...I fear I don't know what you mean."

"You know *exactly* what I mean."

She took a pace back. Joy was hunched at her side, looking all but ready to pounce, but Elio Krator paid the cat no mind. He stepped forward to close the gap between them.

"I know who you are," he said. "You are the bastard child of Leila Nemati, the princess I was fated to wed. You are the child that Safina hid from me for the wrath I would have brought on her. You are the child sent away to save you from my clutches. You are the child that might, in another life, have been *mine*."

Saska shook her head for all the good it would do. "No, I'm not," she said in a panic. "I'm nothing, nobody. A servant and a slave, that's all I am."

"Do not lie to me!" he shouted, a fury rising in his voice. "I see it in your face! I see Leila, twenty years ago, soft skinned and young. I see the girl who would have given me a crown, mixed with the blood of the north!" A snarl ripped across his face. "And I see that *boy*, that *slave*, who stole into her bed and raped her. I see him in you too. In those eyes. You have *his* eyes."

She wasn't understanding. None of that made sense. "My father wasn't a slave!" she came back. It was all she could think of to say. "He was Bladeborn. *Royal*. Old Hob, he...he said so. He came here during the war and fell in love with the princess. He would never have raped..."

"So you admit it? You admit who you are?"

"No. I...I don't know who I am. Not for sure. I don't..."

"You came to take your place at your grandmother's side," Lord Krator broke in, seeming not to hear her. "You came here to rule when she dies." He waved a hand. Saska sensed guards moving in. "Do you deny it?"

A sense of panic tore through her. "Yes! Yes I deny it! I came here to meet her, that's all. She's meant to tell me what to do next. I don't want to rule. I'm not Aramatian. I can't even speak the language!"

Elio Krator wasn't listening. "You will be returned to your room under guard, until I decide what to do with you. If you behave I will permit you to walk the grounds with an escort. Your friends Mellio and Pig will stand before me in court, but I sense they will face execution for this. As will Sir Ralston. He will be brought to the palace to face the charge of attempted assassination. He was caught breaking into the city and my own estate to kill me. Our heaviest penalty will surely follow."

"But that's not true!" Saska wailed. "You're lying!"

"The truth is what I make it. This is *my* city, child, *my* land. I will not see the bastard spawn of a northern slave and rapist strip me of my right to rule. For the love I once bore your mother, I may spare you. Consider that a mercy. But the others who have colluded to bring you here must die. And this cat..."

"*NO!*" Saska dropped to her knees, wrapped her arms around Joy's neck. She only realised then that she was weeping, her eyes blurry with tears. It had gone wrong, so horribly wrong. *Rolly...what have I done?* "No, you can't..."

Elio Krator was looking down at her in contempt. "As you wish. The cat will be spared. She is a fine animal and the *light* in you must be respected." He flicked a hand. "Now stand up. This needn't be any more difficult than you are making it."

"Don't kill him," Saska whimpered, still kneeling. "Please! Rolly... Sir Ralston, he has done nothing wrong. He has only ever tried to protect me."

"Nothing wrong, you say? And what of the men he slaughtered at the river? Oh yes, I know all about that. Your friend Mellio was only too willing to speak in order to save his own tongue, though his reprieve will only be temporary. These were *my* men, Patriots of this land, and your guardian butchered them like pigs. For this alone he deserves to die." She went to argue but he held up a hand. "No, I will hear no more of your pleas. Stand up."

Saska stood on shaking legs. Joy nuzzled into her side. Several soldiers stepped in. "My lady," one said quietly. "You will accompany us to your chambers."

He took her arm. She pulled away. "My father," she bit, turning on the sunlord. "He isn't what you say. You're *lying*! You're trying to trick me. I'm a Bladeborn of royal blood. My father was *not* a slave."

"He was." Elio Krator yawned. His golden feathers fluttered as he lifted his arm to wave her away. "He was a slave and a rapist both." He gave the lead guard a nod, and he reached for Saska again. "And Bladeborn? Who can say? Slaves here in Aram do not typically have access to godsteel." A laugh ran through his lips. "But I suppose you can ask him, if you want. I shall happily arrange a meeting."

Saska's eyes widened. *Meet him?* "He's here?"

"Of course. He has been here for many years." Elio Krator smiled that cold empty smile of his. "Come with me, I will show you."

He escorted her into the residence with a cohort of guards and sunwolves to flank her. Joy's name seemed wholly inappropriate now. The cat loped along forlornly in mimic of Saska's tread. She knew already that this was some cruel trick. Her father wasn't here, was he? If so he'd be in chains, she had no doubt, no more than a shell of a man, beaten and abused and humiliated for twenty long years. Thinking of that made her want to turn back. "I can't," she said, as they pressed down a long wide hallway. She tried to stop but they drew her on. "I don't want to."

Elio Krator ignored her. "Just through here. We're almost there."

The guards pushed through a set of heavy oaken doors, and they entered a large room full of artefacts and ornaments. It seemed its only purpose was to display them. The walls were covered from low to high with paintings and tapestries and trinkets and trophies. More sat atop small ornamental tables and lecturns. There were several stands with great dusty tomes laid atop them that reminded Saska of the fake Book of Thala in that chamber in the palace. She saw rare feathers and horns and scales and skins, indigenous artworks from strange and distant lands, musical instruments, pipes and rocks and poisonous plants in pots. The room was such a wonder that Saska momentarily forgot why she was there. Then Lord Krator's hand came down upon her shoulder. "Here," he said. "Meet your father."

He turned her to a small stand tucked away to one side. It was a simple podium, chest height, made of dull grey stone. Saska stared at the trophy positioned atop it. The hollow eyes. The pale white dome. The lipless mouth and rows of broken teeth.

"Isn't he handsome," said her host. "And he was once, that I will admit. A very handsome young man. Though not when I was done with him."

Saska stared at the skull of her father. The slave, the rapist, Elio Krator had said. There were cracks in his jaw, his cheeks, his head, inflicted as he was beaten to death. A heavy grief swallowed her up. *Is this truly it? Is this truly him? Is this what I came here to see?*

Suddenly King Godrin's words felt empty. Suddenly they made her angry. *You're exactly where you're meant to be.*

It had all been a rotten lie.

46

Janilah

"This was the cell of Ranulf Shackton," intoned King Janilah Lukar, as he paced back and forward before the rusted iron bars. "He was a guest here for some months, rotting away in the cold and the darkness, but his resolve never did wilt. I suppose I should give him credit for that. Those Rasals really are a defiant people."

He stopped and turned, peering into the dank space within, heavy with the scent of damp and mould. There was a single wooden bench, no more than a crumbling mess of splinters and rot, a pile of soiled hay that passed for a pallet bed, a pail for a chamberpot, and a man, hidden in the deepest shadows that pooled in the far corner, away from the light of the lantern that burned low and lazy in Janilah's grasp.

The king looked at that man and smiled. "Shackton eventually escaped, a matter that didn't concern me at the time, though has since come back to haunt me. I could say the same about many things of late." A hundred setbacks went through his mind. The boy Jonik. The turncoat Vesryn. The missing page in the Book of Thala. Godrik's betrayal. Gerrin and the Bloody Traders and the Bull and the Oak who'd failed in their task last night. He turned from that final thought with a grunt and looked into the shadows, where Elyon Daecar sat, two silver-blue eyes gleaming like a cat. "Shackton had help when he got out of here, a man named Reggie Warren whose throat I cut open myself for that oversight. But you...no, you won't get out of here, Elyon, save from my command, nor will you last so long as Shackton did lest you tell me what I want to know." He paused, glowered. "And you know what that is, of course? You know what will buy your freedom?"

Elyon Daecar said nothing. Janilah had expected that. He continued to pace, back and forth, back and forth, holding the lantern at his side, creaking as it swung. Shadows danced about him with every step, twisting upon the walls, menacing.

"There will be no trial, Elyon, not like you had at Harrowmoor. There were no witnesses when you killed Sir Griffin Kastor, but plenty of them here. And those bruises you left on Lady Melany's neck? The bite marks on your hand? Oh, the poor girl must have fought, and fought hard, but what could she do to a man like you? No woman would stand a chance."

He stopped, turned, regarded the shadow of the boy. Still he said nothing. Still he didn't stir.

"Your friends won't be able to save you this time. They can claim your innocence all they like, but the evidence speaks for itself...and that dreadful red ruin you made of Melany's body..." He shook his head, tutting. "Is that what you want, boy? To be remembered as a brutal killer? First Griffon Kastor, now Melany Monsort, both butchered in your rage, their heads near cleaved from their shoulders. Is that the reputation you're willing to die with, Elyon? Is it truly worth it? Is it...just to protect the location of the Windblade?"

Elyon finally shifted at that, his eyes as pits of molten silver as they regarded Janilah with a smouldering hate. Yet on his face was a smile. A smile that said, *I won*.

The first embers of ire sparked to life inside Janilah Lukar. "You'll be dead in days, boy," he growled. "Hanged for the sport of the crows. You murdered a noble girl, the lady-in-waiting of a princess, nay a queen, on the night of her wedding. A scandal of such profundity cannot be left to fester, not when the truth of what happened is so plain for all to see. Do you wish to spend your final hours in silence? In defiance of..." He paused. "Of *what*, exactly? Do you even know why I want those blades, why they are so important to me? Do you have any idea *why* I've been doing what I'm doing!"

"I know," Elyon hissed.

The words took Janilah off guard. He raised the lantern, lighting up Elyon's face, that smile that still lingered on his lips. "You know?"

"I know you'll never have them, *traitor*. The rest...spare me. Spare me your demands. Spare me your words. Spare me the sight of your treacherous face, old king."

"You dare..." Janilah began, but Elyon cut him off, laughing.

"Dare? Dare what? Speak the truth? Tell you to your face what a tyrant you've become?" He narrowed his eyes into a lupine glare. "There's a madness in you, Janilah, one even a blind man could see. So spare me your threats, and spare me your demands. I may die with my reputation sullied, perhaps, but not by those who matter. And you, *kingkiller*? You'll be remembered as a mad tyrant, a cautionary tale of greed and obsession, pitied and reviled through time. So do your worst, and kill me if you must. I'll die knowing you've failed to gather those blades. And for that...I'll die smiling." He leaned into the light, grinned widely, then sunk back into the shadows, silent.

Janilah stared, flint-eyed. A whisper spoke out in his head. *Kill him. Kill the boy. Kill him, kill him, kill him...* "I will give you two days to think on it," the King of Tukor said. "To think on your sister, your auntie, your father, your friends. You call me mad, call me a tyrant. Perhaps that's so. Perhaps that's what is needed to win the War Eternal." He was starting to realise that now. Starting to give in to what he was.

"You had your chance to win the War Eternal last time," Elyon came back. "Yet it's my father who was named the Hero of the North, not you, *cruel king*."

Janilah gave a disdainful laugh. "Cruel king. Kingkiller. Traitor. Do you think these slurs offend me? I'm sure much worse is being said of me across the taverns of White Shadow, and in this very palace, no less. A king learns to ignore the prattle of men who do not matter. And you, Elyon Daecar, do not matter anymore. Two days hence you will be hanging from the gibbet, for all the north to see. And I will be left behind. With your auntie. And your *sister*."

Elyon snarled at that, lurching to his feet. "If you touch her..." He began toward the bars, dressed in rotting rags and stinking. Flecks of Melany's blood were still crusted upon his face.

"Then what?" Janilah asked him. "Just what can a dead man do to me?"

"My father..."

"Is dead, I hear. Dead like your mother and brother, so Hadrin tells me." Janilah didn't believe a word of that, in truth, given the Rat King's feeble insights thus far. Still, it was useful fuel to feed the fire of fear in the boy. And he could see that plain enough in Elyon's face. *He believes it*, he saw. *A part of him, at least, truly thinks his father dead.* "There will be no vengeance against me, leastways not from a Daecar. Your brother and father are gone, Elyon, and you are soon to follow. And your sister..."

"Don't speak of her!"

"Your sister," Janilah went on, calmly, "will soon be a Lukar. The last of a great branch of Daecars will simply be absorbed into my own line." He smiled to that, and broadly. "Your house, Sir Elyon, will perish, lest you tell me what I want to know."

"I'll not."

"Then the Daecars will be no more, the latest of the greathouses to wither away and die. It has happened before and will happen again." The house of Manfrey came to mind, unbidden. Last Janilah knew, the exiled lord, Emeric Manfrey, was still riding with the boy Jonik far away to the south, counselling him in whatever rogue adventure they were taking. Manfrey had once been a great house too, built off the back of the legendary Sir Oswald's exploits, and had been stout and staunch supporters of Galin Lukar when he marched to conquer Tukor. A part of Janilah felt saddened to see House Manfrey dwindle and die, as a part of him would with House Daecar, a house as great and ancient and storied as any before or since. *But fall they must,* he thought, *else they'll continue to stand in my way.*

"I don't know where it is," Elyon Daecar said. "I don't know what you're talking about."

Janilah regarded him closely. "A lie."

The boy's head went side to side, his black hair matted with blood at the base of his skull. He'd been knocked out by a fierce crack with a cudgel, Janilah had been told by Cecilia. Cecilia, who'd spun her web so well. "It's the truth," Elyon claimed, lying again. "I don't know where it is. I had nothing to do with what happened."

Janilah looked at the earnest expression on the young knight's face, an expression that might have fooled another. *But not me.* No, he knew the truth of what had happened last night. He'd grown suspicious when Amara and the oaf Kanabar had done their double-act on stage, and that suspicion had swiftly evolved into confirmation when Sir Fredrick Ruxmond arrived with his report.

"Sire, the Windblade...it's gone," he'd said, as Janilah moved to the side of the feast hall. By that point all were toasting the sweet new couple Robbert and Lillia, and even King Godrik and Prince Dalton had delayed in their departure to raise a cup. "I found Sir Owen and Sir Kevyn knocked unconscious in a storeroom, just down from Swiftwater's quarters. They had an empty chest with them. Both were still out cold, but I got Sir Owen to come around. He mumbled something about an attack. Thieves. Said there were five or so, all dressed in black and hooded. They must have taken it, though he doesn't know where."

"How long ago was this?"

"Not long. I've ordered word spread to search for them. And the chest, I've had it hidden, sire, and Sir Owen and Sir Kevyn taken off." He'd glanced to Prince Dalton. "At least he's still here. Seems no one knows the blade's been stolen yet, except us."

"He'll know soon enough," Janilah said, controlling his thunderous frustration. "And when he finds the blade gone he and his father will be sure to blame me."

"There's no doubting that, sire," Sir Fredrick said. "But, I'm at a loss...who took it?"

Janilah had looked at Amara and Kanabar, with those secret grins they'd been wearing all night. He'd thought of Elyon's drunken departure with that redheaded girl a little earlier. He'd thought himself paranoid for having Sir Fredrick follow him, but it seemed his instincts had been correct. "I have an idea," he had merely said to the Ram's question. "You posted a boy outside Elyon's room?"

"I did, sire, when he went there with that girl." Sir Fredrick frowned. "You think he's involved?"

"I know it. Go see this boy, Sir Fredrick. I want to know if he's seen anyone go in or out of Elyon's chambers. And send me my daughter. She's down there somewhere, mingling." He waved a hand.

The hall was too hot and smokey for Janilah to see its more distant occupants clearly, but the Ram of Ruxmond didn't take long to track down his spider. She crept her way around to the rear of the stage, red-faced from the evening's frivolities, and joined her king father behind the royal table. She'd given an exaggerated curtsy. "You honour me,

Father, to invite me to this hallowed side of the hall. Deary me, if anyone should spot the Bastard Bitch of Blakewood back here..."

"I have no time for japing, Cecilia. I have a problem you may help solve."

"Elyon," she said at once. "He's stolen the Windblade, hasn't he?"

Janilah found himself less than shocked. "Your instincts do you credit, Daughter."

She flicked a dainty wrist. "The Ram mentioned something, and I knew you had plans to take it yourself tonight. It seems others did too..." She turned her keen green eyes in the direction of Amara, laughing uproariously amid the crowds. "That harpy is behind it, no doubt. Tell me how I can help you, Father."

Janilah had given her the broad strokes of what had happened. His bastard had been swift on the uptake, as ever, and quickly confided her plan. "I'll see young Elyon in chains for you at once," she'd promised him, smiling that venomous smile of hers. "And you're sure your *pet* will oblige? It takes a special soul to lay down their life, even to save their own family."

Janilah had looked over to see the Lady Melany Monsort sitting doleful at a table, alone amid all the merrymaking. There had been a moment - just a moment - when he'd doubted his command. But it was fleeting, no more than a wisp of smoke in the wind, quickly gone. "She'll see it done," he said. "The Monsort girl knows too much, and has failed me more than once. Tell her her brother and father will be dead by morning lest she completes this final duty."

"It would be my pleasure," Cecilia tittered, devious. She'd never liked Melany any more than she had Elyon. "A word in her ear, and we'll kill two birds with one stone tonight. Quite literally." She'd laughed to herself in delight and sauntered off to enact her plan.

And successfully, Janilah thought now, as he looked Elyon Daecar direct in his cold blue eyes. As he listened to him deny all involvement in the heist. "Your memory has clearly been impacted by that blow you took to the head," he said. "More rest may heighten your powers of recall. When I return, I hope you have something better for me. Two days, Elyon. Two days or your house will fall."

Janilah turned to leave. Elyon cut him off with a scoff. "You think you can command me as one of your subjects? You think you can threaten me as you did Melany? I will *not* yield, Janilah. If I have to die here, so be it. I will die with my pride intact."

Janilah spun. "Pride kills far too many good men, Sir Elyon. Die now and you'll sit at a lowly place at Varin's Table, far from your father and grandfather, and all the great men of your house..."

"I'll sit with Aleron," Elyon hissed. "The brother that *you* had killed."

Janilah had no immediate reply to that. The boy's eyes were ice and fire all at once, cold and burning. Eventually, he broke the sour silence and said, "Your brother's fate was regrettable. I never wished him dead."

"You did it to free Amilia's hand for Hadrin, I know. And so the Sword of Varinar might go to my uncle, to hand it to you, in time." He stared, sneering. "The latter didn't go so well for you, did it. No Sword of Varinar. No Nightblade. I've seen fit that you'll never get the Windblade either." He neared the bars, pressing into the light. Janilah had never seen such hatred on a man's face. "You *will* be judged for all you've done, Your Majesty," he said. "In this life, and the next, you will face retribution for everyone you have murdered and betrayed."

Janilah withdrew a step, taking the light of the lantern with him, leaving Elyon to recede back into the shadows. "That is the burden I bear." He gave the young knight a single nod. "A burden a man like you will never understand."

He took another step away and turned. His lantern was the only light within that dark stone corridor. *Only I hold the torch*, he thought. *Only I light the way.*

It was the mantra of a man lost to his delusions.

For all about Janilah was darkness now.

47

Elyon

He woke to the whine of rusted hinges and the soft scuffing sound of leather boots on stone. A shadowed figure entered his cell as Elyon sat up, blinking through the bright light of the lantern held in his grasp.

Janilah, was his first thought. *The king has come again.* He'd come a day or two ago, though judging time here in the pitch darkness was difficult. Elyon squinted against the glow of the burning oil, but the man's shape...no, this wasn't Janilah. Nor was it the heavy-bellied gaoler who occasionally came bearing sparse rations of water. *No, too small,* Elyon realised, shielding his eyes from the sudden light. He cleared his throat and made to speak, but the intruder got there first.

"Get up, Elyon," said Prince Rylian Lukar. "I'm putting an end to this farce."

Rylian drew the lantern aside so the glare wasn't quite so fierce. Elyon stood on weak tremulous legs, hunger ripping through his gut. "Rylian, what...what are you..." His throat felt dry, voice hoarse, and the ache in the back of his head wasn't going away. "Janilah...your father... he..."

"Knows nothing of this, and the longer we keep it that way, the better. We don't have much time, Elyon. Here, put this on."

The Prince of Tukor tossed him a bundle of clothes, tied up in string. Elyon had been wearing rags during his short imprisonment, having been dragged from his room wearing nothing but his breeks after the horror of Melany's suicide. *Breeks and blood,* he thought. The feeling of Melany's ichor spraying across his face and chest and arms and abdomen was not one he'd soon forget. "My armour...my blades..."

"Are with Lord Kanabar," Rylian told him. "He's taken possession of your things and you'll retrieve them in due course. Now come, get out of those rags. There's a heavy snow falling outside."

Elyon did as the prince bid him, peeling away the reeking woollen rags and drawing on clean breeches, boots, tunic, jerkin, gloves and cloak and cowl, bedecking himself all in black. He felt weak from lack of food, from the throb in his head where that cudgel cracked his skull, and confused by this sudden reprieve. Once dressed he stood and faced the prince, who waited patiently at the mouth of the cell. "Melany," he said. "What...what happened. You know..."

"I know it wasn't you. I know my father is holding you here without cause. And I know I'll not allow it." Rylian looked Elyon straight in the eye. "The north needs House Daecar, Elyon." He drew a length of leather, thrust it into Elyon's hands. "And take this."

Elyon examined the scabbard and blade within. "My dagger..."

"Retrieved from your room," said the prince. "A Bladeborn should always have a godsteel dagger on his person. The rest of your arms and armour are with Wallis, as I say, but that...you may need it."

Elyon wasted no time in hitching the sheath to his swordbelt, took a grip of the haft to feel his blood-bond. Power rushed into his veins, driving away his hunger and hurt, the ache in his head, the throbbing pain from where Melany had bitten him. All that had swirled about his mind on never-ending repeat as he lay here in the darkness; Melany's wild wriggling in his grasp, those crazed screams that erupted from her throat, the burning bite of her teeth as they dug deep through his skin and flesh, drawing blood...and that look...that look in her eyes as she said, "I'm sorry for everything, but I have no choice," and plunged her blade deep into her neck.

He gulped and turned from all that, clinging to his godsteel dagger for strength. Melany had sewn her own fate by serving Janilah, and had profited from that service. *And she poisoned Aleron,* he reminded himself, tightening his grasp, grimacing. *Forced or not, that's not something I can forgive. Like Jonik. And he'll die for that one day too.*

He looked at Prince Rylian. "I'm ready."

Rylian turned, ushered Elyon out of the cell, shut the door, turned the key. He didn't need to tell Elyon where he'd gotten it. At the end of the dim stone corridor a figure lay slumped on the floor; the thick-waisted, balding jailer who'd brought Elyon his meagre measures of water, served without fail with a side of insults and slurs and spitting.

"Is he dead?" Elyon asked.

"Unconscious. A few others are too, but they'll wake. Best we be gone when they do."

A few was putting it lightly. Beyond the heavy wooden door that marked the entrance to the cells, almost a dozen other guards lay in heaps of leather and wool and steel on the floor, their faces bruised, lips split, noses broken, all bloodied and beaten. Some wore godsteel armour, breastplates and gauntlets, members of Janilah's palace guard serving beneath his Six. Yet none had troubled Rylian, clearly, who looked unmarked and unhurt.

"This way." The prince led him on, down a stone corridor toward a set of spiral steps. At the bottom they came to another dim-lit hallway, cut with small windows along one side that gave a view out into the mountains, the shadows of high peaks just about visible through the snows. Rylian was right, they were falling heavily, as they'd done so often of late.

"Where are we?" Elyon asked. These dungeons felt atypical; built high rather than low. In Varinar, all dungeons were below ground, often cut into the bellies of the palaces and keeps and castles that sprawled imperious atop the ten hills. Elyon could see few structures beyond the windows; only a couple of thin towers spearing up into the cold black skies, a few blocky shapes further down within the pale white mists.

"My father keeps his most valuable prisoners up in these high cells," Rylian answered. "We're in the palace's northernmost wing, where it breaks into the mountains. There are ways out that will lead you through the foothills to the west, down into the Mistwood."

The Mistwood. Carly Flame Mane. Elyon thought of the sellsword's cunning smile, her keen and watchful eyes. She'd taken a path westward into the foothills of the Southern Hammersongs that would bring her down into the Mistwood and into Vandar, along with Crowfoot and Will Red and Sally Scarlet and the rest of her redheaded band of rogues. Elyon looked the prince in the eye, wondering if he knew about that. There was something in the man's expression that said he did. "How much do you know of what happened at the wedding?" Elyon asked him as they walked.

"Enough," Rylian said. "The Windblade. These sellswords your auntie hired. The details of your plot. Amara told me everything." He gave a sigh. "My cousin can connive and conspire as well as anyone, but she clearly didn't see Melany Monsort coming, or my scheming sister. Amara had no choice but to come to me and explain all, and hope that I might be able to help you."

The Bastard Bitch of Blakewood, Elyon could still see that twisted smile on Lady Cecilia's face as she stood outside his room when he was struck with that cudgel. *Vengeance,* he knew. *Vengeance for taking Saska away from her. For tricking her back in Harrowmoor.* He put the woman from his mind. There was other concerns more pressing. "For which I'll always be in your debt, Your Highness. Truly. Always."

Rylian waved a hand to that, dismissing it. "Your house have suffered enough. I'll not see its last son and heir hanged for a crime he didn't commit. You deserve more than that, Elyon. You won't be seeing your end swinging on a length of rope, not so long as I live."

Elyon might have thanked him again, but could see Rylian wouldn't have it. His mind went back to King Janilah's visit, the threats that had slipped off his tongue, the dark madness in his eyes. He stopped a moment in the corridor. "I have to know, Rylian, my family... are they safe?"

The prince put a hand on Elyon's shoulder. "Your sister is bound to my son by pact of marriage, ratified and witnessed by all the north. Her protection is ensured. Amara left with her for Ilivar this very morning, with your household knights and some of Lord Kanabar's men as escort. Your grandfather Brydon will take good care of them."

Elyon nodded his relief. It had been their plan all along for Amara and Lillia to head for Ilivar after the wedding. *But with me imprisoned?* He didn't imagine either would have left willingly, without knowing what fate awaited him. The answer didn't take long to come to him, though. "Amara made you promise that you'd free me, didn't she?"

"Of course she did, and by godsteel oath no less. Not everyone takes those seriously, but I do, Elyon. I agreed without hesitation, and have promised Amara that I'd send a rider with news of your escape as soon as I can." He began walking on. "Your squire left with them, you should know. He wanted to return to your service, but your sister didn't seem willing to part with him. She clearly cares for the boy, and I think it's fair to say that feeling is reciprocated. I do hope you cautioned him not to make any advances on her, now that she's to wed my son?"

"You needn't worry about that, my lord. Jovyn...well, I'll not deny he has developed a youthful infatuation with her, but he knows not to act upon it."

Rylian seemed satisfied. "As you say. She is strikingly similar to your mother, when she was that age. There was a time when every man in the north fell in love at the sight of Kessia Amadar, before your father stole her heart and put a stop to the dreams of a thousand high-born men. My new son-in-law was among them. My son-in-law who's half a dozen years older than I am." He gave a bitter snort, and chose to say nothing more on that.

They walked on in silence for a moment. Then Elyon asked, "What about King Godrik and Prince Dalton? Do they know the truth of what happened?"

Rylian shook his head. "The Taynars continue to believe my father plotted the theft, at least for now. Like everyone else, they saw you leave with that redheaded girl, and were quite convinced of your insobriety. And later...with what happened with Lady Melany...well, the alibi is a good one, is all I'll say." He gave Elyon a supportive pat on the shoulder. "It can't have been pleasant, all that. I know you cared about Melany once."

"Once," Elyon agreed, darkly. *Until I found out she'd been spying on me,* he thought. *Until I found out she helped murder my brother.*

They continued on down the dimly lit hallway, past the windows, reaching a door. It lay ajar; Rylian had clearly come this way. Another pair of guardsmen lay unconscious outside, palace guards with their polished armour and green capes. Rylian stepped over a particularly large man, sprawled upon the stone with a puddle of blood gathering about his head. "Might have struck this one a little harder than I thought," he said. Good man that he was, Rylian Lukar knelt to check his pulse, then nodded and stood. "He'll be fine. Men who serve my father should not be bound to his treachery, or fate."

"And what fate is that?" Elyon asked.

"Death," said Rylian, marching on. He caught the look on Elyon's face, then said, "But not by my hand, if that's what you're thinking. I would not want my name uttered in the same breath as Hadrin's, as kin and kingkiller." The thought of that brought a scowl to his handsome face. "No, my father will have his due in time, but for now...he can sit and rot here, for all I care. Perhaps a bit of time alone will let him reflect on what he's become. He was a great man once, proud and noble, a brilliant warrior and war strategist and inspirational leader. He is a grim shadow of that now, corrupted by his ambition and obsession and the creatures he keeps in his counsel. I am done with him, Elyon. *Done.* Were we not at war with the south I would take steps to remove him for his treacheries, but alas times are too perilous for that now. Curse me for saying it, but he still commands the support of Hadrin and his lickspittles, Kastor and his, and even Taynar, despite their tensions and troubles. In time I will sever these bonds and work to wash away the blight my father has fostered, but that time is not now." He paused. "Trust me, Elyon. All will be well. But first we must get you free of here, and for that, we cannot wait." He turned and hurried on down the corridor. "Come, they'll be waiting."

They turned out to be about the only pair of knights in the city whom Elyon Daecar would willingly trust and travel with. Sir Lancel and Sir Barnibus awaited them beyond a door that let out into a pass between two mountains, with high cliffs of frosted rock rising black and sheer either side. Both were buried beneath thick fur cloaks, armed with their godsteel swords and daggers and with travel packs heaped on their backs. "Good. You made it," said Rylian, moving out to them through the falling snows. "Did you have any trouble getting here?"

"Some," shrugged Barnibus. "Had to knock out a few palace guards, but made sure not to kill anyone, as you said."

"Your directions were clear, Your Highness," Lancel added, dipping his head into a bow. He smiled broadly at Elyon. "El, gods...we feared for you, all of us. After Aleron, the idea of losing you too..."

"He's not going anywhere just yet," Rylian declared. "Aleron will have to wait to see his little brother again."

"A bloody long time, let's hope," smiled Barnibus, chubby cheeks red from the wind, hood already covered with a thin layer of snow. He glanced skyward. "Sorry, Al, but we'll be keeping him down here for now."

"I'm sure Aleron would approve." Rylian turned back to the door. The exit they'd reached seemed distant from the heart of the palace and wider grounds, a few shadowed towers barely visible away to the southeast of where they stood. Through the door, the long dark corridor they'd travelled remained quiet and empty of guards. No pursuit. That was good. "You'd best not linger," Rylian said. "It won't take long for one of the guards to wake and report the breakout." He turned, gestured between the rugged cliffs. Further on, they opened out into what appeared a wider pass, where the Hammersongs rose high and endless in a series of lofty white peaks. "There's an old path that way that'll take you west and down through the foothills. Keep an eye out for it; it'll be tricky to spot in this snow, but if you're keen, you'll see it." He looked to Elyon's companions. "You brought provisions?"

"Plenty, and he looks like he needs a meal." Lancel gestured to Elyon. "They didn't feed you in your cell?"

"Not a mouthful. A bit of water, that's all."

"My father hoped it might weaken you, I suppose. Make you more compliant. I thought he knew more about Daecar defiance than that."

Pride, you mean, Elyon had to think. "*Pride kills far too many good men,*" the king had said to him, and how true that was. *Was I really willing to die just to hide the Windblade from him?* Elyon had laboured over that question since his meeting with Janilah, though in the end, hadn't found an answer. *And now I don't need one, thank the gods.* "I'll repay you for this one day, Your Highness," he told the prince with all the grace and gratitude he had in him. "You saved my life, and..."

"You'll use it wisely." Rylian smiled, gripped his forearm. "Master that blade for starters, and perhaps you can come visit me at Eagle's Perch during the siege. It's said the old kings of Vandar used to fly between kingdoms and castles to seek counsel and bring tidings, or just to share a drink or two with old allies and friends. Well, a short flight over the Bay of Mourning shouldn't be too onerous for you, not once you've learned the Windblade's mysteries." He withdrew his hand, clapped him on the shoulder. "I'll expect to see you soon, Sir Elyon, soaring in from the skies. That's the only repayment I need."

Elyon bowed his head. The idea of learning to fly seemed a ways off yet, given how much effort it had taken just to lift the blade to his shoulder. Still, he hid his doubts and said, "I'll do my best, my lord."

"And your best will be plenty, I know it. You are your father's son,

Elyon, every bit of him." Rylian gave him a final bracing look, then turned to the others. "Dawn isn't far off, so best not waste this head start. Go, all of you. I'll be in contact soon."

A shiver of unease went through Elyon Daecar as he watched the prince fade into the shadows of the palace, returning to that nest of snakes. Behind him, he could hear the others beginning to move off, feet crunching on snow. He took a last look at Rylian as he drained from sight, forever grateful, forever in the man's debt. "I'll master that blade for you, my prince," he whispered in promise. "I'll not forget what you've done for me here."

With that, he turned and followed.

They passed through the passage between the cliffs and emerged onto the white plains beyond, moving at such a pace as they could manage given the depth of the snow. All clutched at their godsteel daggers to give them strength. The winds were white and roaring beyond the high cliffs, blowing in between a set of nearby peaks, and the snows were coming hard. "This heavy fall is good," Lancel called out. "The snow will soon cover our tracks."

"Not soon enough, if they're quick to make chase," Barnibus replied. "I think I see that track Rylian mentioned." He pointed west. "Come, follow me."

Sure enough, amidst a field of scattered stone and boulders were signs of an old paved path, visible where the rocks rose high and offered a buffer against the snow. It gave them a starting point at least, and instinct did the rest, guiding them down the slope and toward the lower foothills beyond. Elyon thought of what Carly Flame Mane had said. A week, she'd told them, to travel across the western foothills and through the Mistwood and reach the great open plains of the Vandarian Heartlands beyond. *That was how long ago now? Two days? Three?* He still wasn't certain how long he'd been locked up within that ink-black cell, in and out of consciousness as he'd been.

He hustled up to Barnibus's side. "How far behind Carly are we?"

"Two days," Barnibus said at once.

That's all it had been. Just the two days in that frigid stone cell. "Might we catch up with her?"

"If we're quick, perhaps. But she left from the south of the palace, and we're to the north. Who knows what difference that makes. Might be that this track eventually merges into the one she took and we'll pick up her trail? Or perhaps this way's longer. I'm not sure in truth, El." Barnibus picked up on what Elyon was wondering then. "You're hoping to get your hands on the Windblade sooner, I suppose?"

"The sooner the better," Elyon said, nodding. "I need to master it, Barn. And anything can happen on the road. We can be sure Godrik and Janilah will have agents out searching for it as we speak."

"Then let's not dawdle," said Lancel, striding to join them, then right past. "Those sellswords were two dozen in number and with the Windblade in tow, they'll be slow."

"Slower than us," Barnibus agreed, "but we'd have to make up two days to catch them. And we have no idea whether we're on the same track. We might come down into the Mistwood twenty miles north of them. Then what?"

"Then we catch up later on. We know they're heading to Dragon's Bane, so what else do we need?" Lancel didn't wait for a reply, driving on forward through the drifts of snow as the others followed in behind.

For a time that's how they went, Lancel and Barnibus swapping the lead and taking the burden of clearing a path through the snow, Elyon remaining to the rear, chomping on bread and cheese and cured cuts of meat taken from his friends' packs in a bid to restore some of his strength. He found his thoughts swirling here, swirling there, often landing on his father. His father out there in the Icewilds, a world much like this, only colder, darker, more deadly and dangerous, a world from which few ever returned.

And will he? Will he return? Perhaps he already had. Or perhaps he was already entombed out there, frozen stiff to the bone one night as he slept, or slain by some tribesman, or feasted on by some beast, or crushed beneath an avalanche of snow or falling rocks, or driven to madness by the endlessness of it, the dread and dark and devilry that lurked and prowled all about him. *Or or or or or.* There were a thousand 'ors' Elyon could think of, a thousand ways to die out there in that bleak white wilderness. *But if anyone can live through it, it's my father,* he thought. Crippled and cursed he might have become, but he was still the Hero of the North. He was still the Slayer of Vallath, the Crippler of Kings, the man some called Varin Reborn, who'd ended a war by the edge of his blade and the mercy he'd shown a prince.

Elyon Daecar smiled defiantly at that, as he pressed on through the whistling winds, the falling snows. For weeks the Rat King's voice had echoed through his head, sneering at him in his dreams, whispering as he woke, an unrelenting repetition of words that had burrowed inside him, deep and deeper still. *Amron Daecar...is dead. Amron Daecar...is dead.*

But enough, he thought now. *Enough! No, he's alive. He has to be alive.* He nodded, casting away Hadrin's hissing voice once and for all. He'd lived beneath the shadow of those words for weeks, giving them more credence than they deserved, but no longer. *Amron Daecar...still lives,* he thought again, trusting it, believing it, knowing it must be true. *Yes, my father lives, and he'll return to us one day soon.*

Elyon Daecar smiled once again, as he strode on through the rugged snowy foothills, toward a brighter dawn.

48

Lythian

Lythian was shaken awake. The narrow dark eyes of Sir Pagaloth Kadosk met him in the dim night air. "Lythian, you must get up. They are returning."

Lythian shook the cobwebs from his head as he scrambled to his feet. The touch of godsteel would typically speed that process. Without it he felt muddy of mind and slow of foot, a shadow of himself. "You're sure?" he croaked.

There was a worrisome look in Sir Pagaloth's eyes. "A sentry just ran down from the hilltop, crying out. He sounded panicked. There has been some disaster, I think."

"*Disaster*?" Lythian was still waking up. Above them the light of a crescent moon was breaking out from behind the clouds, dawn some hours away. "Talasha?" he asked, in half a panic. "She isn't..."

"I don't know," Pagaloth said. "The sentry only called out to wake the camp. He shouted for the healer." The dragonknight marched over to a stack of weapons as Lythian threw on his roughspun cloak, pulling it over his boiled leathers. Pagaloth fetched a sword and sheath and returned. "Put this on your belt," he said, in a voice heavy with caution. "We may find trouble out there."

Lythian didn't have time to question him. His fears were fixed on Talasha. He hitched the sheath to his belt as swiftly as he could before the pair moved straight off down the slope into the main camp, Pagaloth's greasy black hair shimmering in the moonlight. Below they found the outlaws being hastily roused from their sleep, emerging from the blankets and the furs on which they slept. A pair of guards in their patchwork armour and dirtied crimson cloaks were calling out loudly, waving for everyone to wake. Some were already up and dressed, moving out into the woods and up the slope.

Lythian and Pagaloth made to follow, but just then Ashun Klo appeared, hurrying through the trees into camp, passing the ruins of the curtain wall. He looked around in a wild panic, roaring out in Agarathi words Lythian didn't understand. "He's looking for the healer," Pagaloth translated.

"Who's wounded, Ashun?" Lythian called to him, rushing over. He felt weak and weary still from the fever that had near killed him, but the adrenaline was giving him strength. "What happened?"

Ashun Klo's purple eyes blazed in the firelight. There was blood spattered across his face. "*You,*" he rasped, his voice raw from shouting. He wore his dual dragonsteel blades, his body wreathed in his rich scale-mail armour, black as night. "You should never have come here. It...it has all gone wrong because of you!"

Lythian clutched the handle of his sword, but didn't draw it. "What happened, Ashun?" he asked again, as calm as he could. "Where is everyone? The princess..."

Ashun Klo's upper lip tore back into a hateful grimace. His hawkish face looked lean and dangerous in the torchlight. "She is all you care about," he snarled. "But she does *not* matter! Tethian, my prince...he....he..." His eyes spun off suddenly as he spotted the old healer come hurrying through from another part of the camp, several of his acolytes trailing him. Ashun growled a few more words in Agarathi, grabbed the man by the arm, and began hauling him roughly through the broken wall and into the woods.

Lythian shared a disquieted look with Sir Pagaloth. Without a word, they gave chase. Others did the same, a tide of drowsy and panicked souls rushing into the darkness, weaving between boles and branches, leaping rocks and roots. Some held torches to light their way, the flames dancing chaotically as they went. Further off to the left and right fireflies buzzed and hovered, and a great host of frogs was croaking loudly from a nearby pond. The slope began to rise up into the hillock that broke out beyond the trees like an island in the ocean, washed in moonlight. Lythian could see shadows and shapes up there, hear the clamor of shouts and screams.

When he reached the top he saw Neyruu immediately, the sleek grey dragon crouched low to one side and furled up in her wings. On the ground a dozen metres away a group were gathered around a body. In the dimness it wasn't easy to gauge who was who. Voices were surging out in a frenzy. Ashun Klo rushed in, barging sentries and guardsmen aside, near throwing the healer to the earth in his haste, barking commands.

As the crowd parted to let them pass, Lythian spotted Kin'rar Kroll on his knees, his silken grey cape shining under the moonlight, trying to staunch the flow of blood from a gash at Prince Tethian's chest. It wasn't the only one. Already bandages had been applied to several other wounds, and half the prince's face looked as though it had been burned clean off the bone, his flesh charred and sloughed away, exposing the white of his skull beneath. Where his right eye had once been was a black pit, his nose melted into a pulp, his ear missing entirely.

Men were retching at the sight of him, women wailing loudly in great ululating tones. Their grief and terror were palpable. Lythian searched through the stricken faces for the princess and saw her there at the front of the crowd, clutching her hands to her heart in despair. Tears ran freely from her eyes as she looked down at the ruin of her cousin's body.

He ran to her. "Talasha, what happened?" His eyes scanned. There was no sign of Lord Marak, no sign of Sotel Dar. There was no sign of Eldur. "Talasha, where are the others?"

She could give no answer, but to shake her head and sob. The white-bearded healer was down beside Kin'rar now, taking over. His acolytes and helpers were handing him out balms and salves and bandages, but it looked to be no use. Tethian was gone. Lythian had seen enough men die to know when there was no hope.

Pagaloth knew it too. He had a grave look on his face, his long beard twirled into a triple braid. "Captain, we should not linger," he warned in a quiet voice. "When the prince dies, it will not be safe for us here."

"Leave?" Lythian rounded on him. "I can't leave, Pagaloth." He took Talasha into his arms, hugged her fierce. "Talasha, where is Sotel Dar?

Where is Marak?" His throat caught as he said the next name. "*Eldur*. What...what happened, Talasha? Did he wake? Did...did it work?"

The princess turned to look at him in a daze, a strange mix of horror and wonder in her eyes. "Eldur," she whispered, nodding. "The Bondstone, it...yes, it...it worked."

Cold fingers clutched tight at Lythian's heart. He felt a shudder of something deep and primal crawl up his spine. He looked down at Prince Tethian as the men worked feverishly, hopelessly, to revive him. "Those are dragonfire burns," he said. "Who was it, Talasha? Vargo Ven? Another of the Fireborn?"

She shook her head fearfully, lips trembling. "He did not know what he was doing, Lythian. He...he...he slept too long, and woke too... too suddenly. It...it all happened so fast. I can hardly think. I can hardly remember."

And Lythian could hardly breathe. "*Eldur* did this?" His voice was disbelieving. "*Why*? How could he..."

"He did not know. It...it was not him, not really. The Bondstone, it...it seemed to...to come alive as he was near. Its energy seemed to flow *into* him, Lythian; no one expected that, not even Sotel Dar. Then he...he spoke words I could not fathom. His voice..." Her head was shaking side to side, locks of wild black hair swishing. "His *voice*, Lythian. It was like a mountain breaking in half. I had to block my ears, and shut my eyes, and...when I next looked up, the dragons were going wild. And Eldur, and the Bondstone...they were gone."

Lythian's heart thundered as he imagined the horror of it. He could scarce believe it. This was his nightmare come to life. He'd aided in the revival of his people's greatest menace.

He looked across the hillside. Neyruu lay quiet and strangely subdued, gently shaking, Lythian now saw. "She did not go wild like the other dragons?" he asked the princess. "She alone carried you back?"

The princess nodded feebly, staring down at her dying cousin with a grimace fixed on her face. "Kin'rar managed to gain control of her. We got Tethian away...but the rest...Sotel and Marak, they...they were left behind. I do not know what happened to them, Lythian." She cringed and continued sobbing.

Cevi and Mirella appeared at that, her handmaids finally arriving from the woods below. They ran tearful to Talasha's side, flanking her, comforting her. Lythian drew a step away. How could they have been so wrong? The wailing and weeping was so loud he could scarce hear himself think. *It's as I feared. I have helped awaken the darkness.* He shuddered in his skin, as a distant rumble of thunder cackled across the world. It seemed to come from the southwest, from the Wings where the spirit of Agarath lingered. *He laughs*, Lythian could only think. *He laughs at the depths of my folly.*

"He takes his final breaths," he heard Sir Pagaloth say at his side. The Varin Knight's eyes went straight back down to the prince and zealot and leader of these outlaws. Tethian was the only reason for any of them to be here, he and his cause. And that cause was dying with him. "They will come for us, Lythian. Kartheck, Racker, Grumlo. There will be no one to stop them now."

Lythian could see each of them, standing amid the crowd, staring down with hollow eyes as their prince spluttered and convulsed at their feet. The healer and his helpers were having no effect, Lythian could plainly see. Above them, Ashun Klo was pacing side to side, screaming orders. His face was hot and red with fear, his words ripping out on ragged stunted breaths. Pagaloth watched him warily. "Now would be a good time to go, Captain. We will not get a better chance."

Lythian shook his head. "I can't leave without Talasha," he insisted.

"You *must*," Pagaloth told him. "Your union was never meant to last, Lythian. Break it now. It will be easier in the long run."

A part of him knew the dragonknight was right, yet all the same, he wasn't going to let her fend for herself here. "No. If we go we're taking her with us."

"Then we must take Cevi and Mirella too," Pagaloth came back. "Talasha will not leave without them."

"Then we'll take them too," Lythian said firmly. "And if we have to fight, we'll fight."

Pagaloth nodded grimly, clutching at his blade. It was dragonsteel, like those wielded by Ashun Klo, the black metal lined with shards of red light where it had been folded over and over during its forging. There was no finer steel in Agarath, yet Lythian himself was woefully ill-equipped. If he had Starslayer, he'd have little to fear, but without his godsteel blade...

He didn't have time to further that thought. At the heart of the crowd, Tethian was beginning to convulse more wildly, men and women gasping out and calling skyward in beseech that the gods might save him. *Their god is Agarath,* Lythian thought, *and he is not listening.* Another rumble of thunder bellowed out across the foothills, and some took that to mean their fire god was responding. They held their hands high and cried out in hope, but when Tethian's body went limp, that hope withered and died with him.

Lythian knew it would be best to withdraw. He gave Pagaloth a nod and they drew back to let the mourners have a moment to grieve. The left side of Tethian's face was blanched white and bloodless, the right a mutilated mess of charred flesh and bone. The healer had dropped to his knees, pumping hard at the prince's chest for all the good it would do, as his helpers stood by, helpless.

But it would all be for nought. Their pious prince and preacher was dead.

As they slipped away to the rear of the rabble, all went suddenly quiet and still. Lythian could see Ashun Klo staring down stark-faced and ghostly, his long face drawn out in a disbelieving anguish. The old white-bearded healer sat back on his heels, defeated, shaking his head. He'd done all he could, Lythian knew, but Tethian's race had been run before he'd even arrived. The old physician shook his head plaintively, let out a long deep sigh, and reached out to close Tethian's remaining left eye.

His wrist was caught by Ashun Klo. The man's purple eyes were suddenly aflame, flooding with burning tears. He pulled the healer harshly to his feet, snarling words in his rough, raw tongue. The crowd murmured. Lythian didn't understand. The healer recoiled, pleading, but Ashun Klo was not for listening. In a sudden motion he reached to his side, jerked out his dragonsteel sword, and plunged it straight through the healer's gut.

Lythian's eyes flared open in shock. The crowd screamed and scrambled back, scattering. The acolytes spun, scurrying away into the darkness as though fearing they'd be next. Their fears were warranted. Ashun Klo screamed a command and at once Rackar and the cutthroat Kartheck gave chase, swinging their swords, cutting them down.

Lythian went to move forward, but the brute Grumlo spun and blocked his way. His eyes were black stones. In his heavy fists he clutched at his long black dragonsteel spear, thumping its butt into the ground. A crack of thunder rumbled through the clouds as it made impact, as though Grumlo was some great god himself. "You will die here this day, Mist Knight!" he bellowed. "And you, traitor! Both of you will die!" He swung his spear forward and charged.

Pagaloth's blade was out in an instant, glinting black and red in the last of the moonlight as the clouds closed in above them. Lythian reached to draw his own sword, but the dragonknight was quicker. He rushed forward to engage the brawny spearman, swinging hard to parry the big man's thrust. Grumlo grunted as steel met steel, his spear knocked aside by the force of Pagaloth's block. He turned and swung in a heavy, flowing arc. Pagaloth ducked, darted closer, stretched out in a long arm jab, but Grumlo was wise to it. He jinked sideways, bringing his spear back to his flank, thrusting again as he backed away, but Pagaloth was too swift. The dragonknight stepped to close the gap, swinging right and left, knocking the spear aside. Grumlo lost his balance for just a moment, his midsection exposed, and Pagaloth slashed hard and fast across his gut, cutting through leather and mail and flesh. Slick pink snakes slid out in a heap, steaming, as Grumlo crumbled to his knees, staring down at his innards as they slithered out onto the cold rock floor.

A rain began to fall, sudden and heavy. Grumlo let out a low grunting bellow that Lythian had heard a thousand times before, as he tried to scoop up his guts. Lythian had seen that too, and more often than he'd have liked. He'd seen men die in a hundred ways on the battlefield, and being gutted and left alive was one of the less pleasant ways to go.

"I didn't want it to come to this," Pagaloth told the dying man. "You forced my hand, Grumlo."

The spearman made to answer, but when he opened his mouth, only a great gush of blood came spewing out. Pagaloth did the honourable thing, and thrust his blade through his throat to finish him.

The hillside was descending into chaos. Dozens of men and women were scattering from the prince's body, rushing away into the darkness. Kartheck and Rackar were dealing with the final acolytes, slaying them for their failure. Ashun Klo was on his knees at Tethian's side, slowly running a hand over the left side of his face. Kin'rar was calling out loudly for order. Talasha and her handmaids stood together, holding one another, weeping, as the thunder and lightning and thick sheets of rain lashed down hard and heavy upon them.

It was not how it was supposed to be. Today was meant to be their day of triumph.

Only hours ago, all had gathered here upon this very hill to see Tethian and the others depart. They had watched in hushed anticipation as Eldur was carried out upon his bier, wreathed in new-knitted robes of crimson marked with his fiery sigil, attended by Tethian and Talasha, blood of his blood. They had gazed on in wonder as he was raised to a special saddle fixed upon Garlath's back, rejoicing that the day had finally come after so many months and years of waiting. This was it. Their noble prince said so. After ten days of failures, he had found the way. They would fly Eldur to the Nest and let him drink in the power of the Bondstone. Agarath's Soul would wake him, Tethian had promised, breathe into him life anew. He would rise, brilliant and blessed, a saviour to all the world. He would cast away the shadow of war and usher in an age of peace.

But that had been hours ago, when the cheers had rung out loud and true as the dragons had taken flight. When the sun had sparkled down from a bright sapphire sky. When all had been hope and joy.

Now the heavens were black and heavy with rain and thunder. Now those cheers had curdled to cries as women wept and men moaned and violence churned about them. Already Lythian could see the breaking of this fellowship, this cult that only Tethian had kept from falling apart. Old animosities had taken no time to spring back to life, with no one here to judge them. From one edge of the hillside a cliff fell to a base of jagged rocks two dozen feet below. It had been used as a means of execution for rapers and wrongdoers, and now Lythian could see men quarrelling there at the edge, fighting to fling their rivals over the side to dash them upon the rocks.

All has fallen to anarchy, he thought, *a bloody crazed anarchy*. "We have to get out of here," he said, turning to Pagaloth. "See to the princess, Pagaloth. Her handmaids favour you. Take them down the hill and away from here."

"I'll not leave you, Lythian. My life is sworn to yours."

"Then you'll do as I command." He drew his sword. "Go. And do not forget who I am. I do not need godsteel to defend myself."

Pagaloth said no more. He turned and rushed away, dashing through the rains.

Lythian went straight to Skymaster Kin'rar Kroll. He was still blaring loudly, trying to restore calm, and failing. "They will not listen, Kin'rar," Lythian called to him. "They have nothing without this cause. Let them be."

Kin'rar looked around. He was a noble man, fiercely honourable, yet knew the truth of what Lythian was saying. Half these men had come here as exiles and outlaws, driven from their lands and lives for crimes they once committed. Some were killers, others thieves and rapists, and would withdraw to base needs and banditry now. *There is no man more dangerous than a man with nothing to lose,* Lythian thought, and everyone here had lost it all.

Kin'rar nodded. "Where do you plan to go?"

"Away from here. Where can be decided later."

The Skymaster looked to his dragon. Someone had dropped a torch nearby, still flaming despite the rains. A gentle orange glow lit Neyruu's face, those wise eyes of hers searching away into the mountains, strangely distant and solemn. She was looking in the direction of the Nest, Lythian realised. "She suffers," Kin'rar said, his voice heavy with regret. "I can sense her confusion. The dragons, Lythian. Something happened to them. Many went wild. Some threw their own riders from their backs, I saw." He grimaced, shaking his head. "Marak is dead, I fear. He tried to confront Eldur. He had the Fireblade. He was the only one of us who could."

"But why?" Lythian still wasn't understanding. "*Why* would Eldur do this? Why would he attack his own people? The very people who had brought him back..."

"Perhaps he didn't want to be brought back," Kin'rar said darkly. "Perhaps this prophesy was wrong all along, Lythian, as you warned. I cannot say. There is much that does not make sense."

Much and more, Lythian thought, but now was not the time to discuss it. "Can Neyruu fly?"

"I do not think so, not yet. She was overburdened carrying us back, and exhausted. I will return you to Vandar when she is recovered."

"That isn't what I meant," the Varin Knight told him. It was the truth. He had no thought of leaving Pagaloth, Talasha, or her handmaids behind. What little news they'd heard of happenings in the north told him that none would be safe should they return with him. He had to think on that. This was no time to be making decisions of such weight. "We have to escape into the wilds for now," he simply said. "Can you rouse Neyruu to come with us?"

Kin'rar looked again at his bonded dragon. "I am not sure. I feel our bond...weakening, somehow, like a fraying thread. She was distressed flying us back here. It took all I had to keep her calm, yet... she grows more wild in my head. I think it best to leave her. She will come to me, when she is ready."

Lythian could hear the anguish in his voice. He remembered his dream, with all the world wreathed in fire, with the dragons swarming the skies. A cold shudder rippled up his spine as a squall of thick rain drenched them. The winds were picking up now, howling wildly, the thunder booming and bellowing. He turned to see that Pagaloth had led Talasha and her maids away down the hill to safety. He would take them back to the ruins of the keep, Lythian knew, so that they might gather their scant belongings. He saw no reason to delay joining them.

He told Kin'rar so and the Skymaster gave a ponderous nod, looking forlornly toward Neyruu. Lythian could only imagine what he was going through. He had left Starslayer behind in hell and felt grief-stricken at that loss, but a Fireborn's bond to a dragon was an altogether more powerful tie.

"Come, Kin'rar, they'll be waiting." He ushered him gently away, soaked to his bones, moving down the hillside into the woods. Here and there people had gotten lost in their mad scramble to safety, clattering frantically through the trees. One skittish young man came upon them all of a sudden, shrieked as though they would cut him through, and went bowling away into the blackness. Elsewhere a woman was wailing, her grief-stricken screams gobbled up by the rains. The thrash of violence still throbbed too, ringing out through the night.

They gave it no mind. They couldn't interfere or delay. *These are not my people,* Lythian told himself. *I have no choice but to leave them to their fates.*

The camp was half deserted when they reached it, a few sneaks and thieves picking through the leftovers in search of anything of value. Many had already taken their things and run, it looked, as though aware of what would follow. *It was all nothing but a facade,*

Lythian thought, *and they knew it too.* All Tethian's preaching. All of Sotel Dar's sermons. Without them there was no bond of brotherhood here, as Tethian had claimed. This was a flock without a shepherd, scattered across the fields. Some sped off in their little groups and pairs; the rest escaped alone with nought but the clothes on their back and a length of steel at their side.

It was one of the saddest things he had ever seen. *So many people, deceived by a lie.*

Pagaloth and Talasha were among the ruins of the old castle keep, as expected. The dragonknight had managed to get them garbed for the wilds in leathers and cloaks. Talasha wore her suit of scale mail armour beneath, the interlinking plates coloured red, purple and black, with her quiver and hunting bow slung over her shoulder. Yet she looked bedraggled, lost, as though unsure still of what was happening. Her handmaids were at her side, shivering. Only Pagaloth had all his wits about him. "Good, you're here. Skymaster, you will join us?"

Kin'rar gave a nod. When Lythian had first landed at Dragonfall with Borrus and Tomos all those months ago, he'd met both of these men at the docks. Sir Pagaloth had been in command of a unit of city soldiers. Kin'rar had been stationed there as Skymaster, to watch for coming threats and report them back to the Nest, where Ulrik Marak was still the sitting Skylord. Lythian had never expected to call these men friend back then. The thought brought a rueful smile to his lips. How far they had come, to find themselves here.

"Then we should go," Pagaloth went on. "I suggest we make for the foothills to the south. If we must, we can travel into Lumara. The salt-flats are home to communities who may be able to provide us with..."

"You killed him," whispered a cold and fractured voice.

Lythian turned. Ashun Klo stood at the broken wall of the bailey, tears running from his gleaming purple eyes. A black-red dragonsteel broadsword shimmered in his grasp. At his sides were Kartheck and Rackar. Kartheck had a grim and eager look on his face, his black eyes swimming with the hope of blood. *More blood,* Lythian knew. He had slain several acolytes already.

"Grumlo charged us with his spear, Ashun," Sir Pagaloth told him. He moved to Lythian's side; Kin'rar was at his other. "His death was just. He brought it upon himself."

"I don't care about Grumlo." Ashun Klo's voice had a dull intensity to it. *A man who has nothing to lose is a dangerous man indeed*, Lythian thought again. The light-haired highborn Agarathi lifted his blade, pointed it at Lythian. "You killed him. *You*. You brought a curse upon us when you came here. I should have let Eldur bathe in your blood. It would have awoken him...it would!" His eyes were wide and unblinking. They were the same haunted eyes as Talasha's, as Kin'rar's. Lythian could scarce imagine what they'd seen. "We should never have gone to the Nest," Ashun went on. "It was wrong...all wrong. *You* killed him, you of Varin's blood. And now I'll see it spilled."

Kin'rar Kroll stepped forward, his own blade tucked into its sheath. He held up his hands as he walked. "Ashun, think about what you're saying. Lythian has only helped us since he came here. Without him we might never have even reached Eldur's resting place. The Fire Father would have remained entombed there forever..."

"And Tethian would still be alive," Ashun Klo said sharply. "I never cared about raising Eldur. I only cared about him. *My prince*."

"Put the blade aside, Ashun," Kin'rar beseeched him. "You are not thinking clearly. None of us are. Put your blade aside and let this lie. There is no reason for anyone else to die."

"There is every reason. We are at war, Skymaster. And this man is my enemy." Ashun Klo stepped forward.

Kin'rar didn't move. "Stop. That is a command."

Ashun kept on coming. "Your commands are meaningless here. You're an exile like the rest of us. Get out of my way, Kin'rar, or I will kill you too."

Kin'rar refused to move. He raised one hand again, reached with the other to his blade. Lythian knew the Fireborn were well trained in the sword, but it was with their dragons that they dealt death, not steel. His grey cape flapped as the breeze took it. A jagged finger of lightning shot down from the skies, brightening the world. In that split second Lythian saw the intent in Ashun Klo's eyes.

No! he thought, moving forward. "Kin'rar, step back!" he shouted.

Ashun Klo thrust his blade into Kin'rar Kroll's belly, driving hard through his dragon-scale armour. The black steel came out the other side lacquered red, exploding through Kin'rar's sodden grey cape. Lythian sucked a breath, blew it out in a bellow. The handmaids started screaming. Talasha was shouting Kin'rar's name.

Pagaloth launched himself forward in a wild fury. Ashun Klo pulled his blade out of Kin'rar's gut, the Skymaster slumping bonelessly to the ground. Blood surged freely from his front and back, rich and red on the cracked stone floor. Lythian knew at once that he was dead. In the distance, a great echoing roar rolled out from the hilltop; the sound of a soul splitting in two.

Sir Pagaloth's blade met Ashun Klo's, the steel kissing in a spray of rain and blood. From the sides Rackar and Kartheck closed in on the Varin Knight. Lythian moved into Blockform, his fever forgotten, his rage enflamed. Rackar was young, well trained, structured in his movement, Kartheck prowling like a cat, his stance wide and ever-changing. In his grip was his kilij sword, curved and cruel and dripping wet. He darted forward in a whip-quick surge as Lythian spun to face him, but it was only a feint. At once Rackar struck at Lythian's exposed left flank, slashing diagonally down with his grey dinted longsword. The Varin Knight was wise to the move, shifting backward from Kartheck, parrying Rackar's cut, turning him so both foes were right before him. He caught a glimpse of Pagaloth and Ashun Klo in a fierce duel, slashing at one another by the light of a burning brazier. Cevi and Mirella had gone to their knees at Kin'rar's side, trying to stem the flow of blood from his gut. They didn't seem to realise that he was already dead.

Rackar came again, his stance neat and tidy, as Kartheck moved behind him like a shadow. They were trying to get in behind him, but Lythian Lindar knew what it took to keep two enemies in his eyeline. His footwork was precise and fleet even without godsteel, his technique impeccable. He kept to Blockform, blade forward, feet split in a defensive stance, turning away Rackar's attacks. A sideslash was parried, a forward prod deftly knocked aside, opening his opponent's right flank. Lythian struck. The tip of his old broadsword went forward, straight as an arrow, in a long-legged lunge. It caught Rackar at the hip, biting through his leather armour, driving an inch into his flesh. Lythian felt the steel jolt against bone. Rackar yelped in pain, stumbling back, clutching at the wound.

Kartheck took his place.

The sellsword sprung from the shadows, slashing swift and sudden in an upward cut. Lythian spun, downcutting against his blade in a shuddering clash. The attack had turned him. Rackar was now at his back. He could sense the man righting himself, preparing to strike. Lythian moved out of Blockform, took flight in Strikeform. He'd mastered both in his youth; in Strikeform there was no one better.

He needed to end Rackar quick. Ignoring the threat of Kartheck he surged forward on the offensive, thrusting and striking at his foe's weakened side. Blood was leaking down his opponent's leg. His strength there was lost. With a series of twirling slashes and cuts he had Rackar's blade tumbling from his clammy fingers, disarming him. He could see the ghostly fear in the man's eyes, the pain and strain on his face. Lythian had seen that look a hundred times. It was the look of a man who knew he was about to die.

Lythian Lindar obliged him. Rackar tried to pull a dagger, but the Varin Knight cut down at his wrist, slashing through flesh and bone. Only a few spare threads of skin and sinew remained, his hand hanging loose, blood pouring from the stump. An ear-piercing shriek erupted from Rackar's lips, until Lythian swung sideways and cut his throat. His wail withered to a ugly choke as he raised his good hand to his neck, flailing backward as blood wormed out between his fingers.

"Lythian!"

He didn't know who gave the call - Talasha or Cevi or Mirella - but it was enough to warn him. He ducked on instinct and performed a sideward roll, body splashing in the rain and mud, and sprung right back to his feet. Kartheck was right behind him, on the hunt. Across the yard Ashun Klo had Pagaloth cornered at a broken section of wall, a dragonsteel blade in each hand. The dragonknight was defending fiercely, though looked to be tiring.

Kartheck was stalking forward, his eyes black and greedy. He'd been a soldier in the war, earning those tattoos around his eyes for the men he'd killed in battle. Since then he'd turned sellsword and assassin, and had more tattoos for those too. A Varin Knight would make a fine addition, Lythian did not doubt. Godsteel or no, he'd boast forever of how he'd slain the Knight of the Vale in single combat. It was written all across his gaunt face, in that glimmer in his eyes as he swerved left and right, in the eager shape of his mouth, hanging half open, tongue licking across his small sharp teeth.

He lurked forward, drawing into his spare hand a long cruel dagger. His motion was odd, crouching up and down on his legs like a bobbing cork, swaying side to side as though trying to confuse him. It was not a fighting style he'd seen, one learned and adapted during his years stalking alleys, striking from the shadows. Lythian's posture was the opposite; fixed and upright and noble, sword out before him, watching carefully with his light golden eyes.

Suddenly, a blaze of lightning struck down from the black skies, and Kartheck took his chance. It was as though he'd been waiting for it. Through the deluge he sprung forward, cutting down from on high. Lythian saw him in time, slipped sideways, blocking. Kartheck swivelled on landing, slashing low. Lythian parried. He drew a step back, making room. His sword was the longer. Kartheck felt dangerous up close, striking quick as a viper. He changed the angle of his strikes irregularly, using his flexibility to dart low and swing high in a fury of straight and diagonal cuts.

Lythian dealt with them all. Yet the fever was telling. He'd been restoring his strength these last few days, yet the embers of his illness were still with him, burning low in his lungs and chest. Kartheck knew it. He grinned as he came again, darting in and darting out, keeping from Lythian's reach. Then suddenly he changed stance, fighting as a traditional swordsman, upright and split-legged, fencing with skill. Lythian held his surprise. He parried and blocked and went on the offensive. The duel took on a more typical frame, yet only for a dozen strikes or so. Then Kartheck was crouching again, spinning around a portion of broken wall and out of sight. Lythian lost him in the darkness. He'd been drawn some way across the old yard, into the gloom beyond the light of the nearest brazier.

Kartheck's territory.

He made to withdraw but his foe came exploding from the fogs to his right. Lythian whooshed around to face him. Kartheck rushed up and over a low pile of rubble, leaping. Lightning flashed. His curved kilij came down. Lythian swung to block, his blade horizontal, but the force of Kartheck's weight and blow had him stumbling back. The stone was loose underfoot, slippery with moss. For a split second Lythian's footing was gone. Kartheck was looming, his scimitar raised to strike. His arm swung down. Lythian had no defence.

A twang of string sounded across the yard. The arrow caught Kartheck clean in the shoulder, punching through his black mail and leather. The cutthroat's swing faltered. Lythian righted his footing and sured his balance. He caught a glimpse of Talasha, bow to hand, nocking another arrow. The Knight of Varin took his chance, driving forward as Kartheck's lips split open into a monstrous snarl.

Kartheck scurried backward, trying to recompose himself, yet the arrow had struck his right shoulder, rendering his sword-arm limp. He tossed aside his dagger and swapped his scimitar to his left. Few men were as good with both. Kartheck wasn't one of them. His swings carried less venom and speed, his accuracy shot. Lythian drove him backward, cutting, slashing, thrusting. That look of fear crawled onto the cutthroats's face, the same look Rackar had had. Lythian drunk it in. He advanced step by step, strike by strike, metronomic, until at last he knocked Kartheck's blade aside and drove him to the ground.

"Yield," the man begged raggedly. "I yield." He held his palms up in supplication. "Your honour...your honour as a knight compels you to..."

Lythian struck his head from his shoulders in a great heaving swing. He spat on the corpse and turned.

The duel across the yard was ongoing. Lythian saw to his relief that Pagaloth was still standing, yet Ashun Klo was too. The pair seemed to have reached an impasse. Talasha had her bow aimed at them, yet could not get away a clean shot. Lythian rushed over. "Hold," he called to her. "You might hit Pagaloth."

He saw Cevi and Mirella still at Kin'rar's side, though they'd given up trying to save him. The handmaids were looking to the skies, fearful. Lythian heard the first *thwump* then, a familiar sound of beating wings. He looked up as a sleek grey shadow emerged from the blackness. "Cevi, Mirella, away!" he bellowed. The girls scrambled to their feet, stumbling and slipping as they ran back from Kin'rar's body. "Talasha! Pagaloth! Above you!"

Talasha gazed up. Sir Pagaloth didn't hear. Nor did Ashun. Their duel continued, the pair thrashing skilfully through the rains. Lythian ran to Talasha. "Get to safety. We don't know what she'll do!"

Neyruu might kill them all, he feared. They would have no defence against her, none. He gripped Talasha's bow and pulled it from her arms, flinging it aside, then did the same with his own blade. The dragon might not attack if they were undefended, he hoped. It was all they had. "Pagaloth! Above you!"

He didn't hear. Not above the clash of conflict, the crash of thunder, the clamour of the falling rains. Lythian could only watch as the great shadow of Neyruu loomed into view above them, her eyes aglow with something maddened and primal. A nearby brazier lit her underside, sparkling in a hundred hues, as her deadly taloned feet swung forward in landing. A last beat of her wide wings steadied her, a beat that blew a wave of air across Pagaloth and Ashun Klo, finally alerting them to her presence. Both men lowered their swords and turned.

"Pagaloth, get back!" Lythian roared. The dragonknight glanced over. He was panting hard, a sharp intensity in his eyes. "Retreat!"

Neyruu was looking at Kin'rar's body. Her eyes were molten amber shot with red. Slowly, surely, she spanned the yard with her gaze, taking in Lythian, Talasha, the handmaids in turn. She looked at Pagaloth in judgement. She saw the dead figures of Rackar and Kartheck. She sniffed the air, long and deep, and a heavy rumbling resonated from her chest.

Her eyes went to Ashun Klo.

He stood no more than a half dozen metres away, his blades held loose at his sides. Lythian thought he saw the man smile, as though to placate the beast. He thought he heard him whisper something. Ashun Klo was of an old highborn line; there was Fireborn blood in him, the blood of Eldur. His lips moved soundlessly, and he dared take a step forward. Neyruu stared down. An amber light was beginning to glow at the heart of her chest. Ashun dropped one of his blades, reached out, went to a knee. Smoke began to swirl from Neyruu's nostrils. Her mouth opened into rows of fierce white teeth. She smelt it, the blood on Ashun's blade. Kin'rar's blood. *Her* blood.

Ashun knew it too. He began to nod, lowering his hand. *I'm sorry,* that gesture said. *I'm sorry for what I've done.* He lifted his chin, slid his second blade back into its sheath. He faced his end bravely, Lythian would admit that at least. And when Neyruu opened her mouth and let out that great spout of molten flame, Ashun Klo made not a sound.

All went quiet and still, but for the wash of the rain, the crackle of burning leather and flesh as Ashun slumped to the ground, wreathed in crimson fire. Pagaloth shaded back in retreat, never taking his eyes off the beast. Talasha stood where she was, at Lythian's side, tearful. "She is heartbroken," the princess whispered. "A part of her has gone dark, forever."

Lythian nodded solemnly as the dragon swung her frame toward her dead rider. She moved forward, slow, almost delicate, her long neck stretching out to sniff at Kin'rar's body. There was something so gentle about her, something timid,, as she nudged at him, dropping her wing as though he might rise up and climb atop her as he had a thousand times before. Slowly, quietly, Pagaloth moved around to where Lythian and Talasha stood. "We should go," he whispered. "Leave her to mourn."

"Should we not wait," Lythian asked. "Should we not...try to bury him."

"Neyruu will cremate him, when she is ready," Sir Pagaloth said. He gestured to Cevi and Mirella. Silently, they crept to join them, until all five were huddled close.

Neyruu never looked at them as they slipped away, not once. She lay down beside Kin'rar's body, opening a wing to cover him from the rain. And that's how they left them. Two halves of the same soul, dragon and rider, lying together as one.

49

Janilah

The dawn broke cold and grim, the city choked in thick grey clouds and a heavy unending fall of snow. Janilah had hardly slept. Beneath the balcony on which he stood, the courtyard below had been erected with a gallows, with canopies set up to give cover from the snows for the guests come to watch Elyon Daecar die.

Yet not today.

Today there would be no execution, as hoped. By some miracle, the boy had escaped, breaking free of his cell in the dead of night. *There is something about that cell,* Janilah thought, a sour smile wrinkling his lips. First Ranulf Shackton had escaped it, and now Elyon Daecar had done the same. *And not without help.* Shackton had poor wretched Reggie Warren. And Elyon...

Behind him, the voice of Sir Fredrick Ruxmond rang out through the hall. "My king, your son is here."

My son, Janilah thought, flexing his fingers. *Elyon had my son.*

He turned slowly, and moved to take his throne, brushing loose flakes of snow from his broad shoulders as he sat. Sir Fredrick waited at the foot of the dais; Sir Owen and the brothers Hunt, Sir Maxwell and Sir Rees, stood sentinel the doors. The remainder of the Six - Sir Lewyn Huffort and Sir Kevyn Bolt - were out on the chase, scouring the paths beyond the palace in search of the boy, though already that felt hopeless. Janilah had been awoken in his bedchamber to the news two hours ago; Elyon Daecar had disappeared and a full dozen men beaten unconscious. Several had broken bones, one a fractured skull, and those who'd regained their wits had spoken of a single assailant, cloaked and cowled, despatching them in turn without so much as breaking a sweat.

A single assailant, Janilah thought, staring hard at the double doors. There were few men who could mete out such justice. Few men who knew where Elyon would be. Few men who could reach him. *Him,* he thought, scowling. *My son.* "Send him in."

The banded bronze doors opened to a great echoing groan. Beyond, the figure of Prince Rylian Lukar appeared, wrapped in supple leathers and a fur-trimmed umber cloak. All was silent but for his footsteps whispering on the stone as he paced between Sir Maxwell and Sir Rees, past the Oak of Armdall, across the marble floor to the foot of the steps.

Janilah watched him come, his eyes hard with displeasure. Cecilia stood beside his throne, all in dark green silks, a sly grin on her lips. And in his head, Janilah could hear her voice, whispering the same warning she'd whispered a hundred times. *He covets your throne, Father. More and more, he wants it.*

"Father." Rylian put himself into a precise but perfunctory bow. He had his godsteel longsword at his right hip, his dagger opposite, no armour, no plate, no mail.

"Rylian. You have something to say to me?"

His son nodded and went right into it. "I come to confess to you what you will consider a crime," he said. "I come to tell you that I let Elyon Daecar go."

Janilah gave no reaction. Silence settled on the room like the snows outside, cold and soundless.

"You know?" Rylian saw.

"I suspected," Janilah said. "You have shown how much you care for the boy. Much as you did his father."

"Much as I *do* his father. Amron Daecar is not yet dead, and nor should Elyon suffer that fate for a crime we both know he did not commit." Rylian glanced at Cecilia, a loveless look in his eye. "You, Sister, should be ashamed of yourself. People's lives are not yours to toy with."

Cecilia's only reply was to grin a little wider.

"It is you who should be ashamed of yourself, Rylian," Janilah said. "I relented with Robbert's betrothal to Lyriss Reynar. I permitted he marry the Daecar girl. I have given you concession after concession, and still you defy me, your father and your king. Elyon Daecar was *not yours to free*. You are *not* king here! I am!"

"And what sort of king are you, Father?" Rylian returned bitterly. "What sort of *man* have you become that you would stage this farce? That you would let a noble young Varin Knight and heir to a greathouse be hanged for something he did not do? Is it not enough that you had his father maimed and crippled, that you had his brother killed? Will your bloodlust not be satiated until all the Daecars are gone?"

"Guard your tongue," called a voice from the rear. "You speak to your king. Do not sully this sacred hall with your vile accusations."

Rylian's eyes were green fire. He turned sharply on Sir Owen Armdall, standing behind him in his glittery mail and mantle of green and brown and white. "Tell me to guard my tongue again, Armdall, and I'll have yours out."

Sir Owen smiled his disdain. "An empty threat. I am sworn to protect and serve your father. Only he can call me to judgement."

"And when I'm king, Sir Owen? What then?"

"You see, Father," hissed Cecilia. "He wants your throne, as I've told you. He and the Daecar boy seek to take the north for themselves."

Rylian spun to face her. "You silence that forked tongue of yours, Cecilia! Is this you? Is this your doing? Making our father into *this*." He threw a hand at Janilah.

"Into what, exactly, Brother?" She regarded Janilah with an adoring smile. "I see before me a great king, taking steps that must be taken in order to secure a full and lasting peace. I see a man who has put the realm before himself and his honour. I see a hero, that is what I see."

Janilah raised a hand to silence her. "What do you expect me to do with all this, Rylian? You defy me, you make marriage pacts and alliances behind my back, you speak of deposing me, of taking my throne. Is that what you want? Do you covet the crown as Cecilia says?"

"No, I do not. I have a war to win first."

First, he thought, and "First," Cecilia whispered. "Then you admit it," Janilah said, eyes narrowing. "You admit you plan to remove me once the war is done and won?"

Rylian shook his head, but he'd outed his intentions now. The Mistblade was whispering in Janilah's head, *kill him, kill him, kill your son, kill him.* The king gripped the stone arm of his chair, shut his eyes tight, turned his head aside. Those whispers were growing louder, louder, and the pumping in his chest growing stronger, stronger. He snatched a look out into the hall and saw the shadow of worry in his son's eyes. *Do not look at me like that,* he thought, as those fiery fingers scratched at his lungs, burning, as they reached to grip his heart, squeezing. He drew a sharp breath, as a sudden wave of dizziness came over him. "Cecilia...my wine. Fetch me my wine."

She dashed to the side table to fill his cup, pouring in his tonic, swirling. Rylian pressed forward. "Father, what is it?"

"Nothing," Janilah barked. He reached out a hand, grasping as Cecilia hurried back with his goblet. He took it in his grip and drank the contents down. Wine inked into his grey-brown beard, staining his tunic. Little by little he could feel the heat and pressure in his chest drain away, allowing him to breathe again, to think, as he blinked the mist from his eyes and looked clearly upon his son.

"You're unwell," Rylian said worriedly, climbing a step. Janilah held out a hand to stop him. "Father, you must tell me if you're ill. How long has this been going on?" He turned to Cecilia when Janilah gave no answer. "How long, Cecilia?"

There was a cast of concern in her eyes now. "Some weeks," she said, glancing at the king. "He has pains, in his chest. The tonic, it helps to..."

"*Silence*, Cecilia," Janilah commanded raggedly. "Did I give you leave to speak!"

Rylian climbed another step. "You cannot keep this to yourself, Father. The realm needs a healthy king, a strong king. If you're ill..."

"Then what? You'll take my place? As you've always wanted!"

"*As I've always wanted?* Father, listen to yourself. I have served you loyally all my life, never questioning your commands, never seeking to defy you. If you have sensed any rebellion in me of late then look in the mirror, and ask yourself *why*. These treacheries you have committed..."

"Were necessary!" Janilah roared. "Amron, Ellis, Godrin, every one of them was necessary! I *had* to secure the north, Rylian, don't you see? Amron would have stood in my way, you know that as well as I. He would have kept us disunited and that I couldn't allow."

"And Ellis? Why Ellis?" Rylian was searching his face. "Was it by your own hand that he died? Was it you who threw him from the balcony? Tell me true."

"Yes! Yes, it was me, is that what you want to hear? It was my judgement to make and my action to take. I took that burden on myself. I wasn't going to put it on anyone else's shoulders."

Rylian's frown deepened. He was shaking his head, struggling to understand. "But why? Ellis was weak, craven, already at your heel. Why kill him? I don't..."

"Because I need the blades! I need them, every one. I need them so I can combine them and win the War Eternal, bring peace to all the realm...north and south, Rylian, north *and* south. *I* hold the torch, *I* light the way. If I succeed in fulfilling King Galin's promise, I'll have a Table of my own, as Varin does. Peace *and* divinity, son, that is what I seek. That is what it has always been about."

Rylian was looking at him like he was a madman. He stared and said nothing but Janilah was glad, glad to finally reveal the truth, to tell his son the sum of it, consequences be damned. He'd wanted him to know. He'd wanted him at his side. But he knew he'd never have agreed to the things Janilah had needed to do. It had ripped this rift between them but now...*now maybe it can be mended?* he thought, in a sudden moment of hope. *Maybe he will see clearly what I've tried to do, what I've had to do? He will see that I'm not a tyrant, as they say. That I only mean to end the war and bring peace, create a new Table for all the Emerald Guards to go to when they die. He should understand that, shouldn't he? Of all people, my great champion should understand...*

"You're sick," Rylian whispered.

Janilah broke from his thoughts. He blinked and looked at his son. "My heart," he said, nodding. He could concede that; there was no hiding it now. "It has given me trouble recently, I will admit. I should have told you, Rylian, I know, but I...I didn't want to worry you. It is temporary, my physicians tell me. I need rest, that is all."

"I'm not talking about your heart, Father." Rylian's voice was dull but steady. There was a stiffness in his pose. His eyes moved about him, disquieted. "I shouldn't have come..." He took a step back. "I'll return when you're rested. We can...talk then."

Janilah sat still in his throne. "You think me mad?" His voice was ice.

Rylian smiled uneasily. He shifted back another pace. Sir Owen moved to block his path, Sir Maxwell and Sir Rees manning the doors. Sir Fredrick's right hand was clutched at the hilt of his blade, its pommel shaped to the head of a ram. Rylian's eyes went sharply from one to the next.

"You think me mad?" Janilah repeated.

All sound fled the air. Outside the snows were falling steadily, straight down through the windless skies. *Kill him,* someone said. Janilah flinched. It was the voice in his head, he realised, the voice he could no longer control. *Kill him. He wants your throne. Kill him. He'll take it.*

He shook his head. The voice sounded like Cecilia's somehow. He turned now to his daughter. She was looking right at him. There was something dark and dangerous in her eyes. He knew what she was thinking. *You just told him everything,* her eyes said. *You told him everything and he thinks you mad. What do you think he will do now? He covets your throne, Father. This will give him leave to take it. He will see it as his responsibility. He will see no other choice.*

"Rylian..." Janilah whispered the word. He linked eyes with his son, his firstborn, his heir, his champion. But not *his* anything anymore. "You have not answered my question."

"How do you expect me to answer, Father?"

"With the truth."

"The truth." Rylian shook his head solemnly. "I don't even know what the truth is anymore. You have kept so much hidden from him. You have pushed me aside."

"Because I had no choice. You would not have understood. Your honour would have blinded you to what I had to do."

"*Had* to do? Like killing kings. Attempting to assassinate Amron Daecar. Having his son, who was to marry my own daughter, murdered."

"Yes. All necessary evils, all stains on my honour, all matters I spared you from knowing."

"We have different opinions on what is necessary, Father. The realm is weaker without Amron Daecar standing guardian to all the north. You talk of unity and peace, but look at us. Vandar is split and on the verge of civil war over who has rights to the throne. The most powerful Bladeborn houses in Rasalan despise their new king, who now calls my daughter wife and queen. You think they will kneel to Amilia when they find out what you have done? And Hadrin? No. The Rasals will rip them out, root and stem, and install a worthy replacement of Thala's line. Already there is talk that Hadrin's cousins are plotting to overthrow him. You think Amilia will be safe in Thalan? Or any child she might bear?" He shook his head. "You have sewn disunity and strife with your plotting. Vandar, Rasalan, Tukor, all three kingdoms are fractured and broken."

"To be healed when the war is won," Janilah said. His voice was weak. His son was right. How could he deny anything he'd said? Much and more had spiralled beyond the designs of Janilah Lukar. Nothing had gone right of late, *nothing*. And now Elyon Daecar was beyond his clutches, soon to claim the Windblade, no doubt. Another Daecar. Another Blade of Vandar. Jonik. Vesryn. Elyon. *I had not the foresight to see,* he thought. And then, unbidden, he thought of King Godrin, laughing down at him from the Eternal Halls, or up from the Ocean Halls of Rasalan, or wherever the old prophet king might be. Either way, he was laughing, loud and true, to see his old rival blunder and fall, to see him lose his way so terribly.

"It pains me to see you like this, Father," Rylian was saying. Janilah looked up tiredly. There was a shame in his son's eyes now, a pity, a sadness. "What has made you into this? You speak of King Galin's promise? You speak of combining the Five Blades? These are bedtime stories told to children. How can you let them drive you?"

"They are not stories, Brother," broke in Cecilia. "Everything our father has spoken is the truth."

"I don't want to hear another word from you," Rylian told her, spiteful. "You've done enough damage as it is."

"I've done nothing but serve, as you have. And more so than you know."

Rylian gave that a curious snarl. "What does that mean?" he demanded.

Cecilia didn't answer immediately. It felt part of an act. Janilah regarded her. *What is her game now?* And then she said, "The Shadowknight is my son, and Amron's. I served our father by birthing him."

Rylian's eyes showed shock. His head went side to side. "No, that isn't true."

"It is true. Goodness, Rylian, you truly know nothing. Look at you, so innocent, so honourable; you can see why Father never included you. Even Vesryn Daecar was part of it. He was the one who brought me to his brother's tent. He helped slip the tonic into Amron's drink, so he'd think I was his dear beloved Kessia when I climbed atop him. I took his seed that night and took his son, and birthed him to be made a weapon. I did that for our father. I did that for the realm."

Rylian was staring directly at Janilah, a wild disbelieving look on his face. "Say it isn't true." His eyes blinked with rage. "You have plotted for this long? Even...even back during the war? *Twenty years*, Father! You've had this in mind for twenty years!"

"Longer," said Cecilia. "*Much* longer..."

Her voice was cut off by the sound of singing steel. Rylian's blade shimmered in the morning light, silver and green, misting. "Another word and I'll have you head! One more word, Cecilia!"

Cecilia tittered. "Such a silly..."

Rylian lunged at her. Cecilia spun back, around the side of the throne. Sir Fredrick was closest. He flew forward with his blade to block off the prince, who saw him out of the corner of his eye, and turned. A bellow erupted from his lips as he drove forward across the steps, Sir Fredrick parrying with a two-handed grip, left, right, left, right. The clash of steel rang out through the hall. Sir Owen surged in from behind, eager, Sir Rees Hunt a moment behind. Beyond, Sir Maxwell was still at the door, calling, "Sire, your command, sire? What should we do!" But Janilah's voice was gone. His mind was gone. He could only hear whispers. *Kill him, he wants your throne, kill him, kill him, kill him.*

"He needs to die," came another whisper. This one *was* Cecilia, hissing in his ear. She'd appeared at his side again, her own godsteel blade to grasp. Shadows were drawn across her face, twisting her features. "This is right, Father. Let it happen. Rylian is a threat now, a very real threat. He cannot be allowed to leave this room. He needs to die."

Janilah opened his mouth to shout, "*No!*", but nothing but a broken croak came out, unheard over the clang of steel, the scuff of feet, the grunting and bellowing as Sir Owen joined the fray, and Sir Rees followed in behind, and suddenly Rylian was battling three sworn swords, each armoured in mail and plate, each carrying dual godsteel blades. *No,* he thought again. "*NO,*" he tried to bellow, but the word got caught in his throat. He slid forward, made to stand, but his body was stripped of its strength, his heart thumping wildly. He crumbled to a knee, as Cecilia dashed away and returned with a fresh cup of wine. "For your heart," she said. "Drink."

Janilah hit the cup aside, lurched back to his feet. Red splashed across the white stone steps, the goblet clattering across the floor. Burning fingers gripped at his heart, twisting, squeezing, and he fell again to his knees, both knees this time, labouring to breathe. Cecilia sped off to fetch another cup. She was replaced in an instant by Sir Maxwell Hunt, who came rushing from the door. "Sire, do I stop this? Your orders, sire!"

Janilah looked up. His vision was blurred. He could see shapes, four of them, dancing through the throne room, moving in and out between the fluted pillars. *Kill him,* shouted the voice in his head. *Kill your son, kill your son.* "My son," Janilah gasped, one hand clutching at his chest, the other propped on the cold stone floor. *Kill your son, kill you son.* "Don't...don't..."

Sir Maxwell leaned in lower. "Sire, I cannot hear you, sire. Your son?"

Don't kill him, Janilah tried to say, but the first word caught in his mouth. The others came out clearly, "...kill him." And in his head the voice was shouting, laughing, *kill him, kill him, kill him.*

Sir Maxwell stood, a shadow cast on his face. Cecilia came rushing back, wine cup in hand. "I will tend him," she said to the knight. "Go. Help them, Sir Maxwell."

"My lady. Your father. He said...he said..."

"Kill him," Cecilia confirmed, with a single nod. "Kill him, your king commands it."

Sir Maxwell drew his blade and sped away.

After that it was all grunts and noise and the taste of spiced wine being poured into his mouth, as a heavy weight crushed down on Janilah's chest, as pain ripped up his left arm, his jaw, his neck and back and abdomen, as his head swam, dizzy, and his eyes fogged, and the whispers hissed and called out, laughing. Through all that he could make out movement, but little more, as bodies twisted and turned through the hall. He could sense the sharp agonised calls of men being cut and wounded. He could see the blur of bloodstains on the floor, red spattered on the marble pillars. He could feel a sudden wind blowing hard outside, snow dancing in through the balcony, white snowflakes glittering in the air.

He blinked and suddenly all went black. He blinked again and he was on his back, rolled there by Cecilia perhaps, who was still pouring wines and tonics through his lips, urging him to drink. He turned his eyes into the hall. Men were still fighting. One was down; he couldn't say who. another looked to be wounded, limping. He reached out with his right arm. "Rylian, my son. S...s...*stop*," he tried to say, but his voice was too weak.

"Shhhh," Cecilia said, stroking his forehead. "Be calm, Father. Be calm. It will pass."

He tried to sit up, tried to stand. The black void took him again and he crumbled to the floor.

When he awoke the next time it had grown quieter, yet still the clatter of battle went on. He could not say how much time had passed; ten seconds, twenty, a minute, two? Yet another figure was lying still, and now three were in battle. Hope flared in him. *Kill them,* he thought. *Kill them all, Rylian.* His head swam, and his eyes flickered again. He tried once more to sit up, but Cecilia urged him back down. The blackness took him once more.

When his eyes peeled open a final time, all was quiet and still. The stink of blood and iron was hot in the air, puddles and patches of red dotted across the floor. There were three bodies down now, three lying still, with another wounded it looked and another two figures standing above him. He blinked and looked up. Cecilia was there, speaking with...speaking with Sir Owen Armdall. Grief gripped at him. "Rylian," Janilah croaked. They looked down at their king. Janilah searched through his blurred vision and saw blood spattered across Sir Owen's rich mail armour, saw an intensity in his eyes, a grimace on his face. "My son..."

"Is gone," said Cecilia. Her voice was cold as ice, emotionless. She gestured uncaringly to a body in the hall. *Leather and fur,* Janilah saw. *No mail, no plate, no armour. No chance.* "As *you* commanded, Father."

My son, he thought, *my champion, my heir.* Tears welled in Janilah Lukar's eyes as they flickered and slid shut.

He prayed they would never reopen.

50

Jonik

Jonik sat at the desk in Captain Turner's cramped cabin, fighting the urge to fetch up the contents of his stomach as Invincible Iris rolled over the waves. Before him were a series of maps and scrolls, a small stack of books, some spare sheets of parchment, ink pots and quills. Not long ago the table had been mostly covered in empty bottles of rum, but Jonik had seen to tidying up. He couldn't abide a messy space. Growing up, he'd been taught to be neat, to be tidy. In his cold little room in the Shadowfort, a single item out of place would have meant the lash. *An orderly room is an orderly mind,* he remembered Shadowmaster Gerrin telling him. It was one of a hundred mantras drilled into him and his brethren once, to better control their thoughts.

Jonik turned his eyes over the map of the world laid out before him. He'd spent much time in here of late, discussing with the captain where best to make land when they reached the northern ports, so that they might disembark the patients. They had men and women from Vandar, Tukor, and Rasalan aboard, and wanted to get each of them as close to home as possible if they could. The planned itinerary would take them to Mudport in the Bay of Mourning, then to the larger ports and harbours along Whaler's Bay in the south of Rasalan. After that they intended to sail the Sibling Strait, north past Rockfall, and make final berth in Blackhearth. From there they'd strike out on foot and hoof to the Shadowfort, stripped down to only those willing and prepared to fight.

But do we have enough? Jonik wondered to himself, idly tapping the nip of a quill pen on the desk. He looked down the list he'd written. Some were for certain, others less so, the latter written with question marks after their names. *Too many question marks*, he thought. Though Vincent Rose had promised them the use of his sellswords, Jonik didn't trust the man to follow through. Far as he knew, he might just disembark at Mudport or Shellcrest or elsewhere and take Sansullio and his Sunshine Swords with him, and his two Bladeborn bodyguards, Harden and Kazil, too. Old Harden of the Ironmoors had shown himself less than fond of his employer, but still, Jonik wasn't going to bet that the old man would join them, not if Rose waved a pouch of coins in his face.

The biggest doubt was Sir Borrus Kanabar, though. The biggest doubt and the biggest loss, he knew, and by some considerable distance. Jonik had freed the Barrel Knight of his life debt to him now, and still felt sure that Borrus would wish to return his friend Sir Torvyn Blackshaw to the Riverlands when they made berth. That said, Sir Torvyn's strength was beginning to return, and he'd even called upon Jonik to thank him personally for freeing him from the pits. As with the others, his gratitude was profound. *Enough to have him swear his sword to me?* Jonik wondered. That was a conversation for another day.

Others were in for a certainty. Big Mo and Cabel had been clear in their intentions from the start. Sir Lenard Borrington was also willing to join them, as was Sir Corbray Walsh, and they had the Silent Suncoat too, all three of them travelling on the other ship. But still, those question marks...*Too many question marks.* If Jonik could somehow scrub each one of them out, he might, just might, have enough to make this work. But if Borrus and Sir Torvyn left, and Rose reneged on his deal and absconded with his men, then where would that leave them?

He looked down the sheet of names. Emeric Manfrey. Maurice. Cabel. Lenard Borrington. Corbray Walsh. The Silent Suncoat. *And me,* he thought. That was the sum of their guaranteed Bladeborn swords, though they had others too who could heft a blade if need be, even if it wasn't godsteel. Jack o' the Marsh. Young Devin. Brown Mouth Braxton. Soft Sid. Captain Turner had said he wasn't much of a swordsman, and Grim Pete was too craven for battle. Then there was old broken-toothed Benjy, and his companions Mugs and Trigger, all of whom could fight. *Bodies in a battle,* Jonik thought. That's all they'd be against Shadowknights and Shadowmasters. *It's Bladeborn we need,* he knew. *And I'm not sure we have enough.*

A groan sounded across the room as Captain Turner turned over in his bed. That was another thing to worry about, this malady that had been going around. The captain had been sick as a dog for some days now, along with half the ship. Borrus, Big Mo, Cabel and most of the Sunshine Swords aboard Invincible Iris had suffered from bouts of nausea, and this weather wasn't much helping.

Outside, the rain was lashing down hard, and the seas were rougher than they'd been in weeks. They were four nights out of Aram now and pushing up beyond the Solapian Channel, the Isles of Tellesh away to the east, the rugged Aramatian coastline just about visible to the west, shadowed by distance and the dark murky skies. Jonik searched through the window for One World, but Vincent Rose's ship was lost in the blackness. That was hardly ideal. The waves weren't so big as to sink them, he didn't think, but the winds were strong and blowing hard, and they could easily lose one another in this weather. If that happened, they'd be sailing solo, with no one to back them up should any more of the crew come down ill.

Turner groaned again, muttering in his sleep. With him laid low, old Benjy had taken the helm, and would be up there at the wheel now, guiding them through these stormy waters. He'd gotten sick of the same illness, he'd told Jonik, when hiding out in Sutrek some weeks ago. "We all did, m'lord," he'd said. "Me, Mugs, Trigger. Each of us got ill, one after the other. Nausea, fever, all that good stuff. Seems we're immune to it now, and thank the gods. Be no one to crew the ship, elsewise."

He wasn't far wrong. Soft Sid had been poorly too, though nowhere near as bad as Turner, and Grim Pete had been seen to be vomiting occasionally from up in the crow's nest, and was in no position to return there just yet.

I'd best get up there, Jonik thought. With the seas getting rougher, he'd need to be on hand to help tonight, he knew. He rose from his chair and made for the door, leaving Captain Turner to his fevered mumblings, stepping out into the dim light of the corridor beyond. The air was thick with the smell of damp and pestilence, little vomit stains here and there from those who didn't make it up onto deck in time. Jonik zigzagged through them, making a mental note to send someone down with a mop and bucket. Once that would have been Benjy but the old Rasal sellsword had more important matters to see to now.

He knocked on Sir Borrus Kanabar's door, peeked his head inside. "Sir Borrus?" The inside of the Barrel Knight's cabin was dark as death, windowless, perfumed with the scent of sweat and sick. He gripped his godsteel dagger and let his eyes drink in the available light, adjusting. On the small cabin bed, the Barrel Knight lay sleeping, breathing steadily beneath the blankets. He had a wooden bucket beside him, which he'd been making good use of, judging by the unpleasant aroma rising from its interior. Jonik decided not to disturb him. He slipped back out and shut the door, quiet as a mouse.

He moved next to the communal quarters, where the patients had been kept apart and quarantined such as they could. Most of them were travelling on One World, a ship cleaner, larger, and more appropriate for conveying the old, ill, and infirm, but some of the younger and healthier prisoners from the pits were kept here, along with the rest of the crew. Jonik scanned the beds and bunks. He'd once been crammed in here himself, when first sailing out of Green Harbour, before that kraken had attacked them and killed all but a few of the crew. Now he chose to sleep in the cargo hold with Shade.

"Cabel," he whispered, stepping to a raised bunk just off to the right. The communal quarters were long and low, with several beams and wooden supports creating partitions of sorts. The able men and sailors were kept to one side, the patients the other, where they might be tended. Jonik had tried his best to ensure that as few of them grew ill as possible, but there was only so much he could do. None had died yet, there was that at least. He wanted to keep it that way.

"Cabel," Jonik said again, prodding at him in the shoulder. He was turned away toward the wall.

"Yes...milord." Cabel turned feebly, the colour drained from his cheeks. Vomit was stained into the short black hairs of his chin.

"You seem worse," Jonik said, studying him. The young man hadn't been so poorly earlier. But that was how it seemed to work. The worst of the sickness could come on suddenly. "Can I count on you to help up top, if the weather worsens?"

Cabel nodded dutifully, though his dark eyes said 'no'. "I'll be there, if you need me," he croaked.

"My thanks. I'm hoping the weather will improve, but just in case..." He left the young man to sleep.

Next he went to Maurice, who occupied a floor space a little further down. The bunks and beds were too small for him, as they were for Sid, so he chose instead to bundle rags and wools on the planks, fashioning himself a mattress of sorts. Jonik knelt. The ship was creaking and groaning down here, wood twisting and bending as the ship went up and over the waves. On the other side, several of the patients were coughing in the dimness, as the healing maids fed them water, mopped their brows, and tended them with soothing words. "Maurice," Jonik whispered, gently shaking at the man's shoulder. He gave no reaction. "Mo," Jonik said, shaking a little harder.

The giant groaned, low and weary. His scarred face looked especially horrific in this light, the right side a ruin of mangled flesh from the morning star that had struck him there once, tearing away his ear and much of his cheek. "W...what?" he managed, his voice slurred from sleep.

"Just seeing how you are."

"Sleeping," said the big man. "Or was."

"And your stomach?"

"Is on fire. I feel like I'm going to shoot from both ends."

Jonik gave that a huffing laugh. "Try to get up top before you do. It smells bad enough down here as it is." He smiled. "I'm going to take the night shift above. If the weather worsens, I may call on you. How's the blade?"

"Helps," Maurice said. He had a huge godsteel greatsword lying beside him, the hilt clutched loosely between his fingers. Jonik had given both him and Cabel godsteel blades from his personal stores. They'd earned them for their service, and godsteel would help brace them against the worst of the illness, he hoped. It had certainly helped him. Without the Nightblade he'd be bedridden like Turner, most like.

"Good. When this pestilence passes, we'll get to training, hone our skills." He was excited to see what Maurice and Cabel could do, though if they were to train with godsteel, they'd need some godsteel armour, and that mightn't be so easy to come by. Otherwise it would be practice swords, as he used with Jack and Devin. Big Mo gave a queasy grunt and Jonik gripped his shoulder. "Sleep," he told him. "With luck the weather will calm."

He stood and looked around. He could see Grim Pete tucked up in his bunk, shivering and muttering in his sleep, like Turner. He'd grown worse over the course of the day as well. The Sunshine Swords aboard were scattered here and there, a couple sleeping, a couple more sitting against the wall with buckets between their knees, occasionally retching, just trying to get through the night. None were sailors. They could perform basic deckhand duties easily enough, but weren't experienced seamen and had little knowledge of sails and rigging. Soft Sid was absent; Jonik supposed he was on deck, taking orders from old Benjy, along with Mugs and Trigger, the only truly healthy sailors aboard. So long as the weather held, those should be enough to manage things. If it worsened, though...

Jonik left the communal quarters and headed for the deck. If it came to it, he'd rouse Captain Turner from his sleep, fever be damned, and have him return to man the helm. Grim too and Mo and Cabel, and that should be enough. As he walked down the creaking corridor, the ship went over another wave, causing him to reach out to steady himself. Jonik's sea legs were excellent now, even without godsteel to grasp. He shifted his footing as Invincible Iris straightened back out, marched toward the stairs, and up into the rains.

The howl of the wind blew hard and harsh in his ears, the rains spitting across the decks diagonally east to west. The skies above were clogged and black, no moonlight or starlight breaking through the swamp. About the ship, the waters churned chaotically, though it was nothing so bad as Jonik had seen before. White crested waves rose and collapsed, spindrift blowing across the deck. Jonik scanned for the remaining crew. He could see no one fore, no one on the main deck or up on the forecastle or rigging, no one manning the sails. The decks looked empty.

Then he saw the body.

It was lying face down, half hidden at the base of the mainmast, a huge heap of pale muscle and limbs that could only have been Soft Sid. Jonik sped across the deck to him, dropping swift to his knees. "Sid!" He gave him a shake, heaved him onto his back. The giant's eyes were fast shut, but his chest was moving steadily, up and down. "Sid, are you all right?"

He mustered no answer. Jonik saw the thin trickle of blood running off a shallow gash at the back his head, draining across the deck in a twisting red rivulet. Had he collapsed from his sickness? Hit his head when he fell? A more disquieting thought came to mind. Jonik stood, turned, and saw figures up on the quarterdeck, three shadows huddled at the wheel, watching. Old Benjy in the middle, Mugs and Trigger to his flanks. He gripped the hilt of the Nightblade, stormed up the steps to join them. "What the hell is going on?" he demanded, flinging a hand in the direction of Sid. "What happened to him?"

"Fell," said Mugs, standing a half foot taller than the others. "Ship lurched and he knocked his head on the mast, m'lord. We tried to move him but..."

"He's big," broke in Trigger. The youth had a neat-featured, plain face, a nervous manner. Or *did*. There was something different in his eyes now. Something calmer. Older.

"Was about to send someone down to tell you, m'lord," Mugs added. His piggish eyes gleamed, black as night, between his ample cheeks. He had round sloping shoulders, covered in a sopping wool cloak. Rain danced as it spattered against the top of his bald dome. "Need help to shift him."

Jonik knew Soft Sid. He knew how strong his legs were, how well balanced he was for a man of his great size. He'd lived all his life at sea and wasn't prone to tripping up or falling, not even in bad weather. During that storm in which the kraken had emerged from the deep, coming up from Daarl's Domain, Sid had been stable, Jonik recalled. Had the sickness weakened him, causing him to lose his footing? Jonik judged the three men before him suspiciously. Or had someone struck him?

He held his right hand beneath his cloak, fingers curled around the black haft of his blade. His eyes went to old Benjy, smiling that broken-tooth smile of his. "The gash is to the *back* of his head," Jonik said.

The old man shrugged. "Aye, he fell backward, m'lord. Slipped on the deck when the ship rocked, as Mugs says. Cracked his head and went down like a sack of spuds. Happened just moments ago."

It sounded plausible, and yet...and yet...Jonik glanced over the men. He'd been watching them more carefully of late, each and every one, and old Benjy most of all. Something had tickled at him. The way Shade had watched him, recoiling to the old man's touch. The way the girl Leshie had prodded and probed and provoked the man into unleashing those spiteful words. *Harlot*, he'd called her. *I hope the Patriots find you,* he'd said. Leshie had deserved it, there was some truth there, yet it was more than that. It was the way the man's lips pulled back into a snarl as he spat out those words. It was the suddenness of it. It was the dark bite to his voice...

And now this. Now this strange tension as he studied them. He turned his eyes down to their cloaks, hanging sodden from their shoulders. Each of them was wearing their swordbelt, he noticed, blades sheathed at their hips. "Why are you armed?" He shifted back another half pace, making room. Each had come to Vincent Rose's manor armed with old dinted blades, worn from use, but he'd not seen them wearing them since they'd left Sutrek. They were sailors here, not soldiers or sellswords. "Speak." He drew the Nightblade.

The three men exchanged glances, curiously calm. An age seemed to pass before Benjy said, "We saw a ship, off yonder, m'lord. Looked like pirates, we thought. Seemed best we arm ourselves should they try to board, what with them Sunshine Swords laid low, and the Bladeborn too."

"Why didn't you tell me?" The Nightblade fogged at Jonik's side, charcoal mists swirling about its edge like smoke rising from a blaze. Trigger was looking at it with a queer look in his eyes. *Old eyes,* Jonik thought again. *Dead eyes. Emotionless...*

"Didn't seem a need," Benjy said. "Was gone before we knew it."

"But you had time to fetch your swords."

"Aye, Mugs went off and got them. We'd have called for you if they'd come closer, to be sure."

Mugs nodded his round bald head. Trigger moved a hand into a pocket.

"Nothing sinister going on, m'lord," said Benjy. "Not sure there's any need to be drawing that blade of yours. Aint't we done enough to have earned your trust?"

More than enough, Jonik thought, and that was what made him suspicious. "Take Sid below," he ordered. "All three of you should be able to manage. I'll supervise."

"And leave the helm unmanned? Beggin' your pardon, m'lord, but that's madness in weather like this."

"Just do it," Jonik ordered.

He saw a slim smile crawl onto Benjy's face. Beyond, his teeth looked...different. Not so crooked and broken. Not so yellow and stained. And Mugs...Mug's wasn't so piggish anymore. His cheeks had thinned, jaw narrowed. Trigger was laughing, an icy sort of sound, like a cold winter wind gusting across the deck. He wasn't a nervous boy anymore. He wasn't a boy at all. Before Jonik's very eyes their features seemed to change and shift, as the illusion was peeled away, as their true faces came through.

And one face...one face he knew.

Jonik looked at old Benjy, his pulse quickening in its beat, adrenaline flooding his veins. "Gerrin," he said, his voice stiff in his throat. "You caught up with me at last."

Shadowmaster Gerrin didn't smile. He *never* smiled. Perhaps that's what had made his ruse as Benjy so effective, smiling all day long, with that mouthful of rotting teeth. But a facade, an illusion, and it was Trigger was the mage.

"You've led us on quite the merry chase, Jonik," Gerrin said. The grim face Jonik remembered was still emerging, those craggy lines about his eyes and mouth, the thin lips made for scowling, the humourless grey eyes. His voice stirred a thousand memories in Jonik's head, dark memories he'd tried to forget.

"Not so merry," growled Mugs. He drew out his blade as the rains flooded down, hard and heavy. It wasn't the dinted iron longsword he'd arrived at Rose's manor with, but a godsteel broadsword, misting a bluish grey, gleaming.

Jonik's eyes narrowed to look at it. "You got into my stocks," he said. "How did you find them?"

"With patience," said Shadowmaster Gerrin. "We just had to wait for the sickness to set in, so that we might search the ship undetected. Always suspected you'd have them hidden in the captain's quarters. I got in there last night, while Turner was sleeping." He looked over at the sword in Mugs' grip. "Fine blades, Jonik. I spoke to Lady Shark, over on Passway Key. She wasn't happy with you, nor Lord Manfrey, for killing her best men, and taking their arms. But don't worry, she'll not be coming after you. I...persuaded her to leave it be."

Jonik didn't care to ask how. Gerrin might have killed her, or not, but either way it didn't matter. Jonik had long forgotten about Lady Shark and those feckless Bladeborn sellswords of hers whom he and Emeric had slaughtered at the beach. He'd had much greater perils to worry about since then, with every cutthroat and assassin in the region trying to sniff him and his allies out, and the Patriots too, and the Shadow Order, who he always knew would catch up with him eventually.

And I always knew it would be you, Gerrin, he thought, looking at the closest thing he'd ever had to a father. The man who'd raised him, taught him, beaten and abused him, made him into what he was. The man who'd trained him in the forms, taught him the ways of the Nightblade, lied and lied and lied some more, twisted him, tortured him, yet was tender with him sometimes too...tender and warm, once in every long while, and that just made it worse. *It gave me a shred of humanity, where my brothers and kin had none,* Jonik thought. Should he thank Gerrin for that, or curse him? It didn't matter. He would kill him all the same.

As the rains came down, as the ship rode the waves, Jonik drank in the power of the Nightblade, and felt his form fade off to black. He watched the eyes of his master and adopted father, his teacher and torturer as he bled away into the night. Gerrin gave no reaction. There was no fear, no worry on his face. He just stood there, unafraid, as his former pupil receded into the shroud of night. A moment later, Jonik found out why.

Trigger pulled his hand from his pocket. His palm was closed around something, something that looked like *light* itself, glowing between his fingers, bright and blinding. Jonik raised a hand to shade his vision, and in that very moment, the sorcerer made a strange cackling sound and flung at Jonik a glittery powder, sparkles of starlight and firelight bursting through the air toward him, silver and scarlet and gleaming gold. Jonik drew back from the nebula of kaleidoscopic dust, but too late, the multi-coloured cloud enrobing him, embracing him, choking him, blinding him, sticking to his cloak and hair and skin.

"We see you," hissed the voice of the mage. "There's no hiding from us now."

Jonik backed away, stumbling across the quarterdeck, half blind.

He coughed and tried to call out, blinked and tried to see. Blurred shapes appeared, prowling toward him, left and right. "We see you," said that voice again, to the left. "I've been itching for this," said another voice, to the right. Neither was Gerrin's. Jonik could make out his outline moving behind them, following, watching, waiting, clad in black.

He reached the stair down onto the main deck, tripped, stumbled, clattered down. The wind was punched out of him as he juddered from step to step, landing heavy in a heap at the bottom. He gasped and scrambled back to his feet, blinking hard to clear his vision. Mugs and Trigger were following him down, Shadowmaster Gerrin behind.

He turned to face them, the Nightblade held out before him. "Another step," he wheezed. "One more step..."

"And what? Don't you see what this is, boy," growled Mugs, now gaunt of face and rough of voice. "No one escapes the Order. No one."

"We see you," cackled Trigger, his blue lips broken with purple veins, skin spotted and split and drooping from his bones. He looked grotesque, even through Jonik's blurred vision, the opposite of the boy he'd been, his back stooped and arms queerly twisted, a great black boil erupting from the side of his neck.

"Monster," he heard himself whisper, his voice catching in his throat from the strange dust the creature had conjured. It was some spawn of the old blood, Jonik did not doubt, like that Whisperer in Russet Ridge. "I took your brother's head, and I'll take yours too!"

The creature cackled louder. Mugs was first to the bottom of the steps. He was tall, rangy, lithe and long-limbed, and Jonik thought he recognised him now. *One of the older Shadowknights,* he thought. *The sort sent out to track down those like me.*

He blinked and backed away, his vision clearing, little by little. The mainmast loomed to his right, the steps to the forecastle behind him. If he could only circle around, dash below, he might be able to wake Sir Borrus and Big Mo and Cabel and the rest. But what help would they be in their state? All were sick, and that was the point. *They waited for their chance to get me alone, and here I am, at their mercy.*

Somehow the strange powder was sticking to him, illuminating his outline even when concealed by the Nightblade's power. He could see it sparkling on his arm as he drew back, a fine dust of dancing particles, beautiful and beguiling to behold. *But deadly to me.* He made to shift out of his cloak, but all of a sudden Mugs was on him, surging forward, swinging. Jonik saw him in time and parried, sidestepped, spun and took flight up the stairs to the forecastle. He felt his opponent hot on his heels, bearing down on him, swift and sticky as a shadow.

Jonik reached the centre of the deck. *My training yard,* he thought, turning. *Invisible or not, I can still best the three of you.* Mugs was right before him, the creature Trigger shambling up the opposite set of stairs. Gerrin followed, slow and methodical. "Do it yourself, coward!" Jonik called to him over the torrent. The winds were bawling, the skies breaking, thunder rumbling quietly in the far off world. "You raised me, trained me, tortured me, so kill me. *You.*" He pointed with the Nightblade. "This is your duty, Shadowmaster. Your burden. Yours!"

Gerrin nodded slowly, stepped forward, drew out the godsteel blade he'd stolen from Jonik's stores. He gave Mugs a glance and the man withdrew a step. The mangled form of Trigger shuffled closer, hissing. "Do you think that wise, Gerrin? You taught the boy everything he knows. What if he should best you?"

"Are you afraid, Parsivor?" Gerrin asked, looking to the twisted thing to his side. "You have performed your illusions, played your tricks. Now let me play mine. Jonik is no match for me."

"If you're sure," Parsivor said, grey skin hanging from his cheeks and chin in great loose folds.

"I'm sure. And we have Valtho as backup. Fear not, mage. All will be well."

Parsivor ran a dark red tongue over his blue and purple lips. His teeth looked rotted to the bleeding gums, face and figure disintegrating with each passing moment as he let the layers of illusion drip away. Jonik looked at him in disgust. "How many of these things are there in the Shadow Order?" he asked, recoiling. "We were never told. You never told me anything, Gerrin."

"I told you what you needed to know."

"You never told me who my father was. You never said it was he I was being sent out to kill."

"Because you didn't need to know. It would only have given you doubt."

"*His death will save the world,* you told me. How? Amron Daecar isn't even dead. Was that just another control? Another shackle around my neck?"

"It was true, in a fashion. Amron was standing in the way of something greater."

"And Aleron? What was he standing in the way of? He was my *brother*, Gerrin! And you wonder why I ran. You wonder why I turned."

"I don't wonder, Jonik," Gerrin said, in a voice as soft as he'd ever heard from him. "I know why you did it. I'd have done the same."

A frown fell over Jonik's eyes. He didn't miss the sideward glances that Parsivor and Valtho gave that comment, the questioning looks in their cold dark eyes. "Sympathy. You're trying to sympathise with me? Before you kill me..."

"I've no intention of killing you, son."

A throaty hiss cut through the sound of the rains. "What are you saying, Gerrin?" asked Parsivor, his flesh seeming to slough off his very bones. "We cannot take him alive."

"I can go below now," broke in the tall figure of Valtho. "Kill the rest of the Bladeborn. Kanabar and the others. We wouldn't need to play out our ruse any longer, Parsivor. We could keep the boy alive as Gerrin says. Return him to the council. To the *king*."

The old sorcerer gave Valtho a deadly look. "The Shadow King cares nothing for this boy. He has bigger concerns. We must kill him now and be done with it, Gerrin. Follow the plan, as agreed."

"And if it doesn't work?" questioned Valtho. "The Barrel Knight might sniff out the lie when he recovers. And Manfrey too, when the boats come back together. That one doesn't miss much."

"He missed us," declared the mage, smiling a bloody smile. "My illusions will hold until we make land in the north. We can take the Nightblade then. It will be neater that way."

Valtho gave a curt nod. "Gerrin, what do you say?"

The Shadowmaster was in quiet thought, looking straight out into the wet black world. Ten long heartbeats passed before he looked Jonik straight in the eye. "I hoped to be a better father to you, Jonik," he said, strangely. "I know you won't believe me, but I never wanted this. I was bound by service, by oath, and had no choice. There's much about my past that you do not know."

"What is this?" growled Valtho, taking a sharp step toward the shorter, older man. "You gone soft now, Gerrin? Now kill him or I will. Parsivor's right. Best be done with him now."

"It's our only chance," added Parsivor, with a haste in his voice. "My powder won't last forever. Already it's fading."

Jonik had noticed that too. He could sense the sparkling motes of light around him blinking out, one by one, and the burning in his eyes and throat was leeching away too. Gerrin still seemed unconcerned, unafraid. "I'm sorry, Jonik, for what I put you through. I know you'll never believe that, but it's true."

I don't believe it, thought Jonik, but he had no chance to say it. Valtho was turning on Gerrin now, anger flaring across his face. "You lost your wits, old man? Sentiment, is it? You raised him, you kill him. There're no friends in the Shadow Order." He looked down at Gerrin, hoping for a reaction. When he got none he shoved forward, closing in on Jonik.

"Stop," said Gerrin.

Valtho halted in place, turned back to face him. He judged him for a moment and then nodded his approval. "Knew you were still in there somewhere, Gerrin. Kill him now and this'll all be forgotten." He looked to the creature Parsivor, who nodded.

"Forgotten," he said, in a voice like a nightmare. "We can forgive a single slip up, Gerrin. Now kill the boy. And be quick about it. Valtho, stay close."

Gerrin faced Jonik again, his expression unreadable. Valtho loomed to the Shadowmaster's right flank, the creature Parsivor a step behind at his left. Jonik could feel the wind gusting through his sodden hair, chilling the back of his neck. The bow of the ship was just behind him. Beyond was empty sea, black and raging. A strike of lightning lit the distant skies.

"You ain't gonna do it, are you?" growled Valtho, as the moment stretched out into seconds, and those seconds became an age. "Parsivor, take note. He'll have to answer to the council for..."

Gerrin spun suddenly, swinging his blade up and through Valtho's face, splitting his chin and jaw in two. It opened like a cracked stone, blood seeping out through the breach, as Valtho slipped and stumbled back in surprise. Gerrin swung again in a sideward slash and Valtho's head went spinning off his shoulders, careening across the deck, his body teetering a moment before slumping to the ground. The old sorcerer was scrambling back, shrieking, wizened hands holding onto the bulwark for support as he moved for the stairs. Gerrin marched after him in cold pursuit. "I've always hated you, Parsivor," he said. "Come, put a curse on me, speak a spell." He pushed him in the back, and the creature fell to the floor, snapping an ankle on impact, yelping. "You can't, can you? Your power is spent."

The mage looked up, fear etched across his ancient eyes. He was almost that nervous boy again, eyes twitching here and there, a bony-fingered hand raised in feeble defence. "Why, Gerrin? Why?"

"Why? You ask me why?" Gerrin's voice was a cold black rage. He pressed the point of his stolen blade to the mage's throat. "Sickness, Parsivor. Your order is a sickness." He pressed, slow and true, as the godsteel sliced easily through the creature's neck. Blood as black as ink bubbled and boiled around the edges of the steel, fizzing and hissing as it spread out across the deck. "Sickness," he said again, in a low whisper, as he watched the darkness flee from the mage's eyes, watched the final layers of illusion wither and die, watched him crumble and collapse into a heap of rotten putrid flesh and bone at his feet. "*You* are a sickness. And so is your king."

Jonik watched, rooted in place, struck dumb by what he'd seen. Withdrawing his blade, Gerrin turned to face him. "I know you'll never trust me," he said, calmly. "And I know you want to kill me." He tossed the bloodied blade to Jonik's feet, the steel clattering dully on the rain-drenched deck. "I leave that up to you, Jonik. Do with me as you will."

A trick, Jonik could only think. *This...this must be a trick.* The ship was swaying now, threatening to spin on the waves as they sloshed and rose against the hull. Some might grow big enough to broadside them, turn them over. His thoughts went straight to his men below decks, to Captain Turner and Sir Borrus Kanabar and Grim Pete, to Soft Sid lying unconscious beside the mainmast, to the Sunshine Swords and sellswords and patients and maids aboard, whose lives were in his hands. "Return to the helm," he said, looking to Gerrin. "As you said, it would be madness to leave it unmanned in this weather."

Gerrin inclined his head. "As you wish, my lord."

Jonik watched carefully as Gerrin turned and moved aft to the quarterdeck. The glitter about him was fading now, his eyes sore but clearing, his heart thumping a heavy careful beat. He held the Nightblade fast in his grasp, yet let its power drain out of him.

A trick, he thought. *This is all an illusion.* He went first to Parsivor to make sure he - *it* - was truly dead, prodding with the Nightblade at the sunken heap of fabric and flesh and brittle bone his corpse had made. Jonik knew something of these creatures. It wasn't just age that ravaged them, but the dark magic they used, each spell another curse on their soul, scarring and desolating their physical forms. This one must have performed much horror in its time, Jonik judged, to have grown so foul. He prodded, poked, kicked at the creature until satisfied. *Dead,* he thought, though until the thing was cast over the side of the ship, he'd not be able to rest easy.

Valtho's mortality was easier to confirm. He lay on his back, a huge pool of crimson blood spread out from his severed neck. His head had made it across the forecastle deck, sitting upright against the starboard rail. His cold black eyes stared out blankly, chin and jaw, mouth and nose split clean in two. He was dead, to be sure. *But it's all a part of his plan,* Jonik told himself, looking over to find Gerrin manning the helm, steering them back on course. *A ploy to gain my trust.* This Shadowknight, this sorcerer...both were expendable. Gerrin's true master was Janilah, Jonik had come to see. *He will lure me home and lead me to the Warrior King's clutches. Better to kill him now.* He made his way to the wheel.

"You'd be wise to wake Captain Turner before you take my head, Jonik," Gerrin said. "I'm sure you didn't fail to note, that I just killed two of your remaining crew."

"Will the others recover?" Jonik asked, keeping his distance.

Gerrin nodded. "They'll be fine, in a day or two, now that Parsivor's dead. It might be wise to join up with Vincent Rose's ship and restock with a couple of your other men, else you'll find yourself shorthanded. These friends you've made, they seem to respect you. You're not the man who left the Shadowfort, all those months ago."

"Experience changes a man, Gerrin. I've been through much of late."

"So I've heard. It's been interesting watching you these last ten days, I will admit. Watching, and listening." He paused, turned his eyes to study him. "So you wish to return, I understand? To the Shadowfort. You wish to drive the darkness away." Gerrin spun the wheel a half turn to port. Jonik had never known he could sail or navigate a ship so well. He knew nothing about him, in fact, save the man he'd been in the Shadowfort. What life he'd led before then, if any, he'd never known.

"I wish to free them," he said stiffly. "Free young men from suffering as I did. At the hands of men like you."

"I was a servant as much as you, boy. Do you think I took pleasure in the role?"

"You seemed to, sometimes."

"Did I?" Gerrin's eyes flattened out. "Or are you misremembering? Are you forgetting the lenience I gave you? Are you forgetting the forbidden tenderness I showed?"

"I forget nothing. Those moments were fleeting. And they only made it harder."

"Then I apologise. I was tasked with a duty I never wanted, Jonik, as you were. These last months have opened my eyes, as they've opened yours. The world is changing, son. The shackles are coming off."

"Not fast enough. And don't call me son."

"As you wish. But know that you're the closest thing I've ever had to a son of my own. Know that I suffered as you have suffered, Jonik. Know that..."

"I don't want to know. I don't want anything from you, Gerrin." Jonik could hear the groans of a man down on the deck now. He turned; Sid was climbing back to his feet, steadying himself against the mainmast with one hand, rubbing at the back of his head with the other. It came back lacquered in blood. He frowned in slow dismay. "Sid," Jonik called out. The simple sailor turned to look up to him, a broad smile splitting his face. "Wake Captain Turner, and Sir Borrus Kanabar. Have them come to deck immediately." The dimwitted giant nodded his understanding and began lumbering toward the stairs. "Are you all right, Sid? The head? Is it OK?"

"OK, OK," the man said in booming tones. Then he frowned up at Gerrin, confused by the stranger at the wheel.

"Don't worry, it'll all be explained later," Jonik told him. "Captain Turner, Sir Borrus. Quickly now, Sid." The giant nodded again and staggered off.

"What do you intend to do with me?" Gerrin asked, in that steady voice of his.

Jonik didn't want to answer that question yet. "Was it you who hit him?"

The Shadowmaster shook his head. "Valtho. He needed to crack him hard to knock him out. That giant is made of rock and iron. Perhaps he knocked some wit into him?"

"Perhaps I'll let him have you," Jonik warned in a growl. "He and Maurice could use you for a tug-of-war, rip your arms clean from their sockets."

Gerrin gave a throaty laugh. "That would be a way to go. No less than I deserve."

"Then you admit to your crimes?"

"I admit to being a tool of people worse than me. I admit to performing horrors at the behest of evil men."

Jonik nodded slowly to that. He might have said those words himself. The seas seemed to be calming a shade, the frothing white waters reduced to a gentle churn, the winds blowing light and breezy, yet cold, colder than he expected so far to the south. Away to the west, the soft rumble of thunder rolled across the skies, and there, far out there, came the occasional flash of lightning, silver on black.

A quiet settled between them, before Sid came lurching back out with Turner and Borrus Kanabar behind him in a blare of puffing lungs and stamping feet. The captain looked sallow and shrunken in the cheek, yet there was a light in his eyes, as only a sea captain could have, when fearing for his ship in poor weather. "Lord," he said, looking up. "Sid, he..." A flaxen frown fell over his eyes. "Now who's this? What...what's been happening, lord?"

Jonik turned to Gerrin. "Sir Borrus, Captain Turner, Sid, I'd like to introduce you to Shadowmaster Gerrin, my former tutor. You knew him before as Benjy. His two companions are on the forecastle, dead."

A wave of bewilderment fanned across the faces of Kanabar and Turner. Soft Sid just looked up, smiling, then grimacing, as he rubbed at the back of his head.

"Mugs and Trigger," Turner eventually said. "Who...who, er, killed 'em, lord?"

"Gerrin did. Captain, are you well enough to resume at the helm?"

Turner looked to be having a hard time catching up. "If I must, aye. Might pass out at any minute, but..." He frowned again. "This is...this is Gerrin, you say? He of the Shadowfolk, who raised you a weapon?"

"Then why is his bloody head still attached to his shoulders?" Borrus Kanabar demanded grumpily, Red Wrath clutched in his fist.

Again, Jonik didn't know how to answer that. "I want him bound and gagged and tied up below, somewhere dark and wet would be best. I'll think about parting his head from his shoulders later. It's been...a long night, Sir Borrus."

"You're telling me. I've thrown up a half dozen times already."

"We can find somewhere cosy for him, down in Iris's guts," Captain Turner said. "Sid, you know the way." The giant nodded enthusiastically. "Fetch that rope there," Turner went on. "Best bind this one tight. Sid's good with his knots."

"Good," breathed the giant. "Good, yes, good."

The rope was thus fetched and Sid went to work, binding Shadowmaster Gerrin hand and foot so that he couldn't walk without shuffling. Turner went to take the wheel, as Jonik accompanied Gerrin below, Sid chaperoning him down and down and down some more into a forgotten storeroom deep in the belly of the boat, one that doubled as a brig for mutineers and troublemakers. It was just as Turner described, dark and damp, with an inch or two of saltwater sloshing about on the floor. "Tie him to the wall," Jonik said, and the giant obliged, fastening the prisoner into an extra set of rusty chains.

"You're thorough," Gerrin said, with iron and rope around his ankles and wrists. A squeak sounded in the air, thin and sharp, as a rat scuttled away into a small hole in the skirting. "At least I'll have company."

"Save your quips," Jonik told him. "I'm sure the dark won't trouble you, Gerrin. You're used to it, after all."

He left him there, Sid shutting and barring the door, plunging the cell into complete and total darkness. Jonik didn't deign to give his former master a final look. He turned abruptly and returned to the top deck, stopping Sid a moment to inspect the cut in the back of his head. The giant had to go to a knee for Jonik to get a proper look. "That looks nasty," he said. "You should go below, see one of the healing maids. She'll sew you up, Sid."

"Sew," huffed the giant, nodding. "Yes, sew, sew."

Jonik continued back out into the wind and the rain. He found Sir Borrus on the forecastle, contemplating the two corpses. "Gerrin did this, you say?" the burly man asked, seeing Jonik approach.

Jonik nodded. "I will say, I did not see it coming," he told the Barrel Knight. *A sickness,* he thought, looking down at Parsivor's foul broken body. *You are a sickness,* Gerrin had said. *And so is your king.* He gave the creature a little kick. "This one was a dark mage. In truth I'd be dead if it wasn't for Gerrin."

"A trick," Sir Borrus intoned, echoing Jonik's thoughts. "He means to weasel his way back into your trust. You should kill him now, Jonik. I'll do it, if it's too close to home. Makes no matter to me. And I've still got that life debt to honour, whatever you say."

"I may hold you to that, Sir Borrus," Jonik said, managing a smile. *But will I? Can I condemn him after what he did, what he said? Lies and lies and lies,* he thought. How to find the truth amidst them? It wouldn't be an easy task, he knew, but for the time being, he could make use of his former master.

You are a sickness. And so is your king.

The Shadow King, Jonik thought. *And Gerrin has the information I need.*

51

Amron

Amron Daecar was losing track of time. *How many days?* he wondered. *How many long hours in this strange eerie place?* He scrambled across the loose stone of the hillside, the grey mists swirling and eddying about him. For the first day or two Amron had tried to be silent as a spider, but no longer did he care for all that. Too long in this land had emptied him of his years. And *empty* was the word. He'd seen no sight or sound of a bird or beast in days. No strange creatures. No monsters of the like the Snowskins had warned. It was dead and desolate, devoid of life. *Because what sort of animal would want to live in a place like this?*

The hill was steep and growing steeper, yet not far away, Amron could see the glow of sunlight burning in the skies above. It urged him onward, around a scarp of rock, past a field of scree and small thicket of pines. He liked to feel the sun on his face every day, if he could, though the window was always short. About thirty minutes, he judged, for him to find some high place and bask in the sunny glow, and plot his path onward through this misted land, for all the good it would do.

Another five minutes of precious sun-time passed before he finally emerged beyond the blanket of fog, clambering onto a shallow hilltop that gave ranging views of the soupy lands around him. He tried to camp out in such places, if he could, though that wasn't always possible. There were many high points here, many hills and stumpy mountains, peaks and prominences, yet most had proven impassable. If he could see properly, he might be able to plot a route, but there was a thing about these mists - they made visibility rather poor. Half the time he found himself having to turn back when he reached a cliff he couldn't climb, or came suddenly upon a great forest or lake that he'd never known was there, forcing him to divert his route.

He found a comfortable looking stone and sat down, performing his daily routine. Food came first. He had packed ample provisions, thankfully, though already his sack was feeling concerningly light. Still, he had enough for now; salted meats and cheese, both courtesy of the greatyaks, hard black bread, a good ration of nuts. As he ate he tried to pick out landmarks on the horizon, orienting himself. It had never been his strength. Amron Daecar was no navigator or quartermaster; those duties he'd always left to other men. His was to lead, to rule, to fight. It was another lesson in humility to find himself so hopelessly exposed, so glaringly out of his depth.

"And perhaps that's why I'm so utterly lost," he muttered to himself. He did that too, to fill the silence. The talking made him feel half-mad, but it helped, because the quiet was unnerving at times. He missed the whisper and rustle of trees and grasses. The caws of birds and buzzing of bees. The myriad sounds that insects made, chittering and chirping and squeaking all day long, especially during summer, and by the gods did he miss that too. *Warmth*. What he'd give to feel warm again, not just this fleeting glow as the sun broke out over the horizon for thirty minutes, but proper warmth, proper heat. "I might just go live in the south after all this," he said, laughing. "A few long decades on the Sunrise Isle might just thaw this cold from my bones."

He gnawed on a heel of hard black bread, looking out over the swampy mists. To the right, the lands rose much higher into a range of mountains that seemed to shallow further to the northeast. The coast was out that way, Amron knew, where the fabled Sea-King was said to have landed. He had veered toward it as much as he could, but it wasn't so easy as all that, with all these hills and ranges blocking his route, turning him left and right. He could only properly navigate by the stars when he climbed up onto these elevated peaks, and reaching them hadn't been so easy as he'd hoped. The forests, lakes, steep slopes and valleys, cliffs and ridges and all else in between had gotten in the way. Only during these rare moments could he see clearly. When he went back down into the soup, he was walking blind.

"So much for Wagga's advice," he grumbled, chewing to moisten his bread, as the sun reached its pitifully low apex and began into its quick descent. Wagga the White had been adamant he make use of the higher ground to get his bearings. Wise counsel in theory but not so much in practice. Up here, Amron could plot his route well enough, but as soon as he plunged back into the mire, well, it was only too easy to get lost again.

He sighed, forlorn. "I should have let Whitebeard come with me after all." Amron was starting to see how the Snowskin heroes and legends of the past had never made it out of here. The tribesmen believed all had fallen to the mythical malice, or some other foul creature, battling heroically to the death as their stories and songs often said, but it seemed more likely to Amron that they'd simply gotten lost and starved to death. Water was plentiful, with all the streams and rivers and springs, but food was greatly more scarce than he'd expected. He'd come upon some fruiting trees, and had found the occasional animal track, suggesting deer and hare and other game did in fact live out here, but catching them...that was another matter. You'd need to be a trapper, he supposed, because hunting with bow and arrow would be impossible. "And you're not much of a trapper," he told himself. "Rogen is, but you're bloody well not. You might just die out here, you know."

He'd intended that as a jest to lighten his mood, but today it hit too close to home. He found himself thinking of Lillia and Elyon as the sun's light began to fade. He found himself wondering how they were, where they were, whether they would survive the coming war. He found himself wondering if he'd ever see them again. Whether he'd see Aleron first, and Kessia, and his father Gideon and mother Nadiya, who'd died when he was a boy. Many were awaiting him now, more than remained on this ephemeral plane. *Lythian*, he thought, *Borrus*. Both dear friends killed for his folly and hubris, last he knew. Others had been lost to him during the war, and since, too many others to count...

Would death be so bad? he had thought, more than once. Varin's scriptures taught that life was but a part of the journey that all men took, the fiercest, brightest, shortest part in which they sowed their seeds and did their deeds and wrote their legacies in sweat and blood. Life was but an antechamber, Varin wrote, an antechamber where all of life's beauties and brutalities played out. Battle through it and you'd make it into the hall beyond, the Eternal Halls where men gained access to chambers and rooms befitting their triumphs and attainments, where the fruits of their life's labours could be enjoyed for all time, where they might reap in death the seeds they sowed in life. Varin's Table was set aside for men of his order, the envy of every hall of the afterlife. *And have I not secured a vaunted seat?* Amron wondered. *Are they not waiting for me now, with open arms, eager to share in my stories and songs?*

And then his thoughts circled back once more to his daughter, and his son, who still had so much to live for, and suddenly he was on his feet, shoving his food back into his bag, slinging it onto his shoulders and shambling back down the hill.

"Follow your heart," he muttered, out loud, as he plunged back down into the dense grey mists. He'd been foolish enough to think that young Svaldar's advice would mean something. He'd been drawn into the mysticism of it, he knew, into the Snowfist's piety, as he had Walter's. But Vandar's Tomb had been an abject failure, and this...this was becoming something worse. He was alone, lost, his rations beginning to dwindle, and how long would it be for madness to set in? How long before he went the way of Bjorga Bonecrusher and Jonas the Giant and Ronja Ironmaid and all the rest? How long before he found himself truly swallowed by this endless blight, never to be seen again?

"Follow your heart," he said again, trying to inject some hope into his voice. He'd taken that to mean he should trust his instincts, and he had, but where had they gotten him? He'd searched high and low, through valleys and forests, over mountains and chasms and in caves and subterranean chambers where only the light of Whitebeard's godsteel blade might guide him. But still he'd covered a mere fraction of this place. He could be here years, decades even, without ranging the entire thing, vast as this tract of land was. How was he to find this malice? Just what was he to do?

"Just keep going," he told himself in answer. There was nothing else for it. He descended the slope.

At the base of the hill he came upon a sweeping valley with a wide river cutting through it, the chill icy water meandering slow and steady toward the northeast. Amron decided to stick to the banks, following it in the hope that it would lead him to the coast. The river was broad and shallow, it looked, with a bed of stones and the occasional boulder sitting imperious in the rush. On its far side, the shadow of a slope ascended toward a high sheer cliff. Near the banks where Amron walked, a thick and twisted forest of spruce and pine and black cottonwood blanketed the world, though how far it went, he couldn't say. The fogs seemed mildly thinner here, the movement of the water perhaps helping to circulate the air somehow. Or perhaps it was the wind that blew down through the valley, knifing through his clothes as he inched once more to the north. Whatever the cause, it was a welcome relief. "I was blind, but now I see," he said. He smiled and marched on, all but whistling a tune.

Some hours later, he saw the first splash in the water. All had been so tranquil and still that it almost made him jump. He stopped and peered into the river. Further upstream, the waters were disturbed again, and this time he saw the cause. A fish, salmon, it seemed to him, swimming upriver. They were known for it, in Rasalan especially, born with some inbuilt homing beacon that had them swimming upstream to spawn in the very place they were born. That usually happened earlier in the year, he knew. *Or later.* The year had surely turned by now, ticking into a new one.

It made no matter. He watched the river for a time, a strange sort of smile on his face, as the water broke and splashed elsewhere, and more sleek shapes could be seen darting over the stony bed, swimming industriously upstream. It made him question his earlier assertion that the fabled heroes must have starved out here. Stegra has said these lands had rivers that teemed with fish and it seemed that he was right.

And then he saw the shapes, emerging from the wood. Amron Daecar drew out his godsteel blade as several hulking brown bears came stalking out from the trees. One was further down from him, another behind, several more further off. They weren't so large as the ice bear Rogen Whitebeard had slain, not by half, but if they caught his scent and made to attack...

But none paid him any mind. It was the salmon they were after, Amron quickly realised. He could see more now, some six, seven, eight, nine of them, taking their places as the fish drove upstream. Some were growling and pawing at one another, fighting for the best spots. Those seemed to be on the elevated shelfs where the salmon would jump. Other bears merely crashed out into the water, leaping and pouncing. Juveniles, Amron supposed, not yet experienced or patient enough to know better. It made him think of all the pages and squires and young knights of his order, all fighting for fame and renown. One old bear was standing on a rock, perfectly still, perfectly calm. He waited, waited, waited some more, and when the first salmon leaped by him, he deftly plucked it from the air, ripping and feasting happily at its flesh.

Amron Daecar smiled at the sight. He felt an affinity with that old grizzled bear. "And I'm starting to understand the appeal of this place," he said, thinking of Stegra.

He turned downstream, and continued on, man and bear in harmony,

Where the valley began to narrow, the river grew wilder. There were more rapids, more little falls, and still the salmon were battling their way up. He decided it best to cross. On his side the woods were thick and foreboding, and running into a bear in there would not be quite so welcome.

He found a shallow crossing where he might ford, weaving between the bears who glanced at him curiously, as though they'd never seen a man before. Quite where all this wildlife had been until now, he couldn't say. Had he crossed a threshold of sorts? Passed some unseen border? Because it wasn't just the bears he saw now, but birds too, crows and ravens in the trees, geese and river ducks on the water, robins nesting in the branches, owls hooting their nightly calls. He even spotted some elk, drinking at the water's edge, and wolves too, which were a little more troubling, and even a huge great moose, gigantic antlers proudly spreading from its head, watching from a nearby clifftop, as though master of all he surveyed.

A curious place, he thought. *Curious indeed.*

Reaching the far side of the river, he continued along the eastern bank, the cliffs high and black to the right. Mist choked the ever-night air but it remained thin and gentle, less pervasive than before. At first they'd been swamp-heavy and still, so thick Amron could almost taste them, yet now they moved and swirled, dancing a rhythm, and at certain points he could even see through them, through little pockets opening overhead, right up into the starry skies above.

Follow your heart, he thought again. This was as close as he'd gotten to that so far. For the first time in days he felt like he was going the right way. He felt...he felt like something was compelling him along this route. "The river is a road," he whispered, taken by a strange urge, "leading me to where I need to go."

The rapids began to ease off again, the river slowing. Amron turned his eyes across to the far bank, where the trees gathered thick and close at the edge, shoulder to shoulder, watching. He gripped his godsteel dagger and searched through the night. The branches were lined with birds, he saw, dozens of them, hundreds, black-winged and black-beaked, black eyes following as he passed.

A shiver climbed up his spine. *I am not welcome here,* he thought. Then he saw the deer, and the elk, and the wolves and the bears, and white foxes, white hares, rabbits and rodents between them. All were watching him. All were still as stone, standing sentinel along the far bank. *This cannot be right. I'm seeing things.* He blinked and looked again. The animals were gone.

A prickle moved across Amron's flesh, a tingle tickling at the back of his neck. A quietness had fallen. He looked to the far bank again. *I must have dreamed it,* he thought. *Food. Perhaps that's it. I'm hungry and need to eat. I've been walking too long without rest...*

"I've been expecting you," said a voice.

Amron spun. It seemed to come from behind him, and in front, and from his left and right all at once. And above. He looked up. There was the shape and shadow of a man upon the cliff, looking down. He near stumbled back in fright, but when he looked again, the man was gone.

"What is this place?" he asked. His voice was choked now by a sudden, juddering fear. "Show yourself!"

Show yourself, echoed his voice, bouncing off the black cliff wall, fading away as it fled downriver, softer, softer. *Show yourself. Show yourself...*

And it seemed to come from the opposite bank too. From the ravens in the branches. *Show yourself,* they called as one. *Show yourself, show yourself.*

I'm hallucinating, Amron knew. There could be no other explanation. The cold and the mist, it was doing something to him, infecting him somehow. He turned downriver and continued marching, refusing to wilt or bow to his fears, to these queer manifestations of the mind. Through the corner of his eyes he could see the birds watching, but they weren't real, no, they couldn't be. Nor the bears there now, nor the wolves, nor the elk, nor the reindeer that had marched out from beneath the branches, all gazing at him as he passed. No, none were real. *None.* He dared look over to make certain, and sure enough, there was nothing there, no beasts on the banks, no birds in the branches. All was quiet and still.

"I need to find somewhere to rest," he told himself. He held his godsteel dagger before him, shimmering with a pale blue light. His hand was shivering, he saw. From the cold. That's all it was. *I'm not afraid. I'm not.* He hastened on, feet crunching on the thin film of ice developing between the pebbles. "And a fire, for warmth." He'd soaked himself to his thighs fording the river, and the chill was reaching through skin and flesh and bone. His right leg was beginning to ache horribly. He'd need dry wood for kindling, some leaves or moss or pine needles to get the blaze alight. "I can find them," he said. "The woods, they'll have what I need."

He looked across the water again toward the haunted snowy forest. Through a break in the mists moonlight was shining down, glimmering on the surface of the river. The water looked deep and dark here, too deep to cross, and strangely still, still as a millpond. Nothing moved. Nothing stirred. Amron blinked. The shadows and shapes were still in his eyes; bears, wolves, deer, elk, ravens in the trees. He felt them there, but every time he looked, they were gone. *What is this devilry, this malice?* He and Walter and Whitebeard had been stalked by a similar menace many weeks ago, down in that system of chasms not far from the Weeping Heights. A shadow with no face, that seemed to disappear every time they turned to face it. It had done them no harm but to unsettle them through those days, and the same was true here, he hoped, he prayed. *This is in my mind,* he knew for a certainty. *A trick in the air, some magic in these mists. I must leave this valley. I must leave this river.*

"But the river is a road," that voice said, that seemed to come from all around him, ahead and behind, above and below, outside and inside his very head. "And what do we do with roads when we don't know the way? We follow them. Follow it, Amron Daecar. Follow the road, follow..."

He followed.

He couldn't say for how long. He couldn't say how he got there. But when he came out of his trance he found himself in an arena of grey stone, tiers of seating cut into the rocks, cliffs rising up and up and up beyond them, high up into the black night skies. The mists floated softly in the air, wisps and curls as thin as flower petals, dancing. Amron turned to find that the river was gone. The trees were gone. The birds and the beasts were gone. The stadium of stone reminded him vaguely of the arena in Varinar, where his son...where his son had died. "Aleron," he whispered.

And "Father," he heard.

He turned to the heart of the arena. "*Aleron...*"

He was dressed in silver plate, layered and lobstered, Vallath's Ruin in his grasp, blue and silver and red. And red too was the colour of Aleron's neck, red the cleaved wound that cut deep through his throat. It wept blood when he spoke, crimson bubbles frothing with each word. "Father, why didn't you tell me?" asked his son; a wheezing, dying sound.

"I wanted to," Amron said desperately, moving forward. "I tried to..."

Liar, called a thousand voices from the tiers. The voices of Elyon and Lillia, Amara and Rikkard, of Vesryn and Lancel and Barnibus and Amilia. Amron found each of them amid the stands, dotted among all the dull and faceless shadows. They glared down at him, rebuking. *Liar*, they all said at once, and Elyon loudest of all. "I told you to tell him, Father. I told you to tell him who the Shadowknight was. I begged you tell him the risks."

"You killed him," said Amilia Lukar, the beautiful princess his son was to marry. "You killed my husband, who would have been father to my sons. You ruined my life. You did that. *You.*" She pointed a shaking finger at him, and wept.

"Is it true, Father?" came a sweet voice in the air. Amron found his daughter's eyes, so much like her mother's, innocent and pure. "Is it true he's your son, the Shadowknight? Is it true you betrayed our mother?"

"No. No, my sweet girl, no it isn't true."

Liar, they said together.

"It isn't a lie. I didn't know. I didn't."

Liar.

"I'm not lying!" He looked at his eldest son, blood gushing down his neck and into the sand at his feet. "Aleron, you must believe me. I would never...your mother...I would never have broken my oaths to her."

"What does it matter? I'm still dead, Father. I'm still dead because of you."

"I'm sorry." Amron fell to his knees. "I'm sorry, my boy, I didn't know, I didn't see..."

"*See*," Aleron broke in bitterly. "I'll never see you again. Not from where I'll be seated at Varin's Table. I was to be great, Father, as you are. I was to be First Blade. I was to be champion. And now I die as nothing. Amron's Echo," he said, in a hiss, and all through the crowds, the faceless shadows took up the call. *Amron's Echo. Amron's Echo.* "That's all I ever amounted to. That's all I'll ever be."

"Aleron..." Amron rose to his feet, staggered forward, but his son turned and walked away, leaving bloody footprints in the sand. "Aleron, please...please, don't go..."

Laughter sounded behind him. He spun and saw a spectre of Janilah Lukar, sitting in a throne of skull and bone. The dead piled up around him, corpses old and new, fresh and rotting. The Warrior King's bearded face was warped by shadow, eyes black and lifeless, yet his smile...his smile was like nothing Amron had ever seen before, twisted and maddened, his laughter a sound of dark thunder, cracking through the skies.

"You," Amron said, drawing out his godsteel blade. It wasn't Whitebeard's dagger any longer, but the Sword of Varinar, glowing gold. Amron's eyes widened to see it in his grasp.

Janilah stared at the golden blade, eager. "Yes, me," he said. "Bring it to me, Amron."

Amron surged forward at the throne of skull and bone, at the broad-shouldered king sitting in it, and swung, but all turned suddenly to dust and mist and air. A great wind swirled about him, spinning him around. When he regathered his feet he looked forward and saw a giant, with a huge great axe upon his back, skin the colour of milk, hair and beard of silky snow. The monster loomed, towering eight feet tall, punching his chest with his fist. "Jonas," he bellowed. "Jonas, Jonas!"

Jonas, Amron thought. *Jonas the Giant.* The giant charged.

Amron shifted his stance to Blockform as that huge great axe came swinging. He darted aside, ducked, and swung through the man's colossal legs. A voice echoed through his head. The voice of Kusto Crowbane. *Go for the legs,* he called out. *Always remember. Go for the legs.*

But when the Sword of Varinar reached the giant's legs, they turned to dust and mist, and suddenly that wind came again, that swirling vortex, spinning him around. He landed, the air stilling, and a new opponent stood before him, a tall fierce woman with dashes of red in her pale white hair. She bore in her hand a great spear of bone. She raised it to throw. "You are not worthy," called out Ronja Ironmaid.

Amron deflected the bone spear with a swift parry of his blade. "I am," he came back. "I am Amron Daecar."

"A cripple!" shrieked the woman. "I could not clear the mist. I could not claim the frost. *You* will not either!" Another bone-tipped spear materialised in her grasp. She threw, and threw, and threw again, five of them, ten, two dozen spears coming for him. Amron deflected them all, every last one. The warrior woman erupted in a shrill roar, and burst into shadow and dust, as the wind turned him again.

Who is this now? he wondered. *What is this cursed place of nightmares and terrors?* The faceless shapes still watched from the stands as a man with eyes of ice stepped forward. His hair was sheared short, jaw tight and clenched, body dressed in a mottled coat of pelts and furs from a hundred different beasts. "Iceheart," Amron said.

The legendary huntsman nodded. "No one leaves this place, Steel Lord. Not even you."

"This place? What is this place?"

"Death," said the hunter. He drew an ashwood bow from his shoulders, painted white, a quiver with a thousand arrows at his back. "Spears you can parry, but arrows?" His fingers reached behind him, plucking the first shaft. "There was never a better shot than me."

"Then why did you die out here?" Amron challenged.

Iceheart's pale lips were drawn in a line, his face impassive. "Everyone dies out here." He nocked the arrow and loosed.

The Sword of Varinar flashed, slicing the thin shaft in two. Iceheart reached again, five arrows in his grasp. He drew each to the string, pulled back, let fly. Amron's arm was lightning, left, right, up, down, diverting one, cutting another, blocking a third, weaving past the rest.

Iceheart smiled. "A hundred, then."

A hundred arrows came at him, singing through the mists. The shadows were watching from the stands, leaning forward, it seemed to him, hoping he'd get struck. *I will not,* Amron told himself. *I am worthy. I am.* The golden blade that had become a part of his arm for twenty years went side to side, flicking, tapping, knocking every dart away. Some hit the earth at his feet, shattering into pennons of wispy grey smoke. Others flew past his ears, whistling as they went. He was young again, strong again, as he'd not been in an age, it felt. A smile ripped across his bearded face, light shining in his silver-blue eyes. The thrill of the fight was in him.

The last arrow he blocked with the shard of Vandar's Heart he held, and it burst into a thin grey powder, a streamer of fog quickly falling. When he looked up, Iceheart was fading away, leaving nothing behind but a smile, and a whisper. "Good," he said. "Very good, Steel Lord."

The world spun again. The arena shifted, changing. He was on an open field, a hundred thousand bodies around him. Sunlight shone off armour and shields and swords. Battle cries rang out. Men on horseback and wolf-back and cat-back surged across the plains. Dragons screamed in the skies, shooting down great gouts of molten fire, orange and yellow and red. Before him loomed the greatest of them. Vallath, with Dulian atop him, young and noble, curly black hair blowing in the wind, rich red cape clasped at his shoulders. "We meet at last," the prince said, as he had that day at the Burning Rock. "I have yearned for this, Sir Amron. Too long have you run from my shadow."

"I never run," Amron said. His voice sounded younger in his ears, as it had been two decades gone by. He was wreathed in full plate armour, his Varin cloak billowing at his back, the great blade of his house in his grasp, which would win two new names that day. "A Knight of Varin does not run. Nor does a Daecar."

"Your house will wilt this day. First I will claim you, then your father." Dulian flicked his eyes west, far across the fields. "He is out there, somewhere, defending your king. I must end you quick, lest Lord Marak claim them first."

"I wish you luck, Prince of Agarath." Amron would not yield to the taunt, nor let himself be drawn to the goad.

"Luck I do not need. I have Vallath, who is Drulgar reborn. He will raze this field, and your armies, and your cities. You have sons, I understand, in Varinar? He will raze them too."

Amron bristled. He recalled that well. *Aleron*, he'd thought, who was just a young boy, *and Elyon*, a toddler, whom he'd not yet even met. The war had kept him busy, and Varinar was far. Kessia had asked to travel to camp with their sons, but he'd forbade it. He would not take the risk. Varinar was a fortress, built to withstand dragon attack, and the road was perilous. But those words from Dulian, they'd stung, cut deep. A fire had erupted within him. "I will kill this dragon of yours," he'd growled, "but not you. You I will let live, Prince Dulian, to fester in darkness and shame."

Dulian smiled, cold and handsome. "Then I extend you the same courtesy, Sir Amron. And wish you luck in the coming bout."

It was then, with all the world falling to chaos...with Lythian leading a host of Varin Knights nearby, and Borrus scything through the Agarathi horde...with Prince Rylian Lukar, bedecked in glimmering green plate, calling other Fireborn down to duel, and his Emerald Guards flinging their godsteel spears to the skies, and the Sunriders and Starriders surging, charging...it was then that Amron had taken the first step forward, toward the hulking mountain of scales and teeth before him. It was then that he'd won his greatest victory. And inflicted his greatest pain.

Liar, came those voices in union. Amron blinked and suddenly the dragon and prince were gone, the thousands of warriors were gone, the shields and spears and swords shining in the sun were gone, the field of dust and blood and death...all gone. The arena spread about him once more, cold and grey, rising beyond his sight, and now the thousands in the stands were many more, tens of thousands, hundreds of thousands, climbing to eternity.

Liar, they all said together. *Liar*, they chanted, and Amron knew what they meant. All the north called it mercy when he let Dulian live, a moment of great humanity in the face of a mortal enemy. They called his blade the Mercyblade and raised him onto their shoulders, a champion, a vision of honour and virtue with the strength of Varin and the wisdom of Ayrin, commanding and compassionate all at once.

Liar, he thought now, to himself. It had never been mercy that Amron showed the prince who would become king, the king who would go mad. Mad from grief and the torment of a stricken soul. Mad from the cruelty shown by a young knight, who would not finish him, even as he begged and pleaded for his end. A young knight who only smiled down at him with cold, pitiless eyes, remembering the taunts and threats the prince had made against his sons, to let him live in darkness and despair for all the rest of his days.

"It was cruelty that drove me that day, not mercy," he whispered. Yet ever since the north had said otherwise. The songs had said otherwise, and the stories and tales told at balls and banquets, feasts and festivals, and in every tavern and town, city and square from the Tidelands to the Stormy Sea. All had said otherwise. All had spread the lie.

Liar, whispered the voices innumerable. *Liar, liar, liar.*

Amron sunk to his knees. This was his hell, he was sure of it. To replay these moments in his life, these moments he'd always regretted. *Varin has forsaken me,* he thought, *as his master Vandar did. One denied me access to his tomb and the other condemns me to have no place at his Table. This is where I'll rest. In this place, for all time.*

He lowered his head away from the staring shapes and shadows. "I am not worthy," he said, in a whisper, and then louder, "I am not worthy," and then he stood up, and looked up, and shouted from the pits of his stomach, "I am not worthy...is that what you want to hear!"

The earth shook beneath him, violent and sudden, as it had at the mountain. A great rending of stone sounded, the breaking of the world, and at the far side of the arena split open a gaping fissure. Amron stood his ground, making no move to step aside. *I was wrong,* he thought. *I will not rest here.* He stared at the rift as it widened and came toward him, a void of light beyond black beneath, down and down and down, for all eternity. *The Long Abyss comes to take me.* And into that void, he fell.

Amron Daecar opened his eyes.

The sound of running water reached his ears, the gentle hooting of an owl, the swaying of branches and leaves in a breeze. He felt pebbles beneath him, and sand. *The riverbank,* he thought, looking up. He ached all over, his left arm stiff and frozen, right thigh of solid stone. With effort he scrambled to his feet, taking in the world. "A dream," he whispered. "It was...all a dream."

Yet the river was different here, widening into an estuary, and the cliffs to the right of him were gone, replaced by a wild and rugged strand and beyond, the open sea. He stared, uncomprehending. *How far did I walk? How far have I come?* A deep hunger churned in his gut, his lips dry and parched from thirst. The ocean was roaring distantly, waves breaking against the coast, floes of ice large and small filling the world beyond. Further out he saw icebergs, monstrous shadows rising from the darkness. And a light, a fierce white light, shining down on the beach.

He raised a hand against its glare. It burned bright as a fallen star, obscuring all around it. Curiosity drove him forward, his cloaked and weary form shambling across the stones and pebbles as crabs scuttled at his feet. To his right, a small thicket of trees sprouted from a patch of grassy earth. An owl was watching him, as those ravens had, and the bears and wolves and elk. "Is this real? Is this the truth now?" he asked the bird, half expecting an answer. The owl only cocked its head queerly, and gave a soft hoot. Amron continued toward the beach.

The light grew brighter as he approached. *I have tasted hell, but is this heaven? Is this my ascent to Varin's Table? Did I pass the test?* A nervousness filled him. He could take little more of these illusions. He breathed long and true, saturating his lungs with pure salty air, and then it came to him. *The mists...the mists are yet thinner here, thin to the point of being gone.* He looked back. They seemed to be retreating, dispersing. Words came to him, the words of the Sea-King's prophesy.

A lord of steel will come and drive the curse away. One great quest will fail, but one greater will light the way. Steel and snow will meet as enemies, but part as allies and friends. In this the frost shall be taken, and the lands grow clear to tend.

Light the way, he thought, staring at the white blaze ahead, ringed in a sparkling halo of frozen dust. *Can it be?* A shape gradually presented itself amid the otherworldly glow, the outline of a rock, sitting alone upon the beach. The white light was radiating from something embedded into it...something driven through its heart. He frowned. The air felt suddenly cold, colder than he'd ever felt before. His breath frosted before him, fogging as his lungs filled and emptied. He pushed on, step after painful step, through the cold, through the shroud, toward the boulder...

...and the blade rising from it.

So this is why I'm here, he thought in wonderment, his breath stilling as he reached the source. His fingers crept out from his cloak, reaching to the frozen hilt. Tentatively, they curled about the handle as a power at once alien and familiar bled into Amron's veins. *One great quest will fail, but one greater will light the way.* He looked at the glyphs, glowing white and silver, written down deep into the ancient godly steel. *This has been the reason for my coming all along. It was always about something...greater.*

With a look of great purpose cast upon his face, Amron Daecar summoned the last of his strength.

"In this the frost shall be taken," he whispered, and pulled the Frostblade from the stone.

52

Amara

The messenger wore a quilted riding jacket with a stiff high collar, sturdy breeches, leather boots laced up to the knee, and a pair of moleskin gloves. One of those gloves reached into a pocket and plucked out a letter. He reached out across the table and handed it to her. "For you, Lady Amara. From His Highness, the prince."

She swiftly inspected the seal. *Rylian's,* she saw at once. *And untampered with.* She broke it, removed the letter, ran her eyes swiftly over the words. Amara Daecar was not a woman prone to nerves, but this news she'd been hoping for for days. She let out a breath. "Good, oh good," she said, more relieved than she could possibly say. Elyon had been much in her thoughts of late, keeping her and Lillia and young Jovyn up all hours, worrying for his fate.

But I knew I could count on my princely cousin, she thought, reading Rylian's words again, to be absolutely sure. By his account, Elyon had been safely removed from Janilah's cells and deposited beyond the palace in the reliable care of Sirs Lancel and Barnibus, with ample supplies to see them safely through the mountains and into the realm of Vandar. Amara could not be more grateful. She had been loathe to leave Ilithor without being certain of Elyon's fate, but alas it had grown too dangerous for her to stay. Lillia would be protected by her betrothal to Prince Robbert, but not her. It had been prudent to leave the city before her sweet king cousin did something rash.

But all is well, she thought. Amara had a certain fondness for scheming, but was keenly aware that plots were like fruit, sweet and delicious...all until they spoiled. Her scheme to thieve the Windblade had almost turned rotten with Elyon's capture, but this...She smiled again, broadly. "Will you take a sip of wine," she asked the messenger. "You look like you could use one."

His eyes were bruised and weary, face windburnt, hair ragged and askew. Yet he shook his head. "My thanks, my lady, but no. I ought not stay."

"You're certain?" The door of the tavern was rattling on its hinges as the winds gusted hard outside. It had been overcast all through the day, the skies threatening rain, though as yet they'd not followed through with that promise. But a deluge was imminent, she had no doubt. "These are no conditions to set back out on the road," she told the rider. "And we have plenty of room here. Please, take a seat at least. You must be weary after riding so far."

"If it pleases you, my lady." The man drew back a chair and sat, joining Amara at the small circular table she occupied in one corner of the tavern. She had before her a platter of meats, breads, nuts and fruits, and a large flagon of wine. The flagon she'd attacked with gusto, the rest left largely untouched. Amara Daecar's preference for liquid dinners was well known.

"It would please me if you didn't stand on ceremony so," Amara said, as the man settled awkwardly into his seat. She could sense some doubt in him, and doubt was weakness. She much preferred direct and assertive action. She poured him a cup of wine. "Come, drink. I shall have a room prepared for you." She waved over the captain of her guard, who broke from his game of dice beside the hearth and came marching over at once. "Sir Connor, see a bedchamber prepared for our guest."

Sir Connor Crawfield was a sullen but dutiful man of thirty six, not unpleasant to look upon, with short tawny brown hair, pale blue eyes, and a large square jaw made perfectly for grinding. He had just missed out on selection for the Varin Knights in his younger days, to his eternal displeasure, and had been forced to satisfy himself instead with becoming captain of the Daecar household guard; a notable appointment in its own right, certainly, but not one that would permit him a hallowed place at Varin's Table. He bowed his head. "I believe the inn is at capacity, my lady. All private chambers are taken."

"Oh?" Amara hadn't realised that. "I do apologise," she told the messenger. "Perhaps a place here in the common room will serve? I know we seem a rowdy lot, but it will soon calm down in here, I assure you."

The weary rider looked through the room. Amara had some dozen of her own men here, as well as a larger host provisioned by Lord Kanabar, to see them safely back to Vandar and the safe comfort of Lord Brydon Amadar's keep. They had appropriated the entire tavern for the evening to give them privacy, paying the innkeeper generously for the pleasure, and as ever it was the Kanabar lot making most of the noise and merriment. The men of the Riverlands seemed to take after their lord in that fashion, drinking in great quantity and eating in similar measures. Many were broad of chest and equally so in the gut, strong stout men who fought as they feasted, with great alacrity. "I will pitch a tent somewhere outside," the messenger decided, studying the boisterous crowd. "I prefer the quiet of the empty road."

Amara shrugged. "As you wish," she said. "Sir Connor, do sit." She waved the letter. "We're celebrating."

"News of Sir Elyon?" asked the captain, seating himself. He didn't raise a smile. Sir Connor didn't have the necessary capacity for joy, Amara had long since decided.

"See for yourself." She handed him the note, and looked to the man who'd brought it. "I didn't get your name."

"Sir Roger of House Wayman, my lady."

"Ah yes, I recognise you now. One of Rylian's household knights." It made sense. Rylian wasn't like to send just anyone with such news. He needed a man he could trust.

"Just so, my lady."

"But not an Emerald Guard?" Amara inferred.

"No, my lady. I chose instead to serve the prince directly."

"Then you and Sir Connor have much in common. He chose to serve House Daecar, rather than join the Varin Knights. Isn't that so, Sir Connor?" She gave the captain a grin.

Sir Connor was unamused. "You know quite well that I had higher aspirations in my youth, Lady Amara."

Yes, and that was the point, she thought, laughing. Gloomy men were always more fun to tease, Amara had always thought, and there were few more glum than Sir Connor Crawfield. Perhaps that was why she liked him so much. Amara's tongue was like a sword; it needed to be kept sharp, and Sir Connor made for an excellent whetstone.

The captain handed back the note. "Fine news," he said. "I trust you know of the letter's contents, Sir Roger?"

"I was present when Prince Rylian wrote it," he confirmed. He was a plain-faced man, and young, no more than twenty-five by the look of him. Amara recalled his family name. The Waymans held lands here, east of the Hammersongs, down near the Vandarian border. Another reason why he was a shrewd selection on Rylian's part. "He returned straight to his solar after releasing Sir Elyon from his cell, put pen to parchment, and had me ride out at once," the knight explained. "He wanted me on my way before he visited with his father."

Sir Connor frowned. "He would confess directly to the king?"

"That was his intention, yes."

"Then he's a braver man than most," Amara chuckled. "I would dearly like to have been there for that, to see the look on Janilah's face."

"Quite," said Sir Roger. "I admit I'd expected to have caught up with you sooner, however, my lady. You left only a day ahead of me, I was told. At the pace I've been going..."

"We have been making some haste of our own," Amara said. "This is no leisurely ride we're on, Sir Roger. I have a wish to reach Ilivar in the shortest possible time."

"We have lost two horses already," Sir Connor complained grumpily. "I am all for riding hard through daylight, but not after dark, and especially not when there's cloud cover. It is far too hazardous for them. We'll be lucky if we reach Ilivar with any horses left at this rate."

"You exaggerate, Sir Connor. He's a natural worrier, as befits his duty. I'm sure you're the same, Sir Roger? Is it not required of you to worry for those you are sworn to protect?

"It is, my lady. I have served the prince near a decade now. I would gladly lay down my life for him and his."

"And does that loyalty extend to his father?" Amara wanted to know.

Sir Roger considered that, unsure of how to answer.

"This isn't a test, sir," Amara told him, laughing. "I'm sure you know my personal feelings for my king cousin. But if you don't, let me put it plainly. I hate him. I hate him with a deep and fiery passion. I hate him so much, in fact, that were we to hold a contest over who detests him the most, I would feel confident of coming out the victor. The Song of He or She Who Hates Janilah Lukar Most Fiercely, we could call it, though I daresay the competition would last for years, given how many people would wish to enter. Even so, I'd be right there until the end, and am starting to think that your prince might well be there too. So please, Sir Roger, don't worry about speaking openly. Every man here would happily put a stake through Janilah's cold black heart. Say you would too, and we'll welcome you with open arms."

All that seemed to confuse the poor young man even more. "I... well I'd not...I'd not want to kill him, my lady. He remains my king, and..."

"And you'd never stoop to such treachery, of course. That does you a service. But your loyalty is to Rylian, clearly, and not his father. You'd not have ridden all this way with news of the prince's defiance otherwise, would you? No, you'd have gone straight to Janilah and confessed of Rylian's crime. But here you are, proof of where your allegiances lie. That's all I needed to know."

She sipped her wine, sparing the man any further interrogations on the topic. "So, are you to join Rylian when he sails for the south? That is the word currently circulating, so far as I understand it. He's to take an armada to Eagle's Perch to try to win the fortress city. A bold move, if somewhat predictable. Eagle's Perch always seems to come in for a good sieging during these Renewals, successful or otherwise. It didn't go so well the last time, when Gideon Daecar tried to win the city. Not after that Moonrider turned up and drove them all back to their ships."

"Justo Nemati," said Sir Connor. "The Moonrider's name. He duelled Lord Gideon outside the city walls, a fierce battle, it's said. Lord Amron told me the bout ended by mutual agreement."

"He told me the very same," said Amara. "But of course the smallfolk say different in their songs, warbling on about some great victory for Gideon when in truth the bout ended in a stalemate. He lost the battle, though, seeing as Justo Nemati broke the siege. But that part never seems to make it into the songs. Curious, isn't it?"

"Not so curious, my lady,' Sir Connor intoned. "We don't like to sing of our failures in the north."

"Well we should. Failures are always more important than victories, Sir Connor. You learn a great deal more from them." She turned back to Sir Roger. "So? Are you to join Rylian when he sets sail, sir?"

"Regrettably no, my lady. The prince bid me return to the palace to watch over his lady wife."

Amara's face screwed up in pity. "Then I feel desperately sorry for you. The Lady Clarris is quite the wretched shrew, everyone knows. I'm sure you'd sooner risk life and limb on the field of battle than watch over that gorgon."

"I go where my prince most needs me," Sir Roger said politely.

Amara laughed. "Tactfully put, but the truth is in your eyes, young man. You mislike the Lady Clarris greatly, it's not so hard to surmise. I'm quite convinced that there's not a single soul in this world who feels any warmth at all toward Clarris Kastor. Not her husband, certainly, and her children seem to avoid her like the plague too, such as I've seen."

"Her brother seems fond of her," Sir Connor offered dourly, pouring himself an ale from a flagon on a side table.

"That doesn't count. I said there's not a *soul* in this world who feels any warmth for her. So you'd need to have a soul first, and that counts Cedrik Kastor out."

Roger Wayman's lips broke open at that. "Quite so, my lady," he said, with a chuckle. "His Highness is not fond of his brother-in-law either." He looked to the flagon of ale. "Might I have one, Sir Connor? I confess myself more drawn to beer than wine."

"Then you're both *proper* men," Amara declared, with no small measure of sarcasm.

Sir Connor poured and Sir Roger took a sip. His smile broadened a little. His was a kind face, Amara decided, not especially handsome, but pleasant in its way. "I recognise the brew. This is my father's own vintage, made not so far from here. They call it Wayman's Roast. My father always thought it his finest work, so decided to put his name to it."

"A lord and a brewer," said Amara. "Your father sounds a well-rounded man."

"Oh he is. A man of many interests. And well-rounded is the right term, my lady. He has grown quite portly in his dotage." He drank down his beer in several long swigs, relaxing into his seat. "You know, it's been some years since I've tasted it. I might just have another, if I may?"

"Have as many as you like, Sir Roger," said Amara. "Are you hungry?"

"Quite famished, if truth be told."

"Then enough of these courtesies. Eat. Drink. Be merry. And for goodness sake, sleep with us this evening. There's a rain coming, and a heavy one. There's no sense in you bedding down outside when it's warm and dry in here."

The young knight was breaking, she could see. "Many thanks for your kindness, Lady Amara. I suppose it would be rude were I to refuse you a second time."

"Most rude, yes. And rudeness is something I just cannot abide, as Sir Connor will tell you." She grinned and raised her cup. "Now a toast. To princes and heirs and the good they will do. To Rylian and Elyon."

"Rylian and Elyon," the knights echoed.

Amara supped down her wine and pushed to her feet. "Well then, all this wine...I have a need for the facilities." It was quite unladylike to openly admit such a thing, but what did she care? "Why don't you two get acquainted. And here's a challenge for you, Sir Roger, one all before you have failed at. Try to get Sir Connor to smile. Believe me, you'll have an easier time felling a dragon."

"I shall give it my best shot," Roger Wayman said, chuckling. "I have a sally or two in mind that might tickle at Sir Connor's humour."

"I daresay Sir Connor is not ticklish in that regard, but I wish you luck all the same."

She left Sir Roger to his gargantuan task, sliding between the tables toward the dark oaken bar. Sir Daryl Blunt was in conversation with the barkeep. He was Sir Connor's second-in-command and quartermaster, and vastly different of personality, as quick to laugh as he was to brawl. And that laugh...well, what a thing it was, a great swelling thunderous sound that could cross mountains and cities, Amara did not doubt. "You'll excuse the interruption," she said, butting in.

Sir Daryl's laughter trailed off. "My lady, is there something you need?" Strangely, his speaking voice was not half so impressive. Sir Daryl Blunt was a man of extremes, and that extended to his physical appearance, with a curiously round body and head and long skinny limbs. He looked like the sort of stick figure a child would draw.

"I'm just enquiring as to the location of the privy," she said, looking to the bartender. You never quite knew what you were going to get in a place like this. When staying in lordly castles and keeps, the facilities were mostly passable, but a lonely tavern off the open road was rather more of a lottery. Oft as not a chamberpot would have to suffice.

The innkeep pointed to the door. "Outside, m'lady. I fear it'll not be up to your usual standards, but tis the best we got 'ere. Though there're piss-pots in the rooms."

"Charmingly put, but I think I'll brave this privy first. Tell me it at least has a roof and four walls." She had a horrible image of a ditch with a plank over it, cut with a hole.

"There're walls, aye, and a roof. Tis a stone shed, really, just off to the right. Can't miss it."

"Would you like me to accompany you, Lady Amara?" asked Sir Daryl. "It's a terribly dark night out there, not a jot of moonlight. I'd not want you to trip or hurt yourself."

"I thank you for the thought, Sir Daryl, but no. I will take the risk of a twisted ankle to better preserve my decency."

"As you will." Sir Daryl looked over to the table she'd vacated. "This stranger. A messenger, is he?"

"One bearing news of Elyon," Amara told him, leaning in. "He's safe, Sir Daryl. Isn't that just wonderful?"

"Oh yes, wonderful...most wonderful, my lady." He truly sounded like he meant it, unlike Sir Connor. "Will we meet him, on our way back to Ilivar?"

"I would hope so, though who can say for sure? Elyon will be making for Dragon's Bane, though we might cross paths as we range west through the Riverlands."

"We can have outriders and scouts search ahead," Sir Daryl said. "These Kanabar men know their lands as well as a wife knows her husband's...well, you know what I mean. They'll track him down if anyone will. I will speak to Sir Mooton, see that it's arranged."

Sir Mooton was the largest of the entire Kanabar host, and its leader, near wide as he was tall, with a dense thicket of a beard and a neck as broad and muscular as any Amara had ever seen. He was a Blackshaw, a Bladeborn house as close as kin with the Kanabars, and a fierce warrior to hear Lord Wallis tell it. He was currently engaged in a drinking contest with several of his men, equally as fierce with goblet to grasp as godsteel, it seemed. "Perhaps wait until tomorrow," Amara suggested.

Sir Daryl unleashed that signature laugh. "Never interrupt a Riverlander when he's drinking," he said.

"Not unless you're intending to join," added Amara. A further gale of laughter blew through Sir Daryl's lips. "Now if you'll excuse me, I must confront this shed. Wish me luck, Sir Daryl. I feel I'm going to need it." She wrapped her sable cloak about herself and shouldered through the door.

A different type of gale greeted her outside, the winds howling loudly and a tad excitedly, she judged, as they swept down from the mountains to the west. The lands about the tavern were mostly flat and open, spotted with snow. Much of it was farm and pastureland, and across the road she could see a great white huddle of sheep, bracing against the wintry air. Were it clearer, she might be able to see the distant shadow of Tukor's Pass, the twin statues of the gods Vandar and Tukor soaring away into the soupy grey skies. But not tonight. The skies were dark as tar, heavy with cloud, and the air tasted of precipitation. Already she could feel the first little droplets beginning to fall. They were as stones that would start an avalanche. A torrent was close at hand, she knew.

She saw the shadow of her quarry to the right, the squat stone privy shed sitting lonely and forlorn some twenty metres distant from the main tavern. Some horses had been stabled in the space in between, enjoying the cover of a wooden awning that jutted out off the inn's southern wall. A pair of lanterns hung there, offering illumination. Amara walked past them, out into the blackness.

The reek of the privy met her almost immediately. "Good gods," she said, gasping and covering her mouth with a sleeve. She marched on wilfully all the same, reaching out and pulling open the creaking wooden door, hinges screaming. The stink was almost overpowering, the interior even more horrific than she'd expected. She gave it a quick scan. "No," she said to herself. "Absolutely not." Her chamberpot would have to do.

She turned back to the tavern, and gasped once more. A man was standing right before her, broad shouldered and all in black, cloaked and cowled. The rains started to fall, suddenly hard, suddenly heavy. Amara stumbled back, straight into the shed. She slipped on something she didn't want to think about and found herself sat down on the seat, just where she'd originally intended. "Stay back," she said, brandishing her finger as though it were a blade. "I have men inside, dozens of them. If I should scream..."

"I should like to hear that, Amara. I have missed your screams."

She frowned. Those words might have unsettled her, but that *voice*...She stared, trying to still her beating heart. "Vesryn? Is...is that you?"

He stepped forward, drawing away his hood. Her husband's lips were in a faint smile, hidden within a thickening beard, grey and black. His hair hung down, unwashed, and even through the stench of the shed she got a whiff of his odor. "You were always a loud lover, Amara," he said. "Those are the only screams of yours I ever want to hear." He reached out with a gloved hand. "Please. This is no place for us to reunite, my lady."

"I can stand by myself." She brushed his hand aside, took to her feet, barged straight out into the pouring rains. She took a pace away from him, then spun. "Bastard," she spat, stepping right back. He stood his ground, preparing for what would come next. "Bastard," she repeated, whipping her palm across his face. The connection was poor. She slapped him again, and better this time, though the twisting hairs of his beard offered too much protection for her liking.

He caught her wrist the third time. "Amara, enough. You'll only tire yourself."

She struggled to pull her hand free. He let go, and accepted a further flurry of attacks and insults. By the end she was puffing and panting.

"Are you done?" he asked, a red sting appearing on both cheeks.

"What are you doing here, Vesryn?" she demanded. The rains were falling ever harder, tumbling down as though the skies had broken open. "Do you have any idea how many people are looking for you? And *us*? If they find you here..."

"They've not found me yet, Amara."

"It's only a matter of time." She couldn't comprehend how he'd gotten here, so far west of where he'd disappeared. Harrowmoor was over a hundred leagues away, as the crow flies. That distance could be covered easily enough at any normal time, but with half the realm on the hunt for you? "How in the blazes did you cross the Sibling Strait?"

"At great cost, and under cover of night. I try not to travel by day unless I must."

"They told me you had Sunsilver with you." She looked around, but could see no sign of Vesryn's magnificent chestnut stallion. "Don't tell me you came all this way on foot. Don't tell me..." She saw the shadow of grief in his eyes. "Sunsilver, he isn't..."

"I told you there was a cost to crossing the strait, Amara. A merchant gave me passage in exchange for him. Discreetly, of course. I had no choice."

She knew how much he'd loved his horse. "It can't have been easy," she said.

"It was necessary. Sunsilver was too recognisable. A man can go unnoticed easily enough in cloak and hood, but a destrier of his size and colouring..." He shook his head. "I could not risk being spotted."

She nodded, studying his face, lit by the soft orange glow radiating from the lanterns hanging nearby. She'd heard a hundred rumours surrounding her husband's disappearance, some absurd, others frankly ridiculous, a few that were rather more believable. Over the last weeks, the ladies of Ilithor had probed relentlessly into the topic, but she'd given them nothing but brittle bones to chew on. *You're his wife, you must know something,* they would say, but she didn't, not really. She knew nothing of where Vesryn might have gone, or what he intended. *And for all those whispers that said he'd gone mad...*"You look well," was all she allowed, studying his eyes for some sign of his mania. "I mean, the stink is unspeakable and your hair and beard need a trim, but beyond that..."

He seemed to understand what she meant. "You were expecting someone more...unhinged?"

"I wasn't expecting anything. I knew you'd turn up sooner or later, but *here*?"

"A chance meeting, if you'll believe it," he said. "But a fateful one, I think. You can imagine my surprise when I turned my eyes through the window of the inn and saw you there." He drew forward a step. "I have missed you so, Amara."

She drew back. "Please, Vesryn, don't get too close. I'd not want to vomit all over you."

"I'm covered in worse, I'm sure." He was wearing his godsteel armour beneath his cloak, she could tell, and can't have taken it off in many long weeks. He took another step forward.

"*Don't*, Vesryn," she said, more sternly. She stared at him, long and hard. "Elyon told me what happened that night at Harrowmoor. He told me how you confessed your sins, your part in Janilah's treacheries."

Her husband stopped in place and nodded. "Sins of which I intend to make up, however much I can."

"Oh? I did not realise the Sword of Varinar had the power to bring people back from the dead."

"I did not know Aleron would die, Amara. I told Elyon as such. I told him..."

Amara raised a hand. She could see it in his eyes; he was about to tell her his full tale, plead his side of the story. She didn't want to hear it. She knew full well what had happened already and needed no repeat. "I have no time to lend you an ear, Vesryn. If I don't return soon, my men will come looking for me. You would do well to be gone when they do."

"I understand, and have no intention of joining your company, if that concerns you. It would only put you in danger, I know, to harbour a fugitive."

"We're near enough fugitives ourselves," she said to that. "I suppose you've been deaf to what has gone on of late, running and hiding as you are."

"Not entirely," he said. "I have kept abreast of the latest rumours, such as I can, eavesdropping in backwater inns and such. You can have no idea how much I wanted to come to Ilithor. To speak with Elyon, and you. To see Lillia again."

"Is that the only reason, sweet husband? To play happy families. I had hoped you would come too, in truth, but for blood, not for love."

"Janilah," Vesryn said.

"Yes Janilah," Amara agreed, and fiercely. "If you seek to make amends then you'd be wise to start there."

"I have considered it..."

"But you're too craven to see it done," Amara spat.

"No, my lady. Too wise. I don't know the White City half so well as you do, and would be cornered and caught for a certainty should I try to infiltrate the palace. How then would that serve our house, to give Janilah what he wants?" He opened his cloak to reveal the great golden sheath at his hip, emitting a soft glow of its own. "He wants it, as he wants them all. I'm not so foolish as to deliver it to his doorstep."

"Then perhaps you are in your right mind after all," she had to admit. Because there was much truth in what he said. He might cut through a hundred knights on the way to Janilah's door, but eventually he'd be overwhelmed. "Where then will you go?"

"West," he said at once. "There are others who have plotted the downfall of House Daecar. My purpose is to restore it, I am a dead man walking, Amara. But until my last breath, I'll work to make this right." He stepped toward her once more, and this time she didn't shrink back. For all his faults, she still loved the old fool. "I have one need of you, if you'll permit it." He looked down at her with a smile.

"If you ask for a kiss..."

"I would ask for more, but I'm certain I smell as bad as that privy."

"Worse, I assure you. What is it you need?"

"A horse," he told her. "I have walked a long way, running and hiding where I must, sleeping as little as I can. I confess myself weary, and have a long way yet to go. I cannot continue afoot forever."

"Can you not steal one? It would be low on your list of crimes, Vesryn."

"I did, some weeks ago, but the horse could not bear me long. I need a special-bred destrier, strong and able to convey a full-armoured Bladeborn knight at speed. I noticed that Sir Connor rides with you. He always had a fine sorrel..."

"And he'll keep that fine sorrel," Amara said sharply. "Connor Crawfield is miserable enough as it is without having his own horse stolen from under his nose. I'll not be party to that."

"I understand. There are others..."

"No." Amara found herself unwilling to support this. "I loved you, Vesryn...gods, maybe I still do, but I cannot allow you to take one of my men's horses. We've lost two already to broken legs and have a need to reach Ilivar as soon as possible. We cannot afford to lose another."

He nodded. "As you say. I will continue on foot for now." He smiled, looked to the inn. "Lillia. How is she?"

"Sleeping," she told him, afraid he might want to see her. They'd near enough raised her as their own daughter, with Amron so often away. She knew how much Vesryn loved her. "She's doing well otherwise, or will be when I speak to her in the morning. We've been waiting on word of Elyon."

"Word? What word? Has something happened to him?"

"Much, yes, though frankly I have little time or energy to tell you of it now. Let us just say he is safe, and will be making his way to Dragon's Bane to join Rikkard. You may hear troubling reports soon enough. Reports that will greatly anger our new King Godrik."

He gave her a searching look. "What have you done, Amara?"

"Me?" she said, all innocent. Then she decided to give up the facade. "Oh all right, I admit I've stirred the pot somewhat. We stole the Windblade from him, though made sure Godrik would point the finger at Janilah first. That won't last, not when men start seeing a certain Daecar soaring the skies. Alas Vandar is splitting in two, Vesryn. Lord Kanabar is adamant he put Amron on the throne. Elyon taking possession of the Windblade...that was only the start."

Something dark festered in Vesryn's eyes. "The Taynars have much to answer for. Consider me aligned in that purpose, Amara. Godrik will not sit the Steel Throne long."

She decided not to probe further, but his meaning was abundantly clear. *Treachery begets treachery,* she thought, *and kings are falling like flies.* "So Varinar," was all she said. "That's where you're headed."

"Rights must be wronged, Amara. I serve nothing but the honour of my house." He dipped his eyes to his hip, where the Sword of Varinar hung. "The blade has shown me the way. It has...corrected my course." He stared down to his side for a long moment, then lifted his eyes, blinking. He reached out, took her hand. "Tell Lillia I love her, will you? Tell her I'm sorry, for all I've done. And Elyon...when you see him next. I hate how we left it, but...I'm glad he knows the truth. And you, my lady. Too long have I lived a lie."

A lump rose in her throat. "Will I ever see you again?"

"I cannot say, my beautiful wife." He smiled sadly. "But a man can dream, can he not?"

And so can a woman, she thought, as her husband kissed the back of her palm and took a step back, receding into the darkness. She watched him go, letting the tears roll down her cheeks to join the rains. And behind her, a light blazed suddenly bright, and the noise of the tavern fogged out into the night.

"My lady?" called out Sir Daryl Blunt. "Lady Amara, are you all right?"

She turned. "Quite all right," she said, her voice half a croak.

He stepped out into the rains. "You're soaking, my lady. Please, get inside or you'll catch a chill. I wondered...you were taking a while, but..."

"But you didn't want to interrupt." She made herself smile. "I thank you for sparing me," she told him. "Sometimes it can take time for the bowels to move."

"Well yes," he said, laughing a little awkwardly. This was no sort of chat to be having with a noble lady. "I have the same problem...from time to time." He sped out, raised his cloak to cover her. "But come, let's get you warmed by the fire." He glanced away in the direction Vesryn had left. "Did I see someone with you? I could have sworn..."

"A local farmer," Amara lied. "He's out searching for his favourite sheep."

"Ah, well that explains it," Sir Daryl said generously. He glanced into the darkness again, frowning. "Come, come, I'll fetch some towels. The men are already celebrating, my lady. About Elyon. I swear to you, I even saw Sir Connor crack a smile."

"Then Sir Roger Wayman is a funnier man than I gave him credit for."

Yet when morning came, whatever shadow of a smile might have crossed Sir Connor's face was well and truly gone. She found him outside, looking at an empty space in the stables, more grim and grumpy than ever. "Brigand," he grunted, when Amara asked him what was wrong. He pointed to the empty stall. "Bastard stole my horse."

Amara Daecar could only smile.

EPILOGUE

The waves crashed against the rocky shore, blowing a soft salt spray across his tan leathery cheeks. Akar Vim watched those waves carefully through a set of old seamed eyes, searching for any flotsam washed ashore by the recent storms. This rugged length of beach was a treasure few knew about, yet Akar had learned the secret from his father, and he from his father before him, and ever since then he'd come down here after storms to see what riches might be found.

He scanned the strand and seas beyond. The storms had been queer of late, black and red and frightening to behold, and some in the village were proclaiming a return to the Days of Dread. Akar didn't believe in all that. He was a simple man of simple faiths who saw no merit in thinking that way. Talk of the Ire of Agarath, of the Last Renewal, of the stirring of the gods...he left all that to more pious men. Akar's trade was the sea, that was all he knew. It gave him bounty enough to satisfy his needs and those of his family, and for a man of modest means, that was all he cared for.

It was the getting here that was the problem, though. The beach was a two hour hike from his village down the coast, clustered at the base of a perilous cliff, and the climb down could be treacherous for those who didn't know the best way. And going back up, well, that was even harder, when his back was burdened by whatever treasures he might have found. Oft as not he'd come upon little of value, but sometimes there would be a trinket or jewel or gemstone of some sort he could sell, or a crate of unspoiled food, or weapons, yes, he'd found many swords and shields and harpoons before, from both fishing cogs and warships that had foundered in the waters.

But his wife told him he was getting too old for it. "You'll fall to your death one day soon, Akar," she would chastise in that haughty tone of hers, "and then what? You'd leave me behind a widow. Is that truly what you want?"

He wouldn't mind leaving her behind, if truth be told, though not as a widow. That would mean his death. He'd sooner be a widower. That wouldn't be so bad at all, in fact, because the cursed woman was always complaining. Calling him old and frail and stupid, condemning him for clambering up and down those cliffs. He was into his fifty sixth year now, not far from six decades deep into life, and had no intention of putting his feet up and retiring, oh no. Coming here gave him some respite from the woman, but it was more than that. It was about the mystery of what he might find, for Akar had always been a curious sort. Not every storm brought a wreckage ashore, no, but oft as not he found *something*.

You just never know what you'll find down here, he thought, turning his eyes over the beach. That was the thrill of it in the end. The excitement of the unknown.

Yet still. Not today, it looked. There were some old rotting planks and lengths of wood caught among the rocks, but those had been here for a while, and elsewhere snags of cloth and broken barrels and other worthless debris lay scattered across the beach. What he really wanted was sealed crates and casks, and bodies were good too. At first it used to turn his stomach to pick through the dead, all bloated and pale and putrid and crawling with crabs, but not anymore. They were the best places to find rings and bracelets and jewellery, after all, especially when a rich merchant or ship captain washed in on the tides.

No corpses today though, he thought, sighing, but perhaps that was a good thing? He tried not to think of who they once were, whether they were leaving wives and kids behind, as he searched them for valuables before leaving them to the crabs and carrion crows. It was easier that way, and he rarely came upon a corpse anyway, in truth. Most were taken by sharks before they got here, and sometimes those that came ashore had already been bitten to bits. He would search them all the same, but it was hardly pleasant work...

He turned westward, moving among the section of the beach where the rocks formed craggy tide pools. Sometimes he found smaller chests and crates in those, though today there were only cockles and crabs and urchins and snails taking up residence. All of those he could sell as well, of course, but that wasn't the reason he came. He was a treasure-hunter, he would tell himself, not a fishmonger. Only on the bad days did he make the ascent with a sackful of shellfish on his back.

A gull gave a sharp call, drawing his eye up toward the cliffs. Above him, high up and away to the west, he could make out the distant shadow of the great watchtower of Dragonwatch, black and grey stone soaring up into the cerulean sky at the top of a looming headland. He was too far away to see the soldiers up there, but knew they'd be standing sentry, watching the seas and twin islands of the Wings, away on the far horizon.

It was said the watchers had strange devices called telescopes that helped to enhance their vision, so they might better watch the dragons that lived on the islands. Akar had long since wished for one himself. *If I did, I could look down from the cliffs and search for treasure before making the climb*, he thought. He'd even travelled to Dragonwatch once to enquire as to whether he might buy one, but the soldiers had shooed him away as a parasite. "Never come here again," the guardsmen at the gate had told him bluntly. "Ours is a holy duty, old man. Come again and you'll be shot." He'd gestured to the bowmen up upon the wallwalk and Akar had beat a hasty retreat.

He'd misliked the men of Dragonwatch ever since, and often wondered if they could see him from all the way up there, picking through the wreckages down on the beach. Perhaps that's why they'd called him parasite? Had they seen him scavenging from the dead? That thought had worried him, and he'd decided not to return for a while for fear they'd put him in chains and whisk him off to some lightless dungeons. But they hadn't, and eventually he'd crept back to resume his treasure hunting. Because that's what he was. A treasure hunter, not a grave robber. He was quite adamant on that point to anyone who might ask.

He scowled up to the fortress, so high up there in the skies. The sentrymen of Dragonwatch thought themselves so noble, but what did they really do? So far as Akar could figure, their role was to watch over the Wings, counting wild dragon numbers as best they could, and alerting the Nest when one of them decided to fly away northeast to be bonded, or when strange occurrences took place out there. *Well what's so difficult about that,* he wondered, bitter. *I could do it just as well.* Indeed his own village was only a few miles southeast along the coast, and from there they could see well enough the scarlet storms and crimson lightning that has filled the world of late, hear the great crash and crackle of thunder as though Agarath himself was climbing free of the earth.

A few weeks ago, Akar had even seen a pair of dragons flying *toward* the Wings, he was sure. That day the storms had been so bad the earth had trembled, and half the village had crept out of their shacks to watch, as the other half hid away. Akar wanted the best view, though, so he climbed the hills away to the east and that was when he saw them, flying right overhead. One had been sleek and grey, he recalled, the other massive, with silver and blue scales. It made him wonder. There had been rumours from Eldurath that the Lord of the Nest had betrayed the new Agarathi king, and that dragon, blue and silver, it looked like Garlath the Grand, Lord Marak's beast. Did the men of Dragonwatch see them too? Somehow he doubted it, seeing how dark the skies had been that day. But was he going to hike there to report it? Oh no. Akar Vim would sooner die than help *those* men do their jobs.

He gave the watchtower a final sneering look, before turning back to the shore. It seemed his search would be in vain today. Sailing through the Dragonwatch Pass was perilous enough at the best of times, but with these red lightning storms and rough, churning seas, and the growing threat of wild dragon attacks...well, it seemed fewer vessels were braving the route.

He was considering making his way back to the cliffs when he saw the old man on the beach.

He was a little further down the shore, dressed in a crimson robe, newly spun it looked, with a strange fiery motif on the back. Akar squinted - his eyes weren't what they were - and raised a hand against the sea-spray, wondering if he was seeing things. But no, the man was still there, standing alone upon the rocks. He held a black wooden staff in his right hand, a full foot taller than he was, its top fitted with a large circular stone that seemed to be glowing a lemony gold, veined with darker threads of amber and red.

"Hello," Akar called to him. "You, on the beach. Are you lost, friend?"

The old man gave no answer. At least, he *must* have been old, given the blanched white hue of his long hair, flowing loose down the back of his head. *Perhaps he cannot hear me over the wind?* Akar began working his way, clambering over the rocks. Half were covered in slippery green seaweed, and he had to choose his step carefully. He'd fallen here too many times to count, skinning knees and palms and had even twisted his ankle once, making the climb back up even harder.

"You there, hello?" he called out as he went, but still the man gave no answer. By the time he drew near his ire was up. "Can you not hear me? *Hello*!"

He must be deaf, Akar decided. What he couldn't work out was how he'd gotten here. He didn't delude himself by thinking he was the only man who knew the way down to this beach, but even so, this wasn't a man he'd seen before, and he knew everyone from the nearby villages. *And few could make the climb even so.* Akar might have been getting old himself, but he was tough and sinewy no matter what his wife said, and he'd scaled these rugged cliffs for thirty years and knew every hand and foothold on the way. *I know the cracks and crevices better than those on my wife's body,* he'd been known to say, when drinking in the village tavern. That one always got a laugh, and it was true as well. He'd fondled these cliffs more often than his wife's ample curves and felt a much closer bond to them too.

He reached the small jutting promontory on which the old man stood, the waves washing in and out upon the slippery grey rocks at his feet. One false move and he could slip and fall in and when the waters were rough, getting out wasn't so easy. Akar would be damned if he'd have to jump in and save him. He'd sooner wait for him to drown, and then take that nice red cloak of his...

"Stranger, if you can understand me, step back from the edge. It's dangerous." The orb atop his staff glowed peculiarly, Akar now saw, strangely mesmerising, red and yellow and orange, like fire. He'd heard it said the Bondstone had similar colouring. His eyes were drawn to it. The colours seemed to shift and move like living mists within the translucent stone. "You don't...want to...fall in..." he whispered, gazing at the orb. "You'll be sure...be sure to drown. I won't be able to...to save you."

He swallowed, blinked, wrenched his eyes away from the swirling colours...and found that the old man was looking right at him. Akar drew back, alarmed. The man's eyes were deep crimson, like nothing he'd ever seen before, his face in some way ancient and ageless all at once. *He has no pupils,* he realised, looking at those eerie red eyes, as a whisper that sounded like a thousand waves breaking ashore slipped through the man's pale lips. "What year is this?"

Akar shook his head, confused. That voice...it was inhuman. "Year? I don't..."

"What age?" the man said.

Akar still wasn't understanding. The man was a loon. "That depends where...where you're from." His voice was shaking, he realised, brittle. "The northerners...they count time differently. Same as those south of the Scales. Here in Agarath we count from the death of Eldur. That was...3352 years ago."

"So long," the man whispered, turning back to look at the sea. He seemed to be restraining his voice somehow. Even so Akar could feel it, trembling through his bones.

"How, er...how'd you get down here? I didn't see you climb, or..." He scanned for a skiff or dinghy, but could see no row or sailboat on the water.

"So long," the man whispered again, seeming not to hear him. He turned his eyes around, half in a daze, and drew the orb of his staff toward his face. Its light unveiled the deep-etched seams in his skin, as cracks in ancient stone. He ran a hand over its surface, staring with those unearthly red eyes. "Master," he whispered, as the veins and shapes shifted. "This is truly what you want?"

Akar slid his right foot back, searching for a good landing. It was time to go, he judged. He'd be no help to a madman like this.

"You are sure it will wake him? He has been sleeping so long, even longer than I..." The madman watched those shifting patterns, licking like tongues of fire, and Akar was sure he saw a face in the orb, wreathed in scarlet flame. "Then I will see it done. For you, my Lord Agarath. I serve you, always."

Agarath? Akar might have laughed if he wasn't so horrified, a deep trembling fear clawing through his veins. He reached his left foot back and felt firm rock beneath his sole, stealing another step away from the lunatic. It was never wise to turn your back on a wild animal, he'd always known. Another few steps and he'd have ground enough to turn and make a dash for it. He felt sure he could outpace the man to the cliffs if he made chase, and there was no man who knew how to scale the scarp better than he. Silently, he put another pace between them, then another, and all the while the loon was gazing into his orb with those strange red eyes, occasionally glancing away to the sea. The Wings were out there, Akar knew, some thirty miles away across Dragonwatch Pass. If this man had a wish to reach them, he'd find nothing but dragons and death and red storms out there.

Let him, he thought, wanting nothing more than to flee. He felt more terrified than he could say, his every limb shivering, a deep throbbing beat pushing through his blood. Yet step by step he was inching away. *One more,* he thought. *One more step and I can run.* He slid his leg back, found firm footing, and he spun...

The dragon before him was immense, a colossal cliff blotting out the sun. How it had crept up behind him he could not say. Hot steaming breath poured from its nostrils, tinged with red flame, and its eyes were red too, red as blood and wild, just like the madman's. The dragon lifted its head, up and up and up. Akar's eyes followed, as though pulled by a string. He wanted to weep. He wanted to run. He wanted to fling himself to the rocks or leap into the sea. But all he could do was watch, as the dragon opened its jaws, and those blue and silver scales caught the sunlight, and glittered.

"Do not be afraid," whispered that voice behind him that sounded like the world tearing open. "The fire is cleansing, child. In time it will cleanse us all." Akar looked up to the dragon, and suddenly he saw another, and another, and another landing on the beach. "They come to their master's call," the man told him, placing his hands upon Akar's shoulders. "Now stand and be cleansed, and join Agarath's Eternal Flame. You will be the first of many, child. Soon all the world will follow. Soon all the world will burn."

You never know what you'll find down here, Akar thought, paralysed, as the silver-blue dragon widened its gaping jaws, and the molten flame came gushing out. *Gemstones, jewels, swords, shields.*

He'd never expected this.

THE END

The Bladeborn Saga will continue in Book Four - ***The Winds of War***

ALSO BY T. C. EDGE

THE ENHANCED SERIES (MAIN SERIES):

The Enhanced (Book One)

Hybrid (Book Two)

Nameless (Book Three)

Assassin (Book Four)

Captive (Book Five)

Renegade (Book Six)

Invader (Book Seven)

Avenger (Book Eight)

Defender (Book Nine)

Nemesis (Book Ten)

Sequel (to main Enhanced series, and Warrior Race series):

The Enhanced: Awakening

The Enhanced: Conquest

The Enhanced: Fractured

The Enhanced: Invasion

THE WARRIOR RACE SERIES (ENHANCED UNIVERSE):

The Warrior Race (Book One)

The Red Warrior (Book Two)

Angel of War (Book Three)

CHILDREN OF THE PRIME SERIES (ENHANCED UNIVERSE):

The Chosen (Book One)

Trial of the Chosen (Book 2)

Blood of the Chosen (Book 3)

March of the Chosen (Book 4)

War of the Chosen (Book 5)

Fall of the Chosen (Book 6)

Rise of the Chosen (Book 7)

Fate of the Chosen (Book 8)

VARIANT SERIES (ENHANCED UNIVERSE)

Variant (Book One)

Initiate (Book Two)

Survivor (Book Three)

Pathfinder (Book Four)

Legend (Book Five)

Prodigy (Book Six)

Worldkiller (Book Seven)

OTHER BOOKS BY THE AUTHOR:

THE WATCHERS SERIES:

The Watchers Trilogy:

The Watchers of Eden (Book One)

City of Stone (Book Two)

War at the Wall (Book Three)

The Watchers Trilogy Box Set

The Seekers Trilogy

The Watcher Wars (Book One)

The Seekers of Knight (Book Two)

The Endless Knight

The Seekers Trilogy Box Set

THE PHANTOM CHRONICLES:

The Last Phantom (Book 1)

Phantom Hunter (Book 2)

Phantom Legacy (Book 3)

Phantom Unleashed (Book 4)

www.ingramcontent.com/pod-product-compliance
Lightning Source LLC
Chambersburg PA
CBHW020720310726
48979CB00004B/995

* 9 7 8 1 0 6 8 5 1 8 2 2 5 *